The Wych Elm

The Wych Elm

TANA FRENCH

VIKING
an imprint of
PENGUIN BOOKS

VIKING

UK | USA | Canada | Ireland | Australia
India | New Zealand | South Africa

Viking is part of the Penguin Random House group of companies
whose addresses can be found at global.penguinrandomhouse.com.

First published in the United States by Viking 2018
First published in Great Britain by Viking 2018
Published in this edition 2019

001

Set in 10.68/13.13 pt Dante MT Std
Typeset by Jouve (UK), Milton Keynes
Printed and bound in Great Britain by Clays Ltd, Elcograf S.p.A.

A CIP catalogue record for this book is available from the British Library

ISBN: 978-0-241-37950-9

www.greenpenguin.co.uk

MIX
Paper from
responsible sources
FSC® C018179

Penguin Random House is committed to a
sustainable future for our business, our readers
and our planet. This book is made from Forest
Stewardship Council® certified paper.

For Kristina

Lord, we know what we are, but know not what we may be.

William Shakespeare, *Hamlet*

I

I've always considered myself to be, basically, a lucky person. I don't mean I'm one of those people who pick multi-million-euro lotto numbers on a whim, or show up seconds too late for flights that go on to crash with no survivors. I just mean that I managed to go through life without any of the standard misfortunes you hear about. I wasn't abused as a kid, or bullied in school; my parents didn't split up or die or have addiction problems or even get into any but the most trivial arguments; none of my girlfriends ever cheated on me, at least as far as I know, or dumped me in traumatic ways; I never got hit by a car or caught anything worse than chicken-pox or even had to wear braces. Not that I spent much time thinking about this, but when it occurred to me, it was with a satisfying sense that everything was going exactly as it should.

And of course there was the Ivy House. I don't think anyone could convince me, even now, that I was anything other than lucky to have the Ivy House. I know it wasn't that simple, I know all the reasons in intimate, serrated detail; I can lay them out in a neat line, stark and runic as black twigs on snow, and stare at them till I almost convince myself; but all it takes is one whiff of the right smell – jasmine, lapsang souchong, a specific old-fashioned soap that I've never been able to identify – or one sideways shaft of afternoon light at a particular angle, and I'm lost, in thrall all over again.

Not long ago I actually rang my cousins about it – it was almost Christmas, I was a little drunk on mulled wine from some godawful work party, or I would never have rung them, or at any rate not to ask their opinions, or their advice, or whatever it is I thought I was looking for. Susanna clearly felt it was a silly question – 'Well, yeah, obviously we were lucky. It was an amazing place.' And into my silence: 'If you're getting hung up on all the other stuff, then personally' – long deft slice of scissors through paper, choirboys sweet and buoyant in the background, she was wrapping presents – 'I wouldn't. I know that's easier said, but seriously, Toby, picking at it after how many years, what's the point? But you do you.' Leon, who at first had sounded genuinely pleased to hear from me, tightened up instantly: 'How am I supposed to know? Oh, listen, while I have you, I meant to email you, I'm thinking of coming home for a bit at Easter, are you going to be—' I got mildly belligerent and demanded an answer, which I knew perfectly well has always been the wrong way to deal with Leon, and he pretended his reception had gone and hung up on me.

And yet; and yet. It matters; matters, as far as I can see – for whatever that's worth, at this point – more than anything. It's taken me this long to start thinking about what luck can be, how smoothly and deliciously deceptive, how relentlessly twisted and knotted in on its own hidden places, and how lethal.

•

That night. I know there are an infinite number of places to begin any story, and I'm well aware that everyone else involved in this one would take issue with my choice – I can just see the wry lift at the corner of Susanna's mouth, hear Leon's snort of pure derision. But I can't help it: for me it all goes back to that night, the dark corroded hinge between before and after, the slipped-in sheet of trick glass that tints everything on one side in its own murky colours and leaves everything on the other luminous, achingly close, untouched and untouchable. Even though it's demonstrably nonsense – the skull had already been tucked away in its cranny for years by that point, after all, and I think it's pretty clear that it would have resurfaced that summer regardless – I can't help believing, at some level deeper than logic, that none of this would ever have happened without that night.

It started out feeling like a good night; a great night, actually. It was a Friday in April, the first day that had really felt like spring, and I was out with my two best mates from school. Hogan's was buzzing, all the girls' hair softened to flightiness by the day's warmth and the guys' sleeves rolled up, layers of talk and laughter packing the air till the music was just a subliminal cheery reggae boom boom

boom coming up from the floor into your feet. I was high as a kite – not on coke or anything; there had been a bit of hassle at work earlier that week, but that day I had sorted it all out and the triumph was making me a little giddy, I kept catching myself talking too fast or knocking back a swallow of my pint with a flourish. An extremely pretty brunette at the next table was checking me out, giving me just a second too much smile when my eye happened to land on her; I wasn't going to do anything about it – I had a really great girlfriend and no intention of cheating on her – but it was fun to know I hadn't lost my touch.

'She fancies you,' Declan said, nodding sideways at the brunette, who was throwing her head back extravagantly as she laughed at her friend's joke.

'She's got good taste.'

'How's Melissa?' Sean asked, which I thought was unnecessary. Even if it hadn't been for Melissa, the brunette wasn't my type; she had dramatic curves barely contained by a tight retro red dress, and she looked like she would have been happier in some Gauloise-ridden bistro watching several guys have a knife fight over her.

'Great,' I said, which was true. 'As always.' Melissa was the opposite of the brunette: small, sweet-faced, with ruffled blond hair and a sprinkle of freckles, drawn by nature towards things that made her and everyone around her happy – bright flowered dresses in soft cotton, baking her own bread, dancing to whatever came on the radio, picnics with cloth napkins and ridiculous cheeses. It had been days since I'd seen her and the thought of her made me crave everything about her, her laugh, her nose burrowing into my neck, the honeysuckle smell of her hair.

'She is great,' Sean told me, a little too meaningfully.

'She is, yeah. I'm the one who just said she's great. I'm the one going out with her; I know she's great. She's great.'

'Are you speeding?' Dec wanted to know.

'I'm high on your company. You, dude, you're the human equivalent of the purest, whitest Colombian—'

'You are speeding. Share. You stingy bastard.'

'I'm clean as a baby's arse. You scrounging git.'

'Then what are you doing eyeing up your woman?'

'She's beautiful. A man can appreciate a thing of beauty without—'

'Too much coffee,' Sean said. 'Get more of that down you; that'll sort you out.'

He was pointing at my pint. 'Anything for you,' I said, and sank most of what was left. 'Ahhh.'

'She is only gorgeous,' Dec said, eyeing the brunette wistfully. 'What a waste.'

'Go for it,' I said. He wouldn't; he never did.

'Right.'

'Go on. While she's looking over.'

'She's not looking at me. She's looking at you. As usual.' Dec was stocky and tightly wound, with glasses and a mop of unruly copper hair; he was actually OK-looking, but somewhere along the way he had convinced himself that he wasn't, with predictable consequences.

'Hey,' Sean said, mock-wounded. 'Birds look at me.'

'They do, yeah. They're wondering if you're blind, or if you're wearing that shirt on a dare.'

'Jealousy,' Sean said sadly, shaking his head. Sean was a big guy, six foot two, with a broad open face and his rugby muscle only starting to soften; he did in fact get plenty of female attention, although that was wasted too, since he had been happily with the same girl since school. 'It's an ugly thing.'

'Don't worry,' I reassured Dec. 'It's all about to change for you. With the . . .' I nodded subtly in the direction of his head.

'The what?'

'You know. Those.' I darted a quick point at my hairline.

'What're you on about?'

Leaning in discreetly across the table, keeping my voice down: 'The plugs. Fair play to you, man.'

'I don't have fucking hair plugs!'

'They're nothing to be ashamed of. All the big stars are getting them these days. Robbie Williams. Bono.'

Which of course outraged Dec even more. 'There's nothing wrong with my bleeding hair!'

'That's what I'm saying. They look great.'

4

'They're not obvious,' Sean reassured him. 'Not saying they're obvious. Just nice, you know?'

'They're not obvious because they don't *exist*. I don't *have*—'

'Come on,' I said. 'I can see them. Here, and—'

'Get off me!'

'I know. Let's ask your woman what she thinks.' I started to signal to the brunette.

'No. No no no. Toby, I'm serious, I'm going to actually kill you—' Dec was grabbing at my waving hand. I dodged.

'It's the perfect conversation starter,' Sean pointed out. 'You didn't know how to get talking to her, right? Here's your chance.'

'Fuck yous,' Dec told us, abandoning the attempt to catch my hand and standing up. 'You're a pair of shitehawks. Do you know that?'

'Ah, Dec,' I said. 'Don't leave us.'

'I'm going to the jacks. To give you two a chance to pull yourselves together. You, Chuckles' – to Sean – 'it's your round.'

'Checking that they're all in place,' Sean told me, aside, motioning to his hairline. 'You messed them up. See that one there, it's gone all—' Dec gave us both the finger and started off through the crowd towards the jacks, trying to stay dignified as he edged between buttocks and waving pints, and concentrating hard on ignoring both our burst of laughter and the brunette.

'He actually fell for that, for a minute there,' Sean said. 'Eejit. Same again?' and he headed up to the bar.

While I had a moment to myself I texted Melissa: *Having a few with the guys. Ring you later. Love you.* She texted me back straight-away: *I sold the mad steampunk armchair!!!* and a bunch of firework emojis. *The designer was so happy she cried on the phone and I was so happy for her I almost did too :-) Say hi to the guys from me. I love you too xxx.* Melissa ran a tiny shop in Temple Bar that sold quirky Irish-designed stuff, funny little sets of interconnected china vases, cashmere blankets in zingy neon colours, hand-carved drawer knobs shaped like sleeping squirrels or spreading trees. She had been trying to sell that armchair for years. I texted her back *Congratulations! You sales demon you.*

Sean came back with the pints and Dec came back from the jacks, looking a lot more composed but still intently avoiding the brunette's eye. 'We asked your woman what she thinks,' Sean told him. 'She says the plugs are lovely.'

'She says she's been admiring them all night,' I said.

'She wants to know can she touch them.'

'She wants to know can she lick them.'

'Stick it up your holes. I'll tell you why she keeps looking over at you, anyway, fuckfeatures,' Dec said to me, pulling up his stool. 'It's not because she fancies you. It's only because she saw your smarmy mug in the paper, and she's trying to remember were you in there for conning a granny out of her savings or shagging a fifteen-year-old.'

'Which she wouldn't care about either way unless she fancied me.'

'In your dreams. Fame's gone to your head.'

My picture had been in the paper a couple of weeks earlier – the social pages, which had netted me a ferocious amount of slagging – because I had happened to be chatting to a long-serving soap actress at a work thing, an exhibition opening. At the time I did the PR and marketing for a medium-sized, fairly prestigious art gallery in the centre of town, just a few laneways and short cuts away from Grafton Street. It wasn't what I'd had in mind when I was finishing college; I had been planning on one of the big PR firms, I'd only gone to the interview for the practice. Once I got there, though, I found myself unexpectedly liking the place, the tall barely-renovated Georgian house with all the floors at weird angles, Richard the owner peering at me through his lopsided glasses and inquiring about my favourite Irish artists (luckily I had prepped for the interview, so I could actually come up with semi-sensible answers, and we had a long happy conversation about le Brocquy and Pauline Bewick and various other people I had barely heard of before that week). I liked the idea of having a free hand, too. In a big firm I would have spent my first couple of years huddled in front of a computer obediently watering and pruning other people's ideas of brilliant social media campaigns, dithering over whether to delete racist troll comments about some horrifying new flavour of crisp or leave them up to generate buzz; at the gallery I could try out whatever I wanted and patch up my learner's mistakes on the fly, without anyone hanging over my shoulder – Richard wasn't entirely sure what Twitter was, although he knew he really should have some, and he clearly wasn't the micromanaging type. When, to my faint surprise, I was offered the job, I barely hesitated. A few years, I figured, a few nice publicity coups to make my CV sparkle, and I could make the leap to one of the big firms at a level I would actually enjoy.

It had been five years now, and I was starting to put out feelers, to a gratifying level of response. I was going to miss the gallery – I had ended up enjoying not just the freedom but the work itself, the artists with their goofy levels of perfectionism, the satisfaction of gradually picking up enough to understand why Richard leaped on one artist and turned another one down flat. But I was twenty-eight, Melissa and I were talking about getting a place together, the gallery paid OK but nowhere near as well as the big firms; I felt like it was time to get serious.

All of that had come pretty close to going up in smoke, over the past week, but my luck had held. My mind was bouncing and dashing like a border collie and it was infectious, Sean and Dec were bent over the table laughing – we were planning a guys' holiday for that summer but couldn't decide where, *Thailand? hang on, when's the monsoon season?*, phones coming out, *when's the coup season?* – Dec kept insisting on Fiji for some reason, *has to be Fiji, we'll never get another chance, not after—* and a fake-subtle tilt of his head at Sean. Sean was getting married at Christmas, and while after twelve years it was hardly unexpected, it still felt like a startling and gratuitous thing to do and the mention of it inevitably led into slaggings: *The minute you say 'I do' you're on borrowed time, man, before you know it you'll have a kid and then that's it, your life's over . . . Here's to Sean's last holiday! Here's to Sean's last night out! Here's to Sean's last blowie!* Actually Dec and I both liked Audrey a lot, and the wry grin on Sean – mock-annoyed, secretly pleased as punch with himself – got me thinking about Melissa and we'd been together three years now and maybe I should think about proposing, and all that talk of last chances made me glance across at the brunette who was telling

7

some anecdote and using her hands a lot, scarlet nails, and something in the angle of her neck told me she knew perfectly well that I was looking and that it had nothing to do with the newspaper picture— *We'll get you seen to in Thailand, Sean, don't worry— Here's to Sean's first ladyboy!*

After that my memory of the evening gets patchy for a while. Of course in its aftermath I went over it a million times, obsessively, combing every thread to find the knot that set the pattern changing beyond recovery; hoping there was just one detail whose significance I'd missed, the tiny keystone around which all the pieces would slot into place and the whole would flash jackpot rings of multicoloured light while I leaped up shouting *Eureka!* The missing chunks didn't help matters (very common, the doctors said reassuringly, completely normal, oh so very very normal): a lot came back along the way and I picked what I could from Sean's memory and Dec's, laboriously pieced the evening together like an old fresco from husbanded fragments and educated inferences, but how could I know for sure what was in the blank spaces? Did I shoulder someone at the bar? Did I talk too loudly, riding high in my euphoria balloon, or throw out an arm in some expansive gesture and catch someone's pint? Was the brunette's roid-rat ex snarling in some unnoticed corner? I had never thought of myself as the kind of person who goes looking for trouble, but nothing seemed out of the question, not any more.

Long buttery streaks of light on dark wood. A girl in a floppy red velvet hat leaning on the bar when I went up for my round, chatting to the barman about some gig, Eastern European accent, wrists bending like a dancer's. A trodden flier on the floor, green and yellow, faux-naïf sketch of a lizard biting its tail. Washing my hands in the jacks, smell of bleach, chill air.

I do remember my phone buzzing, in the middle of an uproarious argument about whether the next *Star Wars* film was inevitably going to be worse than the last one, based on some intricate algorithm Dec had come up with. I jumped for it – I thought it might be something to do with the work situation, Richard wanting an update or maybe Tiernan finally returning my calls – but it was just some Facebook birthday-party invitation. 'Story?' Sean wanted to know, raising his eyebrows at my phone, and I realised I had grabbed at it a little too urgently.

'Nothing,' I said, putting the phone away. 'And anyway how about the *Taken* series, the daughter started out as the victim and next time she turned into the sidekick—' and we went back to the film argument, which by this point had gone off on so many tangents that none of us remembered what anyone's original stance had been. This was what I had needed from the night, this, Dec leaning forwards over the table gesticulating, Sean throwing out his hands in incredulity, all of us trying to shout each other down about Hagrid— I pulled my phone back out and set it to silent.

The trouble at work hadn't been my fault, actually, or at least only very tangentially. It stemmed from Tiernan, the guy in charge of exhibitions, a lank, long-chinned hipster with vintage horn-rimmed glasses and two main topics of conversation: obscure Canadian alt-folk bands, and the injustice of the fact that his art (meticulous oil portraits of ravers with mindlessly glaring pigeons' heads, that kind of thing, produced in his parent-funded studio) hadn't achieved the prominence it deserved. The year before all this, Tiernan had come up with the idea of a group show of representations of urban spaces by disadvantaged youths. Richard and I had both leaped on it – the only way that could have been easier to publicise was if some of the disadvantaged youths were also Syrian refugees and ideally trans, and Richard, despite his general air of unworldly vagueness and ragged tweed, was well aware that the gallery needed both status and funding in order to stay open. Only a few days after Tiernan first floated the idea – offhandedly, at the monthly meeting, picking crumbs of doughnut sugar off his napkin – Richard told him to get started.

The whole thing went like a dream. Tiernan scoured the dodgiest schools and council flats he could find (in one place a bunch of eight-year-olds pounded his fixie bike into Dalí with a lump hammer, in front of him) and came up with a collection of satisfyingly scuzzy youths with low-grade criminal records and scruffy-edged drawings involving syringes and tattered blocks of flats and the occasional horse. To be fair, not all of it was that predictable: there was one girl who made small, sinister models of her various foster homes out of materials she had pilfered from derelict sites – a tarpaulin rag-doll man slouched on a sofa chipped from a lump of concrete, with his arm draped around a tarpaulin little girl's shoulders in a way I found kind of disturbing; another kid made Pompeii-esque plaster casts of objects he found in the stairwell of his block of flats, a crushed lighter, a pair of child-sized glasses with one twisted earpiece, an intricately knotted plastic bag. I had taken it for granted that this show would be trading entirely on its moral superiority, but a few things in there were actually pretty good.

Tiernan was especially proud of one discovery, an eighteen-year-old known as Gouger. Gouger refused to talk to anyone but Tiernan, give us his real name or, frustratingly, do any interviews – he had been in and out of the juvenile system for most of his life and had developed complicated networks of enemies, who he was afraid would come after him if they saw him getting rich and famous – but he was good. He layered things, spray paint, photographs, pen and ink, with a ferocious slapdash skill that gave them a sense of urgency, look fast and hard before something comes roaring in from the side and smashes the picture to shards of colour and scrawl. His *pièce de résistance* – an enormous whirl of howling charcoal teenagers around a spray-paint bonfire, heads thrown back, neon arcs of booze flying from waved cans – was called *BoHeroin Rhapsody* and had already had interest from several collectors, after I put it up on our Facebook page.

The Arts Council and Dublin City Council practically threw money at us. The media gave us even more coverage than I had expected. Tiernan brought in his youths to shuffle around the gallery, nudging each other and sniping in undertones and giving long unreadable stares to the 'Divergences' show of mixed-media abstracts. Various distinguished guests responded to our invitation saying that they would be delighted to come to the opening. Richard pottered around the gallery smiling, humming bits of light opera interspersed with bizarre stuff he'd picked up somewhere (Kraftwerk??). Only then I went into Tiernan's office without knocking, one afternoon, and found him crouched on the floor touching up the detail on Gouger's latest masterwork.

After the first stunned second I started to laugh. Partly it was the look on Tiernan's face, the mixture of scarlet guilt and puffy defensiveness as he flailed for a plausible excuse; partly it was at myself, for having bounced cheerfully along through all of this without a single suspicion, when of course I should have copped months earlier (since when were underprivileged youths even on Tiernan's horizon?). 'Well well well,' I said, still laughing. 'Look at you.'

'Shhh,' Tiernan hissed, hands coming up, darting his eyes at the door.

'My man Gouger. In the flesh.'

'Jesus shut *up*, please, Richard's—'

'You're better-looking than I expected.'

'Toby. Listen. No no listen—' He had his arms half-spread in front of the painting so that it looked ridiculously as if he was trying to hide it, *painting? what painting?* 'If this gets out, I'm *dead*, I'm, no one will ever—'

'Jesus,' I said. 'Tiernan. Calm down.'

'The pictures are good, Toby. They're *good*. But this is the only way, no one'll ever look twice if they come from me, I went to *art* school—'

'Is it just the Gouger stuff? Or more of them?'

'Just Gouger. I swear.'

'Huh,' I said, peering over his shoulder. The picture was classic Gouger, a thick layer of black paint with two savagely grappling boys sgraffitoed into it, through them a wall of minutely pencilled balconies with a tiny vivid scene unfolding on each one. It must have taken forever. 'How long have you been planning this?'

'A while, I don't—' Tiernan blinked at me. He was very agitated. 'What are you going to do? Are you . . . ?'

Presumably I should have gone straight to Richard and told him the whole story, or at least found an excuse to pull Gouger's work from the show (his enemies were on his trail, something like that – giving him an OD would just have made him even more of a draw). To be honest, I didn't even consider it. Everything was going beautifully, everyone involved was happy as a clam; pulling the plug would have ruined a lot of people's day for, as far as I could see, no good reason at all. Even if you wanted to get into the ethics of it, I was basically on Tiernan's side: I've never got the self-flagellating middle-class belief that being poor and having a petty crime habit magically makes you more worthy, more deeply connected to some wellspring of artistic truth, even more real. As far as I was concerned, the exhibition was exactly the same as it had been ten minutes ago; if people wanted to ignore the perfectly good pictures right in front of their eyes and focus instead on the gratifying illusion somewhere behind them, that was their problem, not mine.

'Relax,' I said – Tiernan was in such a state that leaving him there any longer would have been cruelty. 'I'm not going to do anything.'

'You're not?'

'Cross my heart.'

Tiernan blew out a long, shaky breath. 'OK. OK. Wow. Got a fright there.' He straightened up and surveyed the painting, patting the top edge of it as if he were soothing a spooked animal. 'They are good,' he said. 'They are, aren't they?'

'You know what you should do,' I said. 'Do more of the bonfire ones. Make it a series.'

Tiernan's eyes lit up. 'I could,' he said. 'That's not a bad idea, you know, from the building of the bonfire right up to the, when it's going down to ashes, dawn—' and he turned to his desk, fumbling for paper and pencil, his mind already brushing the whole episode away. I left him to it.

After that little wobble, the show went back to rolling smoothly towards its opening. Tiernan worked flat out on Gouger's bonfire series, to the point where I was pretty sure he wasn't sleeping more than a couple of hours a night, but if anyone noticed his dazed, grimy look and constant yawning, they had no reason to connect them with the pictures that he lugged in with triumphant regularity. I spun Gouger's anonymity into a sub-Banksy enigma, with plenty of fake Twitter accounts arguing in semi-literate textspeak over whether he was your man from down the flats who had stabbed Mixie that time, because if so Mixie was looking for him;

the media dived on it and our followers skyrocketed. Tiernan and I did discuss, semi-seriously, getting an authentic skanger to be the face of the product, in exchange for enough cash to support his habit (obviously we would need one with a habit, for maximum gritty authenticity), but we decided against it on the grounds that a junkie skanger would be too short-sighted for reliability: sooner or later he would either start blackmailing us or start wanting creative control, and things would get messy.

I suppose I should have been worrying about what if it all went wrong – there were so many ways it could have, a journalist getting all investigative, me screwing up the slang on Gouger's Twitter account – but I wasn't. Worrying had always seemed to me like a laughable waste of time and energy; so much simpler to go happily about your business and deal with the problem when it arose, if it did, which it mostly didn't. So it caught me completely off guard when, a month before the exhibition was scheduled to open and just four days before that night, Richard found out.

I'm still not sure how, exactly. Something about a phone call, from what little I could gather (pressed against my office door, staring at the dinged-up white paint, heart rate building slowly to an uncomfortable thump at the base of my throat), but Richard threw Tiernan out so fast and on such a searing gust of fury that we didn't get a chance to talk. Then he came into my office – I jumped back just in time to avoid a door to the face – and told me to get out and not come back till Friday, when he would have decided what to do about me.

One look at him – white-faced, collar rucked up, jaw tight as a fist – and I had more sense than to say anything, even if I had had a chance to come up with anything coherent before the door slammed behind him with a bang that spun papers off my desk. I packed up my stuff and left, avoiding Aideen the accountant's round avid eyes through her door-crack, trying to keep my footsteps easy and jaunty on my way down the stairs.

I spent the next three days being bored, mainly. Telling anyone what had happened would have been idiotic, when there was a good chance that the whole thing would blow over. I had been startled by just how angry Richard was – I would have expected him to be annoyed, of course, but the depth of his fury seemed totally out of proportion, and I was pretty sure he had just been having a bad day and would have settled down by the time I went back to work. So I was stuck at home all day, in case anyone spotted me out and about when I shouldn't have been. I couldn't even ring anyone. I couldn't spend the night at Melissa's place or ask her over to mine, in case she wanted to walk in to work together in the morning – her shop was only five minutes beyond the gallery, so we mostly did walk in after a night together, holding hands and chattering like a pair of teenagers. I told her I had a cold, convinced her not to come over and look after me in case she caught it, and thanked God she wasn't the type to decide I was cheating on her. I played an awful lot of Xbox, and put on work clothes when I went to the shops, just in case.

Luckily I didn't live in the kind of place where I swapped cheery waves with my neighbours on our way out to work every morning, and if I missed a day someone would call round with cookies to make sure I was OK. My apartment was on the ground floor of a slabby, red-brick 1970s block, jammed eye-jarringly between beautiful Victorian mansions in an extremely nice part of Dublin. The street was broad and airy, lined with enormous old trees whose roots rucked up big patches of the pavement, and the architect had at least had enough sensitivity to respond to that; my living room had great floor-to-ceiling windows and glass doors on two sides, so that in summer the whole room was a glorious, disorientating tumble of sunshine and leaf-shadows. Apart from that one stroke of inspiration, though, he had done a pretty lousy job: the outside was sourly utilitarian and the corridors had the hallucinatory, liminal vibe of an airport hotel, long line of brown carpet stretching off into the distance, long line of textured beige wallpaper and cheap wooden doors on either side, dirty cut-glass wall sconces giving off a curdled yellowish glow. I never, ever saw the neighbours. I heard the occasional muffled thump when someone dropped something on the floor above me, and one time I had held the door for an accountant-looking guy with acne and a lot of M&S shopping bags, but apart from that I might have had the whole block to myself. No one was about to notice, or care, that instead of going to work I was at home blowing up emplacements and inventing cute gallery stories to tell Melissa on the phone that evening.

I did do a certain amount of panicking, off and on. Tiernan wasn't answering his phone, even when I rang from my unlisted landline, so I had no way of knowing how thoroughly he had ratted me out, although the lack of contact didn't feel like a good sign. I told myself that if Richard had been planning to fire me he would have done it straight out, the same way he had to Tiernan; most of the time this made total, comforting sense, but every now and then there was a moment (middle of the night, mostly, eyes snapping open to the slant of pale light sweeping ominously across my bedroom ceiling as a car passed near-silently outside) when the full potential of the thing thumped down on top of me. If I lost my job, how would I hide it from people – my friends, my parents, oh God *Melissa* – until I could get a new one? In fact, what if I couldn't get a new one? All the big firms I had been carefully cultivating would notice my sudden departure from the gallery, notice how the star of the big hyped summer show had abruptly dematerialised at the exact same time, and that would be it: if I wanted a new job I would have to leave the country, and even that might not do me much good. And on the subject of leaving the country: could Tiernan and I be arrested for fraud? We hadn't sold any of Gouger's paintings, thank God, and it wasn't like we had been claiming they were by Picasso, but we had taken funding under false pretences, that had to be some kind of crime . . .

Like I said, I wasn't used to worrying, and the intensity of those moments took me aback. In facile hindsight it's tempting to see them as a premonition gone awry, a wild danger signal propelled to me by the force of its own urgency and then scrambled, ever so slightly but fatally, by the limitations of my mind. At the time I just saw them as a nuisance, one that I had no intention of allowing to freak me out. After a few minutes of spiralling panic I would get up, shock my mind out of its loop with thirty seconds under a freezing shower, shake like a dog and then go back to whatever I had been doing.

On Friday morning I was a little jumpy, enough that it took me several tries to find an outfit that felt like it sent the right message (sober, repentant, ready to get back to work) – eventually I settled on my dark-grey tweed suit, with a plain white shirt and no tie. All the same, when I knocked on Richard's door I was feeling fairly confident. Even his curt 'Come' didn't put me on edge.

'Me,' I said, putting my head diffidently around the door.

'I know. Sit down.'

Richard's office was a riotous nest of carved antelopes, sand dollars, Matisse prints, things he'd picked up on his travels, all precariously balanced on shelves and stacks of books and each other. He was sifting aimlessly through a large pile of papers. I pulled up a chair to his desk, at an angle, like we were going to be looking through brochure proofs together.

He said, when he had waited for me to settle, 'I don't need to tell you what this is about.'

Playing innocent would have been a bad mistake. 'Gouger,' I said.

'Gouger,' Richard said. 'Yes.' He picked up a sheet from his pile, gazed at it blankly for a second and let it drop. 'When did you find out?'

Crossing my fingers that Tiernan had kept his mouth shut: 'A few weeks ago. Two. Maybe three.' It had been a lot longer than that.

Richard looked up at me then. 'And you didn't tell me.'

Cold undertow in his voice. He was furious, really furious, still; it hadn't worn off at all. I dialled up the intensity a few notches. 'I almost did. But by that time, by the time I found out, it had just gone too far, you know? Gouger's stuff was out there, on the website, it was on the *invitation* – I know for a fact he was the reason the *Sunday Times* said yes, and the ambassador—' I was talking too fast, gabbling, it made me sound guilty. I slowed down. 'All I could think was how suspicious it would look if he vanished so close to the show. It could have cast doubt on the whole thing. The whole gallery.' Richard's eyes closed for a second against that. 'And I didn't want to throw the responsibility onto you. So I just—'

'It's on me now. And you're right, it's going to look incredibly suspicious.'

'We can fix it. Honestly. I've spent the last three days working it all out. We can have it sorted by the end of today.' *We, we*: we're still a team. 'I'll get on to all the guests and the critics, explain that we've had a slight change in the lineup and we thought they might want to know. I'll tell them Gouger got cold feet – he thinks his enemies might be sniffing around, he needs to keep a low profile for a while. I'll say we're very optimistic that he'll sort out his personal problems soon and bring his work back to us – we need to keep them hopeful, let them down gradually. I'll explain that this is a risk you take when you work with people from that kind of background, and while we're obviously sorry it's gone wrong, we don't regret giving him a chance. It would take a monster to have a problem with that.'

'You're very good at this,' Richard said wearily. He took off his glasses and pressed the bridge of his nose between finger and thumb.

'I need to be. I need to make it up to you.' He didn't react. 'We'll lose a few of the critics, and maybe a couple of guests, but not enough to matter. I'm pretty sure we're in time to stop the programme going to press; we can redo the cover, put Chantelle's sofa assemblage on it—'

'All of that would have been much easier to do three weeks ago.'

'I know. I know. But it's not too late. I'll talk to the media, make sure they keep it low-key, explain we don't want to scare him off for good—'

'Or,' Richard said. He put his glasses back on. 'We could send out a press release explaining that we discovered Gouger was an impostor.'

He looked up at me, mild blue eyes magnified and unblinking.

'Well,' I said carefully. I was heartened by the 'we', but this was a really awful idea and I needed to make sure he got that. 'We could. But it would almost definitely mean cancelling the whole show. I mean, I suppose I could try to find a way to angle it, maybe highlight the fact that we pulled his work as soon as we knew, but it's still going to make us look gullible, and that's going to raise questions about the rest of the—'

'All right,' Richard said, turning his face away and raising a hand to stop me. 'I know all that. We're not going to do it. God knows I'd love to, but we're not. Go do the other thing, all the stuff you talked about. Get it done fast.'

'Richard,' I said, from the heart. Looking at him, the sudden tide of fatigue dragging at his body, I felt terrible. Richard had always been good to me, he had taken a chance on grass-green me when the other woman at the final interview had had years of experience; if I'd had any idea it would hit him this hard I would never have let things go this far, never— 'I'm so sorry.'

'Are you?'

'God, yes, I am. It was an awful thing to do. I just . . . the pictures are so good, you know? I wanted people to see them. I wanted us to show them. I got carried away. I'll never make that mistake again.'

'All right. That's good.' He still wasn't looking at me. 'Go make your phone calls.'

'I'll sort it out. I swear.'

'I'm sure you will,' Richard said flatly, 'now go,' and he went back to rearranging his pieces of paper.

I took the stairs down to my office at a run, jubilant, already mapping out the storm of speculation and doom-mongering from Gouger's Twitter followers. Richard was obviously still pissed off with me, but that would wear off once he saw everything fixed and back on track, or at the very latest once the exhibition went off beautifully. It was a shame about Tiernan's pictures – I couldn't see any way for them to do anything but moulder in his studio, after this, although I wasn't ruling out the possibility that I'd come up with something down the line – but he could always make more.

I needed a pint, in fact I needed a few pints; in fact, I needed a full-on night out. I was missing Melissa – we usually spent at least three nights a week together – but what I needed was the guys, the slaggings and the impassioned ridiculous debates and one of those endless sessions we hadn't been having as much lately, where everyone crashes out on someone's sofa around dawn after eating everything in his fridge. I had some really nice hash at home – I had been tempted to break it out a few times that week, but I didn't really like getting drunk or high when things weren't going well, in case it just made me feel worse; so I had saved my stash for the happy-ending celebration, as a gesture of faith that there would be one, and I had been right.

And so: Hogan's, checking out beaches in Fiji on our phones, reaching over now and then to tug on one of Dec's hair plugs ('Fuck *off*!'). I hadn't been planning on mentioning the week's events, but I was light-headed and bubbling with relief and somewhere around the fifth pint I found myself telling them the whole story, only skipping the late-night flashes of panic – which, in retrospect, had been even sillier than they had felt at the time – and throwing in extra flourishes here and there for laughs.

'You gobshite,' Sean said, at the end, but he was shaking his head and smiling a little wryly. I was slightly relieved; I've always cared about Sean's opinion, and Richard's reaction had left a residue of unease at the back of my mind.

'You are a gobshite,' Dec told me, more pointedly. 'That could've blown up in your face.'

'It did blow up in my face.'

'No. Like properly blown up. Like losing your job. Maybe even getting arrested.'

'Well, it didn't,' I said, irritated – that was the last thing I wanted to think about right then, and Dec should have realised that. 'What world do you live in, anyway, where the cops care whether a picture is by some random nobody in a tracksuit or some random nobody in a fedora?'

'The show could've been shut down. Your boss could've pulled the plug.'

'And he didn't. And even if he had, it wouldn't exactly have been the end of the world.'

'Not for you, maybe. What about the kids doing the art? There they are, pouring their hearts out, and you're taking the piss out of their lives like they're a joke—'

'How was I taking the piss?'

'—their one big chance has finally come along, and you're risking it all for a laugh—'

'Oh for God's sake.'

'If you'd scuppered it, that would've been them stuck in the muck, for the rest of their—'

'What are you talking about? They could have gone to *school*. Instead of spending their time sniffing glue and breaking the wing mirrors off cars. They could have got *jobs*. The recession's over; there's no reason for anyone to be stuck in the muck unless they actually choose to be.'

Dec was staring at me, wide-eyed and incredulous, like I'd poked a finger up my nose. 'You haven't got a clue, man.'

Dec got into our school on a scholarship; his dad drove a bus and his mother worked in Arnotts and none of them had ever been arrested or addicted, so he had no more in common with the ex-hibition kids than I did, but occasionally he liked to play up the wrong-side-of-the-tracks angle, when he wanted an excuse to get chippy and self-righteous. He was still in a snit about the hair-plug thing. I could have pointed out that he was living proof that his own sanctimonious bullshit was just that – he wasn't huddled in a squat huffing shoplifted spray paint, instead he had put in the time and effort and ended up with an excellent IT career, QED – but I wasn't in the mood for playing along with him, not that night. 'It's your round.'

'You actually haven't got a clue.'

'It's actually your round. Are you going to go up and get it, or do you need me to sub you because of your deprived background?'

He kept up the stare for another moment, but so did I, and even-tually he shook his head ostentatiously and went up to the bar. He didn't even bother dodging the brunette this time, not that she noticed.

'What the fuck?' I demanded, when he was out of earshot. 'What was that all about?'

Sean shrugged. I had brought back a few packets of peanuts with the last round – I hadn't had dinner, disentangling the Gouger situ-ation had kept me too late at the office – and he had found one with something dubious on it; most of his attention seemed to be on that.

'I didn't *hurt* anybody. Nobody got *hurt*. He's acting like I punched his *granny*.' I had reached the earnest stage of the night; I was leaning forwards across the table, maybe a little too far forwards, I couldn't tell. 'And anyway look who's talking, for Christ's sake. He's done stupid stuff before. Plenty of times.'

Sean shrugged again. 'He's stressed out,' he said, through the peanut.

'He's always stressed out.'

'He was talking about getting back with Jenna.'

'Oh Jesus,' I said. Jenna was Dec's most recent ex, a noticeably crazy schoolteacher several years older than us who had once rubbed my thigh under a pub table and, when I glanced over astonished, winked at me and stuck her tongue out.

'Yeah. He hates being single, though. He says he's getting too old for first dates and he can't handle all this Tinder crap, and he doesn't want to be the forty-year-old saddo who gets invited to dinner parties out of pity and sat next to the divorced one who spends the whole night bitching about her ex.'

'Well, he doesn't need to take it out on me,' I said. I could in fact see Dec ending up exactly like that, but it would be his own fault if he did, and as far as I was concerned right then, he deserved it.

Sean was settled back in his seat, watching me with an expression that could have been amusement or just mild interest. Sean has always had this air of comfortable detachment, of being – without either effort or smugness – a little more on top of the situation than anyone else. I always vaguely attributed it to the fact that his mother died when he was four – a fact that I regarded with a mixture of recoil, embarrassment and awe – but it could just have been because he was such a big guy: in any situation involving alcohol, Sean was inevitably going to be the least drunk person there.

When he didn't answer: 'What? Do you think I'm some kind of evil Thatcherite Fagin bastard now, too?'

'Honestly?'

'Yeah. Honestly.'

Sean shook the last of the peanut dust into his palm. He said, 'I think it's kid stuff.'

I couldn't work out whether to be insulted or not – was he

dissing my job, reassuring me that this was no big deal, what? 'What are you talking about?'

'Fake Twitter accounts,' Sean said. 'Imaginary skanger wars. Sneaking stuff in behind the boss's back, keeping your fingers crossed it'll all be grand. Kid stuff.'

This time I was genuinely injured, at least a little bit. 'For fuck's sake. It's bad enough Dec giving me hassle. Don't you start.'

'I'm not. Just . . .' He shrugged and upended his glass. 'I'm getting married in a few months, dude. Me and Audrey, we're talking about having a baby next year. It's hard for me to get too excited about you pulling the same old stunts.' And when I drew my eyebrows down sharply: 'You've done stuff like this ever since I knew you. Got caught sometimes. Sorted it out every time. This is the same old same old.'

'No. No. This is—' I made a wide, slicing arm motion that ended in a dramatic finger-snap; it felt like a pure and complete statement in itself, but Sean was still looking at me inquisitively. 'This is different. From those other times. This is not the same thing. At all.'

'How is it different?'

I was miffed by this; I knew there was a difference, and I felt it was ungenerous of Sean to demand that I explain it after this many pints. 'Never mind. Forget I said anything.'

'I'm not giving you hassle. I'm asking.'

He hadn't moved, but there was something new and sharpened in his face, an unblinking intentness, as if there was something important he wanted from me; and I felt an obscure urge to explain myself to him after all, explain about Melissa and being twenty-eight and the big firms and getting serious, tell him how occasionally these days – I would never have admitted it in front of Dec, had never mentioned it even to Melissa – I pictured a tall white Georgian house overlooking Dublin Bay, me and Melissa snug under one of her cashmere throws in front of a roaring fire, maybe even two or three little blond kids tumbling with a golden retriever on the hearthrug. A couple of years earlier the image would have given me the screaming heebie-jeebies; now it didn't actually seem like a bad idea.

I wasn't really in the right state to describe incipient epiphanies to Sean – there was no way I could even have pronounced 'incipient epiphanies' – but I did my best. 'OK,' I said. 'OK. All the other times you're talking about, yeah, that was kid stuff. For the laugh, or because I wanted free pizza or a chance at snogging Lara Mulvaney. But we're not kids any more. I know that. I get that. I mean, we're not like *adult* adults, but we're definitely heading that way – well, Jesus, who am I telling? I know we were taking the piss out of you there, but honest to God, what you and Audrey have, it's great. You're going to be . . .' I had lost my train of thought. The bar was getting louder and the acoustics couldn't handle it, all the sounds were blurring into one sourceless stuttering roar. 'Yeah. And that's what this was all about, the Gouger thing. That's what it was *for*. I'm going after the big stuff now. Not free pizza. The real stuff. *That's* the difference.'

I sat back and looked at Sean hopefully.

'Right,' he said, after what felt like half a second too long. 'Fair enough. Good luck with it, man. I hope you get what you're after.'

Maybe it was my imagination or the heaving noise all around us, but he sounded remote, almost disappointed, although why? He even looked farther away, as if he had deliberately receded a few steps down some long passageway, although I was pretty sure that had to do with the booze.

The part he didn't seem to be getting, frustratingly, was that the Gouger stuff really had been precisely about making those changes – the better the show did, the better my chances with those big firms, the better a place I could afford to get with Melissa, and so on and so on – but before I could find a way to articulate that, Dec was back with the pints. 'Do you know what you are?' he asked me, setting the glasses down and managing to slop only a bit onto the table.

'He's a gobshite,' Sean said, tossing a beer mat onto the spillage. That sudden gleam of intensity was gone; he was back to his usual placid, easy self. 'We established that earlier.'

'No. I'm asking him. Do you know what you are?'

Dec was grinning, but the note had changed; there was an unreliable, staticky glitter to him. 'I'm a prince among men,' I said, leaning back spread-legged in my seat and grinning right back at him.

'There you go.' He pointed at me triumphantly, like he'd somehow scored. 'That's what I'm talking about.' And when I didn't take him up on it, he demanded – pulling his stool closer to the table, settling in for the fight – 'What would've happened to me, if I'd pulled a stupid fucking stunt like that at work?'

'You'd be out on your ear.'

'I would, yeah. I'd be ringing my mum right now, asking if I could move back home till I got a new gig and could afford rent again. Why aren't you?'

Sean sighed heavily and sank a good third of his pint. We both knew Dec in this mood: he was going to keep needling away at me more and more aggressively, jab jab jab, till he either got to me or got drunk enough that we had to load him into a taxi and give the driver his address and his fare.

'Because I'm a charmer,' I said. Which was sort of true – people tended to like me, and that did tend to get me out of trouble – but it was totally beside the point and I was only saying it to annoy Dec. 'And you're not.'

'Nah nah nah. You know why it is? It's because you're not renting. Your parents bought you the gaff.'

'No they didn't. They put down the deposit. I pay the mortgage. What the hell does that have to do with—'

'And if you were really up against it, they'd pay your mortgage for a couple of months. Wouldn't they?'

'I haven't got a clue. I've never needed—'

'Ah, they would. Your ma and da are lovely.'

'I don't *know*. And anyway, so what if they would?'

'So' – Dec was pointing at me, still smiling, a smile that could have passed for friendly if I hadn't known better – 'so that's why your boss didn't give you the heave-ho. Because you didn't go in desperate. You didn't go in panicking. You went in knowing that, no matter what happened, you'd be grand. And so you were grand.'

'I was *grand* because I went in there and apologised and told him how I could fix it. And because I'm good at my job and he doesn't want to lose me.'

'Just like in school.' Dec was really into this: leaning over the

24

table at me, pint forgotten. Sean had taken out his phone and was swiping, checking the news headlines. 'Like when you and me robbed the toupee off Mr McManus. The pair of us did it. The pair of us got spotted. The pair of us got brought in to Armitage. Right? And what happened to us?'

I rolled my eyes. I had no idea, actually; I remembered leaning over banisters to hook the toupee, McManus's panicky bleat fading below us as we hurtled away laughing, toupee swinging from my dad's fishing rod, but I couldn't remember what had happened after that.

'You don't even remember.'

'I don't *care*.'

'I got *suspended*. Three days. You got detention. One day.'

'Are you serious?' I gave him an incredulous stare. I was getting sick of this; the air was leaking out of my shiny happy balloon of relief, and I felt like I deserved to hang on to it for at least one evening, after the week I'd had. 'That was like fourteen *years* ago. You're still pissed off about it?'

Dec was waving a finger at me, shaking his head. 'Not the point. The point is, you got a slap on the wrist and the scholarship kid got a kicking. No, hear me out, I'm talking here' – when I flopped back in my seat, eyes to the ceiling. 'I'm not saying Armitage did that out of badness. I'm saying I went in there petrified that I was going to get kicked out, wind up down the shithole community school. You went in there knowing that even if you were expelled, your ma and da would just find you another lovely school. That's the difference.'

He was getting loud. The brunette was losing interest in me – too much electricity in the air around me, too much hassle, on which I totally agreed with her. 'So,' Dec said. 'What are you?'

'I don't even know what you're *talking* about any more.'

'Get it over with,' Sean said, not glancing up from his phone. 'For fuck's sake.'

Dec said, 'You're a lucky little prick, is what you are. That's all. Just a lucky little prick.'

I was looking for a smart retort when all of a sudden it caught me, warm and buoying and irresistible as a thermal current: he was right, he was speaking the absolute truth, and it was nothing to get annoyed about, it was pure joy. I took what felt like my deepest breath in days; it came out in a rush of laughter. 'I am,' I said. 'That's exactly what I am. I am one lucky bastard.'

Dec was eyeing me, not done yet, deciding where to take this next. 'Amen,' said Sean, putting his phone down and raising his glass. 'Here's to lucky little pricks, and to just plain little pricks,' and he tilted his glass at Dec.

I started laughing all over again and clinked my glass against his, and after a moment Dec laughed loudest of all and clashed his glass against both of ours, and we went back to arguing over where to go for our holiday.

I'd gone right off the idea of bringing them home with me, though. When Dec was in this mode he got unpredictable as well as aggressive – he wasn't brave enough to do anything really disastrous, but still, I wasn't in the mood. Things still felt a bit precarious, wobbly at the joints, as if they shouldn't be prodded too hard. I wanted to lie back on my sofa and smoke my hash and melt nicely into a giggly puddle, not keep an eye on Dec while he buzzed around my living room collecting things to use in a makeshift game of bowling and I tried not to glance at anything fragile in case it gave him ideas. Deep down I still hold this against him: twenty-eight is old enough to have outgrown that particular brand of stupid crap, and if Dec had managed to do that, he and Sean would have come home with me and and and.

After that things go fuzzy again. The next thing I remember with any clarity is saying goodbye to the guys outside the pub, closing time, loose noisy clumps of people arguing over where to go next, heads bending to cigarette lighters, girls teetering on their heels, yellow-lit taxi signs cruising past – 'Listen,' Dec was telling me, with hyperfocused drunken sincerity, 'no, listen. Joking aside. I'm delighted that it all worked out for you. I am. You're a good person. Toby, I'm serious, I'm over the moon that it—' He would have gone on like that indefinitely, only Sean flagged down a taxi and steered Dec into it with a hand between his shoulder blades, and then gave me a nod and a wave and strolled off towards Portobello and Audrey.

I could have taken a taxi, but it was a nice night, still and cool, with a soft easy edge that promised more spring in the morning. I was drunk but not to the point of unsteadiness; home was less than a half-hour walk away. And I was starving; I wanted a takeaway, something spicy and pungent and enormous. I buttoned my over-coat and started walking.

A flame-juggler at the top of Grafton Street whipping up his straggly crowd to a rhythmic clap, drunk guys roaring unintelligible encouragement or distraction. A homeless guy curled in a doorway, wrapped in a blue sleeping bag, out cold through the whole thing. While I walked I rang Melissa; she wouldn't go to bed until we'd had our good-night phone call and I didn't want to keep her up any later, and anyway I couldn't wait till I got home. 'I miss you,' I said, when she answered. 'You're lovely.'

She laughed. 'So are you. Where are you?'

The sound of her voice made me press the phone closer to my ear. 'Stephen's Green. I was in Hogan's with the lads. Now I'm walking home and thinking about how lovely you are.'

'So come over.'

'I can't. I'm drunk.'

'I don't care.'

'No. I'll stink of booze and I'll snore in your ear, and you'll dump me and go off with some smooth-talking billionaire who has a pod machine to purify his blood when he comes home from the pub.'

'I don't know any smooth-talking billionaires. I promise.'

'Oh, you do. They're always there. They just don't swoop until they see their chance. Like mosquitoes.'

She laughed again. The sound of it warmed me all over. I had hardly expected her to sulk or pout or hang up on me for neglecting her, but the ready sweetness of her was another reminder that Dec was right, I was a lucky bastard. I remembered listening with slightly self-congratulatory awe to his stories of elaborate drama with exes, people locking themselves or each other into or out of various unlikely places while everyone sobbed and/or yelled and/or pleaded – none of that stuff would even occur to Melissa. 'Can I come over tomorrow? As soon as I'm human again?'

'Course! If it's nice again, we can have lunch out in the garden and fall asleep in the sun and snore together.'

'You don't snore. You make happy little purry noises.'

'Ew. Attractive.'

'It is. It's lovely. You're lovely. Did I mention you're lovely?'

'You are drunk, silly.'

'I told you.' The real reason I didn't want to go over to Melissa's – actually I did want to, very badly, but the reason I wasn't going to – was, of course, that I was drunk enough that I might find myself telling her about the Gouger episode. I wasn't worried that she would dump me, or anything extreme like that, but it would have bothered her, and I cared a lot about not bothering Melissa.

I wanted as much of her as I could get before I hung up, though. 'Who bought the steampunk armchair?'

'Oh, Toby, I wish you could have seen them! This couple in their forties, all in yacht-club gear, she had one of those stripy Breton tops, you'd never expect— I thought *maybe* a blanket, if the colours weren't too wild for them, but they went straight for the armchair. I think it must have reminded them of something; they kept looking at each other and laughing, and after about five minutes they decided they didn't care whether it went with anything else in their house, they had to have it. I love when people are unexpected.'

'We'll have to celebrate tomorrow. I'll bring prosecco.'

'Yes! Bring the one we had last time, the—' A yawn caught her off guard. 'Sorry, it's not the company! I'm just—'

'It's late. You shouldn't have waited up for me.'

'I don't mind. I like saying good night.'

'Me too. Now go to sleep. I love you.'

'I love you too. Night-night.' She blew me a kiss.

'Night-night.'

For some reason this is the mistake – hardly a mistake, really, what's wrong with having a few pints on a Friday night after a stressful week, what's wrong with wanting the girl you love to think the best of you? – this is the choice to which I return over and over, picking at it compulsively as if I could somehow peel it off and throw it away: one less shot of whiskey with the lads, one less pint, a sandwich at my desk as I re-jigged the exhibition programme, and I would have been sober enough that I would have trusted myself to go over to Melissa's. I've thought about that might-have-been night so much that I know every moment of it: spinning her off her feet in a hug when she opened her door, *Congratulations! I knew you'd do it!*; the soft breathing curl of her in bed, her hair tickling my chin; lazy Saturday brunch in our favourite café, walk by the canal to see the swans, Melissa swinging our clasped hands. I miss it as ferociously as if it were something real and solid and irreplaceable that I somehow managed to mislay and could somehow, if only I knew the trick, salvage and keep safe.

'You didn't hang up.'

'Neither did you.'

'Night-night. Sleep tight.'

'Safe home. Night-night.' Kisses, more kisses.

Baggot Street was silent and near-deserted, long rows of massive Georgian houses, the fabulous wrought-iron whorls of old street-lamps. Smooth tickticktick of bicycle wheels coming up behind me and a tall guy in a trilby skimmed past, sitting very erect with his arms folded neatly across his chest. Two people kissing in a doorway, fall of smooth green hair, ruffle of lilac. I must have picked up Indian food somewhere although I can't imagine where, because the air around me was rich with coriander and fennel, making my mouth water. The street felt warm and strange and very wide, full of some odd coded enchantment. An old man in beard and flat cap doing a shuffling half-dance to himself, fingers spread, among the great trees in the centre divider. A girl across the street walking fast, black coat swirling around her ankles, head down over the phone that shone blue-white in her hand like a fairy-tale jewel. Delicate dusty fanlights, golden glow in a tiny high window. Dark water under the canal bridge, glitter and rush.

I must have made it home without incident – although how do I know, how do I know what was going on just beyond the corner of my eye, who might have been watching from the doorways, what might have detached itself from a shadow to pad soft-footed behind me? But at any rate I must have made it home without anything happening that set off warning bells. I must have eaten my Indian food and maybe watched something on Netflix (although wouldn't I have been too drunk to bother following a plotline?), or maybe played some Xbox (although that seems unlikely; after the last few days I was sick to death of my Xbox). I must have forgotten to turn on the alarm – in spite of being on the ground floor, I only bothered with it about half the time; the kitchen window was a little loose and if the wind was in the wrong direction it rattled and set the alarm shrieking hysterically, and it wasn't like I lived in some crime-ridden urban jungle. And at some point I must have changed into my pyjamas and gone to bed, and fallen drunkenly and contentedly asleep.

•

Something woke me. At first I wasn't sure what; I had a clear memory of a sound, a neat crack, but I couldn't tell whether it had been inside my dream (tall black guy with dreadlocks and a surfboard, laughing, refusing to tell me something I needed to know) or outside. The room was dark, only the faintest streetlamp glow outlining the curtains. I lay still, the last of the dream still cobwebbing my mind, and listened.

Nothing. And then: a drawer sliding open or closed, just on the other side of the wall, in my living room. A soft thud.

The first thing I thought was the guys, Dec sneaking in to mess with me as revenge for the hair-plug thing, one time in college Sean and I had woken him to our bare arses pressed up against his bedroom window, but Dec didn't have a key – my parents had a spare, maybe some surprise but surely they would have waited till morning – Melissa? couldn't wait to see me? but she hated being out alone at night— But some animal part of me knew; I had sat bolt upright, and all the time my heart was laying down a grim relentless beat.

A brief murmur from the living room. Pale swish of a torch-beam past the crack under the bedroom door.

On my bedside table was a candlestick that Melissa had brought over from the shop a few months back, a beautiful thing made to look like the black wrought-iron railings outside old Dublin homes: barley-sugar-twist stem and graceful fleur-de-lys swoops at the top, the centre prong sharpened to hold the candle (stub of melted wax, a night with wine in bed and Nina Simone). I don't remember getting up but I was on my feet with both hands wrapped tight around the candlestick, testing the heft of it and feeling my way softly towards the bedroom door. I felt like an idiot, when obviously nothing bad was happening, I would terrify poor Melissa, Dec would never let me live this down—

The door to the living room was half open, a beam of light wavering through the darkness inside. I smashed the door back with the candlestick and slapped the light switch, and the room flared into brightness so that it was a blinking half-second before I could see.

My living room, espresso cup from that morning still on the coffee table, papers strewn on the floor beneath open drawers, and two men: both with tracksuit tops pulled up high over their mouths and baseball caps pulled down low over their eyes, both frozen in mid-motion to stare at me. One was turned towards my open patio door, hunched clumsily around my laptop; the other was stretching up behind my TV, reaching for the wall mount, his torch still poised in the other hand. They so clearly and utterly didn't belong there that they looked ludicrous, superimposed, a bad Photoshop job.

After the first stunned instant I yelled, 'Get out!' The outrage slammed through my whole body like rocket fuel, I'd never felt anything like it, the sheer nonchalant audacity of these scumbags coming into my home— 'Out! Get the fuck out! Out!'

Then I realised they weren't running for the door and after that things get a bit confused, I don't know who moved first but all of a sudden the guy with the torch was halfway across the floor to me and I was launching myself at him. I think I got in a pretty good crack to his head with the candlestick, that at least, but our momentum threw us both off balance and we grappled at each other to stay standing. He stank, body odour and something strange and milky – I sometimes still catch a whiff of it in a shop and find myself gagging before I understand why. He was stronger than I had expected, wiry and twisting, he had me by the candlestick arm and I couldn't get another swing – I was jamming short furious punches into his stomach but I didn't have room to get any force behind them, we were pressed too close, stumbling. His thumb stabbed into my eye and I yelled and then something hit me in the jaw, blue-white light splintered everywhere and I was falling.

I landed on my back on the floor. My eyes and nose were

streaming, my mouth was filling with blood and I spat a mouthful, my tongue was on fire. Someone shouting, *stupid cunt you*— I was up on my elbows and pushing myself backwards away from them with my feet *think you're fucking great* and trying to pull myself up by the arm of the sofa and

Someone was kicking me in the stomach. *I'll fucking burst you*— I managed to roll away, retching in great raw heaves, but the kicks kept coming, into my side now, solid and systematic. There was no pain, not exactly, but there was something else, worse, a hideous jarring sense of wrongness. I couldn't breathe. I realised with a terrible detached clarity that I might die, that they needed to stop right now or it would be too late, but I couldn't find the breath to tell them this one unbearably important thing

I tried to scrabble away, flat on my stomach, fingers clawing uselessly. A kick to my arse driving my face further into the carpet, and another and another. A man's laugh, high and amped up and triumphal.

From somewhere:

—*anyone else*—?

Nah or they'd

Have a look. —*girlfriend*—

The laugh again, that laugh, with a new avidity driving it. *Ah yeah man.*

I couldn't remember whether Melissa was there or not. On a fresh wave of terror I tried to push myself up off the ground but I couldn't, my arms were weak as ribbons, every breath was a thick ragged snuffle through blood and snot and carpet fibres. The kicking had stopped; the hugeness of the relief washed away the last of my strength.

Scraping sounds, grunts of effort. The candlestick, rolled away under an overturned chair. I couldn't even think about reaching for it but somehow it clicked a piece into place in my jumbled brain, *night-night sleep tight*, Melissa safe at her place, thank God— The light jabbing my eyeballs. Crash of tumbling objects, again, again. The green geometric pattern of my curtains, stretching upwards at an unfamiliar angle, fading and clearing and fading

That's it

—has any—
—fuck it. Go
Hang on is he?

A blur of dark moving closer. A sharp jab to my ribs and I balled up, coughing, pawing feebly against the next kick, but it didn't come. Instead a gloved hand came down into view and curled around the candlestick, and I had just time to wonder dizzily why they would want that before a vast soundless explosion blotted out the air and everything was gone, everything.

•

I don't know how long I was out. None of the next part holds together; all I have is isolated moments, framed like slides and with the same lucent, untethered quality, nothing in between them but blackness and the harsh click of one rotating away as the next drops into place.

Rough carpet against my face and pain everywhere; the pain was astounding, breathtaking, but that didn't seem particularly important or even particularly connected to me, what mattered the terrifying part was that I was blind, utterly, I couldn't

click

trying to push myself up from the floor but my arms were juddering like a seizure, went from under me and face-first onto the carpet

click

lunatic swipes and dabbles of red on white fabric, rich metallic reek of blood

click

on hands and knees, vomiting, warm liquid spilling onto my fingers

click

ragged blue chunks of china, scattered (in retrospect I figure these must have been the remnants of my espresso cup but at the time my mind wasn't working that way, nothing had any meaning or any essence, nothing was anything except there)

click

crawling through an endless field of debris that shifted and crackled, my knees slipping, the edges of my vision seething

click

the corridor, stretching away for miles, brown and beige and pulsing. A flick of movement far far away at the end, something white

holding myself up against the wall, staggering forwards jerkily as if all my joints had been unstrung. A terrible cawing noise coming from somewhere, rhythmic and impersonal; I tried desperately to speed up, to get away before it could attack, but I couldn't break out of nightmare slow-motion and it was still there, in my ears, at my back, all around me (and now of course I'm pretty sure it was my own breathing, but at the time etcetera etcetera)

click

brown wood, a door. Scrabbling at it, grate of my fingernails, a hoarse moaning that wouldn't form into words

click

a man's voice urgently demanding something, a woman's face skewed with horror, mouth wide, pink quilted dressing gown, and then one of my legs went liquid and the blindness came roaring back in and I disappeared.

2

After that came a long period – about forty-eight hours, as far as I can reconstruct events – where nothing made much sense. Obviously there are big dark patches where I was out cold, and I'm unpleasantly aware that I'm unlikely ever to know exactly what went on during those. I did ask my mother once, but she got a white, tight look around her mouth and said, 'I can't, Toby,' and that was the end of that.

Even when I started to wake up off and on, my memories are dislocated fragments arranged in no particular order. People barking at me, demanding things from me; sometimes I tried to do what they wanted – *squeeze my hand*, I remember, and *open your eyes* – to make them happy so they would leave me alone, but sometimes I just ignored them and eventually they went away again. My mother slumped in a plastic chair, silver-blond hair straggling loose and a green cardigan falling off one shoulder. She looked terrible and I wanted to put an arm around her and tell her that everything would be fine, she was getting wound up over nothing, all I had done was jump out of my grandparents' tree and break my ankle; I wanted to make her laugh till her slim rigid shoulders relaxed, but all I could manage was a clumsy grunting sound that sent her hurtling from the chair towards me, mouth stretched wide, *Toby oh sweetheart can you*— and then more darkness. My hand, with a chunky, shocking arrangement of needle and tube and bandage attached to the back of it, embedded deep in my flesh like some grotesque parasite. My father leaning against a wall, unshaven and baggy-eyed, blowing into a paper cup. There was an animal pacing silently back and forth in front of him, a long-muscled tan creature that looked like some kind of wild dog, maybe a jackal, but I couldn't focus on it properly enough to be sure; my dad didn't seem to have noticed it and it occurred to me that maybe I should warn him, but that would have felt silly when quite possibly he had brought the animal himself, to cheer me up, which it wasn't really doing but maybe later it was going to curl up on the bed with me and that would do something about the pain— The pain was so huge and diffuse that it felt like an element intrinsic to the air, something to be taken for granted because it had always been there and would never go away. And yet it's not what I remember most vividly when I think of those first couple of days, not the pain; what I remember is the sensation that I was being methodically pulled apart into gobbets, body and mind, as easily as a wet tissue, and that there was nothing at all I could do to resist.

When the parts of me actually managed to reassemble themselves, tentatively and to whatever extent and in whatever form, it was night. I was flat on my back in an uncomfortable bed in an unfamiliar room, some part of which was partitioned off by a long pale curtain. I was much too hot. My lips were parched; my mouth felt like it was lined with dried clay. One of my hands was tethered to a tube that ran upwards into shadow. Window blinds ticked fitfully in a draught; a machine beeped faintly and regularly.

It occurred to me, gradually, that I must be in a hospital. This seemed like a good idea, given the kind of pain I was in. Just about everything hurt. The epicentre seemed to be a spot just behind my right temple; it felt full to bursting with a dark, hideous, liquid throbbing that made me too afraid to put up my hand and feel it.

The rush of sheer terror, once started, wouldn't stop. My heart was racing so frantically that I thought I might be having a heart attack; I was panting like a runner and every breath flared pain through my left side, which set the terror rising even more wildly. I knew there had to be a button somewhere nearby that I could press for a nurse, but I couldn't afford to do that: what if she gave me something that knocked me out, and I never managed to struggle back up again?

I lay very still for a long time, gripping fistfuls of bedsheet and fighting not to scream. Thin stripes of grey light slid between the slats of the window blinds. Somewhere beyond the curtain a woman was crying, quietly and terribly.

At the heart of the fear was the fact that I had no idea how I had got there. I remembered something about Hogan's and Sean and Dec, walking home, phone kisses to Melissa or had that been another night? and then nothing. If someone had tried to kill me – and it certainly felt like they had, and had come pretty close to getting the job done – then what was to stop them coming after me in here, what was to stop them being behind the curtain right now? Sore, weak, shaking, staked down by tubes and God knew what else, I wasn't going to be much use against a merciless determined killer— The blinds clicked, and a spasm of fear nearly shot me out of the bed.

I don't know how long I lay there, trawling doggedly and desperately through the ragged shards of my mind. The woman in the other bed was still crying, which was at least slightly reassuring: as long as she kept going, I could be fairly sure there was no one creeping up on her side of the curtain. I was pretty close to tears myself by the time I finally managed to come up with one image: my living room, sudden blaze of light, two men frozen and staring at me.

Maybe this sounds strange, but it came as a huge relief. Burglars had beaten me up: it could happen to anyone, and now it was over and I was safe; they were hardly going to track me down in hospital to finish the job. All I had to do was lie there and get better.

Slowly my heart rate calmed. I think I even smiled, through it all, into the dark. That's how convinced I was, you see, how utterly and blessedly certain, that it was all over.

•

In the morning a doctor came to see me. I was awake, more or less – the noise level out in the corridor had been building for a while, brisk voices, footsteps, the sinister rumble of trolley wheels – but I could tell from the pale, head-cracking blast of light through the window that it was early. Behind the curtain someone was telling the woman in the other bed, with the cool, heavily emphasised firmness you would use on someone else's tantrumming toddler, 'You'll just have to accept that everything we've done has been within best-practice guidelines.'

I must have made some sound, because there was a rustle off to the side and a voice said gently, 'Toby.'

I flinched, sending pain crashing everywhere, but it was my father: leaning forwards in a chair, rumpled and red-eyed. 'Toby, it's me. How are you feeling?'

'OK,' I said blurrily. Actually I was feeling a lot less Zen than I had when I went to sleep. Everything hurt even worse, which wasn't supposed to be happening; I was supposed to be getting better, and the possibility that things might not be that straightforward set the panic scritch-scratching at the edges of my mind again. I managed to get up the courage to touch two fingertips gingerly to the spot behind my right temple, but it seemed to be covered in a thick pad of gauze, which didn't tell me anything useful, and the movement ratcheted up the pain another notch or two.

'Do you want anything? A drink of water?'

What I wanted was something to put over my eyes. I was trying to pull together the focus to ask for it when one edge of the curtain twitched aside.

'Good morning,' said the doctor, putting his head through the gap. 'How are you today?'

'Oh,' I said, struggling to sit up and wincing. 'OK.' My tongue was about twice its usual thickness, and sore on one side. I sounded like some bad actor playing handicapped.

'Are you feeling well enough to talk?'

'Yeah. Yes.' I wasn't, but I urgently needed to know what the fuck was going on.

'Well, that's a big step,' the doctor said, closing the curtain behind him and nodding to my father. 'Let me give you a hand there.' He fiddled with something and the head of my bed lifted, with a displeased wheezing sound, so that I was half-sitting. 'How's that?'

The movement made my vision swoop and dip like I was on a fairground ride. 'Good,' I said. 'Thanks.'

'Good good.' He was a young guy, only a few years older than me; tall, with a round, bland face and a receding hairline. 'I'm Dr Coogan' – or it may have been Cregan or Duggan or something totally unrelated, who knows. 'Can you tell me your name?'

Just the fact that he was asking, like I might actually not know, was disturbing. It brought back a churning flash of chaos, loud voice snapping in my ear, bright light swinging and bouncing, my whole body convulsing with dry retches— 'Toby Hennessy.'

'Mm-hm.' He pulled over a chair and sat down. He was holding a sheaf of cryptic-looking paper that I assumed was my chart, whatever that meant. 'Do you know what month it is?'

'April.'

'It is indeed. Do you know where you are?'

'In a hospital.'

'Right again.' He made some kind of note on the chart. 'How are you feeling?'

'OK. Kind of sore.'

He glanced up at that. 'Where's the pain?'

'My head. It's pretty bad.' This was an understatement – my head was pounding so hideously that it felt like my brain was actually rocking with the force of every heartbeat – but I didn't want him to go off in search of painkillers and leave me without any explanations. 'And my face. And my side. And' – I couldn't think of the doctor-appropriate term for 'right above my arse', I knew there was one but it wouldn't come out – 'here?' The movement pulled an involuntary noise out of me.

The doctor nodded. He had small, clear, shallow eyes, like a toy's. 'Yes. Your tailbone is cracked, and so are four of your ribs. There's nothing we can do to help with those, but they should all heal on their own with no lasting damage; nothing to worry about. And I can certainly get you something for the pain.' He held out a finger. 'Can you squeeze my finger?'

I did. His finger was long and a bit chubby and very dry, and there was something nasty about touching it that intimately.

'Mm-hm. And with the other hand?'

I did it again with the other hand. I didn't need medical training to tell the difference: my right hand felt the same as always; my left had a dreamlike cotton-wool quality that terrified me. My grip was soft as a child's.

I glanced up at the doctor, but he gave no sign that he'd noticed anything. 'Very good.' He made another note. 'May I?'

He was indicating the bedsheet. 'Sure,' I said, disorientated. I had no idea what he wanted to do. My father was watching in silence, elbows on his knees, fingers steepled in front of his mouth.

The doctor flipped back the sheet, expertly, revealing my bare legs – I had a couple of ugly bruises – and the rucked-up skirt of the hospital gown, which was a greying white with a discreetly perky print of little blue diamonds. 'Now,' he said, placing the palm of his hand to the bottom of my foot. 'Can you point your foot against my hand?'

Flex, extend, other foot, left weaker than the right again, although not as badly, surely the difference wasn't as big— There was something horrifying about being exposed and handled so efficiently and impersonally. He was acting like my body was meat, not attached to a person at all. It took all my willpower not to jerk my foot away from his hand.

'Good,' he said. 'Now I want you to lift your leg against the pressure of my hand. All right?'

He tweaked my gown straight and put a flat palm on my thigh. 'Wait,' I blurted out. 'What's wrong with me?'

I half-expected him to slap me down like he had the woman in the other bed, but she must have just been neurotic or a pain in the arse or something, because instead he took his hand off my leg and sat back in the chair. 'You were attacked,' he said gently. 'Do you have any memory of it?'

'Yes. Not all of, the whole thing, but— I mean, that's not what I mean. Do I have a, a—' I couldn't come up with the word. 'My head. Did they break it? Or what?'

'You were hit in the head at least twice. Once probably with a fist, here' – he pointed to the left side of his jaw – 'and once with a heavy sharp object, here.' That spot behind my right temple. I heard a tight breath from my father. 'You had a concussion, but that seems to have resolved well. You also have a skull fracture, which caused an extradural haematoma – that's a bleed between the skull and the outer covering of the brain, caused by a ruptured blood vessel. Don't worry' – I wasn't really following a lot of this, but at that my eyes must have widened, because he raised one hand reassuringly – 'we corrected that surgically, as soon as you came in. We drilled a small

40

hole in your skull and drained the blood, and that relieved the pressure on your brain. You were very lucky.'

Some vague part of me felt that this was a fairly outrageous thing to say to someone in my situation, but a bigger part seized on the comfort of it – lucky, yes, I was lucky, the guy was a doctor after all, he knew what he was talking about, I didn't want to be like the whiny woman in the other bed. 'I guess,' I said.

'You were indeed. You had what we call a lucid interval, after the attack. It's fairly common with this kind of injury. We're estimating that you were unconscious for an hour or more, due to the concussion, but then you came to and were able to call for help before you lost consciousness again?'

He blinked at me inquiringly. 'I guess,' I said again, after a confused moment. I couldn't remember calling anyone. I still couldn't remember much of anything, actually, just dark seething flashes that made me not want to look too closely.

'Very lucky,' the doctor repeated, leaning forwards to make sure I understood the seriousness of this. 'If you hadn't managed to get help, and the haematoma had been left untreated for another hour or so, it would almost certainly have been fatal.' And when I stared at him blankly, unable to do anything at all with that: 'You nearly died.'

'Oh,' I said, after a moment. 'I didn't realise.'

We looked at each other. It felt like he was waiting for something from me, but I had no idea what. The woman in the other bed was crying again.

'Now what?' I asked, managing to keep most of the fluttering panic out of my voice. 'I mean, my hand. My leg. Are they going to—? When are they going to—?'

'Too soon to know any of that,' the doctor said briskly. He wasn't looking at me any more, he was doing something with his notes, and that made the panic surge higher. 'The neurologist will be around to have a—'

'I just want a, a, a—' I couldn't come up with the word, and I was afraid this was where he would put on that toddler-quelling voice and tell me to stop asking questions and behave myself—

'We understand you can't give us any guarantees,' my father said, quietly but firmly. 'We'd just like a general idea of what to expect.'

After a moment the doctor nodded and folded his hands on top of the notes. 'There's often some damage after an injury like this,' he said. 'Yours seems to be relatively minor, although I can't say anything definitive based on a bedside assessment. One common effect is seizures, so you'll have to be watchful for those, but they usually peter out over time. We'll be referring you to a physical therapist who can help with the left-side weakness, and there are occupational therapists available if you find yourself having trouble with concentration or memory.' His tone was so matter-of-fact and reasonable that he actually had me nodding along, like all of this – *seizures, occupational therapist*, stuff straight out of some melodramatic medical show light-years away from my real life – was perfectly normal. Only some tiny peripheral part of me began to understand, with a sickening drop, that this was in fact my real life now. 'You can expect most of the improvement to come over the next six months, but it can continue for up to two years. The neurologist will . . .'

He kept talking, but out of nowhere I was swamped by a tidal wave of exhaustion. His face doubled and blurred to nonsense; his voice receded into a faraway meaningless gabble. I wanted to tell him that I needed those painkillers now please, but summoning up the energy to talk seemed impossibly hard, too much for anyone to expect of anyone, and the pain went with me down into a thick treacherous sleep.

•

I was in the hospital for just under two weeks. It wasn't that bad, all things considered. The evening of my chat with the doctor, they (apologetically, with some autopilot mumble about overcrowding) found me a single room, which was a relief: the neurotic woman in the other bed kept crying and it was starting to grate on me, drill its way into my dreams. The new room was bright and airy and quiet, and I gave myself a mental pat on the back for having good health insurance even though I hadn't expected to need it for decades.

I did a lot of sleeping, and when I was awake there was usually someone with me. During the day it was mostly my mother, who had ditched work and thrown everything into the department's lap – she teaches eighteenth-century history at Trinity – as soon as she got the phone call. She brought me things: a fan because the room was mercilessly hot, endless bottles of water and juice and Lucozade because I needed to stay hydrated, art postcards and bunches of tulips, snacks I had liked as a kid (Monster Munch, cheesy popcorn that smelled violently of vomit), cards from my aunts and uncles, a baffling assortment of books, a pack of cards, a hipstery Lego-plated Rubik's Cube. I touched almost none of it and within a few days the room was getting a weird overgrown look, as if random stuff was popping up on every available surface through spontaneous generation and sooner or later the nurses would find me buried under a heap of cupcakes and an accordion.

I'd always got along well with my mother. She's smart and spiky and funny, with a keen sense of beauty and a lovely, expansive capacity for happiness, someone I would have liked even if we weren't related. Even when I was a mildly rebellious teenager, my fights (standard-issue stuff, why can't I stay out later and it's so unfair that you give me hassle about homework) had been with my father, almost never with her. Since I'd moved out of home I had rung her a couple of times a week, met her for lunch every month or two, out of genuine affection and enjoyment, not duty; I picked up odd little presents for her now and then, texted her funny things Richard said that I knew she would appreciate. Even the look of her warmed me, her long-legged unselfconscious stride with coat flapping, the wide fine arcs of her eyebrows quirking together and up and down in tandem with whatever story I was telling. So it came as a nasty surprise to both of us when her hospital visits drove me crazy.

For one thing she couldn't keep her hands off me: one of them was always stroking my hair or resting on my foot or finding my hand among the bedclothes, and even aside from the pain I was finding that I loathed being touched, so intensely that sometimes I couldn't stop myself from jerking away. And she kept wanting to talk about that night – how was I feeling? (Fine.) Did I want to talk about it? (No.) Did I have any idea who the men had been, had they followed me home, maybe they'd spotted me in the pub and realised my coat was expensive and— At this stage I spent most of the time foggily but firmly convinced that the break-in had been Gouger and one of his Borstal buddies, getting revenge on me for having him booted out of the exhibition, but I was still much too confused about the whole thing to explain it to my mother even if I had wanted to. I retreated into grunts that got ruder and ruder until she backed off, but an hour later she would circle back to it, unable to help herself – Was I sleeping all right? Was I having nightmares? Did I remember much?

The real problem, I suppose, was that my mother was badly shaken up. She put a lot of willpower into covering it, but I knew the artificial, over-calm cheerfulness from childhood crises (*OK, sweetheart, let's get the blood cleaned off so we can see whether you need to go to Dr Mairéad for the blue glue! Maybe she'll have stickers again!*) and it set my teeth on edge. Occasionally the façade slipped and a terrible, raw horror showed through, and that sent me into paroxysms of sheer fury: obviously she had had a bad couple of days, but now I was out of danger and she had nothing to worry about, her hands were both working perfectly, her vision wasn't stuttering and doubling, nobody was giving her speeches about occupational therapy, what the hell was her problem?

All I wanted to do, almost the moment I saw her, was pick a fight. Whatever else the head injury had done, it didn't stop me doing that – on the contrary: most of the time I could just about form simple sentences, but going on the attack seemed to unleash a new and ugly fluency. All it took was one misstep from my mother, one phrase or look that flicked me on the raw – and even at gunpoint I couldn't have justified why certain things counted as missteps, but they did – and we were off.

'I brought you peaches. Will you have one now? I can wash them in the—'

'No. Thanks. I'm not hungry.'

'Well' – dialling up the cheery note, bending to rummage in the stuffed plastic bag beside her chair – 'I brought pretzels, too. How about those? The little ones that you—'

'I *said* I'm not hungry.'

'Oh. All right. I'll leave them here for later.'

The soupy, martyred forbearance on her face made me want to throw up. 'Jesus, that look. Can you stop giving me that look?'

Her face tightened. 'What look?'

'*Oh, poor dear Toby, he's not himself, must make allowances, the poor thing doesn't know what he's saying—*'

'You've been seriously hurt. Everything I've read says it's normal for you to be a bit—'

'I know exactly what I'm saying. I'm not a fucking *vegetable*. I'm not drooling into my puréed prunes. Is that what you're telling people, that I'm *not myself*? Is that why no one's been in? Susanna and Leon haven't even rung me—'

My mother was blinking rapidly, staring past my ear into the light from the window. I had a horrible feeling that she was trying not to cry, and an equally horrible one that if she pulled that crap I was going to throw her out of my room. 'All I've said is that you might not be feeling well enough yet. You haven't seemed like you want to talk to people.'

'You didn't bother to ask me what I thought? You just decided that I was too *not myself* to make a great big decision like that all on my own?' It was a relief to be able to blame this on my mother. I didn't in fact want to talk to my cousins, but we had grown up together, and although by this stage we weren't living in each other's pockets any more – I saw Susanna a few times a year at Christmas and birthdays, Leon maybe once a year when he was over from Amsterdam or Barcelona or whichever city he was currently drifting around – it had still stung when they didn't bother.

'If you want to see everyone, I can—'

'If I want to see them, I can tell them myself. Or do you think I'm too brain-damaged for that? You think I'm basically a toddler now, I need Mummy to set up my playdates?'

'OK' – with maddening care, hands clasped tightly in her lap – 'then what would you like me to tell them, when they ask about you?

They've all been Googling head injuries, and of course there's such a wide range of outcomes that they have no idea what to—'

'Don't tell them anything. *Nothing.*' My family swarming and picking like ants over my carcass, I could just see it – my aunt Louisa pulling soppy compassion-faces, Aunt Miriam debating which of my chakras would need unblocking, Uncle Oliver pontificating about some blather he'd picked up on Wikipedia and Uncle Phil nodding sagely through it all— It made me want to punch someone. 'Or I know, I've got a genius idea, tell them I'm fine and to mind their own fucking business. How's that?'

'They're worried about you, Toby. They just—'

'Oh, shit, I'm sorry, is this hard on them? Are they having a *hard time* with this?'

And so on and on. I had never been cruel before, never, even in school where I had been one of the cool kids and could have got away with anything I had never once bullied anyone. Finding myself doing it now gave me a rush of savage, breathless glee and of wretchedness – glee because it was a new weapon although I'm not sure exactly how it was supposed to protect me (next time I ran into burglars I could totally flay them with sarcasm, I suppose) and wretchedness because I had liked being a kind person and now I couldn't find my way back to that, it seemed lost for good in some dark expanse of smoking rubble, and altogether by the time my mother left every day both she and I were exhausted.

In the early evenings my father came. He was a solicitor, always up to his ears instructing barristers on some impenetrable financial case; he came straight from work, bringing with him the same unflappable, esoteric atmosphere of expensive suits and half-secrets that used to sweep in the door with him every evening when I was a kid. Unlike my mother, he could tell when I wasn't in the mood for chitchat, and unlike with my mother I had no urge to goad him into no-winner fights. Mostly he would ask a few polite questions about how I was feeling and whether I needed anything, then pull a rolled and battered paperback from his coat pocket (P. G. Wodehouse, Thomas Keneally), settle himself in the visitor's chair and read quietly for hours on end. If I had been capable of finding anything restful or comforting, I think it would have been that: the regular rhythm of his page-turning, the occasional soft huff of laughter, the clean lines of his profile against the darkening window. Often I fell asleep while he was there, and those were the only sleeps in that place that weren't ragged and precarious, shadowed by tainted dreams and by the possibility of never waking up.

Melissa came whenever she could find someone to mind the shop, even for an hour, and again in the evenings. To be honest, the first time she came, I was horrified. Even to myself I reeked of sweat and nameless chemicals, I was still wearing a hospital gown, and I knew I looked like shit. When I had dragged myself to the bathroom and looked in the mirror, it had been a shock. I was used to being, frankly, good-looking, in an easy, straightforward way that didn't require much thought from anyone concerned; I have thick smooth fair hair, very blue eyes, and the kind of open, boyish face that instantly makes both guys and girls want to like me. The guy in the flyspecked mirror was a whole other story. My hair was a stringy, dirty brown and there was a big shaved patch on the right side of my head, with an ugly red wound-line running across it, studded with thick, brutal staples. One eyelid had an ugly, stoned droop, my jaw was puffy and mottled with purple; a big chip was missing from one of my top front teeth, and I had a fat lip. Even in those few days, I had lost weight; I'd been on the lean side to start with, and now there were hollows under my cheekbones and jaw that gave me a startling, starved urgency. Several days' worth of stubble made my face look unwashed, and my eyes were bloodshot and had an unfocused middle-distance stare that put me somewhere halfway between dumb and psycho. I looked like the lowlife in a zombie movie who isn't going to make it past the first half-hour.

And there was Melissa, airy gold head and whirl of flowered dress in the opening door, a fairy creature from some faraway world of butterflies and dewdrops. I knew she would take one look at this grim place and me – anything worthwhile deliberately, methodically stripped away, nothing left but the basest mechanics and fluids and stenches of life obscenely exposed – and she would never see me the same way again. I didn't expect her to turn and run – for all her softness, Melissa has a straight-backed, unwavering code of loyalty that I knew would not include dumping your brain-injured boyfriend before he even got his IV out – but I braced myself for the jolt of horror across her face, the clench of determination as she set herself to do her duty.

But instead she came flying across the floor without even a second's pause, arms reaching – 'Oh Toby, oh darling—' just stopping herself at my bedside in case she hurt me, hands fluttering inches from me, white face and round stunned eyes as if she had only that moment heard what had happened – 'Your poor face, oh Toby—'

I laughed out loud with sheer relief. 'Come here,' I said, managing not to sound too thick-tongued, 'I'm not breakable,' and I wrapped my arms around her (shot of agony through my ribs, but I didn't care) and squeezed her close. I felt her tears hot on my neck, and she laughed through a sniffle – 'So silly, I'm just so *glad*—'

'Shh,' I said, cupping her soft head, stroking her back. The honeysuckle smell of her, the delicacy of her neck under my hand – I felt a breathtaking rush of love towards her, for being there and for breaking down so that I was the strong one comforting her. 'Shh, honey. It's OK. It's all going to be fine.' And we stayed there like that, sweet spring breeze stirring the blinds and the sun throwing ovals of wavering light through the myriad water bottles, my tailbone killing me and me ignoring it, until she had to go open the shop again.

That was how we spent a lot of her visits, the best of them: together on the narrow bed, not talking, not moving except for the rise and fall of our breathing and the steady rhythm of my hand on her hair. Sometimes, though, it didn't work out that way. There were days when the thought of anyone touching me made my flesh leap, and although obviously I didn't put it that way to Melissa (I told her I hurt all over, which in fairness was true) I could see that it caught at her to feel me shift away after a brief hug and kiss – *So how was today, did you sell anything good?* She hid it well, though: pulled up the visitor's chair and chattered away, funny stories from work, gossip about her flatmate's latest drama (Megan was a petulant, nit-picky girl who managed a chichi organic-raw-kale-type café and couldn't work out why everyone she met turned out to be an arsehole; only Melissa could have lived with her for any length of time): dispatches from the outside world, so I would know it was still there and waiting for me. I appreciated what she was doing and I tried my best to listen and to laugh in the right places, but my concentration was shot, the nonstop flow of talk made my head hurt, and – I felt ungrateful and traitorous, but I couldn't help it – her stories seemed like such trivial fluff, so minuscule and weightless, next to the vast dark mass that filled my mind and my body and the air around me. I would end up drifting, finding pictures in the folds of the rumpled sheet or picking compulsively at my memory of that night in search of new images, or just plain falling asleep. After a while Melissa's voice would trail off and she would murmur something about getting back to work or getting home, lean over to brush a gentle kiss on my bruised mouth, and slip away.

When I had no visitors I did, basically, nothing. My room had a TV, but I couldn't follow a plotline for longer than a few minutes, or have the sound up to a normal volume without getting a splitting headache. I got a headache if I tried to read, too, or mess about on the internet on my phone. Normally this kind of inactivity would have had me jiggling like a kid and asking anyone who came within earshot when I could go home or at least go for a walk or do something, anything; but I found myself eerily willing to just lie there, watching the fan blades turn lazily and the stripes of light through the blinds make their slow way across the floor, shifting position every now and then when my tailbone ached too badly. My phone beeped and beeped – texts from friends (*Hey dude just heard, how fucked up is that, hope you're on the mend and the arseholes who did it get banged up for life*); from my mother, asking whether I wanted a jigsaw puzzle; from Susanna, *Hey just checking in, hope you're doing well, let me know if you need anything or if you fancy some company*; from Sean or Dec, asking if they could come visit; from Melissa, *Just to say I love you*. Sometimes it was hours before I got around to picking up the phone and reading the texts. Time had lost its solidity, in that arid, airless room haunted by faint electronic noises and smells of dissolution, it puddled and scattered like mercury. The only thing that gave it any cohering thread was the inexorable cycle of my pain meds kicking in and wearing off. Within a few days I knew the signs in fine-grained detail, the gradual ominous build of the throbbing above my ear, the thinning of the kind fog that kept the world at a manageable remove; I could tell almost to the minute when the pump on my IV would let out the smug, piercing beep that meant I could push the button for another dose.

The pain wasn't the worst part, though, not by a long shot. The worst part was the fear. A dozen times a day, more, my body would do something that it patently should not have been doing. My vision would split and wobble, and it would take a frantic burst of hard blinking to reset it; I would reach for a glass of water with my left hand, unthinking, and watch as it tumbled from between my fingers and went bouncing across the floor, water slopping everywhere. Even though the tongue swelling had gone down, my speech still had that thick village-idiot slur to it; when I went to the bathroom, my left foot dragged across the sticky greenish floor so that I hobbled along like Quasimodo. Every time sent me into a fresh tailspin: what if I could never see/walk/talk properly again? what if this was the first of those seizures the doctor had warned me about? if not this time, what if it was the next time or the next or the next? what if I never got another day in my life when I was normal again?

Once the fear took hold, I was fucked. I'd never known anything like it could exist: all-consuming, ravenous, a whirling black vortex that sucked me under so completely and mercilessly that it truly felt like I was being devoured alive, bones splintered, marrow sucked. After an eternity (lying in bed with my heart jackhammering, adrenaline firing me like a strobe light, feeling the last few threads that held my mind together stretch to snapping point) something would happen to break the vortex's hold – a nurse coming in so that I had to make mechanical cheerful chitchat, an uncontrollable rush of sleep – and I would clamber up out of it, shaky and weak as a half-drowned animal. But even when the fear receded for a while, it was always there: dark, misshapen, taloned, hanging somewhere above and behind me, waiting for its next moment to drop onto my back and dig in deep.

•

About a week in, two detectives came to talk to me. I was lying in bed watching TV with the sound off – a bunch of cartoon trucks were trying to comfort a truck in a pink cowboy hat, who was crying big cartoon tears – when there was a tap at my door and a guy with neatly trimmed greying hair stuck his head in.

'Toby?' he said. I knew straightaway, from his smile, that he wasn't a doctor; I'd already got the hang of the doctors' smiles, firm and distancing, expertly calibrated to tell you how much time was left in the conversation. This guy looked genuinely friendly. 'Detectives. Have you got a few minutes for us?'

'Oh,' I said, startled – which I shouldn't have been, obviously this was going to involve detectives at some point, but I had had other things on my mind and it hadn't occurred to me. 'Yes. Sure. Come in.' I found the bed-lift button and whirred myself upright.

'Great,' said the detective, coming in and pulling the chair to the side of the bed. He was maybe fifty, or a little over it; at least six foot, with a comfortable navy suit and a solid, unbreakable-looking build, like he had been cast all in one slab. There was another guy behind him – younger and skinnier, with ginger hair and a slightly flashy retro tan suit. 'I'm Gerry Martin, and this is Colm Bannon.' The ginger guy nodded to me, settling his backside against the windowsill. 'We're investigating what happened to you. How're you getting on?'

'OK. Better.'

Martin nodded, cocking his head to examine my jaw and my temple. I liked that he was straight-up inspecting me, matter-of-fact as a boxing coach, rather than pretending not to notice and then sneaking glances when he thought I wasn't looking. 'You look a lot better, all right. You got a bad doing-over. Do you remember me from the night?'

'No,' I said, after a disorientated second – it was disturbing to think of them there that night, seeing me in whatever condition I'd been in. 'You were there?'

'For a few minutes, only. I came in to have a word with the doctors, see what state you were in. For a while there they were afraid they might lose you. Nice to see you're tougher than they thought.'

He had a big man's voice, easy and Dubliny, with a comforting rumble running along the bottom of it. He was smiling again, and – even though a part of me knew it was pitiful to feel so grateful to this random guy for acting like I was a normal person, not a patient or a victim or someone to be handled with kid gloves in case he fell to pieces – I found myself smiling back. 'Yeah, I'm pretty happy about that part too.'

'We're doing everything we can to find out who did this. We're hoping you can give us a hand. We don't want to stress you out' – Flashy Suit shook his head, in the background – 'we can go into more depth once you're out of the hospital, when you're ready to give us a full statement. For now we just need enough to get us started. Are you able to give it a shot?'

'Yeah,' I said. The slurring to my speech, I didn't want them thinking I was handicapped, but I could hardly say no— 'Sure. But I don't know how much use I'll be. I don't remember a lot.'

'Ah, don't worry about that,' Martin said. Flashy Suit got out a notebook and a pen. 'Just give us what you've got. You never know what might point us in the right direction. Will I top that up for you, before we get started?'

He was pointing at the water glass on my bedside table. 'Oh,' I said. 'Thanks.'

Martin extracted my water jug from the jumble on the trolley table and filled my glass. 'Now,' he said, putting the jug back on the table. He hitched up his trouser legs more comfortably and leaned his elbows on his thighs, hands clasped, ready for conversation. 'Tell us: is there any reason why anyone would want to do this to you?'

Luckily I knew there was some pressing reason why I shouldn't mention my Gouger theory to the cops, even though I couldn't remember what that was. 'No,' I said. 'No reason at all.'

'No enemies?'

'No.' Martin was looking at me steadily, out of small pleasant blue eyes. I looked back, grateful for the meds, which would have stopped me getting twitchy even if I had tried.

'Any hassle with the neighbours? Arguments over parking spaces, someone who thinks you play your stereo too loud?'

'Not that I can think of. I don't really see the neighbours.'

'That's the best kind. See this fella here?' To Flashy Suit: 'Tell him about your man and the lawnmower.'

'Jesus,' said Flashy Suit, raising his eyes to the ceiling. 'My old neighbour, yeah? I'd always cut the grass on a Saturday – at *noon*, like; not even early. Only your man next door, he liked to sleep in. He gave me some grief about it, I told him to buy earplugs. So he *recorded* me cutting the grass and played it up against the bedroom wall, all night long.'

'Jesus,' I said, since he clearly expected something from me. 'What'd you do?'

'Flashed the badge, had a chat with him about antisocial behaviour.' They both chuckled. 'That settled him. The point is, but, not everyone's got a badge to flash. That's when things can turn nasty.'

'I guess I've been lucky,' I said. 'Plus the stuff, the' – I was looking for *insulation* – 'the walls in our place are pretty good.'

'Hang on to those neighbours of yours,' Martin advised me. 'Worth thousands, neighbours with no hassle. Do you owe anyone money?'

It took me a second to catch up. 'What? . . . Not like that. I mean, me and my friends, if we're on a, a night out, maybe someone subs someone twenty quid? But I've never owed anyone *money* money.'

'Wise man,' said Martin, with a wry half-smile. 'D'you know something, you'd be amazed how rare that is. I'd say at least half of the burglary cases we get – half?'

'More,' Flashy Suit said.

'Probably more. The fella owed someone money. And even if that had nothing to do with what happened, we have to convince him to tell us about it – people don't realise, we're not out to fuck over the victim here; if you like the odd bit of coke and you got behind with your dealer, that's not our problem, we're only interested in closing our case. And once the fella does tell us, we have to track down the lender and eliminate him. And that's all wasting time we could be using to catch the actual guys. I'm always delighted when we don't have to go through all that rigmarole. Nothing like that here, no?'

'No. Honestly.'

Flashy Suit wrote that down. 'How's the love life?' Martin asked.

'Good. I've got a girlfriend, we've been together three years—' Somehow I knew this wasn't news to them, even before Martin said, 'We've talked to Melissa. Lovely girl. Any hassles there?'

Melissa hadn't mentioned anything about detectives. 'No,' I said. 'God, no. We're very happy.'

'A jealous ex on either side? Anyone's heart get broken when the two of you got together?'

'No. Her last ex, they split up because he was, he' – I wanted *emigrated* – 'he went to Australia, I think it was? It wasn't a bad breakup or anything. And Melissa and I didn't even meet till months after. And I don't really see any of my exes, but we didn't have bad breakups either.' I was finding all this kind of unsettling. I had always considered the world to be basically a safe place, as long as I didn't decide to do anything actively dumb like getting hooked on heroin or moving to Baghdad. These guys were talking like I had been happily bopping along through a minefield where all you had to do was break up with your girlfriend or mow your lawn and boom, curtains for you.

'What about since you two got together? Anyone been giving you the eye? Anyone you had to knock back?'

'Not really.' There had been an artist a few months back, a very pretty hippie-type from Galway, who kept finding reasons why she needed to discuss the publicity campaign for her show in person; I had enjoyed the attention, obviously, but once she started touching my arm too much I had moved things to email, and she had got the message straightaway. 'I mean, people flirt, sometimes. Nothing serious.'

'Who flirts?'

I wasn't about to sic these guys on the artist, when she had clearly had nothing to do with this and the embarrassment factor would have been sky-high all round. 'Just, like, random girls. At parties or wherever. In shops. No one in particular.'

Martin left that there for a few seconds, but I drank my water and looked back at him. My eyes still weren't always tracking right; every now and then part of Martin's head would disappear, or there would be two of him, until I managed to blink hard enough to reset my focus. I felt a small pathetic rush of gratitude towards these guys for taking up my attention, leaving no room for the terror to take hold.

'Fair enough,' Martin said, in the end. 'Ever followed through with any of them?'

'What?'

'Ever cheated on Melissa?' And before I could answer: 'Listen, man, we're not here to get you in hassle. Whatever you tell us, if we can keep it to ourselves, we will. But anything that might have pissed anyone off, we need to know.'

'I get that,' I said. 'But I haven't cheated on her. Ever.'

'Good man.' Martin gave me a nod. 'She's a keeper. Mad about you, too.'

'I'm mad about her.'

'Aah,' said Flashy Suit, scratching his head with his pen and giving me a grin. 'Young love.'

'Anyone else mad about her?' Martin asked. 'Anyone been hanging around her that you didn't like the cut of?'

I was so used to saying no to every question that I was about to say it again, automatically, when I remembered. 'Actually, there was. Back, um, before Christmas? This guy, he came into her shop and got chatting to her, and then he kept coming back and not leaving for ages. And trying to get her to go for a drink. Even after she said no. It made her pretty—' Un-something, unhappy, no— 'She didn't like it. His name was Niall Something, he's in finance at the—'

Martin was nodding. 'Melissa told us about him, all right. We'll be checking him out, don't you worry. Give him a bit of a scare while we're at it, wha'?' He winked at me. 'Do him good, even if he's not our fella. Did you have any run-ins with him? Warn him off?'

'Not a run-in, exactly. But yeah, after a few goes of this, I told Melissa to text me next time he came in. And then I ran down from work and told him to get lost.'

'How'd he take it?'

'I mean, he wasn't pleased. There wasn't any, we weren't shouting or shoving or . . . but he got pretty stroppy with both of us. He left, though. And he didn't come back.' I had no compunction about siccing the Guards on Niall Whatever. He had been a ridiculous, puffy-faced wanker who informed me that if Melissa had actually wanted to get rid of him, she would have done it, *ergo* the fact that he was there meant that she wanted him to be. I would have laughed – he obviously wasn't dangerous, he was all hot air – if it weren't for Melissa's tense white face, the hunted strain in her voice when she'd told me about him. The fierce surge of protectiveness had been so strong that I didn't care if she was overreacting; I was actually disappointed that I hadn't needed to punch the little prick.

'Sounds like you handled it. Fair play to you.' Martin resettled himself more comfortably, one ankle propped on the other knee. 'You said you went down from work to run him off. You work in an art gallery, am I right?'

'Yeah. I do the PR.' The mention of the gallery made my stomach do a small sideslip. If they had talked to Melissa, they might have talked to Richard – maybe I should just come clean, before they sprang something on me? but I really didn't think Richard would want to get me into trouble, and anyway I was too muddled to be clear on what exactly I had done, I knew Tiernan and I had fucked up and got Gouger thrown out but—

'Ever bring home any of the art?'

'No. Never.'

'Any reason someone might think you did? Does anyone ever bring it out of the gallery? To show a buyer, maybe?'

'It doesn't work that way. If a buyer gets a, a private viewing, it's in the office. We're not insured to carry the art around.'

'Ah,' Martin said. 'The insurance lads; of course. Get their noses into everything. Never thought of that. Anyone at work that you don't get on with?'

'No. It's not that kind of place. Everyone gets on fine.' Or had, anyway, but—

'What about at home? Have you got anything valuable that they might have been after?'

'Um—' The barrage of questions was starting to disorientate me; he kept switching topics, and it was taking all my concentration to keep up. 'I guess my watch – I have this antique gold watch that used to be my grandfather's, he collected them? And I didn't get like the, the fanciest one, because one of my cousins is older than me, Leon? he doesn't look like it, but he's actually . . .' I had lost track. It took me an agonisingly long time, while the detectives watched me with polite interest, to remember what I was supposed to be talking about. 'Right. Yeah. I think mine could be worth maybe a grand.'

'Beautiful, those old watches,' Martin said. 'I don't like the modern stuff, all those Rolex yokes; no class. Do you wear it out and about? Would people have seen it on you?'

'Yeah, I wear it. Not always – mostly I just check the time on my phone? But if, for an opening or a, a meeting or . . . then yeah.'

'Were you wearing it the other night?'

'No. I mean' – meeting with Richard, a little extra gravitas –'yeah, I think I had it on that day. But then I probably, when I went to bed, it should be on my bedside table— Did they take it?'

Martin shook his head. 'Couldn't tell you for sure. I'll be honest, I don't remember seeing a gold watch, but that doesn't mean it wasn't there.' The thought of these guys rummaging around in my apartment sent a twist through my stomach, and then a much colder and more urgent one: I had that hash, and – *shit* – hadn't there been some coke left over from that Paddy's Day party? But surely if they had been planning to give me hassle over that, they would have mentioned it by now— 'How about your car?' Martin asked.

'Oh,' I said. My car hadn't even occurred to me. 'Yeah. It's a BMW coupé – I mean, it's a few years old, but it's probably still worth— Did they take it?'

'They did, yeah,' Martin said. 'Sorry. We've been keeping a lookout for it, but no joy yet.'

'The insurance'll sort you out, no problem,' Flashy Suit told me comfortingly. 'We'll give you a copy of the report.'

'Where were the keys?' Martin asked.

'In the living room. On the, the' – word gone again – 'the sideboard.'

He blew air out of the side of his mouth. 'In full view of the windows, man. Ever leave the curtains open?'

'Mostly. Yeah.'

Martin grimaced. 'You'll know better next time, wha'? Did you have them open last Friday evening?'

'I don't—' Getting home, going to bed, everything in between, it was all blank, a black hole big enough that I didn't even want to get near it— 'I don't remember.'

'Did you have the car out that day?'

It took me a moment, but: 'No. I left it at home.' I had figured that, whatever happened with Richard, I was going to want a few pints.

'In the car park in front of the building.'

'Yeah.'

'Do you drive it most days?'

'Not really. Mostly I walk to work, if the weather's OK, save the hassle of parking in town? But if it's raining or, or I'm running late, then yeah, I drive. And if I go somewhere at the weekend. Maybe two days a week? Three?'

'When was the last time you had it out?'

'I guess—' I knew I had stayed home for a few days before that night, couldn't remember exactly how long— 'The beginning of that week? Monday?'

Martin lifted an eyebrow, checking: *You positive?* 'Monday?'

'Maybe. I don't remember. Maybe it was over the weekend.' I got where he was going with this. The car park was open to the road, no gate. Martin thought someone had scoped out my car, clocked me getting into it, watched the windows till he identified my apartment, and then come looking for the keys. In spite of the element of creepiness – me sprawled contentedly on my sofa eating crisps and watching TV, eyes at the dark crack between the curtains – I liked that theory, an awful lot better than I liked my Gouger one. Car thieves weren't personal, and they were hardly likely to come back.

'Anything else valuable?' Martin asked.

'My laptop. My Xbox. I think that's it. Did they—'

'Yeah,' Flashy Suit said. 'Your telly, too. That's the standard stuff: easy to sell for a few bob. We'll keep the serial numbers on file, if you've got them, but . . .'

'What we're trying to figure out,' Martin said, 'is why you.'

They both looked at me, heads cocked, expectant half-smiles.

'I don't know,' I said. 'Because I'm on the ground floor, I guess. And my alarm wasn't on.'

'Could be,' Martin agreed. 'Crime of opportunity. That definitely happens, all right. But there's plenty of other ground floors out there. Plenty of other people who don't set their alarms. At this stage, we have to keep asking ourselves: could there be any other reason why they picked you?'

'Not that I can think of.' And when they kept up the mild, expectant, matching gazes: 'I haven't *done* anything. I'm not involved in, in *crimes* or anything.'

'You're sure. Because if you were, now would be the time to get ahead of it. Before we find out some other way.'

'I'm *not*.' This was starting to freak me out: what the hell did they think I had been doing? dealing drugs? selling kiddie porn on the dark web? 'You can ask anyone. Check me out whatever way you want. I haven't *done* anything.'

'Fair enough,' Martin said agreeably, settling back in his chair with one arm looped easily over the back. 'We have to ask.'

'I know. I get that.'

'We wouldn't be doing our job if we didn't. Nothing personal.'

'I know. I'm not— I'm just telling you.'

'Perfect. That's all we want.'

Flashy Suit flipped a page. Martin arched his back – the crappy plastic chair creaked under his weight – and adjusted his waistband with his thumbs. 'Jaysus,' he said. 'I need to lay off the fry-ups; the missus is always telling me. Now, Toby: tell us about Friday night. Start when you left work, say.'

'It's kind of patchy,' I said doubtfully. This was an understatement. What memories I've got came back in fits and starts, over months; at this stage, depending on where I was in the pain-meds cycle, I was sometimes convinced that I was back in college and I had got way too drunk at the Trinity Ball and whacked my head falling off the Edmund Burke statue outside Front Arch.

'You just give me as much as you can. The more the better. Even if it doesn't seem relevant. Will I get you more water, before you start? Some of that juice?'

I told them what I remembered, which at that point was basically a few flashes of the pub and the walk home, that one image of the two guys staring at me across my living room, and then a couple of bad moments when I'd been on the floor. Martin listened with his hands folded over his belly, nodding and occasionally interrupting to ask a question – could I describe anyone who'd been in the pub? anyone I'd seen on the walk home? had I felt like anyone was following me? could I remember turning my key in the outer door of the building, had there been anyone nearby? Behind him, the TV sputtered with endless bright jerky images, cartoon children throwing their arms out in a dance routine, perky presenters with eyes and mouths stretched wide, little girls holding up dolls whose sparkling practised smiles matched their own. Flashy Suit shook his pen, scribbled hard, then went back to writing.

Once we got to the central part of the night, the questions got more detailed and more insistent. Could I describe the guy reaching up to the telly? Height, build, colouring, clothing? Any tattoos or marks? What about the guy holding my laptop? Had they said anything? Any names? nicknames? What were their accents like? Anything unusual about their voices, a lisp, a stutter? High-pitched or low?

I told them what I could. The guy by the TV had been about the same height as me, so five eleven? skinny, white, acned; maybe around twenty, as near as I could guess; a dark tracksuit, a baseball cap; no tattoos or marks that I'd noticed. The one holding my laptop had been a few inches shorter, I thought, a bit stockier; white; something in the way he held himself had made me think he might be older, mid-twenties maybe; dark tracksuit and baseball cap; no tattoos or marks. No, I couldn't see what colour their hair was, the baseball caps had hidden it. No, I couldn't see whether they had beards or moustaches, their tops had hidden the lower halves of their faces. No, I didn't remember them saying any names. Both of them had had Dublin accents, nothing distinctive about their voices that I remembered. No, I wasn't a hundred per cent positive (Martin had gone back to each question two or three times, wording it a little differently every time; after a while I couldn't tell, any more, what I actually remembered and what I was confabulating for the sake of an answer); more than fifty per cent; eighty? seventy?

I was starting to lose my grip on the conversation. Talking about that night was doing things to me, more on a physical level than on an emotional one: a dark relentless fluttering in my stomach, a growing constriction in my throat, my hand or my knee leaping like a tic. And my pain meds were starting to wear off. The colours on the TV were harshening; the detectives' voices and mine scraped at the inside of my skull. With a weak, sick urgency that was swelling with every second, I wanted this to be over.

Martin must have noticed. 'Right,' he said, straightening up in his chair and throwing Flashy Suit a glance. 'That'll do us for today. Plenty there to keep us going. You did great, Toby.'

'Here you were worried you didn't remember enough to be any use,' Flashy Suit said, flipping his notebook closed and sliding it into his jacket pocket. 'We get plenty of people who weren't hit in the head, still don't manage to give us that much. Fair play to you.'

'Right,' I said. My head was shimmering; all I wanted to do was keep it together till they were out of the room. 'That's good.'

Martin stood up, arching his back with a hand to his spine. 'My Jaysus, that chair. Any longer in that and I'd be in the bed next door. The doctor said you'll be out of here sometime next week, yeah?' It was the first I'd heard of it. 'You can have a look round your apartment then, let us know if there's anything else missing, anything there that shouldn't be. OK?'

'Yeah. No problem.'

'Great. If anything happens before then, we'll make sure and update you.' He offered me his hand. 'Thanks, Toby. We know this can't have been easy for you.'

'It's OK.' His hand was huge, enveloping, and even though his shake wasn't crushing, it set off a fizzle of pain all the way up my arm. I was still smiling and nodding like an idiot, trying to calibrate the smile to polite friendliness and positive I was veering off into a grim rictus or a crazed leer, when I realised they were gone.

•

Sean and Dec had both texted me a bunch of times to ask when they could come visit, but I hadn't wanted to see them, or more accurately hadn't wanted them to see me. After the cops' visit, though, things seemed a little different; the car-thieves theory stripped away at least one layer of fear, the unreasoning terror that the men were still watching me from some nebulous darkness, unblinking and avid, biding their time till I got out of hospital and they could seize on their next chance. If Martin and Whatshisface were right – and they were detectives, experienced professionals, Martin looked like he had been doing this since before I was even born; they would know, wouldn't they? – then all I had to do was buy a crappy Hyundai and keep my curtains closed, and I could handle that. The whole mess felt a small but solid notch clearer and more manageable; even the physical stuff seemed like it might, just possibly, be temporary. I texted Sean and Dec the next morning and told them to come in.

They came straight from work, in suits and ties, making me fiercely glad that I had got a nurse to unhook my IV so I could take off the terrible hospital gown and (locked in the bathroom, bubbling with impotent anger, biting my lip till I tasted blood when my left leg refused to obey me) battle my way into the tracksuit bottoms and T-shirt my mother had brought in. They knocked gently at the door and practically tiptoed into my room, all braced to stay steady and neutral in the face of almost anything – 'Jesus Christ,' I said cheerfully and snarkily, 'it's not a bloody funeral. Come on in.'

Both of them relaxed. 'Good to see you, man,' Dec said, breaking into a smile. He crossed fast to my bed and gave me a long, two-handed handshake. 'Really good.'

'You too,' I said, matching the handshake and the grin. It really was good to see them, good but strange; it felt like it had been a long time, like I should be asking them what they were doing with themselves these days.

'Yeah, great to see you,' Sean said, shaking hands and giving me a very careful clap on the shoulder. 'How're you getting on?'

'Not bad. I was pretty sore for a few days there' – the mushy slur in my voice made me flinch, but my jaw was still bruised and puffy, surely they would blame it on that – 'but it's wearing off. Have a seat.'

Sean pulled up the visitors' chair and Dec sat – gingerly, checking for IV lines – on the edge of my bed. 'Loving the hair,' he said, pointing at my head – by this time I was showering and shaving (although both took a long time, and I sometimes had to sit down on the shower floor for a while when a dizzy flash hit), so the zombie-movie vibe had faded a bit, but I hadn't got around to doing anything about my hair. 'You could get into all the cool clubs, looking like that.'

'You should shave off one eyebrow to go with it,' Sean said. 'Start a hipster fad.'

'I'm thinking of going for a' – I found the word just in time – 'a mohawk. Think Melissa would like it?'

'I think you could get away with just about anything with Melissa, right now. Go for the mohawk.'

Dec had been absently tugging the edge of my blanket straight, and watching me. 'You seem all right, man,' he said. 'I mean, not all *right* all right, like I wouldn't advise you to go entering the Ironman or anything. But we were scared you were, like, fucked up.'

'Jesus,' Sean said. 'You're a real sensitive guy, you know that?'

'Come on, he knows what I mean.' To me: 'We couldn't tell what shape you were in, yeah? Melissa kept saying you were basically grand' – which was nice to hear – 'but I mean, Melissa; she's always positive about everything. Which is great, don't get me wrong, but . . . we were worried. It's just good to see you're OK.'

'I am OK,' I said. Which I was, right then, or as near as possible: I had carefully timed my Pavlov-button dose of painkillers, holding off for more than an hour after the beep, through the spine-grating ache building in my head, to make sure I would be at the perfect point in the cycle when they arrived. 'I have to get this tooth fixed, but apart from that I basically just need to take it easy for a while.'

'Jesus,' Dec said, examining the tooth with a grimace. 'Bastards.'

'Did the cops get them?' Sean asked.

'Nah. They think the guys were mainly after my car, so they're keeping an eye out for that. But I'm not holding my breath.'

'Hope they drive it off a bridge,' Dec said.

'Fuck it,' Sean said. 'You can buy another car. Just take it easy and get better. Speaking of which—' He held up a big, stuffed paper bag and passed it to me. 'Here.'

Inside were a sheaf of magazines – *Empire*, the *New Scientist*, *Commando* – a Bill Bryson book, a sudoku book, a book of cross-word puzzles, a little model-airplane kit, and half a dozen packets of fancy crisps in a variety of surrealist flavours. 'Hey, thanks, guys,' I said, touched. 'This is great.' I could no more have done a sudoku puzzle or built a model airplane than piloted a fighter jet, but the fact that they thought I could warmed me right through.

'No problem,' Sean said, giving the chair a baffled look as he tried to get comfortable. 'Keep you occupied.'

'We figured, if you actually were all right, you'd be bored off your tits,' Dec said.

'I am bored off my tits. Any news?'

'Oh yeah, there's news,' Sean said, forgetting about the chair. 'Guess what he's gone and done' – jerking a thumb at Dec, who was managing a nice blend of sheepish, defensive and delighted with himself.

'You're pregnant.'

'Ha ha.'

'Worse,' Sean said darkly.

'Oh Jesus,' I said, realisation dawning. 'You haven't.'

'He fucking has.'

'Jenna?'

Dec had his arms folded and his chin out, and he had gone a fetching shade of pink. 'I'm happy. Is that all right with you?'

'Dude,' I said. 'Did you get hit on the head too? Remember what happened last time?'

Sean turned up his palms: *Exactly*. Dec and Jenna had gone out for less than a year, during which they had broken up like six times. The last time had been a dramafest of epic proportions involving Jenna showing up at Dec's work four days running to beg him through sobs to try again, cutting the letters 'FUCK YOU' into a T-shirt he'd left at her place and couriering him the remains, and shooting off furious incoherent wall-of-text messages to all his Facebook friends including his parents.

'That was last *year*. She was going through a lot. She's sorted her head out now.'

'He's going to wake up one morning with his dick in his mouth,' Sean said.

'He should be so lucky,' I said. 'He's going to wake up with a thing, a positive pregnancy test in his face.'

'Do I look thick? I use johnnies. Not that it's any of your—'

'She's not thick, either. All it takes is a pin and boom, who's the daddy now?' I was loving this, every second of it. For the first time since that night I felt almost normal, I felt like an actual real person. I hadn't realised just how rigid with tension my whole body was till some of it melted away, and the dissipation was so ecstatic that I could have laughed or cried or kissed them both.

'Fuck off,' Dec said, aiming a middle finger at each of us. 'The pair of yous. I'm happy. If it all goes tits-up, then you can say *I told you so*—'

'We will,' Sean and I said, together.

'Be my guests. Until then, if you can't say anything nice, don't say anything at all. And you' – me – 'you need to be extra nice to me. Want to know why?'

'Don't go changing the subject,' Sean said.

'You shut up. Here,' Dec said to me, leaning in, with one eye on the door and a grin lurking. 'What meds are you on?'

'Why? You want some?' I tilted my IV bag invitingly in his direction.

'Ah, deadly. Just give us a quick sip.'

He pretended to reach for it; I swiped his hand away. 'Fuck off. I'm not sharing.'

'Seriously. What's in there?'

'Painkillers. The good stuff. Why?'

'See?' Sean said, to Dec. 'Told you.'

'He didn't say what *kind* of painkillers. It could be—'

'What are you on about?' I demanded.

Dec reached for his inside jacket pocket and, with that eye on the door again, produced a silver hip flask. 'We brought you another present.'

'*He* brought you another present,' Sean told me. '*I* said he was a fucking eejit. Mix that with serious meds, you could kill yourself.'

'What's in there?' I asked Dec.

'Macallan's, is what's in there. Sixteen years old. Cask strength. Only the finest for you, my son.'

'Sounds like the business,' I said, holding out my hand.

As soon as it came to crossing the line, of course, Dec looked taken aback. 'You sure?'

'Jesus, dude, you're the one who brought it. Or are you just, just prick-teasing?'

'I know, yeah. But would you not Google the meds first, see if—'

'What are you, my mum? Hand it over.'

He threw a dubious glance at the IV bag, like it was an untrustworthy dog that might go for my throat if it was disturbed, but he passed me the flask. 'He's right,' Sean told me. 'For once. Google the interactions.'

I uncapped the flask and took a deep sniff. The whisky filled my nose, rich with raisins and nutmeg, with reckless late nights and helpless laughter, idiotic stunts and long earnest meandering conversations, everything that stuck up a middle finger in the face of this godawful place and all the last godawful week. '*Oh* yeah,' I said. 'Dec, dude, you're a genius.' I tipped my head back and took a huge swallow. It burned beautifully, generously, all the way down. 'Hah!' I said, shaking my head.

The two of them were staring at me like I might spontaneously combust or fall over dead at any moment. 'God,' I said, starting to laugh. 'You should see your faces. I'm fine. Here—' I held out the flask. 'You pair of pussies.'

Surprisingly it was Sean who, after a moment, let out a laugh and took the flask. 'All right,' he said, raising it to me. 'Here's to living dangerously. A bit less dangerously from now on, yeah?'

'Whatever you say,' I said, still grinning, as he swigged. The booze had hit my system and whatever it was doing in there, it felt great.

Sean came up blowing like he'd been underwater. 'Jesus! That's beautiful. If it kills him, I'd say it's worth it.'

'Told you,' Dec said, reaching for the flask. 'To living dangerously.'

And when he lowered it, smiling beatifically: 'Ahhh. *Chapeau* to me, if I say so myself.' But when I held out my hand, he didn't pass it back to me. 'Save the rest, yeah? In case you need a little pick-me-up later on. This place would have anyone browned off.'

'I'm not browned off. I get to lie around all day with women in, in nurse outfits bringing me breakfast in bed. Would you be browned off?'

'Still. There's not a lot left; hang on to it. Just stick it in here—' He started shoving stuff aside on the shelf of my bedside locker.

'Oh Jesus, not like that. Give me it.' I grabbed the flask off him and started rooting through the locker for something to wrap it in. 'The nurse in charge, or whatever they call it, she's batshit crazy. I had a fan, right? She took it off me because she said it would *spread germs*. If she catches me with this she'll, I don't know, give me detention or—'

The locker was on the right side of my bed, and in order to reach it more easily I had switched the flask to my left hand. I felt it slipping free, grabbed wildly for it, and watched powerlessly as it slid through my fingers like they were made of water, bounced off the blanket and thudded dully onto the floor. The cap was loose; a trickle of whisky spread on the rot-green flooring.

There was an instant of frozen silence: Sean and Dec wide-eyed and uncertain, me unable to breathe. Then Sean leaned sideways to pick up the flask, tightened the cap and passed it back to me. 'Here,' he said.

'Thanks,' I said. I managed to get the flask bundled into a plastic bag and stuffed into the bedside locker, with my shoulder turned to the guys so they wouldn't see how hard I was shaking.

'They get your hand?' Dec asked, easily. Sean found a paper napkin on the trolley table, tossed it on the floor and started wiping up the spill with his foot.

'Yeah. A kick or something.' My heart was skittering out of control. 'It's fine. The doctors say there's some, like, some nerve damage, in my wrist? but no big deal. A couple of months of physio and I'll be fine.' The doctors had in fact said nothing of the kind. The neurologist – a flabby, ponderous old guy with the clammy pallor of someone who had been held in a basement for several years – had refused, smugly and flatly, to tell me anything at all about whether or when or to what extent I might expect to get better. Apparently that depended on a lot of factors, which he had of course no intention of listing for me. Instead – talking over me every time I stumbled or slurred, eyes sliding off me like I was beneath his attention – he had drawn me helpful cross-sections of my head with and without haematoma, informed me that my residual disabilities ('that means the problems that haven't gone away yet') were 'really very minor' and that I should consider myself lucky, told me to do my physical therapy like a good little boy, and then left while I was still trying to find some way of getting it through to him that this was actually my business. I still got light-headed with fury just thinking about him.

Sean nodded, balling up the wet napkin and looking around for a bin. After a moment Dec said, 'At least it's not your wanking hand.' The burst of laughter from all three of us was just too loud and too long.

By the time they left we were finishing off a bag of crisps and laughing easily again; Sean and I were advising Dec to take advantage of being in the hospital to get himself checked out for whatever lurid diseases Jenna had given him, and he was threatening to rat me out to the head nurse for drinking if I didn't shut my gob; from the outside everything would have looked fine, completely fine, three great pals shooting the breeze and having a grand old time. But a while later, when I pulled out the hip flask – getting really fucked up felt like an excellent idea, and whatever the booze-and-meds cocktail ended up doing to me, I was fine with it – it looked ridiculous, its cocky silver curves ludicrously out of place amid all the uncompromising functionality and institutional hospital colours. It looked like a joke, a sneer straight in my face for actually thinking – *stupid, pathetic* – that all it would take was a few slugs of booze and ta-da! everything would be totally back to normal! The sour reek of the whisky turned my stomach, and I put it away again.

•

A few days later they let me go home. They had taken a staple-remover to my head, leaving behind a long red scar surrounded by red dots where the staples had gone in, and disconnected me from my painkiller IV – I had been a bit nervous about that, but the pills they had given me instead were working OK, and anyway my ribs and my tailbone were a lot better and even the headache wasn't constant any more. I had had a visit from a physiotherapist, who had given me a bunch of exercises that I had promptly forgotten and a card with an appointment time for some clinic somewhere, which I had promptly lost. I had also had a visit from a social worker or a counsellor or something, a scrawny woman with enormous glasses and a gooey smile who had given me a huge sheaf of brochures about Brain Injury And You (very very simple block-figure covers in bright monochrome, diagrams of a block figure putting things into his Memory Filing Cabinet and taking them out again, explanations of why I should eat plenty of colourful vegetables, 'At first I didn't want to take naps after lunch, but they really help. I still get tired but I feel much better' – James from Cork, plus lots of helpful planners – Important Things to Do Today; Things That Went Well Today) and suggested that if I felt anger I should hang a towel from my washing line and whack it with a stick.

I had also had another visit from the shitbird neurologist, which had been fun. All my questions (When can I go back to work? when can I go for a few pints? have sex? go to the gym?) had been either ignored completely or met with the same offhand, infuriating 'When you feel ready,' which of course was exactly what I was asking to begin with: when was I going to feel ready? The exception was When can I drive? which it hadn't even occurred to me to ask: the neurologist (pasty chins tucked down, eyebrows raised forbiddingly over his glasses, he just stopped short of wagging a finger in my face) had informed me that I was absolutely not allowed behind the wheel of a car, in case of seizures. After six months, if the seizures hadn't materialised, I could come to him for a check-up and ask nicely if please sir I could have my licence back. I was trying very hard not to think about the possibility of seizures, but at that moment my entire remaining brainpower had been concentrated on how passionately I wanted to kick the neurologist in the nads, so I had made it through the conversation without spiralling into horror (*Things That Went Well Today!*).

My mother was due to come pick me up in an hour and I was wandering uselessly around my room, trying to make up my mind what the hell to do with the accumulation of stuff heaped on every surface. I didn't think I wanted any of it (where had a blue plush rabbit even come from?) but maybe some of the food would look more appetising when I was home and didn't feel like going to the shops, and surely I would be up to reading some of this stuff at some point, and my mother's flowers were in vases that she might want back . . . Two weeks earlier I would have cheerfully dumped the whole lot in the bin, told my mother I had no idea where her vases had gone, and bought her new ones.

I was staring helplessly at the plush rabbit in my hands (would Melissa really have brought me this thing? would she expect me to keep it?) when there was a tap at the door and Detective Martin stuck his head around it.

'Howya,' he said. 'Gerry Martin; remember me?'

'Oh,' I said, seizing gratefully on the opportunity to forget about the rabbit. 'Sure. Did you find the guys?'

'Jesus, man, give us a chance. This stuff doesn't happen overnight.' He scanned the trolley table. 'That's a lot of Monster Munch you've got there.'

'I know. My mother . . .'

'Ah, the mammies,' Martin said indulgently. 'Can't beat 'em. Can I have a packet, can I? You've got enough there to feed an army.'

'Sure. Take your pick.'

He dug out a packet of roast-beef flavour and pulled it open. 'Lovely. I'm only starving.' Through a mouthful: 'We heard they were turning you loose, came in to give you a lift home. Bannon's downstairs with the car.'

'But,' I said, after a befuddled second. 'My mother's coming to get me.'

'We'll give her a bell, sure. Explain the change of plans. How long till you're ready? Few minutes?'

'But,' I said again. I couldn't figure out a polite way to say *But why?*

Martin picked up on it anyway. 'We said before: we need you to have a look round your place, see what's missing, if there's anything that's not yours that they left behind. Remember?'

'Oh,' I said. I remembered, all right, but I had assumed they meant like a day or two after I got home. 'Now?'

'Oh, yeah. Now's when you'll notice anything out of place. And you'll want to get the gaff back in order, and you can't do that till you've done the look-round.' *Back in order*— It hadn't even occurred to me to think about what shape my apartment might be in. Overturned furniture, carpet spiky with dried blood, flies buzzing— 'Get it over with now, go back to normal. Easier all round.' He threw a few more Monster Munch into his mouth.

'Right,' I said. The thought of walking into that with Martin and Flashy Suit sharp-eyed at my shoulder was bad, but it was a lot better than having my mother there, all big compassionate eyes and arm-squeezes, plus I was pretty sure she was planning to spend the car ride trying yet again to convince me to move back home for a while. 'Yeah, no problem.'

'Beautiful. Here' – picking up the holdall my mother had brought me and swinging it onto the bed – 'you'll want the books, and that vase there looks like it cost someone a few bob. The rest can go in the bin, am I right?'

•

Going back into my apartment was worse than I had expected. It wasn't the horror-film extravaganza I had been picturing: in the living room the furniture was perfectly arranged, the carpets and the sofa had been cleaned (although I could still make out the shadows of bloodstains and spatters, across a shockingly wide area), every surface was immaculate and glossy, not a speck of dust anywhere; the drawers from my sideboard were neatly stacked in a corner, next to carefully aligned piles of the papers and cables and CDs that had been inside them; there was even a big vase of curly purple and white flowers on the table. Sun and leaf-shadows poured over it all.

It was the air that was wrong. Without realising it, I had gone in there reaching for the faint, familiar smell of home – toast, coffee, my aftershave, the basil plant my mother had given me, the fresh-cotton scent of the candles Melissa sometimes lit. All that was gone, wiped away; in its place was the thick scent of the flowers and a throat-coating chemical underlay, and I was sure that at the back of my nose I caught the sweaty, milky odour of the guy who had rushed me. The place didn't smell abandoned; it smelled intensely, feverishly occupied, by someone who wasn't me and didn't want me there. It was like stretching out a hand to your dog and seeing him back away, hackles rising.

'Take your time,' Martin said, at my elbow. 'We know this is tough on you. Need to sit down?'

'No. Thanks. I'm fine.' I braced my left leg harder; if it buckled on me now, I was going to rip the bloody thing right off—

'Your mam must've done a cleanup,' Flashy Suit said. 'We didn't leave it in this good nick. Fingerprint dust everywhere.'

'They had gloves,' I said, mechanically. I had just realised that half the drawers were broken, shards of wood sticking out, sides hanging loose.

'Sure,' Martin said, 'but we didn't know that then. And anyway, they could've taken them off at some stage, while you were out cold. Better safe, amn't I right?' He arranged himself comfortably against the wall by the living-room door, hands in his pockets. 'Have a look around, tell me if you spot anything missing. In your own time.'

'The TV,' I said. I'd been expecting it but it still looked impossible, the big blank space on my wall, as though if I blinked hard enough my TV would surely be back in its place. 'And the Xbox. And my laptop, unless someone put it away somewhere – it was probably on the coffee table—'

'No laptop,' Martin said. 'Anything on it that anyone might have wanted?'

'No. I mean, my credit-card numbers would have been on there somewhere, but they could have just taken my—' The top of the sideboard was bare. 'Shit. My wallet. It should be, I keep it right over there—'

'Gone,' Flashy Suit said. He had his notebook out again, pen poised and ready. 'Sorry. We've cancelled the cards and put a flag on them, so we'll be notified if anyone tries to use them, but so far no dice.'

'Oh,' I said. 'Thanks.'

'Anything else?' Martin asked.

My eye kept being pulled back to the bloodstain-shadows on the carpet. The memory caught me like a singeing crackle of electricity: clogged snuffle of my breath, pain, green curtains, a gloved hand reaching down— 'The candlestick,' I said – I was glad to hear that my voice sounded normal, even casual. 'I had a candlestick. Black metal, about this big, shaped like one of those twisted railings with a, a, a petal thing at the top—' I couldn't make myself tell them how I had brought it out of the bedroom with me, the big hero all ready to smash the living shit out of the bad guys. 'It was there, on the floor.'

'We've got that,' Martin said. 'Took it for forensics. We think it's what they hit you with' – indicating his temple. 'We'll get it back to you once the Tech Bureau's done with it.'

The scar on my head itched, suddenly and viciously. 'Right,' I said. 'Thanks.'

'Anything else? Anything here that shouldn't be?'

I looked around. My books were all wrong in the bookshelf; I didn't want to ask whether it was the burglars who had spilled them out, or the detectives searching. 'I don't think so. Not that I can see.'

'Those drawers there,' Martin said, pointing. 'They went through those pretty hard. When we got here, the papers and that were all over the floor.' Another fizz-zap of memory, crawling through rubble that rustled and slid under me— 'Any idea what they might've been after?'

The top right drawer was where I had had my hash and the left-over coke. Apparently the burglars had been considerate enough to take those, unless Martin was bluffing to see if I would lie to him – that affable, neutral face watching me, I couldn't read anything off him— 'No,' I said, pushing at what was left of my hair. 'I mean, not that I can remember? Mostly it's just stuff that doesn't really belong anywhere else. Paperwork, the restore disks from my laptop, I'm not even sure what else was in there . . .'

'Have a look through it anyway,' Martin suggested, only it wasn't really a suggestion. 'Maybe something'll ring a bell.'

Nothing did. Fish food from when I'd had a tank years back, a T-shirt I'd meant to return to the shop but had forgotten about, why would I have a Radiohead CD, had someone lent it to me, was someone out there bitching about how I had never given it back? I kind of thought there had been an ancient digital camera in there, but I couldn't be sure and certainly couldn't remember, when Martin asked, what photos had been on it – pre-college holiday in Mykonos with the guys maybe, long-ago parties, family Christmases? The sun was turning the room into a terrarium and the chemical smell was giving me a headache, but I didn't want to suggest opening the patio door when the detectives weren't complaining and anyway there was a new lock on it, shiny and not quite covering the pale splintered wood where the old one had been broken out, and I didn't have the key. I had changed my mind about these guys being better company than my mother. At least I could have told her to leave.

They took me through the apartment methodically, ruthlessly, room by room, drawer by drawer. My clothes were put away wrong, too. My grandfather's watch was in fact gone: I gave the detectives a description, they promised to check the pawnbrokers and the antique shops and the cash-for-gold places. My condoms were gone too, but we all felt there was less chance of tracking those down, not that I wanted them back, if it would prevent those guys from reproducing I was happy to donate to the cause, we all had a good laugh about that. My head was killing me.

'Right,' Martin said, at long last, giving Flashy Suit a glance that made him flip his notebook shut. 'We'll leave you to settle back in. Thanks for doing this, Toby. We appreciate it.'

'Have you,' I said. We were in the bathroom: sparkly clean, bottles perfectly lined up, too small for the three of us. 'Have you got any ideas? About who they were?'

Martin scratched at his ear and grimaced. 'Not really. I'm feeling a bit guilty about that, to be honest with you. Normally, by this time? we'd have a fair idea who we're after: this fella always gets in using the same method, that fella empties the fridge onto the floor and has a shite in the bed, the other fella has a tattoo that matches a witness description . . . Not saying we'd always be able to put them away for it, but mostly we'd be pretty sure who they were. This time . . .' He shrugged. 'Nothing's ringing any bells.'

'They might've been new on the job,' Flashy Suit said, a bit apologetically, tucking his pen away. 'That'd explain why they lost the head so easily, too. Rookies.'

'Could be,' Martin said. 'How about you, Toby? Anything come to mind since we last talked?'

By this time my head had cleared enough that I no longer suspected Gouger of being behind the break-in, but I did wonder about Tiernan. I'd heard enough of his rants (sheeple gallery owners without the guts to take on an artist till someone else had given him the stamp of approval, conniving female artists using their wiles and their tits to get gallery and media space over far more talented men, mindless trend-follower critics who wouldn't recognise groundbreaking art if it introduced itself) to know that he was the type to find someone else to blame for his problems and then get pouty and obsessed about it, and he had presumably met plenty of dodgy guys with burglarising experience during his travels for the exhibition. I still wasn't about to tell the cops the whole saga, specially when I had nothing more than a vague suspicion, but I did wish I'd paid more attention to Tiernan's youths when he brought them into the gallery. 'No,' I said, easily enough. 'I've gone back over everything, I don't know how many times, but I'm not coming up with anything new.'

Martin stayed put, watching me amiably, swinging the hand-towel ring back and forth with one finger. 'No?'

I couldn't tell what that meant, whether he was just hoping to jog my memory or whether he was telling me he knew I was hiding something. Both of them felt enormous suddenly, in the small cramped space, I was backed up against the bath with no way out— 'No,' I said. 'Nothing.'

After a moment Martin nodded. 'Right, so,' he said cheerfully. 'You've got our cards. Yeah?'

'I guess—' I had some vague memory of them leaving me little cards, that first time in the hospital. I looked around the bathroom like they might have teleported into my sink.

'Here you go,' Martin said, fishing in his pocket and handing me a white card, big clear type, fancy Garda seal. 'You be sure and let us know if anything comes to you. Yeah?'

'Yeah. I will.'

'Great. We'll be in touch. You relax, now; get some decent grub into you, have a couple of cans, leave the unpacking till later.' To Flashy Suit: 'Will we head?'

•

My mother arrived practically as soon as the detectives left, of course, with bags of inexplicable shopping (the basics, bread and milk and whatever, mixed in with stuff like a knobbly beige object that she informed me was ginger, 'just in case'). She didn't stay long, and she didn't make any helpful offers to find a carpenter to fix the sideboard drawers or anything. She was adapting, gradually and carefully, to this new landmined world where I was trapped, and I didn't know whether to be grateful or to hate her for the implication that she thought it was permanent. She managed not to ask whether I would be all right on my own; when she hugged me at the door, I managed not to flinch.

After work Melissa came over, hauling a huge fragrant bag of Thai takeaway. She was so irrepressibly and touchingly delighted about me being home – spinning around the living room laying out cutlery like she could barely keep her feet on the ground, flicking on the sound system to some radio station full of peppy sixties girl groups, flinging a kiss my way every time she passed me – that I couldn't help feeling a little more cheerful. I hadn't been hungry since that night, but my fiery beef stir-fry actually tasted good, and Melissa gave me the whole saga of how she had spent the last week persuading my mother not to get me a dog (my parents loved Melissa; fortunately they weren't the type to drop heavy hints about weddings and grandchildren, but I could see them thinking it): 'She was totally set on it, Toby, she said you could never have a dog when you were little because of your dad's allergies but this was *perfect*, it would be extra security *and* it would cheer you up – your dad kept going, "Lily, it's not going to work, the management company—" but she just went, "Oh, Edmund, who cares about them, I'll talk them round!" And Toby' – giggles starting to break through – 'the one problem she could see, the *only* one, she thought you wouldn't hoover and the whole place would be covered in dog hair. So she' – Melissa was giggling harder and I found myself laughing too, even though it hurt my ribs – 'she decided to get you one of those great big poodles. Because they don't shed. She was going to have it here waiting for you, she said it would be the perfect welcome-home surprise—' The image of me and the detectives walking into the apartment and coming face to face with a poodle in full pompom resplendence had us laughing so hard that I was startled to find myself trembling. It had been a long day.

As the evening wore on, though, I got edgy. Melissa – shoes kicked off, snuggled drowsily against me on the sofa – obviously assumed she was staying the night. As far as I was concerned, this was unthinkable, absolutely out of the question. I couldn't even let my mind touch on what would have happened if she had been there that night, when clearly I would have been utterly unable to protect her. I started stretching and yawning and dropping hints about how it was going to be weird being back in my own bed and I might be kind of restless, so maybe since she had to get up in the morning . . . Melissa picked up on this quickly, ungrudgingly – yes, getting sleepy too, better go now before I doze off right here. 'Soon,' I said, tracing a finger down the back of her neck as she bent to pull on a shoe.

'Yes,' she said, and turned fast to kiss me fiercely, '*soon*.'

I got her a taxi on my phone, so I could watch the little car icon tick towards her place, holding my breath every time it paused or took an odd turning. And there I was: on my own at last, in this apartment that felt so much like mine and yet in some insidious way not like mine at all, with my holdall dumped by the door like a long-distance traveller and with absolutely no idea what I was supposed to do with that night, or the next day, or the next.

•

The next couple of months were bad. It's hard to say whether it was the worst time of my life, given everything that came after, but it was definitely the worst I'd had at that point, by a long shot. I was restless as a tweaker, but I didn't want to go out during the day – I still had an underfed, off-kilter look, I still limped, and although my hair was growing back and I'd shaved the rest to match it, the Frankenstein scar still showed. I had some idea of going for long walks late at night, roaming the shadows of Ballsbridge in a Phantom of the Opera kind of way, but as it turned out I couldn't do that either. I had been walking home at all hours of the night since I was a teenager, and it had never once occurred to me to be afraid; wary, sure, when I spotted a junkie on the scrounge or a pack of drunk guys looking for hassle, but never this thick miasma of nonspecific fear polluting the air, corrupting everything into a threat – every shadow could be hiding an attacker, every walker could be waiting for his moment to lunge, every driver could be an instant from flooring it straight over my body, how would I know and what would I do? I got about thirty metres from my gate before adrenaline was juddering me like an electric current, I was panting for breath, and I turned tail and gimped as fast as I could back to my apartment, which although it hardly counted as safety did at least have manageable boundaries that I could keep an eye on. I didn't try again. Instead I walked up and down my living room, for hours on end, shoulders tight, hands dug deep into the pockets of my dressing gown. I can still feel the terrible rhythm of it, step and drag, step and drag, every pace driving it home all over again, but I couldn't stop; somehow I believed that as long as I was up and moving, no one would break in, I wouldn't have a seizure, at least nothing would get worse. Sometimes I kept walking until grey light filtered around the edges of the curtains and outside the birds started chirping.

When I did force myself to go to bed, I was, predictably, having a hard time sleeping. While I was in hospital my parents had thoughtfully had a monitored alarm installed, with a panic button and all (I could picture my mother looking around at the damage, knuckles pressed to her mouth, groping for some way to go back in time and stop it happening), and while I saw their point and knew it was probably a good idea, part of me wished they hadn't. The panic button was a rectangular thing about the size of a matchbox, in a brisk medical shade of red, and it was set near my bed but low down, just out of reach. I spent hours frozen in bed, holding my breath and straining to catch the follow-up to some minute click or scrape, heard? imagined? about to explode into hoarse shouts and crashes? should I dive for the button now and risk crying wolf and not being taken seriously when the danger was real, or should I hold off for ten more excruciating seconds, ten more, ten more, and risk being too late, scrabbling frantically to cross those unbridge-able few inches as the blows crunched into me? The button devel-oped a life of its own, swollen with symbolism, a single chance at salvation pulsing redly in the corner and if I blew it too soon or left it too late then I was lost. I developed a habit of sleeping balanced precariously on the edge of the bed, with my arm hanging over so my fingers would be as close as possible to the button. Once or twice I fell out and woke up on the floor, yelling and flailing.

Texts from friends, from my cousins, from work connections. *Hey dude how you doing, barbecue at my place Saturday week are you on for it?* . . . *Hi, not to hassle you but you might want to pick up when my mum rings, otherwise she tells your parents that she thinks you're uncon-scious on your floor* – Susanna, with a little eye-roll emoji thrown in. Memes and gifs and bits of internet chaff from Leon, presumably meant to give me a laugh. *Hi Toby, this is Irina, I heard what hap-pened and just hoping you are feeling OK now and we will see you soon . . .* I mostly didn't answer, and gradually the texts got sparser, which left me unreasonably miffed and self-pitying. Richard rang; when I didn't pick up, he left a message telling me – awkwardly, delicately, with real warmth – that everything at work was absolutely fine, the show was going beautifully, a major collector had bought Chan-telle's sofa assemblage, and that I shouldn't worry about anything, just concentrate on getting better and come back to work whenever I felt ready. Texts from Sean, from Dec, will we call round? how about tomorrow? at the weekend? I didn't want to see them. I didn't feel like I had anything at all to contribute to a conversation, and I couldn't stand the thought of them leaving in a cloud of inarticulate pity, waiting till they were well away from my door before they spoke: *Jesus. He's . . . Yeah, he is. The poor bastard.*

Physically, I was getting better, at least to some extent. My face went back to normal – except for the chipped tooth, which I knew I should get fixed at some stage – and my ribs and my tailbone healed up OK, although I still got the odd twinge. I didn't have any seizures, as far as I could tell, which was nice, although the neurologist had informed me smugly that they could start months or even a year or two after the injury. Sometimes I went four or five hours painkiller-free before the headache kicked in again; I liked life a lot better on the pills, which blurred the edges till things were just about bearable, but I was going easy on them in case – I didn't even want to think too hard about this possibility – the doctors refused to renew the prescription once I ran out.

The mental stuff was a different story. I had a good all-round selection of the symptoms from the social worker's helpful brochures: my Memory Filing Cabinet appeared to be well and truly fucked (standing blank-headed in the shower trying to remember whether I had already washed my hair or not, in mid-conversation with Melissa groping for the word *instant*), I was constantly exhausted just like James from Cork, and my organisational skills were shot to the point where making breakfast was a major and incredibly frustrating challenge. In practical terms all this was less of a problem than it might have been, I suppose, given that I wasn't even trying to do anything complex like work or socialise, but that didn't make me feel any better about it.

Overall, being home was worse than being in the hospital. At least in that cockeyed, dislocated limbo my symptoms hadn't seemed out of place, while here in the real world they were glaringly, repellently wrong, they were obscenities that should never have been allowed to exist: grown man standing slack-jawed in his kitchen trying to figure out *duhhh how me make fried egg*, on the phone with the credit-card company fumbling for his date of birth, drooling moron, defective, freakshow, disgusting— And down again into that all-consuming vortex, only it had deepened, it was spreading: not just fear any more, now it was roiling fury and loathing and it was a depth and breadth of loss that I had never imagined. Only a few weeks ago I had been a normal guy, just a guy, tossing his jacket on in the morning, humming the Coronas through a slice of toast caught between his teeth, deciding where he was going to take his girlfriend for dinner; now every second was part of an inexorable tide drawing me farther and farther from that guy whom I had every right to be and who was gone for good, left behind on the other side of that unbreakable sheet of glass. And whereas in the hospital I had been able to tell myself that things would be better once I was home, now that that had turned out not to be true, I couldn't find any reason to think that anything would get better ever.

It wasn't only myself I raged at, of course. My mind churned out epic, elaborate fantasies in which I tracked down the two burglars (recognised a voice in the street, a pair of eyes across a pub, kept my cool with awe-inspiring self-control as I stalked them through their seedy haunts) and destroyed them in Tarantino-esque ways much too embarrassing to recount. I lived those scenarios over and over, amplifying and refining each time, till I knew each step and twist of them far better than I knew the details of the actual event. Even at the time, though, I knew exactly how feeble and pathetic they were (zit-ridden asthmatic loser locked in his bedroom furiously fantasising, under his collection of scantily clad anime posters, about kung-fu-kicking the school bullies into next week) and in the end the rage always turned back on myself: mutilated, useless, physically and mentally incapable of a trip to Tesco never mind action-hero revenge, a fucking joke.

Calls from my mother, who – since Melissa had managed to convince her that I didn't need a poodle – had switched back to suggesting, with infuriating persistence, that what I really needed was a few weeks at home. 'You'd be amazed what it can do for you, a different setting— We promise to stay out of your way, you'll barely know we're there—' And, when I made it clear that nothing on earth would induce me to move back home: 'Or I know! What about the Ivy House? Uncle Hugo would love to have you, and it's so peaceful – just try it for a weekend, if you don't like it you can go back to your apartment—' I put that idea down a lot more viciously than I needed to. I couldn't even think about being at the Ivy House, not like this. The Ivy House, twilight hide-and-seek among the moths and the silver birches, wild-strawberry picnics and ginger-bread Christmases, endless teenage parties with everyone lying on the grass gazing up at the stars— All that was unreachable now; that night was a flaming sword barring the way. The Ivy House was the one place that, more than any other, I couldn't bear to see from this far shore.

Unidentifiable ready-meals congealing to lumpy glue on my cof-fee table. Dust thickening on the bookshelves, crumbs on the kitchen counters – I had texted my cleaner to tell her I wouldn't be needing her any more, partly because I knew the clattering and hoovering would give me headaches, more because I very strongly didn't want anyone (except Melissa) in my apartment. Bird-shadows skimming across my living-room floor, making me leap.

Melissa was a problem, actually, a big one. I loved her coming over, she was the only person I genuinely wanted to see, but the thought of her staying the night still sent me into a firework fizzle of panic that I could barely hide. I could have gone to her place, in fact I did try that once, but there was Megan the awful flatmate, hanging around with her thin lips all primmed up and just waiting for Melissa to leave the room so she could make bitchy jabs about how that one time when she got mugged she had been totally trau-matised and she was actually much more sensitive than most people but *she* had actually managed to get *over* it in like a couple of *weeks*? because she had really set her *mind* to it? and someone as special as Melissa actually deserved someone who would make that actual *effort*? I made my excuses (headache) and left when I realised I was on the actual verge of actually punching Megan's face in. I'd never had a temper before, I'd always been the easy-going type, but now tiny ludicrous things would send me, out of nowhere, into an uncontrollable fury that took my breath away. One time I couldn't get a frying pan to fit back into the tangled mess that was my kitchen cupboard; I smashed it down on the counter over and over, with utter methodical concentration, until the pan bent and the handle cracked apart and the whole thing went flying in various directions. Another day, when my toothbrush fell out of my hand for the third time, I slammed my stupid fucking useless left fist into the wall, over and over, I was trying to smash the vile thing to pulp so they would have to cut it off me but – the irony – my muscles didn't have the strength to do any real damage; all I ended up with was a big purple bruise that made my hand even more useless for the next few days and that I had to remember to hide from Melissa.

I knew awful Megan was right, of course. I knew that Melissa, the unfailing, unforced sweetness and patience of her – never a word of complaint, always a joyful hug and a full-on kiss – was far more than anyone could have expected in the circumstances, far more than I deserved. I knew, too, that even Melissa's optimism couldn't be bottomless, that sooner or later she would realise I wasn't going to magically wake up one morning as my old sunny self. And then what? I understood that the only decent thing to do was to break it off now, save her all the squandered time and energy and hope, save both of us the terrible shatter and slice of the moment when it finally hit home; let her go on her way free of the heavy belief that she had abandoned me when of course that wouldn't be true, not at all: I was the one who had abandoned her. But I couldn't do it. She was the one person who seemed to believe, to take for granted, that I was the same Toby she had always known; a bit bruised and battered, sure, in need of extra nuzzles and funny stories and of having my coffee brought to me on the sofa, but not changed in any essential way. Even though I knew that was rubbish, I couldn't make myself give it up.

I was aware that I was in big trouble here, but there didn't seem to be any way out. At the dark heart of the horror was the knowledge that it was inescapable. The thing I couldn't bear wasn't burglars or blows to the head, wasn't anything I could beat or evade or set up defences against; it was myself, whatever that had become.

•

So when I say that I was lucky to have the Ivy House, I don't mean that in some airy-fairy abstract way, ooh so lucky! to have such a lovely pretty place in my life! For better or for worse, the Ivy House saved me, in the most concrete of ways. If I hadn't gone back there that summer, I'd still be pacing my apartment all night, getting skinnier and paler and twitchier by the month, having long muttered conversations with myself and never answering my phone; that or else – which seemed like a better and better idea as the weeks wore on – I would be dead.

Susanna rang me on an evening in mid-August, daylight lasting and lasting, barbecue smell and gleeful kid-game shouts filtering in even through my closed windows. The voice message she left – 'Ring me back. Now' – sparked enough curiosity in me that I actually did; considering the low level of hassle she had given me over the past few months, I was pretty sure she didn't want to pressure me about moving home or make sure I was eating.

'How're you doing?' she asked.

'Fine,' I said. I had the phone a few inches from my mouth, hoping the slurring wouldn't come across. 'Still kind of sore in places, but I'll live.'

'That's what your mum said. I wasn't sure – you know how she always puts a positive spin on stuff. But I didn't want to bug you.'

The rush of gratitude to my mother caught me off guard – she had actually done it, covered for me like I had asked her to, she hadn't spread out the full extent of my wreckage for them all to pick and cluck over. 'Nah, she's right. It sucked for a while there, but it could've been a lot worse. I got lucky.'

'Well, good for you,' Susanna said. 'I hope they catch the bastards.'

'Yeah, me too.'

'Listen,' she said, tone shifting. 'I've got bad news. Hugo's dying.'

'What?' I said, after a second of total blankness. 'Like, *now*?'

'No, not *now* now. But this year, probably. No one wanted to tell you yet, in case it upset you or something. Which . . .' A flick of unreadable laughter. 'So I'm telling you.'

'Wait,' I said, struggling up from the sofa. The galvanising rush of anger at the rest of my family was distracting; I made myself shove it aside for later. 'Hang on. Dying of what?'

'A brain tumour. A few weeks back he was having trouble walking, so he went to the doctor, and a bunch of tests later: cancer.'

'Jesus.' I turned in a circle, scrubbing my free hand through my hair. I couldn't get a grip on this, couldn't be positive whether Susanna had actually said what I thought she had or— 'What are they doing about it? Did they operate yet?'

'They're not going to. They say the tumour's too involved with his brain; it's got tentacles everywhere, basically.' Susanna's voice, level and clear. Even as a kid, she had always got harder to read in crises. I tried to picture her: leaning against one of the old brick walls of the Ivy House, sun scouring the clean pale angles of her face to translucence, ivy bobbing at her red-gold hair. Scent of jasmine, hum of bees. 'And they say chemotherapy wouldn't make much difference, so there's no point in wrecking his quality of life for his last few months. They're going to do radiotherapy. That might give him an extra month or two, or it might not. I'm working on getting a second opinion, but for now, that's the story.'

'Where is he? What hospital?' My room, the polluting smell of it, the soft patient ticking of the blinds in no obvious breeze—

'He's home. They wanted to keep him in, "in case of unforeseen developments", but you can imagine how that went.' I laughed, a startled, painful bark. I could see the exact drop of Hugo's shaggy eyebrows, hear the mild, inflexible firmness with which he would put down that suggestion: *Well, as far as I can tell, the main unforeseen development you're worried about is me dropping dead, and I think I can do that much more comfortably at home. I promise not to bring you to court if I turn out to be wrong.* Unless—

'How is he? I mean—'

'Like, apart from the whole dying thing?' That flick of a laugh again. 'He's OK. He can't walk too well, so he's got a cane, but he's not in pain or anything. They said that might come later, or not. And his mind's fine. For now, again.'

I had been wondering why my aunts had quit leaving me voicemails, why my cousins' texts had dried up. I had figured, with a hot scraped soreness, that it was because they were sick of me not answering and had decided not to bother any more. It came as a shock, cut with a bit of shame and a bit of outrage, to realise that it had had nothing to do with me.

'So,' Susanna said. 'If you want to see him, like while he's still in decent enough shape to have conversations, you might want to go stay with him for a while.' And when I didn't answer: 'Someone needs to be there. He can't keep living by himself. Leon's going to fly over as soon as he sorts things with work, and I'll come in as much as I can, but I can't exactly dump the kids on Tom and move in.'

'Oh,' I said. Leon was living in Berlin and didn't come home a lot. It was dawning on me that this was actually serious. 'Can't your parents, or I mean maybe my parents could, or—'

'They all have work. From what the doctors said, this could go to shit any time; he could collapse, or have a seizure. He needs someone there twenty-four-seven.'

I wasn't about to tell her that I might do much the same thing. The image of me and Hugo having synchronised seizures sent a jagged ball of laughter rising in my throat; for a second I was terrified I was going to burst into lunatic giggles.

'It wouldn't be actual nursing – if he needs that later on, we can get someone in. But for now it's just being there. Your mum said you're taking a couple of months off work—'

'OK,' I said. 'I'll try and go.'

'If you're not well enough, then tell me and I'll—'

'I'm fine. That doesn't mean I can just, just dump everything and *move*.'

Silence on Susanna's end.

'I said I'll try.'

'Great,' Susanna said, 'you do that. Bye.' And she hung up. I stood in the middle of my living room for a long time, phone held in mid-air, dust motes weaving through sunlight, kids screaming somewhere in excitement or terror.

As Susanna had gathered, I had no intention of going anywhere. Even leaving aside the way I felt about the Ivy House, just making the decision seemed well beyond my capabilities, never mind actually doing it (how would I get there? how the hell would I even pack?), never mind looking after a dying man when I couldn't even look after myself, never mind the daunting prospect of having to spend however long coping with my whole extended family bopping in and out – normally I got along great with every one of them, normally I would have been already throwing stuff into that holdall, but now . . . The thought of Susanna and the rest seeing me like this snapped my eyes shut.

And of course, underlying all that: it was Hugo; Uncle Hugo, dying. I wasn't sure I could cope with that, not right now. All through my childhood he had been there, a constant as fixed and taken for granted as the Ivy House itself – even when my grandparents were alive he had lived there, the bachelor son leading his own peaceful existence parallel to theirs, gradually and without fuss slipping into the role of carer as they aged and then, when they died, back into his own well-worn contented rhythms. Hugo padding about in his sock feet with a book open in his hand, peering and swearing ('Well, hell's bells and buckets of blood') at the Sunday roast that never once in all my childhood did what was expected of it, putting paid to cousin-bickering with half a dozen brisk words (why hadn't he done that to the doctors, informed them in that mild tone that allowed for no argument that of course it wasn't incurable, nipped this nonsense in the bud?). The world was slippery and incohesive enough as it was; with him disintegrating, it might fly apart into a million pieces.

I did get that I had a responsibility to at least go see him, but I couldn't fathom how I was supposed to do it. The only possible way to get through this, on what minimal resources I had, seemed to be to pull my head deeper into my cave, slam everything shut as tightly as possible, take plenty of painkillers and refuse to even think about the whole thing until it was over.

I was still standing there with the phone in my hand when the buzzer made me shy sideways: Melissa, with a massive cardboard pizza box and a funny story about how the Italian guy in the restaurant had been in genuine pain at the thought of putting pineapple on her half. And, since I couldn't find a way to tell her what had just happened, I laughed and put my phone away and started on my pizza.

But my appetite was gone again, and after one slice I gave up and told her. I expected shock, hugs, compassion – *Oh Toby, that's all you needed, are you OK?* Instead Melissa surprised me by saying, instantly, 'When are you going?'

She looked like she was ready to jump up and start packing for me. 'I don't know,' I said, shrugging and focusing on my pizza. 'Maybe in a few weeks. Depends on how I'm doing.'

I thought for sure that would be the end of that, but out of the corner of my eye I could see Melissa sitting up very straight, cross-legged – we were on the sofa – pizza forgotten, one hand cupped in the other like a supplicant. She said, 'You should really go. Like, right away.'

'I know that.' I almost managed to keep the flash of irritation out of my voice. 'If I can go, I'll go. Right away.'

'No. Listen.' The barely controlled urgency made me look at her. 'That night, when your mother rang me—' A quick intake of breath. 'It was five in the morning. I threw on clothes and got a taxi. No one knew what was going on. No one knew if you were going to—'

Her eyes were too bright, but when I reached for her she put my hands aside. 'Wait. I need to finish this, and if you hug me I'll . . . I was in the taxi and I was screaming at the driver to go faster, actually screaming at him – I was lucky he was so nice, he could easily have put me out on the side of the road, but instead he just went faster. Everything dark, and no one on the roads, and we were going so fast the wind was roaring at the windows . . . And all I could think was that I couldn't bear it if I was too late. If you woke up and wanted me and I wasn't there, and then . . . It was pure selfishness, I knew you probably wouldn't even know whether I was there or not – I just couldn't bear going through the rest of my life knowing I hadn't been there when you needed me.'

When she blinked, a tear ran down her face. I reached out and brushed it away with my thumb. 'Shh. It's OK; I'm right here.'

This time she caught my hand and held on tight. 'I know. But if you don't go see your uncle, Toby, that's what it's going to be like. You're so shaken up right now, it might not sink in till you're feeling

88

better, but by then it could be too late.' Squeezing my hand tighter, when I started to say something: 'I know you can't even think about what things will be like when you're OK again. Believe me, I understand that. But I can. And I don't want you to be left feeling that for the rest of your life.'

It went straight to my heart, her total and ludicrous faith in me, in a future where I was OK again. I had to swallow back tears too – that would be just great, the two of us sitting on the sofa bawling into our pizza, like a pair of teenage girls watching *Titanic* at a sleepover.

'Even if you think I'm talking rubbish, can you just trust me on this one thing? Please?'

For my sake more than hers, I couldn't tell her that this magical future wasn't going to materialise. And with that realisation something surged up in me, a confused reckless swirl of defiance and destructiveness: fuck it, everything was wrecked anyway, what the hell was I trying to salvage? why not go for broke, gun the motorcycle straight for the burning bridge, bring the whole doomed mess tumbling down? At least it would be my call this time; and at least it would make Melissa happy, and Hugo—

Out of nowhere, before I even knew I was thinking it, I said, 'Come with me.'

The surprise stopped her crying; she stared at me, lips parted, hand loosening on mine. 'What? You mean . . . like, for a visit?'

'For a few days. Maybe a week. Hugo won't mind. You got on great at my birthday thing.'

'Toby, I don't know—'

'Why not? We've always had people in and out of that house. One time Dec had a fight with his parents and stayed for basically the entire summer.'

'Yes, but now? Do you think your uncle really wants anyone but family around?'

'It's so big, he'll barely even notice you're there. I bet Leon brings his boyfriend, who, God, I can't even remember his name. If he's not a problem, neither are you.'

'But—' My rush of giddy energy had caught her; she was almost laughing, breathless, wiping her eyes with the back of her wrist. 'What about work?'

It was hitting me that maybe it hadn't been a crazy thing to say, after all. Maybe with Melissa there, my small shining amulet, I could handle the Ivy House, maybe— 'There's a bus straight into town. It'd only add like ten minutes each way. Not even.' And when I saw her wavering: 'Come on. It'll be like a holiday. Only with shitty weather. And brain cancer.'

I already knew she was going to say yes: to keep me like that, fired up about something, joking even, she would have said yes to almost anything. 'I mean, I suppose – if you're sure your uncle won't—'

'He'll be delighted. I swear.'

With a watery laugh, she gave in. 'OK. But next year we're going to Croatia.'

'Sure,' I said, and a part of me almost meant it, 'why not?' And before I knew it, Melissa was singing to herself as she tidied away the pizza things and I was pulling up Hugo's phone number, and just like that, I was going back to the Ivy House.

3

The drive to the Ivy House, that Sunday afternoon, felt a lot like an acid trip. It had been months since I'd been in a car or been anywhere much outside my apartment, and the sudden torrent of speed and colours and images was way more than I could handle. Patterns kept popping up everywhere, frenetic and pulsing, dotted lines leaping out at me from the road, strobing rows of railings zooming past, grids of apartment-block windows replicating themselves manically into the air; the colours were all too lurid and had a shimmering electronic zing that made my head hurt, and the cars were all going much too fast, whipping past us with a ferocious whoosh and smack of air that made me flinch every time. We were in a taxi – Melissa's car was somewhere else or being fixed or something, she had explained but the explanation had been too complicated to stay in my head for any length of time – and the driver had the radio up loud, some talk show with a woman getting hysterical about being housed in a hotel room with her three kids while the host tried to make her cry harder and the taxi driver shouted an outraged running commentary over it all.

'Are you OK?' Melissa asked in an undertone, reaching over to squeeze my hand.

'Yeah,' I said, squeezing hers back and hoping she wouldn't notice the cold sweat. 'Fine.' Which was sort of true, at least on some levels. As soon as the initial rush of reckless abandon wore off I had started wondering what the fuck I had got myself into, but luckily I had managed to get an appointment with my GP and ask for a top-up on painkillers and a hefty Xanax prescription – which he had had no problem writing, after he skimmed my hospital records and I whipped out the full-colour heartrending story of my sleep woes. I had zero intention of taking downers as long as I had to spend nights in my apartment, but I had made sure to swallow the first one right before we got into the taxi, so I would be good and spacy by the time we reached the Ivy House. It was kicking in: while the thought of walking in there like this still broke my heart, I found that I didn't much care, which made a refreshing change.

'Wait,' Melissa said suddenly, leaning forwards. 'Isn't the turn around here?'

'Shit,' I said, sitting up straight. 'That one, that left—'

We had missed it; the taxi driver had to do a U-turn, with plenty of sighs and grunts. 'Jaysus,' he said, ducking his head to peer down the road. 'Never even knew this was here.' He sounded miffed, as if the street had insulted his professional expertise.

'Down at the far end,' I said. Hugo's road has that effect; it gives the impression of being there only on alternate Thursdays or to people with the mysterious talisman in their pockets, invisible the rest of the time and instantly forgotten once you leave it. Mainly it's the proportions, I think; the road itself is much too narrow for its tall, terraced Georgian grey-bricks and its double line of enormous oaks and chestnuts, making it easy to miss from the outside and giving the inside its own micro-climate, dim and cool and packed with a rich unassailable silence that comes as a shock after the boil of city noises. As far as I could tell it had been inhabited entirely by old couples and fiftysomething women with scruffy dogs ever since I was born, which seemed demographically unlikely, but I had never seen a single kid there except me and my cousins and later Susanna's kids, and the only teenage parties had been ours.

'Here,' I said, and the taxi pulled to a stop in front of the Ivy House. I fumbled to pay fast before Melissa could take our suitcases from the boot, I got them out somehow (left elbow hooked through the handle, right hand hauling furiously), and then the taxi had ground through a multi-point turn and zoomed back up the road and we were standing on the pavement outside the Ivy House, next to our cases, like lost tourists or like travellers coming home.

The house's official name is Number 17; one of us – Susanna, I think – called it the Ivy House when we were little because of the thick drifts of ivy that practically covered all four storeys, and it stuck. My great-grandparents (from prosperous Anglo-Irish families, lots of solicitors and doctors) bought it in the 1920s, but by the time I came along it was my grandparents'. They had raised their four sons there, the younger three had moved out and got married and had kids of their own, but the house was still the family hub: Sunday lunch every week, birthday celebrations, Christmases, parties that wouldn't fit in our own suburban houses or gardens; by the time Leon and Susanna and I were seven or eight, our parents were dropping us at the Ivy House for large chunks of the holidays so the three of us could run wild together, under our grandparents' and Hugo's benign neglect, while our parents drove around Hungary in camper vans or headed off around the Mediterranean on someone's boat.

Those were wonderful times, idyllic times. We got up when we felt like it, made ourselves bread-and-jam breakfast and had the run of the place, dawn till bedtime, occasionally answering the call to a meal and then running off again. In a top-floor spare room we built a fort that started with a few bits of discarded plywood and grew, over months, into a multi-level structure that we spent endless afternoons capturing back and forth and fitting out with spyholes and trapdoors and a contraption that dumped a bucketful of rubbish on the enemy's head. (There was a password, what was it? *incunabula, vestiary, homunculus*, something like that, some esoteric word that Susanna had picked up God knows where and chosen for its musty, incense-trailing mystique rather than because she had any clue what it meant. It bothers me more than it should, that I've forgotten it. Sometimes, when I can't sleep, I've tried using up the night by scrolling down page after page of online dictionaries, hoping something jumps out at me. I suppose I could try ringing Susanna and asking her, but I prefer not to come across as that crazy guy any more than I really have to.) We rigged a spiderweb of pulleys across the garden so we could shuttle stuff between trees and windows; we dug a pit and filled it with water and used it as a swimming hole, even when it degenerated into a mud wallow and we had to rinse each other off with the garden hose before we could go indoors. When we got older – when we were teenagers, after my grandparents had died – we would lie out on the grass after dinner, drinking illicit booze and talking and laughing as the owls called in the darkening sky and Hugo moved back and forth across the lit windows. Often there were other people there with us – it was true, what I'd told Melissa: Sean and Dec and the rest of my mates were always in and out, so were the others' mates, sometimes for afternoons, sometimes for parties, occasionally for weeks. At the time I took the whole scenario for granted as a happy near-necessity of life, something everyone should have and what a shame that my friends had somehow missed out, but at least they could share mine. It's only now, much too late, that I can't help wondering if it was ever really so simple.

The ivy was still there, lush and glossy with summer, but the house was more dilapidated than it had been in my grandparents' time; nothing dramatic, but there were rusty patches on the iron railings where the black paint had flaked away, the spiderweb fan-light was dusty and the lavender bushes in the snippet of front garden could have done with pruning. 'Here we go,' I said, hefting our cases.

Someone was standing in the open door. At first I barely recognised it as a person; stripped of substance by the bright sunfall through the leaves, flutter of white T-shirt, confusing gold swirl of hair, white brushstroke face and dense dark smudges of eyes, it had something illusory about it, as if my mind had conjured it from patches of light and shadow and at any moment it might break up and be gone. The smell of lavender rose up to meet me, spectrally strong.

Then I got closer and realised that it was Susanna, holding a watering can and watching me, unmoving. I slowed down – I'd discovered that if I concentrated and kept it slow, I could sort of disguise the leg thing as an indolent, too-cool-to-care stroll. Even through the Xanax, the feel of her eyes on me made my jaw clench. I had to stop myself from reaching up to smooth down the hair over my scar.

'Holy shit,' Susanna said, as we reached the bottom of the steps. 'You made it.'

'Like I said I would.'

94

'Well. More or less.' One corner of her wide mouth quirked up in a smile I couldn't read. 'How're you doing?'

'Fine. No complaints.'

'You got skinny. Watch out for my mum. She's got a lemon poppy-seed cake and she's not afraid to use it.' When I groaned: 'Relax. I'll tell her you're allergic.' And to Melissa: 'It's good to see you.'

'You too,' Melissa said. 'Susanna, is it really OK, me being here? Toby says he's sure it's fine, but—'

'He's right, it's fine. Better than fine. Thanks for doing it.' She upended the watering can over the nearest lavender bush and turned back into the house. 'Come on in.'

I dragged our cases up the steps, gritting my teeth, and left them inside the door, and somehow, before I really knew what was happening, I was inside the Ivy House. Melissa and I followed Susanna over the familiar worn tiles of the hall – wayward breezes blowing everywhere, all the windows had to be open – and down the steps towards the kitchen.

Voices rose up to meet us: my uncle Oliver's emphatic declamation, a kid yelling in outrage, my aunt Miriam's big throaty laugh. 'Oh Jesus,' I said. Somehow it hadn't even occurred to me. 'Shit. Sunday lunch.'

Susanna, up ahead, didn't hear that or ignored it, but Melissa's face turned to me. 'What?'

'On Sundays everyone comes here for lunch. I didn't think – I haven't gone in forever, and with Hugo sick, I never figured— *Shit*. I'm sorry.'

Melissa squeezed my hand for a second. 'It's fine. I like your family.'

I knew she hadn't bargained for this any more than I had, but before I could answer we were into the big stone-flagged kitchen and the room hit me like a fire hose to the face. Hubbub of voices, the fly and strike of sunlight through the open French doors, meaty casserole smell catching the back of my throat and turning me somewhere between starving and nauseated, movement everywhere – I knew there could only be a dozen people there, maximum, apart from me and Melissa, but after months of near-solitude it felt like a football crowd or a rave, much too much, what had I been thinking? My father and Uncle Oliver and Uncle Phil all talking at once and pointing their glasses at each other, Leon leaning over the kitchen table on his elbows playing some hand-slap game with one of Susanna's kids, Aunt Louisa dodging about clearing plates— After the silted-up debris and dust of my apartment the whole place looked unnaturally clean and colourful, like a stage set freshly constructed in preparation for this moment. I thought about grabbing Melissa and backing straight out of there, before anyone noticed we had arrived—

A cry of 'Toby!' and my mother popped out of the mass of bodies, glad-faced, catching my hand and Melissa's and talking nineteen to the dozen – I couldn't take in a word – and that was it: we were trapped, too late to run for it. Someone shoved a glass into my hand and I took a big gulp, prosecco mimosa, I could have done with something a lot stronger but that would probably have been a bad idea with the Xanax and at least it was booze— Miriam throwing her arms around me, in a cloud of essential oils and hennaed hair, and congratulating me on the exhibition ('Oliver and I have been *meaning* to get to it, now that Leon's home we can all go together, a family excursion – Hugo can come too, a bit of art would do him good— What happened to that boy who was all over your Facebook page? Grunger?') and on being alive, which was apparently an indicator of my exceptional resistance to negative energy. Tom, Susanna's husband, pumping my hand like we were at some kind of religious meeting and giving me a great big earnest smile full of empathy and encouragement and all kinds of good stuff that made me hope Susanna was banging his best friend. Oliver landing a back-slap that doubled my vision, 'Ah, the wounded warrior! I'd say you gave as good as you got, though, am I right? I'd say there are a couple of burglars out there questioning their career choice—' and on and on, punctuated with belly-shaking chortles, until Phil must have caught my increasingly wall-eyed look because he cut in with some question about my opinion on the housing crisis, on which frankly I had had no opinion even before I got clocked on the head but at least it distracted Oliver. My mother regaling us with the saga of some byzantine department feud that had climaxed with one medieval-studies professor chasing another down a corridor, whacking at him with a sheaf of documents ('in front of the students! It was on YouTube within ten minutes!') – she tells a story well, but my mind kept cutting in and out, skidding off on tangents (child's drawing stuck to the fridge and I couldn't work out what it was meant to be, dinosaur, dragon? had Leon had that platinum-streaked forelock last time I saw him, it looked ridiculous, he looked like a My Little Pony, could I have forgotten that? how was I going to lug Melissa's and my cases up the stairs?) and by the time my mother finished the story I couldn't remember how it had started. I laughed when Melissa did and talked as little as possible – the slur in my speech had faded a bit but not enough, unless I was super-careful I still sounded handicapped. The Xanax didn't stop me from longing to get out of that room, to just about anywhere that didn't have my mother's eyes skipping to me too often and Leon elbow-ing me in the back every time he gestured; it just stopped me from imagining any conceivable way to do it.

'I'm very glad you came,' my father said, suddenly at my shoulder. His sleeves were rolled and his hair was rucked up in tufts; he looked like he'd been there a long time. 'Hugo's been looking forward to seeing you.'

'Oh,' I said. 'Right.' Getting to this point had taken so much concentration that I'd practically forgotten why I was there to begin with. 'How's he feeling?'

'He's all right. He had his first radiotherapy session on Wednesday and it's left him a bit tired, but apart from that he's himself.' My father's voice was level, but the undercurrent of pain made me look at him properly. He seemed somehow thinner and puffy at the same time, a slight sag under his eyes and his jawline that I didn't remember being there before, bones showing under the loose skin of his forearms. I had a sudden flash of deep, premonitory terror – it had never really hit me before that my father would get old, so would my mother, someday I would be hanging around their kitchen waiting for one of them to die. 'You should go say hello.'

'Right,' I said, downing my mimosa. Melissa had been nabbed by

Miriam. 'I probably should,' and I threaded my way through the press of bodies, flinching at every touch, towards Hugo.

I had been dreading seeing him, pretty badly, actually – not out of squeamishness, simply because I had no idea what it might do to my head and I really couldn't handle any more surprises. Hugo was the tallest of the four brothers, well over six foot, with the wide-shouldered, rangy build of a hill farmer and a big, shaggy head with big, messy features, as if the sculptor had given the clay a rough general shape and left the detail for later. I had had nightmare visions of him emaciated, glassy-eyed, huddled in a chair with his long fingers picking fitfully at the covering blanket— But there he was at the old stove, stirring a chipped blue enamel saucepan, eyebrows down and lips pushed out in concentration. He looked so exactly like himself that I felt silly for having got all worked up.

'Hugo,' I said.

'Toby,' he said, turning to me, breaking into a smile. 'How lovely.'

I braced myself for his pat on the shoulder, but somehow it didn't trigger the savage surge of repulsion that any non-Melissa physical contact set off in me. His hand was warm and heavy and simple as an animal's paw or a hot-water bottle. 'It's good to see you,' I said.

'Well, I didn't do this to get you all here, but it's a pleasant side effect. Does this look ready to you?'

I looked into the saucepan. Creamy amber swirl with a smell straight out of my childhood, caramel and vanilla: Gran's famous ice-cream sauce. 'I think it needs a couple more minutes.'

'So do I.' He went back to stirring. 'Louisa kept insisting that I shouldn't bother, but the children love it . . . And how are you? You've been having adventures of your own.' Tilting his head to examine my scar; when I tensed, he turned back to the stove immediately. 'We have matching war wounds,' he said. 'Although luckily yours is part of a very different story from mine. Does it hurt?'

'Not much any more,' I said. Till he mentioned it, I hadn't noticed the shaved patch and the raised red line on the side of his head, among the too-long salt-and-pepper hair.

'Good. You're young; you'll heal well. And have you recovered?'

That sharp skimming glance, from his grey eyes. None of us had ever been able to get anything past that glance. Sunday lunch, that glance sweeping across the cousins and catching on sixteen-year-old me expertly concealing a hangover: *Hm.* And later, in my ear, with a quirk of a smile: *One fewer next time, I think, Toby.* 'Pretty much,' I said. 'How are you doing?'

'Disorientated,' Hugo said. 'More than anything else. Which seems silly; I'm sixty-seven, after all, I've known for years that something like this could be sprung on me at any moment. But to have it become solid fact, and imminent, is inexpressibly strange.' He raised the spoon out of the sauce and inspected the long thread that trailed from it. 'The counsellor at the hospital – poor woman, what a job – did a lot of talking about denial, but I don't think it's that: I'm well aware that I'm dying. It's that everything seems altered, in fundamental ways, everything from eating breakfast to my own home. It's very dislocating.'

'Susanna said something about radiotherapy,' I said, 'didn't she? Couldn't that fix things?'

'Only if it were combined with surgery – and probably not even then – but the doctor says that's not a possibility. Susanna's trawling the internet, researching the top specialists in order to get a second opinion, but I don't think I can afford to put too much stock in that.' He pointed at the vanilla bottle, on the counter near me. 'Could you pass me that? I think we could do with a drop more.'

I handed it over. Propped against the counter beside it was my grandfather's old silver-headed walking stick, ready to hand.

'Ah,' Hugo said, catching the direction of my eyes. 'Yes, well. I can't manage the stairs without it any more; even walking is a bit of a problem, off and on. No more mountain hikes for me, I'm afraid. It seems like an odd thing to be bothered by, in the circumstances, but in some ways it's the trivial things that are the most upsetting.'

'I'm sorry,' I said. 'I really am.'

'I know. I appreciate that. Could you put this back in the cupboard?'

We stood there for a while, watching the rhythmic turn of the spoon in the saucepan. A soft breeze, rich with earth and grass, wandered in at the French doors; behind us, Leon's voice rose to a punch line and everyone burst out laughing. The creases and sags of Hugo's face gave him a dozen familiar expressions at once, made him unreadable.

I felt as if there was some crucial question I should be asking him; some secret he knew that could change everything, illuminate the last terrible months and the ones to come in a new undreamed-of light that would turn them not just bearable but harmless, if only I knew how to ask. For a startling, vertiginous moment that was gone almost as soon as I recognised it, I found myself on the verge of tears.

'There,' Hugo said, moving the pan off the heat. 'That should do it. Really we should let it cool for a while, but—' Turning to the room: 'Who'll have ice cream?'

•

The whole afternoon was very strange. There was a bizarre festive quality to it – maybe just the overlay of all those remembered celebrations, maybe the fact that so many of us hadn't seen each other in months or years. Bowls of curly blown yellow roses everywhere, the special silverware with some forgotten ancestor's initials on the scuffed handles, Gran's big-occasion emerald earrings swinging and sparking from Aunt Louisa's ears; waves of laughter and ring of glass on glass, *Cheers! cheers!*

In spite of the familiarity, though, there was something off-kilter about it all. People were doing the wrong things, those earrings on Louisa, Tom instead of Hugo laying out the ice-cream bowls while Hugo – a sudden grey layer of fatigue veiling his face – sat at the kitchen table, nodding at whatever Tom was gabbling about; two little blond kids who weren't us running around among people's legs making airplane noises and grabbing stuff off each other, Susanna quelling them with a glare exactly like the one Louisa used to throw at us; and there I was with another mimosa in my hand, nodding while my uncle Phil meandered on about the ethics of corporate tax breaks. It felt like being in one of those horror films where unspeakable entities take over the supporting characters' bodies but not quite well enough, our hero spots the slip-ups and tumbles to the plot unfolding under his very nose— At first this was just unsettling, but as the afternoon wore on and on (the ice cream and caramel sauce, coffee, liqueurs, I didn't want any of it and it just kept on coming) it set off an awful, swelling riptide deep inside me. Louisa bearing down on me with a gargantuan chunk of lemon poppyseed cake and a determined eye, Susanna smoothly intercepting her with a shocked 'Mum! Toby's allergic!', Melissa gallantly vowing that lemon poppyseed was her favourite, Oliver blowing his nose cacophonously into a vast handkerchief and glowering darkly at the roses: they all looked utterly alien, these people who were supposed to be my nearest and dearest, collections of jerking limbs and colours and gurning faces that added up to nothing at all, certainly nothing to do with me. Every jostle of my elbow or movement in the corner of my eye made me leap like a spooked horse, and the constant adrenaline spikes and plummets were exhausting. I could feel that vortex opening at the base of my brain, the tension starting to build like a storm front in my spine. I had no idea how I was going to get through the rest of the day.

Somehow the plates were cleared and rinsed and loaded into the dishwasher, but no one seemed to be leaving; instead we all moved into the living room, and someone made a fresh round of mimosas. Everyone was knocking them back a little too hard. Leon was re-enacting a spectacular face-off between a drag queen and a punk that he swore he'd seen in a Berlin club and that had my mother and Tom and Louisa in gales of laughter, *Leon, she didn't! Oh God, stop, my stomach hurts* . . . I caught a glimpse of my father knuckling his eye and looking utterly exhausted, but the next moment Miriam turned to him and he snapped into animation, smiling down at her as he said something that made her hoot and whack his arm. Phil was leaning in at Susanna, talking too fast and gesticulating so forcefully that he rocked back and forth a little on his feet with the momentum. The high-ceilinged room jumbled all the voices into gibberish and the whole thing had a precarious, unmoored feel to it, a knees-up in some Blitz-time basement as bombs whistled overhead, the hilarity brittle as an ice sheet and on the verge of skidding wildly out of control, that's the spirit, faster and higher and faster until boom! all gone!

I couldn't stand it any more. I glanced about for Melissa, but she was ensconced on one of the sofas with Hugo, deep in conversation; there was no way we could slip unobtrusively away. I went back down to the kitchen, ran myself a glass of cold water and took it out onto the terrace.

After the babble of noise and colour inside, the garden had a stillness that was almost holy. The thing I always forget about the Ivy House garden, the one that catches me afresh every time, is the light. It's different from anywhere else, grained like the bleached light in an old home movie of summer, as if it were emanating from the scene itself rather than entering from any outside source. In front of me the grass stretched on and on, overgrown, rough with tall ragweed and bright with poppies and cornflowers; under the trees, the patches of shadow were pure and deep as holes in the earth. Heat shimmered over it all.

Voices, clear as robins', making me jump. There were children playing, down at the bottom of the garden: one swooping crazy patterns on a rope-swing, flicking in and out of existence as it arced from shadow to light and back again, one rising out of the long grass with hands held high and wide to scatter something. Thin brown limbs in ceaseless movement, white-blond hair shining. Even though I knew they were Susanna's kids, for a sliding second I thought they were two of us, Leon and Susanna, me and Susanna? One of them called out, sharp and imperious, but I couldn't tell whether it was meant for me. I held my glass against my temple and ignored them.

The garden had the same look of low-level unkemptness as the front of the house, but that wasn't new. For a city garden it's enormous, well over a hundred feet long. It's lined along the side walls with oak trees and silver birches and wych elms, behind the rear laneway by the back of an old school or factory or something – adapted into a hip apartment block during the Celtic Tiger – five or six storeys high; all that towering height gives the place a secret, sunken feel. Gran was the gardener; in her time the garden was artfully, delicately crafted till it felt like somewhere out of a fairy tale, slyly revealing its delights one by one as you earned them, look, behind this tree, crocuses! and over here, hidden under the rosemary bush, wild strawberries, all for you! She died when I was thirteen, less than a year after my grandfather, and since then Hugo had loosened the reins a lot ('Not just laziness,' he told me once, smiling out the kitchen window at the summer confusion of growth; 'I prefer it running a bit wild. I don't mean dandelions, they're just thugs, but I like getting a glimpse of its true colours'). Gradually plants had strayed and tangled, long tendrils of ivy and jasmine trailing from the wall of the house, tumult of green leaves on the unpruned trees and seed-heads poking up among the long grass; the garden had lost its enchanted air and taken on a different quality, remote and self-possessed, archaeological. Mostly I felt that I had liked it better before, but that day I was grateful for the new version; I was in no mood for whimsical charm.

The smaller kid had caught sight of me. She stood for a while examining me from amid the Queen Anne's lace, swaying a handful of stems back and forth with absent-minded persistence. Then she drifted over.

'Hi,' I said.

The kid – it took me a second to find her name: Sallie – regarded me with opaque, feline blue eyes. I couldn't remember how old she was; four, maybe? 'I have dolls in my shoes,' she said.

'Oh,' I said. I had no idea what she meant. 'That's nice.'

'Look.' She balanced herself with a hand on a big geranium pot and turned up the sole of one trainer, then the other. An inch-high doll, encased in a thick bubble of clear plastic, gave me a stupefied leer from each one.

'Huh,' I said. 'That's cool.'

'I don't know how to get them out,' Sallie said. For a moment I was afraid she was expecting me to do something about that, but just then her brother – Zach, that was it – followed her over and stood beside her. He was a head taller, but apart from that they were a lot alike, the same pale tangled curls and fine egg-brown skin and unblinking pale-blue eyes. Together they looked like something out of a horror movie.

'Are you going to be living here?' he asked me.

'For a couple of weeks. Yeah.'

'Why?'

I had no idea what Susanna had told them about Hugo. I had a vision of me saying the wrong thing and both of them exploding into piercing howls of trauma. 'Because,' I said. And when they kept staring: 'I'm visiting Hugo.'

Zach was holding a stick; he swished it through the air, making a fine, nasty hissing sound. 'Grownups aren't supposed to live with their *uncle*. They live by them*selves*.'

'I don't *live* with him. I'm *visiting* him.' Zach had struck me as a little shit before. One Christmas Susanna had had to take him away from the dinner table for spitting in his sister's turkey because it looked better than his.

'My mum said you got hit in the head. Are you special needs now?'

'No,' I said. 'Are you?'

He gave me a long stare that could have meant anything, although probably not anything good. 'Come on,' he said to Sallie, flicking her on the leg with his stick, and he headed off down the grass with her trailing after him.

My leg was starting to judder – too much standing. I sat down on the terrace steps. Stretch of grass by the camomile patch where Leon and Susanna and I had pitched a tent and camped for a week one summer, giggly and eating biscuits and scaring each other with spooky stories all night, heavy-eyed and ratty all day, redolent of camomile where we had rolled over onto the plants. Over there the tree where in the dizzying darkness of Leon's fourteenth birthday party I had had my first real kiss, a slight sweet blonde called Charlotte, illicit cider taste of her tongue and the softness of her breasts against me, cheers and whoops from the lads somewhere *Go on Toby you legend* and the unending soft whoosh of the breeze in the leaves overhead. This terrace where we had sprawled the first time we smoked hash, stars overhead bouncing into tantalising coded patterns and the smell of jasmine strong as music in the air, and I had with total solemnity convinced Leon that Susanna had turned into a tiny fairy and I had her cupped in my hands, him trying to peer between my fingers *Hey babes talk to me are you OK in there?* while Susanna was right beside us and there had been someone else there too, Dec, Sean? someone at my shoulder and shivering with laughter in the darkness, who? Holes in my mind, blind spots shimmering nastily like migraine aura. All these landmarks, close enough to touch and miles out of reach. Now, great big grown-ass man me, I could no more have mustered the courage to sleep in that tent than I could have flown.

'Oh my God,' Leon said, behind me, slamming the terrace door with a flick of his wrist. 'What a *nightmare*.'

'What?' I asked. The slam had made me leap like a startled cat, but Leon didn't seem to have noticed; he was fishing a pack of Marlboro Reds out of the pocket of his jeans, which were black and shredded in weird places and so tight that he had trouble getting the smokes out. He was also wearing a Patti Smith T-shirt and Docs the size of his head.

'The whole thing. Like some lovely family re*union* and we'll all be sent off on a scavenger hunt any minute. It's grotesque. But I guess that's Hugo, isn't it, keep calm and carry on—' He bent his head to the lighter. 'Which, yeah, respect, he's got guts and whatever, but still. Jesus.' Tossing back his forelock as he straightened: 'Is that vodka?'

'Just water.'

'Shit. I left my drink on the windowsill and now my mother's there, and if I go back for it she'll start asking me about some amazing cultural *event* she read was on in Berlin and have I been to it and what do I think? And I honest-to-God can't.' He inhaled deeply and thirstily.

Leon and Susanna were the ones who had been on my mind the most, over the last few days. When I was a kid, the aunts and uncles – not Hugo, he was different, but Oliver and Miriam, Phil and Louisa – had been basically an amorphous cloud of adulthood that occasionally fed us and mostly needed avoiding in case they made us stop doing something, and even when I grew up I had never really put in the attention to bring them into sharp focus. But

Leon and Susanna: they had been, to all intents and purposes, my brother and sister; we had known each other with the same complete, matter-of-fact intimacy with which we knew our own hands. Some tiny inchoate part of me had been hoping, against all reason, that just being around them would magically bring together all my pulverised fragments, that with them I couldn't be anything but myself. The rest of me had been dreading meeting them, with an awful churning terror that they would take one look and see straight through all my pathetic concealments, to every fine detail of the damage.

'Here,' I said, holding out my hand. I was still thrumming with adrenaline. 'Give me one of those.'

Leon glanced over, one eyebrow arched. 'Since when?'

I shrugged. 'Off and on.' In fact I'd barely smoked a cigarette in my life until a month or two back, but I wasn't about to say that in case he interpreted it as some dramatic lunge towards self-destruction, which it wasn't. The head-injury thing had done something weird to my sense of smell; I kept picking up improbable scents (reek of disinfectant off my microwave pasta, sudden rush of my father's cologne as I pulled the curtains closed for night-time), and since the awful warnings about smoking always waxed ominous about how it destroyed your sense of smell, I figured it was worth a try. So far I had managed to hide it from Melissa, but I felt safe enough; she was hardly likely to ditch Hugo and come looking for me.

Leon passed me a cigarette and his lighter. Of us three, he was the one who had changed most. When we were little kids he had been sparky and mischievous, in constant motion, but somewhere around the time we hit secondary school that had changed. We were in different classes, but I knew he had taken a certain amount of hassle – small, slight, suspiciously delicate-featured and gentle, it had been inevitable; I'd done what I could, but when I caught a glimpse of him in the corridors he had always been hurrying along, head tucked down, shrunken and self-contained. He was still a couple of inches shorter than me, and he still had the elfin look and the ragged dark hair falling in one eye – although now the raggedness had clearly taken about an hour and a metric ton of hairwax – but I had trouble overlaying either of those memories on this slim guy slouching against the wall, jiggling one foot and looking cool enough to imply that your whole life was an exercise in missing out.

'Thanks,' I said, passing back the lighter.

Leon had relaxed enough to look at me properly – I had to stop myself turning away. 'Sorry I didn't ring you more,' he said abruptly. 'When you got hurt.'

'You're fine. You texted me.'

'Just, your mum said all you needed was peace and quiet and not to be hassled, so . . .' A one-shouldered shrug. 'Still, though. I should have rung. Or come over.'

'Jesus, no. No need for that.' I couldn't tell whether my voice sounded casual enough, too casual— 'I just, all I wanted to do was chill out and, and take it easy. Like, shitty daytime telly in my pyjamas, you know? I wouldn't have been great company.'

'Still,' Leon said. 'Sorry.'

'You're here now, anyway,' I said. I didn't want to talk about this any more. 'Are you staying here?'

'Oh *hell* no. I'm at my parents'. God help me.' He wiggled the lighter into his pocket. 'I'd actually way rather be here, except once I moved in, boom, I'd be the designated carer and I'd never be able to leave because then it would be all my fault if Hugo collapsed and died alone, and no thank you very much. I love Hugo, I want to spend time with him while I can and I'm happy to help out for a few weeks, but I can't make any big long-term commitments. I've got a job' – Leon worked for some achingly hip indie record label, I couldn't remember the name – 'I've got a relationship, I've got a *life*. And I'd like to keep them.'

I didn't much like the sound of this – I had no intention of being the designated carer, either – but then Leon had always been kind of a drama queen, and it sounded like someone had been leaning on him pretty hard. 'Pressure?' I asked.

He rolled his eyes to heaven. 'Don't even get me started. My mother *and* my father. They've been tag-teaming me, like a pair of *interrogators*, every single day. First she'd call to go on about poor Hugo spending his last days alone and bring on the violins, then he'd call with a big pompous speech about how good Hugo's always been to me and wouldn't it make sense to give a little of that back, then she'd call to tell me how they have *total* faith in me to be able to *handle things* just for a *little while*, and after that I don't know who would say what because that's when I'd stop answering my phone. I'm hoping they'll back off now that I'm at least in town, but I don't know, they might step it up and hope that if they drive me mental enough I'll move in here just to get away from them. Which I won't.'

He was a little drunk, but not enough that most people would have noticed. 'I'm staying here,' I said.

His face whipped around to me, eyebrows sky-high. *'You?'*

The incredulity – like I was a chimpanzee put in charge of a rocket launch – set my teeth on edge. 'Yeah. Me. Is there a problem?'

After a moment Leon let his head fall back against the wall and started to laugh, up at the sky. 'Oh. My. God,' he said. 'This is beautiful. I can't *wait* to see this.'

'What's funny?'

'Our Toby, the angel of mercy, sacrificing himself to care for those in need—'

'For a couple of *weeks*. I'm not planning on being the designated carer either.' And when that turned the laugh into a dry, knowing snort: 'What?'

'Surprise surprise.'

'What are you bitching at me for? You just said there's no way you'll move in even for—'

'Because once I was in I'd never get out. While you'll just prance off, won't you, the minute you've had enough—'

The cigarette and the booze and the whole fever-tinted afternoon were making me feel sick; I really wasn't in the mood for this. 'It's not my fault if you don't have the, the' – I was looking for *cojones* – 'the balls to stand up to your parents—'

'—and we all know that won't take long. I give you a week. Ten days, max.'

The snide flick in his voice, like I was some pampered prince who had never dealt with anything tougher than a hangover— If only he knew, Mr Cool with his faux-meaningful leather bracelets and his carefree all-night-clubbing life, if he had the faintest clue— 'What the fuck are you babbling about? You don't think I'm able for it?'

I was at least semi-deliberately asking for trouble. Leon always did get defensive easily; the snap in my voice was the perfect way to turn him nasty, especially when he was already on edge. It wasn't that I was aiming to get into a knock-down-drag-out fight on the terrace – although I could think of worse ways to spend the time; it sounded like someone inside had started singing – but I did, with a vicious, self-flagellating intensity, want Leon to lose his cool and tell me exactly what he thought about this new version of me.

He brought up his cigarette and took a long pull. 'You're not exactly at your best right now,' he said, on a sideways stream of smoke. 'Are you?'

The rush of anger almost felt good. 'What? I'm *fine*.'

A glance under his eyelids. 'If you say so.'

'What the fuck is that supposed to mean?'

I couldn't tell how close I was to punching him, but he didn't seem worried. One corner of his mouth curled upwards. 'Oh, *please*. How many words have you said today? A dozen? How many bites did you eat in there, like two?'

I laughed, a startled yelp that echoed off the high walls. I had been expecting something about my walk, my inability to follow the thread of a conversation, the agonising pauses as I fumbled for words: a deft, pitiless slice straight to the jugular that would leave me bloodied and reeling. In its place I had got a snippy little finger-wag about not being chatty enough and not eating my greens, and I was practically light-headed with relief.

'Today sucks,' I said, still laughing. 'Like you said. I can't be arsed making the effort to pretend everything's great. If you can, away you go. I'll watch.'

'Now that's the Toby I know and love,' Leon said. There was an edge to his voice; he didn't like being laughed at. 'Leave the dirty work to everyone else.'

'I'm not making you do anything, dude. I'm just doing my own thing. Nothing wrong with that.' It came out so naturally, so exactly the way the old me would have said it, and the fast upwards jerk of Leon's chin made it so clear that I was getting to him, I couldn't stop laughing.

'That's bullshit,' he snapped. '*Dude*. Have you seen your eyes? Just because you can slip it past them' – toss of his head towards the house – 'that doesn't mean you're actually doing an amazing job of hiding it. You're off your tits on something.'

This made me laugh so hard that smoke went down my nose. I doubled over, hacking. '*And* you're hysterical,' Leon said sourly, moving away from me. 'Whatever you're on—'

'Heroin, man. All the cool kids are taking it. You should really—'

'You know what would be great? If you would just shut up. Just finish your cigarette – *my* cigarette – and go inside and leave me alone.'

'Oh, here you are,' Susanna said, ducking surreptitiously out of the back door with a fast wary glance behind her. 'Your dad's singing "Raglan Road", Leon. I said I'd go find you guys, since obviously you wouldn't want to miss that. I think it might take me a while, though. What's so funny?'

'Toby's lost his mind,' Leon said, grinding out his cigarette viciously under his heel. 'What there was of it.'

'Jesus,' I said, catching my breath. My heart was skittering. 'That was worth this entire shitty afternoon.'

'Thanks a lot,' Susanna told me. 'You've been great company too.'

'The company's been' – I was looking for *scintillating*, couldn't find it – 'gorgeous. Dazzling. But you've got to admit, given a choice of ways to spend the day, this comes right below a, a root canal.'

'Tell me you brought booze,' Leon said to Susanna. 'I can't face going back in there till I've had more drink.'

'I thought you had some. Hang on' – turning, eye to the crack of the door – 'OK, it looks clear. I'm going in. If I get nabbed, you come get me, right? I'm serious.' She vanished back into the kitchen.

'Sorry about that,' I said. I was feeling a lot warmer towards

Leon, and not just because he thought the only thing wrong with me was a few too many party favours. We hadn't been close in a long time, not since we left school – new friends, widening social lives, plus he had come out and had made sure everyone noticed by going through an over-the-top phase of the kind of stereotypical drugs and clubs that definitely weren't my scene, and we had never really made our way back from that – but there was something very heartening about the discovery that I could still push his buttons with practically no effort. 'Just, for a second there it sounded like you thought I was banging up or something. It was beautiful.'

Leon lit another cigarette, without offering me one.

'It's just painkillers. I still get the odd headache from the concussion. No big deal. I just didn't feel like coping with today and a headache at the same time.'

'Whatever.'

'Did anyone else notice?'

He made a dismissive *pfft* noise. 'Nah. Even if they did, they'll just think you're still shaken up. My mother says you need yoga classes to re-centre your energy.'

That pulled a snort of laughter out of me, and after a moment he gave a reluctant half-grin. 'Wonderful,' I said. 'I'll be sure and ask her for recommendations.'

'Just be careful,' Leon said, glancing after Susanna and lowering his voice. The edge had gone out of his tone. 'I had a friend who . . . well, anyway. All I'm saying is, whatever you're taking, just because you get them from a doctor, that doesn't mean they're harmless little Smarties. Don't get cocky.'

'Who, me? Never.'

Leon's mouth twisted, but before he could say anything Susanna nipped back out the door, holding a bottle of wine. 'Score,' she said. 'We're definitely going to need supplies. Your dad's doing "Spancil Hill" now, Leon.'

'Oh Christ.'

'I couldn't get Melissa out,' Susanna told me. 'Your mother's got her arm around her.'

'I should go in there,' I said, without moving.

'She looks OK.'

'She is OK. Melissa would be OK anywhere. That's not the point.'

'You won't believe this,' Leon told Susanna. Flicking his chin at me: 'He's staying here.'

Susanna sat down next to me on the steps, produced a corkscrew from her back pocket and held the bottle between her knees. 'I know. I asked him to.'

Leon's eyebrows shot up. 'You never said.'

'Well, I didn't think he'd actually do it. But' – a flash of a smile to me, as she wrestled with the cork – 'looks like I underestimated him.'

'It's so easy to do,' Leon said, out to the garden.

The cork came out with a pop. Susanna took a swig, with a relish that startled me – part of me still thought of her as an eight-year-old – and passed the bottle to me. 'Ignore him,' she said to me. 'He's had a shit day.'

'Haven't we all,' I said. The wine was red, heavy and late-summery, and I could tell even before it hit my tongue that it was strong. 'How are you doing?'

'About how you'd expect,' Susanna said, tilting her head up and massaging the back of her neck. She had changed a lot less than Leon. Her hair was in a wavy chin-length tumble instead of the two thick childhood plaits or the graceless teenage flop, and her old bony plainness had settled into something arresting in its serene aura of permanence, its implication that she would look much the same in twenty years, or fifty; but having babies had softened her long-legged angularity only a little, she was wearing faded jeans and almost no makeup, and she still sat the way she had as a kid, cross-legged and unselfconscious. 'Tom's turning into the back-rub king. How about you?'

'Fine.'

'Honestly?'

'Well, I don't have Tom's back-rubs. But apart from that, I'm fine.' I caught Leon's sardonic glance and ignored it.

'Whatever that means right now,' Susanna said, reaching for Leon's cigarette. Someone, presumably one of the kids, had drawn some kind of bug on her hand in purple marker. 'Give me a drag of that.'

'You can have your own. Here—'

'I don't want my own. I don't want the kids seeing me smoking.'

She was a bit drunk, too; now that I came to think of it, so was I. 'Give me one,' I said to Leon. 'I'll share with Su.' The kids were down at the bottom of the garden poking something in the grass with sticks, and they didn't appear to be taking any interest in us, but I've always been a little protective of Susanna, even though she's only three months younger than me. I can remember being about five, picking her up around the chest with a mighty effort and waddling frantically away from the wasp that had been circling her. I lit the cigarette, took a deep drag and passed it to her.

'My dad's not fine,' she said, on a stream of smoke. 'We were over there the other day and I walked in on him crying. Sobbing his heart out.'

'Jesus,' I said.

'Yeah.' She glanced sideways at me. 'He's got some present for you. To make up for missing your birthday party. I think it might be some awful family heirloom. If it's shit, be nice about it.'

'Sure.'

'Because I don't think he could handle even one more tiny— Zach!' Susanna called across the lawn, to where Zach was clambering up into a big wych elm. 'Get out of that tree! How many times have I told you?'

'We used to climb those trees all the time,' I pointed out. Zach was pulling himself farther up the tree, totally ignoring her.

'Right, and then you fell out of that exact one and broke your ankle, you were in a cast for— Zach! Get down right now. Do I have to come over there?'

Zach dropped from a branch, did an exaggerated slump with his head thrown back to inform his mother what a moron she was, and then charged off across the grass to hassle Sallie.

'He's a little bollix sometimes,' Susanna said. 'And Tom's parents don't help. They let him get away with anything, and when they see us making him behave, they're all, "Oh, leave him alone, boys will be boys!" And you know what Hugo's like, "Just let them run wild, they'll turn out fine in the end" – which was great when it was us, but it's not as much fun from the other side.'

I didn't point out that that part of the problem, at least, was likely to take care of itself fairly soon. I wasn't interested in discussing Zach's issues. 'I can't even remember the last time I saw your dad,' I said.

I realised almost instantly, from the surprised silence, that I had put my foot in it. I rummaged frantically in my mind for whatever I was missing; all I could come up with was calling Uncle Phil when I got completely hammered and lost my wallet at some teenage disco and Hugo wasn't answering his phone, the wry look on his face in the car as he advised me to be very quiet on my way into my house, but obviously I had seen him since then—

'But they were here at Christmas,' Susanna said. 'Remember? They gave Zach that dagger thing, and he stabbed the sofa?'

'Oh,' I said. The sharp, intent way she was looking at me, like something was just dawning on her, made my gut clench. 'Duh. I guess my mind was on other stuff at Christmas, I had like a lot on at work? and all the Christmases kind of blur together, right, specially since a lot's happened—' Leon snorted, just loudly enough to be obvious. The sofa-stabbing didn't sound like the kind of thing that would blur easily.

'You,' Susanna said, with finality, 'are drunk.'

'Yeah,' I said. 'I really am.' I was so grateful to her for the out, so pierced by her infinitely kind and innocent world where nothing worse than a few mimosas could possibly be wrong with anyone's mind, I could have cried.

'Give me that,' Leon said, reaching for the bottle. 'You've had plenty.' The arch of his eyebrow at me said *What with the other stuff.*

'I have, yeah. And I'm planning to have plenty more.'

'Melissa's such a lucky girl. Is she staying here too?'

I shrugged. My heart was hammering: sooner or later I was going to really fuck up, say or do something so moronic that no amount of naïveté could gloss over it, I should never have come here— 'For a few days, yeah.'

'Doesn't want you out of her sight?'

'What can I say, dude. She likes my company. Your guy didn't make it, no?'

'Carsten's got a job. He can't just take off whenever he feels like it.'

'Ooo. He sounds important.'

'I wish this was over,' Leon said, suddenly and fiercely. 'I know that's awful, but I do. What are we supposed to *do*? Are we supposed to pretend it's not happening? There should be a *manual*.'

'I bet in some cultures there is,' Susanna said, taking the bottle off him. 'Rituals you do, when someone's dying. Chants. Dances. Burning herbs.'

'Well, I wish I lived there. Shut up' – to me, when I rolled my eyes – 'I do. What you're supposed to do *after* someone dies, that's all mapped out, wakes and funerals and wreaths and the month's-mind mass. But the part where you're waiting for them to die is at *least* as bad, and there's fuck-all to tell you how to do that.'

'Speaking of when it's over,' Susanna said. 'Does anyone know what happens to the house, afterwards?'

There was a small, intricate silence. Leon pulled a stem of jasmine off the wall and spun it between his fingers, not looking at either of us.

'I mean, it might not come to that,' Susanna said. 'We're getting a second opinion. But if.'

'Jesus,' I said. 'Is it not a bit early to, to go divvying up his stuff?'

Both of them ignored that. Leon said, 'Granddad and Gran's will said Hugo gets to live here.'

'And then what?'

'You mean,' Leon said, 'is it going to be sold.'

'Yeah.'

'Not if I get a say in it.'

'Well, *ob*viously,' Susanna said, with a touch of exasperation. 'What I'm asking is if anyone knows whether we do get a say. If it goes to our dads, and they want to sell it and split the money . . .'

Another silence, this one longer. This whole issue had never occurred to me, and I had no idea what I thought about it. It sounded like Susanna and Leon were not just set on hanging on to the place but also taking it for granted that I felt the same way, although I had no idea what they thought we would do with it: rent it out? share it, all of us together in one great big happy commune, taking turns to cook lentils and tie-dye organic hemp? A few months back I would have been all for selling up – any fraction of the house would have been a big step towards that white Georgian overlooking the bay – but now that whole daydream stabbed like a humiliating joke, it made me feel like one of those deluded caterwaulers babbling about superstardom on *The X Factor*. It was made worse by the paranoid sense that the other two were thinking things I wasn't in on, invisible signals zipping back and forth past my face like insects; I felt like an unwanted outsider, like they would be happier if I made some vague excuse and went inside, or even better if I hauled my bags into another taxi and drove straight back to my apartment.

'Can't you ask your dad what the story is?' Leon said to Susanna. He had taken his lighter out and was flicking the flame at the jasmine stem, blowing it out when it caught.

'Why can't you ask yours?'

'Because you're closer to yours.'

'Just because we live in the same country doesn't mean we're close.'

'It means you *see* him. Which makes it an awful lot easier to casually slip the question into conversation, oh by the way Dad, do you happen to know—'

'Hello? You're *right here*. You're actually *living* with yours.'

Leon blew out the jasmine viciously. 'Which means I've got more than enough on my plate right now, thanks, without—'

'And I don't?'

'Why don't you do it?' Leon said to me. 'You're just sitting there, assuming one of us will—'

I was finding this bickering weirdly comforting, actually, with its familiarity and its implication that I wasn't the *persona non grata* here, that maybe everyone was just stressed and out of joint. 'I'm living with Hugo,' I pointed out. 'I can't exactly ask him: hey, Hugo, just wondering, when you kick the bucket—'

'You could ask your dad.'

'You're the one who brought it up. If you're so desperate to know—'

'You're not?'

'Of course he's not,' Susanna said. 'Duh.'

'What's the big deal?' I demanded. 'We'll find out when he dies, what difference does it—'

'*If* he dies—'

'All *right*,' Leon snapped. 'I'll do it.'

Both of us turned to look at him. He shrugged, against the wall. 'I'll ask my dad.'

'OK,' Susanna said, after a moment. 'You do that.'

He dropped the jasmine on the terrace and twisted his heel on it. 'I will.'

'Wonderful,' Susanna said. 'So we can quit bickering. I have to listen to that all day long; I don't want to *do* it too. Is Oliver still going?'

I cocked an ear towards the door. 'Yep. "She Moved Through the Fair."'

'Jesus,' Leon said, rubbing a hand over his face. 'Give me that bottle back.'

Susanna let out a breath precariously near to laughter or tears. '*Last night she came to me,*' she sang softly, '*my dead love came in . . .*'

Oliver's voice, eroded to veil-thinness by distance, fell on hers like an echo. *My dead love came in . . .* Out over the grass, among the Queen Anne's lace and the leaves.

'Oh, perfect,' Leon said, and tilted the bottle to his lips. 'Let's all see how morbid we can get.'

Susanna hummed a few bars of some tune I couldn't put my finger on, till Leon let out a snap of laughter and sang along, in a tenor that was surprisingly rich coming out of someone so slight: '*Isn't it grand, boys, to be bloody well dead? Let's not have a sniffle—*'

I started to laugh. '*Let's have a bloody good cry,*' Susanna joined in, and we all finished it together in style, cigarettes and bottle raised high: '*And always remember the longer you live, the sooner you'll bloody well die!*'

A sound behind us, in the kitchen: cupboard door closing. After one horrified second all three of us collapsed with laughter simultaneously, as if we'd been sandbagged. Leon was doubled over, Susanna had choked on the wine and was whooping, banging herself on the chest; I felt tears run down my face. The laughter felt uncontrollable and terrifying as vomiting. 'Oh, God,' Leon gasped. '*Look at the coffin, with golden handles—*'

'Shut *up, Jesus*, if that's Hugo—'

'Wow,' Tom said, appearing in the doorway. 'So this is where the real party is.'

We took one look at him and collapsed again. 'What?' he said, bewildered. When none of us could answer: 'Are you smoking something?'

The question was jocular, but just enough of a serious undertone sneaked through that Leon straightened up and gave him a wide-eyed paranoid look, hand to heart. 'Oh my God. Does it show?'

Tom blinked at him. Tom is medium height and medium stocky and medium blond and medium handsome and extremely sweet, and he brings out the irresistible urge to warn him about drop bears and dihydrogen monoxide. 'Um,' he said. 'What . . . ? Like, what is it?'

'It's just a bit of bingo,' Leon said. 'Have you ever tried it?'

'Bingo?'

'Oh, you should,' I said. 'I bet bingo would be the biggest thrill of your life.'

Tom – worried, eyebrows pulled down – was glancing back and forth between us and Susanna, who had hit the point where all she could manage was to flap a hand helplessly in his direction. 'I don't—'

'It's totally legal,' Leon said reassuringly.

'Well,' I said.

'Well. More or less.'

'Do you want a hit?' I offered Tom my cigarette.

'Um, no thanks. *Su,*' Tom said, rubbing at his neck. 'I mean, the kids. If they—'

This obliterated Susanna all over again. 'Oh, they're fine,' Leon said. 'They're *miles* away.' He waved to the kids.

'If they notice anything,' I said, 'we'll talk to them about it. Give them the facts. In today's world, the sooner you educate your kids about bingo the better, right?'

'I guess. But I mean, I don't think—'

I'd never really got Tom. When Susanna met him, in our first year of college, everyone was delighted. She had been having some kind of ornate teenage crisis over the past year and had first gone into emo mode, lank hair and oversized jumpers and no social life and lots of music about too-passionate spirits crushed by the cruel unfeeling world, and then done a 180 and turned into a full-on wild child, Alice-in-Wonderland clothes and pop-up clubs in secret locations, disappearing for weeks except for a handful of vague giggly texts from someone's camper van in Cornwall and never handing in her essays. To me it all looked like standard teenage-girl stuff, but her parents were worried enough that Aunt Louisa kept buttonholing me to ask whether I thought Susanna was cutting herself (how would I know?) and whether I thought she took drugs (definitely, but then so did I), and I knew they had tried a few times to get her to see a therapist. Tom – sturdy, peaceful, pleasant, unremarkable in every way – seemed like the perfect antidote; once she got together with him, Susanna settled down and, almost overnight, went back to her old untroublesome well-behaved self. I didn't bother developing much of a relationship with him, since I assumed she would move on once he had got her solidly back to normal, and I was completely gobsmacked when instead, before they had even finished college, they decided to get married. Within a couple of years they had two kids and much of their conversation revolved around toilet training and school choices and various other things that made me want to get a vasectomy and go on a coke binge. Basically, while Tom seemed like an OK guy, I didn't see what he was still doing in our lives.

'You,' Susanna told us, finally getting her breath back. 'Stop fucking with Tom. I like him.'

'We like him too,' I said. 'Don't we, Leon?'

'Looove him,' said Leon, giving Tom a lascivious lash-flutter.

'You bollixes,' Tom said, red and grinning.

'We're only playing,' I said.

'Play with someone else,' Susanna told us. 'Jesus, I needed that.'

'Mummy!' Sallie dashed across the grass and skidded to a stop in front of Susanna. 'There are dolls in my shoes and I can't get them out and Zach says if we leave them in there they'll die!'

'Let me see,' Susanna said. She scooped Sallie onto her lap, deftly whipped off one shoe, pulled out the inner sole and popped the doll into Sallie's hand.

'Whoa,' Sallie said, wide-eyed. 'Cool.'

Susanna did the same with the other shoe, wriggled them back onto Sallie's feet and slid the kid off her lap. 'There,' she said, 'away you go,' and saw Sallie off with a light slap on the rear. Sallie galloped off down the garden, a doll held high in each hand, yelling, 'Zach! Look! They're out! HA-ha!'

'That'll shut Zach up,' Susanna said. 'Do him good.'

'Babes,' Leon said, leaning over to throw one elbow around Susanna's neck and give her a big smacking kiss on the cheek. 'I've missed you.' And over her head, to me: 'I might have actually missed you, too.'

•

Finally – it can't have been after nine o'clock, but it felt much later – the party, or whatever it was, broke up. I think my mother had some wistful idea that the five of us would cosy up in the living room for a late-night chat ('I could use a nightcap – Hugo, what happened to that odd bottle of stuff that we brought you from Sicily? Or Melissa, would you rather some—'), but my father – baggy-eyed, fumbling at a cufflink – put a stop to that: he needed to go to bed, he said gently but definitively, family was the best thing in the world but also the most tiring, and if the rest of us had any sense we would do the same. Hugo, with me and Melissa at his shoulder, waved from the top of the steps as the others got into their cars and drove off, chatter and laughter and car-door slams dissolving upwards into the dusky sky. I was glad of the dimming light; the day had exhausted me to the point where my leg was wobbling almost uncontrollably, and when I waved my hand flopped like spaghetti.

At some point when I wasn't looking, someone – one of my parents, presumably – had hauled our cases upstairs, which would have infuriated me if my head hadn't been too full and whirling to have space for anything more, or if the Xanax had finished wearing off. Instead I let myself go along with Melissa's wave of delight at seeing my old holiday room, which had been my father's room when he was growing up and which was still more or less how I had left it the last time I'd stayed there, the summer before college – 'Toby! did you draw this? I didn't know you could draw . . . Oh, the fireplace, it's beautiful, those flower tiles . . . Was this yours? You did not use to like Nickelback! . . . I love imagining you as a little five-year-old looking out this window . . . Oh my God, is this your school rugby jersey?'

Through her eyes, the room lost the secretive, desiccated feel of some little-seen exhibit – too many years of sun fading streaks into the unmoving curtains, of the furniture legs wearing dents into their fixed spots on the floor – and took on a shy, bittersweet charm. As she skimmed around, she flicked things out of our cases – she had packed for me, so unobtrusively that I had barely realised what was happening – and glanced to me for permission to put them in place, here? here? so that by the time she came to rest the room was fresh and lively and ours, her hairbrush and my comb side by side on the old chest of drawers, our clothes neatly hung in the wardrobe with its cartoon-car stickers scraped patchily off the doors. 'There,' she said, with a quick look at me, half pleased, half anxious. 'Is that all OK?'

'It's great,' I said. I had been leaning against the wall, watching her, both because I enjoyed it and because I was too shattered to move. 'Can we go to bed now?'

Melissa sighed, satisfied. 'Definitely. Bedtime.'

'So,' I said, as she pulled her dress over her head – wonderful vintage dress, pale blue and twirly, it had spun among the shining oak and worn Persian carpets of the house as if it had been made for the place. 'How was your day?'

Melissa turned to me, dress in her hands, and I was startled by the glow of happiness on her face. Melissa had always romanticised my family – she didn't have much of a family life; her mother drank, not flamboyantly but with real dedication, and much of her childhood had been made up of isolation and damage control. To her, the cheerful chaos of my family and the Ivy House had been like something out of a fairy tale; she used to ask me for stories about them, listen enthralled with her fingers curled in mine. 'It was lovely. They're all so *nice*, Toby, it's such a hard time for you all but they made me feel so welcome, like they're genuinely glad to have me here— Did you know your aunt Miriam was in the shop, last year? She bought a set of those plates with the deer on them. She never realised it was me!'

Yellow light from my little bedside lamp shone velvety on her cheek, the turn of her bare shoulder, the supple curve of her waist into her hip. Her hair was a golden haze. 'Come here,' I said, reaching for her.

She let the dress fall to the floor and kissed me back, strongly and joyfully. 'What about you?' she asked, drawing away to look up at me. 'Did you have a good day?'

'Absolutely,' I said. 'And this is the best part of all.' I slid my hand down her back and pulled her closer.

'Toby!'

'What?'

'Your *uncle*!'

'We'll be quiet.'

'But he's right behind that—'

'Vewy vewy quiet. Like we're hunting wascally wabbits.' And sure enough, she laughed and her body relaxed against mine.

I had had girls up in that room before, and for some reason it was the first one who my mind went to – a breathless little blonde called Jeanette, we were fifteen and I'd given Hugo some story about a history project which in retrospect of course he hadn't believed for a second – and although Jeanette and I hadn't actually had sex or even come particularly close it felt the same, the giddy giggles muffled in each other's neck, the breathtaking sense of bounding into something risky and marvellous, the frantic grabs for the headboard at every squeak, *Shh!* You *shh!* It wasn't the first time Melissa and I had had sex since that night but it was the first time it had felt like the real thing, rather than some tense, unhappy, confused compulsion. Afterwards I lay on my back with Melissa's hair fanned across my chest, listening to her soft contented breathing and gazing up at the familiar cracks running across the ceiling, and startled myself by thinking that this might actually have been a good idea.

4

We woke early; my Ivy House bedroom, high above the garden, let in a lot more light than the one in my apartment. Melissa had work. I got up with her, made us breakfast – Hugo was still asleep, at least I hoped he was just asleep – and walked her to the bus stop. Then I made myself another cup of coffee and took it out onto the terrace.

The weather had changed in the night; the sky was grey and the air was cool and still and saturated, ready to rain. The garden, beneath the great lines of trees, looked as if it had been abandoned for centuries. The big pots of geraniums on the terrace burned a crazed, frenetic red against it all.

I sat down at the top of the steps and found my cigarettes (those I had managed to remember for myself, hiding them in my jacket pocket from Melissa). It had been a long time since I'd done anything like this, just sitting outside on my own, and it felt weird and exposed and risky in an inchoate way that made me twitchy. I smoked a cigarette with my coffee and buried the butt in a geranium pot.

I didn't feel like doing very much, or anything really. I'd actually slept properly, for the first time in months – logically I should have been much edgier at the Ivy House, seeing as it didn't even have an alarm system, but somehow it was impossible to picture anyone breaking in, even if they could find the place – but instead of energising me it had left my mind smeared and foggy, incapable of getting a handle on anything. Already after ten minutes, though, I was too restless to sit still any longer. I could feel the terrible rhythm starting to pulse in my head, step and drag, step and drag, back and forth across my sweet old holiday room until Melissa came home.

I went inside. Hugo was in fact alive, apparently: somewhere along the way he had surfaced, I could hear him in his study rattling computer keys and humming and occasionally saying severely, 'Hm.' I tiptoed past his door and into my grandparents' old bedroom.

Patchwork quilt still on the bed, big jar of seashells from long-ago travels still on the mantelpiece, empty wardrobes and faint smell of lavender and dust. The rain had started, a light unobtrusive patter, its shadows down the windowpane mottling the sill and the bare floorboards. I stayed there for a long time, watching the drops merge and course down the glass, picking two and betting on their race to the bottom, the way I had when I was a kid.

On the top floor the room where we had built our fort was a tumble of old furniture covered in dusty sheets, here and there a carved arm or a battered claw-foot poking out, dramatic festoons of cobweb in the high corners. In Susanna's old room the bed was made up and there was a scattering of objects – stuffed rabbit splayed on the floor, Spider-Man mask and a tangle of small bright clothes on the dresser – that said she had been reviving the family tradition and dropping her kids with Hugo for a night here and there. Leon's room was empty except for the stripped bed and a pile of what looked like folded curtains in one corner. This whole trip no longer felt like such a good idea. My own ghost was everywhere, muffling laughter in the fort, leaning over the banisters to call to Leon, sliding a hand up Jeanette's top, agile and golden and invulnerable, utterly clueless about the anvil waiting to fall on his head and crush him to pulp. Outside the garden was lush and silent under the rain, leaves hanging with the weight of it, long grass bowed into hummocks and everything a luminous shadowless green.

I had been standing on the stairs for a while, staring at a painting on the wall (late-nineteenth-century watercolour, picnic by a lake, I couldn't read the signature but I certainly hoped some ancestor had painted it rather than paying money for it), when Hugo's study door opened.

'Ah,' he said, peering benignly at me over his glasses, apparently not at all surprised to find me standing there. 'Hello.'

'Hi,' I said.

'I was about to make some lunch. It's actually quite late, isn't it, I got carried away . . . Will you join me? Or have you eaten?'

'OK,' I said. 'I mean, no, I haven't eaten. I'll join you.'

I was moving aside to let him go ahead of me when I realised: the walking stick in his hand, the breath of preparation when he looked down the long flight of stairs. 'I'll make lunch,' I said. Here I was supposed to be at the Ivy House to help Hugo out. Some job I was doing. I could just hear Leon's derisive snort of laughter: *Knew it.* 'And bring it up here.'

A flash of chagrin crossed Hugo's face, but after a moment he nodded. 'I suppose that's a good idea. There's some of yesterday's casserole in the fridge, in the blue dish; I was just going to put it in the oven for a few minutes. Thank you.'

I hadn't been planning on anything more ambitious than bread and cheese for lunch (making breakfast for Melissa and myself had been an adventure: she clearly hadn't been keen on rooting around in Hugo's kitchen, so I had spent what felt like an hour standing in the middle of the floor paralysed by the question of what to get out first, the bread? the butter? mugs? plates? start the coffeemaker? and that was before I even got into the whole issue of remembering what was kept where), but somehow I got the casserole heated and found a tray to load up with the plates and cutlery and two glasses of water, and managed to very carefully balance the whole thing back up to Hugo's study in an awkward curl of my right arm. It occurred to me, with a spurt of something between astonishment and hope, that the constant fatigue might not be yet another sign of how fucked up my brain was; it could be just because everything took about ten times more effort than normal.

The study hadn't changed since I was a kid. Hugo was a genealogist, which I couldn't imagine paid particularly well, but then with his lifestyle – no mortgage, no rent, no family, no expensive habits – I supposed it didn't need to. His study had a Georgian writing desk, a fat battered leather armchair, dark oak floorboards, exuberant heaps of paper teetering on impractical surfaces; there were built-in bookshelves everywhere, crammed with huge leather-bound volumes stamped in ornate gold – *Thom's Irish Almanac and Official Directory, Pettigrew and Oulton's Dublin Almanac* – and odd knick-knacks, a French carriage clock lacquered in a pattern of leaves and dragonflies, a corner of some ancient Roman plaque incised with a few stray letters, a little huddled rabbit carved from olive wood. Leon and Susanna and I had spent a fair bit of time there, as kids. Hugo used to let us pick up extra pocket money by helping him with his research, lying on our stomachs on the worn rug running our fingers down rows of wobbly old-fashioned type or beautiful near-illegible handwriting; Susanna, who had learned calligraphy at school, had a lucrative sideline drawing up frameable Celticky family trees for Americans. I had always liked the study. The lining of books wrapped it in an extra layer of silence, and the odd objects gave it a quality of low-level, mischievous enchantment; you expected a friendly mouse to poke its head out of a hole in the skirting board, or the clock to whirr and spin its hands backwards and strike thirteen. It reminded me a bit of Richard's office, at the gallery. In fact – it had never occurred to me until that moment – Richard reminded me a bit of Hugo, all round. I wondered all of a sudden if that was why I had been so charmed by that first interview, why I had taken the job, why – a dizzying sense of things spiralling around me, shaping themselves into patterns I had no chance of keeping up with – why everything had unrolled the way it had.

'Ah,' Hugo said, looking up from his desk with a smile. 'Lovely. Here—' He moved his laptop aside so I could put his plate on the desk. On the screen: scanned image of a yellowed form, *1883, marriage solemnised at the Parish Church in* . . .

'You're working,' I said, nodding at it.

Hugo looked at the laptop as if faintly surprised by its existence. 'Well, yes,' he said. 'I am. I did think about taking off on some mad fling through the South American jungle, or at least the Greek islands, but in the end I decided there's a reason why I haven't done that already. This suits me much better – whether I like to admit it or not. And besides' – his wide smile lightening his whole face – 'I've got quite an interesting mystery going on, and I don't want to go anywhere without seeing how it turns out.'

I sat in the armchair and pulled over the little side table to hold my plate. 'What's the story?'

'Ah,' he said, leaning back in his chair. 'A few months ago a lady called Amelia Wozniak contacted me from Philadelphia, looking for help tracing her Irish roots. Which did sound a bit unlikely' – he laughed, polishing his glasses on a frayed edge of jumper – 'until I found out her maiden name was O'Hagan. She'd done a certain amount of work herself, come up with a pretty comprehensive family tree as far back as the 1840s, in Tipperary, mostly. But then it all went a bit wonky.' He laid the glasses aside and took a large bite of the casserole. 'Mm. This overnighted pretty well, don't you think? – She submitted DNA to one of the big databases, and up popped a whole assortment of cousins in Clare who, according to her research, really shouldn't have been related to her at all. McNamaras, and she hadn't come across that name anywhere. So she called me in.'

'And?' As a kid I had never been particularly interested in Hugo's 'mysteries'. Leon and Susanna liked them, but I didn't get the fascination: the answers weren't going to change anything, there was never a throne or a fortune or anything at stake, what difference did it make? I had been involved purely out of companionability, and obviously for the extra cash.

'Well, I don't know yet. One possibility is a non-paternity event: somewhere along the line a woman stepped out on her husband, or was raped, and with or without her husband's knowledge raised the child as his.'

'Jesus,' I said. 'Lovely.'

'Another possibility' – he was ticking them off on his fingers, fork waving – 'is a second family. It happened quite a bit in those days, you know, with all the emigration. A man goes over to America to look for work, planning to send for his wife and children as soon as he's saved up the passage money; but that's easier said than done, next thing he knows it's been years, he's lonely, he doesn't know what his children look like any more . . . So easy to fall for someone in your new world, so much easier not to mention that other life back in the old country – and before you know it you've got a skeleton in the family closet, safely hidden away for centuries, perhaps, until new technology comes along.'

I was trying to pay attention, but my mind had started sliding.

Hugo was right, the casserole was good, rich with herbs and full of big hearty chunks of beef and potato and carrot. His feet stretched out in their worn brown wool slippers, could they be the same old ones? A line of dark wooden elephants marching along the mantelpiece, from largest to smallest, I didn't remember those—

'And then there's the possibility of a child who was given up, or kidnapped. Oh, not the nasty man in the white van' – at my startled look – 'but Ireland even a couple of generations back wasn't a good place to be an unmarried mother. So many of them ended up in those terrible homes for fallen women, the Magdalene Sisters, you know. Enormous pressure to give up the baby, not to wreck its life with the taint of your own sin. Very often the Sisters didn't even bother with that, they simply abducted the child: told the mother it had died, sold it to a well-off American couple. Quite possibly kept the mother imprisoned for life, working in their laundry to expiate her sin.'

'I'm going to bet on someone's wife hooking up with the guy next door,' I said. The villainous nuns would have made better TV-movie fodder, but they sounded like a pretty big stretch to me. 'Just playing the odds.'

Hugo didn't grin back; instead he gave me a long, thoughtful look. 'Perhaps,' he said, turning his attention back to his food. 'I'd like to think so, too. So much less uncomfortable to think about. But until I know, you see, I have to pursue all the avenues.'

He ate with the thorough, methodical enjoyment of a labourer, leaning forwards over his plate. 'I'm not a DNA specialist,' he said, between mouthfuls, 'but I can make a decent fist of analysing results – or at any rate better than someone like Mrs Wozniak, who's never done it before. She was born in 1945, and the percentage of matching DNA puts the McNamara connection two or three generations back. So we're talking about somewhere between, say, 1850 and 1910. It would be easier if I had the census records, but . . .'

An exasperated, familiar shrug. A combination of government logic, World War I paper shortage and fire destroyed basically all the nineteenth-century Irish census records; I had heard Hugo complain about it plenty of times before. 'So I can't just go and check if one of the ancestors was on the census with a wife and three children before he emigrated, or if someone vanishes from the home address and pops up in a Magdalene laundry, or if the next-door neighbour happened to be a McNamara. Instead I'm going at it sideways. Parish records, mostly, but I've also been checking the passenger lists of emigrant ships—'

I was losing hold of the conversation – too many possibilities and tributaries, the words had stopped meaning much – but the run of Hugo's voice was peaceful as a river. The standing lamp, on against the dim underwater light, gave the room a sanctified golden glow. Rain pattering at the windowpane, bindings worn at the edges. Bird-dropped twigs in the grate of the little iron fireplace. I ate and nodded.

'Would you like to give me a hand?' Hugo asked suddenly.

He had straightened up and was blinking hopefully at me. 'Well,' I said, taken aback, 'um, I don't know how much use I'd be. It's not really my—'

'It's nothing fancy. Just the same stuff you and your cousins used to help me with: going through records looking for the right names. I know it's not very exciting, but it does have its moments – do you remember that nice Canadian whose great-grandmother turned out to have run off with the music teacher and the family silver?'

I was trying to come up with a good excuse – I couldn't read a news article without forgetting what was going on halfway through, what were the chances I could keep track of half a dozen names while I deciphered page after page of Victorian handwriting? – when I realised, duhhh, with a sharp prickle of shame: Hugo wasn't charitably trying to keep the poor unfortunate gimp busy. He wanted to know the answer to Mrs Wozniak's mystery, and he didn't have a lot of time to find it. 'Oh,' I said. 'Yeah, sure. Absolutely. That'd be great.'

'Oh, marvellous,' he said happily, pushing his empty plate aside. 'It's been too long since I had company at this. Do you want anything else to eat, or shall we get stuck in?'

We cleared the plates ('Oh, just put them in that corner for now, we'll take them downstairs later' – I had a sharp flash of wondering whether Hugo had noticed my dragging leg and wanted to spare me the stairs, but his face was turned away from me as he stacked the tray, I couldn't find anything there) and he set the printer to churn out a stack of ships' manifests while he fixed me up with the armchair and the side table and a year-old phone bill to run down the pages so I wouldn't miss a line. 'Check all the names, won't you, not just the ones marked as Irish? You never know, there could be an error, or someone could have found a way to pass himself off as English – being Irish wasn't exactly an advantage back then . . .' When I wrote down the names I was looking for and put the piece of paper beside the stack, he didn't comment. 'Ah,' he said, turning his chair to his desk and pulling the laptop closer with a sigh of satisfaction. And then – exactly like when we were kids, blast from the forgotten past: 'Happy foraging.'

It was very peaceful. In my spaced-out state, my mind couldn't manage to snag on my problems or Hugo's, or on anything really except the lines of type appearing like magic above the moving edge of the phone bill: *Mr Robt Harding 22 M Gent England, Miss S. L. Sullivan 25 F Spinster Ireland, Mr Thos Donahue 36 M Farmer Ireland . . .* The rhythm, once I found it, was hypnotic: three lines of the list, eyes swinging right to remind myself of the names I wanted, left again to the list for three more lines, tick tock tick tock, steady and solid as a pendulum. When I got down to steerage class, the passengers lost their titles and the occupations changed: *Sarah Dempsey 22 F Servant Ireland, George Jennings 30 M Labourer Scotland, Patk Costello 28 M Ironmonger Ireland . . .* I could have stayed there all day, all week, lulled by the quaint old terms – *Hostler, Dye Sinker, Furman* – only half-hearing the rain and the clicking of Hugo's keyboard. It came as a shock when I heard the cheerful rat-a-tat-tat of the door knocker, downstairs, and – lifting my head notch by notch on my stiff neck, blinking at the reappearing room – realised slowly that the light had shifted; that that must be Melissa at the door; that I had spent hours like this, without either my concentration or my head or my eyes going to shite; that, for the first time in a long time, I was starving.

•

Somewhere during the evening before – while I was out on the terrace with my cousins? – Melissa and Hugo had apparently become friends. They had met before, at my family birthday party back in January, and had liked each other, but now all of a sudden they were easy as old pals, sharing in-jokes – Melissa pulling a bag of sweet potatoes out of one overloaded shopping bag to brandish it at Hugo, 'Look, see? I *told* you!' and Hugo throwing back his shaggy head in a big crack of laughter; him resting a hand briefly on her shoulder as he passed her, the same way he did to me.

'I like Hugo,' Melissa said, later, leaning against my bedroom window to look out at the garden. The bedroom light was off; she was only a silhouette against the faint colourless glow of the outside. 'A lot.'

'I know,' I said. I went to stand beside her. The rain was still going, a steady busy patter working away in the darkness. 'Me too.'

Melissa took one hand off the windowpane and held it out to me, palm up. I put my hand in hers and we stood there like that for a long time, watching the light from Hugo's window illuminating a slanted rectangle of pale grass and weeds far below, the fine rain falling on and on through the beam and vanishing into the dark.

•

From there we slipped easily into a routine. Hugo would have breakfast ready when Melissa and I got up – 'I wish he wouldn't go to all that hassle,' I said, as Melissa and I got dressed to the smell of frying sausages curling up the stairs; 'maybe I should—' but Melissa shook her head: 'Don't, Toby. Let him.' After I walked Melissa to the bus stop, Hugo and I would potter about for a bit – wanders around the garden, washing-up, laundry, showers (I hovered on the stairs while he took his, just close enough that I would hear the thud of him falling; I sometimes wonder if he did the same for me). Sometimes one of us would end up having a doze, on the sofa or if it was sunny in the hammock. At some point we would drift to his study and start foraging.

Sunlight melting across the floorboards, smoky smell from the chipped blue teapot, small birds arguing in the ivy outside the open window. In our breaks Hugo told me long, absorbed stories about when he and his brothers were little (apparently my father had run away from home once, although only as far as the garden shed, where the other three had kept him supplied with food and sleeping bags and comics until he got bored enough to go back inside) or, in other moods, talked about his work. 'The thing is,' he said once – turning from the cluttered desk, leaning his head back to massage his neck with one big hand – 'it's a different job now. I don't mean all the computer stuff, the digitisation; I mean the tone of it. People used to get in touch with me out of curiosity – they wanted to know the family history, they'd got as far as they could on their own, they were hungry for more. I was like a fairy godfather, dropping unexpected gifts into their laps: *Look, here's a copy of the letter your grandfather wrote to his sister during World War I! Look, here's your great-grandmother's birth certificate! A photo of the old family farm!*'

He poured the tea, held out a mug to me. 'But now, with DNA analysis, it's more complicated. People are coming to me because their analysis didn't turn out the way they expected. "But I'm supposed to be a hundred per cent Ashkenazi Jewish, why does this say twelve per cent Irish? Why are my third cousins coming up as second cousins?" They're unsettled and they're frightened, and what they want from me isn't the lovely presents, any more; it goes much deeper. They're afraid that they're not who they always thought they were, and they want me to find them reassurance. And we both know it might not turn out that way. I'm not the fairy godfather any more; now I'm some dark arbiter, probing through their hidden places to decide their fate. And I'm not nearly as comfortable in that role.'

'It's not that bad,' I said. I didn't want to minimise what he did, especially not now, but all of this seemed like a bit much, a streak of melodrama that I hadn't spotted in Hugo before, and it made me uneasy. Any anomaly in Hugo unsettled me: just a quirk I'd never noticed, or the first step into some nightmare downslide? 'I mean, they're the same people, no matter what you find out.'

That long look, thoughtful and interested, over his glasses. 'It wouldn't bother you? If you found out tomorrow that you were adopted, say, or that your grandmother was actually the child of some unknown man?'

'Well,' I said. The tea was mouth-puckeringly strong – I'd lost count of the spoonfuls of tea leaves – but Hugo didn't seem to have noticed and I wasn't about to point it out. 'Being adopted would bother me, sure. A lot. But if Gran's mother shagged around . . . I mean, I didn't know her; it's not like I've got any respect for her to lose. And it doesn't make any difference to me. So no, I wouldn't care.'

Hugo smiled. 'Well, then,' he said, reaching for a biscuit, 'you've got nothing to worry about. One look at your profile and anyone could tell you're a Hennessy.'

When Melissa came home we would put the work away and help her make dinner – exuberant, experimental dinners full of ingredients I didn't know how to pronounce, let alone what to do with (galangal? teff?). Melissa was happy; I could see it, in the unguarded glow of her face when she looked up at me, the skip of her step between the cooker and the counter. Although it baffled me, I was glad of it: I knew she shouldn't be there at all, shouldn't be dealing with any of this, but I needed her, and that glow let me dodge the looming sense that I should really get her out of there. After dinner Hugo would light a fire in the living room – 'I know it's not a cold night,' he said simply, the first time, 'but I love wood fires, and I can't afford to wait for the winter' – and we would play rummy or Monopoly, among the faded red damask armchairs and old Italian engravings and worn Persian rugs that had been the same all my life, until Hugo got tired and we all went to bed. We mentioned Hugo's illness only incidentally – planning for his appointments, passing his cane. What had happened to me never came up at all.

Little rituals. Me brushing Melissa's hair by the bedroom window, morning sun transforming it to pure light streaming through my hands. The neat tap of sheaves of paper on tables, me and Hugo squaring off edges before we got stuck into the day's work. The debate over which CD to put on while we cooked dinner, *No way, we had your French bistro whatever last night, it's my turn!* Looking back, I'm amazed by how quickly they took shape, those rituals, how solid and smooth and immutable they felt after only a few days; how quickly it came to feel as though we'd been there for years and would be there, all of us, for years more.

It's difficult to give a clear description of my state of mind during those weeks; even harder to imagine how it might have developed, if things hadn't gone the way they did. It wasn't that I was getting better, exactly. In some ways and to some extent, I was – the weird vision glitches had subsided a lot, so had the leaping at shadows, and although I couldn't bear to have faith in this I thought the droop in my eyelid might be receding – but I was no nearer feeling like myself again, or even really like a human being. It was more that that didn't seem to matter as much, at least not in any immediate way. Every day included plenty of things that should have sent me into a full-on spiral – mugs falling through my fingers to shatter on the floor, forgotten words leaving me gabbling – and yet I wasn't a shaking wreck pacing my room and gnawing at my revenge fantasies; although I did feel like a meltdown was the only, the inevitable response, I also felt like it could wait till some other time. I suppose it was a bit like being mauled to rags by a savage animal, and then somehow dragging myself to a safe place and slamming the gates: I could still hear the animal padding and snuffling outside, I knew it had no intention of leaving and sooner or later I would have to go out there again, but at least for now I could stay in shelter.

The rest of the family came in and out. On Sundays there was lunch, and during the week Oliver or Louisa or Susanna drove Hugo to doctor's appointments and radiotherapy sessions and physiotherapy; my mother and Miriam brought over armloads of shopping bags; my dad, sleeves rolled up, hoovered the rugs and scrubbed the bath. Phil played endless games of draughts with Hugo (and brought me the late birthday present Susanna had warned me about: an indescribable gilt construction that he informed me was my great-great-grandfather's pocket-watch holder, and that I had no idea what I was supposed to do with). Leon brought over ultra-hip takeaways for lunch and stayed for the afternoon, making Hugo laugh with stories about the time he and Carsten had been landed with an up-and-coming ska-punk band spending a week on their living-room floor. Hugo's friends came, too, more of them than I would have expected: dusty, courteous old guys who could have been antiques dealers or handymen or college professors, smile-lined women with confident walks and surprisingly elegant clothes. I always left them to it in the living room, but I could hear the voices coming up through the floor, absorbed and overlapping, punctuated by bursts of real laughter.

I liked it best when it was just the three of us, though, me and Melissa and Hugo. My dad and my uncles were so wretched that their misery stampeded into the house with them like some rampaging animal, upending all the delicate balances that Hugo and Melissa and I had constructed. My aunts were jumpy, losing weight, heads ceaselessly whipping back and forth as they tried to make sure everyone was OK. Louisa kept rearranging stuff, and under stress Miriam was turning into a parody of herself, covertly reiki-ing Hugo behind his back while he sat at the kitchen table obliviously eating apricots and Leon doubled over biting one knuckle in an extravagant cringe-mime, and Susanna and Melissa and I huddled over the cooker to hide the giddy giggles.

I was actually getting on better with my mother. Finding out she had covered for me with the family had shifted something; that terrible urge to pick fights with her was gone. She had too much sensitivity to try and do anything useful inside the house, so instead she went at the garden, dead-heading and weeding and cutting back for autumn. I didn't really get the point – it wasn't like Hugo cared whether the garden got scraggly – but I sometimes joined her anyway. I'm not a gardener; mostly all I did was follow her around with a bag, picking things up, but my mother is a sociable person and she seemed to like the company. Either she thought I was all better or she was putting in some superhuman effort of will, because she had quit trying to lure me home or buy me emotional-support guard poodles. Mostly we talked about books and her students and the garden.

'We're getting there,' she said one afternoon. We were digging out the dandelions that had grown tall and muscular among the flowerbeds. It was still warm as summer, but the light was starting to shift, turning long and low and gold towards autumn. In the kitchen, Melissa and Hugo were starting on dinner; it was Melissa's turn to pick the music, the Puppini Sisters' version of 'Heart of Glass' was bopping cheerfully through the open doors. 'It's not going to look like it did in your grandparents' day, but it'll do.'

'It's looking good,' I said.

My mother sat back on her haunches, swiping hair back from her face with one arm. 'I get that Hugo doesn't care that much either way, you know,' she said. 'But there's nothing I can do, so I'm doing what I can.'

'He'll be happy,' I said. 'He hates dandelions.'

'And I feel like I owe this place. Even though it's not my ancestral home.' She tilted her head back to look up at the house, shielding her eyes against the light. 'It meant a lot to me, you staying here during the holidays.'

'Thanks a lot,' I said.

She made a face at me. 'Not just because I wanted you out of the way so we could hang out in Sicily getting drunk on dodgy grappa. Although that too.'

'I knew it. Here you told us you were going to museums.'

My mother laughed, but only for a moment. 'We worried about you being an only, you know,' she said, 'your dad and I. We would've loved a couple more, but there you go. Your dad was just sad about you missing out on everything he'd had with his brothers, but I . . .'

She bent to the dandelions again, wiggled a long root carefully out of the ground and tossed it into the bag. 'I worried that maybe you spent too much time being the centre of the world,' she said. 'Not that you were selfish, you've always been generous, but there was something . . . I thought it would be good for you to have Susanna and Leon as sort-of siblings, at least part of the time.' With a quick up-glance at me, questioning: 'If that makes any sense.'

'Not really,' I said, grinning at her. 'But that might be too much to ask.'

She wrinkled her nose at me. 'Disrespectful child. Are you calling me flaky?'

Strands of pale hair falling out of her ponytail, streak of dirt on her cheek: she looked young, she looked like the dauntless laughing mother I had adored as a kid, whose direct blue gaze had been a sweet shot right to my heart. *I'm sorry*, I wanted to say, not for teasing her but for everything, for being an arsehole over the last few months and for the terror she must have felt and for her only child being such a spectacular disaster area. Instead I said, 'Hey, if the shoe fits,' and she waved her fork threateningly in my direction, and we stayed out there together, weeding, till my leg was wobbling and I could barely hide the exhaustion and Melissa called from the kitchen door to say dinner was ready.

•

My cousins were a different story. We did manage flashes of the old closeness, but too much of the time we just pissed each other off. They were different from how I remembered them, and not in good ways. I knew it had been a long time since we'd hung out together, people change and grow apart and yada yada yada, but I had liked them a lot better before.

Leon had always been mercurial, so it took me a while to notice that there was more than that going on now: his moods weren't just changeable, they were elaborately, deliberately layered and coded. I followed him out to the terrace for a smoke one afternoon – by this point I was pretty sure Melissa and Hugo both knew I had started smoking, but given everything else that was going on, I figured they were unlikely to stage an intervention. Leon had brought over cartons of fiery, complicated noodle dishes and spent lunch trying to convince Melissa, whom he liked, to move to Berlin – 'All that stuff in your shop, the Germans would go mad for that, they love anything Irish – shut up, Toby, Melissa and I are having a conversation here. And oh my God, German guys. They're all about seven feet tall and they don't spend their entire lives in the pub, they actually *do* things, parties and nature walks and museums and— Tell me again, what do you see in this big ugly lump?'

When I went out onto the terrace, though, he was sitting on the steps, a thin thread of smoke rising from one hand, not moving. It was late afternoon; the shadow of the apartment block was starting to slant across the garden, slicing it sharply into a bright half and a dark, small pale butterflies appearing and vanishing again like a magician's trick as they flitted back and forth. 'Hey,' I said, lighting my cigarette and sitting down beside Leon. 'Quit trying to make my girlfriend dump me.'

Leon didn't turn. The hunch of his shoulders startled me; all the effervescent charm had fallen away like a dust sheet, leaving him a dense dark huddle on the steps. 'He's getting worse, you know,' he said.

It took me a second to realise what he meant. 'No he isn't,' I said. I was already starting to wish I had stayed inside.

Leon didn't even look at me. 'He is. Today when I came in, he said, "My goodness, it's been a while!" Big smile.'

Leon had spent the whole afternoon there two days earlier. 'He was joking,' I said.

'He wasn't.'

There was a silence. 'Are you staying for dinner?' I asked. 'I think we're making ravioli with—'

'And his fucking leg,' Leon said. 'Did you see him going down into the kitchen? Three stairs, and his leg was shaking like jelly. I didn't think he was going to make it.'

'He had radiotherapy yesterday. It tires him out. By tomorrow he'll be stronger.'

'No he won't.'

'Look,' I said. I really, badly wanted Leon to shut up, but I knew him well enough to keep that out of my voice. 'I'm with him all the time. OK? I know the, the, the patterns. After radiotherapy, he's worse for a day or two, then he gets better.'

'A few more weeks and he's not going to be able to manage on his own. What happens when you go home? Has anyone got anything planned? Home care, or hospice, or—'

'I don't know when I'm going home,' I said. 'I might hang on here for a while.'

That made Leon turn to look at me, leaning back like I was some bizarre creature that had suddenly appeared in his field of vision. 'Seriously? Like how long?'

I shrugged. 'I'll see as I go.' For the last few days I had been wondering, idly but persistently, how long Melissa would be on for staying at the Ivy House. I did have doubts about how much longer I could get away with convincing my family that the only thing wrong with me was an extra glass of wine or a fondness for painkillers, and the thought of any of them realising just how fucked up I was made me flinch like someone jamming a finger into an open wound; in some ways I felt like I should get out soon, while I was still ahead. On the other hand, going back to my apartment and the panic button and the nightly horrors was unthinkable. 'I'm in no hurry.'

'What about work? Are you not going back?'

'I am back. I'm doing stuff from here.' I hadn't been in touch with Richard in months; I had no idea whether I still even had a job. 'They know the story. They're fine with me working from home for a while.'

'Huh,' Leon said, eyebrows still up. 'Lucky you. Then what happens when it gets to be more than you can handle? No' – lifting a hand, when I started to say something – 'I'm actually not being bitchy. You've been a trouper, I appreciate it more than I can tell you, and I apologise from the bottom of my heart for saying you wouldn't be able for it. OK? But are you on for, I don't know, lifting Hugo out of the bath? What about wiping his arse? Giving him his pain meds every four hours, day and night?'

'Oh for fuck's sake,' I said. My voice was rising, I heard it but couldn't stop it. 'None of this has actually *happened*, Leon. Can I worry about it when it does, yeah? *If* it does? Is that OK with you?'

'Not really, no. Because when it does get to be too much for you, there needs to be a plan all ready to go. You can't just walk out and leave him to look after himself till—'

'Then make a fucking plan. I don't care what it is. Just *leave me out of it.*'

I expected Leon to snap my head off, but he gave me one unfathomable look and turned back to his smoke. The shadow had inched farther across the garden and the butterflies were gone, which to me in that mood seemed gratuitously and cheaply symbolic. I finished my cigarette as fast as I could and crushed it out under my shoe.

'I asked my dad,' Leon said suddenly. 'About what happens to this place.'

'And?'

'I had it wrong. It's not just Hugo's to live in; Gran and Granddad left it to him, straight up. Oldest son.' He ground out his cigarette on the step. 'So the question is what Hugo's will says. If he has one.'

His eyes had slid sideways to me. 'Oh hell no,' I said. 'I'm not asking him.'

'You were going on about how you spend all that time with him, you know him so well—'

'And you were going on about how you've got a life in Berlin and God forbid you should have to move back here. What do you care if—'

'Do you actually *want* the place sold?'

'No,' I said, swiftly and definitely, startling myself. After the last few weeks, losing the Ivy House was unthinkable. 'God, no.'

'Hugo wouldn't, either. You know he wouldn't. But my dad says Phil and Louisa are all gung-ho about it: give Su and Tom a few bob for the kids' education, for a better house, all that stuff. Susanna doesn't want it, but try telling them that. And Phil's the next oldest. Hugo could easily leave it to him, and boom, gone. If you talk to Hugo, you can explain that. Make sure he leaves it to someone who'll hang on to it.'

'OK,' I said, after a moment. 'OK. I'll talk to him.'

Leon went back to staring at the garden, arms clasped around his knees like a kid. 'Make it soon,' he said.

I buried my cigarette butt in the geranium pot and went inside, to Hugo and Melissa looking up smiling from the old photo album he had dug out to show her. But it was too late: my head was pounding savagely and there was no way I could face an evening of ravioli and rummy and chitchat, watching Leon watch Hugo's every move. I said something about a headache, went upstairs and took a

Xanax and a couple of painkillers – fuck Leon, anyway – and went to bed with the pillow over my head.

Susanna had got a lot pricklier, too. She had been a sweet kid, earnest and bookish and quirky – sometimes to the point of cluelessness; I had spent a fair bit of our teenage years explaining to her why she needed to make an actual effort with clothes and hair and whatever, unless she wanted the shit slagged out of her – with an unexpected sharp sense of humour. In spite of the various shifts she had gone through since then, a part of me was still expecting that kid, and it came as an unpleasant surprise when that wasn't what I got at all.

'I've got hold of the guy,' she said, one afternoon, in the kitchen. She had just taken Hugo to his radiotherapy session; he had come back exhausted and shaky, and we had helped him into bed and were making tea and buttering scones to take up to him. 'For the second opinion. He's in Switzerland, but he's *the* guy for this cancer, worldwide. I rang him up and he says he'll take a look at Hugo's file.'

'I thought like three doctors had already seen him,' I said. 'At the hospital.'

Susanna pulled open the fridge and rummaged for the butter. 'They have. So one more won't hurt.'

'So a fourth opinion. What do you want a fourth opinion for?'

'In case the first three were shit.'

I was at the sink, filling the kettle; all I could see was her back. 'How many are you planning to get? Are you going to keep chasing doctors till one of them tells you what you want to hear?'

'Just this one.' A cool skim of a glance at me, as she turned back to the counter. 'How come you don't like the idea?'

What I didn't like was the implication that Hugo's doctors might have missed a trick. It raised the horrible possibility that mine might have done the same thing, left something undone that could have magicked me straight back to normal if only they had bothered— 'I just don't want Hugo getting his hopes up for nothing.'

'Better than having him give up when he doesn't need to.'

'What do you think is going to happen? This Swiss guy is going to come back and say hey, surprise, he doesn't have cancer after all?'

'No. But he might come back and say hey, we could try surgery and chemo after all.'

'If there was any chance of that, I think at least one of the first three guys would have mentioned it.'

'They're all buddies. They're not going to contradict each other. If the first one says there's nothing they can do—'

'I was in the same hospital,' I said, 'and my doctors were *great*. They did absolutely everything anyone could have done. Everything.'

'Good. I'm glad. I'm sure they did.'

I had just taken out the tea bags before the teapot and I couldn't work out what to do with them while I looked for it, and I really wasn't in the mood for that cool flat tone. I knew I should probably be encouraging her, or at least I should prefer all this no-stone-unturned stuff to Leon's doom and gloom, but what I actually wanted was for everyone to fuck off and leave us alone. 'So why are you looking for a fourth opinion?'

'Because,' Susanna said, buttering half a scone with one hard neat sweep, 'Hugo's not you. He's sixty-seven, and he's obviously not some rich powerful big shot – he doesn't even have health insurance, did you know that? He's been going public. And let's face it, he's vague enough and scruffy enough that if you weren't paying a lot of attention, you could easily write him off as a batty old loser. At least he's a guy and he's white and he's got a posh accent, so he's got those going for him, but still: just because they went all out for you, that doesn't necessarily mean they're going to pump the same resources into some half-senile old geezer who's probably going to die soon anyway.'

The rush of anger took me by surprise. 'Well that's just *bullshit*,' I said, after a moment where I couldn't even talk. 'For fuck's sake, Su. You seriously think they're deliberately letting Hugo die, just because he's old and scatty and not a millionaire? These are *doctors*. I don't know what kind of social-justice-warrior shite you've been reading, but their *job* is to make people *better*, if they can. Which sometimes they can't. That doesn't mean they're evil villains rubbing their hands and looking for ways to fuck up people's lives.'

Susanna pulled the teapot out of a cupboard, whipped the tea bags out of my hand and dropped them in. 'Remember when Gran got sick?' she asked. 'Horrible stomach pain, for weeks, all bloated up? She went to her GP three times, she went into A and E twice, and they all said the same thing: constipation, go home and take a nice senna tablet, good girl. No matter how many times she told them that wasn't it.'

'So they made mistakes. They're human.' I didn't actually remember any of this. I had been thirteen, head humming with girls and friends and rugby and bands and school; I had visited Gran at least a couple of times a week while she was sick, used my pocket money to buy her favourite fruit-and-nut chocolate as long as she could eat and her favourite yellow freesias when she couldn't, but I hadn't paid a lot of attention to all the ancillary stuff.

'Basically,' Susanna said, 'they took one look at Gran and decided she was just a batty old lady looking for attention. Even though ten seconds of actually listening to her would've told them she wasn't like that at all. You know what it took before they bothered to even check for stomach cancer? My dad finally went in and gave her GP a massive bollocking. *Then* he sent her for tests. And by that time it was too late to do anything useful.'

'It might have been too late anyway. You don't have a clue.'

'Yeah, it might've. Or it might not. That's not the *point*. Move.' She leaned across me, grabbed up the kettle and poured the tea, roughly enough that a few drops of water splashed onto the countertop. 'The point is, if your doctors went all out for you, great. But not everyone gets to live in the same world as you.'

'Oh for God's *sake*,' I said. 'Listen to yourself. It's not like they have a, have some, some—' I knew exactly what I meant, couldn't find the words to get it into Susanna's head, bit down hard on the inside of my lip— 'They don't have some secret *score* card where they take points off you for having a skanger accent or being over sixty-five, and then you only get as much treatment as your points can buy. That's ridiculous. You're going to have to trust that they're doing their best.'

Susanna had the tray ready. She started tidying around it: crumbs swept into her hand and flung into the bin, milk and butter shot into the fridge, door flicked shut, deft economical movements with a snap to them.

'Having Zach wasn't fun,' she said. Her voice was very level, but there was a tightly controlled undercurrent to it. 'The consultant did some stuff to me – I mean, I'll spare you the details, but basically there were a few options and I really didn't agree with the one he wanted to go with. So I said no. And he told me, quote, "If you try to get feisty with me, I'll get a court order and send the police to your door to bring you in."'

'He was winding you up,' I said, after a startled second.

'He was dead serious. He told me all about the times he'd done it to other women, in detail, to make sure I knew he wasn't winding me up.'

'Jesus,' I said. I wanted to know what the fuck Tom had been doing while someone talked to his wife like that. Presumably he had been nodding inoffensively and pondering which cringe-worthy baby-carrier to schlep the kid around in. 'Did you file a complaint?'

Susanna turned, butter knife in hand, and gave me an incredulous stare. 'About what?'

'He can't do that.'

'Of course he can. If you're pregnant, you don't have the right to any say about your health care. He could do whatever he wanted to me, whether I agreed to it or not, and it would be totally legal. Did you seriously not know that?'

'Well,' I said. 'I mean, in theory he could. But in practice, I really doubt it works out like—'

'It works out *exactly* like that. I should know. I was there.'

I didn't particularly want to get into a fight about this, plus I felt like we were getting a little off topic here, given that Hugo was unlikely to be pregnant. 'That consultant was a shithead,' I said. 'I'm really sorry that happened to you. And I can totally see why you'd be gun-shy about doctors. But just because you ran into a bad one, that doesn't mean—'

'Jesus fucking *Christ*,' Susanna said. She threw the butter knife into the sink with a clatter, picked up the tea tray and left.

•

Normally I would have handled that conversation a lot better. After all, it wasn't like Susanna had transformed into an entirely different person; she had always liked getting up in arms about injustices, real and imagined, and I'd never done anything but roll my eyes cheerfully and let it go. The same with Leon: he had always been a moody little bollix, I knew better than to let it get to me, normally I would have walked off and left him to it long before his mood could rub off on me. Now, apparently, minor variations on their usual bullshit had the power to knock me sideways.

It's tempting to blame it on the stress of Hugo dying, or on the cracks, neurological or psychological or whatever, from that night, but if I'm honest I think it was a lot more mundane and pathetic than that. The truth, I suppose, is that I envied Leon and Susanna. The sensation was so unfamiliar that it took me a while to recognise it; I'd spent my life taking it for granted that, if anything, it was the other way around. Social stuff had always come easily to me – not that I was some charismatic leader type, but I was always effortlessly part of the cool crowd, invited to everything, secure enough in my footing that Dec had been accepted into the fold in spite of his accent and his glasses and his atrocious rugby skills, simply because he was my friend. Leon had spent school as the kind of kid who got regular wedgies, and while Susanna (in our sister school, next door) hadn't exactly been a reject, she and her friends had been a bunch of generally ignored Lisa Simpson types who did stuff like selling handmade candles to raise money for homelessness or Tibet or something; if the two of them got included in anything remotely cool, it was because of me. Even once we grew up, Leon had dropped out of college after a year and ricocheted around the world picking some crop or other in Australia and living in a squat in Vienna and never holding on to a job or a boyfriend for longer than a year or two, and Susanna had turned into Mrs Stay-at-Home Mummy and spent her time pureeing green beans or whatever, while I had got straight on track for a snazzy career and pretty much the perfect life. It honestly wasn't that I looked down on them, ever – I loved them, I wanted them to have every good thing in the world – just that I was aware, in the back of my mind, that if they were to compare their lives with mine, mine would come out on top.

But now: they ran up the front steps two at a time, juggled multiple threads of conversation without missing a beat; Leon told scurrilous stories about nights out with bands I had actually heard of, Susanna had just dusted off her degree and got into a prestigious master's programme on social policy and was sparking with excitement about it; and then there was me. I was functioning fine, give or take, within my new miniature simplified world, but I knew perfectly well there was no chance I could handle even a single day in my old job or my old life. I envied them, hard and shamefully, and it felt against the natural order of things. It made it impossible for me to see their foibles and flaws with the old warm, amused tolerance. Stuff that a few months ago would have had me grinning, shaking my head, set my teeth on edge to the point where I could barely keep back a roar of rage. It was always a relief when they left, and Melissa and Hugo and I could slip back into our gentle, crepuscular world of rustling pages and card games and hot cocoa at bedtime, of delicate unspoken agreements and accommodations; of – and I only see it now, really, for the rare and inexpressibly precious thing it was – mutual, grave, tender and careful kindness.

•

Leon was right, though: Hugo was getting worse. It was subtle enough that most of the time we could almost convince ourselves it wasn't happening. A sudden wild buckle of his leg, me or Melissa grabbing at his elbow, oops! mind the rug! but it was happening more and more often and there wasn't always a convenient rug to blame. The dazed, tractionless gaze skidding around the room sometimes when his head came up from his work, *What . . . ? what time is it?* and then his eyes lighting on me with such a total lack of recognition that it took a lot not to back right out the door, to say instead *Hey, Uncle Hugo, it's almost three, want me to make the tea?* and he would blink at me, coming back into his eyes little by little, and finally smile, *Yes, I think we've earned it, don't you?* The occasional snap of irritability that verged on anger, out of nowhere – *No, I don't want more vegetables, I'm perfectly capable of serving myself, don't rush me!* The drag at one corner of his mouth, subtle enough to look like a wry deprecating quirk of expression, except that it didn't go away.

One evening he fell. We were in the middle of making dinner – empanadas, I can still smell the rich greasy mix of chorizo and onion suddenly hitting the back of my throat. We had Chopin waltzes playing, Hugo had gone upstairs to the toilet and Melissa and I were rolling out dough on the countertop and debating how big the discs should be, when we heard a confused scuffle, a thick terrible thud, a tumble and clatter; and then silence.

We were out of the kitchen and calling Hugo's name before my mind had time to understand what I had heard. He was half-sprawled on the stairs, white and wild-eyed, clutching the banisters with one hand. His cane was far below him and there was something awful about the flung angle of it, earthquake, invasion, everyone fled—

Melissa got to him first, kneeling on the stairs beside him, hands on his arms to hold him down – 'No, stay still. Don't move yet. Tell me what happened.'

Her voice was brisk and unfazed as a nurse's. Hugo was breathing fast through his nose. 'Hugo,' I said, catching up, trying to squeeze in beside him. 'Are you OK? Does anything—'

'Shh,' Melissa said. 'Hugo. Look at me. Take a deep breath and tell me what happened.'

'It was nothing. My cane slipped.' His hands were shaking violently and his glasses were askew halfway down his nose. 'Stupid. I thought I had the hang of it by now, got careless—'

'Did you hit your head?'

'No.'

'Are you sure?'

'Yes. I'm fine, really I—'

'What did you hit?'

'My backside, obviously. I bounced down a few stairs, I'm not sure how many— And my elbow, that's actually the worst— Ouch.' He tried to move his elbow, grimaced in pain.

'Anywhere else?'

'I don't think so.'

'A doctor,' I said, finally coming up with a contribution to the situation. 'We need to call a, or an ambulance, we—'

'Wait,' Melissa said. Deftly, matter-of-factly, she ran her hands over Hugo, turn your head, bend your elbow, does that hurt? what about this? Her face was intent and detached, a stranger's; her hands left smudges of flour like long-settled dust on his brown cords, his misshapen jumper. In the kitchen Chopin was still playing, the 'Minute Waltz', demented frenzy of trills and runs speeding on and on and I wanted savagely to make it shut up. Hugo's breathing, fast and laboured, was setting off some frantic alarm at the base of my brain. It took everything I had to stay there.

'All right,' Melissa said in the end, settling back on her haunches. 'I'm almost positive you haven't done anything serious. Your elbow's not broken, or you'd never be able to move it like that. Do you want to go to A and E? Or shall we get the doctor on call to come have a look?'

'No,' Hugo said. He struggled to sit up straight. I grabbed his hand, much bigger than mine and so bony, skin sliding, he had lost weight and I hadn't even noticed— 'Honestly, I'm fine. Just a bit shaky. The last thing I need is more doctors. I just want to lie down for a bit.'

'I really think you should get checked out,' I said. 'Just in case—'

His hand tightened in mine. With a flash of annoyance that was almost anger: 'I'm an adult, Toby. If I don't want to see a doctor, I won't. Now help me stand up and get me my cane.'

He was shaking too hard for the cane. We got him upstairs and into bed, one of us on each side with our shoulders braced under his arms, Chopin whirling and looping crazily in the background, the three of us tangled into one big ungainly creature moving with infinite care, up! OK, up again! Once he was settled, Melissa and I brought him a cup of tea and started making tinned chicken soup and toast for dinner. None of us wanted the empanadas any more.

'He really didn't do any damage, you know,' Melissa said, in the kitchen. 'And it could have been just what he said: his cane slipped.'

It hadn't been, and I didn't want to talk about that. I was pretty shaky myself; my heart was racketing, my body didn't believe the emergency was over. 'How did you know? How to check him over?'

She stirred the pan of soup, caught a drop on her finger to taste. 'I took a course, ages ago. My mother has falls sometimes.'

'Jesus,' I said. I wrapped my arms around her from behind and kissed the top of her head.

She took my hand off her waist, pressed it to her lips for a second and put it aside to reach for the herb shelf. The leftovers of that cool detachment still hung about her, and I wanted it gone; I wanted to take her to bed and strip it off with her clothes, burn it off like mist. 'No, it's good. You'd be surprised how many times it's come in useful.'

'Still,' I said. I had heard enough over the years to know that I would never be able to meet Melissa's mother without wanting to punch her face in, but this was the first time I'd recognised the grim irony here: all Melissa's childhood soaked up by taking care of her mother, she finally got away and found a guy who would take care of her instead, and all of a sudden, hey presto, she was right back in carer mode, only now she was stuck looking after two people instead of one. 'This isn't what you signed up for.'

She turned to look at me, herb jar in her hand. 'What isn't?'

'Being Hugo's carer.'

'I only checked him over.'

'You're doing a lot more than that.'

Melissa shrugged. 'I don't mind. I'm not just saying that; I honestly, truly don't mind. Hugo's wonderful.'

'I know. But this was only supposed to be for a few days.' We had been at the Ivy House for over three weeks by this point. Melissa had made a couple of trips to her place and mine, to pick up more clothes, but somehow the subject of moving back had never come up. 'Maybe you should go home.'

She leaned back against the counter, eyes scanning my face, soup forgotten. 'Do you want me to?'

'It's not that,' I said. 'I love you being here. It's just that' – saying it to her felt like a commitment somehow, one I wasn't sure I was ready to make, but it was too late – 'I've been thinking I might stay on for a while longer.'

Melissa's whole face lit up. 'Oh, I've been *hoping* you would! I didn't want to ask— I know someone else could take over, but Hugo loves having you here, Toby. It means the world to him. I'm so glad— And of *course* I'll stay. I want to.'

'It's one thing now,' I said. 'But it's going to get worse. And I don't want you dealing with that.'

'As long as you're here, I'm here. Oops—' She whirled around to the soup, which had started to hiss and foam ominously, and turned down the gas. 'This is ready. Did you put the toast on?'

'It's not just Hugo,' I said, with incredible difficulty; the words hurt coming out. 'You've done a fair bit of taking care of me, this last while.'

That made her smile at me, over her shoulder. 'I *like* taking care of you.'

'I don't like you having to do it. I hate it. Specially what with your mother.'

'That's not the same thing,' Melissa said instantly, turning from the cooker, and there was an absolute, iron inflexibility to her voice that I'd never heard there before. 'You didn't do this to yourself. Any more than Hugo did. It's completely different.'

'It comes to the same thing, though. This isn't what you should be doing. When we're eighty, sure, but now . . . you should be out dancing. Going to festivals. Having picnics. Sun holidays. All the stuff we—' My voice shook. I'd had this conversation in my head a thousand times, but I'd never had the strength to do it out loud and it was just as tough as I'd thought it would be. 'This isn't what I want for you.'

'Well, if I could pick anything in the world, this isn't what I'd want for you, either,' Melissa said matter-of-factly. 'But it's what we've got.'

'Believe me, this isn't what I want for myself, either. Jesus, this is just about the last thing—' My stupid voice cracked again. 'But I don't have a choice. You do.'

'Course I do. And I want to be here.'

All this unruffled composure wasn't what I was used to from Melissa – I had held her while she freaked out about Niall the pathetic semi-stalker, for God's sake, when she burst into tears over refugee kids on the news or starved puppies on Facebook – and it was kind of disconcerting. When I'd had this conversation in my head, I had been the steady one, comforting her.

'I want you to be happy,' I said. 'And there isn't a way for that to happen while you're here. While you're' – I had to take a breath for this – 'while you're with me. I'm supposed to make your life better. Not worse. And I think, I really think I used to do that. But now—'

'You *absolutely* make my life better. Silly.' She reached out to put a hand to my cheek, kept it there, small and warm. 'And so does being here. It's not just because of Hugo that I'm glad we're staying, you know. Being here is—' A quick breath of a laugh. 'It's been so good for you, Toby. You're getting better. Maybe you don't notice it yet, but I do. And that's the happiest thing that could happen to me.'

In my head this conversation had always ended with goodbye, with her going weeping back up into the sunlight like Orpheus, leaving me alone to dissolve into the thickening dark. That didn't really seem to be on the cards. The shift left me feeling very strange, light-headed and deflated all at once, scrabbling for footholds. I couldn't find a way to explain to Melissa all the things she had all wrong. 'No,' I said, pressing her hand against my cheek. 'Listen. You don't—'

'Shh.' She tiptoed to kiss me, a proper kiss, hands clasping at the back of my neck to pull me close. 'Now,' she said, smiling, when she leaned away. 'We need to feed Hugo or he'll faint from hunger, and then you *will* have something to worry about. Put the toast on.'

•

By the next morning, Hugo seemed fine; stronger than he had in days, actually, humming as he pottered around the living room looking for some book he wanted to reread and was sure he'd seen just a couple of years ago. I went out to the bottom of the garden – I had taken to drifting down there for my cigarettes, so we could all keep pretending I didn't smoke – and lay on the grass under one of the trees. Outside my patch of shadow the sun was blinding; gold coins of light spilled over my body, grasshoppers zizzed everywhere, yellow poppies bobbed.

I felt like talking to Dec, or even better, Sean. I hadn't actually spoken to either of them since that visit in the hospital; they had kept the texts coming, and I had even managed to text them back once or twice, but that was as far as things had gone. I was starting to notice that I missed the pair of bollixes. When I had finished my smoke I rolled over onto my stomach and pulled out my phone.

Sean picked up almost instantly, and there was an urgency to his 'Hello?' that startled me. 'Dude,' I said. 'How's tricks?'

'Fuck me,' Sean said, and it was only with the rush of glad relief in his voice that I got it: when my number came up he had been scared shitless, that I was ringing to say goodbye, that it was my parents ringing to break the news— It occurred to me that I had been kind of a dick to Sean and Dec. 'The man himself. What's the story?'

'Not a lot. You?'

'Grand. Jesus, dude, I haven't talked to you in— How're you doing?'

'Fine. I'm down at my uncle Hugo's. He's sick.'

'He OK?'

'Not really, no. It's brain cancer. He's got a few months.'

'Ah, shit.' Sean sounded genuinely upset; he had always liked Hugo a lot. 'Man, I'm sorry to hear that. How is he?'

'OK, considering. He's at home. He's kind of weak, but nothing too bad so far.'

'Tell him I was asking for him. He's a good man, Hugo. He was good to us.'

'You should come over,' I said; I hadn't known I was going to say it till I heard the words. 'He'd love to see you.'

'You sure?'

'Definitely. Come.'

'I will. Audrey and I are going to Galway for the weekend, but I'll come first thing next week. Will I bring Dec?'

'Do, yeah. I'll ring him. How's he getting on? Jenna stab him yet?'

'Fucking hell.' Sean blew out a long breath. 'Like six weeks ago, yeah? when they've been back together about five minutes? she decides they need to move in together. I tell Dec he'd be bloody insane to do it, which he totally agrees with. Right up until Jenna throws a screaming wobbler and says he's just using her for sex, and somehow by the end of the conversation Dec's decided he has to prove she's wrong by moving in with her.'

'Oh Jesus. We'll never see him again. She won't let him out the door.'

'Wait. It gets better. So they go apartment-hunting together, right? They pick out a nice little place in Smithfield, put down the security deposit and the first month's rent, few grand. Dec gives notice on his place. And a week later—'

'Oh no.'

'Yeah. She breaks it to him that she was just *punishing him* for *toying with her feelings*, she's got no intention of moving in with him, in fact she's dumping him. Bye.'

'Shit,' I said. 'How's he doing?'

'He's not great. I've been trying to get him out for a few pints, but he says he can't be arsed. You ring him. He'll do it for you.'

I rang Dec, but he didn't answer. I left a voice message: 'Hey, you fucking idiot. Please tell me you're not in the middle of a make-up shag. I'm at my uncle Hugo's. Sean says he's going to call round next week. You should come too. Give me a bell.'

I like to imagine that, if things had gone differently, Melissa and I would have stayed and stayed, at least as long as Hugo was alive, maybe longer. Sean and Dec would have come down for that visit (Hugo blinking and smiling, *My goodness, both of you all grown up, I'll have to stop thinking of you as scruffy teenagers with an overdeveloped sense of mischief – although I hope you've still got that . . .*) and stayed for a long leisurely barbecue, all of us stretched on the grass, slagging Dec about that time back in fifth year when Susanna's friend Maddie spent an entire evening hitting on him and he never even noticed. The steady aplomb with which Hugo was facing death would have raised me to some kind of enlightened state wherein I would have realised that what had happened to me was not only survivable but surmountable, just a rough grain of sand in the ocean of life. My cousins and I would have got each other through the tough times – black humour, arms around shoulders, long drunken late-night talks – and come out the other end sadder but closer, our old childhood bond reforged and bright again. Melissa would have coaxed me into going to physical therapy. At some point I would have got my hands on a ring and gone down on one knee among the Queen Anne's lace, and we would have run up to the house hand in hand to give Hugo the news, a star of promise in the encroaching darkness, the line continuing, irrepressible life spinning on. And in the end I would have hired some estate agent to sell the apartment for me, without ever setting foot in it again, and headed off to that white Georgian house on the bay. Of course it didn't play out that way, at all; but sometimes, when I badly need rest, I like to pretend that it could have.

•

As things turned out, this lasted for just under four weeks. On the Friday morning I was in the garden again, having a smoke under the trees. It was starting to be autumn, yellow birch leaves trickling down to land in my lap, elderberries turning purple so that small birds flew over to give them experimental pecks, a cool clean tinge to the blue sky. Someone was using a lawnmower, far enough away that it was just a comfortable homey buzz.

When the shape caught my eye I nearly jumped out of my skin: a lopsided bulk blurry amid the slanting light, coming towards me slow and inexorable as a messenger through the tall grass. It took me a second to realise it was Hugo, leaning heavily on his cane. I jammed out my cigarette and swept some dirt over it.

'May I join you?' he asked, when he reached me. He was a little out of breath.

'Sure,' I said. My heart was still hammering and I wasn't sure what was going on. Hugo never came out to me in the garden;

catching me smoking would have violated one of the unspoken pacts that kept our delicate balance working. 'Have a seat.'

He lowered himself jerkily onto the grass – biting his lip and bracing himself with the cane, one sharp shake of his head when I held out a hand to help him – and arranged himself leaning back against an oak tree, legs out in front of him. 'Give me a cigarette,' he said.

After a startled second I fished out my packet, handed him a cigarette and flicked the lighter for him. He inhaled deeply, eyes closed. 'Ahhh,' he said, on a long sigh. 'My goodness, I've missed that.'

'You used to smoke?'

'Oh God, yes. The hard stuff: Woodbines, a pack a day. I quit twenty years ago – partly because you lot had started staying here and it didn't seem like a good example to set, but mostly for my health. Which turned out to be the wrong call, didn't it?' I couldn't tell whether the twist in his half-smile was bitterness or just the drag at the side of his mouth. 'I could have spent those twenty years happily smoking my head off, and it would have made no difference to anything at all.'

Another pact broken: we never talked about the fact that he was dying. I had no idea what to say. This conversation felt bad, threatening in ways I couldn't catch hold of. I lit myself a new cigarette and we sat there, watching sycamore helicopters spin through the air.

'Susanna rang,' Hugo said, eventually. 'Her Swiss specialist fellow had a look at my file. He agrees with my doctors: there's nothing more that can be done.'

'Oh, shit,' I said, flinching. 'Shit.'

'Yes.'

'I'm really sorry.'

'I really believed I wasn't getting my hopes up,' Hugo said. He wasn't looking at me; he was watching the smoke of his cigarette curl out into the sunlight. 'I really did.'

I could have punched Susanna. Selfish little bitch, so in love with her seat on the high horse, her self-righteous victim bullshit about evil doctors, she had put Hugo through this when anyone with half a brain would have known it was pointless— 'That was a shitty thing for Susanna to do,' I said. 'A fucking stupid fucking shitty thing.'

'No, she was right. In principle. The specialist said that, in around three-quarters of the cases that come his way from these parts, he actually does disagree with the original doctors and recommend surgery – mostly it isn't a cure, the cancer comes back sooner or later, but it gives people an extra few years . . . I just happen to be in the wrong quarter. Something to do with the location of the tumour.'

'I'm so sorry,' I said again.

'I know.' He took a final deep drag on the cigarette and put it out in the dirt. His thick locks of hair shifted as he bent, showing the bald spot on the side of his head where the radiotherapy waves had gone in or out. A blur of leaf-shadows and sunlight whirled over his thin-worn shirt. 'Could I have another one of these?'

I found him another smoke. 'I should try everything,' he said. 'Speed, LSD, the lot. Heroin. There wasn't much of anything around when I was young; I smoked hash a few times, didn't really take to it . . . Do you suppose Leon would know where to get LSD?'

'I doubt it,' I said. The thought of babysitting Hugo on an acid trip was mind-boggling. 'He probably wouldn't know anyone in Dublin.'

'Of course not. And I probably wouldn't take it anyway. Ignore me, Toby. I'm babbling.'

'We'd like to stay here,' I said. 'Me and Melissa. As long as . . . as long as we're any use. If you'll have us.'

'What am I supposed to say to that?' A sudden harsh burst of bitterness in Hugo's voice, his head going back— 'I know, I should be thanking you on my knees – yes, I should, Toby, the thought of leaching away the last of my life in some hellish hospital— And of course I'm going to say yes, we both know that, and of course I'm grateful beyond words, but I would have liked to have a *choice*. To invite you to stay on because I love having you both here, rather than because I'm in desperate need. I would like' – voice rising, the heel of his hand slamming down hard on a tree root – 'to have a bloody *say* in some of this.'

'Sorry,' I said, after a moment. 'I didn't mean to . . . like, force your hand. Or anything. I just thought—'

'I know you didn't. That's not what I'm talking about. At all.' Hugo rubbed a hand over his face. The surge of energy had ebbed out of him as suddenly as it had come, leaving him slumped against the tree. 'I'm just sick and tired of being at the mercy of this thing. Having it make all my decisions for me. It's eating my autonomy as well as my brain, eating me right out of existence in every way, and I don't like it. I would like . . .'

I waited, but he didn't finish. Instead, when at last he took a breath and straightened: 'I would love to have you stay on,' he said, clearly and formally. He was looking out at the garden, not at me. 'You and Melissa both. On condition that you promise me you'll feel free to change your minds. At any point.'

'OK,' I said. 'Fair enough.'

'Good. Thank you.' He searched for a bare patch of dirt and twisted out his cigarette in it. 'I need to ask you another favour. I'd like to be cremated, and I'd like my ashes to be scattered here, in the garden. Could you see to it that that gets done?'

'You should have a,' I said. This conversation was becoming more and more unbearable, like some carefully calibrated form of torture that ratcheted up one precise notch every time I managed to catch my breath. I wondered idiotically if I could claim that I heard the phone ringing indoors, if I could pretend to fall asleep right there in mid-sentence, anything to make it stop. 'You should have a will. To make sure. In case anyone argues about, you know, wants to do something different—'

'A will.' Hugo snorted bleakly. 'I should, shouldn't I. I've been telling myself every day: *This week, I must get it sorted out this week, I'll get Ed or Phil to recommend a good solicitor—* And then I look at their faces and think, *I can't do that to them, not today, I'll find a day when they're in better form* . . . And before I know it another week's gone past. It seems that counsellor woman in the hospital was right all along, wasn't she? Denial. A part of me must have been still hoping.'

Until that moment, I'd forgotten all about asking Hugo what would happen to the house. It was the will stuff that brought it back. 'The house,' I said. 'If you're making a— I mean, if you want to, to be here' – I made some kind of shapeless gesture at the garden – 'then the house should stay in the family. Right?'

He turned his head and looked at me, a long intent look under those shaggy eyebrows. 'Do you want it to?' he asked.

'Yeah,' I said. 'I really do.'

'Hmf.' The eyebrows twitched. 'I didn't realise you were so attached to the place.'

'I didn't either. I mean, maybe I wasn't, I don't know. It's just . . . now. Being back here.' I had no idea how to explain myself. 'I'd hate it to go.'

He was still looking at me; it was starting to make me itchy. 'And your cousins? What do they think?'

'Yeah, them too. They'd really like to, to hang on to it. I mean, we're not all trying to grab the house for ourselves, it's not like that, at all—' The slight frown on his face, I had no clue what he was thinking— 'Just, it's the family home, you know? And they're kind of worried that Phil would want to, like, sell it, not that he doesn't care about it, but—'

'All right,' Hugo said abruptly, cutting me off in mid-gibber. 'I'll sort it out.'

'Thanks. Thank you.'

He took off his glasses and polished them on the hem of his shirt. His eyes, gazing unblinking out over the sunlit garden, looked blind. 'If you don't mind,' he said, 'I'd appreciate a few minutes to myself.'

'Oh. Right.' For a minute I hovered, dithering – was he pissed off with me? had I fucked up, offended him by talking about his death as a *fait accompli*? was he going to be able to get up without my help? – but he ignored me completely, and in the end I gave up and went inside.

●

He was out there for well over an hour, just sitting, so still that the small birds foraging on the grass came within feet of him (I was hanging around the kitchen to keep an eye on him, staying well back from the windows). When he came in, though, he was brisk and a bit distant, impatient to get to work – he had done some incomprehensible DNA triangulation and turned up something on Mrs Wozniak, more cousins or cousins' cousins in Tipperary, he had explained it to me the day before but it hadn't stuck. There was no mention of the conversation outside, and part of me wondered with a horrible sinking feeling whether he had forgotten the whole thing.

The next morning over breakfast, though, he announced cheerfully that Susanna's lot and Leon would be coming over that afternoon. 'Let's make apple-and-walnut cake. Not the children's favourite, I know, but it's mine, and I think now and then I should be shameless about using the situation to get my own way. And' – with a flash of a smile at me – 'apple-and-walnut cake is much less trouble than LSD, isn't it?'

And so: Saturday afternoon, tea and cake in the living room. Warm smell of apples and cinnamon all through the house, still grey sky outside the windows. Tom earnestly explaining how he had finally got through to the most apathetic kid in his fifth-year history class, something improbable about *Game of Thrones* but it seemed to make him happy; Susanna and Melissa bonding over some new band they both liked, Leon rolling his eyes and offering to make them a playlist of *real* music, Hugo teasing us all for not appreciating the Beatles. It all looked like a nice cosy family afternoon, but this wasn't in the routine and we all knew it; I could feel everyone wondering and waiting, covert question-mark glances zipping back and forth. I ignored them. I still had the nasty feeling that I had fucked up that conversation with Hugo, in some nebulous but important way, and everything was getting ready to go all wrong.

Susanna's kids weren't helping. Their attention span had lasted about as long as their cake, and by the time Tom and Leon cleared the plates Zach was buzzing around the living room like a hornet, nudging things with his toe and flicking bits of paper at people and joggling my elbow every time he passed. 'Uncle Hugo!' he demanded. He was swinging off the back of Hugo's chair by his armpits, like a chimpanzee. 'Can I take out the demolition set?'

'Zach,' Susanna said sharply, from the sofa, where she and Melissa had been mooning over some phone video of their new pet band. 'Get off Hugo's chair.'

Zach made a violent barfing noise and collapsed onto the floor in disgust, narrowly missing Sallie, who was lying on her stomach pushing some toy around the rug and talking to herself. 'Uncle *Hugo*,' he said, louder, from there. 'Can I—'

Hugo turned, creakily, and reached down to lay a hand on his head. 'Not now. I need to talk with your parents and the rest of this lot. You and Sallie go outside.'

'But—'

Hugo leaned over, beckoned till Zach knelt up, and whispered something in his ear. Zach's face broke into a big grin. 'Oh *yeah*,' he said. 'Come on, Sal,' and he zoomed off towards the back garden with Sallie in his wake.

'What did you say to him?' Susanna asked, a little suspiciously.

'I told him there's treasure hidden in the garden, and if they can find it they can keep it. Presumably it's not even a lie; there must be all kinds of things out there that have been dropped over the years. They'll be fine.' Hugo settled carefully back into his armchair. 'I do need to talk to all of you. Susanna, would you mind getting Leon and Tom in here for a moment?'

Susanna went, darting one sharp unfathomable glance at me along the way. We settled obediently as schoolchildren, Melissa and me on one sofa, Leon and Susanna on the other, Tom planted in the armchair across from Hugo with his hands on his knees and a St Bernard's look of generalised faint worry on his face. A cool-edged breeze, and the sound of Zach yelling orders, strayed in through the open kitchen door.

'Toby pointed out to me,' Hugo said, 'that we need to clarify what will happen to this house when I die.'

'Oh. I didn't—' Melissa stood up. 'I'll keep an eye on Zach and Sallie,' she said to Susanna.

'No,' Hugo said, instantly and firmly, reaching out to touch her arm. 'Stay, my dear. I need you to be here. You're part of this too.'

With a faint wry smile: 'Whether you like it or not.' Melissa hesitated for a moment, unsure, but he gave her a smile and a tiny, reassuring nod, and she sat down again.

'Good,' Hugo said. 'Now. Toby tells me that he and you two' – Susanna and Leon – 'think this house should stay in the family. Is that right?'

Both their backs straightened. 'I do,' Susanna said.

'Definitely,' Leon said.

'And you're worried that Phil and Louisa might sell it, if it were to go to them.'

'They would,' Susanna said. 'All this stuff about giving the kids *advantages*.'

Hugo cocked an eyebrow. 'You don't want advantages?'

'We're fine. It's not like we'll be out on the street without that money. The kids don't need fancy holidays or sailing lessons or a massive house with a cinema room. I don't even *want* them to have that crap. But my parents don't listen.'

Hugo glanced at Tom, who nodded. 'Your parents,' he said to Leon. 'How do they feel about it?'

Leon shrugged. 'My dad's not mad about the idea of this place going. But you know what he's like. If Phil turns up the pressure . . .'

'Oliver will give in, in the end,' Hugo said. 'Yes. And yours, Toby?'

'I don't have a clue,' I said. This whole thing had an unreal tinge, a scene from some TV drama, carefully staged, the clan gathered in the drawing room to hear the patriarch's dying wishes. 'I mean, my dad loves this place, but . . . I haven't talked to him about it.'

'Ed's the sentimentalist,' Hugo said. 'Deep down.' He rearranged his legs, carefully, nudging the weak one into place with his hand. 'Here's the thing. If the place stays in the family, what are you planning to do with it? Do any of you want to live here?'

We all looked at each other. I had a sudden unsettling vision of me in forty years, pottering around the Ivy House with a cup of lapsang souchong and a pair of knee-sprung cords.

'Well, I'm in Berlin,' Leon said. 'I'm not saying that's forever, or anything, but . . .'

'We might,' said Susanna, who had been having a complicated private exchange of glances with Tom. 'We'd have to talk about it.'

'The inheritance tax would be pretty stiff,' Hugo pointed out. 'Would you be able to pay it?'

This was feeling more and more surreal, Hugo's calm business-like tone as he sat there in the armchair discussing a time just a few months away when he wouldn't exist any more, all of us going along like it was perfectly sane— The air tasted thick and sour, subterranean. I wanted to get out.

'We could sell our house,' Susanna said. 'We should get enough.'

'Hm,' Hugo said. 'The only thing is, that doesn't seem very fair to the boys. It's not as if I have anything else to leave them – certainly nothing that's worth anywhere near as much as the house.'

'I don't care,' Leon said. He was lounging in his corner of the sofa, too cool for school, but his fingers were drumming a tense fast rhythm on his thigh; he wasn't any happier than I was. 'Su can give me my share someday when she wins the lotto. Or not. Whatever.'

'Toby?'

'I don't know,' I said. Way too many factors crashing into each other, my head felt like an old computer logjammed by too many programs running. 'I haven't— I never thought about it.'

'We could . . .' Tom said tentatively. For a savage instant I wanted to punch him in the gob, what was he doing shoving his nose into this conversation? 'I mean, only if the guys were OK with it. It could belong to all three of them, and we could live here and pay the guys rent on their two-thirds?'

'*If* we wanted to live here,' Susanna said, with a swift warning side-glance at him. 'I'm not sure yet.'

'Well, yeah. If. And obviously we'd need to work out all the—'

Out in the garden, Zach screamed. He and Sallie had been yelling off and on the whole time, but this was something else: this was a hoarse, raw shriek of pure terror.

Before I managed to register what I had heard, Susanna was on her feet and throwing herself out of the room. Tom was close behind her. 'What the fuck—' Leon said, and then he and I and Melissa were up and after them.

Zach and Sallie were standing at the bottom of the garden. Both of them were rigid, arms out in shock, and by this time both of them were screaming, Sallie's piercing inhuman high note rising above Zach's ragged howls. My feet thumping on the ground, my breath loud in my ears. Wave of birds lifting from the trees. And on the bright green grass in front of Zach and Sallie a brown and yellow object that, although I had never seen a real one in my life, I understood without the need for a single thought was a human skull.

In my memory the world stopped. Everything hung motionless and weightless above the slowly turning earth, suspended in a vast silence that went on and on, so that I had time to take in every detail: Susanna's red-gold hair frozen in mid-swing against the grey sky, Zach's mouth wide, the slant of Leon's body as he skidded to a stop. I was reminded, strangely, of nothing so much as the moment when I had flicked on the light in my living room and the two burglars had turned to stare at me. One blink, one glance to the side, and when you look again everything is different: the trees and the garden wall and the people all looked like themselves, but they were made of some new and alien material; the world looked unchanged, and yet somehow I was standing in an entirely different place.

5

Susanna swooped Sallie onto her hip, grabbed Zach's arm in the same movement and hustled the pair of them back up the garden, talking firm reassuring bullshit all the way. Sallie was still screaming, the sound jolting with Susanna's footsteps; Zach had switched to yelling wildly, lunging at the end of Susanna's arm to get back to us. When the kitchen door slammed behind them, the silence came down over the garden thick as volcanic ash.

The skull lay on its side in the grass, between the camomile patch and the shadow of the wych elm. One of the eyeholes was plugged with a clot of dark dirt and small pale curling roots; the lower jaw gaped in a skewed, impossible howl. Clumps of something brown and matted, hair or moss, clung to the bone.

The four of us stood there in a semicircle, as if we were gathered for some incomprehensible initiation ceremony, waiting for a signal to tell us how to begin. Around our feet the grass was long and wet, bowed under the weight of the morning's rain.

'That's,' I said, 'that looks human.'

'It's fake,' Tom said. 'Some Halloween thing—'

Melissa said, 'I don't think it's fake.' I put my arm around her. She brought up a hand to take mine, but absently: all her focus was on the thing.

'Our neighbours put a skeleton out,' Tom said. 'Last year. It looked totally real.'

'I don't think it's fake.'

None of us moved closer.

'How would a fake skull get in here?' I asked.

'Teenagers messing around,' Tom said. 'Throwing it over the wall, or out of a window. How would a real skull get in here?'

'It could be old,' Melissa said. 'Hundreds of years, even thousands. And Zach and Sallie dug it up. Or a fox did.'

'It's fake as fuck,' Leon said. His voice was high and tight and angry; the thing had scared the shit out of him. 'And it's not funny. It could have given someone a heart attack. Stick it in the bin, before Hugo sees it. Get a shovel out of the shed; I'm not touching it.'

Tom took three swift paces forwards, went down on one knee by the thing and leaned in close. He straightened up fast, with a sharp hiss of in-breath.

'OK,' he said. 'I think it's real.'

'Fuck's *sake*,' Leon said, jerking his head upwards. 'There's no way, like literally no possible—'

'Take a look.'

Leon didn't move. Tom stepped back, wiping his hands on his trousers as if he had touched it.

The run down the garden had left my scar throbbing, a tiny pointed hammer knocking my vision off-kilter with every blow. It seemed to me that the best thing we could do was stay perfectly still, all of us, wait till something came flapping down to carry this back to whatever seething otherworld had discharged it at our feet; that if any of us shifted a foot, took a breath, that chance would be lost and some dreadful and unstoppable train of events would be set in motion.

'Let me see,' Hugo said quietly, behind us. All of us jumped.

He moved between us, his stick crunching rhythmically into the grass, and leaned over to look. 'Ah,' he said. 'Yes. Zach was right.'

'Hugo,' I said. He seemed like salvation, the one person in the world who would know how to undo this so we could all go back inside and talk about the house some more. 'What do we do?'

He turned his head to look at me over his shoulder, pushing up his glasses with a knuckle. 'We call the Guards, of course,' he said gently. 'I'll do it in a moment. I just wanted to see for myself.'

'But,' Leon said, and stopped. Hugo's eyes rested on him for a moment, mild and expressionless, before he bent again over the skull.

·

I was expecting detectives, but they were uniformed Guards: two big thick-necked blank-faced guys about my age, alike enough that they could have been brothers, both of them with Midlands accents and yellow hi-vis vests and the kind of meticulous politeness that everyone understands is conditional. They arrived fast, but once they were there they didn't seem particularly excited about the whole thing. 'Could be an animal skull,' said the bigger one, following Melissa and me down the hall. 'Or old remains, maybe. Archaeology, like.'

'You did the right thing calling us, either way,' said the other guy. 'Better safe than sorry.'

Hugo and Leon and Tom were still in the garden, standing well back. 'Now,' said the bigger guy, nodding to them, 'let's have a look at this,' and he and his mate squatted on their hunkers beside the skull, trousers stretching across their thick thighs. I saw the moment when their eyes met.

The big one took a pen out of his pocket and inserted it into the empty eyehole, carefully tilting the skull to one side and the other, examining every angle. Then he used the pen to hook back the long grass from the jaw, leaning in to inspect the teeth. Leon was gnawing ferociously on a thumbnail.

When the cop looked up his face was even blanker. 'Where was this found?' he asked.

'My great-nephew found it,' Hugo said. Of all of us, he was the calmest; Melissa had her arms wrapped tightly around her waist, Leon was practically jigging with tension, and even Tom was white and stunned-looking, hair standing up like he'd been running his hands through it. 'In a hollow tree, he says. I assume it was this one here, but I don't know for certain.'

All of us looked up at the wych elm. It was one of the biggest trees in the garden, and the best for climbing: a great misshapen grey-brown bole, maybe five feet across, lumpy with rough bosses that made perfect handholds and footholds to the point where, seven or eight feet up, it split into thick branches heavy with huge green leaves. It was the same one I'd broken my ankle jumping out of, when I was a kid; with a horrible leap of my skin I realised that this thing could have been in there the whole time, I could have been just inches away from it.

The big cop glanced at his mate, who straightened up and, with surprising agility, hauled himself up the tree trunk. He braced his feet and hung on to a branch with one hand while he pulled a slim pen-shaped torch from his pocket; shone it into the split of the trunk; pointed it this way and that, peering, mouth hanging open. Finally he thumped down onto the grass with a grunt and gave the big cop a brief nod.

'Where's your great-nephew now?' the big cop asked.

'In the house,' Hugo said, 'with his mother and his sister. His sister was with him when he found it.'

'Right,' the cop said. He stood up, putting his pen away. His face, tilted to the sky, was distant; with a small shock I realised he was thrilled. 'Let's go have a quick word with them. Can you all come with me, please?' And to his mate: 'Get on to the Ds and the Bureau.'

The mate nodded. As we trooped into the house, I glanced over my shoulder one last time: the cop, feet stolidly apart, swiping and jabbing at his phone; the wych elm, vast and luxuriant in its full summer whirl of green; and on the ground between them the small brown shape, barely visible among the daisies and the long grass.

●

Susanna was on the sofa, with an arm around each kid. She was even paler than normal, but she looked composed enough, and the kids had stopped screaming. They gave the cop matching opaque stares from the safety of Susanna's arms.

'Sorry to disturb you,' the cop said. 'I'd like a word with this young man, if he's feeling able for it.'

'He's fine,' Susanna said. 'Aren't you?'

'He is, of course,' said the cop heartily. 'He's a big boy. What's your name, sonny?'

Zach wriggled out of Susanna's arm and looked at the cop warily. 'Zach,' he said.

'And what age are you?'

'Six.'

The cop pulled out a notebook and squatted awkwardly by the coffee table, as close to Zach as he could get. 'Aren't you great for finding that yoke out there? That's a big tree for a little fella like you to be climbing.'

Zach rolled his eyes, not too obviously.

'Can you tell me what happened?'

Zach, however, had apparently decided he didn't like this guy. He shrugged and dug his toe into the rug, watching the pile ruck up.

'What was the first thing you did when you went out into the garden, say? Did you go straight for the tree? Or were you doing something else first?'

Shrug.

'Were you playing a game, yeah? Were you being Tarzan?'

Eye-roll.

'Zach,' Susanna said evenly. 'Tell the Guard what happened.'

Zach drew a line in the rug with his toe and examined it.

'*Zach*,' Tom said.

'That's all right,' the cop said easily, although he didn't look pleased. 'You can talk to the detectives when they get here, if you'd rather do that.' The word *detectives* sent a flicker through the room; I heard a quick catch of breath, couldn't tell where it came from. 'What about this young lady here? Can you tell me what happened?'

Zach shot Sallie a vicious look. Her chin started to wobble and she buried her face in Susanna's stomach.

'Right,' the cop said, cutting his losses and straightening up. 'We'll leave that for later; they're a bit shaken up, sure, who wouldn't be. Was it you they came to, Mrs . . . ?'

'Hennessy. Susanna Hennessy.' Susanna had one hand on the back of Sallie's neck and the other on Zach's shoulder, tight enough that he squirmed. 'The rest of us were in here. We heard them scream, so we all ran out to the garden.'

'And that yoke out there. When you ran out, was it where it is now? On the grass near the tree?'

'Yes.'

'Did anyone touch it? Apart from your son?'

'Sal,' Susanna said gently. 'Did you touch it?' Sallie shook her head, into Susanna's top.

'Anyone else?'

We all shook our heads.

The cop wrote something in his notebook. 'And are you the resident here?' he asked Susanna.

'I am,' Hugo said. He had moved slowly and carefully around the rest of us to lower himself into his armchair. 'These three are my niece and my nephews, Tom is my niece's husband, and Melissa is Toby's girlfriend. The two of them are staying with me at the moment, but usually it's just me.'

'What's your name, sir?'

'Hugo Hennessy.'

'And how long have you been living here?'

'All my life, with the odd gap here and there. It was my parents' house, and my grandparents'.'

'So it's been in the family since when?'

Hugo considered that, rubbing absently at one of his radiotherapy bald spots. '1925, I think. It might have been 1926.'

'Mm-hm,' the cop said, examining what he'd written. 'Would you have any idea how old that tree is? Did you plant it?'

'Goodness, no. It was old when I was a child. It's a wych elm; they can live for centuries.'

'And that yoke out there. Any idea who it might be?'

Hugo shook his head. 'I can't imagine.'

The cop looked around the rest of us. 'Anyone else? Any ideas?'

We all shook our heads.

'Right,' the cop said. He closed his notebook and tucked it away in a pocket. 'Now, I have to tell you, we might need to be here for a while.'

'How long?' Susanna asked sharply.

'No way to know at this stage. We'll keep you informed. And we'll try to minimise the disturbance. Is there any other entrance to the garden, besides through the house? So we don't have to be coming in and out on you?'

'There's a door in the back wall of the garden,' Hugo said, 'leading out onto the laneway. I'm not sure where the key—'

'Kitchen cupboard,' Leon said. 'I saw it last week, I'll get it—' and he slipped away as swiftly as a shadow.

'That's great,' the cop said. His eye moved around the room and stopped on Tom. 'Mr . . . ?'

'Farrell. Thomas Farrell.'

'Mr Farrell, I'm going to ask you to make us a list of the name and contact details of everyone here. We'll also need a list of who's lived in this house, as far back as any of you know, and the dates – doesn't need to be exact at this point, just "Granny Hennessy lived here from, we'll say, 1950 till she died in 2000," that kind of thing. Can you do that?'

'No problem,' Tom said promptly. Even in the middle of all this, it sent a sharp flare of outrage through me – fair enough, Hugo was obviously not well and Leon looked like a refugee from a Sex Pistols tribute band and Susanna was covered in kids, but I was standing right there, I was family and Tom wasn't, why the fuck was this guy skipping over me?

Leon came back with the key. 'Here,' he said, holding it out to the cop. 'I don't know if it'll work, no one ever uses that door so it might have gone all—'

'Thanks very much,' the cop said, pocketing it. 'I'm going to ask you all to stay in this room here for a while. If you need to use the toilet or the kitchen, obviously, that's no problem, but the garden'll be off limits until further notice. The detectives will fill you in a bit more when they arrive. Are you all able to wait here for them? Does anyone have an appointment, anywhere you need to be?'

Nobody did. 'That's grand, so,' the cop said. 'We appreciate your cooperation,' and he headed off, closing the living-room door a little too firmly behind him. His heavy footsteps thumped down the stairs to the kitchen.

'Well,' Hugo said. 'He was a bit . . . , wasn't he? A bit clumsy; callow, is that the word I'm looking for? I was expecting someone more – I don't know, polished. Too many detective novels, I suppose. Do you think he knows what he's doing?'

Leon said, 'There's that tape all round the garden. That blue and white stuff. It says "CRIME SCENE NO ENTRY".'

No one said anything. After a moment Melissa sat down on the other sofa and reached for the pack of cards on the coffee table.

'I think we could be here for a while,' she said. 'Does anyone want to play rummy?'

•

It took a very long time for the detectives to arrive. I fetched paper and pen from Hugo's study, and Tom did up his lists – when did your granddad die again, Su? Hugo, do you remember what year you moved back in? do we put in the summers you guys stayed here? blah blah blah, like some awful lickarse aiming for best class project. Melissa and Hugo and I played hand after hand of rummy, very badly; Leon joined in, off and on, but he could barely stay still for one round before he gravitated back to the windows, where he pressed himself against the wall and stared furtively out at the road like a PI peering around a street corner. Susanna played some game on her phone with Sallie, a low nonstop current of blips and electronic music and sharp cartoony giggles. Zach was so hopped up on adrenaline that he'd gone full tweaker: manically circling the room, climbing furniture, making a furious variety of clicking and tocking and sucking noises that were driving me bananas. I was itching to stick out a foot and trip him up.

For some reason it seemed impossible to say a single word about the skull. It felt like there were a thousand questions I wanted to ask and angles I wanted to discuss, but I couldn't put my finger on a single one, and the longer I left it the more unsayable it all seemed and the more dreamlike the entire situation felt, as if we had been in that room forever and would never be able to leave. 'Toby,' Leon said. 'Your deal. Come on.'

The doorbell rang. We all froze and looked at one another, but before any of us could do anything sensible we heard boots tramping up the hall and the front door opening. Male voices swapping brief unemotional comments, crackle of a radio, confusion of footsteps going back down the hall; then the kitchen door slamming.

'I'm *hungry*,' Sallie said, not loudly but for at least the fifth time.

'You just had cake,' Susanna said, without looking at her. Out in the garden, brusque voices were calling back and forth, too distant for us to catch any words.

'But I'm *hungry*.'

'OK,' Susanna said. She rummaged in her bag and pulled out a little plasticky orange pouch with a spout on it. 'Here.'

'I want one!' Zach demanded, popping up from the floor, where he had been drumming his feet on the fireguard and trying to beatbox.

'You hate them.'

'I *want* one.'

'Are you going to eat it?'

'What about medical students?' Tom said suddenly, perking up. He had been hovering around the living-room door, clutching his precious lists, looking for his big chance to hand them in to Teacher.

'What,' Leon said, cutting him a withering glance without bothering to turn his head. He was slouched sideways in an armchair with his knees hooked over the arm, jiggling one foot in a fast insistent rhythm that I was trying not to look at.

'The' – flapping his lists in the direction of the garden – 'that. You know that apartment block behind the laneway? It's got lots of students, right? And medical students, they've got a messed-up sense of humour. If a couple of them nicked a skull and mucked about with it for a while, scaring their mates, and then they couldn't figure out how to get rid of it, they could have tossed it down the tree.' He looked around triumphantly.

'They'd want to have some aim,' Leon said sourly. 'To get it through all the branches and all the leaves and straight down a hole that has to be, what, a couple of feet across. A medical student who's also a world-class basketball player: that should narrow it down.'

'Maybe they weren't aiming for the tree. They were trying to throw it into the garden, to freak people out, and they missed.'

'And got it through all the branches. And all the leaves. And straight down a hole that has to be—'

'I don't want this,' Sallie said. She was holding the packet out from her body and she looked like she was on the verge of tears.

'You love that,' Susanna said. 'Eat it.'

'There's snabbits in it.'

'What are snabbits?'

'They're in there.'

'No they aren't. It's carrots and apples and some other thing, parsnips or something.'

'I don't *like* snabbits.'

'OK,' Susanna said, taking the pouch out of her hand. 'I'll get you a new one.' She headed out to the kitchen.

'I'm just saying,' Tom said. 'It's not necessarily anything sinister. It could be just—'

'A hippogriff could have dropped it,' Leon said. 'On its way to the Forbidden Forest.'

'That *would* be sinister,' Tom said, aiming for jollity. 'The Forbidden Forest at the bottom of the garden.' No one laughed.

My head was still throbbing, faintly but persistently, and my vision was glitching; I couldn't tell what was in my hand, sevens and nines looked the same, eights and tens. 'Oo,' Melissa said, laying down a fan of cards. 'Rummy.' She smiled up at me and gave me a small, steadying nod. I tried to smile back.

Susanna came back with what looked to me like the same orange plastic pouch. 'Here,' she said. 'I got you one with no snabbits.' Sallie grabbed the packet, retreated to a corner of the sofa and started sucking feverishly on the spout.

'The garden's swarming,' Susanna said to the rest of us, low, glancing over at Zach and Sallie to make sure they weren't listening. 'Guys in white boiler suits and hoods and *face* masks, like in some sci-fi movie where the virus just got out of the lab. Taking photos. They're putting up a thing, a canvas gazebo thing. With plastic sheets on the ground. Down by the strawberry bed.'

'Jesus Christ,' Leon said. He tossed down his cards, swung himself out of the armchair and started circling the room. 'This is fucked up. What the fuck are we supposed to do? Are we supposed to set up camp here until they finish whatever the fuck it is they're doing out there?'

Tom was making frantic warning grimaces and jerking his head sideways towards Zach and Sallie. 'Oh for *fuck's sake*,' Leon said.

'Knock it off,' Susanna said. 'And relax. This is not the end of the world.'

'Don't tell me to relax. Of all the stupid bloody things to say—'

'Go have a smoke.'

'I *can't* go have a smoke. There are *cops* all over the—'

'Yuck,' Zach said, shoving his orange pouch into Susanna's hand. 'Don't tell me yours has snabbits too.'

'There's no such thing as snabbits. It's just disgusting.'

'I *asked* you if you were going to eat it. You said—'

'If I eat it I'll *puke*.'

'Oh, for God's sake—'

There was a tap at the door, and a man stuck his head in. 'Afternoon,' he said. 'I'm Mike Rafferty; Detective Mike Rafferty. Sorry about all this hassle.'

We all came up with some shapeless polite nonsense. Leon had stopped pacing; Melissa's hand was suspended in mid-air, cards fanned.

'I appreciate that,' Rafferty said. 'I'm sure this isn't how you were planning on spending your Saturday afternoon. We'll be out of your way as soon as possible.'

He was maybe in his early forties; tall, a bit over six foot, with a thin, rangy build that managed to look strong and agile all the same, as if he was a black belt in some obscure martial art that we weren't cool enough to have heard of. He had rough dark hair and a long, lean, bony face carved deeply with smile-lines, and a discreetly excellent grey suit.

'I just have to ask you a few questions, if that's all right. Everyone OK with that? Anyone feeling a bit too shaken up right now, prefer to wait till later?'

Now was apparently fine with everyone. Leon leaned against the window frame, hands stuffed deep in his pockets; Susanna took up her place on the sofa again, an arm around Sallie, murmuring something in her ear. Melissa swept the cards into a pile.

'Great,' Rafferty said. 'That'll help us out a lot. OK if I sit here?' He turned Leon's armchair to give a good view of us all, and sat down.

His presence was doing bad things to me. On the surface he was nothing at all like Martin or Flashy Suit, but still there was something, something about the economy of movement and the easy friendly tone leaving no option of refusal and giving away absolutely nothing, that brought it all back: polluting hospital air burrowing into every pore, my head clogged with pain and with a thick haze like demolition dust, the pleasant blank faces watching me and waiting. My hands were shaking. I clasped them between my knees.

'As you've probably gathered from all the action,' Rafferty said, 'that's a human skull out there in your garden. So far we don't know a lot more than that. These two were the ones who found it?'

'My son,' Susanna said, 'and my daughter.' Sallie was pressed against her, the pouch thing still firmly stuck in her mouth. Zach was hanging over the back of the sofa, staring.

Rafferty nodded, examining them. 'Which of them's more likely to be able to tell me how it happened? Kids this age, some of them make great witnesses, better than adults: good observers, good clear account of events, no messing about. Other kids, they're so busy playing cute or shy or stubborn, they can barely make a sentence, and when they do it's mostly rubbish. Which of your two—'

'Me,' Zach said loudly, scrambling over the back of the sofa and nearly kicking Susanna in the face. 'I'm the one who found it.'

Rafferty gave him a long look. 'This isn't like explaining to your teacher why Jimmy hit Johnny in the playground. This is serious business. You think you can manage to give me a clear account?'

'Course I can. I'm not *stupid*.'

'Right,' Rafferty said, pulling out a notebook and a pen. His hands seemed wrong for a detective, long and muscular, with scars and heavy calluses like he spent a lot of time sailing in hard weather. 'Let's hear it.'

Zach arranged himself cross-legged on the sofa and took a breath. 'OK,' he said. 'So Uncle Hugo told us to go out in the garden and look for treasure. So Sallie went and looked in the strawberry patch, which, duhhh, we go in there all the time so if there was treasure there we would have found it already? And I went to look in the hole in the tree.'

Rafferty was nodding along, grave and intent. 'That's the big elm tree? The one right next to where you left the skull?'

'Yeah.'

'Had you been up that tree before?'

'We're not allowed.'

'So why today?'

'All the grownups were having some big serious talk. So . . .' Zach grinned, at Susanna, who made a wry face at him.

Rafferty let the edge of a matching grin slip out. 'So you knew you wouldn't get caught.'

'Yeah.'

'And?'

'And I stuck my arm down the hole—'

'Hang on,' Rafferty said, lifting his pen. 'If you'd never been up that tree before, how did you know it had a hole in it? You can't see the hole from the ground.'

Zach shrugged. 'I tried climbing that tree a load of times before, only my mum or Uncle Hugo always yelled at me to get down. A couple of times I got high enough up that I saw the hole. And one time I saw a squirrel come out of it.'

'Ever notice anything in there? Apart from the squirrel?'

'Nah.'

'Ever put your hand in there before? Or a stick, or anything?'

'Nah.'

'Why today?'

'Because I was looking for *treasure*.'

'Fair enough,' Rafferty said. 'So you stuck your arm down the hole . . .'

'Yeah. And first there was just all leaves and muck and wet stuff, like hairy stuff—' Zach's eyes snapped wide as he realised.

'Moss, probably,' Rafferty said easily. 'What next?'

'And then there was something big, like smooth. It felt weird. And there was a hole in it so I stuck my fingers in the hole and pulled it out, and at first I thought it was like a big eggshell, like from an ostrich egg? And it smelled like dirt. And I was going to throw it at the wall so it would smash. Only then I turned it around and there were *teeth*.' Zach shuddered from head to feet, an irresistible spasm. Susanna's hand went out towards his shoulder and stopped. 'Actual teeth.'

'Yeah,' Rafferty said. 'There are. What'd you do next?'

'I threw it. Onto the grass. Not trying to smash it; I just wanted to get rid of it. And I yelled and I got down out of the tree, I fell the last part but I didn't get hurt. And Sallie started screaming and then Mum and everyone came.'

He was hunched over, hands tucked tight into the crooks of his knees, eyes flicking away from the memory. For a second I actually felt sorry for the little bastard.

'Well done,' Rafferty said, giving Zach a nod. 'You were right: you're a good witness. At some point I'll get this typed up and I'll need you to sign it, but for now, that's exactly what I need. Thanks.'

Zach took a deep breath and relaxed a notch or two. Rafferty had a good voice, rich and warm with a windswept tinge of Galway, like some rugged islandman in an old movie who would probably end up with Maureen O'Hara. I was willing to bet that this guy got more hoop than he could handle. To Sallie: 'Now let's see you give it a try. Can you remember what happened?'

Sallie was snuggled in tight against Susanna, watching the whole thing with solemn unreadable eyes over her orange pouch. She took it out of her mouth and nodded.

'Off you go.'

'I was looking for treasure and Zach was up the tree and then he threw a thing on the grass. And he was yelling. And it was a skull and I yelled too because I was scared it was a ghost.'

'And then?'

'Then everyone came and Mummy took us inside.'

'Well done,' Rafferty said, smiling at her.

'Is it a ghost?'

'*Duhhh*,' Zach said, under his breath. 'There's no such thing as ghosts.' He seemed to have recovered.

'No,' Rafferty said gently. 'We've got a special machine that tells us exactly what something is, and we've gone over every bit of that skull. There's no ghost there, any more than there is in this.' He touched his notepad. 'It's only a piece of bone.'

Sallie nodded.

'You want to check this for ghosts?' He waved the notepad at her.

That got a head-shake and the tip of a smile. 'Phew,' Rafferty said. 'I left my machine outside. When was the last time anyone else was up that tree? A gardener, maybe? Someone trimming the branches?'

'No gardener,' Hugo said. 'I don't exactly keep the place in show condition – well, you've seen that for yourself. What little I want doing, I do myself. I don't trim the trees.'

'We used to climb it,' I said, enunciating carefully to keep the slurring down. I felt like I needed to make some kind of mark on this conversation. 'Me and Susanna and Leon' – pointing – 'when we were kids.'

Rafferty turned to look at me. 'When were you last up there?'

'I broke my ankle jumping out of it. When I was nine. After that our parents didn't let us climb it any more.'

'Mm,' Rafferty said. His eyes – deep-set and an odd light shade of hazel, almost golden – rested on me thoughtfully. That look, practised and assessing and opaque and so familiar, made my spine curl. I was suddenly viciously aware of my droopy eyelid. 'Did you?'

'I don't—' A flicker of memory, swinging my legs on a branch in semi-darkness, can of beer, someone laughing, but everything felt so dislocated and unreal that I couldn't— 'I'm not sure.'

'Yeah, we did,' Susanna said. 'When our parents weren't there. Hugo' – a fleeting smile between them – 'always let us away with a lot more.'

'It's not like we were up there every day,' Leon said. 'Or every week. But now and then, yeah.'

'When was the last time?'

Susanna and Leon looked at each other. 'God, I don't remember,' Leon said.

'Some party when we were teenagers, maybe?'

'That time when Declan was singing "Wonderwall" and someone threw a can at him. Weren't we all up there?'

'Was that that tree?'

'Had to be. The three of us and Dec, and wasn't that girl there too, Whatshername who he liked? We wouldn't all have fit in any of the other trees.'

'Declan who?' Rafferty asked.

'Declan McGinty,' I said. 'He's a friend of mine.'

Rafferty nodded, writing down the name. I thought I could smell him, a keen outdoorsy tang like split pine. 'Any idea what year that would've been?'

'I think that was the summer we left school,' Susanna said. 'So ten years ago. But I'm not sure.' Leon shrugged.

'Ever do any exploring down the hole in the middle?'

Leon and Susanna and I looked at each other. 'No,' Susanna said. 'I mean, I glanced in a couple of times, when I was up there, but it looked manky; all wet dead leaves. I wasn't going to go rooting around.'

'I think I poked a stick in there once,' Leon said. 'When we were kids, like eight. Just to see how deep the hole was. I didn't feel anything like . . . anything.'

'How deep was it?'

'Oh, God, I don't remember. Deep enough.'

Rafferty glanced at me. 'I don't . . .' I said. My memory was fluttering and sparking; I was blindingly aware that I sounded like an idiot. 'I don't think so. Maybe.'

'What about you, Mr Hennessy?' He meant Hugo. 'Did you ever climb that tree, when you were a child?'

'Heavens, yes,' Hugo said. 'The four of us – my brothers and I – we were up and down it all the time. I think we may even have hidden things in that hole, but I wouldn't swear to it. My brothers might have better memories than I do.'

'We'll check with them, so,' Rafferty said. 'Do any of you have any ideas on who it could be? Now that you've had time to think it over?'

'I thought . . .' Tom said, tentatively. 'I wondered about medical students. In the apartment block that backs onto the laneway. Taking a skull from college for a laugh, and throwing it down there.'

Rafferty nodded, apparently giving that serious consideration. 'We'll look into that. Any other ideas? Anyone you can think of who went missing in the area? Or maybe a houseguest who left without saying goodbye, a tradesman who didn't come back to finish the job? It doesn't have to be recent. That's an old tree.'

'There was a homeless man,' Hugo said suddenly. 'This is going back, oh, twenty-five years, maybe more— He used to sleep in the laneway, occasionally. He'd call to the door, my mother would give him sandwiches, fill his flask with soup, and then he'd set up camp. At some point he stopped coming. We didn't think much of it at the time, he was never a regular visitor, but . . .'

'Can you describe him?'

'In his fifties, I'd say – although it's hard to tell, isn't it, with people who've had a rough life. Medium height, maybe five foot ten? Grey hair. Midlands accent. I think his name was Bernard. He was usually fairly drunk, but never aggressive or unpleasant, nothing like that.'

'Did he ever come into the garden?'

'Not that I know of. But the back wall isn't exactly impregnable. It's high, but if someone really wanted to get over, he could probably find a way.'

'Bernard,' Rafferty said, writing. 'We'll look into that. Any other possibilities?'

We all shook our heads. 'Right,' Rafferty said. He closed the notebook and slid it into his pocket. 'I'm sorry to be the bearer of bad news, but that tree's going to have to come down.'

'Why?' Leon asked sharply.

Rafferty transferred his gaze to him and gave him a long thoughtful look. 'There are some other things we're interested in, down that hole.'

'Like more bones?' Zach demanded, wide-eyed. 'A whole skeleton?'

'We won't know till we get in there. I've been trying to find a way around cutting down the tree, but no dice. We've got to document everything, record every step; we can't just pull out whatever's in there by the handful.' He saw the looks on our faces. 'I know it's like we're smashing a family heirloom, but we don't have a choice. There's a tree surgeon on the way.'

'In for a penny . . .' Hugo said, half to himself. And to Rafferty: 'That's fine. Do whatever you need to do.'

'Can you tell when it's from?' Leon asked. He was still leaning against the window frame, seemingly at ease, but something in the line of his shoulders told me that every cell of him was practically shorting out with tension. 'The skull?'

'Not my area,' Rafferty said. 'But we've got the state pathologist out there, and we're bringing in a forensic archaeologist. They'll be able to tell us more.'

'Or what happened to it? I mean, was it, was the person . . . ? How did they . . . ?'

'Ah,' said Rafferty, giving him a startlingly charming smile that crinkled his eyes into invisibility. 'That's the million-euro question.'

'Do we need to stay here?' Susanna asked.

He looked surprised. 'Oh, God, no. You can go wherever you like – apart from the garden, obviously. Was someone making a list of names and phone numbers? In case I need to get in touch with any of you again?'

Tom produced his lists, and Rafferty was appropriately impressed. 'Thanks very much for your time,' he told us all, folding them carefully away and standing up. 'I know this is a nasty situation, and it's been a big shock, and I appreciate you helping us out in the middle of it all. If you'd like to talk to anyone about it, I'll put you in touch with our Victim Support advocates, and they can find you someone who—'

None of us apparently felt the need for professional assistance to unpack our feelings about finding a skull in the back garden. 'Here,' Rafferty said, putting a small neat stack of business cards on the coffee table. 'If you change your minds about that, or you think of anything, or you want to ask me anything, give me a ring.'

Hand on the door, he turned, remembering. 'That key, the one to the garden door. Are there any more copies we could borrow? Would a neighbour have one, or your brothers maybe?'

'There used to be another one here,' Hugo said. He was starting to look tired. 'It went missing, somewhere along the way.'

'Any idea when?'

'Years ago. I couldn't even begin to narrow it down.'

'No problem,' Rafferty said. 'If we need extras, we'll get them cut. I'll keep you updated.' And he was gone, closing the living-room door gently behind him.

'Well,' Hugo said, on a deep breath, after a moment of silence. 'This should be interesting.'

'I told you,' Leon said. He was gnawing his thumbnail again, and his nostrils flared with every breath. 'I *told* you we should dump it in the bin and forget the whole bloody thing.'

'You can't do that,' Tom said. 'There could be a family out there, wondering—'

'I thought you thought it was med students.'

'The detective's nice,' Melissa said. 'Was he more like what you expected, Hugo?'

'Definitely.' Hugo smiled at her. 'And much more confidence-inspiring than the other ones. I'm sure he'll get all this sorted out in no time. Meanwhile' – glancing around – 'you three should let your parents know what's happened, shouldn't you?'

Leon and Susanna and I, by unspoken but wholehearted agree-ment, hadn't rung our parents, but I realised with a sinking feeling that Hugo was right, it wasn't like we could keep this contained within the house forever. 'Oh God,' Susanna said. 'They're going to want to come over.'

'I'm *starving*,' Zach said.

'Jesus,' Leon said, in a stunned voice that sounded suddenly very young. 'There's people out there *filming*.'

There was a general rush to the windows. Sure enough, stand-ing with her back to our front steps was a brunette in a snazzy coral trench coat, talking into a microphone. On the pavement across the road, a skinny guy in a parka was huddled over a video camera pointed at her. A restless wind had come up, tossing the trees into bewildering whirls of green.

'Hey!' Zach yelled, banging a palm on the windowpane. 'Get lost!'

Susanna caught his wrist, too late: the cameraman said some-thing and the brunette turned to look at us, hair whipping across her face. 'Get back,' Leon said sharply. Susanna reached out and slammed the shutters, heavy bangs reverberating up through the empty rooms of the house.

•

Around this point Zach and Sallie went into full whine overdrive about how hungry they were. Their bitching finally drove us all out to the kitchen, where Hugo and Melissa rummaged through the fridge and discussed options and decided on pasta with mushroom sauce. Susanna was on the phone to Louisa, trying to convince her not to come over ('No, Mum, he's fine, anyway what would you do that we're not doing already? . . . Because there are *reporters* out the front, and I don't want them nabbing you and interrogating— Well then, watch it on the news tonight, and you'll know as much as we do. No one's telling us anything . . . No, Mum, I don't have a clue who it—') and holding Sallie back from the biscuit tin with her free hand. Tom was rattling on about some kiddie movie they'd seen, trying to draw Zach into the chat; Zach, drumming his hands on the counter and keeping a calculating eye on the biscuit tin, wasn't biting.

Leon and I stood at the French doors, looking out at the garden. The big uniformed cop was on the terrace with his hands clasped behind his back, looking official and presumably guarding the crime scene, but he was ignoring us and we ignored him. Down by the wych elm, Rafferty was deep in conversation with another suit and a stocky guy in a dilapidated overall who, judging by the gestures, was the tree surgeon. The skull was gone. There was a stepladder beside the tree and a person in a hooded white boiler suit on top of it, leaning sideways at a precarious angle to point a camera into the hole. The door in the back wall stood open – I hadn't seen it opened in years – on the laneway: stone apartment-block wall, the other uniformed cop in the same official pose, glimpse of a white van. People moved in and out, between the laneway and the tree and the white canvas gazebo, with its festive pointed roof, that had materialised beside the strawberry bed. Bright blue latex gloves, hard plastic black case like a tool kit open in the grass, grey sky. Snap of wind in the crime-scene tape and the canvas.

'All that stuff about the key to the garden door,' Susanna said in a low voice, at my shoulder. 'That wasn't because they need more copies. That was him finding out whether anyone else could get into the garden, or whether it's just us.'

'There was another one,' Leon said. 'I remember it.'

'Me too,' I said. 'Didn't it use to be on a hook beside the door?'

Susanna glanced behind us at Zach and Sallie, whom Melissa and Hugo had somehow convinced to help slice mushrooms; Zach was making karate-chop noises as he slammed the knife down, and Sallie was giggling. 'Someone took it, one summer. Wasn't it Dec, when he stayed here?'

'Dec didn't need to sneak in the back. He came in the front door. What about that friend of yours, the weird blonde who kept showing up in the middle of the night? The cutter?'

'Faye wasn't *weird*. She had shit going on. And she didn't have a key. She'd text me and I'd let her in.'

'What happens,' Leon said. He was watching a small sturdy woman with greying hair and combats stumping out of the tent to join the conference beneath the tree (the state pathologist? the forensic archaeologist? I had only a hazy idea of what either of those should look like, or for that matter what they did). 'What happens if they find some evidence that the person was killed? What do they do then?'

'Just going by experience,' I said, 'they'll show up a couple of times when we least want to see them, they'll ask a shit-ton of questions about how it might be our fault that someone dumped a skull in our tree, and then they'll disappear and leave us to pick up the pieces.'

The vicious edge to my voice startled me. I hadn't realised, till that moment, just how intensely I loathed having Rafferty and his pals there. It startled Leon and Susanna, too: their faces turning sharply towards me, uncertain silence. My hands were shaking again. I shoved them into my pockets and kept looking out at the garden.

'Well,' Leon said, after a moment, 'I don't know about you, but I've got no problem with them disappearing. The sooner the better.'

'At least they're being polite about the whole thing,' Susanna said. 'If we were all on the dole and crammed into a council house . . .'

'They've been out there for ages,' Melissa said, at the sink, hands full of lettuce. 'We should see if they want tea.'

'No,' all three of us said in unison.

'Fuck them,' Leon said.

'They probably have Thermoses,' I said. 'Or something.'

'Maybe we should offer them some pasta,' Tom said.

'*No.*'

'One of the downsides of being young,' Hugo told us all, apparently apropos of nothing, 'is that you worry too much. Really, you do. It's all going to be fine.' He laid a hand on Sallie's curls, smiling at us. 'Worse things happen at sea, as they say. Now, where shall we eat?'

We ate in the dining room – the thought of crime-scene dinner theatre, as Leon put it, was well over everyone's weirdness limit. The glossy old mahogany table was almost never used except for Christmas dinner, and I had to wipe off a film of dust. Susanna had closed the shutters on the garden and the overhead light was weak, leaving the room a smeared, confusing yellow. Nobody said very much; even Zach was subdued, picking through his pasta and pushing the mushrooms to one side without bitching about them. Sallie was yawning.

'We should go, after this,' Susanna said, glancing at Tom. 'Will you guys be OK?'

'We'll be fine,' Hugo said. 'And I'm sure they'll be packing up for the night soon enough, too. It's you I'm worried about, leaving. Is that reporter woman still there?'

'I doubt it,' Tom said. He slid open the doors to the living room, went to the window and put one eye to the crack between the shutters. 'Gone,' he said, coming back to the table.

'For now,' Leon said darkly.

Somewhere, a sound started up: a low, nasty, animal snarl that built rapidly till it vibrated all through the air, making it impossible to tell where it was coming from. One by one, our heads lifted; Hugo laid down his fork. It took all of us a moment to recognise it for what it was: a chainsaw, out in the garden, setting to work.

•

When the daylight went, around eight, the cops went too. Rafferty came in to give us our update first, just like he had promised: 'The tree surgeon hates my guts,' he said ruefully, picking chips of bark off his trousers. 'That tree's over two hundred years old, apparently, and there aren't a lot of them left; Dutch elm disease got most of them. When I asked him to cut down a perfectly healthy one, I thought he was going to walk out on me. Didn't blame him, either.'

'Is it done?' Hugo asked.

'Ah, God, no. We have to go slow: document everything, like I said. But we should have it done by the end of tomorrow. We'll leave an officer here overnight.' At our blank stares: 'It's not that we think you're in danger, nothing like that. We're just ticking the boxes: we have to be able to say we had our eye on that tree the whole time. He'll stay out in the garden, won't be in your way at all.'

The thought of one of these guys wandering around the garden while we slept made my teeth clench – I had been checking my watch more and more obsessively, maybe at six o'clock they would fuck off and leave us to ourselves again, maybe at seven, surely to Jesus they had to knock off by eight – but we very obviously didn't have a say in this. 'Does he need anything?' Melissa asked.

'No, he'll look after himself. Thanks very much.' Rafferty dropped the chips of wood into his jacket pocket and gave us a nod and the charm-smile, already turning towards the door. 'See you in the morning.'

Hugo almost never turned on the television, but we watched the nine o'clock news that night. The story was fairly high up, below the incomprehensible EU machinations and the Northern Ireland political spat but above the sports: the brunette in the coral coat doing her sombre voice in front of our steps, human remains found in a Dublin garden, Gardaí are at the scene; a shot of the laneway, looking bleak and run-down with wind twitching the forlorn clusters of dead leaves at the bottom of the wall, white figure climbing out of the white van, crime-scene tape across the garden door; anyone with any information please contact the Gardaí.

'There,' Hugo said, when the newsreader moved on to football. 'It's all very interesting. I never thought I'd have a ringside seat at a criminal investigation. There are an awful lot of people involved, aren't there?' He manoeuvred himself up off the sofa, joint by joint, and reached for his cane. He seemed a lot less unsettled by the whole thing than the rest of us, which I supposed made a certain amount of sense. 'If it's going to start all over again in the morning, though, I need to get some sleep.'

'Me too,' I said, switching off the telly. Melissa and I had started going to bed whenever Hugo did – we didn't let him do the stairs by himself any more, if we could help it, and we liked to be within earshot when he was changing for bed – but although those made a convenient excuse, I couldn't help being aware that I was also more exhausted than I'd been in weeks.

On the landing outside our bedrooms we stood for a moment looking at one another, in the dim glow of the stained-glass pendant lamp, as if there was some crucial thing that needed to be said and we were all hoping someone else knew what it was. It had occurred to me a few times by this point that it would make sense to ask Hugo whether he had any idea who the skull could be, but there didn't seem to be any way to do it.

'Good night,' he said, smiling at us. 'Sleep tight.' For a second I had the crazy impression that he was thinking about hugging us, but then he turned and went into his room and closed the door.

'He seems OK about all this,' I said to Melissa, in our room, as we put away the pile of clean clothes I had brought up and left on our bed that morning. It felt like weeks ago.

She nodded, rolling my socks into neat balls. 'I think he is. It's taking his mind off being sick.'

'What about you? Are you OK with it? I mean, this *really* isn't what you signed up for.'

She thought about it, hands moving deftly, eyes down. 'I'm not sure what I am,' she said, in the end. 'I suppose it depends a lot on whether there are more bones in the tree or not.'

'Baby,' I said. I stopped sliding T-shirts into a drawer and put my arms around her from behind, pulling her close. 'I know it's creepy as hell. But whatever's in there, they'll get rid of it tomorrow. You should've gone back to your place for the night.'

Melissa shook her head, a quick decisive snap. 'It's not that. They're just bones. I don't think I believe in ghosts, and even if they're out there, I don't think the bones make any difference. I'd just like to know. A skull could have got there loads of ways. But a whole skeleton . . .'

'Rafferty said the tree's over two hundred years old. Even if there's a skeleton in there, it's Victorian or something.'

'Then would it really be the Guards doing all this? Wouldn't it be archaeologists?'

'They might not be able to tell the age straight off. They probably have to do tests. And there is an archaeologist. Rafferty said so.'

'You're probably right.' She leaned back against my chest, hands coming up to cover mine. 'I'd just like to know what we're dealing with. That's all.'

I kissed the top of her head. 'I know. Me too.'

She tilted her head back to examine my face, upside down. 'And you? Are you OK with all this?'

'I'm fine.' And when her face stayed upturned, waiting for more: 'Well, it's not what I had planned for the weekend. And yeah, I'd love them to just disappear. But it's not a problem. Just a pain in the arse.'

Apparently I sounded convincing, or at least convincing enough. 'Good,' Melissa said, smiling, and reached up an arm to pull my head down and kiss me, and then she went back to rolling socks.

None of us slept well, though. Over and over, I twisted looking for a comfortable position and caught the dark shine of Melissa's open eye, or was jolted out of a half-doze by the creak of a floorboard or the close of a drawer through the wall, in Hugo's bedroom. At some point I got out of bed, too restless to stay still another second, and went to the window.

Yellowish city-dark clouds, no stars, one golden rectangle of light in the towering wall of the apartment block. The wind had died down to a covert stirring in the ivy. Uncanny blue-white glow like a will-o'-the-wisp, below me: one of the uniformed cops, I couldn't tell which, was leaning against an oak tree, wrapped in a big overcoat, doing something on his phone. On the other side of the garden, there was a fresh, shocking gap in the silhouette of the treeline: the wych elm's whole crown was gone, only the trunk left, thick stubs of branches poking out obscenely. It should have looked pathetic, but instead it had a new, condensed force: some great malformed creature, musclebound and nameless, huddled in the darkness waiting for a sign.

I fumbled in a drawer as quietly as I could for my Xanax stash, and swallowed one dry. 'Are you OK?' Melissa asked softly.

'Fine,' I said. 'Just checking that Chief Wiggum isn't pissing in the flowerbeds,' and I slid back into bed beside her.

6

The cops and the tree surgeon and the rest of the posse were back in the garden bright and early on Sunday morning, eating dough-nuts and drinking out of Thermoses ('See?' I said to Melissa, at our bedroom window, 'Thermoses') and squinting up through fine driz-zle at a thick grey sky. I wondered how hard it would have to rain to make them go away.

We got dressed before breakfast, instead of going down in our bathrobes – no pretty little hair-brushing ritual today, Melissa gave her hair a fast going-over and pulled it back in a ponytail. In the kitchen Hugo was at the French doors, also dressed except for his slippers, his back to us and a mug steaming in his hand. 'It's incred-ible how fast they work,' he said. 'That tree'll be gone by lunchtime. Two hundred years, and: poof. I don't know whether it's terrifying or impressive.'

'The faster they get it down,' Melissa pointed out, aiming for cheerful, 'the sooner they'll go away.'

'True, of course. There's porridge on the cooker, and coffee.'

Melissa poured our coffee; I scooped porridge into bowls and threw in handfuls of blueberries. I was having trouble struggling up out of the Xanax, viscous fog dragging at my mind and my limbs, and the cops prowling the garden like a pack of feral dogs in the corner of my eye were more than I could handle; I wanted to get out of that room as fast as possible.

'Hugo,' I said. 'Do you want porridge?'

Hugo hadn't turned from the doors. 'I spent a while looking up wych elms, last night,' he said, between sips of coffee. 'I'd never thought much about them before, but it seemed inappropriate to know nothing about them now, somehow. Did you know that the Greeks believed there was one at the gates of the Underworld?'

'No,' I said. The combats woman stuck her head out of the tent and said something, and the cops all vanished inside, ducking in one by one like clowns into a clown car. 'I didn't know that.'

'They did. It sprang up where Orpheus stopped to play a lament after he'd failed to rescue Eurydice. "In the midst," Virgil says, "an elm, shadowy and vast, spreads its aged branches: the seat, men say, that false Dreams hold, clinging beneath every leaf."'

Melissa shivered, a small violent movement that made her clench' the coffee mugs harder. 'Lovely,' I said. 'I feel better about this one being cut down.'

'Apparently "the decoction of the bark of the root fomented, mollifieth hard tumours"', Hugo informed us. 'According to Culpeper's *Complete Herbal*. I suppose I should try it, seeing as I'll have plenty of root bark to hand, but I'm not sure how to decoct or foment, never mind how I would get it in there to do the mollifying. The elm also "cureth scurf and leprosy very effectually". If you should ever need it to.' I wondered if I could turn around and go back to bed.

The tree surgeon fired up the chainsaw. 'Goodness,' Hugo said, wincing. 'I think that's our cue to leave.'

.

I thought it would have been fairly obvious that Sunday lunch wasn't a good plan, but around noon people started showing up, my parents (my mother hauling a plant pot containing an enthusiastic sapling as big as she was: 'Red oak, he says it's fast-growing so there won't be a horrible gap for long, and in autumn the leaves should be wonderful—'), Phil and Louisa (bags of M&S food), Leon and Miriam and Oliver (an enormous and disorganised bouquet), thank God Susanna had apparently decided to keep her lot away. I couldn't tell whether they were all there because they thought they were providing emotional support, or because they needed to see for themselves what was going on, or just out of Pavlovian reflex: Sunday, Hugo's, go! It felt like the doorbell never stopped ringing, everyone in turn crowding to the French doors to gape out at the carnage – huge branches strewn across the grass, sawdust flying, white-suited figures going up and down stepladders – and go through the same round of inevitable exclamations and questions, oh no look at the tree!! did they find anything else in there? they look awfully sinister, don't they, those white outfits— do they know who it is yet?

Finally they had all satisfied their curiosity, or else the bursts of noise from the chainsaw got too much for them, and we could move to the living room. Obviously we were expected to come up with lunch, but there was no way in hell I was going to cook up a nice roast or whatever in that kitchen, and Hugo and Melissa clearly felt the same way. We dug through the shopping bags and dumped baguettes, cheese, ham, tomatoes and whatever else on the dining-room table, along with all the clean plates and forks we could find.

The room had a skittery, unsettled fizz to it. None of us had any idea what we were supposed to be thinking or feeling or saying in a situation like this one, and everyone had seized, with a messy combination of relief and shame, on the chance of focusing on something other than Hugo. Everyone had a theory. Miriam was telling my mother, at ninety miles a minute, about Celtic boundary rituals and human sacrifice, although it wasn't clear how she thought the Celts would have got a skull into a two-hundred-year-old tree; my mother was countering with something about the Victorians' complicated relationship with vigilante justice. Leon – not eating, hyper to the point where I wondered whether he had got his hands on some speed – was winding Louisa up with an ornate story about a local hurler who had sold his soul to the devil, via an improbable ceremony, in exchange for champion-level skill ('No, I *swear*, I heard it *years* ago, just no one knew where the skull had landed—'), while Louisa gave him a jaded look and tried to decide whether to call him on it. Even my father, who as far as I knew hadn't strung together more than two sentences since Hugo got sick, was earnestly explaining to Melissa just how far a fox could drag a heavy object.

I wasn't as into this as the rest of them. I wasn't really capable of seeing detectives as an intriguing distraction, and the fact that the others had that luxury was making me feel increasingly sour and left out. Phil and Louisa had brought Camembert, which was stinking up the whole room. My appetite was gone again.

'Clearly,' Oliver said, pointing the tomato fork at me, '*clearly* it must date from before 1926. Your grandparents were avid gardeners, you know, out there planting and pruning and whatnot all year round, and your great-grandmother was the same. Not to be crude about it, but if there had been a body in the garden in their time, *decomposing*, they couldn't have missed it. But the previous owner was an old woman, bedridden for years. When my grandparents bought the place, the garden was in a terrible state – brambles and nettles up to here, my grandmother used to tell me how when they came to view the house she shredded her best polka-dot stockings, ha! A whole army could have rotted away out there, and no one would have noticed. D'you see?'

'We don't know that it was an entire body,' Phil pointed out from across the table, reaching for the Camembert. 'Or that the tree is where it decomposed. For all we know, someone had a skull they wanted to get rid of—'

'Then where did the rest go? If you find a skull lying about, you call the Guards – the peelers, the bobbies, whatever they were called back then. Exactly like Hugo did. The only reason you'd *get rid of it* is if you had a whole body that you weren't supposed to have. And what was going on, not long before 1926? Who might have found themselves in possession of a dead body?'

I was losing track of all this: like Hugo's genealogy mystery, too many tributaries of possibility and inference, I couldn't hold on to all of them at once. The crowded room wasn't helping, bodies and movement everywhere, unpredictable roars from the chainsaw making me jump every time. Melissa caught my eye, over my father's shoulder, and gave me a tiny encouraging smile. I managed to grin back.

'The Civil War,' Oliver said triumphantly. 'Guerrilla warfare; summary executions. Someone got caught informing, vanished amid the general *Sturm und Drang*. I'd put money on it: that body dates from 1922. Anyone fancy taking that bet? Toby?'

My phone buzzed in my pocket: Dec. 'Sorry,' I said to my uncles, 'I have to take this,' and escaped to the kitchen.

Hugo, hip braced against the counter, was sliding a large sponge cake out of its box. Out in the garden, chunks of splintered wood were everywhere, the cops were clustered at the door of the tent, and the wych elm was down to a stump.

'Hey,' I said, into the phone.

'Hey,' Dec said. Hearing his voice actually made me smile. 'Long time.'

'I know. How're you doing? Sean told me about Jenna.'

'Yeah, well. It's not great, but I'll live. And yeah, before you say it, I fucking know you told me so.'

'We fucking did. Just be glad you got out with all your organs. Did you ever wake up in a bath full of ice?'

'Fuck off. How've you been getting on?'

'Fine. Chilling, mostly. Richard's letting me take a bit of time off, so I'm just hanging out here.'

'Sean said about Hugo. I'm really sorry, man.'

'I know.' I moved farther away from Hugo, who was painstakingly slicing the cake, knife held in an awkward curled grip that made me tense up. 'Thanks.'

'How's he doing?'

I made some kind of noncommittal noise.

'Tell him I was asking after him.'

'Will do.'

'Come here,' Dec said, in a different tone. 'Was that Hugo's gaff on the news?'

'Yeah.'

'Jesus. I thought it was, all right, but . . . What the fuck?'

'You know that old elm tree? The big one, down towards the bottom of the garden? Susanna's kid found a skull in there. Down a hole in the trunk.'

'Jesus!'

'Yeah. I mean, it's probably old. They say the tree's like two hundred years old; the skull could've got there any time. They're cutting down the tree, though. There's Guards all over the place.'

'Fuck,' Dec said. 'Are they giving you hassle?'

'Nah. They've been fine. They asked us a bunch of questions, but we don't know anything about it, so now they're basically leaving

195

us alone. It's a pain in the hole, but whatever. I guess they've got to do their job.'

'Listen, me and Sean were going to come down this week. Do you still want us to? Or do you not need anyone else buzzing around?'

Actually I very badly wanted to see them, but I knew I didn't have enough bandwidth to cope with them as well as a garden full of cops; I would end up stammering, losing the thread of the conversation, making an idiot of myself. I felt a fresh stab of annoyance with Rafferty and his buddies. 'Maybe wait till the cops go. With any luck they'll be out of here soon; I'll give you a bell then and we can plan, yeah?'

'No problem. It's not like I'm doing anything else. Sean's been great, him and Audrey have been inviting me over for dinner and all, but seeing them all lovey-dovey and happy, you know what I mean? It just makes me—'

There was a tap at the French doors: Rafferty, peeling off a pair of thin latex gloves. 'Gotta go,' I said to Dec. 'I'll let you know about this week,' and I hung up and went to the door.

'Afternoon,' Rafferty said, smiling at us and dusting his hands together. 'So: the tree's done. We'll get rid of the wood for you; the tree surgeon's going to take it away.'

'Did you find anything?' Hugo asked, polite as a shop owner, *Have you found everything you need?*

'It was useful, yeah.' He scraped his feet carefully on the door-mat and came inside. 'Before I forget: we tracked down your homeless fella, the one who used to doss down in the laneway? I asked around, found a couple of lads who used to work this area. One of them remembered him. Bernard Gildea. I'd love to be able to tell you he got his life back on track, lived happily ever after, but he wound up getting taken into a hospice. Cirrhosis. He died in 1994.'

'Oh, no,' Hugo said. He looked genuinely distressed. 'He seemed like a decent man, underneath the drink. Well-read – occasionally he would ask if we had a book to spare, and I'd find something to give him – he liked non-fiction, World War I stuff. He always seemed to me like someone who, if just one or two rolls of the dice had gone differently . . .'

'Sorry to be the bearer of bad news,' Rafferty said. 'And I'm afraid I've got more. The garden's going to have to come up.'

'Come up?' Hugo said, after a blank moment. 'What do you mean?'

'We're going to have to dig it up. Not the rest of the trees, and we'll try to put back whatever plants we can, once we're done, but we're not gardeners. You might be able to apply for compensation—'

I said, a lot louder than I expected, '*Why?*'

'Because we don't know what we might find there,' Rafferty explained, reasonably. He was still talking to Hugo. 'Probably, I'll be honest with you, we'll find nothing relevant at all, and you'll be left cursing us out of it for wrecking your beautiful garden for no reason. But look at it from our side. There were human remains in that tree. We've got no way of knowing if there are other human remains somewhere else in the garden, or maybe a murder weapon. Probably not, but I can't run an investigation on "probably not". I can't go back to my gaffer with "probably not". I've got to know for certain.'

'That radar machine,' I said. The thought of the garden, razed, bare dirt rucked up like a bomb site, tangles of roots reaching for the sky— 'That archaeologists use, on those shows. The one that—' I mimed a sweeping motion. 'Use that. If it finds anything, go ahead and dig. If it doesn't, then you can leave the garden alone.'

Rafferty turned his eyes on me. They were golden as a hawk's and with the same impersonal, impartial ruthlessness, a creature simply doing what he was for. I realised that I was terrified of him. 'Ground-penetrating radar,' he said. 'We do use that, yeah. But that's when we're sweeping a large area, like a field or a hillside, for something big – a gravesite, say, or a cache of weapons. Here, we don't know what we're looking for; it could be something this size.' Thumb and finger an inch apart. 'If we go in with the GPR, we'll be digging every time it picks up a rock, or a dead mouse. It'll work out the same in the end; it'll just take a lot longer.'

'Then no,' I said. 'No way. We haven't done anything *wrong*. You can't just come in here and, and *wreck* the whole place—'

Hugo sat down, heavily, at the table.

'It's bloody unfair on you, all right,' Rafferty said, gently, so that my voice turned into pathetic bluster. 'I see it all the time, in this job: people who did nothing wrong, just happened to be in the wrong place at the wrong time, and all of a sudden we're showing up and ruining their day – or their garden. And you're right, it's not OK. Thing is, we don't have a choice. There's someone dead here. We need to figure out what happened.'

'So find other ways to do it. It's not our fault he's dead, or she, or—'

'I can get a warrant if you'd rather,' Rafferty said, still just as mildly, 'but that won't be till tomorrow, and I'll need to leave someone here till then. It'll just stretch out the whole thing. If you give us the go-ahead to start now, we can aim to be out of here within a couple of days.'

'I would appreciate it very much,' Hugo said, cutting me off – I wasn't sure what I had started to say – 'if you could wait an hour or two before getting to work. The rest of the family is here for lunch, and they won't be any happier about this idea than Toby and I are. It would make things simpler for everyone if you could wait until they leave.'

Rafferty transferred that gaze to him. 'I can do that,' he said. 'We need to go find ourselves some lunch anyway, sure. How would half-three suit you? Would they be gone by then?'

'I can make sure they are.' Hugo reached for his cane and leaned the other hand on the table to heave himself upright. There were dark bags under his eyes. 'Toby, would you carry in the cake plate, please?'

•

At three o'clock Hugo announced that he was getting tired. It took what felt like hours for everyone to get the hint – let me help with the washing-up, no really I want to, are you sure you'll be all right with all of *them* hanging about – 'Honestly, Louisa,' Hugo finally said, with a hint of exasperation, 'what do you think the Guards are going to do, start cracking heads? And how much help do you think you'd be if they did?' But finally all the food had been covered with clingfilm and organised carefully in the fridge, and Hugo and Melissa and I had been given full lawyerly instructions on exactly what to do if the cops did this or that or the other, and they all flooded out the door, still talking, and left us alone.

The three of us stood together at the French doors and watched the cops work. They started at the back wall. There were five of them, Rafferty and two uniformed guys and a uniformed woman and someone in a boiler suit, all of them with wax jackets and wellies and shovels. Even through the glass and the distance I thought I could hear the crunch of blades into earth. In a shockingly short time the strawberry bed was a ragged heap, great clumps of Queen Anne's lace and bellflowers tossed aside, pale roots straggling, and there was a wide strip of dark churned-up earth across the bottom of the garden. The cops moved back and forth along it, stopping to pick something up and examine it and confer over it and drop it again, in no hurry. Above them, clouds hung thick and grey, unmoving.

'This,' Hugo said, 'I didn't see coming.' He was leaning one shoulder against the door frame at an angle that made him look at ease, even cocky, but I could see his bad leg wobbling. 'I should have.'

A head popped up over the back wall; then a hand, holding a phone, flailing slightly as the guy tried to keep his balance on whatever he was standing on. 'What the hell?' I said.

'Reporter,' Hugo said grimly. 'There were a couple out front this morning, before you two came down. One of them tried to interview Mrs O'Loughlin next door, on her way out, but she was having none of it.'

My first thought was to charge down there and make the guy fuck off, but the cops were in the way, and they were ignoring him completely. The guy managed to steady his arm long enough to snap a couple of photos, and dropped down behind the wall again. After a moment a different head appeared, complete with arm and phone.

'They're taking turns giving each other a leg up,' Melissa said, moving back from the window.

'Little *rats*,' Hugo said, with real anger. 'Out the front is one thing; this is private. Can't the Guards get rid of them? Are they just going to stand there?'

The second guy got his shots and disappeared. We waited, but apparently that was it for the moment. The cloud had lowered and the light was changing, turning dim and bruised, uneasy.

The cops finished going over their strip of earth and started digging up a fresh one. It took them a while to uproot the biggest rosemary bush, but they got there in the end. After a while Rafferty came loping over and asked us, pleasantly and without feeling any need to give us a reason, if we could find somewhere else to be.

·

All Monday it rained, dense vertical uncompromising rain. I had taken another Xanax the night before and it had given me fucked-up dreams – the big uniformed guy on overnight guard duty had somehow got into my and Melissa's room, he was sitting on the chair in the corner playing with his phone, face puffy and unhealthy in the blue-white light; I kept jerking awake looking for him, drifting back into an unsettled doze-dream where Melissa and I gave up and moved to the spare room, only to find the cop waiting there, lounging against our old fort, phone in hand.

Walking Melissa to the bus stop, heads bent against the rain, not talking. Faffing aimlessly around the house with Hugo, loading the dishwasher and unloading the washing machine, while in the background the cops (cocooned in their wax jackets, rivulets streaming off their sleeves and the brims of their hoods) jammed shovels into the earth and tugged at daisy clumps with grim endurance. The dryer was broken, which hadn't been a problem when we could hang washing out on the line, but now the line had been taken down and hung in sad loops from a hook on the garden wall, the end drooping into the mud below. Hugo only had one drying rack and when that filled up we draped the rest of the wash on chair-backs and radiators, giving the dining room a downtrodden tenement feel. It was a long time before we finally managed to get it together to head up to his study and start work.

I was going through the 1901 census on Hugo's laptop – some

Australian guy couldn't find a great-grandmother who should have been living somewhere near Fishamble Street, I was checking the original forms to see if it was a transcription problem. At his desk, Hugo turned pages in a slow rhythm, with long gaps where I couldn't tell whether he was considering something or getting distracted by the faint shovel-thwacks and sporadic voices from below the window (louder all the time, as the cops worked their way up the garden), or whether he had just forgotten what he was doing. My eyes were glitching again, fatigue or the Xanax or whatever, the words on the page kept doubling. Neither of us was getting a lot done.

Around lunchtime there was a knock on the door: Leon, with fancy Italian sandwiches from some place in town. I thought for sure he would lose the plot when he saw the garden – almost half gone now, the canvas tent marooned in a sea of mud – but he just shook his head, jaw tight, and threw the sandwiches onto the kitchen counter with a little too much force. 'Fuck's sake,' he said. 'This is getting way out of hand.'

I got down three plates and passed them to him. 'No shit.'

'We should tell them to fuck off.'

'I did. They said they'd get a warrant.' I was in no mood for Leon giving me hassle. 'What would you have done?'

'Oh, chill. I'd have done exactly the same thing. Of course.' A quick, disarming smile. 'How's Hugo dealing?'

I wondered if he was there to nudge Hugo about making his will – the skull had knocked the whole house thing right out of our heads, and no one had brought it up since. 'OK. Pissed off.'

'What I'd love to know' – Leon shook a sandwich out of its paper bag – 'is what he thinks this is all about.'

A sideways glance at me. 'I don't know,' I said, finding water glasses. 'That homeless guy he was talking about, the cops tracked him down. It isn't him.'

'And? Has Hugo got any other ideas?'

'We haven't really talked about it.'

'You haven't asked him?'

'No. Why would I?'

Leon shrugged. 'He's the one who's been living here for however long. If anyone has a clue about this, it's probably him.'

'It was probably before he was even born. Your dad thinks it was some informer in the Civil War.'

Leon rolled his eyes. 'Course he does. He's hoping this is some major discovery and we'll end up in the textbooks for changing the narrative of Irish history yada yada.' Another sideways glance, as he arranged the plates on the tray. The sandwiches were probably wonderful, but I hadn't been hungry since the cops showed up and to me they just looked gross, all those folds of dark-red meat and globs of pale sweaty cheese. 'What about you? What do you figure?'

The truth was that I didn't have a theory, not even the germ of one. This had been bothering me, a lot, actually: everyone else had entire sagas, it felt like a glaring defect in my mind that it couldn't come up with anything at all. I had tried, but every time I thought of the skull my mind ran aground on the flat, stunning, unbudging reality of it; there didn't seem to be any way to think beyond or around it. It reminded me, with a deep sickening lurch in my stomach, of my few memories from right after the attack: disconnected images stripped of any context or meaning, only and vastly and unthinkably themselves. 'I don't have a clue,' I said. 'Neither does anyone else. We don't even know what they've found out there, how are we supposed to know how it got there?'

'Well, obviously we don't *know*. I just mean ideas. Possibilities.'

'I don't have ideas,' I said, putting down the glasses on the tray a little too hard, 'because I don't actually give a damn what happened. I just want those guys' – a jerk of my chin at the sodden cops outside – 'to fuck off and not wreck Hugo's last few months. That's all I care about. OK?' Which shut Leon up, just like I had known it would.

I was expecting him to quiz Hugo, over the sandwiches, but maybe what I said had got through. Instead he babbled cheerfully about Ivy House memories from our childhood; after we finished eating, he took half of Hugo's paper heap and lay face-down on the carpet with it, kicking his heels like a kid, occasionally waving a page to get our attention ('Oh my God, listen to this, this guy was named Aloysius Butt, I bet school was hell for him . . .'). When I came back up from making coffee, halfway through the afternoon, I heard their voices from the stairs, but by the time I opened the door they were peacefully absorbed in their work, Leon sucking the end of his pen with a contemplative whistling sound.

•

By Tuesday morning the garden was almost completely obliterated, one vast solid expanse of churned mud, with a last strip of grass and bobbing poppies at the very top like a bitter joke. It looked like some old battlefield, World War I, flung heaps of dirt and lopsided holes, thin cold rain falling; unrecoverable, nothing to be done except leave it alone in its silence and wait for the grass and poppies to grow back and cover it all.

Rafferty was missing, which somehow made things worse, like his guys were going to be there forever so there was no need for him to hang around. We made coffee and toast and got out of the kitchen as fast as we could; when I got back from walking Melissa to the bus stop, Hugo and I went straight to work, with the study door closed and the curtains pulled. The study lights weren't bright enough and it amplified the wartime feel, blackout, us hunched over and cold-fingered, flinching at every sound from outside.

Sometime around eleven, when I was starting to rub at my cricked neck and wonder if I could be arsed facing the kitchen to make coffee, there was a knock at the study door and Rafferty stuck his head in.

'Sorry to interrupt,' he said. 'Toby, could I have a quick word?'

He was wearing another very nice suit, but he looked rough around the edges, hair rucked up and a heavy dark shadow on his jaw. For some reason that stubble unsettled me – the implication that he had been up all night, doing vital detective things that he wasn't about to let me in on. 'OK,' I said.

'Thanks. Will we go down to the sitting room? So we don't disturb your uncle's work?'

Hugo nodded, vaguely – I wasn't sure he really got what was going on – and turned back to his desk. I made a note of where I was in the census and followed Rafferty.

'What do you do?' he asked companionably, on our way

downstairs. He was leading the way, which I was glad of, since it meant he couldn't see me take the stairs, clutching the railing, foot lagging. 'Yourself and your uncle?'

'He's a genealogist. You know, like tracing people's family trees? I'm just helping out while I'm here. I'm actually in PR.'

'Great study he's got there,' Rafferty said, opening the living-room door for me. 'Like something out of Sherlock Holmes. We should've given him a proper look at that skull, let him tell us if it came from a right-handed pipe welder with marriage problems and a Labrador.'

There was another man in the living room, settled comfortably in Hugo's armchair. 'Oh,' I said, stopping.

'This is Detective Kerr,' Rafferty said. 'My partner.' Kerr nodded to me. He was short and stocky, big-shouldered, with an under-hung bulldog face and buzzed hair not quite hiding the bald spot, and a suit that looked like he shopped in the same place as Rafferty. 'Have a seat.'

He was already moving towards the other armchair, which left me on a sofa, knees up to my chin, gazing up at them. Kerr or someone had opened the shutters, which we had been keeping closed in case any more reporters showed up; they hadn't, at least not right then, but the slice of street in the corner of my eye made me edgy. I tried to ignore it.

'You've been very patient about all of this,' Rafferty told me. 'All of ye. We know it's been a pain in the arse; we do get that. We wouldn't put you through this if it wasn't necessary.'

'I know,' I said.

'So' – he settled into the armchair – 'let me tell you what we've been at, the last few days. You're owed that much, amn't I right?'

I made some meaningless noise.

'First off: we're done with the garden. Bet you're glad to hear that.'

Glad wasn't exactly the right word. 'Great.'

'Do you want us to try and put some of the plants back where they were? Or would you rather do it your own way?'

'We'll deal with it,' I said. All I wanted was these guys gone. 'Thanks.'

'Fair enough.' Leaning forwards, wide-legged, hands clasped between his knees, getting down to business and that was when I felt the first far-off blip of wariness: 'So here's the thing. There was a full human skeleton in your garden. You probably figured that out already, yeah?'

'I guess,' I said. I wasn't sure what I had figured out. The thought of a whole skeleton, which should probably have made my skin crawl, seemed completely impossible, way too far outside reality for my mind to process.

'Don't worry, it's gone. The pathologist's got it now.'

'Where was it?'

'Most of it was down the tree. We were missing one hand, so that looked interesting, but we found it buried under a bush – so we didn't dig up the garden for nothing, if that's any comfort. One of the uniform lads' – Rafferty couldn't hold back a grin – 'he was all into the idea that it was some Satanist thing, the Hand of Glory, yeah?' Kerr snorted. 'He's new. The pathologist found toothmarks on the hand, so she figures a rat dragged it off to work on it.'

'Scanlon doesn't,' Kerr said, aside to Rafferty. 'Now he figures it was *cannibal* Satanists.'

'Jesus,' Rafferty said, finger to his mouth half-hiding the grin. 'Poor little bastard. When he realises what this job is actually like, he's going to be devastated. So' – brisk again – 'first thing we needed to do was figure out who the skeleton belonged to. The pathologist said it was a white male, aged between sixteen and twenty-two at the time of death – they can narrow that down pretty well, in young people: they go by the teeth, the ends of the long bones. He was a big guy, somewhere between six foot and six foot three, and he'd probably been physically active – something about the places where the ligaments would've been attached to the bone; it's amazing what they can work out. She said he'd broken his collarbone at some point, but it was well healed up, nothing to do with his death.'

He looked over at me hopefully, like I might have something to contribute. I didn't. I was starting to be bothered by the fact that these guys were talking to me on my own: why? why not everyone at once, like last time? sure, not everyone was around, but Hugo was right upstairs, there was no reason why he shouldn't be in on this, unless—

'And,' Rafferty said, 'he had modern dental work. Done sometime in the past fifteen years.'

Another pause. I had had myself almost completely convinced that my mother was right and this was some Victorian taking out his embezzling business partner, or the moustachioed villain who had seduced his daughter. I didn't like the way this was going at all.

'So that made our job a lot easier. We keep a database of missing persons; we went in there, searched for tall young white males who went missing from the Dublin area fifteen years ago or less. That narrowed it down to five. After that, all we had to do was compare dental records. I'm just after getting the results.'

He pulled out his phone, swiped and tapped: leisurely, at ease, elbow resting on the arm of the chair. 'Here,' he said, leaning across the coffee table to hand me the phone. 'Does this fella ring any bells?'

The guy in the photo was wearing a rugby jersey and grinning, arm thrown around someone who had been cropped out. He was maybe eighteen, broad-shouldered and good-looking, with rough fair hair and a cocky slouch and yes, I knew him straightaway but clearly there had been some mistake—

'That's Dominic Ganly,' I said. 'But that's, it's not him. I mean, the tree guy. It's not him.'

'How do you know this fella in the photo?'

I was suddenly ferociously aware of Kerr, watching me, a notebook somehow materialised in his hand and his pen poised. 'From school. He was in my class. But—'

'Were you good mates?'

'Not really. I mean' – I couldn't think, this didn't make any sense, they had it all wrong – 'we got on fine, we hung out with the same, the same crowd, but we weren't *friends* friends? Like we didn't do stuff just us, or—'

'How long did you know him?'

'Hang on,' I said. 'Wait.'

Two bland, interested faces, turned towards me.

'Dominic *died*. I mean, not like that, not in our— He killed himself, the summer after we left school. He jumped off Howth Head.'

'How do you know?' Rafferty asked.

'Everyone said it,' I said, after a baffled silence. I knew there had been something about his phone, text messages, something, couldn't remember the details—

'Looks like everyone was wrong,' Rafferty said. 'His body was never found; the Howth Head assumption was just based on the information they had at the time. His dental records are an exact match to our guy in the tree. And your friend Dominic, he broke his collarbone during a rugby match, when he was fifteen' – I remembered that, suddenly, Dom lounging in the back of the classroom with his arm in a sling – 'and the X-rays on that match as well. We're running DNA, just to be sure, but it's him.'

'Then what the hell—' But I was sure I had been at Dominic's funeral, positive: school choir singing, sniffles from the pews, a scrawny blond mother turned grotesque by the tug-of-war between weeping and industrial quantities of Botox; rugby jersey spread carefully on the rich mahogany of the coffin— 'What happened to him? Why was he, why, how did he get into our *tree*?'

'That's what we'd love to know,' Rafferty said. 'Any ideas?'

'No. I haven't got a— It's *crazy*.' I ran my hands over my head, trying to clear it. 'Are you— I mean, do you think someone *killed* him?'

'Could've done,' Rafferty said matter-of-factly. 'We don't know the cause of death; all we can say is his head wasn't bashed in – you probably noticed that yourself, sure. So he could've gone down that tree himself, one way or another. Or not. We're keeping open minds for now; just finding out a bit more about him, seeing if that gives us a clearer picture. You hung out with him, yeah?'

'Yeah. Sometimes. Sort of.' There had been maybe a dozen of us who ran as a loose crowd, basically because we were in the same class and we were all popular or cool or whatever you want to call it. I had been at one end of the group, Dominic had been at the other; we had hung out by default rather than by active choice, but there was no way I could have come up with the words to explain that. My brain was stuttering, over and over, computer in a loop of crash and reboot and crash: skull on the grass, clot of dirt and roots in the eye socket, Dominic yawning at his desk with his head down over his phone, skull on the grass—

'What was he like?'

'I don't know. Just a regular guy.'

'Was he smart? Thick?'

'Not really. I mean, not either one. Like he didn't do great in school, but not because he was seriously thick? He just, he couldn't be arsed.' Skull, dirt clot, yawn, I had been sitting under that tree just a few days before—

'Nice guy? Sound?'

'Yeah. Definitely. He, Dominic was a good guy.'

'Did he get on with people?'

Kerr was writing all this down and I had no idea why, what had I even said that was worth recording? 'Yeah. He did.'

'He was popular? Or just harmless?'

'Popular. He was I guess really confident? Out, out—' *Outgoing*, I meant, couldn't find it— 'Always on for a laugh or, you know, action, like a party or whatever. And he was good at rugby, so that always helps, but I mean it wasn't just that—' The rhythm of this was getting to me, no let-up, every answer seized and turned straight into a new question; like being back in the hospital, trapped in the bed, my head throbbing and Martin and Flashy Suit asking on and on—

'Anyone you can think of who didn't get on with him?'

Actually I had a vague memory of Dominic taking the piss out of Leon, but a lot of guys had taken the piss out of Leon back then, and under the circumstances I didn't think I should go into this. 'Not really.'

'What about girls? He do well there?'

'Oh yeah. They threw themselves at him. It was kind of a, a thing? Like a joke? Whatever girl we were all into, Dom was the one who'd get with her first.'

'We all know that guy,' Rafferty said, grinning. 'The bastard. He piss anyone off with that? Rob anyone's girlfriend, maybe?'

'No way. Like I said, he was a good guy. He wouldn't have hit on anyone's girlfriend – bro code, you know? And the rest, the way girls were all into him . . . like I said, that was kind of a running joke. No one got upset about it.'

'Easy for you to say, man, if you weren't on the wrong end of it. Dominic ever get a girl you were into?'

'Probably. I don't remember.' This was true. I had been into just about every girl who was pretty or hot or both, back then; odds were Dominic had hooked up with at least some of them, but then I had done OK myself, so it hadn't bothered me.

'Did he stick to the hit-and-run stuff? Or did he have a girlfriend of his own?'

'Not when he . . . Not that summer. I think he was maybe going out with someone for a while, like the year before? Maybe some girl from St Therese's, that's our sister school? But it wasn't, like, a big serious thing.'

'When did it end?'

I saw what he was getting at, but— 'No. Ages before he— And I think he dumped her. Either way, he wasn't torn up about it or anything. That wasn't why . . .' I stopped. I was getting mixed up.

'About that,' Rafferty said. 'When you heard he'd killed himself. Did that make sense to you? Or were you surprised?'

'I don't—' My bedroom upstairs, rolling over with a grunt to grab my insistent phone, Dec's voice: *Did you hear? About Dominic?* 'I mean, yeah, I was shocked. He didn't seem like the type, at all. But everyone knew he hadn't got the course he wanted, like for college? He wanted to do Business, I think, but he didn't get the points in the Leaving Cert. And he was pretty upset about that. So he'd been kind of off, that summer.'

'Depressed?'

'Not really. More like angry, a lot of the time. Like he was taking it out on the rest of us who'd got into the courses we wanted.'

'Angry,' Rafferty repeated thoughtfully. 'That cause any problems?'

'Like what?'

'Dominic get into any fights? Piss anyone off?'

'Not exactly. Mostly he was just kind of a bollix, like getting nasty with people out of nowhere? But nobody held it against him. We all got it.'

'That's pretty understanding,' Rafferty said. 'For a bunch of teen-age boys.'

I did some kind of shrug. The truth was that I at least hadn't thought very much about Dominic, that summer, except for the odd moment of pity tinged with smugness. My mind had been on college, freedom, a week in Mykonos with Sean and Dec; Dominic's strops (pinning Darragh O'Rourke against the wall and shouting in his face, after some harmless comment, then storming off when the rest of us broke it up) had been low on my priority list.

'Looking back, do you think he might have been in worse shape than you realised? Teenagers, they don't always know how to spot the signs that someone's in real trouble. They're all half mental anyway; even when someone's falling apart, they just figure it's more of the same.'

'I guess he could have been,' I said, after a moment. 'He was def-initely . . .' I couldn't come up with the right way to describe it, the raw, splintered, unpredictable energy that had made me start avoid-ing Dominic that summer. 'He was off.'

'Put it this way. If one of your friends right now started acting the way Dominic was that summer, would you be worried?'

'I guess. Yeah. I would be.'

'Right,' Rafferty said. He was leaning forwards, hands clasped between his knees, gazing at me like I was making some valuable contribution to the investigation. 'When did he start acting out of character? Ballpark, even.'

'I don't . . .' It had been years since I'd thought about any of this. 'I mean, I wouldn't swear to this. At all.' Rafferty nodded understandingly. 'But I think it sort of started around the Leaving Cert orals, so April? And then it got way worse in June, with the written exams. He knew he'd fucked up. Like, most of us? we were all stressing about how we'd done, except a few nerds who knew they'd got a million points; one day we'd be all "Yeah, I should be fine" and the next we'd be like "Oh shit, what if . . ." But Dominic was like, "I'm fucked." End of. And it was obviously wrecking his head. And when the results came out in August and yeah, he actu-ally had done as badly as he thought, then he got even worse.'

'Why'd he do so badly? You said he wasn't thick.'

'He wasn't. He just hadn't studied. He' – hard to explain – 'Dominic's parents were rich. They kind of, I guess they spoiled him? Like he always had everything, cool phones and cool holidays and designer gear, and before sixth year they bought him a BMW?' Sudden vague memory of resentment, my dad had laughed in my face, *Better start saving*— 'I think it just, like, genuinely never occurred to him that he might not get something he wanted. Including whatever course he wanted. So he didn't bother studying. And by the time it hit him, it was too late.'

'Did he ever do drugs?' And, wryly, when I hesitated: 'Toby. It's been ten years. Even if I was looking to bang people up for a bit of hash or a few pills, which I'm not, the statute of limitations ran out years back. And I haven't cautioned you; anything you say wouldn't be admissible in evidence. I just need to get a feel for what was going on in Dominic's life.'

'Yeah,' I said, after a moment. 'He did drugs sometimes.'

'What kinds?'

'I know he did hash, and E. And coke, sometimes.' Dominic had liked coke, a lot. It hadn't been all that common, back in school, but when there was some around it had been his more often than not, and he had been good about sharing with the host: clap on my shoulder during a party, *C'mon over here, Henno, I need a word*, sneaking to the bottom of the garden snickering and swearing as our feet sank into mud, lines chopped out on a rusty little garden table. 'There could've been other stuff, I don't know. That's all I saw him with. And he wasn't some junkie, or anything. Just . . . when it was going.'

'Your basic teenage experimenting,' Rafferty said, nodding. Kerr was writing away. 'Any hassle there, do you know? A dealer he didn't pay, someone who ripped him off, anything like that?'

'Not that I know about. But I probably wouldn't have known anyway.'

'That's right. You weren't *friends* friends.' He left that there for a moment that made me vaguely uneasy. 'Was Dominic ever at this house?'

'Yeah,' I said. This felt like something I shouldn't admit, but there didn't seem to be much choice. 'Me and my cousins, we used to stay here during the holidays? And we'd have parties? I mean, not like mad raves or, I mean Hugo was right here, but he'd stay upstairs – we'd just have a bunch of mates over, put on music, hang out and talk and maybe dance—'

'And drink,' Rafferty put in, grinning. 'And the other stuff. Let's be honest here.'

'Yeah. Sometimes. We weren't, like not a drug den or orgies or anything, but . . . I mean, this wasn't when we were like *twelve*, I'm talking when we were sixteen, seventeen, eighteen? Mostly it was just a few cans, or someone would have a bottle of vodka or – and I guess sometimes people would have hash or whatever—'

I knew I was stammering and babbling, I could see Kerr's face getting a subtle look of very sympathetic understanding like it was dawning on him that I was a bit unfortunate. I wanted to grab him by the collar and shout in his face, get it into his thick head that that was nothing to do with me, it was all because of two worthless skanger pricks and he should be fucking giving them that look, not me. Everything inside my head was ricocheting.

Somewhere in there, although I can't pinpoint it exactly, had been the moment when all this turned real. Up until then it had been basically an outrageous pain in the arse – horrible, sure, obviously, and grotesque, presumably this poor guy (or girl, whatever) hadn't planned on having his skull fished out of a tree and God knew what kind of tragic story had gone on there, but it would have been really fucking nice if he had picked some other tree; but, apart from in the geographical sense, nothing to do with us. Even through the first half of this conversation, I had had the same feeling, even when Rafferty said the skeleton wasn't old, even when he showed me the photo – *Dominic, Jesus Christ, didn't see that coming, how the fuck did he wind up in there?* It had taken a while to sink in that we weren't spectators any more; we were, somehow, inside this.

'And Dominic came to these parties?' Rafferty asked.

'Yeah. Not always, but I guess most of them.'

'How many?'

I had no idea. 'Maybe we had three or four parties that summer, and he came to two or three? And around the same the summer before that, and the one before that. But I don't, I mean I'm just guessing?'

'Fair enough. It's been a long time; we don't expect anyone's memory to be perfect. Just give us what you've got. If you don't remember, that's grand, go ahead and say that.' Rafferty smiled at me, all easy and reassuring. 'Who would've invited him to the parties? Would that have been you? Or was he closer to one of your cousins?'

'Me, probably. I'd just send out a group text to all the guys.'

'Was he ever here apart from the parties? Like, did he ever call round on his own? Or with a few of your mates?'

'I'm not—' What flashed up in my mind was me and Leon and Susanna on the terrace, the first time we got stoned, the three of us giggling like maniacs and I was almost positive another laugh in the darkness, had that been Dominic's catching chuckle, hadn't it? 'I think so. I can't remember any, any specific times, but I think he was over now and then.'

'Would you remember the last time he was here?'

Dominic lying back on his elbows in the grass grinning across at Susanna, had it been Susanna? Dominic shouting with laughter, in the kitchen, over the shards and splatter of a dropped beer bottle. 'I don't know,' I said. 'Sorry.'

'What about the last time you saw him?'

'I don't have a clue. I don't think it was right before he went missing, because I would remember that' – maybe – 'I mean, it sounds like the kind of thing I'd have been telling people, afterwards, right? "Oh my God, I just saw him that day and he looked fine"? And I don't remember doing that. So . . .'

'Makes sense,' Rafferty said, which was charitable of him. 'The last time Dominic was seen was – let's see here' – reaching for his notebook, flipping – 'the twelfth of September. That was a Monday. He was working a part-time summer job at a golf club; he finished up there around five, got home around six and had dinner with his family. They all went to bed around half-eleven. Sometime during the night, Dominic snuck out, and he never came home.' A glance up at me: 'Any idea what you were doing that day? Whether you were in the country, even?'

'I was staying here. Me and Susanna and Leon, we'd been here most of the summer. But I don't—'

Kerr shifted, chair creaking. 'Why?' he asked.

I stared at him blankly. 'Why what?'

Patiently: 'You stayed here for the summer. How come?'

'We always did.' And, when he kept looking at me: 'Our parents go travelling together.'

'You were eighteen that summer, but. Would you not have rathered stay on your own at your parents' house? Free gaff, no uncle keeping an eye on you. Party time.'

'Yeah, no, I could've. But—' How could I explain? 'We all liked it here. And it was more fun with three of us. We were all single, that summer, so it's not like we wanted to play house with our girlfriends or boyfriends. We just wanted to hang out.'

'Sounds like they did all right for parties even with the uncle around,' Rafferty told Kerr, grinning. 'Amn't I right, Toby?'

'Right.' I managed a weak smile. 'But I don't have a clue whether we were here that actual day. We all had summer jobs, so probably we were at those?'

'Unless you were too hungover, right? Been there. Where were you working?'

'I was' – it took me a second to get my summers straight – 'I was in the, the post room at the bank where my uncle Oliver works. Susanna was volunteering for a, one of those non-profits, I can't remember which one. And Leon was working at a record shop in town.'

'What time would you have finished up there?'

'I think I finished at five? And then probably we came back here for dinner, that's what we mostly . . . Maybe we might have gone out afterwards, or people might have come here, but if it was a Monday then probably not . . . But I don't actually remember.'

'That's OK. We'll ask around, see if any of your gang kept a diary.

Check out social media – Myspace, wouldn't it have been, back then? – see if anyone posted about their day.' Rafferty straightened up, hands on the arms of the chair: winding this up. 'Since the dead person had links to this house,' he said, 'we're going to need to search it.'

The fireball of outrage took my breath away. 'But,' I said, and stopped.

'That's one reason why I wanted to talk to you on your own,' Rafferty said, apparently not noticing. 'Your uncle. I hope I'm not putting my foot in it here, but is he all right?'

'No,' I said. 'He's dying. Brain cancer. He's got maybe a few months.'

If I hoped this would be some kind of get-out-of-jail-free card, I was wrong. Rafferty grimaced. 'Sorry to hear that. I'm glad I talked to you first; maybe you can help me come up with a plan to make this as easy on him as possible. We'll do our best to work fast, but realistically, it's going to take us the guts of today. Is there anywhere the two of you could go for the day? Somewhere your uncle would be comfortable?'

'No,' I said. Actually I had no idea whether Hugo would mind clearing out for the day, but I minded, for him and for myself, with a savagery that made no sense but I didn't give a fuck. 'He needs to be here. He can barely walk. And he gets confused.'

'The thing is,' Rafferty explained, very reasonably, 'we don't have any choice about searching the house. That needs doing. We've got a warrant and all. And you can see how we can't have the two of you hanging over our shoulders.'

We looked at each other, across the coffee table. The terrible part was that I knew, with total and wretched certainty, that just a few months ago I would have been able to talk them round: easy-peasy, no problem to me, charming smile and some perfect solution that would make everyone happy. The gibbering mess I was now couldn't have talked round a five-year-old, even if I had been able to come up with a solution, which I couldn't: the only thing I could think of was going all Occupy Ivy House and telling these guys that they would have to handcuff me and drag me out, and even apart from the cringe factor I had a feeling they would cheerfully do exactly that if they had to.

'Tell you what,' Rafferty said, relenting. 'Split the difference. You and your uncle clear out of our way for, what, say an hour?'

He glanced at Kerr. 'Hour and a half, maybe,' Kerr said. His notebook had vanished.

'Hour and a half. Go get some lunch, do the shopping. While you're out, we'll do the study and the kitchen. Then when you get back, you can stick to those rooms – get your work done, make yourselves a cup of tea if you want one – and we won't be in each other's way. How does that sound?'

'OK,' I said, after a moment. 'I guess.'

'Great,' Rafferty said cheerfully. 'Sorted, so.'

When I stood up, he did too. At first I didn't understand why. It was only as he followed me up the stairs to Hugo's study that I got it, and that I realised: *Since the dead person had links to this house, we're going to need to search it. We've got a warrant and all*; but a few minutes earlier, he had made it sound like he had only just that moment found out who the dead person was.

•

I wasn't supposed to drive, but Hugo clearly couldn't, and there was no way in hell I was going to make him walk the streets till Rafferty and his pals finished doing their thing. His car was a long white 1994 Peugeot, rust spots and duct tape everywhere, but actually a nice drive once I started getting the hang of its quirks. The hard part was the surroundings, out on the main road: speed and coloured lights and moving things everywhere, like being yanked up from the depths of still green water into way too much of everything. I hoped to God I was driving OK; I really, really couldn't handle any more cops right then.

I badly wanted a cigarette. I hadn't been smoking long enough to build up a serious addiction, but what with the situation – cops to the left of me, journalists to the right, and there I was, stuck in the middle with my nonsmoker act – I hadn't had one since the night before, and it had been a bastard of a day already. I pulled off the main road and turned corners till I found a cul-de-sac lined with spindly trees and little old-person cottages. 'Can we just hang on here for a minute?' I said, switching off the ignition, already fumbling for my cigarettes. 'I really need one of these.'

'I almost punched him,' Hugo said, startling me. He had taken the news and the plan quietly, just a nod and a careful note on his papers before he put them aside, barely a word on our way out the door or on the drive. 'That Rafferty man. I know it's not his fault, it has to be done, but still. The thought of him and his men prodding and peering through my house – not that I have anything I want to hide, but that's beside the point, it's *our home*— Just in that second, when he said it, I very nearly—' The sudden rise and roll of his shoulders: for a fleeting moment I saw the size of him, the breadth of his back, the reach of his arms. 'A part of me wishes I had.'

'I did try to stop them,' I said, although I wasn't sure this really counted as true. 'From searching the house. Or at least from throwing us out.'

Hugo sighed. 'I know. It's all right. Probably it's good for us to get out of the house for a bit.' He leaned his head back against the headrest and ran a hand over his face, roughly, eyes squeezed tight. 'I couldn't tell what the detective was thinking, not a glimmer. He's very hard to read, isn't he – which I suppose is his job. What did he ask you?'

'Just about Dominic. What he was like. How much time he spent at the house.'

'He asked me the same.' Rafferty had talked to Hugo in the study, while Kerr made pleasant chitchat with me in the living room (genealogy, leading into Kerr's great-uncle who had had some involvement or other in the 1916 Rising) to gloss over the fact that he was supervising me. It had taken long enough that I had got violently, unreasonably twitchy, what the hell were they talking about up there while Kerr – apparently oblivious – droned on and on and on? 'I barely remember him, though, this boy Dominic. God knows I've been trying. I don't know whether he just didn't leave much of an impression, or whether my memory . . . I think it was a bit frustrating for the detective.'

'That's his problem,' I said. The cigarette was improving my mood, but I still wasn't feeling very charitable towards Rafferty.

'The photo rang a bell, but not much more than that. I do remember one of your class committing suicide the summer you all left school, but I didn't think it was someone who was particularly close to any of you.'

'He wasn't. He hung around with the same crowd as me, was all.'

'What was he like?'

'He was a good bloke, basically. Kind of a party animal. He wasn't over at the house a lot, I don't think. Probably that's why you don't remember him.'

'Poor boy,' Hugo said. 'I'd really like to know the story behind him ending up in that tree. I'm not being prurient, at least I don't think I am; but there he was, and here I am, with his death getting right in the middle of mine. Maybe it's childish, but I do feel as if I've got a bit of a right to know what happened.'

'Well,' I said. 'If the cops do their job, we should all know the story soon enough.'

A wry twist of his mouth. 'Not necessarily soon enough for me.'

'You've got time,' I said, ludicrously. 'I mean, the doctors didn't, it's not like they gave you a *deadline*. You're not getting worse, or . . .' I couldn't keep it up.

Hugo didn't look at me. His hair had grown: it was down to his shoulders, thick rumpled locks streaked dark and grey. His hands lay on his lap, huge square capable hands, loose as rubber gloves.

'I can feel it, you know,' he said. 'Just this last week or so. My body turning away from all this. Focusing its energy on doing something else, some new process. Something that I don't understand and have no idea how to go about, but my body knows and is busy at it. At first I told myself it was psychological – from hearing that Susanna's Swiss expert couldn't do anything – but it's not.'

There was nothing I could say. I wanted to reach out and take his arm, physically hold him there, but I knew I wasn't solid enough myself to make any difference.

After a moment he drew a long breath. 'Well, there you are. Give me one of those, would you?'

I held the lighter for him. 'On the other hand,' he said in a differ-ent tone, cocking an eyebrow at me as he bent to the flame, 'it's good to see you on the opposite trajectory. Even in these few weeks, there's been a real change.'

'Yeah,' I said. I had finished my cigarette; I threw the butt out of the window. 'Well.'

'No?'

'I guess. But' – I didn't know I was going to say it till I heard the words, today was all out of whack, still that dazzled feel like being in a simulator, everything too brightly coloured and hanging in mid-air – 'even if stuff gets better, like my leg or whatever, so what? Because that's not the point. The point is, even if I end up running a *marathon*, I'm not the same person any more. *That's* the point.'

Hugo thought about that for a while. 'I have to say' – he blew smoke carefully out his window – 'you seem pretty much yourself to me.'

'Well,' I said. This was nice, inasmuch as it meant I was doing a decent job of faking it, but given Hugo's condition it was hard to put too much weight on it. 'That's good.'

'No, I know you're putting in the effort. I can see that – no, not that anyone else would notice, it's only because I'm living with you and I've known you all your life. But that's not what I mean.' It took him two tries to get the cigarette out the window to tap ash. 'Fun-damentally, under all that, you still seem like Toby. Battered and cracked, of course, but essentially the same person.'

When I didn't say anything: 'Do you really feel so very different?'

'Yes. Jesus, yeah, I fucking do. But it's not even that.' I had never put this into words before, and even trying was making my hands shake; I could hardly breathe. 'It's not the actual ways I've changed. Probably I could handle those – I mean, they're utterly shit, I fuck-ing hate them, but I could . . . But it's the *fact* of it. I never thought much about my, my personality before, but when I did, I took it for granted that it was *mine*, you know? That it was me? And now it's like, I could wake up in the morning a, a, a Trekkie, or gay, or a mathematical genius, or one of those guys who shout at girls on the street to get their tits out? And I'd have no way to, to know it was coming. Or to do anything about it. Just . . . bam. There you go. Deal with it.'

I stopped talking. My adrenaline was through the roof; every muscle was trembling.

Hugo nodded. We sat there, not talking, for a while. When he moved, for a horrible second I wondered if he was going to put his arm around me or something, but instead he threw his cigarette out the window and bent to a cloth bag on the floor between his feet – I had vaguely registered him going into the kitchen (Rafferty trailing him unobtrusively) and coming back with it, on our way out, but I hadn't paid much attention. 'Here,' he said, coming up with a clingfilm-wrapped bundle. 'You do need to eat, you know.'

It was the leftover cake from Sunday's pick-up lunch. He had even brought a knife. He spread out the clingfilm on his lap and sliced the cake into two neat halves. 'There,' he said, handing me mine, on a paper napkin.

We ate in silence. The cake was jam sponge and it tasted start-lingly, almost humiliatingly delicious, childhood rush of sugar and comfort. It was still raining, wind blowing small erratic spat-ters at the windscreen. A woman went by with a little kid in a bright yellow raincoat, the kid jumping in puddles, the woman shooting us a suspicious look from under the hood of her puffy jacket.

'Now,' Hugo said, brushing crumbs and powdered sugar off his jumper into his hand. 'Do you want to ring your cousins and let them know?'

'*Shit*,' I said. Somehow this hadn't even occurred to me, but of course, Rafferty would be zooming over to interrogate them as soon as he finished fucking up the Ivy House. 'Yes. I should do that now.'

'Here,' Hugo said, balling up the clingfilm and the napkins and handing the whole thing to me. 'You can find a bin for this, while you're at it – don't forget the cigarette butts. I might close my eyes for a moment. We've got a while, haven't we, before we can go home?'

He turned the radio on to Lyric FM – something peaceful, string quartet – and leaned his head back against the headrest. I got out of

the car, turned up my jacket collar against the rain and went looking for a bin while I rang Susanna.

She picked up fast. 'What's up?'

'There was a whole skeleton in there. In the tree. And the cops
found out who it is. Remember Dominic Ganly?'

Silence.

'Su?' I didn't remember Susanna being remotely matey with
Dom, she hadn't been his type, but given the effect he had had on
girls— 'Are you OK?'

'Fine. I just didn't expect it to be someone we knew.' In the background, horrible cacophony of someone banging on a piano—
'Zach! Knock it *off*! —Do they know what happened to him?'

'No. Not yet, anyway. They say maybe he could have been' – the
word felt unreal, a bright migraine flare rippling out dangerously
across everything – 'he could have been murdered.'

Sharply: 'Could have been? Or he was?'

'Could have been. They don't know. What he died of, even.'

A second of silence. 'So they think he could have got in there by
himself.'

'That's what Rafferty said. It sounds crazy to me, how the fuck—'

'Well, plenty of ways,' Susanna said. Zach was still smashing the
piano, but faintly now, farther away; she had left him to it. 'Maybe
he was up the tree, he slipped and he broke his neck falling into the
hole. Maybe he was off his face on something and thought he had
to go down there to look for dwarf treasure, and then he couldn't
get out and he, I don't know, suffocated. Choked on vomit.'

'The detectives asked that. Whether he ever did drugs.'

'There you go. What did you say?'

I turned my shoulder to the rain, trying to keep it off my phone.
'I said yeah. I wasn't going to fuck about. They would've found out
anyway.'

'Right,' Susanna said. There was an absent note to her voice; she
was thinking hard. 'Or maybe he actually did kill himself.'

'Why the fuck would he kill himself in our tree? And how?'

'Overdose, maybe. And I haven't got a clue why. I barely knew
him. That's not our problem; the detectives can figure it out.'

'Yeah, that's the other reason I'm calling. They interviewed me, or interrogated me, or whatever they call it. And Hugo. And now they're searching the house. They threw us out.'

That got Susanna's attention. 'Searching the *house*? What for?'

'How would I know?' I had finally managed to find a bin; I jammed the rubbish into it. 'Because Dominic "had links to" it, they said. I'm just giving you the heads-up: whenever they get finished, they're probably going to show up at your place.'

'Those pricks threw you *out*? Where are you? Where's Hugo?'

'Only for an hour and a half. We're just hanging out in the car. Hugo's having a nap. It's fine.'

A second while she decided whether to get really pissed off or save it. In the end: 'What did they ask you?'

'About Dominic, basically. What he was like, how well I knew him. Whether he was depressed that summer. How much he was at the house. Stuff like that.'

Susanna went silent again. I could practically hear her mind whirring.

'They weren't shitty about it, or anything. It was fine. I just thought you'd want to know before they show up on your doorstep.'

'I do, yeah. Thanks, Toby. Seriously.' A breath. Briskly: 'Listen. I'll let you know when they've been and gone. Then we can take it from there.'

I wasn't sure what she was talking about – take what where? what exactly did she think we could do about any of this? 'Yeah. OK.'

'Got to go. See you later, or tomorrow. Meanwhile, just remember: they're allowed to lie to you. And they're not your buddies.'

I wanted to ask why exactly she thought her knowledge of cops beat mine, but— 'Su. Hang on.'

'Yeah?'

'The first time the three of us got stoned. On the terrace. Remember?'

'You told Leon I'd turned into a fairy. He was freaking out.'

'Yeah. Was Dominic there too?'

'No. Why would he be?'

'I couldn't remember who it was. I thought maybe him.'

'There wasn't anyone else there,' Susanna said. There was a note in her voice that I couldn't read; bafflement, curiosity, what? 'It was just the three of us.'

No it wasn't, I almost said, but the ugly twist in my stomach stopped me. 'Right,' I said. 'I guess that stuff was stronger than I thought.'

'I think it must've been pure skunk or something. *I* even started believing I'd turned into a fairy. I was getting worried about how I'd turn back, except I figured you probably had a plan and you wouldn't let me get stuck that way.'

'God, no.' That actually got a smile out of me. 'I had the antidote all ready.'

'There you go. Talk later. Bye.'

Leon's phone was busy. I had wandered far enough in search of the bin that it took me a while to find my way back to the car – indistinguishable wet shabby side streets, tiny empty gardens, I had a nasty mental image of having to ring Hugo to ask him where he was – but when I finally found it he still had his head back on the headrest, eyes closed. He looked asleep. I leaned on someone's garden wall and lit another cigarette before I tried Leon again. This time his phone rang out.

It was half-one. I figured surely to Jesus the cops had finished whatever they were doing in the study by now, and even if they hadn't, that was their problem. I threw my cigarette into a puddle and headed for the car.

•

Rafferty met us at the door like a host – come in, great timing, just finished the study, up you come! shepherding us down the hall past a glimpse of some uniform squatting to rifle through the coffee-table clutter, sweeping us up the stairs and into the study, there you go, we'll keep you updated! And he was gone, with a firm click of the door behind him.

The study looked subtly, undefinably off-kilter, the wooden elephants lined up too neatly on the mantelpiece, the patterns of book spines all wrong on the shelves, everything half an inch out of place. It made me want to back out the door. 'Well,' Hugo said, after a moment, blinking at the pile of paper he had left behind. 'Where were we?'

I went through the census PDFs like an automaton: pick a street, pick a house number, click on original census form, skim the names, back button and move on to the next house. I had no idea what I was seeing. Footsteps thumping back and forth overhead, in my room; thud of a drawer closing. Somehow it hadn't sunk in till then what *search the house* actually meant, and the thought of Rafferty pawing through Melissa's underwear sent me into an impotent rage that almost stupefied me, left me staring at the laptop screen, blind and panting.

Scrapes of furniture being moved, muffled voices through walls, feet going up and down the stairs. It went on and on. I knew I should be hungry and so should Hugo, but neither of us suggested making lunch.

At some point, after what felt like days, Rafferty knocked on the door. 'Sorry, quick question,' he said. He had an armful of large brown paper bags with clear windows running down the sides. 'Who owns these?'

He spread out the bags on the rug for us to inspect. 'I think this is mine,' Hugo said, pointing at what looked like a heavy khaki jacket, big pockets, worn and dirt-smudged. 'I haven't seen it in years. Where was it?'

'Do you remember when you got it?'

'Goodness . . . twenty years ago, it must be. I used to wear it for gardening, back when my parents were alive and we took that stuff more seriously.'

'When did you see it last?'

'I have no idea,' Hugo said tranquilly. 'A long time ago. Do you need it?'

'We're going to have to take all of this, yeah.' Rafferty watched to see what we thought of that. His stubble had darkened, giving him a dashing renegade look. When neither of us said anything: 'We'll give you a receipt. Any of the rest ring a bell?'

'That was mine,' I said, pointing to my old rugby jersey. 'Back in school. And that' – a red hoodie – 'that could've been mine too, I'm not sure? And I think those' – grubby pair of thick-soled black creepers – 'were maybe Leon's? And that was sort of everyone's' – a cobwebby blue sleeping bag. 'For when we slept out in the garden, when we were kids, or later for if friends stayed over. I don't know about that' – a maroon wool scarf, dusty and bobbled. 'I don't remember seeing it before.'

'Nor do I,' Hugo said, holding on to his desk so he could lean over to examine it more closely. 'It might have been Leon's, I suppose. Or it might have belonged to one of your friends. Teenagers strew things everywhere they go, don't they?'

'We'll ask around,' Rafferty said. 'The good news is, we're done here. The lads are packing up, and then we'll be out of your hair. Thanks for all your patience over the last—'

Downstairs, the front door slammed and Melissa's voice, fresh as summer, called out, 'Hi, I'm home! Oof, this rain, it—' There was a startled silence.

'That's Melissa,' I said, standing up. 'I'd better—' and while I was getting down to her and trying to explain what was going on, the cops came clumping down the stairs with their evidence bags and their cameras and whatever else, and Rafferty and Kerr shook all our hands on the doorstep and made more meaningless noises about how much they appreciated our cooperation, and then the door closed behind them and they were gone, leaving the three of us finally alone in the sudden high-ceilinged emptiness of the house.

We went out onto the terrace to face the damage. The rain had stopped, just a haze in the air and the occasional leaf-drip rattling through a tree. That last strip of grass and poppies was gone: the garden was mud, nothing left but the lines of trees backed up against the side walls in what looked like a doomed last stand, broken by the jagged crater – shockingly wide and deep – where the wych elm had been. The uprooted bushes were lined up considerately along the back wall, in case we had plans for them. In one corner of the terrace was a neat pile of stuff the cops had apparently found along the way: shards of old china glazed in pretty blue and white patterns, a dirt-caked Barbie, a plastic seaside spade, an ornately whorled iron bracket thick with rust. The smell of turned earth was overwhelming, almost too rich and wild to breathe. In the furrows, tiny movement everywhere: worms curling, woodlice scurrying, ants clambering. At a safe distance from us, a couple of blackbirds and a robin darted and pecked.

'We'll replant the bushes tomorrow,' Melissa said. 'And I can ring the garden centre and have them come and put in grass, the sod or whatever they—'

'No,' Hugo said gently. 'Leave it.'

'Toby and I will look after it, you won't have to—'

He reached out and put a hand on her head, lightly. 'Shhh. We've had enough comings and goings.'

After a moment she took a breath and nodded. 'We'll do the bushes. And get some new plants.'

'Thank you, my dear. That would be wonderful.'

We stood there for a long time, while the birds and the insects went about their business and the leftover raindrops ticked in the trees. The air was thin and chilly and the light was turning grey, but none of us could seem to find a reason to move.

7

Halfway through the next morning Leon showed up, and Susanna not long after. Hugo had gone for a nap and I had been wandering around the house picking up knick-knacks and putting them down again, unable to settle to work or anything else, so I was relieved to see them, but that didn't last. Rafferty and Kerr had been to see Susanna that morning and Leon the night before; they were both on edge, in their different ways, and for some reason I couldn't work out Leon was in a bad mood with Susanna. 'I rang you,' Susanna said to him, slinging her jacket over the back of a kitchen chair. 'Like five times. I was going to give you a lift here.'

Leon was unloading the dishwasher, banging plates down on the counter with unnecessary force, and didn't look up. 'I got the bus.'

'I thought you wanted to talk to me.'

'I *did*. Last *night*. So I could tell you what the cops asked me.'

'Sallie had had a nightmare. I was dealing with that. And I didn't need to know what they'd asked you. It wouldn't have made a difference.'

'It would have made a difference to me. I wanted to *talk* to you.'

'Well, we can talk now,' Susanna said coolly. 'Outside, though. I want a smoke. Is that coffee still hot?'

'Yeah,' I said, passing her a cup from the cupboard where I was putting the dishes away. 'Jesus, Leon, keep it down. You'll wake Hugo.'

'No I won't. He's miles away.' But he toned down the banging. 'What does Tom think about all this?' he asked Susanna. 'Is he having fun?'

Susanna poured herself coffee from the pot on the stove and headed to the fridge for milk. 'He's fine with it.'

'I bet he's going out of his tiny mind. This is probably the scariest thing that's ever happened to him, isn't it, except for the time he went wild and went an extra stop on the bus without paying and the inspector got on and he nearly shat himself—'

'You,' Susanna said crisply, without turning from the fridge, 'don't have the faintest clue about Tom. It would take a whole lot more than this to make him lose his mind. Unlike some people.'

'*Ooo*,' Leon said, into the chilly silence that followed.

'How's Carsten doing?' I asked. Whatever this was, I didn't feel like dealing with it. Between the bad nights and the Xanax I was exhausted, a thick leaden exhaustion that I'd thought I'd left behind in my apartment, and my head hurt in a petty nagging way that wasn't quite worth a painkiller.

Leon grimaced. 'He keeps wanting to come over. I keep saying no, because I'm not having him anywhere near this mess. He'd go all overprotective and get stroppy with the cops.' A snide look under his lashes at Susanna, who was unlikely to suffer from spousal overprotectiveness and who ignored him. 'I've never gone this long without seeing him. Not since the day we met. I hate it.'

'You can just go home, you know,' Susanna pointed out. 'Any time you want.'

'No I can't. Not now. It'll look like I'm doing a runner because I've got something to hide.'

'It'll look like you're going home. To your boyfriend and your job. Like you were going to anyway.'

'No thanks.'

'Well then.' Susanna dug a packet of Marlboro Lights out of the depths of her bag. 'Come on.'

The rain was still holding off, if only barely. A lean grey cat, which had been stalking a blackbird among the ridges of mud, streaked away and scrambled over a wall at the sight of us. 'What a mess,' Susanna said. She had brought out an old dishtowel; she dropped it on the terrace and scuffed it around with her foot, soaking up leftover rain. 'We should replant all that stuff, before it dies.'

'Melissa and I are going to do it when she gets home,' I said.

'How's Melissa with all this?'

'Fine. Glad they're out of our hair.'

'Well,' Susanna said. She tossed the towel towards the door and dropped down to sit at the top of the steps, moving over to make room for me beside her. 'More or less.'

'Oh, God,' Leon said, sinking down on her other side. The week's events had apparently hit him right in the fashion sense: his forelock hung over his face in a childish, neglected flop and he was wearing a misshapen grey jumper that didn't go with his edgy distressed jeans. 'I hate cops. I didn't like them even before I got arrested, and now I swear to God, just the sight of them—'

'You got *arrested*?' I said. 'What for?'

'Nothing. It was years ago. In Amsterdam.'

'I didn't know you even *could* get arrested in Amsterdam. What'd you do?'

'I didn't do anything. It was stupid. I had a fight with— You know what, it doesn't even matter, it all got sorted out in a couple of hours. The point is, I could really do with a nice big spliff right now.'

'Here,' I said, tossing him my cigarette packet. 'Best I can do.' I was kind of enjoying this, actually, after all Leon's little jabs about how there was no way I could cope with a tough situation; not that I had handled the detectives like a champ or anything, but at least I wasn't having the vapours and practically demanding smelling salts. 'Just breathe. You'll be fine.'

'Don't fucking patronise me. I'm so not in the mood.' But he took a cigarette and bent his head to his lighter. His hand was shaking.

'Were they mean to you?'

'Just fuck off.'

'No, seriously. Were they? They were fine with me.' A little too fine, actually – the thought of Kerr's slowed-down sympathy still twisted my stomach – but that was none of Leon's business.

'No, they weren't *mean*. They don't have to be. They're *detectives*. They're scary no matter what.'

'They were totally considerate to me,' Susanna said. 'They gave me a ring in advance and everything, to check what time I'd have the kids out of the way. What did they ask you?'

Leon threw my smoke packet back to me. 'What Dominic was like. How I got on with him. How everyone else got on with him. How much he was over here. Stuff like that.'

'Me too. What did you say?'

Leon shrugged. 'I said he was around every now and then, he was your typical loud rich rugby-head, but I don't remember a lot about him because I basically didn't give a fuck about him. He was Toby's friend, not mine.'

'He wasn't my *friend*,' I said.

'Well, he definitely wasn't mine. The only reason we knew him was through you.'

'It's not like Dominic Ganly would've normally hung out with the likes of me and Leon,' Susanna said. 'God forbid.'

'He wasn't my bloody *friend*. He was a guy I knew. Why does everyone keep—'

'Is that what you said to the cops?'

'Yeah. Basically.'

An approving nod. 'Smart.'

What? 'It's not *smart*. It's *true*.'

'I'm just going to keep saying I don't remember anything about anything, ever,' Leon said. He was smoking his cigarette fast, in short sharp drags. 'I don't care; they can't prove I do. The less we give them, the better. They're looking to pin it on someone, and I'd rather it wasn't me, thanks very much.'

'What the fuck have you been watching?' I wanted to know. The coffee and the cigarette were helping my headache and my fatigue and the overall sense of low-level prickling unease, but not a lot. ' "Pin it on someone" – pin *what*? They don't even know what happened to him.'

'On the news they said "treating the death as suspicious". And "anyone with any information, contact the Guards".'

'It is suspicious,' Susanna said. She didn't look particularly worried about it: comfortably cross-legged, hands wrapped around her coffee cup, face tilted to the sky as if it were a beautiful day. 'He was down a bloody *tree*. That doesn't mean he was murdered. It just means they want to find out how he got there.'

'They told me they think he was murdered,' Leon said.

'Course they did. They wanted to see what you'd do. Did you freak out?'

'*No*, I didn't *freak out*. I asked them why they thought that.'

'What'd they say?'

'They didn't. Of course. They just asked me if I knew any reason why anyone would want to kill him.'

'And?'

'And I said no. *Obviously*.'

'Did you?' Susanna asked, with mild surprise. 'I said he was kind of upsetting people, that summer. He was a nice guy, but something was obviously going on with him. That could cut either way – it could be a reason why someone would kill him, or a reason why he'd kill himself – but that's Rafferty's problem to figure out, not mine.'

'I told them the same thing,' I said.

Leon threw up his hands. 'Oh, *great*, now they're going to think I was lying—'

'No they're not,' Susanna said. 'They're not stupid. People remember different things; they know that. Did they ask if you remembered the night he went missing?'

'Oh yeah,' Leon said. 'I said no, nuh-uh, nothing. They kept on pushing, they were giving me these worried looks, like that was really suspicious – *Are you sure, come on, you must remember something, think back* . . . Who remembers some random night ten years ago? If I had, *that* would've been suspicious.'

'I said yes,' Susanna said serenely, finding a cigarette. 'I remember it because it wasn't some random night, it was the night Dominic went missing. So afterwards everyone was talking about what they'd been doing – *OhmyGod, I was just sitting in bed texting my BFF and poor poor Dominic was out there feeling so alone, if only I had rung him then maybe blah blah blah* . . . The four of us were here. We had dinner and watched telly, and then Hugo went to bed and the three of us stayed up talking for a while, and then we went to bed around midnight.'

'Wait,' I said. I had just managed to put my finger on something that had been bothering me. 'How come they thought he'd killed himself back then? And now they don't? I mean, if there were good reasons at the time, then why do they think—'

'He sent a text to everyone in his phone, remember?' Susanna said. 'The night he went missing; late, like three or four in the morning. Just saying, "Sorry." You must've got one. I even did – I don't even know why Dominic and I had each other's number, maybe from when I was tutoring him for the French orals? I remember because it woke me up and I had no idea what he was talking about, so I just figured he'd texted the wrong person and went back to sleep.'

I did have some kind of muddled memory of this, or at least I thought I did, not that that was worth very much seeing as I also remembered Dominic's funeral. 'I think I got one,' I said.

'It was a huge deal,' Leon said. 'Who'd got that text and who hadn't. Personally I think about half the people who claimed they'd got one were bullshitting so they could pretend they'd been best buddies with Dominic. Lorcan Mullan? Please. No way did Dominic Ganly even know Lorcan *existed*, never mind have his number.'

'Oh, God,' Susanna said. 'And everyone claiming that as soon as they saw it they just *knew*, they had OMG a total *premonition*! Isabelle Carney was swearing to anyone who'd listen that she saw Dominic standing at the foot of her bed, *glowing*. I like to think that even Dominic would've had better taste than to waste his big apparition moment on an idiot like Isabelle Carney.' She tipped up her coffee cup to get the last of it. 'Now presumably the cops figure, if someone killed him, they sent the text to make everyone think it was suicide. And it worked.'

'But the whole Howth Head thing,' I said. 'Everyone thought that. Where did that come from?'

'They tracked the phone there,' Susanna said. 'That was where the text was sent from, or where the phone last pinged a tower, or something. So everyone just assumed.'

'Which *means*,' Leon said, 'now the cops think he was murdered because if he just killed himself in our tree, God knows why he would do that but if, then how did his phone end up on Howth Head?'

His voice was starting to rise again. 'Chill out,' Susanna said. 'Plenty of ways. He was going to jump off Howth Head, but then he couldn't go through with it, so he threw the phone away and came back here and did whatever in the tree—'

'Why here?'

She shrugged. 'Because here has more privacy than his place did, maybe. How would I know? Or else he never went to Howth at all, he just killed himself here – or OD'd or whatever – and then someone freaked out and did the phone thing so it wouldn't be connected to them—'

'Oh, great. Even if they do think that – which they won't, because they're *cops*, it's not their job to think up innocent explanations – but *if.* They're going to think it had to be one of us. What with it being *our garden.*'

'No they're not. If Dominic could get into the garden, then he could bring along someone else. Who could have watched him OD, or fall into the tree, or whatever, and then freaked out. Or who could've killed him, if you want to go that way.'

Leon dragged his hands over his face. 'Fucking hell,' he said.

'How *did* he get into the garden?' I wanted to know. 'Because the wall, I mean, remember the time Jason O'Halloran and that guy from Blackrock got into a fight, at the Halloween party? And Sean and I threw them out? Jason tried to climb over the wall and get back in, but he couldn't do it. And he was a big guy. Even bigger than Dominic.'

'Well, I suppose Dominic could have found a crate or something to stand on, or brought something along. But . . .' Susanna drew on her cigarette. Her profile, upturned to the grey sky, was clean and calm as a plaster saint's. 'I'm betting he didn't. Remember how the cops were looking for extra keys to the garden door? And Hugo said there used to be one hanging beside the door, but it went missing? It disappeared sometime that summer. Like, a month or two before Dominic died.'

'How come you didn't say that to the cops when they asked?' I said. 'Or to us?'

'I didn't remember then. Afterwards I went away and thought about it. What you said about Faye? My "weird blond cutter friend"?' Sidelong eyebrow-lift at me. 'That reminded me. At the beginning of that summer, I used to sneak her in through the garden – I figured the less Hugo knew the better, he didn't need her horrible parents giving him shit, plus I was eighteen so the less adults knew the better in general. By the end of the summer, though, I had to let her in the front, because the key was gone and I didn't want to ask Hugo where he kept the spare.'

'Did you say that to the cops today?' Leon asked.

'Course.' Susanna put out her cigarette on the step and tucked the butt back into the packet. 'I couldn't give them an exact date, obviously, but still, they were very interested. Who knows; maybe Dominic was making plans.'

'Oh, God,' Leon said, doubling over like his stomach hurt. 'I really, really want that spliff. Have either of you got any?'

'No,' Susanna said. 'And neither will you, if you're smart. Rafferty and his pals are going to be asking around about us. Possibly keeping an eye on us.'

'So what?' I wanted to know. 'You've been going on about how they don't have any reason to think we did anything—'

'They don't. So don't give them one. You especially.'

'What? Why me?'

'Because you're the one who knew Dominic. If they get it into their heads that he came here to meet someone, who do you think they're going to be looking into?' And when I rolled my eyes to the sky: 'I know you're all "Oh, the Guards are our friends, if you haven't done anything wrong then you've got nothing to worry about." But just for now, it might be a good idea to pretend that's not necessarily true. Just be boring for a while.'

'That's all right for you,' Leon said bitchily. 'Some of us have more to our lives than kiddies and nightmares and—'

'And that's the other thing,' Susanna said. 'Don't say anything over the phone that you don't want the cops hearing. Our phones could be tapped.'

'Oh for God's *sake*,' I said.

'Hang on,' Leon said, head snapping around. '*That's* why you wouldn't talk to me last night? And you're telling *me* to stop being paranoid?'

'They probably aren't. But better safe than sorry.' I realised, with a small shock, that on some level Susanna was enjoying herself. Back in school, she had always been the smart one, the one who aced every exam effortlessly while I cruised happily along with my string of B's and Leon didn't seem to care one way or another, the one for whom teachers kept predicting great things. I had never thought much about it, except to cheerfully congratulate her when she did something impressive and to raise a mental eyebrow when she ditched the big PhD plans for a life of nappies and snot; but it occurred to me all of a sudden that that ferocious intelligence of hers had probably been craving a challenge for years.

'Shit,' Leon said, suddenly whispering and wide-eyed. 'What about the house? They could've planted anything, while they were searching—'

I snorted. Susanna shook her head. 'Nah. Apparently it's a lot easier to get a warrant to tap someone's phone than to bug someone's house. They'd need something solid on us, which of course they don't have.'

'How do you know this stuff?' I asked.

'The miracle of the internet.'

'Remember last month?' Leon said, pressing his fingers into his eyes like they hurt. 'I'd just got into town, and the whole mob was over for lunch, and we were sitting out here freaking out about Hugo? Here we thought we had problems then.'

'We don't have problems,' Susanna said. 'Not any more than we had then, anyway.'

Leon buried his face in his hands and started to laugh. There was a hysterical note to it.

'Oh, get a grip. So detectives talked to you. The world didn't collapse. And then they went away.'

'They'll come back.'

'Maybe. And unless you say something incredibly thick, they'll go away again.'

Leon wiped his hands over his face. He had stopped laughing. 'I want to go home,' he said. 'Give me a lift.'

'In a bit, yeah.' Susanna stood up and brushed off the seat of her jeans. 'Come on. Let's go replant that stuff.'

•

'They'll come back,' Leon had said; except they didn't, and I didn't know what to think about that. I was constantly waiting for them, braced and listening for the knock at the door, and it made it impossible to sink back into our gentle green underwater world. There was something off about the sounds in the house: too loud, naked and raw, as if the windows had thinned and every bird-chirp or gust of wind or clatter of the neighbours' bin was right inside with us, making me jump – I had gone back to shying like a wild horse at unexpected sounds. For a bad couple of days I was sure my hearing was going weird, before I realised: the acoustics of the garden had changed, wind and sounds barrelling unchecked through the space where the wych elm had been, across the flat expanse of mud.

They didn't come back but they didn't feel gone. We kept finding their spoor everywhere, pans stacked wrong in the kitchen cupboards, clothes misfolded, bottles changed around in the bathroom cabinet. It was like having some hidden interloper in the house, a goblin behind the skirting board or a sunken-eyed intruder crouched in the attic, sneaking out to wander the house eating our food and washing in our bathroom while we slept.

Three days, four, five: no Rafferty on the doorstep, no phone call, nothing on the news even. The reporters had moved on; the flurry of messages on the alumni Facebook group (*Jesus what's the story there, I thought he went off howth head??? . . . Guys just so you know a couple of detectives called round to talk to me, don't know what's going on but they were asking all sorts about Dom . . . RIP buddy I'll never forget that third try against Clongowes good times . . . What's the story on the garden where he was found whose house is it?*) had died down or gone offline. 'Maybe the trail's gone cold,' Leon said hopefully. 'Or whatever they call it. They've put it on the back burner.'

'You mean they've ditched the whole thing,' I said. 'Too difficult, let's go work on something we can actually solve so we'll look good to our boss.'

'Or,' Susanna said, slicing open a huge bouquet of ragamuffiny crimson ranunculus flowers – we were in the kitchen; Hugo was napping – 'that's what they want people to think.'

'Oh my God, you're a little fucking ray of sunshine,' Leon snapped. 'Do you know that?'

'Just saying. Ignore me if you want.' She spread out the flowers on the counter. 'Who brought these?'

'Some woman in a red hat,' I said. 'Julia Something.'

'Juliana Dunne? Tall, with dark curly hair? I think she and Hugo had a thing going for a while, back when we were kids.'

'They did not,' Leon said. He was sitting on a countertop, picking at a bowl of nuts and swinging one heel against a cupboard door. I wanted to tell him to stop, but in this mood it would only have made him worse.

'They totally did. They had this huge fight, one time when we were like fourteen – well, Hugo didn't fight exactly, because Hugo, but he actually raised his voice, and Juliana was yelling, and then she stormed out and slammed the door. That's a couple fight.' To me: 'Remember that?'

'Not really,' I said. The whole thing sounded unlikely. I had a paranoid moment of wondering if Susanna was making it up to fuck with my head.

She rolled her eyes, slicing stems. 'Oh, you. I swear by the next *week* you'd forgotten it ever happened. Typical: anything you feel bad about just falls straight out of your head. We were up in Leon's room, and they were in the hall? And we commando-crawled out onto the landing to eavesdrop? And then Juliana slammed out and we were holding our breaths, waiting for Hugo to go, but he looked up and snapped, "I hope the three of you have had your entertainment for the day," and then he went back into the kitchen and banged the door. And we were so ashamed of ourselves we stayed upstairs for the rest of the evening, and all we had for dinner was this Mars bar Leon had stashed somewhere. You seriously don't remember that?'

'I don't,' Leon said flatly, rummaging through the nut bowl.

'Maybe,' I said. It did sound sort of familiar, the more I thought about it – dust from the landing rug tickling my nose, Susanna's quick breathing next to my ear; the three of us, afterwards, sitting on Leon's floor staring guiltily at each other— 'I guess so. Sort of.'

'Huh,' Susanna said. Her glance at me had an unexpected sharp assessment that reminded me unpleasantly of Detective Martin. But before I could say anything she turned away, rapping Leon across the knuckles with a flower – 'Quit doing that, other people like the cashews too, plus it's disgusting' – and they were off into another round of bickering.

Susanna was there because she had taken Hugo to radiotherapy – his last session, which somehow came with a shock of betrayal, the doctors blandly waving goodbye and turning away as the quicksand pulled him under; according to Susanna they had tried to push hospice care, but Hugo had shut that right down. I wasn't sure what Leon was doing there. He was around a lot more these days, bouncing in with sushi just when Hugo and Melissa and I were in the middle of cooking dinner, hovering around the study half the morning tinkering with Hugo's knick-knacks, flopping down on the floor and searching name lists for all of five minutes before popping up like a meerkat with some conversation opener, *OhmyGod did my mother tell you she wants to learn the violin, it's going to be horrendous, I bet the neighbours sue, I'll have to go back to Berlin I don't even care what the police think . . . Toby you know my friend Liam from school, well I ran into him yesterday turns out he's editing this new magazine it'd be the perfect place for a piece on Melissa's shop . . .* There was a feverish, manic quality to it all that made me wonder if he was on something, although uppers seemed like an odd choice in the circumstances. 'He's having a difficult time,' Hugo said, when the door knocker banged yet again and I made some exasperated comment about ignoring him until he went away. 'He's highly strung to begin with, and all this at once . . . He'll be fine in the end. Just bear with him meanwhile.'

Which was more or less what Susanna said, too, except in less comforting terms. She and I were in the kitchen, cleaning up after Sunday lunch – which was getting more of a lunatic vibe every time: no one had managed to come up with new theories to replace the Civil War informer and the Celtic boundary sacrifice, or at least not theories that they liked enough to share, so everyone was putting a lot of energy into pretending the whole thing had never happened. To make sure there was never a second of tricky silence, my dad and all the uncles were laboriously dredging up childhood-escapade memories, and everyone else was laughing too hard. Leon sounded like something out of a monkey house; the reason I was doing clean-up was because I couldn't stand being in the room with him any longer. 'I thought you told Leon not to do drugs for a while,' I said, when another frenetic whoop filtered through from the living room.

'He's not.' Susanna was covering leftovers, with one eye on Zach and Sallie, who were happily digging a trench in the battlefield out back.

'Then what's his excuse?' I was rearranging the fridge, trying to make room. There were a lot of leftovers. No one except Oliver had eaten much.

'He's just tense. And you're not helping. Quit picking on him.'

'I'm not doing anything.'

'Come on. Rolling your eyes every time he opens his mouth—'

I shoved out-of-date cheddar to the back of a shelf. 'He sounds like fucking Whatshername out of *Friends*. He's giving me a headache.'

'Listen,' Susanna said, scooping potatoes into a smaller bowl. 'You want to be careful with Leon. He's scared enough of the cops already. You making snide comments about "I hope you keep it together better than this around Rafferty" isn't helping.'

I hadn't thought anyone had overheard that. 'I was joking, for God's sake.'

'I'm not sure he's really in a funny-ha-ha mood.'

'Well, that's his problem.'

That got a flick of her eyebrow, but she said easily enough, 'Sure. But when Leon gets too stressed . . . Remember that time, we were like nine, and he broke that weird old barometer thing my dad had on his desk? And you kept poking at him, *Oh my God, you're in so much trouble, Uncle Phil loves that thing, he's gonna be sooo mad*— Remember that?'

I wasn't sure. 'You make me sound like a total little shit. I wasn't that bad.'

'Nah, not a little shit. You were only messing; you never worried about getting in trouble – you always talked your way out of it anyway – so I don't think you got that Leon worried about it a lot. By the time my dad got home Leon was in a total panic, and he took one look at my dad and yelled, "Toby ate the mints out of your desk drawer!" Do you seriously not remember?'

I thought I did, sort of, maybe. Leon's open mouth and his hands uselessly scrabbling to piece broken edges together, Susanna picking fragments of glass out of the rug, me breathing clouds of extra-strong mint as I watched – except surely I had gone to find glue, I had tried to help, hadn't I? 'Sort of,' I said. 'What happened in the end?'

'You talked your way out of that one, too.' Wry glance over her shoulder. 'Of course. The adorable sheepish grin and "Oh, I was pretending I was you, Uncle Phil, I was going to sit at your desk and write a brief saying it was against the law for my teacher to give homework, but I know you always need to eat lots of mints when you write briefs . . ." And Dad laughed, and then of course he couldn't give out. I have to say, though, you put him in a good enough mood that he didn't actually get too pissed off about the barometer. So it all worked out in the end.'

'So what's your point?' Another screech from the living room, Jesus— 'You think if Leon, if I wind him up, he's going to, what? Sic the *cops* on me?'

Susanna shrugged, deftly ripping clingfilm. 'Well, not on purpose. But he's not thinking straight. If you get him scared and pissed off enough, who knows what he might come out with. So you probably want to bear that in mind, and lay off him. Because you might not be able to talk your way out of that one.'

'Oh come on.' I laughed; she didn't react. 'He wouldn't. This isn't kids with mints; this is real shit. Leon knows that.'

Susanna turned, a bowl in each hand, and gave me a straight look on her way to the fridge. She said, 'You know, Leon doesn't always like you that much.'

What? 'Well,' I said, after a moment. 'That's not my problem, either.'

Susanna's eyebrow went up, but before she could say anything

Tom stuck his head in the door. 'Hey,' he said cheerily. 'Come back in, you have to hear this, your dad was telling us about—' And then, his eyes going past us to the garden: 'Oh Jesus. Su. Look at that.'

Zach was getting up from a full-length fall, or maybe a dive, into their trench. He was grinning and coated from head to toe in muck. Sallie wasn't much better. She pulled a length of muddy hair in front of her face and examined it with interest. 'Mummy!' she yelled. 'We're dirty!'

'Holy shit,' Susanna said. 'That's impressive.'

'How are we going to get them home? The car's going to be—'

'Bath,' Susanna said. 'And there's spare clothes upstairs. We'll have to carry them up, or they'll get muck all over— Kids! Enough dirt for today!'

Zach and Sallie did the predictable bitching and begging, until finally Su and Tom scooped them up at arm's length and lugged them towards the stairs, Sallie giggling and pawing muddy streaks onto Susanna's cheeks while Susanna laughed and tried to dodge, Zach giving me a blank stare over Tom's shoulder and reaching out to swipe a nice set of fingermarks right down the sleeve of my white T-shirt. 'Well *that* looks fun,' Leon said, sliding past them into the kitchen. 'Not. Shit, did I miss cleaning up?'

'Yep.'

'Oopsie.' Fingertips to rounded mouth. He was medium drunk. 'I totally meant to help, I swear. But your dad is a funny, funny fucker. You thought we got up to stuff behind our parents' backs? We were *amateurs*. This one time, right, they dressed up the neighbours' dog as—'

'Yeah, I've heard that one.' My dad actually hated that story, I couldn't remember why. If he was digging it out, he was getting desperate. 'And all the other ones.'

'Ooo,' Leon said, shaking the ice in his glass and giving me a look that, under the drunken glaze, seemed surprisingly sharp. 'Who rattled your cage?'

'I'm just not in the mood.'

'Was Susanna saying things?' And when I didn't answer: 'Because I love her to bits, but OMG, when she wants to she can be *the* biggest headwrecker—'

'No,' I said, and I brushed past him and headed back to the living room to find Melissa and see if she had any ideas about how to make all these people go away.

•

The Sunday lunch, the hours in Hugo's study, the evenings in front of the fire: to a passing glance, Hugo and Melissa and I would have looked like we'd fallen effortlessly back into our routine. Hugo had even got a step farther with Mrs Wozniak's McNamara mystery: he had tracked down the new crop of cousins, one of whom had turned out to have a whole bunch of some ancestor's illegible nineteenth-century diaries that we spent hours trying to decipher, mostly coming up with bitchy rants about stew quality and the guy's mother-in-law. 'Ah,' Hugo said with satisfaction, pulling up his chair to the stack of small battered volumes: yellowed pages, faded ink, brown leather binding rubbed at the edges. 'I'm so much more at home with the old-school stuff. Centimorgans and megabases are all very well, but the software cuts out so many of the irrelevancies, and I *like* the irrelevancies. Give me a good messy old document that needs hours with a fine-tooth comb, and I'm a happy man.'

But it wasn't the same. Hugo was getting worse: not the final downslide, not yet, but it was getting close enough that its form was starting to coalesce, we could see the hulking outline of what it would be when it finally stepped out of the shadows. Melissa and I were doing more and more of the cooking – Hugo couldn't stand for longer than a few minutes, couldn't grip a knife strongly enough to cut anything tougher than butter, we found ourselves tacitly planning meals (stir-fries, risotto) that wouldn't force him to sit at the table sawing clumsily away. When Phil called round they didn't play draughts any more, and it took me longer than it should have to understand why not. There were times when I would become aware that the quiet rhythms of movement from Hugo's side of the study had stopped, and when I glanced up I would see him staring into space, hands limp on his desk. Once I sat watching him like that for fifteen minutes; when I couldn't stand it any longer and said, 'Hugo?' it took me three tries before he finally turned – infinitely slowly, like someone drugged to the eyeballs – and looked at me with the same incurious, affectless gaze he would have given to a chair or a mug. Finally something switched on in his eyes, he blinked and said, 'Yes? Did you find something?' and I came up with some babble, and gradually he found his way back. There were mornings when he came down in the same clothes he had been wearing the day before, crumpled into deep slept-in creases. When one evening I suggested tentatively that maybe I could help him change, he snapped, 'Do you think I'm a fool?' and the glare he hit me with – a blast of pure undisguised disgust – shocked me so badly that I stammered something incoherent and buried my face in my book. The excruciating silence went on for what felt like forever before I heard his steps dragging out of the room and up the stairs. I was half afraid to go downstairs the next morning, but he turned from the cooker and smiled as if nothing had happened.

It wasn't just Hugo. Around him, Melissa was her usual happy self (and even now he never turned on her, with her his voice was always gentle, to the point where I actually found myself getting absurdly jealous); but when my family came over she went quiet, smiling in a corner with watchful eyes. Even when it was just the two of us, there was a subtle penumbra of withdrawal to her. I knew something was bothering her, and I did try to draw it out of her, a couple of times, maybe not as hard as I might have: I wasn't really in the right form for complex emotional negotiations myself. I was still hitting the Xanax every night and now occasionally during the day, which at this point made it hard to be sure whether my array of resurfacing fuckups – brain fog, smelling disinfectant and blood at improbable moments, a bunch of other predictable stuff way too tedious to go into – was cause or effect, although obviously I had a hard time going for the optimistic view. Hugo and Melissa pretended not to notice. The three of us manoeuvred carefully around one another, as though there was something hidden somewhere in the house (landmine, suicide vest) that at the wrong footfall might blow us all to smithereens.

Even though I knew it made no sense, I blamed the detectives. They had ripped through the place like a tornado, questioned us as if we were criminals, thrown us out into the street, all that stress had clearly fucked with my head and it had to have given Hugo a hard shove towards that downslide; they had wandered off and left us with a variety of pretty disturbing questions that they clearly had no intention of bothering their arses to answer; when you came down to it, we had been doing fine before they came, and now we weren't. They had done something, as yet unclear, to the foundations, and now the whole structure was creaking and twisting around us and all we could do was brace and wait.

•

A week, ten days, and nothing. And then one evening – a cold, gusty evening, Halloween weather, torn leaves tumbling against the windowpanes and thin clouds scudding across a thin moon – there was a knock at the door. I was in the living room, in front of the fire, reading an old Gerald Durrell book that I'd found on a shelf and discovered I could actually follow, since there wasn't much in the way of plot arc. Melissa was at some trade fair; Hugo had gone to bed straight after dinner. I put down my book and went to the door before whoever it was woke him up.

A torrent of wind hurled itself in and down the hall, knocking something off the kitchen table with a clatter. Detective Martin was on the doorstep, bundled and blowing, shoulders hunched.

'Jaysus,' he said, his face brightening at the sight of me. 'The man himself. You're a hard man to find, Toby, d'you know that?'

'Oh,' I said. It had taken me a moment to recognise him. 'Sorry. It's my uncle's house – he's sick, I'm staying here to—'

'Ah, yeah, I know that bit. I'm talking about the road. I'm after spending half the evening going in circles looking for it – and my car's in the shop. I've frozen the knackers off meself.'

'Do you want to come in?'

'Ah, beautiful,' said Martin, heartfelt, heading past me, cold striking off him. 'I was hoping you'd say that. Just for a few minutes, thaw out a bit before I head back out into that. In here, yeah?'

He was already halfway into the living room. 'Can I get you something to drink?' I asked.

I was about to offer tea or coffee, but he said cheerfully –

shouldering off his coat, nodding at my glass of whiskey on the coffee table – 'I'll join you, yeah, if you've got any to spare. Might as well get a silver lining out of the car being down.'

I went to the kitchen and found another glass. My mind was spinning – *I know that bit*? how had he known that bit? and what was he doing here, anyway? 'Lovely gaff,' Martin said, when I got back; he had settled into the armchair nearest the fire and was looking around appreciatively. 'My missus likes everything shiny, know what I mean? Lots of chrome, lots of bright colours, everything put away all nice. It's great, don't get me wrong, but me, if I was a single man' – he patted the arm of the ratty old damask chair – 'I'd be living like this. Or as near as I could get, on my salary.'

I laughed automatically, handing him the glass. He lifted it. 'Cheers.'

'Cheers,' I said, sitting down on the edge of the sofa and reaching for my own glass.

Martin threw back a big gulp and blew out air. 'Ahhh. That's a gorgeous whiskey, that is. Your uncle's a man of taste.' He had put on a little weight since spring, and cut his hair closer. Ruddy from the cold, legs stretched out to the fire, he looked right at home, some prosperous burgher relaxing after a hard day's work. I hoped fervently that Hugo wouldn't pick this moment to wake up and wander downstairs. 'How've you been keeping?'

'OK. I've been taking some time out to look after my uncle.'

'Nice of your boss, giving you the time off. He's a sound man. Fond of you.'

'It's not for long,' I said, idiotically.

He nodded. 'Sorry to hear that. How's the uncle doing?'

'As good as he can be, I guess. He's . . .' The unstrung hands, the void before something behind his eyes came back and found me. The word I was looking for was *diminishing*, but I couldn't find it and wouldn't have used it anyway. 'He's tired.'

Martin nodded sympathetically. 'My granddad went the same way. It's tough, the watching and waiting. It's a bastard. The only thing I can tell you is, he never had any pain. Just got weaker and weaker, till one morning he collapsed and' – one soft snap of his fingers – 'just like that. I know that's not a lot of comfort, man. But compared to what we were afraid of . . . It could've been a lot worse.'

'Thanks,' I said. 'We're just taking it day by day.'

'That's all you can do. Come here, before I forget' – groping inside his coat, slung casually over the arm of the chair – 'here's what I came for.' He pulled out a twisted plastic bag and leaned across, with a grunt, to hand it to me.

Inside was Melissa's cast-iron candlestick. It felt heavier than I remembered, colder and less easy in my hand, as if it were made of some different and unfamiliar substance. I almost asked him if he was sure he had the right one.

'Sorry for the delay,' Martin said, rearranging himself in the armchair and taking another swig of whiskey. 'The Tech Bureau's always backlogged, and something like this – no one died, no suspects on the radar – it's not going to get priority.'

'Right,' I said. 'Did they . . . ? I mean, am I allowed to ask? Did they find anything on it?'

'Ask away; sure, if it's not your business, whose is it? No prints; you were right about the gloves. Plenty of blood and a few bits of skin and hair, but it was all yours – don't worry, I had the Bureau give that a good wash.' A small fierce pulse twitched through my scar. I caught myself before I put my hand up to it.

'Thanks,' I said.

'I want to reassure you here, man. This doesn't mean we're giving up. Nothing like that. Me, doesn't matter how long it takes, I clear my cases. New leads come in all the time. And it's not like these fellas were criminal masterminds.' He grinned, a big hard confident grin. 'Don't you worry: we'll get them.'

'Yeah,' I said. 'That's good.'

'You all right there? Didn't mean to open up a can of worms.'

He was watching me over the glass, apparently casually, but I caught the glint of alertness. 'Fine,' I said. I wrapped the candlestick back up in the bag and put it on the floor beside me. 'Thanks again.'

'I wasn't sure whether to bring it back now, or leave it for a while. You've had a rough enough couple of weeks as it is.' And when I glanced up sharply: 'What with the . . .' He tilted his head towards the back of the house, the garden.

'Oh,' I said. 'Yeah.' I supposed it made sense, that he would know about Dominic; it fit with my vague ideas about detectives, shouting salty accounts of their day at each other across desks heaped with coffee mugs and illegible paperwork.

'Last thing you needed, I'd say. A shock like that.'

'It's been weird, all right.'

Martin pointed a finger at me like I'd said something insightful. 'No shit, Toby. *Weird* is the word. Inside, what, five months? you're burglarised, you're nearly killed, and a skeleton turns up in your back garden? What are the odds?'

'The burglary and nearly getting killed were part of the same thing,' I said, more sharply than I meant to. 'Not two separate things. And the skeleton wasn't in my garden.'

To my surprise, Martin leaned back in the chair and laughed. 'You're in a lot better nick than you were,' he said. 'Aren't you?'

For some reason I felt like I shouldn't admit it. Bloody Susanna, with her dark hints about The Man being against us; I'd rolled my eyes, but some of it must have seeped in. 'I'm doing OK,' I said.

'Good good' – heartily, slapping the arm of the chair – 'I'm only delighted. Still, but: you see where I'm coming from, right, Toby? If you were some skobe from down the flats, this'd be all in a day's work to you: burglary, assault, dead body, that'd be just your average year. A decent young fella like yourself, but, never been near the cops before except for those speeding tickets' – why would he have bothered finding out about my speeding tickets? years back, but I still felt a rush of guilt, snared! – 'that's a different story. It could be a massive coincidence, all right. But I've got to ask myself: what if it's not?'

After a moment where I stared at him, with no idea what to say to this: 'You're the one who said it, Toby. You hit the nail on the head there. It's weird.'

'Wait,' I said. There was a strange sensation going on inside my head, like the vertiginous zoom of going through a tunnel too fast, too close to the walls— 'You think— Wait. You think someone, someone killed Dominic—'

'That's the way the lads're thinking at the moment. Nothing definite, yet, so that could change, but that's what they're looking at for now.'

'—and then the, the, the person, they came after me?'

Martin swirled his whiskey and watched me.

'But. I mean, *why*? Ten years later? And why would they anyway, to begin with, why would they want to—'

'We don't know why Dominic was killed yet,' Martin pointed out reasonably. 'If he was killed. Once we figure that out, we might have a better idea what they would and wouldn't want to do. Any ideas there?'

'No. The other guys, the other detectives, they already asked me about him. I told them everything I can remember.' That rushing feeling was building. I took a big swig of my whiskey, hoping it would clear my head. It didn't.

'Anything you were both involved in that might've upset someone?'

'Like what?'

Shrug. 'Giving the class loser a bit of hassle, maybe. We've all done it, sure: only messing, no real harm in it. But that type tends to hold a grudge, get obsessive . . .'

'I wasn't like that. I didn't bully people.'

'Dominic did?'

'A bit. Sometimes. No worse than a lot of other guys.'

'Mm.' Martin considered that, rearranging his legs at a better angle to the fire. 'How about drugs?'

'Like what?'

'Like a deal that went bad, say. Or someone got into the hard stuff, or had a bad trip or an OD, and blamed the two of ye for it.'

'No,' I said. 'I never sold anything. And there was never—' This didn't feel like a conversation I wanted to have with a detective. 'Nothing like that.'

'Right enough.' Martin lifted his glass to his eye and squinted at the fire through it. 'The other possibility,' he said, 'is revenge.'

'Revenge?' I said, after a second of utter bafflement. 'For what?'

'Rafferty heard you had a few problems with Dominic Ganly.'

'What? No I didn't.' And when he lifted a sceptical eyebrow: 'Who said I did?'

'The lads've been hearing it around,' Martin said, with a vague wave of his hand. 'It's been coming up in the interviews, here and there. One of those things where everyone heard it from someone else, no one's sure where it started.'

'I *never* had problems with Dominic. We weren't best buddies or anything, but we got on *fine*.'

'Fair enough,' Martin said equably. 'Fact is, though, if the Murder lads heard that – true or not – someone else might have heard it too. And believed it.'

'And . . .' I wasn't keeping up here, car-crash pileup of new information jamming my brain— 'And what? Someone thought it was my fault Dominic killed himself? So they came after me?'

'Could've done. Or else they didn't think he killed himself.'

'They thought I *killed* him?'

Martin shrugged, eyes on me.

'That's *crazy*.' And, after a long moment when he said nothing and I couldn't think of a single thing to say: 'No. Their accents, the guys who hit me. They were skangers. Dominic didn't know anyone like that. Definitely no one who would have been close enough to him to want *revenge*. No way.'

'He knew people who could've hired someone.'

'But that's crazy,' I said again. 'Ten years later? Why would they, all of a sudden, how would they even know how to—'

Martin sighed. 'Maybe I've just been in this game too long,' he said. 'I've seen it happen to other fellas: too many years always looking for the link, they start seeing links everywhere. This one guy, yeah? Totally convinced that his murder case in Sallynoggin was connected to a bar fight in Carlow. Would've bet his house on it, like. Hundreds of hours interviewing the shite out of the poor Carlow fuckers, checking alibis, prints, getting warrants for DNA, the lot. All because both cases had a Budweiser baseball cap found nearby. His nickname's still "Bud".'

I couldn't grin back. 'Am I a,' I said. The word felt both too ludicrous and too explosive even to say, a big red cartoon button that at one touch might detonate the whole house. 'Do they think I *did* this? The other detectives?'

Glancing up from the fire, perplexed: 'You mean are you a suspect?'

'I guess. Yeah. Am I?'

'Course you are. If someone killed Ganly, it was someone who had access to this garden. Only a handful of people had access within the time frame. They're all going to be suspects.'

'But,' I said. My heart was pounding horribly, shaking me right through; I was sure he would hear it in my voice. I'd known all that, somewhere in the back of my mind, obviously I'd known, but to hear it said straight out like that— 'But I didn't *do* anything.'

He nodded.

'Do they think I did?'

'Haven't a clue. To be honest with you, I don't think they're that far along. They're just throwing theories around and seeing what sticks; they haven't settled on one yet.'

'Do *you* think I did?'

'Haven't thought about it,' Martin said cheerfully. 'It's not my case; I don't get paid enough to have theories on other people's. I only care if it's got something to do with my burglary-assault.' And when I couldn't stop staring at him: 'Come on, man. If I thought you were a murderer, would I be sitting here drinking your whiskey and having the chats?'

'I don't know.'

He stared back at me. Aggrieved, on a rising note of belligerence: 'Hang on. I'm out in the rain, on my night off, doing you a *favour* ' – he was pointing at the candlestick bag, which I had completely forgotten – 'and you're accusing me of bullshitting you?'

'No,' I said. 'Honestly. Sorry.'

I wasn't entirely sure what I was apologising for, but after another moment of the stare, Martin relented. More gently: 'Two favours, actually. That there' – the candlestick – 'I could've posted that out to you. But I think you're a decent young fella, and you've had a bad enough time the last while. So I figured you deserved a heads-up – off the record, like. If you didn't have any beef with Ganly, then you need to have a good think about why someone would be going around saying you do.'

'I don't know why. I don't even know *who* would—'

But he was shooting his cuff to look at his watch, levering himself out of the chair: 'Jesus, it's later than I thought. I'd better be heading, before the missus decides I've run off with some young one – ah, no, only messing, she knows me better than that. She'll think I've run off to the sunshine, Lanzarote or somewhere. I can't be doing with this weather, it wrecks my head—' Glancing across at me, swinging his coat on: 'What was that?'

'I don't get it. All of it. What's going on.'

Martin stopped patting his pockets and looked at me. 'If you had nothing to do with this,' he said (*if?*), 'then at least one of your family or your mates did. And they're trying to drop you in the shit. And if I was you, I'd be putting all my time into finding out who and why. Like, starting right now.'

•

After he left I spent the next hour or so pacing in circles around the living room – not the awful step-and-drag treadmill, this was fast and jumpy and I wished I could smoke inside. Hugo hadn't come downstairs, and I was praying he would stay asleep and Melissa's trade fair would last a very long time. I needed to think.

You'd assume the part where I was a murder suspect would have been at the top of my agenda, but actually that didn't seem like the most important thing, not now that the initial startle had worn off. After all, Martin had a fair point, anyone who could have got to that tree had to be on the suspect list, and I really doubted I was about to be banged up for murder just because someone had told someone that someone said I had had unspecified problems with Dominic. But gradually the rest of what Martin had said was sinking in, and the more I thought about it the more it seemed obvious, inescapable, vibrating with a truth so vital it pulled like a great magnet: what had happened to Dominic was, had to be, connected somehow to that night.

251

What I couldn't fathom was how. I still couldn't think of any way that either the misguided-revenge thing or the same guys coming back for me would make sense – after all, I had been out cold on the floor, if they had been there to kill me they could have done it easily (my feet shied away from the candlestick, a misshapen lump crouching in its plastic bag). But clearly there was someone out there – presumably the same someone who was trying to drop me in the shit – who knew exactly what the connection was. And, like Martin had said, the list wasn't that long. The mates who could have taken the spare key to the garden door, sometime that summer – I wished I could narrow it down. My cousins. Hugo.

None of them seemed remotely plausible, either as murderers or as Machiavellian frame-up artists. And yet; and yet. More and more clearly it was dawning on me (and Martin must have known, all along) that the old story about the burglars being after my car didn't make sense. I had been out of my apartment all that day and half of that night, my car and my car keys had been right there for the taking; if they had been casing my place, then why would they have waited till I was home?

Those drawers there, they went through those pretty hard. That old camera I'd got for my eighteenth birthday, gone. Photos of long-ago parties.

They had been looking for something that had to do with Dominic's death. The car, the TV, the Xbox, all that had been so much smoke and mirrors – look, just a bog-standard burglary, nothing to see here! They had waited till I was at home so that, if they couldn't find what they were after, they could get it out of me – I didn't want to think about how. Only I had woken up and come out fighting, and everything had gone wrong.

Normally we'd have a fair idea who we're after. This time, nothing's ringing any bells. I'm feeling a bit guilty about that, to be honest with you . . . Martin had known from the start. Not about Dominic, obviously, but that this was no random burglary; those men had come to me not by chance, but by careful design.

It should have felt even more horrifying this way – targeted, stalked, hunted down – but it didn't. If they had come after me specifically, for something I'd done or something I had, then I wasn't just roadkill, not just some object to be mown down because it happened to be in their way: I was real, a person; I had been the crucial factor at the heart of the whole thing, rather than a meaningless irrelevance to be ignored, tossed aside. And if I was a person within all this, then I could do something about it.

My mind was working more clearly than it had in months, a stark crystalline clarity that took my breath away like snowy air. I had forgotten what it was like to think this way.

I could hardly track down the burglars and force them to spill the story, my badass Liam Neeson fantasies notwithstanding. But the other end of the thread, the end that lay somewhere here in the Ivy House: that one I could find, maybe, and follow.

Weather or no weather, I needed a cigarette. I threw on my coat and went out to the terrace. Wind roaring high in the trees, the light from the kitchen throwing the hillocks and valleys of mud into stark, distorted shadow. Leaves scuttling, rain shining on the terrace tiles. My heart was beating high in my throat and for some reason I caught myself grinning.

•

'What's that?' Melissa said, nodding at the plastic bag – later, when she had got in cold-cheeked and windblown, and I had tucked her up on a sofa with blankets and hot chocolate, and I was listening to her trade-fair stories and rummaging through the bag of samples she had brought home.

'Oh,' I said, looking up from what appeared to be a tiny knitted condom. 'It's your candlestick. The one the police took away. That detective, Martin, he brought it back.'

'Why?' Melissa asked sharply.

'They're done with it. The forensic people.'

'Why'd he come himself? Why not post it?'

I didn't want to tell her anything, not yet, not till I had something solid. 'I think he was in the area,' I said.

'What did he want to talk about?'

She was sitting up straight, hot chocolate forgotten. 'He didn't,

253

really,' I said, going back to the sample bag. 'He just dropped it off and left. Is this a leprechaun condom?'

Melissa laughed, relaxing. 'It's a finger puppet, silly! Look, it's got a face, when did you ever see a condom with—'

'I've seen weirder. I bet you can get—'

'It's *wool!*'

With a little zap of panic I spotted the two empty whiskey glasses, which I had of course forgotten to take away, but Melissa either didn't notice them or assumed Hugo and I had had a night-cap together. 'So, kinky leprechauns,' I said. 'What kind of trade fair was this, anyway?'

'Oh, wild. People swinging from hand-blown chandeliers.'

She was happy because I was joking around, and I only realised then just how deeply I had frozen at the first sight of Rafferty and Kerr, just how far I had receded back into some dark echoing space. 'Filling Jacuzzis with organic bilberry-elderflower champagne,' I said. 'I knew it.'

'We're a crazy bunch.'

'Thank God for that,' I said, leaning across to kiss her, 'or you'd never put up with me,' and felt her smile against my mouth.

We went back to poking through the samples so I could take the piss out of the weirder ones, and after a few minutes Hugo came clumping downstairs in his dressing gown, knuckling his eyes, and we made him a hot chocolate and Melissa dug a packet of sustainable oat-based biscuits out of the bag. Neither of us mentioned Martin's visit. The next morning, opening the bin to toss something in, I saw the candlestick: sticking out of the rubbish where it had been shoved deep and hard, plastic bag twisted around it tight as a garrotte.

•

I walked Melissa to work, hung around within earshot while Hugo took his shower, installed him in the study and then told him I was going for a wander around the garden to clear my head. He gave me a vague smile and a wave and turned back to his desk. I wasn't positive he had registered what I had said, or even who I was.

The wind had died down, leaving rumpled drifts of leaves against the walls. The replanted bushes and the stuff Melissa had brought from the garden centre looked disgruntled and out of place; some of them were starting to wither. My mother's sapling leaned at a dispirited angle in a corner, still in its pot– so far no one had worked up the nerve to plant it in that gaping crater. I hadn't taken my Xanax the night before and everything felt jagged and discordant, every branch too savagely outlined against the grey sky, the breeze setting off sharp mechanical rattles among the dead leaves. I put a big oak tree between me and Hugo's study window, and pulled out my phone.

I hadn't held out much hope that I still had a number for Susanna's razor-happy blond friend Faye – I had flirted with her for a while, that summer when she was in and out of the Ivy House, even snogged her a couple of times, but I had carefully backed away when I spotted the crazy – but there it was, somehow, transferred down through all the phones I'd had over the past ten years. I leaned against the tree trunk and dialled. It was like being a teenager with a crush, hands sweating, heart racing through my back against the rough bark, praying she hadn't changed her number.

'Hello?'

'Faye?' Warm but diffident, just enough pleasure without eagerness: 'It's Toby, Toby Hennessy. Susanna's cousin. I don't know if you remember me—'

'Course I do. Toby. Wow. Hi.' Friendly, but with distance. I couldn't tell whether my name had come up on her phone or whether I'd been deleted along the way.

'It's been a while. How're you doing?'

'Great, yeah. Everything's good. How've you been?'

She sounded a whole lot more together than I remembered. In the background, a phone ringing, a man's brisk voice reeling off some business patter: she was at work. 'Yeah, good here, too.' And into the neutral silence that followed: 'I'm just ringing because – well, I'm pretty sure you know all the stuff that's been going on at my uncle Hugo's house.'

'Pretty much, yeah. I saw bits on the news. And then a couple of detectives came to talk to me about it.'

Not Susanna; the two of them were out of touch, then, which

gave me more leeway. 'Me too. That's actually why I called you. They mentioned they were going to talk to you, and I mean, they're pretty intimidating guys. I didn't like the idea of them giving you hassle. I just wanted to check that you're OK.'

That thawed Faye's voice a notch or two. 'Ah, yeah. It was fine.'

'Are you sure?'

'Really. They weren't intimidating at all. Maybe because I was in France with my parents for most of that September, so it's not like I knew anything about whatever happened. They mostly wanted to know about me spending nights at your uncle's house, do you remember that? I wasn't getting on with my parents, and when we fought I'd sneak out my window and come over?'

'Oh, yeah. I remember.' Putting a touch of amused tenderness in my voice. 'And we'd all stay up half the night talking, and be late to our jobs in the morning. It was worth it.'

She laughed, a little. 'Yeah. Well. The detectives, I guess they're interested in the key to the garden door? That went missing that summer? They wanted to know how Susanna would let me in; when I had to start coming in the front.'

'They asked me all that stuff, too. I haven't got a clue. I felt like a total idiot. Did you remember?'

'Sort of. I know the key went missing at a party, because Susanna tried to let me in the day after and she couldn't, and she was all freaked out – I was like, "Don't worry, some eejit probably just took it for a laugh," but she was all, "Now we're going to have to change the locks, except Hugo won't get around to it and whoever it was will be able to wander in whenever he feels like it . . ." I don't have a clue when the party was, though, so I'm not sure how much help I was.'

'More than me, anyway,' I said, with a rueful grin. I couldn't believe how light I sounded, how at ease; I felt like some ice-cool private investigator. 'I think I was a complete waste of their time. No wonder they got kind of stroppy with me. I'm glad they were nice to you.'

'Oh, no! Are you all right? And Susanna?'

Faye had always been sweet, flaky but sweet, unlikely to ask about your problems but deeply concerned about them if you reminded her they existed. 'More or less,' I said. 'I mean, it's a bit of a headwrecker, obviously, thinking about Dominic being there all this time. And we'd love to know why he ended up there, of all the places in the world.'

'It's beautiful, that garden. A really peaceful place. I can understand that part.'

No hesitation, no uncertainty: she still took for granted it had been suicide. The detectives hadn't said anything to her about murder. They had saved that for us, which wasn't reassuring. 'Jesus, all the same,' I said. 'Poor Dominic. Whatever was going on in his head, I wish he'd found a better way to deal with it. He was a good guy.' And waited.

A small pause. 'You think?'

I wondered if Dominic had hooked up with her and then dumped her – she had been pretty, in a fragile skittery way, wide blue eyes that could barely hold yours for a moment before her head ducked away with a delicate flick that I had found very sexy. Or— 'Well, yeah. I mean, he wasn't a saint, but I don't remember having any problems with him.'

'No, I know you guys were friends. Just, I thought . . .'

'What?'

'Never mind. It's been so long, I've probably got it all mixed up.'

What? 'Look,' I said – quieter, little bit unsure, little bit vulnerable. 'I should probably tell you something. I had an accident a couple of months back; I took a pretty bad bang on the head. Ever since then, my memory's not . . . I mean, there's stuff that I should remember, but I don't.'

'Oh, God.' Faye's voice had changed, gone all shocked and compassionate; I had her. 'I'm really sorry. Are you OK?'

'Basically, yeah. The doctors say it'll sort itself out, but till then, it's kind of scary, you know? Just . . . if I'm forgetting something, help me out. Because I really don't – I mean, this isn't the kind of situation where you want to be in the dark. And I'm pretty lost here.'

I threw in all the heartfelt stumbling appeal I could, and it worked. 'I just got the impression Dominic had been a bit of a bastard to your cousins. Is all. And I assumed you wouldn't be happy about it. But I don't know the ins and outs, maybe you—'

'A bastard to my cousins? Like how?' And when she didn't answer: 'Faye, I really need a hand. I don't want to put my foot in it with Susanna or Leon – never mind the detectives. Please.'

'I don't remember the details. Honestly. I had a lot of stuff of my own going on, that year.'

Softening my voice, a note of pain: 'I know you did. I wish I'd been more help. I really wanted to be, but I didn't know how, so I just froze up. Teenage guys are idiots.'

'Ah, no, you were fine. I'm just saying, I should have been paying more attention to Susanna's issues – specially when she was being so kind, letting me come over all the time; it's not like we were best friends or anything, just that your house was closest and your uncle didn't really stick his nose in the way someone's parents would have . . . But I was so wrapped up in my own problems, you know? I just have this vague memory of Dominic giving them hassle. I thought he hit Leon, or something? And Susanna was upset? But like I said, I could have it all wrong—' The male voice in the background, asking some question. 'Toby, I've got to go. Ring me anytime if there's anything else I might know. OK?'

Under all the new composure and cheer and whatever else, she was still the same Faye. She totally meant it, but within half an hour she would have forgotten all about me, which was fine with me. 'I will,' I said. 'Thanks a million, Faye. You're a star – as always. And you sound like you're doing great. It's good to hear.'

'I am, yeah. Thanks. And I hope you feel better soon.'

My hands were shaking so hard that it took me three tries to get my phone into my jeans pocket. I had never done anything like this before. The cunning maverick striking out on his lone enterprise had never been my thing; I had always been happy to drift along in someone else's wake, joining in on whatever looked interesting and leaving the rest alone. It felt strange enough doing this to begin with, but I'd been unprepared for how well I would make it work, or for how good it would feel. And what made it even murkier and more confusing was how much of myself it had brought back: my old ease, my old charm, my old persuasiveness, but transformed in fundamental ways, strange distorted flashes reflected through a dark mirror.

I could have used a Xanax, but I needed my head clear. I lit a cigarette and took a very deep drag instead. A blackbird stopped pecking at the mud and turned one sharp merciless eye on me; I blew a long stream of smoke at it, and it took off in a riot of wings and skimmed away over the wall.

I knew we had thrown a party at the beginning of July, that summer, once the Leaving Cert was done and our parents went off travelling and the three of us moved into Hugo's. There had been one for Leon's birthday, so that had to have been around the third week of August; and there had been another one sometime in September, a last hurrah before everyone went off to college at the beginning of October. That one was too late, if Faye had spent September in France. The first one was too early; we had only just moved in, she wouldn't have had time to start showing up. That left Leon's birthday.

Leon hadn't had a lot of friends to invite, but I was pretty sure a decent handful of my mates and Susanna's had shown up, and probably some people who didn't actually count as any of our mates – everyone knew the Ivy House parties were good ones. Sean and Dec would have been there, whichever of the other guys happened to be around, Susanna's gaggle and likely a few of the cooler girls from her school who fancied bagging a rugby player. And Dominic, I was positive he had been there, for whatever that was worth: Dom laughing, glitter of moonlight and coke in his eyes, Leon in a headlock scrabbling uselessly at his arm, smell of jasmine and happy raucous singing everywhere in the swaying dark, *For he's a jolly good fellow!*

Which was the other thing. What Faye had said about Dominic giving Leon and Susanna hassle: could that possibly be what Martin had been on about? Faye had told Rafferty I wouldn't have been happy about it, Rafferty had translated that into me having some big vendetta against Dominic? It felt like a stretch, but it was the closest I had to something that made sense.

And: assuming Faye hadn't imagined or misinterpreted the whole thing, what exactly had been going on between Dominic and my cousins? I couldn't remember him ever paying much attention to Susanna – Dom hadn't gone for the nerdy type: he had occasionally cracked some dirty joke or tossed out some sexist comment so he could laugh at her Outraged Feminist mode, but he had hardly been the only person who did that. I did remember him giving Leon shit now and then, but again, it had been routine shit, the kind Leon had been taking from plenty of people ever since we were about twelve – fag jokes, lisps and limp wrists; when I happened to be around I had told the guys to back off, but it hadn't seemed like a particularly big deal. Given the state Dominic had been in that summer, though, who knew: could he have ramped things up a level or two? Although surely Leon would have told me, surely I couldn't have missed or forgotten that—

I wasn't about to ask either Susanna or Leon the story. Martin's visit had shifted, very subtly, the way I thought about them, about our positions on this new surreal chessboard where we had somehow found ourselves; even though I knew that was probably exactly what Martin had been aiming for, I couldn't help it. Instead I rang Sean and asked him when would suit him and Dec to come over.

•

They came the next evening, which moved me more than I could have told them even if I had wanted to. I got the message across by giving Sean shit for having gained a few pounds and giving Dec shit about Jenna – 'Man, there's what, half a million women in Dublin? At least one of them has to be single and sane, but no—'

'And have low standards,' Sean pointed out.

'There's that.'

'What are you on about?' Dec demanded, injured. 'I'm employed and I've got all my hair. That's more than a lot of blokes.'

'You're a narky bollix,' I told him. 'I wouldn't put up with you.'

'I'm not a— Melissa. Honestly, now. Am I a narky bollix?'

'You're lovely.'

'See?'

260

'What else is she going to say? She's a nice person, you're sitting right there—'

The kitchen table where we had spent so many teenage evenings, loaded now with bright-patterned serving bowls – pasta, salad, Parmesan – and scraped plates and half-full wineglasses, tousled orange flowers and tarnished silver candlesticks. Hugo was laughing, chin propped on his woven fingers, candlelight flickering in his glasses, '—they've always been like this—' aside to Melissa, who was laughing too, sunshiny in a yellow dress. I threaded my fingers through hers on the table and gave her hand a squeeze.

'At least I'm not a fat bastard,' Dec said, to Sean.

Sean stuck out his belly and gave it an affectionate pat. 'All muscle.'

'Jesus, dude,' I said. 'You'd want to get on to that or you won't fit into your wedding dress.'

'He won't fit into the wedding *photos*—'

They had brought Hugo presents, the same way they had brought me presents in the hospital: fancy chocolates, books, DVDs, Armagnac – even I had forgotten that he liked Armagnac, but Dec had a long story about how when we were fifteen we had raided the booze cupboard and practically killed ourselves on swig after massive swig of it, no one willing to be the one who backed out: 'Toby looked like he was about to explode, bright red, tears coming out – I called him a big pussy-boy, excuse the language, and went for it, right? next thing I know the room's actually going round, I thought I was having a brain haemorrhage— I know you knew, Hugo, the three of us were gee-eyed, but fair play to you, you never said a word—'

'Well,' Hugo said, smiling, leaning sideways to fumble the bottle out of the present bag, 'now you can have all the Armagnac you like, and enjoy it properly. Toby, would you fetch glasses?'

Sean and Dec got up with me, to clear the table. 'The garden's in bits,' I said, nodding towards the doors as I passed. 'We've been trying to put stuff back in, but I think we might actually be making it worse.'

'It'll grow back,' Sean said. 'A load of grass seed, bunch of wildflower seeds . . .'

We hadn't mentioned Dominic all evening. Sean and Dec had stayed far from it: asked Hugo about how he was feeling and how his treatment was going, told funny stories about work, Sean had pulled up phone snaps of his and Audrey's engagement party ('Oh my goodness, look at her, all grown up, I'm still picturing a little slip of a thing with braces . . .'). I had been biting my tongue hard, twitching with impatience for the right moment, and I couldn't afford to wait any longer: for all I knew Sean and Dec were planning on leaving right after the Armagnac. 'That hole there,' I said. 'That was the tree where . . . That big elm, remember?'

Dec paused, with a handful of plates, to look out. 'Sort of. The detectives asked me that. Someone told them I'd been up there, at a party? Singing "Wonderwall"?'

'Probably Susanna,' I said.

'Tell her thanks a bunch from me. I remember being up a tree singing, all right – Jesus, I must've been fluthered – but I'm not an arborist, know what I mean? It could've been an elm or an oak or a bleeding Christmas tree for all I know.'

'I think that must've been Leon's birthday,' I said – I had no idea whether that was true or not. 'The detectives went on about it a lot. They wanted to know who was there.'

'I don't think I've ever had Armagnac,' Melissa said, leaning towards Hugo to examine the bottle. 'What's it like?'

'I'll tell you what it's like,' Sean said, over his shoulder from the sink. 'It's like a gorgeous woman, right? absolute stunner? who has a black belt in karate. If you treat her right, she'll make you feel like you're the king of the world. But if you don't give her proper respect, she'll kick seven shades of shite out of you. I can still feel the hangover.'

Hugo was laughing. 'If you've had cognac,' he said to Melissa, 'it's a bit like that, only richer; earthier. It's powerful stuff, all right, if you're fifteen and swigging right out of the bottle, but this is a wonderful one; bound to be smooth as butter. These boys don't do things by halves.'

They didn't want to talk about Dominic. 'I was shag-all use to the detectives,' I said. 'I got the feeling they thought I was messing them around, but actually the problem is I haven't got a clue about the party, due to my memory being pretty thoroughly fucked.' In the sudden stillness I gave a small wry shrug, keeping my eyes on the glasses I was putting in front of Hugo, so I wouldn't have to see anyone's face. It made my stomach lurch even to touch on this, it was humiliating and disgusting and unsafe, but now that I had finally found an upside to my fuckedupness I had every intention of milking it for all it was worth. 'Yeah. Probably I should've just told them that, but . . .'

And sure enough, after the smallest flicker of silence: 'That was the one where Audrey's mate Nessa spent half the night crying in the jacks,' Sean said easily. He was rinsing plates, ready for the dishwasher. 'Because she'd snogged Jason O'Halloran a couple of days earlier, and he was blanking her. It wasn't one of the big ones, not a lot of people there – it was like a few days after the Leaving Cert results and the college offers, so everyone was partied out. There was the three of us and your cousins, and Audrey brought Nessa and Lara—'

'Leon had those three emo mates of his,' Dec said, grinning. 'Sitting in a corner playing Dungeons and Dragons or whatever they were at. And a few of Susanna's shower turned up – the little blond one, and the mouthy one with the mad hair?'

'And a few of the lads,' Sean said. 'Dominic was there, all right. And Jason, obviously. And I remember Bren was giving out because Nessa was taking up the jacks, and if Bren was there then I'd say Rocky and Mal were too—'

Melissa had gone quiet, one foot curled under her, eyes dark in the dim light and moving back and forth among us. 'That rings bells, all right,' I said. 'Nessa locking herself in the jacks. And didn't we make Leon a hash cake?'

'Yeah,' Sean said, face lighting up with pleasure – look, we're helping, Toby's getting better before our very eyes! 'It turned out crap, it didn't even look like a cake, but it did the job. One of the emo mates ate like four slices and couldn't stop giggling about the floor tiles.'

Hugo was still fumbling with the bottle, trying to uncork it but his grip kept slipping. Melissa reached out a hand and he passed it to her, with a small tight grimace.

'Hang on, but,' Dec said. 'Why are the cops even asking about that party? That was ages before Dominic went missing.'

'Something about the key to the door in the garden wall, I think,' I said. 'It went missing at the party; they want to know who could've taken it.'

'They asked me about the key, yeah. If I knew where it was kept – they knew I was staying here off and on, the summer before that. Did you tell them?'

'No,' I said. 'It wasn't hidden or anything, though, the key; it was just on a hook by the door. Anyone who went down there would've seen it.'

'I remember it, all right,' Sean said. 'On a big keyring with a black dog on it. Metal.'

'That's the one. I've been going mental trying to remember if I saw anyone with it, at that party, but . . .' I shrugged. 'Yeah. Well.'

Dec and Sean looked at each other. 'I didn't,' Sean said. 'If I'd seen anyone messing with it, I'd've stopped them.'

'Me neither,' Dec said. 'Wasn't that the party where we couldn't even go down that end of the garden? It was all dug up and mucky? Hugo, you were putting something in, rocks—'

Hugo glanced up as if Dec had startled him, but he said readily enough, 'The rock garden, it must have been. I'm sure that was that summer – you three helped me, do you remember?' I did remember that, vaguely, hauling rocks in happy summer sun, chart music bopping from the open windows, Hugo cocking his head, *Maybe a little more to the right, what do you think*— 'It turned out pretty well, in the end.'

'That'll be it,' Dec said. 'Bren tried to go down there, and he tripped over into a hole and got his lovely expensive jeans all mucky, so after that we all stayed up this end. That's why Bren was pissed off about Nessa hogging the jacks: he wanted to take off his jeans and give them a rinse.'

'In the end he did it in here, remember?' Sean said, grinning. 'Waving the jeans like' – stripper whirl, hip-swing – 'and the girls

264

all screaming, and then Rocky and Mal grabbed the jeans off him and threw them up a tree.'

'My goodness,' Hugo said, smiling. 'I missed all the excitement. I had a large stockpile of industrial-strength earplugs, back then. Thank you, my dear—' to Melissa, who had poured the Armagnac and was passing glasses.

'So the cops think, what?' Dec asked. 'Dominic robbed the key and then came back here to do himself in? Or someone else robbed it and brought him here?'

'I don't have a clue what they're thinking,' I said. 'I don't think they even know.'

'At least,' Sean pointed out – taking his seat, brushing water off his hands – 'if they're asking about the key, they think it was someone from outside. They're not thinking one of you guys let him in and killed him. Which is nice.'

That hadn't occurred to me, and while I liked the thought, I had a hard time believing it was quite so simple. 'I don't think anyone killed him,' I said. 'Dominic Ganly, for God's sake. Why would anyone want to?'

That was for Dec: he always loved having something to contradict. He went right for it. 'Seriously? I mean' – pulling his chair up to the table, energised by the prospect of an argument – 'I mean, OK, it's unbelievable to think we know someone who might've possibly been murdered. But seeing as we do, right? seeing as, let's face it, apparently we do, are you really that surprised that it was Dom?'

'You're not?'

'Being really honest,' Dec said, 'no. Nobody wants to speak ill of the dead, or anything. But it's been long enough now that we can probably say it, yeah? Dominic was kind of an arsehole.'

'Come on. We were all kind of arseholes. We were eighteen.'

Dec was shaking his head vigorously, shoving his forelock out of his face. 'Nah nah nah. Not the same way.'

'Dec's right,' Sean said. 'For once. He was a douche.'

'He gave me hassle about my accent every single day. He used to pretend he couldn't understand me.'

'We all gave each other hassle,' I said. 'And nobody understands you anyway.'

'It wasn't funny, man. Not at the time. The whole of first year, I was scared to open my gob if Dominic was around, because I knew he'd have everyone laughing at me. In the end Sean told him to fuck off' – he raised his glass to Sean, who nodded and raised his own – 'and it got better after that, but still. Remember that time in third year, stuff was getting robbed out of the locker room? Dominic spread it around that it was me, because I was a skanger, right, and you know what they're like, I was probably selling the stuff to buy gear . . . People *believed* him. People stopped asking me over to their gaffs, in case I walked out with their Xbox up my jumper.'

'Jesus,' I said. This didn't fit the way I remembered Dominic at all – he hadn't been a saint, or anything, but this kind of dedicated nastiness . . . 'You're sure it was him, who spread that around?'

'Yeah, I am. I called him out on it. He laughed in my face and asked me what I was going to do about it. Which obviously' – Dec was smiling, but not with a lot of humour – 'what with him being twice my size, was nothing.'

I couldn't help wanting to ask again, was he positive, all those years ago, maybe he had got mixed up— I had always taken it for granted that Dominic was just a regular decent guy, but when I got right down to it I wasn't sure why. A few weeks earlier I would have said without a thought that I knew Dominic pretty well; now thinking about him felt like thinking about a stranger, someone I had sat opposite for years on a train to work, without ever having an actual conversation. 'Jesus,' I said again. 'I didn't know.'

'Well, yeah. I didn't want you knowing. The whole thing was humiliating enough, yeah? without you guys feeling like you needed to step in and rescue me.'

'I didn't have a clue either,' Sean said quietly, aside to me. 'I thought it had stopped after I told him to get fucked. No one would've said it to us.'

'I'm not saying this to bitch about Dominic,' Dec said. 'It's not like I'm scarred for life, or anything; I'm not crying into my Armagnac – which is gorgeous, by the way, Hugo, and I'm finally properly ashamed of the way I treated yours back in the day—'

Hugo nodded. He was sipping his drink and watching us quietly; there was something about him and Melissa, the stillness, the eyes moving in shadow, that gave them a strange kind of resemblance. 'I'm saying it because it wasn't just me. There's people, *plenty* of people, who Dominic did a lot worse to. And I'm not saying any of them killed him – I actually don't think anyone killed him, I think the Leaving Cert was the first time in his life that Dom couldn't buy his way or bully his way into getting what he wanted, and he couldn't handle it. I'm only saying: the idea of someone *wanting* to kill him isn't actually that incredible.'

'The way I remember it,' I said, 'I always got on totally fine with him. The only thing is' – I wasn't faking the suck of breath before I could keep going, this wasn't easy – 'I might not remember. And I feel like, I kind of think with everything that's going on, I need to know.'

'I don't remember you ever having any problems with him,' Sean said, stretching to top up glasses. 'I didn't either. Not saying I liked him, but he never did anything to me personally.'

'I thought,' I said. 'I don't know if I'm imagining it, or— Did he give Leon a bit of hassle?'

'Oh yeah,' Dec said. 'Dominic was a prick to Leon; way worse than he was to me. I think he beat the shite out of him a couple of times.'

Hugo moved, a sharp wince, covered it by raising his glass to his mouth. 'Do you remember anything like that?' he asked me.

'No,' I said, a little louder than I should have – not that there had been any accusation in his voice, he had sounded perfectly neutral, but still, the idea that I would have stood by while Leon got beaten up— 'All I ever saw was a bit of slagging, the usual stuff, nothing like—'

'I could have it all wrong,' Dec said. 'I didn't actually see anything. I'm just talking rumours, yeah?'

'What about Susanna?' I asked. 'Dom never picked on her, did he?'

Dec shrugged. 'I don't remember him ever picking on girls. And it's not like he even saw her that much.'

'I think he might've actually tried chatting her up, at one stage,' Sean said, 'but she put the kibosh on that fairly quick. Susanna's sharp.'

'I think,' Hugo said, 'it's time I was going to bed. No' – gently but very firmly, a hand coming down hard on my shoulder as I went to follow him, my mouth opening on some excuse about the jacks – 'not tonight.' And when Sean and Dec stood up: 'No, no, I'm not throwing you out. Stay and talk to Melissa and Toby; they could do with the company, cooped up here with a rickety old man like me.' He gave each of them a brief one-armed hug, smiling into their faces. 'Thank you so much for coming. It's been a wonderful evening, and it's meant the world to me. Good night. Safe home.'

We listened in silence to the slow thud and drag of him going up the stairs – 'Hang on,' I said, lifting a hand, when Dec started to speak – and to the flickers of movement as he got ready for bed: crack of floorboards as he crossed the landing to the toilet, muffled thumps of footsteps back and forth in his room, finally the creak of bedsprings, all so faint that I would barely have heard them if I hadn't known exactly what I was listening for. 'OK,' I said, at last. 'I think he's fine.'

'Did we tire him out?' Dec asked – he had been sitting up straight, alert, eyes going back and forth between me and Melissa, trying to figure out whether to worry. 'Is that why he headed up early?'

'He mostly goes to bed around this time,' Melissa said. 'We keep an ear out, just in case.'

'You didn't do him any damage,' I said. 'He was delighted you were here.'

'We'll come back again,' Sean said. 'Soon.'

I hadn't realised, not really, not till I saw Hugo through their eyes: the painful shuffle, the stoop over his walking stick, the hollows under his cheekbones and the new sharpness of his nose. 'Yeah,' I said. 'That'd be good.'

'Did the doctors say anything?' Dec asked. 'Like, how long they think he's got?'

'A few months, probably. This summer they were saying four to six, so by the end of the year; but he responded really well to the radiotherapy, so maybe a little extra. No guarantees, though. Apparently they made a big deal of that. He could last till spring, or he could have a stroke tomorrow.'

'Jesus,' Dec said softly.

'Yeah.'

'We'll come back,' Sean said again.

'Come here,' Dec said to me, lower, leaning in and glancing at the ceiling as if Hugo might somehow hear him. 'I didn't want to say it before because Hugo was looking a bit iffy, but Dominic was a genuine mega-prick to Leon. It got bad, like. He used to tell people Leon had AIDS, so no one would go near him. And one time, yeah? Dom and a couple of others got Leon in the showers, they stuffed his jocks in his mouth to keep him quiet and tried to shove something up his arse – I heard it was a Coke bottle, and then they were going to make him drink it. I don't know how far they actually got, but . . .' And at the look on my face: 'Do you not remember any of that, no?'

'No,' I said, which was true. This had nothing in common, not only with the Dominic I remembered but with the entire world I remembered; it sounded like something out of a totally different school from mine, or maybe out of some horror-tinged English boarding-school movie with a hard-hitting message about the dark heart of humanity. 'Are you positive you got the real story? I mean, dude, that's some seriously crazy shit. I never saw anything like that in school. Like, nothing within a million *miles* of that. And I love Leon, but he exaggerates like hell.'

Dec was looking at me with a new expression on his face, or more like a lack of expression, so complete it was like a flat rejection. 'School wasn't paradise, man. It wasn't just jolly japes and then everyone has a good laugh together. Sometimes it got hardcore.'

'Come *on*. Not like that. I was there. My memory might be fucked, but it's not that fucked.' I glanced involuntarily at Melissa – I didn't usually swear around her – but she was pinching a piece of candle wax into shapes, eyes down, and didn't look up.

'I'm not saying it's your memory. I'm not even saying you're wrong. School was genuinely never like that, for you. That doesn't mean it wasn't like that for anyone else.'

'I'm not totally oblivious. I'm not *thick*. If this shit had been going on all around me—'

'*Around* you, not in your face. You're not a shithead, you're a good guy, so no one would've tried to get you in on it. And they wouldn't've tried it on you, either; you're not the type that gets picked on. But someone like Leon—'

'Leon is a fucking drama queen. He'll take some tiny little nothing and blow it up into the *apocalypse*. I've seen him do it my whole *life*. I've been *grounded* because he—'

'I didn't hear the Coke bottle thing from Leon,' Dec said. 'I heard it from Eoghan McArdle. He was there, but he was scared to do anything in case they went after him as well, so he legged it. He said he went and got a teacher – maybe he did, I don't know. Eoghan wasn't a drama queen. At all. And he was really shaken up. That's why he said it to me: he knew I was mates with you, so he thought I might've heard what had happened in the end.'

I couldn't say a word. Partly it was outrage, at Dominic and, ludicrously, at Dec – I had liked school a lot, had remembered it with real fondness and an inner grin at all the stuff we had got away with, and now apparently the school I had liked so much had never existed. But overriding that was a much sharper sizzle of excitement, because it was all starting, just barely, to make sense.

'I did try feeling you out about it,' Dec said. 'Delicately, you know what I mean? I thought Leon might've told you. But you didn't seem like you had a clue. So I figured maybe Leon felt the same as me, didn't want anyone knowing – let's be honest, it's not the kind of story you want to share, yeah? So I kept my mouth shut. I figured it should be Leon's call.'

'He should have told me,' I said. My heart was going high and fast in my throat. 'I would've done something.'

'Listen,' Dec said – leaning across the table to catch my eye, pointing his glass at me for emphasis. 'I'm not accusing Leon of anything. OK? We all know he did nothing to Dominic. He's a good guy, Leon. And let's face it, even if he wanted to, it would've been like a chihuahua trying to take out King Kong.'

'I know.'

'I'm just telling you because it's probably a good idea for you to be aware of all that stuff. Yeah? If the detectives come back asking more questions.'

'God, yeah. Thanks, man.' I knew my voice sounded weird, tight and breathless, but that was OK, there were logical reasons for that— 'You didn't say it to them, right?'

'Fuck, no.'

'Good. Like you said, Leon wouldn't . . . So there's no reason to go sending the cops down the wrong track.'

Dec was nodding away. 'Right.'

Leon. Leon desperate not to let the house be sold: a new owner might have decided to cut down the trees, and surprise! Leon wanting to throw the skull away and forget all about it, Leon like a cat on hot bricks about the detectives. Leon, after all that huffing and puffing about having to get back to his job and his boyfriend, still here weeks later: no way to leave while this was still up in the air. Leon with excellent reasons to want Dominic dead. And Leon who would have remembered me taking photos on that camera at his birthday party, who might have had reasons to worry about what was on there—

Sean and Dec and Melissa were all watching me, identical concerned expressions, and I realised what my face must look like. 'I should've known,' I said.

'How?' Sean said. 'Dominic wouldn't have pulled any of that crap when you were around. It's not like you're psychic. I didn't know either.'

Melissa slipped her hand into mine, on the table. 'Or maybe Leon did talk to you,' she said softly, 'and you did make Dominic leave him alone. You might not remember.'

'Yeah,' I said, with a small huff of a laugh. I seriously doubted it. Leon making snide little jabs about how easy I had it. Leon, who would have seen the Dominic thing as a totally valid reason to hold a grudge against me, to nudge the cops in my direction – I had been the one who people actually listened to, I should have done something, should have stood up for him; to someone like Leon, it would make no difference that I hadn't had a clue what was going on.

'True enough. That's some best-case scenario.' She squeezed my hand.

'The memory'll come back,' Sean said. 'Give it time. You seem like you're doing a lot better already.'

'I am.'

'He is,' Melissa said, when Sean glanced at her.

'That thick head came in handy for once,' Dec said.

'That night,' I said, and had to take a breath again. 'The night it happened. That basically got knocked right out of my head, yeah? A lot of it's come back, but there's still big chunks missing. It's been driving me mental.'

'Same as the time I got concussion,' Sean said easily. 'The Gonzaga match, remember? That prop they had, size of a moose; I tackled him and knocked myself out? I played the whole rest of the match, and I don't remember a single thing about it.'

'You,' Dec told me, pointing a finger at me, 'you spent that evening giving me shite about my hair. Because you're a bollix. Your fella, right?' – to Melissa – 'your fella, he notices me admiring this very beautiful woman at the next table. Which should've been fair enough, right? seeing as I was single at the time? But he starts accusing me, at the top of his lungs, of having hair plugs—'

Bit by bit – all to Melissa, as if they were telling the story for her sake, to make her laugh – they reconstructed the evening for me (or at least most of it: they skipped delicately over the brunette giving me the eye, and the work trouble). As they talked, my memory twisted and flicked into life – fitfully, almost playfully, filling in a vivid sweep of images here and just a brushstroke there and then skimming away, leaving behind tantalising patches of shadow and blankness. Sean pointing at Dec, '—where to go for our holiday, and Toby and I are all on for Thailand, but this contrary git here, right? he just has to be different, he keeps banging on about Fiji—' and a flash of me waving my phone at Dec, *Look, look at this, this guy says the beaches in Fiji are covered with wild dogs, you want to get eaten?* I laughed along with Melissa, but every flash went through me like a zap of electricity.

Except – I realised with a slow sinking, as Sean and Dec worked their way through the evening – there was nothing there. I had been hoping for the vital fragment that would bring all the pieces together; instead I was getting a lads' night out, unremarkable in every way except for the cheap filter of hindsight that gave everything a sinister foreshadowing loom. Worse: I'd been so focused on that hope that I'd forgotten to consider what it would do to me, hearing about that night. It felt like they were talking about someone else, someone I had been close to a long time ago; a favourite brother maybe, cocky and laughing and innocent enough to break your heart, at ease with all the world and his place in it, and now lost. The longing to have him back was like a physical force sucking my guts out, leaving me hollow.

The thing that saved me was, weirdly, the fact that I had brought it on myself. The vortexing sensation was as strong and as hideous as ever, but for the first time, it hadn't been slammed into me out of nowhere; I was using it, riding it, for my own reasons. The Leon revelation might not be enough but it was something, a start, and I had pried it out myself. I was running this evening, and it felt good. It had been a long time since I had felt capable of running anything more complex than the microwave.

'So then we poured Dec into a taxi,' Sean said. 'Before he could start telling us he loved us.'

'In your dreams. I'll do it at your wedding, how's that? Just so all your new in-laws can see you welling up like a great big—'

'Who says you're invited?'

'We're your best men, you tool. You want me to do it by Skype?'

'I do, yeah, that'd be great—'

'Did you guys go to Thailand, in the end?' I asked. 'Or Fiji?'

'Nah,' Dec said. 'This big sap' – a nod at Sean – 'wanted to wait for you. I was all on for leaving your sorry arse behind, only—'

'He said he didn't have the dosh,' Sean told me. 'Meaning he wanted to wait for you, only he didn't have the balls to say it. We'll go next year.'

'If Audrey lets you out of the gaff,' Dec said.

'She'll be delighted to see the back of him by then,' I said. 'Probably push him out the door.' I had had a fair bit to drink, what with the wine and the Armagnac. That and the candlelight wrapped the two of them in a deep golden glow, like heroes out of legend, timeless and steadfast. I wanted to reach out across the table and grip their arms, feel the warmth and solidity of them. 'Cheers, guys,' I said instead, raising my glass. 'Thanks. For everything.'

'Ah, Jaysus,' Dec said in disgust. 'Not you too.'

•

'It was good to see them,' Melissa said, when Sean and Dec had left and we were tidying up. It was late, candles burned down to stalagmite stubs, old crooner radio station playing low enough that we would hear Hugo if he called. An unsettled wind was moving around the garden. 'Wasn't it?'

'Huh?' I had been loading the dishwasher, humming along to the music – I should have been fading from booze and fatigue, but instead I felt like I was speeding. Half my mind was working on how to get Leon over to the Ivy House, and what to say to him once I had him. If he was somehow behind all this, a part of me was almost impressed: I wouldn't have thought he had the organisational drive to mastermind something that elaborate. The part I couldn't work out was the timing on the break-in. If he had been after the camera, why not tell his scumbag pals to go in during the day, when I would be out at work and they could hunt for it in peace? Unless the nighttime part had been their own addition, easier to walk out with a big flat-screen in the middle of the night – or unless Leon had actually wanted me to run into them, wanted me shaken up, even beaten up: some bitchy poetic-justice thing, *see how you like it*— 'Oh. Yeah. It was great.'

'Sean's so excited about the wedding, isn't he? He was trying to act all blasé about it, but it's lovely. And Dec's in better form than I thought he'd be, after Jenna.' Melissa had tried very hard to be friends with Jenna, but even she had her limits.

'He's way better off. He knows that, deep down.'

Melissa swept crumbs off the tablecloth into her hand. 'And you had a good time?'

That was twice she'd asked. 'Oh yeah,' I said cheerfully. And when I caught her quick glance: 'What, did it not seem like I was?'

'Oh, yes! Almost all the time. Just . . . all that about Dominic. And Leon.'

'Well,' I said, with a grimace: pained but not upset, everything in perspective. 'Yeah. That was nasty stuff. But it was a long time ago. And I guess you guys were right: I did everything I could. I'm not going to beat myself up over it.'

'Good.' A fleeting smile, but there was still a tiny worried crease between her eyebrows. After a moment she said, picking a blob of candle wax off the tablecloth: 'You were asking Sean and Dec a lot of questions.'

I was lining up glasses in the dishwasher, fast neat rhythm, even my hand-grip felt stronger. 'Was I? I guess.'

'Why?'

'I figured they'd remember Dominic a lot better than I do. Apparently I was right, too.'

'Yes, but why does it matter? Why do you want to know about him?'

'I'd like some clue what's going on,' I said, reasonably enough, I thought. 'Seeing as we've somehow ended up in the middle of it.'

Melissa's eyes came up to meet mine, fast. 'You think they know something about what happened? Sean and Dec?'

'Well, not like that.' I laughed; she didn't. 'But yeah, they might know something that they don't realise means anything. Probably not, but hey, it's worth asking, right?'

'The detectives are doing that.'

'Sure. But they might not tell us what they find out, or they might not find out fast enough. Hugo wants to know; he says he feels like he's got a right. You can see his point.'

She brushed her handful of crumbs into the bin, not looking at me. 'I guess.'

'And there's stuff I might be able to find out that the detectives can't.'

A moment's silence. Then: 'So you're going to keep asking. Trying to find out what happened.'

I shrugged. 'I haven't really thought about it.'

Melissa swept the cloth off the table in one swift neat motion and turned to face me. She said flatly, 'I wish you wouldn't.'

'What?' I hadn't seen this coming. If anything I would have expected her to be all encouragement and support, anything that Hugo wanted, anything that got me amped up and interested— 'Why not?'

'Dominic might have been *murdered*. It's not a game. The detectives are professionals; it's their job. Leave it to them.'

'Baby, it's not Agatha Christie. I'm not going to get stabbed in the library with a letter opener for getting too close to the truth.'

She didn't smile. 'That's not what I'm worried about.'

'Then what?'

'You don't know what you might find out.'

'Well, that's kind of the point.' And when she still didn't smile back: 'Like what?'

'I don't know. But how could it be anything that would make you happy? Toby' – her hands tightening on the tablecloth – 'you've been getting so much better. I know how hard it's been, but you have, and it's wonderful. And now this . . . this seems like something that isn't going to take you good places. Even tonight, that upset you, I could tell . . . The next while isn't going to be easy, with Hugo' – and over me, as I started to speak – 'and that's all right – no, it's not all right, but it just *happened*, we can deal with it. Whatever that takes. But *deliberately* getting yourself into something that you know is going to hurt you, doing it to *yourself* – that's not the same thing, Toby. It's not all right. I really wish you'd just leave it.'

I looked at her, standing there all fragile and earnest in the middle of my uncle's rickety kitchen clutching his worn old tablecloth, tiny reflected candle-flames wavering in the dark French doors behind her. All I could see in my mind was me bringing her the answer to all of this, impaled on my spear and carried high, to be laid at her feet in triumph. The image went through my blood like a tracer shot, like another great big beautiful swig of that Armagnac. All these months of her patience, her loyalty, her stunning and full-hearted and completely unwarranted generosity: this was the only way in the world that I could – not repay it, nothing would do that, but justify it.

'Baby,' I said, leaving the rest of the dishes and going to her. 'It's fine. I swear.'

'Please.'

'I'm not going to wreck my head over it. I'm just interested. And I'd love to get Hugo some answers. I know I'll probably find out bugger-all, but what the hell, you know?'

Melissa looked half convinced, but only half. The radio was playing 'Little Green Apples', Dean Martin's voice turning the happy words somehow mournful and nostalgic, a song for a long dark road far from home; all of a sudden I wanted her close. 'Come here,' I said, taking the tablecloth out of her hands and tossing it back on the table. 'Dance with me.'

After a moment she drew a long breath and her body relaxed against mine. I tightened my arms around her and we swayed in slow circles. Candle-flames fluttering and winking out one by one, wind moving through the invisible treetops with a ceaseless sea-sound and nudging at the door.

We could get married in the garden, a good landscaper would have it knocked into shape inside a week. I knew from Sean that you had to give a few months' notice to get married but Hugo could hang on that long, I knew he would, with that to keep him going, or maybe they had some kind of exemption for emergencies? My mother would cry her way through the whole thing, my father would be smiling for the first time in months; Sean and Dec would gleefully slag the shite out of me, Zach would find a way to smash the wedding cake, Carsten would turn out to be an eight-foot Uncle Fester type who made sombre pronouncements in an incomprehensible accent; Miriam would perform some chakra-based ceremony to guarantee a long and happy marriage and we would all dance till dawn. We could invite the detectives, Martin's missus could disapprove of the decor and Rafferty seemed like the type who would disappear early with someone's exotic second cousin . . . Melissa sighed against my shoulder. I buried my face in her hair.

8

And then, finally, the detectives came back. They came the next morning, while I was fighting with the radiators – the autumn chill had come in hard, Hugo felt the cold badly, all the radiators needed bleeding but of course no one knew where the key was so I was struggling with a wrench and some old towels and I was covered in dust and WD-40. Rafferty and Kerr on the doorstep were ironed and smooth-shaven, spic-and-span and ready to take on the world.

'Morning,' Kerr said cheerfully. 'I'd say you thought we'd abandoned you, yeah? Did you miss us?'

'He's only messing,' Rafferty told me. 'No one ever misses us. We're used to it; doesn't even sting any more.'

'Oh,' I said, after an idiotic pause. 'Come in. My uncle's upstairs working, I'll just—'

'Ah, no,' Rafferty said, wiping his feet on the doormat. 'Leave him to it. We only need a few minutes, sure; we'll be gone before you know it. Will we go into the kitchen?'

I offered them tea or coffee, got them glasses of water instead, washed the dirt off my hands and sat down at the table opposite them while Kerr got out his notebook and Rafferty surveyed the garden (dead leaves everywhere, thin chilly sunlight glittering on scraps of plastic blown in by the night's wind) and bullshitted me about how great it looked with the new plants in. The sight of them had hit me with the old full-body flinch, but this time it hadn't left me paralysed. If they were back, it had to be because they had something new, and if my luck was in and I played this right, they were going to share it.

'Just to confirm,' Rafferty said, once we were all nice and settled. 'We took this away with us the other week, remember? You said it was yours?'

He swiped through his phone and held it out to me: a photo of the old red hoodie, spread out on a white surface beside its paper bag. Someone had attached a labelled tag to it, which felt somehow both sinister and ridiculous.

'It might have been,' I said. 'I mean, I had a red hoodie, but I'm not sure it was exactly—'

'Your cousins both say you had one like this.'

'I guess. Lots of people had red hoodies, though. I can't say for sure if this one was—'

'Hang on,' Rafferty said, taking the phone back. 'This might help.' He swiped again and held out the phone.

Me, sitting among daisies with my back against a tree trunk and a can of something in my hand, smiling up at the camera. I looked so young – slight, floppy-haired, open-faced – I had to close my eyes for a second. I wanted to yell at that guy to run, far and fast, before I caught up with him and it was too late.

'That's you,' Rafferty said. 'Right?'

'Yeah. Where did—'

'About when, would you say?'

'That's the garden here, in summer. It might be the summer after we left school. Where did you get—'

'That'd match the date stamp, all right. See what you're wearing?'

Jeans, white T-shirt under an unzipped red hoodie. 'Yeah.'

'Would you say that's the same hoodie we took with us?'

'I don't know. It could be.'

'Same-shape pockets,' Rafferty pointed out, leaning over to swipe between the two photos. 'Same-width cuffs. Same leather tag on the zip pull. Same little round logo there on the left breast. Same binding at the base of the hood, see inside there? The white with the black stripe?'

'Right,' I said. 'Yeah. It looks like the same one.'

'Not exactly like, though,' Kerr said. 'Spot the difference.'

I already knew I wasn't going to find whatever it was they were talking about. They waited patiently while I swiped back and forth, feeling stupider every second. 'I don't have a clue,' I said finally, handing the phone back to Rafferty.

'No?' He kept it in his hand, turning it deftly like a conjuror's deck. 'No problem. It's only a small thing. I'd say we can go ahead and confirm that that's your hoodie, yeah?'

'I guess,' I said, eventually. 'Probably.'

Kerr wrote that down. 'It's not a trap, man,' Rafferty said, amused. 'We're not going to arrest you for possession of a controlled hoodie. Your cousins were the same way: I don't know, might be his, might not, lot of hoodies out there, have you checked how many of this model were sold in Ireland . . . They're pretty protective of you, aren't they?'

That wasn't the word I would have used, at least not that week. 'I guess so,' I said.

He pointed a finger at me. 'Don't be saying that like it's no big deal. That's a wonderful thing to have. Friends are great, but when the chips are down, it's blood that counts. Look at you, sure, moving in here to look after your uncle when he needs you. That's what it's all about: sticking by your family.'

'I do my best,' I said, moronically.

Rafferty nodded approvingly. 'That's what your cousins say, all right. It means a lot to them, you being here, you know that? They're not surprised, though: they say you've always been pretty protective of them, too.'

That seemed unlikely, at least from Leon, although who knew what he was playing at— 'I suppose. I try.'

'Good man.' With a finger-snap, remembering: 'Speaking of looking after your uncle, I meant to say to you: maybe have a bit of a look at the security in this place, yeah?'

'What? Why?' Flash of animal terror, Martin's hints about revenge, my patio door splintered and gaping open—

'Ah, no, we're not thinking anyone's planning on coming after you.' Kerr snorted. 'But we found a load of other stuff down that tree, as well as the remains. Lots of acorns, hazelnuts – I'd say you've got a few pissed-off squirrels out there, trying to work out what happened to their stash. Half a dozen old lead soldiers, did you have those as a kid?'

'No. I don't think so.' The adrenaline was subsiding, leaving me feeling slightly sick.

'Jesus,' Rafferty said, grinning. 'I'm dating myself. They must've belonged to your dad, then, or one of your uncles – they all remember stashing stuff down there, when they were kids. The soldiers were all together, with a bit of rag round them, might've been a cloth bag before it rotted away; one of the four of them hiding his best stuff from his brothers, looks like. I'll have to find out who to give them back to. There's a bunch of marbles, too. And this. You know what this is?'

The phone again. That same white surface; a long brass key, crusted with bits of dirt and attached to a keyring, along with a black metal silhouette of a German shepherd.

'That's the key to the garden door,' I said, 'or anyway it looks like it. The one that went missing, that summer. It was down inside the tree?'

'It was, yeah,' Rafferty said. 'And it fits the garden door. That's what I'm telling you: your uncle should've changed that lock when the key went missing. If he didn't bother, then who knows how many other keys to the other doors are floating around out there? The last thing he needs right now is a burglary.'

'Right,' I said. 'OK. I'll get on to that.'

'Good idea. Not that I'm complaining; it made our lives a lot easier, being able to check this key against the lock. The interesting part, right?' – leaning forwards, elbows on the table, getting into this – 'the interesting part is where the key was. Dominic's clothes were in tatters – time, mildew, animal and insect activity, they were mostly rags. The key was down near the side of his leg, but there's no way to tell whether it was in his jeans pocket and fell out when the material rotted, or whether it was never in there to begin with. You can see how that makes a difference.'

They both watched me: curious, assessing, waiting to see if I could do it. Kerr had a tiny smirk on his face. 'Of course I can,' I said, too loud: their eyebrows went up. I flattened the bubble of rage and said, enunciating as clearly as I could, 'If the key went into the tree separately from Dominic, then someone else was there when he died – unless he dropped the key by accident, while he was up the tree for some reason, and climbed in to get it. But if it was in Dominic's pocket, then it points towards him getting into the garden and into the tree on his own.'

'Well done,' Rafferty said, smiling.

'Huh,' Kerr said. 'You got there quicker than our fella Scanlan did, the one who thought this was cannibal Satanists, remember? I explained that to him three times, and he still didn't get it.'

You think someone killed Dominic, I'd said to Martin; and he'd said, *That's the way the lads're thinking.* 'So,' I said, 'he could have got in there by himself?'

Rafferty shrugged, one corner of his mouth turning down wryly. 'Just going by the remains, it could go either way. There was a load of muck in there with him, but that could be someone trying to cover him up or it could be just ten years' worth of falling leaves and what-have-you. There's no way to tell whether he went in dead or alive – he hadn't been dead long enough for rigor mortis to set in, or it would've been impossible for anyone to get him into that hole, but that's as much as the pathologist can say. No unhealed injuries to the skeleton: he wasn't beaten to death, if he was shot or stabbed it didn't even nick the bone. Drug overdose is a possibility, specially since you told us about him experimenting – don't worry, you weren't the only one, plenty of his other mates said the same.' A hand going up, reassuring or quelling, although I hadn't opened my mouth. 'And he was in an odd position, down there. Legs bent up, arms jammed in front of him, neck vertebrae curled over like his head was tucked down – as far as we could tell, anyway: there was a bit of slippage, but most things held together OK. It could've been positional asphyxia: someone gets himself into a position where he can't breathe properly – maybe because he was going after the key, like you said, or maybe he's just off his face on something – he can't get out of it, he suffocates. It was a tight space, specially for such a big fella.'

He left a silence, waiting either for me to say something or for those images to get me good and rattled. 'Jesus,' I said obligingly.

'Or,' Rafferty said, 'he could've died by himself, but had a hand getting into the tree. Say he ODs. Whoever he's with – or maybe they're not even with him, they just find him when it's too late – they panic. Scared they're going to get locked up for drugs, blamed for him dying. So they do something stupid – because they're teen-agers, and let's face it, stupid shite is what panicked teenagers do – and they hide the body and hope it all goes away.'

'Eejits,' Kerr said. He was doodling what looked like a county crest on his notepad. 'That's an offence, concealing a body. The statute of limitations probably expired years back, but, and it's a lot less of an offence than murder.'

'If you've got any reason to think it might've gone that way,' Rafferty said – glancing up at me, startling flash of gold – 'any rea-son at all, even an inkling, then you need to tell me now. Today. Because right now, yeah? everyone's got an open mind on what happened here. If someone steps up and explains that what we've got is an OD and a scared kid or two, then we're all ready to take that on board. But if this drags on for a while, and my lads get it fixed in their heads that this was murder? It's going to be a lot harder to convince them that it wasn't.'

He sounded so easy and reasonable, all of us on the same side working it out together, I almost wished I could give him what he was after. 'I don't know,' I said. 'I haven't a clue.'

'You're sure. Because this isn't the time to muck about.'

'I don't. I'm not.'

Rafferty left that for a minute, in case I changed my mind. When I didn't, he sighed regretfully. 'All right. Then, like I said, we've got nothing to say whether it was accident, suicide or murder. Except we also found this. Near his right arm.' He swiped at his phone again and laid it on the table in front of me.

White background, a right-angled ruler in one corner. In the middle was a long, complicated black squiggle. It took me a moment to work out what it was: some kind of cord, tied in a loop at each end.

'What is it?' I asked.

He shrugged. 'No way to know for sure. Any ideas?'

The first thing that sprang to mind was our childhood creations, complicated rigs for shuttling notes and supplies, hours of climbing and arguing and testing and one time a branch had broken and an entire illicit apple tart had landed smack on Susanna's head . . . 'We used to rig up ropes across the garden,' I said, 'when we were kids. Like, to pass stuff between windows and trees and our tent? That could have, maybe that fell down the hole?'

Kerr made a faint noise that could have been a snort, but when I looked over he was doodling away. 'Could have,' Rafferty said, politely. 'Except if this went in there years before Dominic did, you'd expect it to be under him. Not up by his arm. Wouldn't you?'

'Maybe. I guess.'

'I would, anyway. Any other ideas?'

'Maybe . . .' I didn't want to say it but it was inescapable, the two loops— 'I mean, it sounds crazy but handcuffs? Like, someone used that to tie Dominic up? Or he was planning on tying up someone else?'

'Not bad,' Rafferty said – thoughtful, rubbing one ear, cocking his head to examine the photo. 'There's about sixty centimetres of cord between those loops, though. That's not going to restrain any- one too well. Unless—' His head snapping up, eureka, finger pointing at me, *Can you get it?*

'I guess it could've gone around his waist?' I said. 'Or around, like, a tree or something?'

Rafferty sighed ruefully, deflating. 'That's what I was thinking, for a second there. Now that I look at it again, though . . . See the knots? For cuffs, you'd want slipknots, right? So that if he struggled, the cuffs would tighten. Those there, those are poacher's knots. Very secure, won't slide, won't pull undone even on a slippery rope, won't shake loose if they're unloaded, won't lower the rope's breaking point. Someone wanted that cord to take a lot of strain, but they didn't want the loops tightening.'

'It's mad, the things you learn on this job,' Kerr said, leaning in for a look. 'I'd never heard of a poacher's knot before.'

'You need to spend more time on boats,' Rafferty told him, grin- ning. 'I could tie a poacher's knot by the time I was eight. You ever sail, Toby?'

'A bit. My uncle Phil and aunt Louisa, they've got a boat; we used to go out with them when we were kids, but I never really got into it—' I didn't like the feel of this. 'What is that thing?'

'No more guesses?'

'No. I'm all out.'

'Like I said, too early to know for sure. But personally,' Rafferty said, reaching out to delicately adjust the phone so it was exactly parallel to the table edge, 'personally, I think it's a homemade garrotte.'

I stared at him.

'One of the loops goes around each of your palms.' He held up his hands, closed them into fists. 'You cross your arms, like this. And then—' Out of nowhere, fast as a leopard, he lunged sideways behind Kerr, flung a loop of imaginary cord over Kerr's head and jerked his fists apart. Kerr clutched his throat, dropped his jaw, bugged his eyes. The whole thing was so brutal and so astonishing that I sent my chair scudding back from the table, nearly going over sideways, before I could stop myself.

'Then if you can take him down backwards,' Rafferty said – over Kerr's head to me, fists still clenched, arms taut – 'even better. A kick to the back of his knee, or just a good pull' – miming it, Kerr following along – 'and he's going down, his chin's folding over the cord, his whole body weight's added to the pressure. And just like that . . .'

Kerr let his head drop limply, tongue lolling. 'The end,' Rafferty said. He opened his hands and relaxed back into his chair. 'Quick, quiet and effective. The victim can't even shout for help.'

'And no blood,' Kerr said, reaching for his water glass, 'not with a cord that thick. A wire would cut his throat, you're left with a whole mess to clean up, but that cord's just going to block off the air flow. Might take a minute longer, but less hassle in the long run.'

'The best part is,' Rafferty said, 'you don't have to be bigger or stronger than your victim. He could be a horse of a man, but as long as you get the jump on him and you've got half-decent upper-body strength, he's fucked.'

They both smiled at me, across the table. 'Honest to God,'

Rafferty said, 'I'm amazed people aren't garrotting each other every day of the week. It's easy as pie.'

'But,' I said. My heartbeat was going like a woodpecker, high in my throat. 'You don't know for sure that that' – the photo – 'even has anything to do with, with Dominic. It could be from when we were kids. Maybe it got snagged on a, something inside the hole—'

Rafferty considered that, turning the phone between his fingers, frowning at it. 'You think that's likely?'

'Well. It's got to be more likely than a, a *garrotte*. All the stuff you said there, I didn't have a clue about any of that. Most people wouldn't. How would anyone even think of it?'

'True enough,' Rafferty said, nodding. 'Fair point. One problem with it being part of your kiddie games, though.'

Swiping at the phone again, long fingers, easy economical movements. 'See this?'

Me leaning back against that tree trunk, cheerfully grinning away. Rafferty tapped the screen. 'There's a drawstring on your hood. Black, looks like paracord. But here . . .'

Swipe. The hoodie they'd taken away, spread on its white table. 'Notice anything?'

He waited until I said it. 'There's no drawstring.'

'There isn't. And' – swipe: the squiggle of cord – 'black paracord. The length is consistent with a standard hoodie drawstring.'

There was a silence. Something had happened to the air in the kitchen: it felt magnetised, charged, humming with a buzz like a microwave's. It took a few seconds for it to sink in: I had gone from a suspect to the suspect.

Rafferty and Kerr were both looking at me, peaceful expectant looks with no urgency, like they could wait all day to hear whatever fascinating things I had to offer.

I said, 'Do I have to keep talking to you about this?'

'Course you don't,' Rafferty said, surprised. 'You are not obliged to say anything unless you wish to do so, but anything you do say will be taken down in writing and may be given in evidence. You can tell us to bugger off any time you like. Only why would you?'

If you're ever uncomfortable with what they're asking, my father had told us all, Phil had told us, over and over, *if it ever sounds like there's even a chance they might suspect you of anything, if they ever caution you, stop talking straightaway and ring one of us.* But if there was anything else these guys might give me, anything at all, I needed it.

'Because,' I said. 'It sounds like you're saying I, that you think I killed Dominic. And I didn't. I never touched him.'

Shaking his head: 'I'm not saying you killed him. I'm saying your hoodie string was used to kill him. You can see how we need to hear what you think about that.'

I felt light-headed and utterly unreal, as if my chair and the tiles under my feet had dematerialised and I was rocking amid that humming air. 'But,' I said. 'But that's all *guessing*. You don't know that drawstring came from my hoodie. You don't know it was meant for a, a garrotte. You don't know anyone used it on Dominic. And even if someone did, that doesn't mean it was me. Because it *wasn't*.'

'True,' Rafferty said, nodding. 'All fair points. We don't know anything for definite, not at this stage. Luckily for all of us, though, most of that is stuff we can prove, one way or the other. It might take a bit of time—'

'I nudged the lab,' Kerr said, aside to Rafferty in a carefully judged undertone. 'They said probably this week.'

'Ah, lovely,' Rafferty said. 'Not that much time, so. The way it works, right? if that cord was wrapped tight around Dominic's neck, he'll have left skin cells on it, all along the centre length. That means DNA. It'll be degraded, obviously, after being down a damp tree for ten years, but our techs are first-rate; they'll still get there, it's just taking them that bit longer. And if someone was pulling on those loops, same thing: he'll have left skin cells all over them.'

'Hang on,' I said. I wanted just a second where I could think without their eyes on me. I wanted a smoke break. 'Wait. If that was my hoodie cord, *if*, then my, my skin cells would be on it anyway. On the ends. Right where the loops are.'

'And,' Rafferty said, ignoring that, 'we've tracked down the hoodie manufacturers. They're finding us the specs on the cord they used for that model, so we can see if it's consistent with what we've got. If it's not, that doesn't mean much either way – maybe there was one odd batch, or maybe the cord got replaced along the way – but if it's a match, that's interesting.'

'That hoodie wasn't— I didn't keep my stuff locked *up*. It was just lying around. Even if it, if that's the cord, anyone could've taken it out. At a party or anywhere. *Dominic* could've.'

'And garrotted himself?' Kerr inquired, with a grin. 'I'm not sure that's a thing, man.'

'We've heard from multiple sources,' Rafferty said, 'that Dominic was a right prick to your cousin Leon. Leon told us himself, sure. He didn't want to, he dodged around it for a while – which is interesting; like we were saying before, ye're protective of each other, right? But he let it slip in the end.'

I just bet he had. I tried to keep my eyes off Rafferty's, find familiar objects that would turn this real. Chipped red enamel teapot on the windowsill, checked tea towel hanging askew from the handle of the oven door. Ruffled orange marigolds in a cracked mug.

'He wasn't a nice fella, this Dominic, was he? The stories people told us . . . I thought I'd seen a bit of bullying at my school, but man, some of this stuff gave me the shivers.' Screwing up his eyes worriedly, rubbing at his jaw: 'How come you didn't tell us that, last time? You said Dominic was "a good guy". Got on with everyone.'

'I didn't know. About the bad stuff. I knew he sometimes gave Leon a bit of grief, but I thought it was just minor crap.'

'Half your *school* told us about it. You're the person who was closest to Leon, and you're telling me you missed the whole thing?'

'Leon didn't tell me. No one told me. I don't read minds.'

Rafferty cocked a wry eyebrow at me: *Come on.* 'D'you feel like shit about it?' Kerr asked me. 'I would.'

'What could I have—' That hum in the air, pressing into my ears. Kerr picking something off a side tooth, hard curious eyes on me. 'What was I supposed to do?'

'Well, put a stop to it,' Rafferty said reasonably. 'I wouldn't say you're the type to stand by and let your cousin take that kind of shite. Amn't I right?'

'Probably not. If I'd known about it. Only I didn't.'

They left that there for a moment. Kerr examined whatever he had found on his tooth. Rafferty balanced his phone carefully on its edge on the table.

'I'd bet,' he said – almost absently, all his attention on the delicate business of the phone – 'I'd bet money that you only meant to give Dominic a scare. You don't seem like a killer to me, not at all, and I've met plenty. You were only planning on shaking him up a bit, nothing serious, just warning him: *Don't you ever fuck with my cousin again.* Which needed doing, and there's not a decent person in the world who'd think less of you for it.' Glancing up at me, golden eyes lit to wildness by a rogue streak of sun: 'I'm serious about that, man. I wasn't just talking, before, when I said sticking by your family is the most important thing in the world. If even half the shit we heard about Dominic was true, then you had to put a stop to it. You had no choice.'

Jasmine creepers swinging dizzily outside the window, back and forth. A watercolour off-kilter on the wall, swallows in a heart-stopping nosedive. Crazy slants of sunlight across the table.

'Only the thing about garrottes is, people underestimate them. Look them up on the internet, every page about them has a million warnings: don't ever try this on a real person, the neck's fragile and easily damaged, even if you think you're just practising or messing about you could kill someone just like that.' He took his fingers off the phone and it fell flat with a bang. 'But teenage boys, they don't take much heed of warnings. They're invincible: *Ah, I know what I'm doing, it'll be grand . . .* And they don't know their own strength. It'd be very, very easy for that to go just a little bit wrong. Pull a tiny bit too hard, for one second too long, and all of a sudden it's too late.'

I stared at him. I couldn't help it; everything else in the room had dissolved into a seething speckled blur.

'If that's what happened,' Rafferty said gently, 'we need to know now. Before the DNA results come back. If we get ahead of it right now, I can keep it low-key: go to the prosecutor, explain the whole story, come back with a manslaughter charge or maybe even assault.

But once we've got DNA, it's out of my hands. Everyone's going to go in with all guns blazing: the prosecutor, my gaffer, the brass, everyone. They're not going to lowball a slam-dunk murder case.'

None of it was sinking in; my mind had seized up, completely and violently as a spasming muscle. I said – my voice felt like it belonged to someone else – 'I want you to leave now.'

There was a long silence, while the two of them watched me. My hands were trembling. Then Rafferty sighed, a long regretful sigh, and pushed back his chair.

'It's up to you,' he said, pocketing his phone. I had expected a fight, and somehow the fact that I wasn't getting one terrified me even more. 'I tried, anyway. And you've still got my card, right? If you change your mind, you ring me straightaway.'

'You fancy giving us a DNA sample?' Kerr asked, closing his notebook with a showy one-handed flip.

'No,' I said. 'Not unless you get a, a warrant or whatever you—'

'No need,' Kerr said, grinning at me. 'The lads took a sample off you back in April, when you got burgled. For elimination purposes. We can use that, no problem. I just wanted to see what you'd say.'

And he touched two fingers to his temple in a salute and strolled off towards the front door, whistling.

'Ring me,' Rafferty said quietly. 'Any time of the day or night, I don't mind. But do it. Yeah? Once this window closes, it's closed for good.'

'Come on, man,' Kerr called from the hallway. 'Places to go, people to see.'

'Day or night,' Rafferty said. He gave me a nod and headed after Kerr.

•

I waited till I heard the front door close; then I went out to the hall-way, tiptoeing for some reason, to make sure they were really gone. Even after I heard their car zoom off – too fast for the street – I stayed there, hands pressed against the cracking white paint of the door, small cold draughts sliding in around its edges to eddy at my neck and my ankles. Here I'd been leaping at the thought of them giving me something new; careful what you wish for.

Now that they were gone and I could think again, I realised Rafferty had been talking bollocks. Slam-dunk murder case, my arse. He had been ignoring me because I was right: even if all his DNA results and hoodie-cord comparisons came back positive, any one of at least a dozen people could have garrotted Dominic with that cord. The fuzzy sort-of-motive he had lobbed at me, Dominic bullying Leon, that pointed at Leon a lot more directly than it did at me. Leon had been a skinny little weed of a kid, but that didn't matter. *The best part is you don't have to be bigger or stronger than your victim. He could be a horse of a man, but as long as you get the jump on him . . .*

The terrible part was that Rafferty had to know all that too; and yet he was sure, sure enough to try strong-arming me into a confession, that it hadn't been Leon, hadn't been any of those dozen people, it had been me. And I understood, with a savage splintering sensation deep inside my breastbone, exactly why. Me six months ago, clear-eyed and clear-voiced, sitting up straight and smart, answering every question promptly and directly and with total unthinking confidence: every cell of me had carried a natural and absolute credibility; accusing me of murder would have been ridiculous. Me now, slurring, babbling, droopy-eyed and drag-footed, jumping and trembling at every word from the detectives: defective, unreliable, lacking any credibility or authority or weight, guilty as hell.

With a rush of fury that took my breath away I wondered if this had been Leon's plan all along: to leave me damaged, drooling into my baby food or beeping into machines; to turn me into something that could so easily and naturally be dumped with the blame, when it came.

It had almost worked. A couple of months earlier, if Rafferty had tapped me on the shoulder and called me by name, I would have gone without a fight: why not? what was there left to save? Plead guilty, walk out of my life and leave all the wreckage behind: it would have come almost as a relief. Now, though, things had changed. I could feel my luck turning, rising, a low slow drumbeat somewhere deep in the fabric of the house. I might not be clear on what exactly was going on here, but I was very clear on one thing, which was that there was no way in hell I was going to lie back and let myself be carted off to jail.

I still couldn't quite believe that Leon was actually planning to take things that far, but it certainly looked that way. That photo of me conveniently wearing the exact hoodie that had provided the garrotte: that had come from somewhere very close to home. And it was a good clear image, none of the pixelated blur off an old dumbphone. None of us had had smartphones, back in school, and the others hadn't had digital cameras, either. But I had. My eighteenth birthday, January of our final year in school, my mother reaching to run her hand over my head, smiling: *Now when we're away this summer you can send us proper photos, promise?* And of course the camera had bounced around Hugo's place with everyone snapping whatever caught their eye, and occasionally I had remembered to upload a bunch of stuff and delete the inevitable shots of somebody's hairy arse and send the most wholesome ones to my mother. And then somewhere along the way I had got a smartphone, and the camera had knocked around half-forgotten until finally it landed in a drawer in my apartment, and there it had stayed until someone decided he needed it very badly.

What Leon had been neglecting was that I knew him very very well and I knew how he worked. He never could keep his mouth shut, not all the way: if something was on his mind he wouldn't tell you straight out but he would skitter around the edges of it, coming back to poke at it again and again, just like he had with Hugo's will. If I gave him enough chances, he would give me hints.

One of the big questions, of course, was where Susanna fit into all this. It was hard to imagine her being in on it. She had been a well-behaved kid, the type who handed everything in on time with footnotes and never talked back to teachers, much more likely to tell a responsible adult about bullying than to start constructing a garrotte. And while she definitely had the organisational drive to mastermind just about anything, she didn't have even Leon's pathetic half-arsed excuse for a grudge against me; I couldn't believe she would have set me up for all these various forms of nightmare just for the hell of it. Equally, though, it was hard to imagine her being quite as oblivious as I had been. Somewhere along the way, she would have spotted something, guessed something.

She had always been much more guarded than Leon, much harder to read or to trick or to wrong-foot, but I knew her too and I knew her weak spot: she really liked being the clever one. If she had known about this and I hadn't, she would have a hard time resisting the chance to rub it in.

And I had one advantage over both of them: they thought I was fucked up – which was true, but not to the extent they imagined, not any more. All those stammers and memory glitches that had infuriated me so much, those were about to come in useful. So much more tempting to let slip a smug little crumb of info to someone who wouldn't remember it, would barely be able to articulate it if he did, would never be believed if he could.

'Was that the door?' Hugo asked, on the stairs behind me – I'd been so focused, I'd missed the shuffle and thump of his approach altogether. 'Is Melissa home already?'

He had on his dressing gown, an old checked thing, over his trousers and jumper. 'Oh,' I said. 'No. It's still early.'

He blinked at the fanlight over the door, cold pale sun. 'Oh. So it is. Then who was that?'

'The detectives.'

In a different tone, eyes going to me: 'Ah.' And when I said nothing: 'What did they want?'

I almost told him. In so many ways it seemed like the natural thing to do, all my childhood rose up in me like a howl of longing to throw it at his feet: *Hugo, help me, they think I killed him, what do I do?* But that was the last thing he needed; and besides – bony wrists sticking out of the dressing-gown sleeves, caved-in slump of his chest, big hands clenched on the cane and the stair-rail – he was frail and he was fading and there was too little of him left to work whatever miracle I was craving. And, maybe most of all, I knew well that whatever he would want to do was very unlikely to have anything in common with what I wanted to do.

'They think someone killed Dominic,' I said.

After a pause: 'Well. That's not too unexpected.'

'With a garrotte. They think.'

That made his eyebrows go up. 'Good heavens. I can't imagine

293

they see that very often.' And after a moment: 'Did they say who they suspect?'

'I don't think they have anyone in mind.'

'They make everything so *difficult*,' Hugo said, flash of frustration, head going back. 'So bloody awkward, all this cloak-and-dagger nonsense, like children playing games and we're forced to play along—' Another draught flooded in around the door and he shivered hard. 'And this *weather*. It's not even October yet, surely I should be able to feel my feet in my own study?'

'I'll finish the radiators now,' I said. 'That'll help.'

'I suppose so.' He leaned a hip against the banisters, with a wince, so he could let go of the rail to pull his dressing gown tighter. 'Shouldn't we be starting on dinner? Is Melissa home yet?'

'It'll be lunchtime soon,' I said carefully, after a second. 'I'll bring something up once I've done the rads, OK?'

'Well,' Hugo said irritably, after a confused pause, 'I suppose you might as well,' and he managed to shuffle around, inch by inch, and hauled himself back up the stairs and into his study and banged the door.

•

By the time I got it together enough to bring lunch he seemed OK again, at least by whatever metric we were using at that stage. He ate his toasted sandwich, anyway, and showed me a couple of pages he'd deciphered from Mrs Wozniak's Victorian relative's boring diary (the cook had burned the roast beef, some kid had shouted a rude word at him on the street, children nowadays were deficient in moral training). The strange thing – I watched Hugo, from my table, as he peered gamely at the next page of the diary – was that although the illness was paring him away with brutal rapacity, he didn't seem smaller. He had lost an awful lot of weight, his clothes hung in folds, but somehow that only emphasised the massiveness of his frame. He was like one of those giant skeletons of elk or bear from an unimaginable prehistoric time, dominating vast museum galleries, alone and unfathomable.

He perked up a bit when Melissa got home, teasing her about the dinner ingredients she'd brought ('Paella, good heavens, you're like a travel agent for the taste buds') and enjoying her story about the happy old eccentric who had shown up in the shop with an armful of totally unsellable handmade scarves in tie-dyed silk and insisted on giving Melissa one to keep. The scarf was enormous, purple and gold, and Hugo draped it around his shoulders and sat laughing at the kitchen table like a magician in a child's game. More and more, Melissa was the one who brought out the best of him.

He knew it, too. 'I've been wanting to tell you,' he said to her – out of the blue, over our rummy game that evening, clutter of cards and mismatched mugs and biscuits on the coffee table, fire crackling merrily – 'how glad I am to have you here. I know what a sacrifice it must be, and I don't think there's any proper way I can put it into words, what it's meant to me. But I wanted to say it all the same.'

'I wasn't sure I should come, at first,' Melissa said. She was curled on the sofa with her feet on my lap; I was keeping them warm with my free hand. 'Showing up on your doorstep, in the middle of all this. And then just staying on. I've wondered dozens of times if I should get out of the way. But . . .' She turned up her palm to the room, a small gesture like releasing something: *Here we are.*

'I'm delighted you're here,' Hugo said. 'It's made me very happy – both you yourself, and also the chance to watch Toby being all grown up and settled in a relationship. It's like the weekends when I had Zach and Sallie: such a lovely progression from all those holidays when Toby and Susanna and Leon would come to stay. The next episode; life moving on. Probably this is fanciful, but I feel as if it's given me just a glimpse into what it might have been like to have children of my own.'

The valedictory tone of all this was making me twitchy; I wanted the subject changed. 'Why didn't you?' I asked. Susanna and Leon and I had speculated on that a few times, over the years. I thought Hugo had better sense than to screw up his serene, ordered existence with a bunch of screaming brats; Susanna thought he had some mysterious semi-detached long-term relationship, maybe with a woman who lived abroad and only came to Dublin every couple of months; Leon, inevitably, thought he was gay, and that by the time the country had grown up enough for him to come out, he had felt like it was too late. Honestly, any of those would have made sense.

Hugo considered that, rearranging the cards in his hand. He had a blanket over his knees, like an old man, in spite of the fire and the fact that I had actually managed to get the radiators working. 'If I'm truthful,' he said, 'it's hard to put my finger on it. Some of it was the oldest cliché in the book – I was engaged, she broke it off, I skulked back home to lick my wounds and swore off women forever. It would be easy to blame everything on that, wouldn't it?' Glancing up at us, a fleeting smile. 'But that happens to an awful lot of people, and mostly they get over it in a year or two. I did too, really – it's not that I've been carrying a torch all these years – but by that time there were your grandparents getting older, your grandfather's arthritis was getting worse, they needed someone to look after them; and I was right there, with no other responsibilities, while all the others had moved out and had wives and little ones . . . I suppose the truth is that I've never been a man of action.' That quirk of a smile again, eyebrow lifting. 'A man of inertia, more like. Don't rock the boat; everything will come right in the end, if you just let it . . . And every year, of course, it got harder to make any changes. Even after your grandparents died, when I could have done anything I wanted – travelled the world, got married, started a family – it turned out that there wasn't really anything I wanted enough to make that leap.'

He picked out a card, examined it, tucked it back. 'The thing is, I suppose,' he said, 'that one gets into the habit of being oneself. It takes some great upheaval to crack that shell and force us to discover what else might be underneath.' And looking up smiling, pushing his glasses up his nose: 'And with all that philosophising, I've forgotten whose go it was. Did I just put . . .'

His voice stopped. When the pause lasted too long I glanced up from my cards. He was staring at the door, wide-eyed, so intently that I whipped around to see if something or someone was there: nothing.

When I turned back Hugo was still staring. He licked his lips, again and again. 'Hugo,' I said, too loudly. 'Are you OK?'

One arm reached out, rigid, fingers grotesquely clawed.

I was off the sofa, cards scattering everywhere, mugs going over as I crashed past the coffee table. Melissa and I made it to him at the same time, threw ourselves on our knees beside him. I was afraid to touch him in case I made it worse. He was blinking and blinking; that distorted arm made great meaningless raking motions in front of him, so taut and determined they seemed almost deliberate.

So this was it: this sudden, one moment pushing up your glasses and considering the king of spades, the next moment gone. After the months of fear and tension and wondering, here it was, this quick and this simple. 'An ambulance,' I said, although I knew they wouldn't make it in time. My heart felt too huge for my chest. 'You ring. Fast.'

'It's a seizure,' Melissa said calmly. She was looking up into Hugo's face, a light, firm hand on his shoulder. 'He doesn't need an ambulance. Hugo, you're having a seizure. It's all right; it'll be over in a minute.'

No way to tell whether he had heard her. Raking, blinking. A line of spit trailed from one corner of his mouth.

It was a few seconds before I could take in that he wasn't dying in front of us. 'But,' I said. Some distant part of me remembered the shitbird neurologist's lecture, small words and a disdainful head-master gaze— 'We're supposed to call the ambulance anyway. For a first seizure.'

'It's not the first. He's been having them for a while now.' At my stunned look: 'Those times when he's staring into space and he doesn't hear you for a minute? I thought you knew.'

'No,' I said.

'I told him to tell the doctors. I don't know if he did.' She was stroking Hugo's shoulder, a slow steadying rhythm. 'It's OK,' she said quietly. 'It's OK. It's OK.'

Gradually the raking movement got looser and vaguer, till his arm fell on his lap, twitched a few times and lay limp. The lip-licking stopped. His eyes closed and his head lolled sideways, as if he had simply dozed off in his chair after dinner.

Merry pop and spit of firewood. Brown puddles of tea spreading across the coffee table, dripping onto the carpet. I was light-headed, my heartbeat running wild.

'Hugo,' Melissa said gently. 'Can you look at me?'

His eyelids trembled. His eyes opened: bleary and drowsy, but he was seeing her.

'You had a seizure. It's over now. Do you know where you are?'

He nodded.

'Where?'

His mouth moved as if he were chewing and for a dreadful second I thought it was beginning again, but he said – scratchy, slurred – 'Living room.'

'Yes. How do you feel?'

His face was white and clammy; even his hands looked too pale. 'Don't know. Tired.'

'That's all right. Just stay put for a bit, till you feel better.'

'Do you want some water?' I asked, finally coming up with something useful I could do.

'Don't know.'

I hurried to the kitchen anyway and filled a glass at the tap, my hands shaking, water splashing everywhere. My face in the dark window over the sink was stunned stupid, mouth hanging open and eyes round.

When I got back to the living room, Hugo looked better: head up, some of the colour back in his face. Melissa had found a paper napkin and was cleaning the trail of drool off his chin. 'Oh,' he said, and took the glass in his good hand. 'Thank you.'

'Do you remember what happened?' I asked.

'Not really. Just . . . everything looked strange, all of a sudden. Different. Frightening. And that's all.' With an edge of fear that he couldn't quite hide: 'What did I do?'

'Not a lot,' I said easily. 'A bit of staring, a few weird arm things. No movie-type flailing around, nothing like that.'

'Have you had ones like this before?' Melissa asked.

'I think so. Once.' Hugo took another sip of water, wiped the corner of his mouth where some of it had leaked out. 'A couple of weeks ago. In bed.'

'You should have called us,' I said.

'I didn't really realise. What had happened. And what could you have done?'

'Still,' Melissa said. 'If it happens again, call us. Please?'

'All right, my dear.' He covered her hand with his for a moment. 'I promise.'

'Did you tell the doctor?'

'Yes. He gave me things. Medicine. Warned me they might not work, though.' He struggled to heave himself straighter in the chair. 'And he started all that about hospice again. I said no, of course. Absolutely not.'

'Do you want to go to bed?' I asked. He seemed practically himself again, almost bizarrely so, but I couldn't really see going back to our game of rummy; even if he was able for it, I wasn't.

'What I'd like,' Hugo said, 'is to sit here for a while. With you two. If that's all right.'

Melissa got a cloth and mopped up the spilled tea; I collected the cards, wiped tea off them with a dampened paper towel and stacked them ready for some other time. Then we went back to our places on the sofa, Melissa curled against me, my arm holding her close, her fingers woven through mine.

We didn't talk. Melissa gazed into the fire, its light throwing warm flickers over the soft curve of her cheek. Hugo stroked the blanket over his legs absently, with one thumb, as if it were a pet. Occasionally he glanced up and smiled at us, reassuring: *Look, I'm fine*. We sat there for a long time, while rain ticked quietly against the windows and a moth whirled half-heartedly around the standing lamp and the fire burned down to glowing gems of ash.

•

I hadn't, I suppose, taken much notice of Melissa's mood that evening. I had vaguely registered that she was quiet, even before the thing with Hugo, but I had more than enough going on already; she was the one blessed thing in my world that didn't seem to require vigilance. So it took me completely by surprise when – after we had seen Hugo safely into his room and tracked the familiar sounds of him pottering about and going to bed, and I was pulling off my jumper in our bedroom – she said, 'The detectives came to talk to me. At the shop.'

'*What?*' I was so startled I dropped the jumper. 'Which

detectives? Like, Martin and, and—' I couldn't remember Flashy Suit's name. 'Or these ones? Rafferty and Thing, Kerr?'

'Rafferty and Kerr.' Melissa had her back to me, putting her cardigan on a hanger. Her reflection – pale hair, pale dress, pale slender arms – rippled like a ghost in the window. 'I never expected them to want to talk to me, since I hadn't even met any of you back when . . . I don't know how they knew where I work. They had me put the Closed sign on the shop door – the scarf woman actually originally came along while they were there and she wouldn't go away, she kept rattling the door handle; I wanted to go tell her I'd be open again in a few minutes, but Detective Kerr wouldn't let me. He kept saying, "No, leave her, she'll give up in a minute," but she was there for ages, she had her face pressed up against the glass peering in—'

Places to go, people to see. 'What the hell did they want?'

'They showed me some photos.'

I could have kicked Rafferty's teeth in. 'Yeah? Of what?'

'A hoodie they found here. And you when you were younger, wearing it. And the drawstring out of it.' Melissa's voice was very clear and controlled. She was looking at the cardigan, carefully straightening the shoulder seams, not at me. 'They found that inside the tree. They think it was—'

'I know, yeah. They showed me the same photos.'

That snapped her head around. 'When?'

'This morning.'

'You weren't going to tell me.'

'I wasn't going to waste your time with that kind of bollocks. Why were they showing you the photos? What did they want?'

'They wanted to know whether you'd ever mentioned Dominic Ganly to me. And whether I'd ever seen you make anything like that, the thing with the loops. Whether you ever make knots like those. And' – eyes on the cardigan as she hung it in the wardrobe, no change in that even voice, only the smallest flicker of her lashes – 'whether I'd ever known you to be violent. I said no, obviously. Never.'

I was, ironically, working hard to stop myself from punching a wall or putting my foot through the wardrobe door or something equally dramatic and pointless. I picked my jumper up off the floor and folded it very neatly.

'They knew about that man last year. The one who wouldn't leave me alone, until you ran him off. They wanted to know exactly what you did: whether you touched him when you were getting rid of him, whether you threatened to beat him up. I said no, but they kept pushing: are you serious, any normal man would be raging, he'd need to get the message across loud and clear, did your fella honestly not have the guts to do that . . . I wanted to tell them to leave, but I was afraid it would look like I was hiding something. They're very— They make it hard to stand up to them, don't they? I just kept saying no, no, no, and trying to keep calm, and in the end they gave up. Or at least they left.'

'Well,' I said, coolly enough, when I could talk again. 'It sounds like you put them back in their box. If they show up again, tell them to get lost. Or ring me and I'll tell them.'

'Toby.' Finally, a shake in her voice, and she turned to face me. 'They think you killed Dominic.'

I laughed, although even I could hear the harsh edge to it. 'No they don't. They don't have any reason to. They don't have even *half* a reason. All they've got is a hoodie cord that anyone could have taken. They're just trying to steamroller someone into confessing, so they can close their case. That's why they hassled you: to put pressure on me. Not because they actually think you know anything, or they actually think I was *violent*—' My voice was rising. I took a breath.

Melissa said, 'They do, Toby. Maybe they don't really think I know anything. But they think you killed him.'

Her face, pale and intent and remote as the ghost in the glass. It hit me, with a stunning thump, that she might think the same thing. I wondered what the detectives had said to her that she wasn't telling me.

I said, 'I didn't kill Dominic.'

'I know,' Melissa said, instantly and forcefully. 'I know that. I never thought you did.'

I believed her. The rush of relief and shame – how could I have thought, even for a second – took some of the tension out of me. 'Well,' I said. 'I guess now you can see how I need to do something about this.'

Her face shut down. 'Like what?'

'Like talk to people. See if I can figure out what the hell actually happened. So we don't have to put up with any more of this crap.'

'No,' Melissa said sharply. I had heard that iron inflexibility in her voice only once before, when she was talking about her mother. 'The only thing you need to do is stay as far as you can from all this awful stuff. Get a solicitor; let him deal with them. It's *not your problem*. There's no reason why you should get all tangled up in it. Leave it alone.'

'Melissa, they straight out accused me of *murder*. I think that pretty definitely makes it my problem.'

'No it's *not*. Like you said, they don't have any proof, and they're never going to get any. All you have to do is ignore them, and sooner or later they'll give up and go away.'

'What if they don't? What if they decide to double down and arrest me, and hope that makes me crack? I don't know about you, but I don't fancy sitting here week after week wondering if today's the day, if they're going to pick the same moment when Hugo has some crisis—'

'What's going to happen when they find out you've been asking questions? They'll think you're trying to find out who knows what because you're nervous. And then they'll go after you even harder, and that'll undo all the good that—'

'Jesus, Melissa!' I didn't care about keeping my voice down any more, let Hugo wake up, fuck it all— 'I thought you'd be *pleased*. A few months ago, I wouldn't have given a damn if I got thrown in jail. I thought you'd be *delighted* that I've got my head together enough to want to fight this. Would you rather I was still sitting on my arse trying to work up enough motivation to make toast?'

That got to her, just like I'd known it would. Her voice softening, the iron note gone out of it: 'You feeling more like yourself, that's wonderful. And *yes*, I'm delighted. But can't you put that into something else? Ring Richard, see if you can do bits and pieces from here – or you always said you wanted to learn scuba diving—'

'Or basket-weaving, or pottery? I'm not *disabled*. I'm not a *mental* patient.' I saw Melissa flinch at my tone, but I kept going. I had never been angry at her before, not once, and it made me even more furious at Rafferty and Kerr and at Leon and even obscurely at Dominic – three years of easy harmony through thick and thin, and now this— 'I don't need a *hobby*. I don't need to *keep busy*. I need to find out why the fuck I just got *accused of murder*.'

'I didn't, Toby, I never said—' I'd picked my angle well: the air went out of her and she slumped back against the wardrobe door. 'I just want you to be happy.'

'I know. Me too. I want *us* to be happy. That's exactly why I'm *doing* this.' The look of defeat on her face – I would have given anything to show her what I was seeing, how this could transform everything— 'Baby, please, just trust me. I can do this. I'm not going to make a balls of it.'

'I know you're not. That's not—' She shook her head, eyes squeezed tight. 'Just don't do things that'll make everything worse. Please.'

'I won't,' I said, going to her. 'I wasn't planning on cornering gangsters in dark laneways with my Colt forty-five. I'm just going to talk to people, and see if they say anything interesting. That's all.' And when she didn't answer, or lean into me: 'I promise. OK?'

Melissa took a deep breath and put a hand up to my cheek. 'I suppose,' she said. And, moving away when I bent to kiss her: 'Let's go to bed. I'm exhausted.'

'Sure,' I said. 'Me too.' Which I should have been, after the day I had had. But long after Melissa's breathing had slowed into the familiar rhythm of sleep, I was wide awake. Not twitching at random noises and adding up the hours since my last Xanax, this time; just watching the subtle gradations of darkness shift across the ceiling, and thinking, and planning.

9

And so, once Melissa was off to work the next morning, I rang Susanna and Leon and invited them over for dinner and a few drinks – stressed out by all this crap, need to blow off some steam, yada yada. None of us mentioned garrottes or hoodies or detectives, which strengthened all my suspicions another notch: Rafferty had made it clear that he'd talked to both of them about that fucking hoodie, and I felt like that was something they should have told me more or less the moment he left, if they were anything like on my side.

Even over the phone their voices sounded different to me that day; they had a glittery, fractured quality that reminded me of the couple of times I'd tried acid. It took me a while to put my finger on what it was: danger. I had always thought of Leon and Susanna as fundamentally harmless. Not in a bad way – mostly it was out of love, we might bicker and bitch but deep down I knew they were good stuff; and also, if I was honest, it had always been hard to take them seriously enough for anything as weighty as danger. With what I knew now, every word and breath hummed with undercurrents and subtexts I couldn't catch. They could be anything; they could be lethal, and I had never noticed.

I had a good feeling about that night, though. It sparkled tantalisingly in front of me like a fourth date, a final interview, the big one with the prize waiting at the end and I was all pumped up and ready to ace it. It wasn't that I was expecting Leon to break down and spill out some lurid confession – although never say never, I could get lucky, who was to say? But if he was holding some grudge against me, I couldn't wait to hear all about it. A couple of drinks and a bit of needling, and I was positive I could get him there; maybe, if I played my cards just right, get him to the break-in.

The big question, of course, was what I was going to do with all that if I got it. It was Leon, for God's sake. One of my first memories was of the two of us sitting in a puddle in this garden, pouring mud on each other's head. I couldn't imagine doing anything that would get him thrown in jail, even if he had been trying to do exactly that to me.

Unless: if he really had been behind the break-in, then all bets were off. I could give him a pass on murder, and on trying to frame me, but the thought of him deliberately or even semi-deliberately turning me into this hit me like a taser every time. I knew that was probably some terrible indictment of my character, but – running up the stairs to tell Hugo the cousins were coming for dinner, mouthful of chocolate biscuit, spring in my step that almost got rid of the limp – I didn't really care.

When Melissa got home I had my clothes laid out on the bed – blue linen chinos and a really nice shirt, soft cream with a tiny blue geometric print, Melissa must have packed it for some reason and it had been months since I'd dressed up for anything and why not? – and I was singing some cheesy Robbie Williams song at the top of my lungs, in snatches, while I shaved. 'Hello, you,' Melissa said, poking her head around the bathroom door. 'How's Hugo been?'

'Fine. Nothing scary. He found out Haskins – the diary guy, Mrs Wozniak's cousins' great-great-whatever? – he hates dogs and fired his maid because she smelled funny.'

'I saw your clothes. What's the occasion?'

'I'm in a good mood. Come here.'

She tiptoed to kiss me around the shaving foam; I grabbed her and rubbed my foamy cheek on her nose, and she squealed and laughed – 'Silly!' – and wiped her nose on my bare chest. 'You're going to be all gorgeous. I'd better dress up too.'

'I seriously need a haircut,' I said, peering into the mirror. 'I look like I should be hanging around a crappy pub in Galway trying to convince tourist chicks that I'm a surfer.'

'Will I trim it for you? I don't know how to do a proper cut, but I could tidy it up a bit, just to hold you till you get to the barber's.'

'Would you? That'd be great.'

'Course. Let me find some scissors.'

'Oh,' I said, when she was halfway out the door. 'Su and Leon are coming for dinner. Do we have enough food? Or will we get takeaway?'

Melissa turned quickly, but she said readily enough, 'Let's order from that Indian place. Hugo loves it, and it's easy for his hand.'

'Lovely. I'm starving; curry sounds great.' Tilting my head to get under the angle of my jaw, not looking at her: 'Listen, about last night. I know it sounds like I'm obsessing over what happened to Dominic. But it's not just that.'

I could see her in the mirror, watching me from the doorway. 'What, then?'

I needed to be careful here. I actually needed a hand from Melissa to make the night go smoothly, and I knew she wasn't going to be crazy about that idea. 'It's tough to explain,' I said. 'I feel like a lot of things are a mess – OK, let's face it, things have been a mess for months, but I was in too bad shape to do anything about it. Now, I don't know if it's because I'm getting better or what, but I feel like I need to clear things up. Dominic, yeah, but not only that.'

She was listening carefully, one fingernail scraping at a stain on the door. 'What else?'

'All the stuff Sean and Dec said, about what Dominic did to Leon. You were right: that's bothering me.'

'It wasn't your fault. You didn't know.'

'Well. That's the question. I honest-to-God don't remember anything like that, but with my memory the way it is . . . yeah. Who knows what that's worth.' I flashed her a crooked half-smile, in the mirror. 'I mean, I seriously don't think I would've let Dominic beat the crap out of Leon, but it'd be nice to be sure.'

Melissa said, 'Does it make a difference now?'

Taken aback, a little pained: 'Well, yeah. Course it does. If I let Leon down, then that's been hurting our relationship ever since, even if I was too thick to realise it. And I know I don't see a lot of him, but him and Su . . . they're the nearest I've got to a brother and sister. Maybe everything's fine and I was the perfect cousin. I hope. But if I wasn't, I need to know, so I can fix it.' With another wry grin, lifting my chin to get at the underside: 'This is what people

306

always say about murders, isn't it? They drag up all kinds of other stuff, and everyone's stuck dealing with it?'

When she didn't answer: 'Look. Probably this doesn't make sense, but . . . this whole getting-attacked thing: I need that to be something. A fresh start. A wake-up call, to get my life sorted out. Otherwise it's just shit – let's be honest, so far it has been just shit. If I can make something good out of it . . . you know?'

And of course Melissa, bless her sunflower heart, couldn't turn away from that. Her face lighting up: 'Yes! Do. That would be wonderful. And tell Leon that. He'll understand.'

'I will.' That was a good idea, actually. 'I need to know what I did to him, though. If I did anything. Could you help me?'

That pulled her eyebrows together. 'Me? How?'

'Could you ask Leon and Susanna what I was like, back then? It's a natural enough question; it's the same as you wanting to look at Hugo's old photos. Obviously they're going to tell you I was a great guy, but could you keep pushing? I'll help things along; I just need you to do the actual asking.'

'Why can't you? Like you said, if you did anything bad, they won't want to tell me. You could ask when I'm not there. I'll go to bed early.'

The truth was, of course, that if I started poking around asking questions Leon was bound to turn wary, and probably Susanna too, depending. 'The thing is,' I said, taking a breath and meeting Melissa's eyes in the mirror, 'I'd rather they didn't know how badly my memory's messed up. I know that's stupid. Obviously they probably have some idea that I'm not a hundred per cent, but I've been working really hard to act at least halfway normal around them, and I'm hoping I've done OK. If I go in there like, "Uhhh, guys, just wondering, any chance you could refresh my memory of, like, our entire teens?" then that's down the tubes. And I just . . . I can't stand the idea of them feeling sorry for me.'

She could hardly shoot that down. 'I understand. I don't think you're badly messed up, Toby, I really don't, but . . .' She saw my wince. 'I'll ask.'

I blew out a breath of relief. 'God, that's a load off my mind. I've spent the whole day going round in circles trying to figure out a way to do it myself – I mean, I bet there is one, but my head . . . If you can do it, that's brilliant. And could you ask about Dominic, too? What he was like? If they won't rat me out, they might say enough about him to give me some idea what was going on. And that won't seem weird, either: God knows he's a big enough part of our lives right now, there's every reason why you'd want to get some idea of him.' It occurred to me, for the first time, to wonder why Melissa hadn't in fact asked anything about Dominic at all.

She said, 'Is this about what happened to him?'

'I don't know,' I said frankly, turning around to face her. 'Let's be honest, there's a chance it could turn out to be connected – I can't see how, but who knows, at this stage. But that's not the main point.'

For a moment I thought she was going to balk, but then she nodded. 'OK. I can ask about him.'

'Leave it till after Hugo's gone to bed. If they do come out with anything awful that I did, he doesn't need to hear about it.' And, of course, it would take me a couple of hours to get Leon good and drunk. I'd been down to the offie that morning for impressive quantities of gin and tonic, and I was going to be doing the pouring.

'No, you're right. I'll do that.'

'And just . . . keep in mind that everything you're asking about, that was ten years ago. OK? I was a stupid arsehole kid. And remember, Su and Leon both exaggerate. If they say I did something really horrific, that doesn't necessarily mean it's true. Whatever comes up, could you give me the benefit of the doubt?'

I meant this part, from the heart – there was, after all, a small but non-zero chance that Leon was going to try hinting that I was a murderer. It must have showed. Melissa came to me, put her hands on my arms and looked up into my face. 'Of course I will,' she said, very seriously. 'Always.'

'Thanks,' I said, and pulled her close for a one-armed hug. 'Thank you so much, baby. It'll all be fine. We're a good team, you and me. Yeah?'

'We are,' Melissa said. 'Now' – a quick breath, a small nod to herself – 'let me go find those scissors.' She tiptoed to kiss me on the nose and left me to it, and I went back to my shaving and my Robbie Williams impression in an even better mood.

•

Tom tagged along with Susanna, which didn't really fit into my plan, but I didn't let it worry me: the night was young, I was pretty sure I could come up with a way to get rid of him. While we waited for the takeaway to arrive, I moved around handing out pre-dinner G and Ts (none of them poured too strong, not yet, no rush) and laughing at everyone's jokes. My haircut had turned out pretty well and the shirt suited me – I had realised, putting it on, that I'd gained back some of the weight I'd lost; I looked better than I had since that night, and I felt it too. I made sure I stumbled just often enough, within earshot of Leon and Susanna (Tom can I get you a drink, oh that's right you're driving, sorry that's the third time I've asked you, haha! ... Yeah, Hugo's work is going great, spent today going through the, you know, the thing, what's it called, Jesus, the state of me, head like a sieve!) – cheerful idiot, harmless, no need to take him seriously. It was Melissa's turn to pick the music, so her French bistro swing was bopping away in the background, all scarlet lips and saucy hip-sway, *Oh that man!* Melissa was dressed up to match, white dress with a swingy skirt and sprays of green flowers, and she was gamely listening as Tom explained some mind-numbing diorama project he had inflicted on his first-years – not going near Leon or Susanna, not yet, biding her time just like I was. The feeling of collusion gave me a delicious burst of triumphant mischief, the two of us on our secret mission, we should have had code words— I caught her eye and winked, behind Tom's back, and after a fraction of a second she winked right back.

Hugo sat in the middle of all this, smiling, drinking his G and T at a careful angle to make sure none of it spilled from the loose corner of his mouth. There was something absent about him, abstracted – laughing at jokes a few seconds too late, 'Hm?' when I asked him what he wanted to eat – that made me edgy. Everything looked like the beginning of another seizure, and apart from the obvious, that would have pretty much put the kibosh on my plans for the evening.

It wasn't until dinner that I found out what was actually going on. All of us were talking a little too fast and too loud; I only noticed that Hugo was trying to get our attention when – as I launched myself into another goofy, stumbling childhood reminiscence – Melissa put a hand on my wrist and nodded at him. 'Oops,' I said. 'Sorry.'

'That's all right,' Hugo said, carefully spooning sauce onto his plate. 'I just want to tell you this before I forget. You'll all be relieved to know that I have a plan for the house. And about time too.'

All of us stopped eating. 'It's going to the whole lot of you,' he said. 'The three of you and your fathers: equal shares. This may seem like I'm passing the buck, leaving you lot to make the big decisions – I probably am – but it's the only way I can think of that allows for all the ways your lives might change. Who might get married or have children, or more children, or move out of the country or back again, or be a bit strapped for cash and need somewhere to live . . . I'd love to be able to picture all the possibilities, but I don't have it in me; I just get muddled. A few days ago' – to Leon, with a wry, painful half-grin – 'I was completely convinced that you had a little girl. Just a baby, with curly dark hair.'

'God forbid,' Leon said, with a shudder of mock horror, helping himself to naan bread. He didn't look great – eyebags, his jumper had been washed too many times and he badly needed a shave, which gave his edgy-young-thing look a jaded, seedy tinge; he was managing perky banter, but the effort showed. 'I'd rather have a rabid chimpanzee. No offence, Su and Tom, your kids are total angels, just saying.'

'I was worried because I knew you weren't with the mother any more,' Hugo explained, 'and I was afraid you wouldn't get time with the baby if you didn't have a good place for her to stay, so I thought you might be the one who needed the house most.'

'I'd pay good money to see Leon with a baby,' I said. I didn't want to listen to this. 'It'd be like some cheesy sitcom where the kid gets left on the wrong doorstep. Wacky adventures ensue.'

'I was trying to think of the baby's name,' Hugo said, refusing to be sidetracked, 'to put her in the will, and of course I couldn't. Then it occurred to me that I couldn't remember you ever actually mentioning the baby, and from there I managed to work out the rest. But you can see why I don't think I'm the best person to make the long-term decisions.' His smile, flashing up at us, was too wide; telling that story had hurt. 'So the house goes to all six of you. That should solve the main problem, anyway: it can't be sold unless all of you agree. Beyond that, it's up to you.'

'Thanks,' Susanna said quietly. 'We'll take good care of it.'

'We will,' I said.

'I won't let the baby fingerpaint on the walls,' Leon said, 'cross my heart,' and Hugo laughed and reached for the rice, and we all went back to talking at once.

I had caught something in Leon's face, though. Later – when Hugo had gone up to bed, and the rest of us were tidying up, me and Leon loading the dishwasher together – I asked, casually, 'Are you not cool with Hugo leaving the house to all six of us, no?'

'It's his house. He can do what he wants with it.' Leon didn't look up. His voice was flat and brittle; now that Hugo was gone, he had dropped the chirpy act. 'I just think it's a horrible idea. That's how you get family feuds.'

'He's doing his best,' Susanna said, over the rush of running water as she rinsed the takeaway containers. She looked a lot better than Leon did, fresh and rested in a soft sage-green jumper that suited her, hair studded with little bright flower clips that I figured had something to do with Sallie. 'We'll work it out.'

'The five of you can work it out. I don't even want to know. Send me a piece of paper to sign when you've all decided what you want to do.'

'What?' I demanded. 'You were the one who was losing your mind about hanging on to the place—'

'That was before a *skeleton* showed up in the garden and fucked up our entire lives. Excuse me if that wrecked my happy associations just a teeny bit.'

Or, more like, that had been back when a new owner with

gardening ambitions could have set off the hidden landmine; now that it had already exploded, there was no need to be territorial any more. As evidence went it wasn't much, but it gave an extra boost to the rising sense that tonight was my night, all its currents running my way. 'Fair enough,' I said agreeably.

'It doesn't bother me,' Susanna said. 'It's gone now. The grounds are a hundred per cent police-certified skeleton-free. How many places can say that?'

Leon shoved another plate into the dishwasher with a clatter. 'Then move in. What part of "I don't care" is confusing you?'

I recognised this mood, restless and electric and contrary, the mood that when we were kids had always ended with the whole three of us getting grounded, or having to hide the broken pieces, or on one memorable occasion being nabbed by a security guard and held in a back room full of cleaning equipment until I managed to talk us out of it by explaining in heartrending detail – while the others, in fairness to them, played along beautifully, Leon rocking and banging his heel off his chair leg while Susanna stroked his arm and made soothing noises – my poor little cousin's disability and what it would do to his ailing mother if he got arrested. Getting anything out of him in this mood would be like pulling teeth. 'What you need,' I said, 'is another G and T. What all of us need, actually. Cucumber or lime, or both?'

'Cucumber,' Susanna said.

'Lime,' Leon said promptly. 'It's too cold for cucumber.'

'What's that got to do with anything? Anyway it's warm, I don't know why I even bothered with a coat—'

'Hang on, let me check, is it June? Are we sitting on a lawn full of daisies? No? Then cucumber doesn't belong in—'

'We've got both,' Melissa said cheerfully. 'I think there are lemons, too, although they might be a wee bit depressed. Everyone can have what they like best.'

'Tom, what's your vote?' I asked.

'Oh,' Tom said. 'Count me out. I think I'll head home.'

'No!' I said, doing deep disappointment. 'It's early. Just have the one.'

'Ah, no. I'm driving—'

'Oh, that's right! You told me! Jesus, my head—'

'—and I don't want to leave my mum with the kids for too long,' Tom explained. 'Zach's been acting up a bit, the last while.'

I didn't blame him for being in a hurry; 'acting up', by Zach's standards, probably involved a SWAT team and a biohazard squad. 'I know Zach's a little bollix sometimes,' Susanna said, reading my expression, 'but we've been working on it. He just needs to get his head round the idea that other people are real too, and he'll be fine. He was doing a lot better, but finding the skull threw him for a total loop. If other people are real, then obviously that means the skull was a real person, and that's way more than he can handle. So his head's wrecked and he's being a pain in the hole.'

'Right,' I said. 'Fair enough.'

'It is, really,' Tom said, patting his pockets and peering around as if he might have dropped something. 'It's a bit of a headwrecker even for us, isn't it, and we're grown adults. He'll be fine in the end. Have a great night' – waving vaguely and benignly at all of us; and to Susanna, who tilted up her face to meet his kiss, 'No hurry. Enjoy yourself.'

'Sorry,' Leon said, to all of us, when he was gone. 'For being bitchy.'

'You're OK,' I said. Melissa smiled and threw him a lime: 'There,' she said. 'To make things better.'

'I'm just a total stress ball today. I got a really pissy phone call from my boss, throwing a massive fit about when I'll be back—'

'In fairness,' Susanna said, slicing cucumber neatly, 'you can see how they might want to know.'

'He didn't have to be a gigantic arsehole about it.' Leon leaned back against the counter and pushed his fingers into the corners of his eyes. 'I don't know why I let it get to me. I'm probably going to move anyway. I'm bored of Berlin.'

'What?' I said, startled, turning with the gin bottle in my hand. 'What about Whatshisname?'

'His name's Carsten. Do I go around forgetting Melissa's name?'

'You probably would if you'd taken a bang or two to the head,' I said. It was getting easier to say stuff like that, which was useful but bothered me all the same.

'I wouldn't,' Leon said, smiling across at Melissa, although it clearly took an effort. 'She's unforgettable. Anyway' – taking the knife off Susanna, starting on the lime – 'Carsten'll survive. I think he might be cheating on me anyway, or at least thinking about it.'

'He's not cheating on you,' Susanna said, like she had said it several times before.

'He keeps mentioning this ex of his.'

'Mentioning him how? Like, "God, I miss Superex so much, lucky I didn't delete his number"? Or like, "Oh, right, I remember that film, I think I saw it with Whatshisname"?'

'Does it matter? He's mentioning him.'

'You're looking for an excuse.'

'I am not. I'm just sick of Berlin, and I'm not going to hang around for someone who can't stop banging on about some other guy. What do you care? You don't even know Carsten – which by the way isn't my fault, I've invited you over like a million times—'

'Totally looking for an excuse. That's why you're still here, too. You're hoping work will get sick of it and fire you.'

'Can we not talk about this any more?' Leon asked abruptly. His voice was a notch too high. 'Please?'

'Your wish is our command,' I said, giving him a clap on the shoulder as I passed – he winced. 'Tonight's about relaxing, remember?'

'That reminds me,' Susanna said. 'Here.' She fished in her jeans pocket, pulled out something small and tossed it to Leon.

He caught it, peered and did a jaw-dropped double take. 'Ohmy-God. Are you serious?'

'Anything for you, babe. Plus if you keep stressing out, you're going to start stressing me too.'

'You *beauty*,' Leon said, with heartfelt awe.

'Skin up. Before you give yourself a stroke.'

'You are a beauty,' I said. This was perfect, exactly what I needed to loosen everyone up. I should have thought of it myself, but the fact that Susanna had done it for me seemed like a gift dropped from the heavens straight into my hands. 'I thought you didn't want to do anything dodgy in case the detectives find out.'

'I don't. But I don't want Leon to give himself a nervous break-down, either.'

'I actually went looking for some,' Leon said. 'Hanging around the jacks in this terrible nightclub – I'd forgotten how shit Dublin clubs are, I might have to go back to Berlin just for some decent nightlife. I got offered several interesting things, but no one had hash. Is there a shortage?'

'Apparently, yeah. I had to go through practically everyone I know to get this.'

'Does Tom know you smoke?'

Susanna raised an eyebrow. 'You make it sound like I'm some hardcore stoner. I only do it a couple of times a year.'

'So he doesn't know.'

'He does, actually. Does Carsten know you're a git?'

'You two stop bickering,' I told them. 'I want to take that stuff outside and get acquainted.'

We took everything outside – glasses, gin, tonic, ice tray, limes, cucumbers, depressed lemons – and laid it out on the terrace. Leon spread out a Rizla and started dismantling a cigarette. Melissa and I brought throws and cushions from the living room – Susanna had been exaggerating; the evening wasn't a cold one, but it was start-ing to get dark and there was a sharp-edged, fidgety breeze prowling the garden, with no plants or long grass to soften it, tugging at branches and jabbing its way into corners. I poured the drinks – good and heavy on the gin for Leon and Susanna – and Melissa added in the bits and pieces. 'There,' she said, putting a glass by Leon's elbow. 'Loads of lime.'

'And loads of cucumber for me,' Susanna said, stretching out on her back and waving her glass at Leon. 'Seeing as it's June on the daisy lawn.'

'Shush, you,' Leon said, holding up a sizeable, expert joint. 'Now. Let's see what we've got here.'

He lit it, took a deep drag and held it. 'Oh sweet mother,' he said in a heartfelt, compressed squeak, eyes watering. 'That's gorgeous stuff. You' – Susanna – 'are a saint. And you' – me – 'you're a genius. Tonight was actually a genius idea.'

'I just figured we all needed a chillout evening,' I said modestly. I settled myself against the wall of the house, legs stretched out, and pulled Melissa in against my chest; she tucked a throw over the pair of us. 'Like Tom said, all of this would wreck anyone's head.'

'They're such a pair of fuckers,' Leon said. He leaned back against the wall and took another drag off the joint. 'The detectives. They really are. I honestly think they're full-on sadist psychopaths; they've just found a way to get paid for it.'

'It's their job,' Susanna said, pulling a throw over herself. 'They need people headwrecked and bickering. So don't fall for it.'

'Look who's talking.'

'Shh. Have more of that.'

'That key to the garden door showed up,' I said. I wasn't going to mention the hoodie cord, not unless they did. 'Did they tell you?'

'Oh God yes,' Susanna said. 'Big dramatic reveal, dun-dun, look what we found in the tree! And then the two of them sit there and give you the headmaster stare: *I'm waiting for an explanation, young lady, and we're all going to stay here until I get one.*'

'Sweet baby Jesus, the stare,' Leon said, passing Melissa the joint. 'I'm petrified I'm going to say something awful. It's like being in church when you're a kid, you know, you start wondering what would happen if you yelled "Ballsack!" right at the most solemn moment, and then you can't stop thinking about it and you're getting more and more terrified that you'll actually do it? Swear to God, if those guys keep giving me the stare, sooner or later I'm going to snap and yell, "Dominic Ganly's ballsack!"'

' "What was your relationship with Dominic Ganly's ballsack?" ' Susanna inquired, in what was actually a pretty good impression of Rafferty's rich, unrufflable Galway. That accent was getting on my nerves more every time I heard it. ' "Did you have any disagreements with Dominic Ganly's ballsack?" '

'Stop it, you.' Leon was getting the giggles. 'Now I'm definitely going to do it, they'll arrest me for being a smartarse and it'll be all your fault—'

' "Was Dominic Ganly's ballsack behaving oddly that summer?" '
I asked. ' "Did Dominic Ganly's ballsack seem depressed to you?" '
Leon doubled over, flapping a hand at me and wheezing with
laughter.

Melissa was laughing too, spluttering – she wasn't much for
hash, or for anything else really, a couple of drinks was her limit.
'Are you OK?' I asked. She nodded, holding up the joint to me over
her shoulder, still speechless.

'Whoa,' I said, when the first wave of it hit me. 'That is good
stuff.'

'Told you,' Leon said, on a happy sigh. He had his head leaned
back against the wall and his eyes closed.

'Back then I thought it was you,' Susanna said, to me. 'Who took
the key.'

Smoke went down my nose. *Me?*

She shrugged. 'It went missing at Leon's birthday party. I'd forgotten, but I've been thinking back, and I'm positive. It was there
that afternoon – remember, Hugo was digging stuff up to put in
the rock garden, and we were taking rubbish out to the laneway?
But the next day, when I went to let Faye in, it wasn't there. And
you and Dominic were the only people who had gone down to the
bottom of the garden during the party. The ground down there
was a mess, someone fell in a hole and got all muddy, so after that
the rest of us stayed up this end, on the grass.'

'Yeah' – I had just about finished coughing – 'I know that. Why
would Dominic and I have been down there?'

'You were doing coke – oh, come on, Toby, I know I was naïve
but you weren't exactly subtle about it. You snuck off down there
together, and then you came back snickering and rubbing your
noses and putting each other in headlocks and talking a mile a
minute. Remember?'

The thing was, I did. *C'mon, Henno, I need a word*; hurrying down
the garden, Dominic swearing as his foot went deep in mud, me
laughing at him, lines chopped out on an old garden table by the
light of my phone. 'Why the hell would I want the key?'

Susanna shrugged, sitting up to take the joint off me. 'How

would I know? I figured maybe since you'd gone off Faye – duh, of course I knew you were hooking up with her – I thought maybe you didn't want me to let her in any more.'

'I didn't give a damn whether you had Faye in and out every night of the week. And I didn't go *off* her. It's not like we were going out. We just— You know what, never mind. Forget it.' I didn't feel like having this conversation in front of Melissa.

'Or else I thought maybe Dominic had tried to rob the key, for a laugh, and you'd taken it off him and lost it— I don't know, Toby, I didn't exactly spend a lot of time analysing the possibilities. I just sort of figured you had it.'

'Well, I didn't. Jesus.'

Susanna shot me an oblique look. 'You don't even remember doing the coke. How do you know for sure you didn't take the key?'

'Because there's no bloody *reason* why I would.'

'Huh,' Susanna said, on a long thoughtful stream of smoke. 'Then I guess it must have been Dominic.'

'Did you say that to the detectives? That you thought it was me? Tell me you didn't.'

'Of course I didn't. I said, "Dominic Ganly's ballsack".' Leon started to giggle again.

'Su, seriously. Did you—'

'*No*, I didn't. I said I hadn't got a clue. Relax.'

The thing I'd almost missed, in the middle of being annoyed with Susanna: she was right. If I hadn't taken the key, and no one else had been down to the bottom of the garden, then Dominic had to have. 'Why would Dominic want a key to our place?' I asked.

Susanna shrugged. 'Beats me. Maybe he was just robbing random stuff because he thought it was funny.'

The joint was kicking in properly; my G and T tasted novel and starry, I could feel every individual bubble popping on my tongue. 'One time Dec robbed Mr Galvin's shopping list for the laugh,' I said. 'Right off his desk, when we were bringing up our homework. It was like, "Ketchup, Heineken, shaving foam, condoms." So Dec took a photo and made it the screensaver for the entire computer room.'

'That was Dec?' Leon said, impressed. 'Everyone said it was Eoghan McArdle.'

'Shh. Nobody has to know.'

'I wish I'd known you all back then,' Melissa said; dreamily, gazing out over the darkening garden, but she had caught the opening I was throwing to her; I felt the shift in her, her body drawing itself together, *ready steady go*. I gave her a tiny encouraging squeeze.

'You don't,' Susanna said. 'Believe me.'

'Why not?'

'No one's at their finest at eighteen. You probably wouldn't have liked us.'

'Don't listen to her,' I said, dropping my head to nuzzle Melissa's hair. 'You would've loved me.' Leon made a faint sound that was just far enough from a snort for plausible deniability. 'And I would have loved you.'

'I imagine you being lovely,' Melissa said. Leon offered her the joint; she shook her head and passed it to me. 'All happy and silly together, having picnics on the grass and staying up all night talking. Toby tells me stories about it, sometimes.'

This time Leon's snort was harder to miss. 'Don't believe a word he says.'

It was clearly meant to sound jokey, but enough edge slipped through that Melissa turned her head to look at him, puzzled. 'But I love those stories. Was it not like that? Was Toby not happy?'

'Oh, he was happy all right,' Leon said. 'Not the angst-ridden type, our Toby.'

'What was he like? Was he nice?'

'I was a saint,' I said. 'I studied twenty-four hours a day and spent my spare time reading bedtime stories to orphans and saving baby seals.'

'Shh, silly. You're never serious about this. I'm asking them.'

'Toby was basically Toby,' Susanna said. 'Eighteen, so he was a bit louder and more obnoxious, but he's always been very much himself.'

'Thanks,' I said. 'I think.'

'Was he loud and obnoxious?' Melissa asked Leon.

'We're probably the worst people to ask,' Susanna said, rolling over onto her stomach to find her glass. 'We know each other too well; we don't really look at each other properly.'

'I'd have loved to have cousins like that.' Melissa had her head snuggled into the hollow of my shoulder, listening with the same milky, wondering gaze she used to have when I told her those childhood stories. 'Mine are nice, but we never saw each other much. It must have been lovely to be so close.'

'Well,' Leon said. 'It's not like we were *close* close. When we were little, yeah, but by the time we were eighteen . . . not so much.'

What? 'Of course we were,' I said. 'We were spending the whole holidays together here—'

'Right, and during term time we barely hung out at all. And it's not like we spent the holidays snuggled up together pouring out our hearts to each other.'

I wasn't sure what to think about this. As far as I was concerned, the old bond had hung on right through secondary school, until college hit and we all went our separate ways – I had felt exactly the same as always about the two of them, I'd assumed they felt the same about me, why wouldn't they? I couldn't tell whether Leon was rewriting history to make himself feel better about whatever he was trying to pull on me, or whether I had genuinely missed some subtle but crucial shift along the way.

'Well, we still loved each other and all that stuff,' Susanna said, see-ing my face. 'We just weren't bestest buddies. That's natural enough.'

'What about you two?' Melissa asked. 'Were you basically the same back then?'

'I was a total nerd,' Susanna said cheerfully. 'And a space cadet. Someone could be mocking me right to my face, or hitting on me, and the whole thing would go straight over my head. I like to think I'm a bit more copped on these days, but then I would, wouldn't I?'

'And I was a loser,' Leon said crisply, flicking ash.

'You weren't,' Susanna said, instantly and firmly. 'You were great. Smart and kind and funny and brave and all the good stuff.'

She was smiling at him. Her face had a warmth, an unconcealed glow of something like admiration, that startled me: Leon? what had been so great about Leon? He smiled back, but wryly. 'Course I was,' he said. 'Unfortunately, no one noticed except you.' To Melissa: 'I was the kid who got his head flushed down the jacks and found shites in his lunchbox.'

'Poor Leon.' Melissa reached out a hand to squeeze his. I couldn't tell whether she was actually a bit tipsy or whether she was putting it on. If she was, she was surprisingly good at it. 'That's horrible.'

He squeezed her hand back. 'I survived.'

'Did Toby take good care of you?'

'He wasn't bad, actually,' Susanna said. 'He brought us along to the good parties. Warned me when some guy chatting me up was a wanker. Basically, he kept me clued in enough that I didn't make a complete tit of myself, at least not too often. He was even fairly tactful about it. Mostly.'

'That's funny,' Melissa said dreamily. 'I wouldn't have expected him to be like that.'

I curled a strand of her hair round my finger. 'What did you expect?'

'I imagined you a little bit thoughtless. So busy with your own things, you wouldn't really notice anyone else's problems.'

'Hey!' I said, mock-wounded.

'I don't mean in a bad way. Just bouncing along, with your head full of so much that there wasn't room to realise . . . Lots of teenagers are like that.' To the others: 'Was he?'

I actually was mildly unsettled by this. It was looking like Melissa was right, but I wasn't clear on how she would know that stuff: even if I had been a self-absorbed teenage brat, that had been years before I met her.

'Well,' Susanna said. 'He was kind of oblivious sometimes. But there was no malice in it. Just being a teenager. Like you said.'

But I had caught her straight warning stare at Leon. He had been about to say something, but instead he shut his mouth tight and concentrated on putting out the joint on the terrace. It was very strange, seeing the two of them as the enemy; unsettling to the core, like suddenly seeing the world through a dark distorting overlay, no way to know which version was the true one.

Melissa had caught that look, too, or anyway she had caught something that told her to move on. 'What about Dominic Ganly? What was he like?'

'We didn't know him very well,' Susanna said. 'Toby saw a lot more of him.'

'Toby says he never thought about him.'

'I didn't,' I said. 'He was just sort of there. Like what you said about not really noticing the people you see all the time. Or maybe you're right and I was a bit oblivious.' I caught the snide arch of Leon's eyebrow – *You think?* – but he kept his mouth shut.

'I keep wondering about him,' Melissa said. 'At first all I could think was *Poor thing, poor boy* – because he was practically a child, wasn't he?'

Leon moved sharply, but he turned it into reaching for the Rizla packet. Melissa was good at this. I hadn't really expected her to be, and it gave me a sweet sharp thrill of triumph: the two of us, in this as a team, invincible.

'Except then,' she said, 'Sean and Declan were over for dinner the other night. And they really didn't like Dominic.' To me: 'Did they?'

'Apparently not,' I said.

'What did they say?' Susanna asked.

'They didn't really go into details,' Melissa said. 'I think they didn't want to speak ill of the dead. But they obviously thought he wasn't a very good person.'

Leon had started working on another joint; he didn't look up from the lighter flame. 'Were they right?' Melissa asked.

'Sean and Dec are no idiots,' Susanna said, fishing a cucumber slice out of her glass to nibble on. 'Or they weren't back then, any-way; I haven't seen them in a while. If they thought he was bad news—'

'Well but,' I said, 'in fairness, teenagers. Everything's black and white. All it takes is one stupid fight, like I don't know over a rugby match, and—'

'Dominic,' Leon said, a little too sharply, 'was a straight-up arsehole.'

'Pretty much, yeah,' Susanna said. 'From what I saw.'

'What kind of arsehole?' Melissa asked.

Susanna shrugged. 'Your basic model. He was big and good-looking and popular and good at rugby—'

'Which at our school,' Leon said, 'meant you could get away with literally anything.'

'Right. So he did. Bullied people, basically. Which didn't make him unique; there was a lot of it about. Even in context, though, I remember him being fairly nasty.'

I waited for Melissa to keep pushing – *Why, what did he do, did he ever bully you* – but she didn't. Instead she sat up, brushing her hair out of her face, and reached for her glass. 'Some people are just bad news,' she said. 'I don't like thinking that, but they are. The best thing you can do is stay far away from them. If you can.' I tried to catch her eye, but she wasn't looking at me.

Susanna laughed a little, up at the sky: dark blue now, a heavy moon hanging above the trees. 'Amen,' she said.

'OK,' I said, lifting a hand to get their attention. 'Question. I've got a question. What's the worst thing you ever did?'

'Oh my God, it's like being ten,' Leon said. He was rolling with enormous care, bent over, nose almost touching his hands. 'Truth or Dare. If I pick Dare, do I have to climb a tree and moon the neighbours again?'

'Jesus, I'd forgotten that,' Susanna said. To Melissa: 'Old Mrs Whatsherface next door was out in her garden, but she didn't have her glasses, so she couldn't work out what she was seeing. She was there peering up at this shiny white arse—'

Leon started to laugh. ' "Princess? Can you not get down? Here, kittykittykitty—" '

'Leon was laughing so hard I thought he was going to fall out of the tree—'

'Knock it off,' I said. 'I'm serious.'

'Jesus,' Susanna said, eyebrows arched. 'What have you done? Have you been arms-dealing out of that gallery?'

'Nothing goes out of this garden. I swear. I just want to know.'

'What brought this on?'

'Well, because. I've been thinking, a lot. What with . . .' I waved a loose arm at the garden and the house and the universe in general. I wasn't as wasted as I was pretending to be, but my arms and legs had an interesting will of their own and the lighted windows of the apartment block seemed to have detached themselves from the walls and were merrily jigging about. 'Because, look, take Dominic. OK? He probably thought he was a good guy. And most people thought so too – I mean, I did, or at least I took it for granted that probably he was, because people mostly are, right? But what you're saying there, and the stuff Sean and Dec were saying – it's like, whoa . . . maybe not so good.' I pretended not to notice the sardonic up-glance from Leon. 'And on the other hand, right, there's Hugo. He's a good person. I don't know if he knows he's a good person, but we do. I mean, there's no guarantee that, once he's gone, there won't be people saying different. But at least we'll be able to tell the world, if we need to obviously, that he was a good man. Because he is. So' – I had sort of forgotten where I was going with this – 'so. You see what I mean.'

'Not really,' Susanna said, topping up glasses and watching me with interest.

'Well' – I found my place again – 'right. So I have to wonder, right? I've always thought of myself as a decent guy. Yeah? But the shit I've done in my life, haven't we all, but the shit I've done, is it bad enough that I don't count as a good person? Or what?' I blinked back and forth between the two of them. 'You haven't been thinking about this stuff? Seriously?'

'Nope,' Leon said, licking the edge of the Rizla in one deft sweep. 'And I'm not planning to, thanks all the same.'

'Well,' I said, after a moment. 'I guess I'm seeing this differently. From a, an angle. Because I don't know if anyone told you guys this, right, but I could have died, back in spring. With that thing, the break-in. I nearly died.'

A small sound from Melissa, a quick breath. I didn't look at her. 'And that really fucks with your head. You know? Because I don't know, if I had died, I don't know whether I would have counted as a good person or not. I'm not talking about heaven and hell, I don't . . . Just, it matters. To me. So I'd really like it if you'd think about it. Just for a few minutes. I'd like it a lot.'

Susanna had turned her head to look at me; the turn shifted half her face into shadow, I couldn't read her expression at all. 'OK,' she said. 'I'll play. If you will.'

'Thanks, Su,' I said, raising my glass to her and managing not to spill any. 'I mean it. You're a, a, a rock star. A trouper. Something.'

'So let's hear it. What'd you do?'

I said, 'You go first.'

'Why?'

'Because. I need to hear other people's first.'

Susanna lay back with her arms behind her head and looked up at the sky. Curve of her throat, drape of the throw around her body, long lines of her outstretched legs, all whitened and chilled by the moonlight: she looked like a statue washed up on some lonely beach, never to be found. 'OK,' she said. 'I might have sort of killed someone.'

Leon, in the middle of lighting the joint, choked and doubled over, hacking. '*What*,' I said.

'*Su—*' Leon managed to wheeze, urgently.

'Not Dominic,' Susanna said to both of us, amused. 'Jesus. Pair of drama queens.'

'What the *fuck*,' Leon croaked, watery-eyed and fanning himself.

'Breathe.'

'I almost had a *heart* attack.'

'Have a sip of that.'

'OK,' I said. 'So who the hell did you kill? Or maybe sort of kill, or whatever?'

'Well,' Susanna said. She arched her back to brush something out from under it, settled herself more comfortably. 'Remember how I told you the consultant who delivered Zach was a total shit?'

I remembered the conversation, all right, even if the details hadn't stuck. 'Yeah.'

'Tip of the iceberg. Basically, he really enjoyed forcing me to do things I didn't want to do, and he really enjoyed hurting me. He did stuff, every appointment— I hadn't had a kid before, and since I was so young none of my friends had either, so at the time I had no idea it wasn't standard. It didn't even occur to me to walk out and find another doctor. But when I was having Sallie I went somewhere else, because fuck him, and duhhh, revelation, apparently the shit he'd been doing wasn't standard after all.'

'You never told me,' Leon said.

'It wasn't exactly coffee chitchat. You really don't want to hear the gory details.'

'I wouldn't have cared. That's *awful*, you dealing with that all by yourself—' He was bug-eyed stoned and looking really distressed. 'Did you at least say it to Tom?'

'Nope. He had enough going on. So did I; I didn't even really think about it myself, not then.' Susanna smiled up at him. 'I was OK, Leon. Honest to God. I knew I could deal with it, once I got a chance.'

'And?' I said, reaching to take the joint off Leon; he had had plenty. I sneaked a glance at Melissa, who was presumably getting a lot more than she had bargained for here, but she was sitting quietly, cross-legged, with the blanket draped over her lap and her glass cupped in both hands, watching Susanna.

'And I dealt with it,' Susanna said. 'Once Sallie was born and things settled down, I had a think about what I wanted to do. Obviously if this guy had done this stuff to me, he'd done it to plenty of others – he was in his fifties, he must've had thousands of patients. So I made an appointment with him, under a fake name so he couldn't go after me – no way was he going to remember my real one, after three years. I told him I'd been a patient of his before and I was going to file a complaint. He laughed in my face – surprise. So I told him I'd tracked down a couple of dozen of his other patients through an internet mummy board, and we were all filing complaints, and eight of them had been recording their appointments on their phones.'

'Whoa,' I said. I could totally see her pulling it off: straight-backed and cool, ticking off points as meticulously as if she were giving a presentation. Susanna always had been a killer poker player. 'What'd he say?'

'He *lost* it. Not scared; furious. That was the amazing part: he wasn't putting it on, he was genuinely outraged. He was jabbing his finger right in my face, threatening to have me committed, call Child Services and have my kids taken away. I told him I could upload that footage to the internet faster than he could make phone calls, and I asked what was he planning to do about the other twenty-six women, have the whole lot of us committed? And all the ones I hadn't found yet, but they'd come forward once they heard about it? So he threw me out of his office. And' – Susanna held out her hand to me for the joint – 'five days later his death notice was up online. I don't know if he had a heart attack or something, or if he did himself in. Either way, though, I'd say there's an OK chance I had something to do with it.'

'You couldn't have known,' Melissa said, although Susanna hardly looked in need of comforting. 'It's not as if you knew he had a heart condition or—'

'Well, I mean' – she held in smoke, waving a hand at us to wait, blew it out over the garden – 'he was kind of fat, and he did get all red in the face a lot. But nah, I didn't know anything for a fact. I thought probably the best I could expect was that he'd quit his job, and more likely he wouldn't even do that but at least he might get spooked and stop pulling that shit on people. I was kind of hoping, though.'

'Why didn't you just file an actual complaint?' I asked.

Susanna laughed out loud, and to my surprise Leon snorted too. Even Melissa was looking at me like I had said something regrettably silly. 'Are you serious?' Susanna asked. 'To a board of his mates? He'd have said I was a hysterical woman making stuff up, end of story. There's a decent chance he genuinely would've got me thrown in a mental hospital, or had the kids taken away. I mean, I guess I could've actually tracked down other people and convinced some of them to record appointments and whatever, but this was quicker and a lot less messy.'

This conversation was turning out to be enlightening in ways I hadn't expected. Apparently my image of Susanna – good girl, follow the rules, if anyone's being bullied run and tell a teacher – was out of date.

'His face was good,' Susanna said, rolling over onto her stomach to pass Leon the joint. 'When I said about uploading the footage. I enjoyed that a lot.'

I couldn't figure out, through the muddle of booze and hash, just how horrified I should be. I felt like there was an excellent chance that she was exaggerating either the doctor's villainy or his dreadful fate, or both, and a non-zero chance that she was making the whole thing up; but either way, the nonchalance got more unsettling the more I thought about it, and either way there was the question of why exactly she was telling this story. The only reason I could see was that she wanted me or Leon or both of us to hear, loud and clear: *If you mess with me, I will fuck you up.*

'OK,' I said. 'So. If you did have something to do with him dying. Do you still figure you're a good person?'

Susanna thought about that, chin on hands. 'Maybe not,' she said, in the end. 'But say I'd decided not to have kids, so I'd never needed to go to him. Or say I'd got lucky and ended up with a decent doctor. Then I wouldn't have done it. But I'd still be the same person; the reason I hadn't done it wouldn't be because I was more virtuous, it would just be dumb luck. Would I be a good person then?'

This was way above my pay grade. Leon had made this joint even stronger than the first one; a weird fizzing sensation was travelling up my arms and I was suddenly very aware of my nose. I felt like there was something wrong with what she was saying, but I couldn't put my finger on it. 'I have no idea,' I said, after a long pause. 'What you're talking about.'

That started Susanna giggling. Once she started, she couldn't stop, and it set the rest of us off too. The windows of the apartment building swung to and fro, bright rectangular pendulums, tick tock tick tock, and that felt somehow irresistibly funny, a marvellous joke straight out of *Alice in Wonderland*. I wondered if Susanna had been joking too, if her whole story had been one great big wind-up, silly me falling for it!

'So,' she said to Leon. 'Beat that.'

Leon held up a palm. 'Oh *hell* no. I'm not playing this game. You three knock yourselves out.'

'You have to play. Or I'm not giving you any more hash and you'll have to go back to wandering around dodgy nightclubs.' She stretched out one leg and poked him with a toe. 'Go on.'

'Stop it.'

'Go. Go. Go.' I started chanting too, 'Go go go,' our voices spilling out across the ravaged garden, Melissa laughing— 'Go go go,' I leaned across and started jabbing Leon in the arm until he couldn't help giggling too, half angrily, slapping my hand away, '*Stop*—' I got him in a headlock and we tumbled over onto Susanna, her elbow jammed into my ribs and Leon's hair in my mouth and it took me straight back to when we were kids scrapping, they even smelled the same— 'OK!' Leon yelled. 'OK! Get off me!'

We disentangled ourselves, breathless and laughing, Leon making a big thing of brushing himself down, 'God, you people are *savages*—' My head was whirling mercilessly; I flopped back onto the terrace and gazed up at the skidding stars, hoping they would settle down. I considered the possibility that we were all still sixteen and getting stoned for the first time and everything since then had been an elaborate hallucination, but this felt way too heavy to deal with and I decided I should probably ignore it. 'Your hair,' Melissa said, laughing, holding out her hands, 'you're all leaves, come here—' and I rolled over to her and put my head in her lap so she could pick the leaves out.

'Fine,' Leon said, fumbling for his cigarette packet. It took me a moment to remember what we were supposed to be talking about. 'The time when we were five and I bit you on the face.'

'Jesus, I actually remember that,' I said. 'You drew *blood*. What the fuck was your major malfunction there?'

'I can't remember. I bet you deserved it, though.'

'I had to start school looking like I'd escaped from Hannibal Lecter,' I told Melissa.

'Poor little Toby.' She stroked my cheek. 'Did you tell the other kids you'd been fighting supervillains?'

'I wish. I probably just said it was the neighbours' cat.'

'So there's mine,' Leon said, noticing just in time that he was about to light the wrong end of his cigarette. 'Toby, you're up.'

'What? No I'm not. That doesn't count.'

'It's what you're getting. Take it and like it.'

'After Su's thing, that's what you come up with? That was crap. Do a proper one.'

He blew smoke at me. 'You do a proper one.'

'I'm not going till you do.'

'I'll go,' Melissa said.

I sat up to look at her face: calm, steady, unreadable. I couldn't tell how stoned she was. 'You don't have to,' I said.

'Why not?' Susanna asked.

'Because she barely even knows you guys. It's not the same thing.'

'Why don't you let her decide for herself?'

'My mum's an alcoholic,' Melissa said. Her voice was clear, almost dreamy. 'One time, when I was twelve, she fell downstairs and broke her leg. I was supposed to be asleep, but she'd been making a lot of noise. She couldn't get up. My dad was working nights, so he was out. She was screaming to me to help her, but I pretended I was asleep. I thought if she had to lie there like that for a while, in an awful lot of pain, it would scare her off drinking. I knew she might choke to death – she was getting sick – but I left her there anyway. I listened to her all night, till my dad came home and found her.'

'Jesus,' I said. I had heard snippets of stories, along the way, but not this one. 'Baby—' I put an arm around her waist and drew her to me.

'It was a long time ago. She was fine; her leg healed up. And she doesn't remember it.' To the others: 'It didn't work. She still drinks.'

'Oh, you poor little *kid*,' Leon said, big-eyed, leaning over to squeeze her hand. 'Of *course* that doesn't make you a bad person.'

'Amen,' Susanna said. 'If it had worked, you would've been a hero.'

'I don't think it does,' Melissa said. 'I hope it doesn't. It was a terrible thing to do, but I was only twelve. I don't think one thing, specially one when you're a kid, can make you a bad person.'

'It doesn't,' I said, pulling her closer and kissing the top of her head. 'You're one of the best people I know.'

That got a touch of a smile. 'Well, probably not that. But . . .' A small sigh, as she leaned her head on my chest. 'Trying my best to make things better. Whatever difference that makes.' And to Leon: 'Your turn.'

He could hardly refuse, after that. I was blown away, yet again, by Melissa. She had to be wondering what the hell I was trying to do, she hadn't wanted me to do it to begin with, and yet here she was throwing herself into the breach, heart and soul, to help me do it.

After a moment Leon said, 'OK.' He gave her hand one more squeeze and moved away to settle his back against the wall, his face in shadow. 'So. Back when I was in Amsterdam, I was going out with this guy Johan – remember him?'

'Yeah,' I said, which wasn't true. Leon always had a boyfriend, none of them ever lasted longer than a year or two, I had given up keeping track.

'I do,' Susanna said. 'What happened there? I thought you guys were serious.'

'We were, yeah. We were talking about getting married. And then one day, while Johan was out at work minding his own business, I dumped all his stuff in the hall outside our apartment with a note telling him we were over, and changed the lock on our door.'

'Why?' Susanna asked. She was lying back on the terrace, dead leaves caught in her hair and a cool shine of moonlight in her eyes. 'What had he done?'

'Nothing. He didn't cheat on me, didn't hit me, practically never even got narky with me. He's an amazing guy, he was mad about me, I was mad about him.'

'Then why?'

'Because,' Leon said, 'it wasn't going to last forever anyway. Shut *up*, Toby, I'm not being dramatic here, I'm just stating the bleeding obvious: for whichever reason, growing apart or fighting or cheating or just getting old and dying, relationships don't last forever.

Not to depress you guys or anything.' A wry, bleak glance at the rest of us, as he mashed out his cigarette. 'And actually, that had never bothered me before. I kind of liked it. It was like, if I do something stupid and make a great big mess of this, no big deal: it wasn't going to last forever anyway. I haven't bulldozed the *pyramids* here. I can just go start over somewhere else.'

He reached for the gin and topped up his glass, not bothering with the rest of us. 'But I was really in love with Jo. And I know how incredibly teenage this sounds, but I genuinely couldn't handle that. It was stressing the fuck out of me. We'd be cuddled up together in bed, or we'd be out dancing and having a laugh, or we'd just be eating breakfast and watching the pigeons on our balcony, and suddenly all I could think about was how one day we wouldn't be doing this together any more. No maybe, nothing I could do to stop it; it was guaranteed. And I'd just want to scream, or run away, or break everything. So in the end I did. It was the ballsack-in-church thing again, only that time I actually did it.'

'What happened when Johan got home?' I asked. For some reason I was picturing Johan as an eternal-postgrad type, thin benevolent face and little wire-rimmed glasses, completely unable to cope with anything coming out of left field like this.

Leon stared at his glass like he wasn't sure what it was. 'Basically what you'd expect. It was horrible. Lots of shouting. Him hammering on the door. Both of us crying. The people in the other apartments sticking their heads out to gawp – the old lady at the end of the hall was screaming at us to shut up, and then her awful yappy dog got out and bit Jo on the ankle . . . In the end he called the cops – not to get me in trouble; because he thought I'd lost my mind. The cops were totally shitty about the whole thing, but since I wasn't actually crazy and it was my flat, in the end there wasn't a lot they could do. I moved anyway. I'd had enough of Amsterdam.'

For some reason I couldn't put my finger on, I didn't like this story at all. I unwrapped myself from Melissa and found my glass, which miraculously hadn't got knocked over along the way.

'So,' Leon said, 'that was the worst thing I've ever done. Breaking Johan's heart.'

I let a snigger escape. 'Is that funny?' Leon snapped, head whipping up.

'No no no' – holding up a hand, half-masking a burp – 'you're fine, dude. Not laughing at you. I'm laughing at myself. All this time I've been related to Mother Teresa, and I never even noticed.'

'What the hell are you talking about?'

'Well – whoops' – as my glass nearly slipped out of my fingers; I saved it and took a long gulp. 'Ahh. That's beautiful gin. What was I . . . ?' With a finger-snap and a point at Leon, who was glaring: 'Right. The thing is, dude, yeah? I know a lot of people. And I don't know *anyone*, like not one person, who can honestly say that the worst thing they've ever done is dumping someone. Maybe my friends are just a shower of arseholes, I don't know. But it's either that or you're a total saint.'

In the corner of my eye I caught a glimpse of Melissa, tugging at a strand of hair and looking worried: my tone was bothering her. I tried to shoot her a covert glance to reassure her that I knew what I was doing, I had a plan, but I was in no state to pull that off and it came out as a cross-eyed leer.

'Johan really loved me,' Leon said. 'God help him. And now, wherever he is, he's stuck for life doing the same thing I did: obsessing about how, sooner or later, whatever he's doing is all going to go tits-up. Like I infected him.' With a defiant stare at me: 'If what you want to hear is that that makes me a bad person, then yeah, I think it probably does. Does that make you feel better about whatever it is you've done?'

'Not really,' I said. 'But then you didn't want it to, did you?'

The thing was, and I wasn't sure what to do about it, I believed him. I hadn't believed Susanna, or not all the way, but every word of this rang true – this kind of self-indulgent emo shite was right up Leon's alley. And I had finally, laboriously, figured out why that story had gone through me like ice. If the worst thing Leon had ever done was hurting specky Johan's feelings, then clearly he hadn't killed Dominic. Whatever was going on here, I had got it all wrong.

'What *have* you done?' Leon demanded. 'This was your stupid idea to begin with, now you're sitting there giving me shite because my ones aren't dramatic enough for you— What's yours?'

It hadn't been Susanna, either. There was no way a skinny teenage girl could have hauled Dominic up that tree. Which meant the reason they were nudging the cops towards me – and they were, I knew they were, one of them? both? not just the hoodie but where else would that photo have come from, who else would have said I had problems with Dominic? – that wasn't to save themselves. Malice, pure and simple? Could they really hate me that much, and I had never noticed? What Could I possibly have done to either of them to make them think I deserved this?

I was on the verge of full stoner paranoia. The apartment windows were tick-tocking back and forth again, but it didn't feel funny this time; it felt sinister, as if they were working up the momentum to rip free from the building altogether and come swooping down at us. I knew if I didn't pull it together I was going to end up rocking and whimpering in some corner.

'Forget it,' Susanna said, on a yawn. She pulled herself up to sitting and knuckled one eye. 'Let's go home. Toby can make his confession next time.'

'No,' Leon said. 'If I'm going to spill my guts, I want to hear his one.'

Melissa was looking at me with her head tilted, questioning and anxious. It was the sight of her that steadied me. After her story, there was no way I could let her down by coming out of this empty-handed; it was unthinkable. There was something here, even if I had been wrong about what it was, and I needed it.

I closed my eyes and took a couple of deep breaths. When I opened them again the windows stayed still, more or less. I smiled at Melissa and gave her a little nod: *Don't worry, baby, everything's going according to plan.*

Susanna was poking Leon with her foot, trying to make him move. 'I'm in tatters. If we don't head, I'm going to crash out right here. How strong did you roll those?'

'Get a drink of water or something. I want to hear Toby's.'

'You go home if you want,' I said to Susanna. Actually, I liked that idea; Leon would be easier to wrangle without her there. 'Zach's probably tied Tom up and set him on fire by now.'

'Leon. Come on. We can split a taxi.'

'No.'

Both of us knew the mulish set of his chin: he was going nowhere. Susanna rolled her eyes and flopped back onto the terrace, but she kept watching us.

'OK,' I said. 'You need to swear you won't tell anyone.'

'Oh for heaven's sake,' Susanna said. 'Mutually assured destruction. You think I want people finding out about me and Dr Mengele?'

'No, I mean it. I could get into serious trouble.'

She gave me an eye-roll and held up her little finger. 'Pinky swear.'

'Whatever,' Leon said. 'Spill.'

'OK,' I said, and took a breath. 'So this spring, right? we had this show going on at the gallery?'

I fumbled and stammered my way through it – which didn't take much acting; this wasn't a story I had wanted to tell Melissa, ever. I kept one eye on her (not happy, clearly: upset, disappointed? angry? what?) and the other on Leon: slouched back against the wall giving me an increasingly disgusted stare, occasionally taking an ostentatiously large swig of G and T when some detail was just too much for him.

'So,' I said, finally, on another very deep breath. 'There's mine.'

I had deliberately picked something relatively innocuous, something that would give Leon every excuse to come after me, especially after the way I'd gone after him. And sure enough: 'Oh. My. God,' he said, lip curling. 'You're trying to claim that's the worst thing you've ever done? *That?*'

'Listen,' I said, rubbing at my nose, properly shamefaced. 'That could have scuppered the whole show. These kids, that was their one chance to make a better life for themselves, and I could have wrecked it. And I was' – what was it Dec had said – 'I was dissing them, their lives. Making a joke out of them. I didn't really get what a big deal it was at the time, but now—'

Susanna was giving me a look of profound scepticism. 'I should have told you,' I said to Melissa. 'I just didn't want to upset you. I was working my way up to it, and then . . .' She shook her head, one brief quick move: *Don't worry about it* or *Don't give me that* or *We'll talk about it later*, I couldn't tell.

'Hold the phone,' Leon said, eyebrows up. 'That's your big moral crisis? You fooled a bunch of people about some paintings? And you gave *me* shite because mine wasn't dramatic enough?'

'Everyone has breakups, man. Not everyone feeds a line of total bullshit to hundreds of people—'

'Total strangers. And no one got hurt.'

'Well, yeah,' I said, mildly miffed. 'Total strangers. I wouldn't do anything to anyone I love. I know you would, you just said that, but—'

'Or,' Susanna said coolly, 'Leon figures the things he's done to people he loves are more serious than the things he's done to total strangers. And you don't.'

Some part of me noticed that she seemed a lot less fucked up than the rest of us, which I didn't like. 'No. No no no.' I waved a finger at her. 'That's what I'm telling you. I don't *do* stuff that would hurt people I love. People who love me.'

I made it good and self-righteous, and sure enough, Leon's head went back. 'Oh. My. God. You are *unbelievable*, do you know that? You're in your own world, it's like talking to an *alien*—'

'Dude, what are you on about? Give me *one* example of me doing something to anyone who—'

'OK. Fine. I, just for *example*, when Dominic bloody Ganly started making my life hell, I went and told you. Do you even remember that?'

He was sitting up straight, glaring at me through his hair like a bristling cat. 'What are you talking about?' I said.

Leon let out an angry laugh. 'I'm not surprised. It's not like you gave much of a fuck at the time.'

'Jesus,' I said, putting up my hands. 'Su, give him some more hash, quick.'

'Leon,' Susanna said.

'No. I don't care if he's messed up or whatever, he's being a total—'

'Whoa whoa whoa,' I said. 'Back up the truck here. Dominic was giving you hassle?'

'*Everyone* gave me hassle. You were right *there*, you saw *plenty* of it, occasionally you'd actually bother to go, "Hey, guys, lay off my cousin," and they'd back off for a while. But Dominic was the only one who actually scared me. The rest were just being Neanderthal idiots, but he was a total sadist. Vicious. He kept it down around you, but when you weren't there, God— So finally I told you. And you' – twist to Leon's lip, almost a snarl – 'you went, "Oh, chill, he's just messing, I'll have a *word* with him." '

'What's wrong with that?' I demanded. 'I was straight in there, ready to help you out. What did you want from me?'

'I didn't want you to *have a word*. I wanted you to get Sean and the two of you knock Dominic's teeth in and tell him you'd rip his head off and shove it up his hole if he ever went near me again. But you said, God you were so *reasonable* about it, you said oh no, that wasn't the way to go about it. You said you couldn't be there minding me all the time, and if you beat Dominic up, he'd find a chance to take it out on me. You said I needed to learn to deal with my problems myself.'

And, at last, there it was. The grudge, spiking through his voice as sharp and bright as if it had been yesterday. 'Well,' I said. My heart was going wild, I couldn't tell how much was the revelation and how much was the hash – stupid, I should have stayed straight for this— 'I had a point, didn't I? What part of that is wrong?'

'*All* of it. It doesn't work that way, it sounds great but— You had your *word* with Dominic, and of course that just made him *worse*, exactly like I'd *told* you it would. Because after that it wasn't just casual stuff in passing, slamming my locker door on my head like he would have to anyone weaker than him; it was targeted. He went *looking* for me. And he knew he could do anything he wanted to me, and all that would happen was a little *chat* where you suggested that maybe he should be nice to me if that was OK please and thank you.'

He was breathing in quick hard puffs, nostrils flaring. 'Jesus,' I said. 'I mean, I'm sorry, man. But this was like, what, fifteen years ago? Maybe it might be time to let go a little, yeah?'

Of course Leon bit on that. Throwing himself back against the wall: 'You are fucking *unbelievable*. My God. Dominic *tortured* me. For years. I thought about killing myself all the *time*. You think getting beaten up fucked with your head— That was *one night*. Imagine what years of it would do to you. I don't know' – raising his voice as I tried to say something – 'I'm never going to know what I would have been like if you had had my back, that time. So, so' – furiously scraping his forelock back from his face – 'so *don't* get all self-righteous about how you would never hurt anyone close to you.'

Melissa was tugging harder at her hair, wrapping it tight around her finger. I knew this was making her unhappy and I wished there had been a way to do it when she wasn't around, but I had to take what I could get; she would understand when I brought her my shining answers— 'But,' I said. 'Jesus. I didn't *know* it was that bad. Fuck's sake, Leon, I don't read minds. You should've *told* me. If I'd known he was getting worse, I would've—'

'You would've been raging,' Susanna said. 'You would've done something.'

'*Exactly*. But I didn't know.'

I had turned to her triumphantly, but there was a look on her face I couldn't read, muddled shadows, darkness tangling with the yellow light through the French doors. 'Are you sure?' she asked.

'What? Of course I am.'

'Because I thought – I mean, Faye said—'

She broke off. 'Faye?' I said. 'Faye what?'

'Nothing specific. Just that you'd been kind of pissed off with Dominic, that summer.'

'I wasn't—' When the hell had Susanna been talking to Faye, why the hell? 'I wasn't pissed off with him.' And when she didn't answer: 'Did you tell Rafferty that? What the fuck, Su?'

'No, I didn't tell him. He already knew.'

'Well,' I said, after a moment. 'Then I guess we all know who did.'

Leon's head snapped up. 'What? You mean me? I never—'

'Of course you did. This is exactly what I'm talking about.' In fact, I was having a hard time keeping track of what I was talking about; the whole thing had the nasty, nightmarish, swimming-through-seaweed quality of all stoned arguments, impossible either to navigate or to escape. 'Me, right? now that you *finally* bother to tell me you had real problems with Dominic, I'm not going to run to Rafferty. Because I don't *deliberately* dump my own cousins in the shit. But you, you blame me for your whole life or whatever it was, and you just *told* us, Leon, you just *said* you don't have a problem fucking over your, your nearest and dearest when it's convenient—'

'That's not the same thing at *all*. I *knew* you wouldn't get it, that's why I didn't want to tell you, I just knew you'd make it into—'

'I don't feel well,' Melissa said abruptly.

She did look awfully white, soft hair rumpled and falling in her face, shoulders slumping. 'Baby,' I said, reaching for her. 'What is it? Are you going to get sick?'

'No. Just a bit dizzy.'

'Oh, shit,' Leon said, round-eyed. 'Did I roll it too strong? You're so tiny—'

'Come on,' I said, slipping an arm round her waist. Her hand clamped hard on my wrist. 'Let's get you to bed.'

She leaned on me through the kitchen, head drooping on my chest, but in the hall she pulled away so abruptly I lost my balance. 'Whoops,' I said, catching the banister rail. 'Are you OK?'

Melissa said, 'I don't want to do this any more.'

'OK,' I said, carefully, after a moment. 'Like, they'll tell me more if you're not around?'

'No. Enough.' She was facing me across the hall like I was dangerous, arms wrapped tight around her chest. 'Let's go home.'

'What?' I said, after a bewildered pause. 'We are home.'

'No. My place, or your place.'

Confusing pale slants falling through the fanlight to stripe her set face, the geometric flowers of the floor tiles; too many patterns everywhere, my eyes wouldn't focus. 'Like, now? Tonight?'

'Yes, now. Or come to bed with me, and we'll go first thing in the morning. Leon can stay with Hugo – I don't want to leave him, you know I don't, but we can come visit—'

I was in much worse shape than I had realised before I stood up. None of this made sense. 'Wait,' I said. 'You're not feeling sick?'

'I want to go home.'

'But,' I said. 'Why? Are you mad about the, the thing at the gallery? Because—'

'No. That wasn't good, you know it wasn't, but right now it's not the— This is terrible, Toby. The three of you. Look what you're doing to each other.'

'Hang on,' I said. 'This is, what, this is because I didn't get Dominic off Leon's back? You're upset about that? I mean I should have, I get it, but I was just a stupid kid, I didn't realise – I'll go back and apologise—'

Melissa shook her head in frustration. 'No. Not that, you can do that some other time, but right now— I can *see* what you're doing. I'm not stupid. But they're doing something too, Toby' – a fierce flick of her head towards the terrace – 'they're trying to do something to you, and I can't tell what it is but it's not good. And we need to go home.'

'No we don't.' I felt I had every right to be indignant about this; she was the one who had insisted we should come here in the first place, I had only gone along with it to make her happy, what was her problem? 'Everything's fine. I know what I'm doing.'

'What? What do you think you're going to get out of this?'

'You heard them out there.' I was still hanging on to the banister, gesturing at the terrace with my other arm, I knew I looked like some wild flailing drunk but I didn't care— 'They know something. I'm going to find out what it is.'

'*Why?* Who cares what they know? What could they know that'll make anything better?'

Even if I'd been sober, I couldn't have put it into words; it surged up inside me, so immense that it almost stopped my throat. 'I'm trying to fix it,' I said. The words felt much too small for something so momentous. 'I'm trying to fix it all.'

Melissa's head went back in frustration. 'You're *not fixing it*. Toby. You're going to make it a million times worse.'

That stung. 'You don't think I can do this? You think, what, I'm too fucked up, I'll make a mess of it and they'll see straight through me—'

'No. You're doing it really well: pretending to be all drunk and stupid, and they're falling straight into it—'

'Then what? You don't think I can handle it? You think I'll find out something I don't like and I'll, what, go to pieces, I'll, I'll be running in circles making chicken noises—'

'I don't *know*! I'm not good at saying things, Toby, I'm doing my best but— All I know is, this whole thing is bad. It's bad stuff. And' – she was drunk too, swaying forwards, small pale hands swooping and whirling like sparklers in the dimness – 'and, and, when something's bad all through, the only thing you can do – not you, anyone – the only thing is to get away. You can't go, "Oh, it's fine, I'll just jump in and *fix* it—" It doesn't *work* like that.' Glint of tears on her face, but when I stepped towards her she put up her hands to keep me off— 'No, *don't*, I'm trying to— If you get yourself all tangled up in whatever's going on here, if you *deliberately* dive right into the middle, it's going to *wreck* you. And I'm not going to sit here and watch while you do that to yourself. Not after how hard you've worked to get better, how hard we've *both*— I'm not. I'm not.' She was crying openly now, and it ripped my heart open. 'I'm going home. Please come with me, Toby. Please.'

'You can't drive,' I said, firmly and ridiculously, as if that were the final word on this whole issue. 'You're too drunk.'

'We can get a taxi. Please. Let's go.'

I would have done it if I could, done it in a heartbeat. I would have done anything else in the world, ripped my own arm off, to stop the tears falling down her face. But this was my one chance of ever clawing my way out of this strangling dark, back up to the warm bright world; this was it.

'Go to bed,' I said. 'I'm way too messed up to even have this conversation. We'll have it in the morning.'

'Come up with me.'

'I'll be there in two minutes. I just have to tell Susanna and Leon we're crashing out.' Soothingly, or as soothingly as I could manage:

'You head on up, baby. Get the bed nice and warm. I'll be right there. OK?'

This time Melissa let me go to her, stroke back her hair and kiss her wet face. 'Shh,' I said, 'shh. Everything's fine,' and she clasped her hands behind my neck and kissed me back, hard. But when she moved away from me and headed up the stairs, her head was down and she had her hand pressed against her mouth, and I knew she was still crying.

I almost went after her. In the eerie grey light of the hall, what I thought of for some reason was that long-ago phone call as I walked home late and drunk, among the wrought-iron whorls of street-lamps and the tantalising smell of spices. *Come over.* How I could have gone to her then; how it would have been, all unknown to me, salvation. For a dizzying and deeply stoned moment, I thought time had folded over and this was my second chance; that if I went up those stairs I would find myself in Melissa's flat, with awful Megan pinching up her lips and making bitchy little jabs about my lack of consideration, while I laughed and headed for Melissa's nest of duvets and a long lazy Saturday morning, pancakes for brunch and a walk by the canal.

Melissa switched on our bedroom light and brightness flooded down the stairs, making me flinch and blink. Then the bedroom door closed with a soft click and the hall was dark again. I stood there for one more minute, leaning against the newel post and star-ing at the tile patterns, trying to make them stop hopping and pulsating. Then I went back out to Leon and Susanna.

Susanna was lying on her back on the terrace, arms behind her head, looking up at the sky. The moonlight hit her full in the face. 'Is Melissa OK?' she asked.

'Just a little bit the worse for wear,' I said. I made my way around her, very carefully, and settled myself on the steps. 'She's going to bed.'

Leon was huddled up with a fist pressed to his mouth; he was clearly much too wasted to cope with this. 'Oh God. We upset her. Didn't we? All that fighting, we upset her, we have to go in and say sorry—'

'I don't think she really wants to see you right now, man. Not after that.'

'Oh *nooo*,' Leon moaned, face going down in his hands. 'Oh, shit . . .'

'Shouldn't you stay with her?' Susanna suggested. 'Like, in case she gets sick or something?'

'She's not *that* bad. She just needs to crash out.' I was impressed with my easy tone, no hint of crisis, nothing like a guy whose girl-friend was walking out on him. The truth was I didn't believe she was, not at all. The things she'd stuck by me through, the roiling nightmare months when I was barely a human being: there was no way she would dump me because I was being a bit too nosy for comfort. By the time I went to bed she would be asleep, curled up still dressed on top of the covers, suitcase open on the floor and a random armful of clothes thrown in there to show me she was seri-ous; I would pull her close and wrap the duvet around both of us, and in the morning when the hangovers wore off we would sort everything out. And oh God if I could come back to her with some-thing solid, something to show her this wasn't pointless and stupid and self-destructive— 'And to be honest, that's OK with me. Because I think we need to talk, Leon, don't we, and I think it's a better idea that Melissa isn't around.'

'What?' Leon's head popped up and he stared at me. 'Talk about what? I didn't say anything to Rafferty, I swear, Toby, I—'

'Not that. Fuck that.' I found my glass, or someone's glass, and took a good swig. 'I want to talk about the break-in at my apartment.'

Susanna rolled onto her side and propped herself up on her elbow to look at me. 'Why?' she asked.

'Well,' I said. 'Those two guys, right? the two guys who broke in? They had a plan. They waited, they specif, spefi—' I was never going to make it. 'They waited *on purpose* till they knew I was home. And then they broke in and took a bunch of my stuff which, you know what, that didn't seem like a huge deal at the time, compared to the rest, although now I'm starting to wonder, you know? But they also beat the living shite out of me. No' – at a movement from Leon – 'shut

343

up, Leon. You have no idea. Whatever you're imagining, what*ever*, it was a shit-ton worse than that. So just shut up.'

Leon curled in on himself, chewing on a thumbnail and breathing too fast. It made me even more positive: guilty conscience, he couldn't even look at me, at last I was on the right track— 'The detective who's looking into it,' I said, leaning closer, 'you know what he told me? He said if it was a random thing, if it was just your basic skanger burglars who fancied my car, right? He would've had an idea who they were, straightaway. He knows all the regulars. But he didn't have a clue. Because *shut the fuck up Leon*' – my voice exploding in a roar, going to wake Melissa, Hugo, the neighbours, I didn't care – 'because *this was personal*. Not random. This was some little *shit* who had a grudge against me and he wanted me *fucked up*, and Jesus Christ he got what he wanted, didn't he? And what I've been trying to explain to you is that people don't *have* grudges against me, because I don't *do* shitty things to people who actually care about me. But *you do*.'

'I hate this,' Leon said – it was almost a wail. 'Can we stop this? Please?'

'You *started* it. All that shite about I didn't take good enough *care* of you, like the whole thing was my problem, like you had no responsibility to look after your fucking self—' This wasn't what I had planned at all, I had meant to coax and charm it out of him, browbeating had never crossed my mind but it felt good and I wasn't sure I could stop even if I wanted to— 'At least I've finally found the one person who's got a grudge against me—'

'Toby,' Susanna said sharply. 'Stop it.'

'The only person who – *look at me you little shit* – the only person who hates me enough to send in a pair of scumbags to beat me half to death. Was that supposed to be, to, to be karma? Because I didn't stop Dominic beating you up?'

'I *didn't*! Toby, what are you talking about, I don't hate you, stop—'

'And now you're telling Rafferty this bullshit—' I got him by a clumsy fistful of jumper, jerking at him, trying to make him look at me but my hand was weak as a kid's and he wouldn't, he just curled

344

tighter. 'You didn't fuck up my life enough the first time, now you're trying to get me *arrested*? What are you, what have you, what the *hell* have you done to me—'

I was about to hit him. I was pulling back my fist, I could already feel the ecstatic smack of it into his face, when Susanna caught my arm. She said, close to my ear, 'Where were you?'

I spun round ready to shout her off, but the sight of her stopped me. Her hair was straggling in her face, clips hanging loose; her eyes were dark and dilated, unfocused.

'What?' I said.

'That night. Toby. Where did you go?'

That night. I thought she meant the gap, the hole in my mind between the pub and my living room. 'I don't know,' I said. My head felt like it was rocking dangerously on my neck. 'I've been trying and trying. It's gone.'

She stared at me, swaying a little, gripping my arm for balance.

'Why?' The paranoia was rising again. 'Do you know? How do you—'

'I went to your room.'

This made no sense at all. 'What?'

'When I got that text from Dominic. It freaked me out. I didn't understand what was going on. I wanted someone else. I went to Leon's room, but he was out cold; when I tried to wake him up he just went "Fuck off" and pulled the sheet over his head. So I went to your room. And you weren't there.'

'No,' I said. I had let go of Leon; he was snuffling somewhere. 'What? That's not what I meant.'

'I sat on my bed for ages, listening for you to come back. Hours. I was scared, I thought maybe Dominic had done something to you and that was what the text was about . . . In the end I fell asleep. In the morning you were back.'

'But,' I said. Her fingers were hurting me. 'You said you just ignored that text. That's what you said.'

'I didn't want to tell anyone. I didn't want to sound like . . . I haven't said it to the detectives. But where were you? How do you not remember?'

345

'That's not,' I said. 'I meant the night I got *hit*. In my *apartment*. The night with Dominic, when Dominic, I was in bed.'

'No.'

'I was.'

'No. I looked.'

I stared at her. She stared back. Somewhere deep in the house, faint and faraway enough that it came to me more as a sensation than as a sound, a door closed.

It seeped in slowly, drop by drop, through all the multiple layers of mess in my brain. Leon and Susanna IDing my hoodie, telling Rafferty I'd had problems with Dominic, giving him the photo: that wasn't some Machiavellian plan to frame me. If they had been out to fuck me up, they could have done a lot better than that. They could have said anything they wanted – the story Susanna had just told, a made-up confession replete with lurid details; I with my smashed memory would have had no comeback. They had pointed Rafferty in my direction because they were scared that he was going to come after them, and – all those little jabs about me getting away with everything – they had no intention of taking the heat for me. They actually thought I had done it.

Which was ludicrous, batshit insane. Me, cheerful oblivious Labrador of a guy, lolloping happily along with the flow: I hadn't been a killer. Beating Dominic up, sure, if I had known the whole story I would have been on for teaming up with Sean to dish out a few smacks. But a garrotte: not just no but oh hell no, nothing in me could ever have come up with that, and they should have known, they of all people should have known me better than to think that of me for a single instant—

'Wait,' I said. 'You think I . . . what?'

'I don't think anything. I don't, Toby. I just want to know.'

'Come on,' I said, quietly enough, I thought. 'All this, this, this dancing around, fuck that. You two have something you want to say to me, you want to accuse me of something, then do it.'

'We're not,' Leon said, his voice high and wobbly. 'Honestly, Toby, we're—'

'You little shit. You haven't done enough to me?'

I was reaching to grab him again, he was flinching back, when I heard it. A noise up on the roof: wild volley of scrabbling, something big on the slates, claws? talons?

'What the hell?' I was off the terrace and backing into the garden before I knew it. Soft earth giving and slip-sliding under my feet, my voice almost a shout: 'The hell was that?'

'What?' Leon hurrying after me, flailing as his ankle turned on a rock— 'Jesus, what?'

'That noise. It's on the roof.'

'Bird,' Susanna said, catching up with us and turning to look. 'Or a bat.'

'No. Look. *Look*.'

High on the roof-peak, black, crouched against the chimney stack. It was shaped like nothing, feathery flicks like wings sprouting from its head, it was shifting, gathering itself, and from the deliberate focus of its movements I would have sworn it was human. Rafferty, spying on us, clinging and listening, anywhere and everywhere— 'That's not a fucking bird, look at the size of it—'

'That's its *shadow*, Jesus, Toby, calm down—'

'Those, on its head, what are those? What kind of bird—'

'Oh God,' Leon moaned, pitch rising. 'Oh God—'

The thing raised itself and spread against the sky, out and out, beyond any bounds of possibility. Then it flung itself into thin air, straight towards us.

Leon and I were both yelling, hoarse strangled screams. I heard the rush of the thing coming at me as I ducked and stumbled, onto my hands and knees in the dirt. I felt the wind of it lift my hair, I smelled it wild and earthy and piney, I flinched from its talons swooping with perfect, merciless accuracy for the back of my neck—

I don't know how long it took me to realise that it was gone. I had stopped screaming; Leon had subsided to a wild, choked panting. Beyond that, the garden was immensely silent.

I pulled myself up to sitting – not easy, I was shaking. The roof-line was bare, nothing in the trees— Susanna was on her knees beside me, doubled over and gasping, and I grabbed at her in a panic, looking for blood. 'Su. Look at me. Are you OK?'

'I'm fine.' It was a second before I figured out she was laughing.

'What the fuck—'

'Oh my God—' Leon was crouched in the dirt, a hand pressed to his chest. 'I can't breathe—'

'Jesus Christ. What *was* that?'

'That,' Susanna gasped, 'that was a long-eared owl. You pair of fools.'

'No,' I said. 'No way. The size of it, the—'

'Have you never seen one before? They're big bastards.'

'It *went for us.*'

'It must've thought you were starting. All that noise you made—'

'Leon. That wasn't an owl. Right?'

The whites of Leon's eyes, in the moonlight. 'My *chest*. I think I'm having a heart attack – guys, please, it hurts—'

'You're having a panic attack,' Susanna said, wiping her eyes with a knuckle and getting her giggles under control. 'Take long slow breaths.'

'I *can't breathe.*'

'That,' I said, 'was not a fucking owl.'

Susanna stared at me for another moment. Her knuckle had left her face streaked with dirt like warpaint. Then she toppled slowly backwards to the ground, hair in the earth, gazing up at the blank sky. Leon sounded like he might be crying.

There was grainy dirt in my shoes and all over my hands; I was sweating and shaking and way, way too stoned. The ugly moonscape all around me looked nothing like the Ivy House that was woven through my life. It hit me, with a freeze of utter horror, that that was because it wasn't the same place at all: this was a fake, a dark mist-formed parallel, some skewed but lethally plausible facsimile that Rafferty had created and tricked us all into, and now we were here there was absolutely no way to get back. It felt like something I'd known all along, deep down, if only I'd had the sense to recognise it. I almost screamed, but I knew Rafferty had to be listening and that tipping him off would lead to some unimaginable disaster.

High whistles of night birds, over the trees. Above us, in my bedroom window, the light had gone out.

'What the fuck,' I said. My voice sounded scraped and hollow. 'Is wrong with you guys. What the fuck.'

Neither of them answered. Leon was sobbing, not bothering to hide it any more.

'You shits. You know that? Fuck you.'

'I want to go home,' Leon said, through tears, wiping his face with his palms. In the faint light he looked grotesque, hair swept into lunatic scribbles, face contorted and dirt smeared everywhere.

'Yeah,' Susanna said. She struggled up to sitting and then to standing, wobbly-legged. 'That's probably a good idea. Come on.'

She held out her hands to Leon. He caught hold, and after some fumbling and staggering they managed to get him vertical. They stumbled off together across the uneven earth, arms wrapped around each other, Susanna's ankles bending at impossible angles. Neither of them looked back at me.

I stayed where I was. Inside the lit kitchen, Susanna slumped against a counter, poking at her phone with glassy, slow-motion concentration; Leon, at the sink, palmed water onto his face and neck, ran himself a mugful and gulped it down. Susanna said something, and he nodded without turning. The air around me was restless and moth-ridden, tiny things fluttering at the back of my neck and crawling on my arms, cold striking up from the earth through my clothes.

After a while Susanna glanced at her phone and said something else: taxi. They groped for coats and dropped them and slung them over their shoulders, and wove their way out towards the hall.

My high was starting to wear off, but the garden still had that terrible alien feel, itself and not itself. The thought of standing up and walking across it, exposed, made my back prickle – who knew what this place had waiting in its secret corners, mantraps, tangling vines, feral dogs and searchlights. But I was shivering, my arse was damp, and even if that thing had been just an owl I didn't like being out here alone with it. In the end I hauled myself to my feet, fought down the head rush and scuttled up the garden like a mouse under a shadow.

It took me a very long time to grope my way up the stairs. Smell of dust, soft even snores from Hugo's room, floorboard creaks making my heart ricochet. I couldn't decide whether to wake Melissa; on the one hand she needed a good night's sleep but on the other hand I needed her to hear this, this bullshit that had pushed us into our one and only fight ever, I couldn't leave it till morning. 'Baby,' I said quietly, or as quietly as I could, into our dark bedroom. 'Are you awake?'

As I said it I knew. The air of the room was chilly and sterile, no breathing, no scent of her, no tinge of body warmth.

I found the light switch. The bed was still made; the wardrobe was open, bare hangers dangling.

I sat down heavily on the bed. My ears were roaring. I found my phone and rang Melissa: it rang out to voicemail. Tried again: same thing. Again: she had switched it off.

I never thought you did, she had said, looking me straight in the eye, and I had believed her because I wanted to. No wonder she had been preoccupied, the last while; no wonder she had been desperate to drag me out of there – middle of the night, drunk, stoned, leave everything behind and run with just the clothes on our backs. She had been trying to protect me. She had been afraid that, if I kept asking questions, I was going to find out what I had done.

Somehow what hurt wasn't the fact that she believed I could be a killer – she hadn't even met me back then, teenagers are scrambled and confused and half off the rails, I could have been anything for all she knew. What made me want to drop my head in my hands and weep was that I had really believed Melissa knew who I was now, knew it so closely and truly that she would be able to hold me together while I didn't even know myself any more, and I had been wrong. I wasn't some callous shithead, some psychopath who could push a murder into a corner of my mind and bounce blithely on with my life as if it didn't exist— And there I was again, here we go round the mulberry bush and come full circle, what made me so sure what type of person I was, what I could and couldn't have done?

Melissa, Leon, Susanna, Rafferty, Kerr. Hugo, for all I knew – in the car that day, *I'd really like to know the story behind him ending up in*

that tree, I do feel as if I've got a bit of a right to know what happened . . .
In hindsight it was obvious that he'd been carefully, delicately inviting me to come clean. Who else? Which of the guys on the alumni Facebook group? Dec, Sean? My own father? My own mother?

Whirls of crimson flowers spread out on a slate countertop, neat rhythmic flash of a knife through sunlight. Susanna's voice, wry and amused: *Oh, you. Anything you feel bad about just falls straight out of your head.*

And with that, finally, it all fell into place. It had taken me a gobsmacking amount of time to notice the one dazzlingly obvious reason why all these people might think I'd killed Dominic: because I had.

The house was utterly quiet, not a creak or a tick of settling wood, not a snore from Hugo. It had the same terrible feel as the garden, a monstrous impostor burgeoning with incomprehensible, unstoppable transformations, wooden floors squelching like moss underfoot and brick walls billowing like curtains with the force of whatever was growing behind them.

That night. Where did you go?

I tried to tell myself that I would remember that. A whack to the head could knock out the word for colander or the last time I'd seen Phil, but not something like this. I had no idea whether that was true.

Faye said you'd been kind of pissed off with Dominic, that summer.

By the time Dominic died, we had all been finished with school, about to head off in our various directions to the rest of our lives. It wasn't like Leon had been facing into another year of Dominic's locker-room shenanigans; all that had been history. Why would he have needed to kill him?

I'd bet money that you only meant to give Dominic a scare. You were only planning on shaking him up a bit, nothing serious.

But surely, I thought (walls rippling queasily, dark pulses at the edges of my vision), surely if that had happened it would have coloured every day of my life since, nightmares, flashbacks, panic attacks whenever I saw a cop or went into Hugo's garden, a head injury couldn't rewrite all that—

We were so ashamed of ourselves we stayed upstairs for the rest of the evening, Susanna had said. *I swear by the next week you'd forgotten it ever happened.* That had had nothing to do with brain damage. My mind – unbroken, back then, wholly and purely itself – had done that.

I felt rotten, not just booze-sick or hash-sick but the all-pervading rottenness of food poisoning or infection, clammy and watery-weak, my whole system revolting. I realised that I couldn't see very much and after a while that I was on my knees and elbows, fore-head pressed to the floor. I breathed slowly and shallowly, waiting to see if I was going to throw up or faint. Some tiny lucid part of me managed to be glad that Melissa wasn't here to see me like this.

My eyes wouldn't open. I couldn't tell whether I was falling asleep or passing out; either one seemed like a blessed mercy. Some-how I managed to grope and clamber my way onto the bed, fingers tangling in the duvet, stomach swinging, before the blackness closed in from every side and I was gone.

IO

I woke up because the sun was hitting me in the face. I managed to open my eyes a slit: light was pouring in around the edges of the curtains, it was late and it was a gorgeous autumn day. Every individual part of me felt like shit in a different way. I rolled over and groaned into my pillow.

The night before came back piece by piece. All I wanted in the world was to go back to sleep, preferably for weeks or months or forever, but the movement had been too much for me. I made it to the bathroom just in time.

The retching went on long after my stomach was empty. Finally I felt safe enough to stand up, swill out my mouth and splash cold water on my face. My hands were trembling; in the mirror I had the same dopey, blotchy look I had had in the hospital.

I was terrified. Being suspected of murder had been one thing when I believed I was innocent: this wasn't some cheesy Hollywood drama, I was hardly going to wind up in prison for something I hadn't done. It was an entirely different thing now that I might be guilty. Rafferty was sharp and experienced and cunning in ways I couldn't begin to imagine; if I had left any evidence – and how could I not have? eighteen, clueless – he would find it. He could talk circles round me, think circles round me, and I didn't even know what to try and hide; I had no idea what had happened, why in God's name I would have done this. It seemed incredible that I could have got away with it for as long as I apparently – possibly? probably? – had.

I desperately needed to think, but my head was pounding much too viciously. I dug through my stuff for my painkillers and swallowed two; I thought about chasing them with a Xanax, but I needed my mind clear, or as clear as I could get it. Then – ignoring the fact that I was still in my snazzy shirt and linen trousers from last night, now smeared with dirt and reeking of sweat and hash – I went downstairs, taking every step gingerly, in search of coffee.

The kitchen was head-splittingly bright; the wall clock said it was past noon. Hugo was at the cooker, in his dressing gown and slippers, keeping an eye on the coffeemaker as it spat cheerily. 'Ah,' he said, turning with a smile. He was clearly having a good day, in fact he was clearly in a lot better shape than I was. 'The dead arise. So it was a good night, yes?'

I sat down at the table and covered my face with my hands. Coffee had been a bad idea; just the smell was making me feel like I might throw up again.

Hugo laughed. 'I was right not to wake you, then. I thought you might need the lie-in. As soon as I heard you moving about, I put the coffee on.'

'Thanks,' I said.

'And I've got a surprise for you, once you're awake enough. Would you eat something? Toast? Scrambled eggs, maybe?'

'Oh God.'

He laughed again. 'In a bit, then.' He peered into the coffeemaker, turned off the gas ring and poured me a very large espresso. 'There' – shuffling over to me, leaning on his stick, my brain didn't come up with the idea of going to him until it was too late. 'Would Melissa have some? Is she still in bed? Or did she make it to work?'

'She's gone,' I said.

'My goodness. I'm impressed.' He poured himself the rest of the coffee, carefully, wrist wobbling. 'What time did you get to bed?'

I considered just not telling him. He loved Melissa; it would break his heart. I could probably get away with it for a day or two, come up with reasons why she wasn't home in the evenings – stocktaking, sick mother – and by that time I might have some clue what I was going to do about all of this . . . I didn't have the energy. 'No,' I said. 'She's gone gone. Permanently.'

'What?' Hugo's head came around sharply and he stared at me. '*Why?*'

'It's complicated.'

After a long moment he put down the coffeemaker, added a dash of milk to his cup and brought it to the table. He sat down opposite me – hands folded around the cup, dressing gown falling open to show flannel pyjamas buttoned up wrong, unblinking grey eyes magnified by his glasses – and waited.

Once I started talking I couldn't stop. It all came out, in a jumble – my memory of the night was pretty hazy, dislocated pieces resurfacing out of any order as I talked, but the gist of it came through clearly enough. The only thing I left out was that last step, that final revelation. Probably Hugo – steadily sipping his coffee, saying nothing – would figure it out, but I couldn't bring myself to say it out loud.

'So' – I was babbling, I had said everything at least twice – 'that was when they went home, or wherever, right after that? And I thought Melissa would be upstairs, but . . . I tried to ring her, I haven't tried yet this morning, but now I don't know if I even should – like obviously I want to fix things, but I mean, I don't know what's going to happen but maybe she's actually better off not being around for it . . .'

I finally managed to shut up. In the immense silence – staring down into my untouched coffee – it dawned on me, too late, what a terrible, shitty thing I had done by throwing all this into Hugo's lap. He only had a couple of months, couldn't I have found a way not to fuck them up with my godawful mess? I couldn't look at him; I was afraid I would see him broken, face stunned and crumpled, tears streaming. I kept my head down and scraped with my thumbnail at a nonexistent stain on the table: soft greyed wood, the place where the grain curved around a dark spot to make a shape like a wide-mouthed cartoon ghost. All the times I'd sat here, toast and jam, geography projects, drunken parties, and now this.

'Right,' Hugo said, putting down his cup with a bang. His voice startled me into looking up: it had the old fullness and authority I remembered from when I was a kid, oak-solid, the voice that had always stopped us in our tracks and put an instant end to our bickering or wrecking. 'This has gone far enough.'

I couldn't say anything. All of a sudden I was humiliatingly close to tears.

'Don't waste another thought on it. I'll sort it out.' He leaned a palm on the table and pushed himself to standing. 'But first, we both need something to eat. We're going to have an omelette – yes, yes you are, I know you don't want it but you'll thank me afterwards. We are going to enjoy it in peace. And then you're going to go take a shower, and I'm going to deal with this mess before it gets completely out of hand.'

I knew it couldn't be done, and yet a part of me couldn't help believing him. Tall and shadow-faced against the flood of brightness through the windows, hand crooked around his cane, hair straggling on his shoulders and robe flowing, he looked like a figure from a tarot card, dense with omens. I still couldn't talk. I wiped the heel of my hand across my eyes.

Hugo hobbled to the fridge and started taking things out: eggs, butter, milk. 'With ham and cheese, I think, and spinach . . . Probably what you really need is a dirty great fry-up, but we don't have the materials.'

'I'm so sorry,' I said. 'I really am.'

He ignored that. 'Come here and chop this. I don't trust my hand.'

I went obediently to the counter, found a knife and started on the ham. The painkillers were kicking in; my head wasn't throbbing as badly, but it felt loose and overrun with drifting things, cobwebs and fog and thistledown.

Hugo broke four eggs into a bowl and started whisking. 'Now,' he said, his voice lightening. 'The surprise; what I was waiting to tell you until you were a bit more awake. You won't believe it.'

I did my best to play along; I owed him that, at least. 'Oh yeah?'

'I think I've cracked Mrs Wozniak.'

The grin on his face was wide and real. 'You're joking,' I said.

'No, I'm pretty sure. Haskins, our diary fellow? In November of 1887, he starts grousing about his wife landing him with her family's problems. He's such a complainer that I didn't take much notice at first, almost skipped the whole section, but luckily I stuck with it. The wife's sister in Clare – yes, can you see why my ears pricked up? – she wants to send her sixteen-year-old daughter to stay with the Haskinses, in Tipperary, for a few months. Haskins's main complaint is that he'll be stuck with the expense of feeding this girl, but he's also puffing up with outrage because she might corrupt his children – who are three, four and seven at this point, so I would have thought fairly difficult to corrupt. Unless . . .' He cocked an eyebrow at me, dropping butter into the frying pan, *Have you got it?*

It took me a while to fish anything out of the morass in my head. 'She was pregnant?'

'Well, it's hard to be positive of anything – Haskins was so furious that his handwriting turns into a complete snarl, double underlining everywhere – but from all the mentions of shame and disgrace and wantonness, I think she was. Pass me the salt and pepper, would you?'

I handed them over. His serenity was starting to freak me out. I wondered if he had forgotten the entire conversation; if we would have to have it all over again that evening, when Melissa didn't come home.

'Thanks. And' – happily salting and peppering away – 'can you guess the niece's surname?'

'McNamara?'

'It was indeed. Elaine McNamara.' He was smiling, squinting at the cooker dial as he adjusted the gas burner just so, but I could see the depth of his satisfaction. 'She hasn't shown up in any of the family trees so far, has she? Or has she?'

'Not that I remember.'

'We'll track her down. So then' – pouring the eggs into the pan, fizzle and hiss – 'I'm afraid I got impatient and started skimming ahead, looking for any mention of any O'Hagans – just to confirm the theory. And sure enough, a few weeks into 1888, Mrs Haskins is suggesting that their lovely neighbours the O'Hagans might be willing to "conceal Elaine's shame". It would have been easy as pie – plenty of lying on birth records, back then: the O'Hagans could just go to the registrar and put down the baby as their own, no need to prove where they'd got him. Our man Haskins isn't mad about the idea – he thinks it would be letting Elaine off too lightly, she won't comprehend the full something, I think it's "magnitude", of her transgression; he wants to send her to a mother-and-baby home. But I think we can be pretty sure his wife won that argument in the end.'

The peaceful run of his voice, the savoury smell of the eggs cooking, bright chill blue of the sky outside the French doors. I thought of my first day back here, the two of us in his study, rain at the windowpane and my mind wandering off among the knick-knacks as he talked.

'And that's as far as I got,' Hugo said, 'before I heard you getting up. All the same, though: a good morning's work, I think.'

His glance at me was almost shy. 'That's amazing,' I said, managing a big smile. 'Congratulations.'

'To you, too. We did it together. We should have a glass of something to celebrate – is there any prosecco, anything like that? Or would that be too much for your head?'

'No, that sounds great. I bet we've got something somewhere.'

'Now, of course' – he sprinkled grated cheese into the pan, a big handful, topped it with the chopped ham – 'I have to work out how to tell Mrs Wozniak.'

'She should be over the moon,' I said. I found a bottle of prosecco in the booze cabinet; not chilled, but what the hell. 'This is what she was after, isn't it? It's not like you've found a murderer in the family tree.'

Hugo gave me a thoughtful glance over his shoulder. 'Well,' he said, 'unless I've got this all wrong, that baby was Amelia Wozniak's grandfather – Edward O'Hagan, the one who emigrated to America. He only died in 1976; it's quite likely that she knew him well. Except with this, it may feel as if she didn't know him that well after all. He wasn't Edward O'Hagan, he was Edward Mc-Namara. An entirely different person, in some ways if not all. And' – scattering spinach into the pan – 'that new person comes with an awful lot of grief attached, a lot of injustice. That sixteen-year-old being sent away from her family in disgrace, having her baby taken away whether she liked it or not, was Amelia's great-grandmother. And all of that grief and injustice is bound up with

Amelia's existence. Without it she might have been Amelia Mc-Namara, or she might never have existed at all.'

'I guess,' I said. I was having a hard time working up much sympathy. I would have swapped my own problems, or his, for Mrs Wozniak's existential crisis any day.

'Well, who knows, maybe she'll see it your way. But I'd rather go about it delicately, just in case.' It took him a couple of tries, but he got the omelette folded over. 'It's not today's problem, anyway. We'll have to decipher the rest of the diary first – I'd like to find out what happened to Elaine in the end, and see if we can get any kind of lead on the baby's father. At some point we can ask Mrs Wozniak whether there are any male-line descendants floating around, for Y-DNA matching; but for now maybe you could start on the parish records, try to find out whether Elaine eventually married? I doubt any husband would have been the baby's father, or why wouldn't she just marry him in the first place – more likely he was ineligible, one way or another – but it's worth looking into.'

'OK,' I said. Apparently we were supposed to go right back to our comfy routine and pretend that none of last night had happened, although I couldn't imagine how Hugo thought that was going to work in practice. Never mind how on earth he thought he was going to sort everything out: I was starting to wonder if his plan had been some illness-generated delusion involving the bat-signal or a Rafferty voodoo doll or something. Was it possible that he hadn't worked out what was going on? That he thought the only problems here were a cousin-spat and a relationship rocky patch, everyone under stress and being silly, just need a good firm talking-to? 'Cheers. Here's to us.'

'And to Elaine McNamara.' Hugo took the glass from me and stepped aside to let me turn the omelette out of the heavy pan. 'Poor child.'

I surprised myself by wolfing down my half of the omelette, fast enough that Hugo laughed at me. 'There are more eggs, if you're still hungry.'

'You were right,' I said. 'I needed that.'

'Of course I was. Maybe next time I tell you something' – smiling at me, over his glass – 'you'll stop fussing and take my word for it.' And as I scraped up the last bite: 'Now go find your cigarettes, would you? Since we're being decadent.'

We sat there quietly, smoking a cigarette and then another, topping up our prosecco glasses. Hugo's head was tilted back and his eyes half closed, gazing up at the ceiling with grave, dreamy calm. Faint trail of cries from wild geese somewhere, carrying all the flavour of autumn, first frost and turf smoke. Hugo's big hand tapping ash into the chipped saucer we were using as a makeshift ashtray, sunlight bringing the battered wood of the table alive with an impossible holy glow.

•

I stayed in the shower for a very long time. The night before was right inside my skin; no matter how hard I scrubbed, I still caught the stench of stale booze, stale hash, garden earth. Finally I gave up and just stood there with the water turned up as hard and as hot as it would go, letting it hammer down on my head.

Now that I was on my own the stoneover had rushed back up, a nasty mishmash of physical and mental, all-consuming sapping despair and a sense of doom that seemed to come not from my mind but from deep inside my stomach and my spine. Melissa had been right all along, going after answers was the stupidest thing I could possibly have done, and now it was too late.

Part of me was still clinging to the slim chance that I had got it all wrong, and if I could just clear my head I would be able to figure out the real story. No matter how hard I scrabbled, though, every trail looped me around to the same place: me with the hoodie, me the only one who could have had the key to let Dominic in, me the only one for whom he would have come when he was called (*Hey dude got a couple of lines, I owe you, want to come over sometime?*), me not in my room that night. And, starker than any of that: who else could it have been? Susanna and Leon both thought it had been me. Hugo: not a chance. There had been no one else in the house. Of course Dominic could have swiped the key and cunningly brought in his own garrotte, and his own murderer, but even in my desperation that seemed a tad implausible and there I was again, looping back around to that same nightmare place.

I had nothing to fight it off with. The only counter-arguments were that I didn't remember it and that I wasn't that kind of guy, and how much were those worth? In court maybe, even probably – come on, ladies and gentlemen of the jury, I know my client's DNA was all over the garrotte but look at him, such a nice blond boy from such a nice rich family, so handsome, never been in trouble in his life, does he seem like a killer to you; if I could do something about the eyelid-droop and keep the slur out of my voice, I might even get away with it. But here, with nothing but the merciless drum of water and the curling steam and the tortured squealing of the pipes, it was different. What was or wasn't in my mind, what I thought I was: those were worthless.

Two hands to turn the key in the rusted lock, whispered *Come on in dude* and Dominic's grin in a slash of moonlight. Bite of the garrotte into flesh, choking sounds, feet scrabbling futilely in the dirt. The impossible weight of a body that had to be dragged across an endless expanse of grass, my own panting terrifyingly loud in my ears, hands slipping, darkness, frantic, *I can't do it*— I had no idea which snippets were memory and which stemmed from some dark hallucinatory process deeper than imagination, involuntary and uncontrollable, simmering with a power and a reality all its own.

Every one of them felt like a violation: alien, lunatic, forced on me. How could I be thinking these things, me? I belonged in a different world, pints with the lads, smartly managed Twitter arguments, croissants in bed with Melissa on lazy rainy Sundays. It took me a while to figure out why the feeling was horribly familiar. I was still standing in the shower staring at nothing – had been standing there for probably half an hour, the water was going cold – when it came back to me: the bland-faced doctor droning away, my first day in the hospital, *neurologist seizures occupational therapist* like those had something to do with me; the slow terrible drop as I began to understand that they did, that this was my life now.

Eventually the water got cold enough that my teeth were chattering. I was drying off when I heard it: discreet rat-tat at the front door; a pause; and then Hugo's even murmur, woven with another voice. The tone was easy and pleasant, no urgency there, but I knew that voice straight through walls and floors, would have known its lightest word anywhere, like a lover: Rafferty.

My legs almost went from under me. So soon. I had known it had to come someday but I had been expecting a few weeks, months, some idiot part of me had actually dared to hope I might get away with it. For a second I thought of doing a runner – Hugo would keep them talking, I could drop out a window and go over the back wall and— Even before I finished the thought I knew how ludicrous it was: and what, go off grid and live in a cave in the Wicklow Mountains? Instead I pulled on my clothes as fast as I could, fumbling buttons, at the very least I didn't need to be shivering in my boxers when they came for me— *Deny*, I told myself, heading down the stairs in what felt like slow motion, so light-headed with terror and nausea and the strangeness of it all that I had to clutch the banister, *deny deny deny and get a lawyer, they can't prove anything* . . .

Rafferty and Kerr and Hugo were in the hall. Their heads turned, sharply and simultaneously, towards me on the stairs. The detectives were dressed for autumn, long overcoats and Kerr had a hat that belonged on Al Capone; Hugo – I half-noticed it without being able to work out what it meant – had changed out of his pyjamas and dressing gown, into sort-of-decent tweed trousers and a clean shirt and jumper. There was something unsettling in the way the three of them were arranged, standing apart, positioned precisely as chess pieces against the geometry of the floor tiles.

'What's going on?' I asked.

'Toby,' Rafferty said – cheerily, completely at ease, as if the last time had never happened. 'I like the haircut. Listen, your uncle's going to come down to the station with us for a bit. Don't worry, we'll get him back to you safe and sound.'

'What?' I said, after a blank moment. 'Why?'

'We need to take a statement,' Kerr said.

'But,' I said. I was confused. All three of them were looking at me as if I had walked in on some private transaction, a business deal, a drug deal, something where I was irrelevant and unwanted. 'You can do that here.'

'Not this time,' Rafferty explained genially. 'It varies.'

I didn't get this; I didn't like it. 'He's sick,' I said. 'He's got—'

'I know, yeah. We'll take good care of him.'

'He's been having seizures.'

'That's good to know. We'll keep an eye out.' To Hugo: 'Do you need any medication for that?'

'I have it here,' Hugo said, touching his breast pocket.

'Hugo,' I said. 'What's going on?'

He pushed his hair off his forehead. It was brushed smooth; that and the good clothes gave its length a sudden ravaged elegance, famous conductor fallen on hard times. 'I rang Detective Rafferty,' he said gently, 'and explained to him that I was responsible for Dominic Ganly's death.'

After a second of utter silence: 'What the *fuck*,' I said.

'I should have done it weeks ago – well, obviously I should have done it years ago. But it would take a certain kind of person to do that, wouldn't it, and apparently I'm not that kind; or wasn't, anyway, until now.'

'Wait,' I said. 'Hugo. What the fuck are you doing?'

He regarded me through his glasses, sombrely, as if from an immense distance. 'At this stage,' he explained, 'it doesn't feel like something I can keep to myself any longer. That seizure the other day, that was a bit of a wake-up call.'

Kerr was shifting his weight, wanting to get moving. 'Remember,' Rafferty said, from where he had melted away to the sidelines, 'you are not obliged to say anything unless you wish to do so, but anything you do say will be taken down in writing and may be given in evidence. You remember that, yeah?'

'I know,' Hugo said. He found his coat on the stand and started shouldering it on, awkwardly, shifting his cane from hand to hand.

'And you're sure about the solicitor. Because I'm telling you now, you should have one for this.'

'I'm sure.'

'I'll call Dad,' I said, too loudly. 'He'll come right down. Don't say anything till—'

'No you won't,' Hugo said – distracted, shoving at a sleeve that wouldn't go right. 'Do you hear me? You won't go bothering your father, or your uncles, or your cousins. Just let me get this done in peace.'

'He needs a lawyer,' I said, to Rafferty. 'You can't talk to him without one.'

He turned up his palms. 'It's his call.'

'He can't make that call. He's not, his mind isn't— He's been getting confused. Forgetting things.'

'Toby,' Hugo said, with a flash of irritation. 'Please stop this.'

'I'm serious. He's, he's not' – the word came back to me – 'he's not competent to make that kind of decision.'

'We don't determine competence,' Kerr said, rolling one shoulder and wincing at the crack. 'That's for the court to deal with.'

'If things go that far,' Rafferty put in.

'Yeah, if. All we know right now is, Mr Hennessy wants to tell us something, so we need to take his statement.'

'But he's imagined the *whole thing*. He didn't *kill* anyone. It's a, some kind of hallucination, it's—' Hugo was fumbling at coat buttons— 'Hugo, *please*.'

'I appreciate the vote of confidence,' Hugo told me, with something between amusement and annoyance, 'but honestly, Toby, I know exactly what I'm doing.'

'If it's a hallucination,' Rafferty told me, 'then there's nothing to worry about. We'll sort it out, no problem, bring him straight home.'

'He's *dying*,' I said, too desperate for tact. 'The doctor said he should be in *hospice*. You can't just throw him in a cell and—'

Kerr laughed at me, a big bark. 'Jesus, man, who said anything about a cell? Relax on the jacks. At this stage we're only going for a chat.'

'Your uncle's free to go at any time,' Rafferty said. 'Worst-case scenario, *worst* case, he'll be home sometime tomorrow.'

'*Tomorrow?*'

'It's not like anyone would oppose a bail application,' Kerr explained, cheeringly. 'He's hardly a flight risk.'

'For heaven's sake, Toby,' Hugo said. 'Everything's fine. Don't fuss at us.'

'You just chill out here,' Kerr told me, moving towards the door. 'Maybe pour yourself a nice little drink, take your mind off things. No point in you getting all het up over nothing.'

Hugo swung his scarf off a hook and wrapped it around his neck. 'Now,' he said. 'Shall we?'

Rafferty opened the door and the wind came flowing in, cold and lush with autumn. Hugo smiled at me. 'Come here,' he said, and when I came, cupped the back of my neck in his hand and gave me a little shake. 'Don't worry. Get to work on that diary, have something interesting for me when I get home. And for God's sake sort things out with Melissa, won't you?'

'Hugo,' I said, but he had already let go of me and was stepping out into the sunlight and the tremble of yellow leaves, with Rafferty and Kerr at his shoulders.

•

I sat down heavily on the stairs and stayed there for a long time. I understood what Hugo was doing, obviously. He had thought it over, calmly done the unbearable maths: he was prepared to bet he had little enough time left that, what with bail and the slow legal system, he wouldn't be going to prison. He had decided it was worth spending a couple of his remaining days in interview rooms, worth going down in history as the Elm Tree Killer or whatever the tabloids came up with, to save me.

On this I didn't really agree with him, but I couldn't imagine what to do about it. I did think about jumping in a taxi and chasing them down to the police station to throw my own confession into the mix, but even apart from the visceral terror of that idea, I couldn't figure out the logistics: I didn't know what station they were at, and I wasn't sure how to confess to something I didn't remember. It felt like the vast majority of my thought processes had shut down.

I didn't for a second consider the possibility that Hugo was telling the truth. Of course no one knows anyone inside out, no matter how much we'd love to believe it, but I did know Hugo well enough to be sure of a few things, one of which was that he wouldn't garrotte anyone. I was a lot more sure of that when it came to him than when it came to myself – which in itself seemed to say everything that needed to be said.

Finally, on obedient autopilot, I went up to the study. The volume of Haskins's diary that Hugo had been working on was open on his desk, a handful of the yellowed pages helpfully tagged with Post-its. Hugo's transcript was laid out beside it. The transcript was patchy, big blank spaces everywhere; he had been skipping around, looking for the exciting bits. I sat down at his desk and got to work filling in the gaps.

It was slow frustrating work any day, but my eyes were blurry and skidding from the hangover and my concentration was shot to hell; every sentence seemed to take about half an hour, all the pages were covered with tiny inkblots jumping merrily. *Heard Georgie read from his schoolbook. His reading is* most satisfactory *but still wants something of liveliness. I demonstrated by reading him a story by – ??? – to both of our great* merriment *. . . A fine day and came home from mass with an appetite, hoped to dine well but . . .* and more bitching about the cook. *Outbreak of measles in the town and we hear that the* – something, Sullivans'? – *youngest child is near death, but* – something something something – *hope . . .*

The afternoon went on and on and on and Hugo didn't come back. At some point, eyes and mind whirling, I rang Melissa – I told myself she deserved to know what had happened, but of course I was actually hoping she would come flying back to be by my side through this fresh crisis. No answer. I didn't leave a message; this didn't feel like the kind of thing that belonged on voicemail.

To-day I expected to travel to Limerick but the rain having flooded the road I could not. I was greatly disappointed and out of – humour? – *with my wife . . .* It was almost six o'clock, surely they should be done taking his statement by now, how much of an epic could it be? I tried Hugo's mobile, but it rang out. I dug through pockets and drawers till I found Rafferty's card and – heart slamming – rang his number: straight to voicemail.

I had got to the Elaine McNamara crisis, and Haskins was working himself into a moral tizzy. *On the one hand we may as Caroline says teach her to become <u>chaste</u> <u>virtuous</u> and* – industrious? *Yet this seems a <u>small</u> <u>penance</u> for her <u>sin</u>* . . . I flipped ahead: this went on for pages.

Dimming sky outside the window, evening chill striking through the glass. Hugo had been very firm about not telling anyone, but I was losing my mind. Susanna was probably still in a snit with me, but she was the only person who might have some sensible ideas about what to do.

It took a few rings before she decided to pick up. 'Toby.' Cool, wary. 'How's the head?'

'Listen,' I said. 'Something's happened.'

When I had finished there was a silence. In the background Sallie was singing, peacefully and slightly off-key: *Itsy bitsy spider went up the water spout . . .*

'OK,' Susanna said eventually. 'Right. Have you talked to Leon?'

'Not yet. Just you.'

'Good. Don't tell anyone else. Leave it.'

'Why?'

Splashing water: Sallie was in the bath. 'Well. I don't know about your dad, but mine's pretty stressed out already. No point in upsetting him more when this could all blow over by morning.'

'You don't think they're going to notice Hugo's been *arrested*?'

'He hasn't been, yet. You're jumping the gun. Here, Sal, put some soap on it—'

'He *confessed*. Of course he's going to be—'

'People make false confessions all the time. The detectives aren't going to just take Hugo's word for it. They check – whether his story matches their evidence, whether he knows things only the killer could know. All that stuff.'

Down came the rainbow washed out all the rain . . . This whole conversation felt wrong, not going the way I had expected— 'So why don't you want Leon knowing? If it's no big deal?'

'Leon's not dealing too well with all this. In case you hadn't noticed. I don't want him freaking out.'

'What? He's not some fragile little flower who we have to *protect* from, from, we're not *kids* any more' – and what if I had tried to protect him, like Rafferty thought, back when we actually were kids? look where that had landed me – 'He's a grown man. If we can handle this, he can too.'

Susanna sighed. 'Look,' she said, lower. 'I don't know if you've realised this, but Leon thinks you killed Dominic.' A small pause to see how I took that. When I said nothing: 'He has from the start, actually. And he has some complicated thing going on where he's pretty pissed off about the idea of you getting away with it.'

'Well he can go fuck himself,' I said, on a surge of anger, my voice rising. 'Did he say that to the cops? Is that why they were giving me shit?'

'No. And he's not going to – don't worry, I've talked to him, he's under control. He doesn't actually want you to go to jail, not really. He just feels like you've always got away with everything and it's not fair.'

'Jesus *Christ*! What are we, six?'

'Yeah, I know. It's stupid leftover kid stuff. But if he hears about this, I don't know what he'll do. And I'd rather not find out unless we have to.'

'OK,' I said, after a moment. I didn't like the sound of this. I had known Leon was stressed, obviously, but Susanna was talking like he was on the verge of an epic meltdown, and I was clearly first in line to be collateral damage. 'What am I supposed to do if he shows up here and wants to know where Hugo's gone?'

'He won't.'

'How do you know?'

'He was pretty upset, last night. I don't think he wants to talk to you for a while.'

'Oh, great,' I said. I didn't particularly want to talk to Leon either, but having him out there in a massive strop with me didn't feel like a good idea. 'That's really fucking reassuring.'

'Don't you start freaking out on me too. Like I said, Leon's under control. Just don't go winding him up and he'll be fine.'

What did that mean? Was I 'under control' too? 'I'm not fucking

368

freaking out. I'm trying to figure out what the hell we do about Hugo.'

'We don't do anything. We just sit tight.'

'He's been there for fucking *hours*, Su. Without a solicitor.'

'So? Even if they believe him, that doesn't mean they've got enough to charge him. And even if they do, it takes what? six months, a year? for a case to get to trial. This isn't a disaster, Toby. I know it's no fun, but in the long run it's not going to make any difference to anything.'

I had finally figured out what felt off about this conversation: Susanna hadn't even bothered registering the fact that Hugo had, according to him anyway, killed Dominic. I said, 'You don't think he did it.'

'Do you?'

'No.'

'Well then.'

Itsy bitsy spider back up the spout again . . . 'It's not just Leon, is it?' I said. 'You think I did it too.'

After a moment: 'Look,' Susanna said. Her voice was clearer, measured and firm, and Sallie's high sweet drone had faded: she had moved away to make sure she could get this into my head. 'The only thing I want here is to make sure all of us stay out of jail. That's it. I don't actually care about anything else. And I think whatever Hugo's doing, it gives us the best shot at that happening. Just leave him to it.' When I didn't answer: 'OK? Can you do that?'

'Yeah. Whatever.'

'What about Melissa? Is she going to be OK with that?'

'She's fine.'

In the background, a sudden wail: 'It went in my *eyes!*' 'Got to go,' Susanna said. 'Just hang in there for tonight; we'll see what happens tomorrow, take it from there – it's OK, sweetie, here's your towel—' and she was gone.

First stars in the window, Hugo's reading glasses at the edge of the desk-pool of lamplight like he had just that moment put them down. I tried to go back to the diary, but my eyes and my brain had both shorted out: it was gibberish. I knew I should probably eat something, but I couldn't be arsed. I told myself I would eat with Hugo when he got home – he would be starving, we could order takeaway. Meanwhile I sat at the kitchen table, smoking cigarette after cigarette and listening to young owls yelping in the darkness outside.

I wanted Melissa, so much I could have howled. I thought of her in her cramped apartment unpacking dresses that still smelled of the Ivy House, tea and wood-smoke and jasmine, while awful Megan hovered and probed and made satisfied little bitchy comments about how she had actually always known I was worthless. I wanted, so intensely that it practically lifted me out of my chair, to get a taxi over there, hammer at the door till she let me in and wrap her tight in my arms; tell her she had been utterly right, I would never argue with her again, we could get on a plane tomorrow and take off for somewhere as far away from this godawful mess as she wanted.

Only I couldn't do it. It had taken this long for it to work its way into my mind: I couldn't go to her, couldn't even ring her, not ever again. I had, almost certainly, killed someone. Even if somehow I got away with it, even if Hugo's plan worked and Rafferty closed the case and went away, I was a murderer.

Melissa – the thought nearly undid me – Melissa hadn't even cared. All she had cared about was protecting me from finding out. If only I had been willing to walk away from this, she would joyfully have walked away with me, hand in hand.

But I cared, a lot. Melissa, sunshiny and bruised and brave, throwing herself indefatigably into making things better: I was something that had no place in her life. She deserved the guy we had both thought I was – actually she deserved better than that guy, too, but I could have been that; I had been on my way to that, had already been making plans. Even after that night, there must have been some tiny fragment of me that believed I might recover. This was different. I couldn't see any way that this could get better, any way I could work my way past it. I was too exhausted and hungover and wretched even to cry.

My phone dinged and I grabbed for it, fumbling and catching like someone out of a sitcom. Voice message.

'Toby, hiya. Rafferty here.' The reception in the Ivy House was patchy, but I was willing to bet he had deliberately rung my voicemail. 'Sorry I missed you earlier. Listen, we're still sorting out a few things, so Hugo's going to stay here overnight. Don't be worrying: we got in pizza, he's taken his medication, he's grand. Just thought you should know so you're not waiting up for him. See you tomorrow.' Click.

I rang Hugo's mobile: voicemail. 'Hugo, it's me. I'm just checking that you're OK. Listen, if you change your mind, if you want me to come pick you up or if you want a lawyer, just ring me or text me, any time' – could he do that, would they let him? did he even have his phone or had they taken it away? – 'and I'll sort it out. OK? Otherwise, just . . . look after yourself. Please. I'll try you again in the morning. Bye.'

I sat there with the phone in front of me on the table for a long time, in case Hugo rang back, which he didn't. I tried Rafferty, with some vague idea of demanding to talk to Hugo, but of course he didn't pick up.

It was getting late. It occurred to me that this was the first time I had spent a night on my own since my apartment. I was so tired I could barely move, but I didn't like the thought of going to bed: asleep, undressed, far enough from all the likely entry points that I wouldn't hear an intruder till it was too late. Instead I got the duvet from my room and stretched out on the sofa, with the standing lamp on. I wasn't expecting to get any sleep – I was jumping at every floorboard crack and radiator burble – but at some point deep in the night I must have dozed off.

•

There was a phone ringing somewhere, but I couldn't drag myself out of sleep properly. It was one of those old black wall-mounted phones with a heavy ornate receiver, in a fuzzy glow of gold light but I couldn't remember where it was, landing maybe? Hugo's bedroom? and my body wasn't working right, I couldn't get to it. It kept ringing and I realised that was probably all wrong, it had to be my mobile— My eyes still wouldn't work, all I could see was a thick fog of grey speckles, but I groped for my phone and swiped blindly. 'Hello?'

'Toby,' said a rich warm voice that for a moment felt almost comforting, a lifeline amid the confusion. 'This is Detective Mike Rafferty. Listen: your uncle's collapsed. He's in an ambulance, on his way to St Ciaran's Hospital.'

'What?' I said, after a moment. I managed to sit up, dizzy and rocking. 'What happened?'

'We don't know yet. Who's his next of kin?'

'What? He doesn't have, I mean—'

'He's the oldest brother, right? Who's next? Your dad?'

'Phil. My uncle Phil.' Gradually my eyesight was clearing, but the room looked wrong, unstable and dangerous: armchairs canting at subtle angles, rug rucked up, grey-tinged darkness that could have been dawn, twilight, storm.

'Can you send me his number? Like now, right away?'

'Is Hugo dead?'

'He was alive five minutes ago, anyway. The paramedics were stabilising him. I'm following them to the hospital' – for the first time I realised there was background noise, engine rush, Rafferty had me on speakerphone as he drove. 'We should be there in ten minutes, if you want to meet us there. Get me that number first.'

'OK,' I said. 'I'm coming,' but he had already hung up.

My phone said it was quarter to seven in the morning. Somehow I texted him Phil's number and ordered a taxi and found my coat and shoes – dazed, heart rattling, unsure whether this was really happening or whether I was still trapped in the dream. Raw wet air, streetlamps still on. The taxi jolting from side to side. Thick vanilla stench of air freshener, the rear-view mirror festooned with rosaries and miraculous medals and yellowed pictures of saints. The driver was a hunched, skinny old guy who hadn't said a word since I got in, and I wanted to lean forwards and tell him there had been a change of plan and I needed to go to Donegal, Kerry, just keep on driving so I would never have to get out.

•

The first step into the hospital hit me like a tidal wave. It was all there, the unceasing blur of noise, the relentless parching heat, but most of all that smell: disinfectant layered thickly over utter pollution, hundreds of bodies and sicknesses and terrors crammed together in too little space. The place felt like a weapon expertly crafted to strip you of all humanity, hollow you to a shell creature that would do anything it was told for the slim chance of someday getting out into the living world again. I almost turned and ran.

Somehow I managed to explain the story to the pancake-faced woman on reception, but I forgot her directions the second I turned away and ended up lost in a maze of corridors and stairwells, miles of rubbery blue floor tiles, people in scrubs bustling past me without a glance, wards jammed with metal beds and jaunty pale-blue curtains and drawn grey faces, things beeping and someone moaning and a guy on crutches dragging himself along with a terrible thousand-yard stare that I knew only too well. I had lost track of what floor I was on and I was fighting a flutter of panic – no way out, trapped here forever – when I turned a corner and saw a lean dark figure at the far end of the corridor, back to me, hands deep in overcoat pockets. Even against the numbing white light I knew it was Rafferty.

In that place he looked like salvation. I limped towards him as fast as I could, and he turned.

'Toby,' he said. He was shaved and crisp and alert, smelling of that sprucey aftershave; the hospital didn't seem to have affected him at all. 'I was waiting for you.'

'Where is he?'

Rafferty nodded towards a set of double doors. Next to them was an intercom with a large sign above it saying 'THE BELLS', which set a bubble of hysterical laughter rising in my throat. I managed to swallow it down. 'They're just getting him into a bed. They said we can go in once he's settled.'

'What happened?'

'Not sure yet. I left him around half-ten last night. He was tired, wanted to get some kip, but he was in good form; joking, even, telling me if he was getting one last weekend away from home he would've rathered Prague. I made sure someone would check on him every half-hour, see if he needed anything, wanted a doctor.' It seemed to me that Rafferty should have sounded at least a little defensive, Hugo had been in his care and now look, but he didn't; he was cool as ice, he might have been filling in another detective on the night's events. 'According to the officer on duty, he got to sleep somewhere between eleven and half past. No complaints, not in pain, not feeling sick, didn't want anything. The last check was at six: he was asleep, breathing fine. I got in at twenty past. He was on the floor, unconscious. We got the ambulance straightaway. I told them about his cancer, and the seizures.'

I couldn't see anything through the double doors, empty corridor, white and blue and chrome— 'What did they say? The doctors?'

'Not a lot. They checked him over in A and E, took him for a CT scan; then when they came out, they said they were heading here to ICU. I'm not family, they can't tell me much. But they said' – Rafferty moved to catch my eye, I couldn't stop jerking my head around, trying to get a handle on the place, all the perspectives seemed off – 'Toby. Mostly, when someone who's in custody gets taken to hospital, we keep an officer right next to them at all times. In case they try to do a runner, or attack someone, or they say something we need to hear. With your uncle, the doctor said no need for that, I could wait out here.'

'But,' I said. He was trying to tell me something, but I wasn't sure I was getting it right. 'If it was a, another seizure, they've got drugs for that. They can do things—'

The door wheezed behind me and I whipped round. It was a stocky white-haired guy in green scrubs, pulling off latex gloves. 'Are you here with Hugo Hennessy?' he asked.

'Yes,' I said. 'I'm his nephew. What happened? Is he, is he OK?'

The doctor waited for me to go to him. He had to be about sixty, wide-shouldered but flabby with it, but he moved like a boxer, that same absolute arrogant control of the space, like everyone else was there only by his permission. His eyes slid over me – droopy eyelid, gimpy leg – with a casual assessment that set my teeth on edge.

'You know about your uncle's brain tumour,' he said. 'Yes?'

'Yes. He was diagnosed a couple of, I think August—'

'He's had a brain haemorrhage. It's fairly common: the tumour disrupts the tissues, erodes through them, and eventually you'll have bleeding. The blood created pressure on the brain. That's what made him lose consciousness.'

'Is he—' I was starting to say *Is he awake yet* or possibly *Is he dead*, but the doctor kept talking like I didn't exist.

'We've stabilised him. A haemorrhage like this can make the blood pressure unstable – his was all over the place, when he came in – so we've given him medication to keep that under control. Now we're just going to keep monitoring and see how he does. We'll hope he wakes up soon. It all depends on how much damage has been done.'

I realised who he reminded me of: the shitbird neurologist, back when I had been in hospital, brushing past my desperate questions like everything about me was too unimportant even to register. 'Is he going to—' *Going to be OK* was wrong, obviously Hugo wasn't going to be OK, but I didn't know how else to—

'We'll have to wait and see,' the doctor said. He punched a code into a keypad by the door, thick blunt fingers. 'You can go in and see him now. Second room on the left.' He held the door for me – and for Rafferty, who hung back, letting me go in ahead – before he nodded and strolled off down the corridor.

Rich stench of hand sanitiser and death, a girl sobbing somewhere. Hugo's room was small and overheated. He was flat on his back; his eyes were a slit open and for a moment I had a wild burst of hope, but then I saw how still he was. His skin was greyish and sagging back from his face, leaving his features standing out too sharply. Wires and tubes poured out of him, fine and flexible and nasty: a tube spilling from his open mouth, another from his bony arm, another from under his sheet, wires sprouting from the neck of his gown. Machines everywhere, beeping, bright-coloured zig-zags running across a monitor, numbers flickering. All of it was horrifying but I clung to it all the same – they wouldn't be bothering with all this stuff unless they thought he had a fighting chance, surely they wouldn't, would they?

A nurse – Indian, soft and pretty, glossy hair in a neat bun – was writing something on a chart. 'You can talk to him,' she said, nodding encouragingly at Hugo. 'Maybe he can hear you.'

I pulled a brown plastic chair to the bed and sat down. 'Hugo,' I said. In the edge of my vision Rafferty moved the other chair into an unobtrusive corner and sat down, settling himself for the long haul. 'It's me. Toby.'

Nothing; not a twitch of his eyelids, not a movement of his lips. The machines beeped away steadily, no change.

'You're in hospital. You had a brain haemorrhage.'

Nothing. I couldn't feel him there. 'You're going to be fine,' I said, ludicrously.

'I'll come back soon,' the nurse said gently, to all three of us, hooking the chart onto the end of the bed. 'If you need me before that, you can push this button. OK?'

'OK,' I said. 'Thanks.' And she was gone, almost soundless on the rubbery floor, the open door letting in a faint trail of sobbing for a moment before closing behind her with a soft whoosh.

Hugo would hate this place, everything about it. Maybe he was deliberately staying in a coma so he wouldn't have to deal with it, I wouldn't blame him— 'Hugo,' I said. 'The sooner you wake up, the sooner you can go home. OK?'

For a moment I thought his mouth tensed as if he was trying to say something, around the tube, but then it was gone and I couldn't be sure it hadn't been my imagination.

There were a hundred things I wanted to tell him, ask him. Maybe one of them would reach him, deep amid the darkness and the wingbeats and the swags of clinging cobwebs. I had been there too, not so long ago; if anyone could find the way through that shifting labyrinth to Hugo and lead him back, surely it would be me.

But there was Rafferty, an angular shadow filling up my peripheral vision, turning everything unsayable. 'What did he say?' I asked, when I couldn't ignore him any longer. 'At the station?'

Rafferty shook his head. 'I can't go into that, man. Sorry.'

Those golden eyes, on me, giving away nothing. I couldn't tell whether he knew Hugo had been lying to him and why, or what he might do about it – arrest me, drag me away for questioning, *Talk and we'll let you go back to your uncle?* I thought about saying it straight out, simple as that, as if we were just two people together in this room: *Look, we both know the story. Let me stay here till this is over, one way or another, and then I'll do whatever you want. Deal?*

I couldn't trust myself to make it work. Instead I turned back to Hugo. One big hand lay loosely on the sheet beside me, and I put mine over it – it seemed like what I was supposed to do. His was cold, somehow bony and rubbery at the same time; it didn't feel like human flesh and mine wanted to jerk away from it, but I made myself stay put because maybe he could feel things in there, maybe I had followed my mother's hand or my father's back to the daylight, who knew? I sat still, watching Hugo's face and listening to the endless even beeping and catching Rafferty's keen split-wood smell with each breath, trying not to move in case it made something happen.

•

I don't have any clear sense of how long we were in the hospital. I remember bits and pieces, but not the order they came in; there was something wrong with the way time worked there, something had fallen out of it so that events didn't link together in any sequence but just drifted round and round, disconnected, in the huge humming white-lit void.

My father was there, shirt collar twisted, hand clasping my shoulder so hard it hurt. I remembered him back when I was in hospital, the long-limbed tan creature that had paced in the shadows around his feet; I almost asked if he had brought it this time but luckily it dawned on me that it probably hadn't been real. The nurse made notes on Hugo's chart, adjusted dials, swapped bags. *I had a go at Haskins's diary,* I told him, *while you were gone. I actually found something he doesn't hate, can you believe it? He loves reading to his kid. I can't work out what he was reading, though; you'll have to do it when you get home, I stuck a Post-it on the page* . . . Hugo's face didn't change. Phil was crying, silently, wiping his eyes with a knuckle again and again.

Two visitors per bed I'm afraid said a different nurse so sometimes I was in a waiting area, rows of black plastic seating and a vending machine humming in the corner, a dumpy middle-aged woman holding hands with a blond teenage girl and both of them staring into space. My mother bent to kiss my head and when I didn't flinch away she held me close, smell of cut grass and cold air, a deep breath before she let me go.

My family yammering questions at me, *Why was he what did he but no no no that's insane of course he didn't what the hell—* I pictured their faces if I told them the truth: *Hey at this stage you should probably know it looks like it was me all along, all my fault, sorry about that guys . . .* For an awful second I thought I might be going to do it, or faint, I wasn't sure which. I sank down into a chair and put my head in my hands, which turned out to be a good move: they backed off and left me alone. Leon stalked the edges of the waiting area, gnawing his thumbnail, not looking at me.

Hugo I meant to ask you, you know what they found down the tree, did they tell you? Leaning in closer, was that a twitch of his hand— *Lead soldiers. Were those yours?* And my father laughing, a startled crack too loud in the dry air: *Those were mine! Oliver was a little brat, whenever any of us had a favourite toy he'd get fascinated by it and try to steal it, so we were always hiding things from him . . . I must have forgotten where I'd put those!* And then silence, while we waited for Hugo to smile, tell us all the things he'd hidden from Oliver and where to look for them.

You should go home and get some sleep someone said to me but that seemed way too complicated; instead I dozed on the plastic chairs, woke bleary-eyed with a hard crick in my neck. Susanna was texting, thumbs flying. There was one nurse who was the image of the pretty brunette who had eyed me in the pub that night, scrubs instead of tight red dress now and face bare of makeup but I would have sworn it was her; her eyes passed over me and I couldn't tell if she had recognised me, I wanted to catch her arm as she went by and ask her but somehow she was always too far away.

On one of Hugo's machines an alarm started up, loud urgent beeping. I fumbled for the call button, heart pounding, my dad shouting beside me, but before I could find it a nurse came in – casual and brisk as a waitress, surely she should have been rushing? – and turned the alarm off. *Let's just turn this up a bit* fiddling with some dial, standing back to watch the incomprehensible coloured lines run across the screen, and then with a small reassuring smile to us: *Now. That's better.*

The light at the windows came and went in unnatural fitful flickers, bright one moment and night the next. *Hugo you have to tell me what to say to Mrs Wozniak, remember? How to break it to her? Should I, I mean, what should I . . .*

And always Rafferty, silent in the corner, waiting. Rafferty still in his overcoat like the heat didn't touch him, its rucked-up folds patterning him with deep shadows at strange angles. One time Oliver was giving out to him, belly puffed and finger pointing, *ridiculous accusations, the decency to give the family some privacy for God's sake.* Rafferty nodded, understanding, sympathetic, in complete agreement, but then Oliver was gone and he was still there, head leaned back against the wall, at ease.

Hugo. Squeeze my hand or something.

Somewhere an old woman sang 'Roses of Picardy', quietly, in a rusty quaver. The alarm went off again, a different nurse bustled in. *What is it?* Phil asked, gesturing at the machines with a hand rigid with tension, *what's happening?* The nurse made mysterious adjustments and notes: *We're just having a little trouble keeping his blood pressure under control. Doctor will talk to you when he comes round.*

Only just as she turned to leave another alarm started going frantically and suddenly things changed, the nurse spinning back to Hugo's bed with her mouth open, Rafferty sitting up straight— *Out* the nurse said sharply, hitting a button, *everyone out, now*— Then we were in the corridor and Rafferty had a hand on my back and one on Phil's, steering us quickly towards the waiting area – me stumbling, my leg had gone to sleep – and as he pulled open the door a voice snapped behind us, just like on TV, *Clear!*

The waiting area, all my family standing up in unison, white-faced, *What what what happened*, Phil explaining in a dead-level voice while Rafferty melted off to some corner. I couldn't look at them. The dumpy woman and the teenager were gone and instead there was an old guy with droopy bloodshot eyes and a suit worn shiny at the knees, who didn't even look up from stirring his styro-foam cup of tea.

For a long long time nothing happened. My father and Phil and Oliver were shoulder to shoulder, a tight pack, pale and somehow all looking alike for once. I wanted to go to my father but I couldn't, not knowing what I did. I wished my mother was there. Leon leaned against the wall with his eyes closed, chewing ferociously at his thumbnail. There was blood on it.

When the white-haired doctor finally came out we leaped to cluster around him, at a respectful distance and keeping our mouths shut till he deigned to speak, like good little petitioners. 'Mr Hennessy's stable,' he said – even, weighted voice, carefully pitched to let us know long before he said the words. 'But I'm afraid it's not good news. We were hoping his haemorrhage would resolve, but instead of improving he's going the other way. He's needing escalating amounts of support.'

'Why?' my father asked, calm and focused, his lawyer voice. 'What's happening, exactly?'

'The brain damage from the haemorrhage is making his blood pressure unstable. We're giving him drugs for that, but we've had to up the dosage several times already, and one of the side effects is heart arrhythmia. That's what happened in there. We've shocked him out of it for now, but if he has multiple episodes, there's really nothing for us to do.'

'Why didn't you drain the blood?' Susanna demanded, sharply enough that I jumped. 'From the haemorrhage?'

The doctor barely glanced at her. 'We're doing everything that's appropriate.'

'Standard procedure is to drain the blood right away, to relieve the pressure on the brain. Why didn't you—'

'For Doctor Google, maybe.' A half-smile, but it was animal and tooth-baring, a warning. 'But when your uncle came in, his prognosis wasn't good. We don't know how long he'd been down before he was found; it could have been anything up to twenty minutes. We managed to get him breathing again, but there's no way to know how much damage was done in the meantime. And that's on top of his pre-existing terminal condition. Even if the haemorrhage resolves, there's a high probability he'll be left in a permanent vegetative state.'

Susanna said, 'He's old and he's dying anyway and he came in from police custody, so he wasn't worth the hassle and resources of surgery.'

The doctor's eyes slid away like she bored him. He said, 'You'll just have to accept that everything we've done has been within best-practice guidelines,' which sounded strange to me, like I had heard it somewhere before; for a second there his voice even sounded different, everything sideslipping— But then he turned his shoulder to Susanna and said in his own voice, to my father and Oliver and especially Phil: 'We need to decide what to do the next time his heart goes into arrhythmia. Do we shock him again? Give CPR? Or do we leave it?'

'"The next time,"' my father said. 'You think it's going to happen again.'

'There's no way to be sure. But almost definitely, yes.'

'And you don't think there's any chance he'll wake up. If you keep stabilising his heart, I mean, to give the haemorrhage time to resolve.'

'Not with any quality of life, no. We've all heard the stories about people coming out of comas after ten years, but that's not going to happen here.'

Silence. Leon looked like he might throw up. Then:

'Leave it,' Phil said. My father nodded, one small jerk of his head. Susanna took a breath and then let it out again.

'We'll keep him comfortable,' the doctor said, almost gently. 'You can go in and see him now.'

We went in and out, one by one, two by two. I knew we were supposed to say our goodbyes and any final messages, but there was nothing I could find to say that wouldn't have been either idiotic or dangerous – Rafferty, stubbled and eyebagged by now, back in his chair – or both. *Hugo,* I said in the end, into his ear. He smelled musty and medical, nothing like himself. *It's Toby. Thank you for everything. And I'm so sorry.* There was something crusted at the corners of his lips; Susanna found a wipe in her bag and cleaned it off, gently, telling him some long story too low and close for me to hear.

Everyone phoning, texting. Oliver pacing the waiting area with his phone pressed to one ear and his finger in the other, talking fast and harshly. Tom bustling in babbling about childcare arrangements to anyone who would listen, which was no one. My mother, Louisa, Miriam with tears pouring down her face as she cast about for someone to hug and the rest of us looked away.

And there we all were, waiting. Far below the window, traffic jammed up in the rain: streaks of light glistening on wet tarmac, pedestrians scurrying, umbrellas flapping wildly.

'They could be wrong,' Leon said, at my shoulder. 'Doctors make mistakes all the time.'

He looked awful, pinched and peaky, with a greasy sheen to his face. 'What are you talking about?' I said.

'He could wake up. I don't like that doctor, the way he bullied our dads into—'

'Even if he does wake up, he'll still have cancer. We'll just have to do this all over again in a few weeks. And he's not going to wake up.'

'I can't think,' Leon said. 'I've been so fucking tense, for so long, my brain won't . . .' He shoved his hair out of his face with the back of his wrist. 'Listen. About the other night.'

'I was a prick to you,' I said. 'Sorry.'

'It's OK. I've probably been a prick to you too, the last while.'

'It doesn't matter.'

He glanced over his shoulder and lowered his voice. 'I think that's what she was aiming for, you know that? She kept telling me to chill out, like, "What's the big panic, they can't even prove he was murdered," but then she'd turn around and be all, "Keep your mouth shut around Toby, you can't trust him . . ."'

'Susanna?'

'"He didn't have your back when Dominic was giving you shit, and now he's all fucked up we don't know what he might do, just watch yourself around him . . ." Was she doing it to you too? About me?'

'Pretty much,' I said. I couldn't even be angry. Whatever Susanna's game had been, she had in fact been right about me: I had been frantically flailing for ways to dump the whole thing on her and Leon. It was nice that at least one person had had a clear sense of what was going on here.

'"Just trust me, I know what I'm doing . . ." Look how that turned out.' Leon drew zigzags in the condensation on the glass. 'At least it should be over now. Shouldn't it?'

'What?'

'If Hugo confessed. That's the end of that. They're not going to keep hassling us.'

'Probably not,' I said. I had no idea – whether Hugo had been convincing enough to fool Rafferty, or what Rafferty could do about it if he hadn't, or what I was going to do either way. I knew I had to come up with some kind of plan, fast, but – in that place, with every remaining brain cell taken up by listening for the alarm – I could no more have done it than I could have flapped my wings and flown away.

Holding up crossed fingers, both hands: 'God, I hope. I can't take much more of *him*.' A violent back-flick of Leon's head, towards THE BELLS and Hugo's room. 'I can't believe he's actually hanging around here. We're in with Hugo, saying good*bye*, and he's sitting there listening to every—' His voice cracked. 'I really need a smoke,' he said. 'Do you want to come for a smoke?'

'No,' I said. The hospital seemed to have sent my body into some kind of unnatural suspended state; I hadn't wanted anything to eat or drink since I got there, never mind a cigarette.

'I should have got a vape,' Leon said, 'or those patches, or— Ring me if anything happens,' and he was out the door at a fast scuttle, already fumbling for his smokes. I kept staring out the window. A cyclist had got into a yelling match with some suit in a Range Rover; the suit was out of his car and they were making sweeping arm gestures at each other. Another cyclist was about to flatten the pair of them.

A swelling, shameful part of me was screaming for this to be over. My father leaning against a wall with his face white and strained, staring at nothing, his hand tense in my mother's: I wasn't sure how much longer he could take. I wasn't sure how much longer any of us could take, come to that. All my circuits were so overloaded with suppressed fight-or-flight that I was practically locked in spasm. My leg was wobbling and I wanted to shift my weight to the other one, but it was like the thought couldn't reach my muscles, nothing happened.

Rain on the window. Nurses coming and going, incomprehensible colour-coded scrubs, brisk soft slip-slap of their shoes. The heat had dried out my eyes till I could barely blink.

'Is Melissa coming in?' my mother asked. She had a bunch of cups of coffee in a complicated cardboard holder.

'She's back at her place,' I said. My lips felt numb. 'It's a long story.'

For an awful moment I thought my mother was going to go off into some spiel, *Oh no Toby what happened?! are you two OK? you're so wonderful together I know whatever happened you can work it out you've both been under so much stress*, or even worse try and hug me. Instead she said, after a second's pause, 'Here. Have one of these. It's not the horrible stuff from the machine; I went out for it.'

'Thanks,' I said. 'Maybe in a minute.' We stood there in silence, side by side. Susanna sang a lullaby, very quietly, into her phone.

When the alarm finally went, it was me and my father in the room. I was past being able to come up with words but my father was leaning forwards with his elbows on his knees and his hands clasped, talking, a low even monologue, very calm. I don't remember most of it – my mind was severing itself from all of this, I felt like I was bobbing somewhere near the ceiling and my body was some bizarrely shaped pouch full of wet sand that had nothing to do with me – but bits drifted across my mind: . . . *let us eat dessert first, always apple crumble because Phil hated Christmas pudding, we'd sit under the tree and . . . followed the music downstairs and found them dancing together, cheek to cheek, I turned around very quietly and . . . And that boat, remember? the old man who would let us take it out every summer, and we would row to the middle of the lake and fish? Never caught anything because Oliver wouldn't stop talking, but I still remember the light, the haze of it over the far edge of the lake, and the sound of the water against the side of the boat . . .* When the alarm started howling, when my father jerked like he'd been electrocuted and Rafferty's chair scraped back hard, it took me a moment to find my way back into my body and realise what was going on.

Rafferty was up and out the door: getting the others, but he wasn't fast enough. It was so quick, after all that waiting. 'Hugo,' my father said, loudly, grabbing his shoulder. 'Hugo.'

More alarms, battering at me, taking my breath away. 'Hugo,' I said, 'can you hear me,' but his grey face didn't change, he didn't move, only the lines on the monitor scribbling out of control to give us a glimpse of what was going on in secret, in the dark inside him.

The nurse was there. She turned the alarms off and stood back from the machines, hands cupped together loosely in front of her, in the sudden ringing silence.

I swear, even though I know it can't be true I swear he smiled at me, that old wonderful smile rich with love; I swear he winked one slitted eye. Then all the sharp intricate peaks on the monitor smoothed out to clean straight lines and my father made a terrible growling sound, but even without any of that I would have known, because the air around us had split open and whirled and re-formed itself and there was one less person in the room.

II

The house was freezing, a solid, all-pervading, damp cold like it had been empty for months instead of a couple of days. I hot-showered myself raw and threw everything I had been wearing into a boil-wash, but I couldn't get the hospital stench out of my nose. Everything smelled of it: the water from the kitchen tap, my shampoo, the inside of my wardrobe. I kept catching the monotonous beeping of the monitors, somewhere just beyond the edge of my hearing.

The only thing I wanted in the world was sleep, but I needed to let Melissa know. *Hi Melissa, I know you don't want to hear from me right now and I understand, but I'm afraid I have bad news. Hugo collapsed and was taken to hospital—* It occurred to me that I should have texted her from the hospital, asked her to come in; maybe her voice would have made it through to Hugo. It had never even crossed my mind.*— but there was nothing they could do. He died late last night—* had it been late night? early morning? *I need to thank you on behalf of all the family for your incredible kindness to him. It meant the world to him. He was enormously fond of you—* It read like I was texting a stranger. I couldn't find how to talk to her; she seemed like someone from another world, someone long lost. *I hope to see you at the funeral, but please don't feel obligated to come if you'd prefer not to. Love, Toby.*

I slept for fourteen hours straight, woke up long enough to eat something and went back to bed. That was how I spent most of the next few days, actually: sleeping as much as I could. Not that I got much rest. Over and over I dreamed that it wasn't Dominic I had killed, it was Hugo: Hugo sprawled on the living-room floor while I stood over him bloody to the wrists, floundering desperately to remember why I had done this; Hugo's skull splitting under the axe in my hands while I moaned *No no no*. Sometimes I was my adult self, sometimes I was a teenager or once even a little kid; often it was in my apartment and I had done it because I thought he was one of the burglars. I would wake sobbing and wander around the house – dark landings, pale blurs of windows, no way to tell whether it was dawn or dusk – till the dream faded enough that I could go back to bed.

Because this was the thing I couldn't stop coming back to, awake or asleep, poking at it like a rotten tooth: Hugo's death was my fault, maybe not the fact that he had died but the way of it. If he hadn't rung the detectives, he would have been at home in bed when the haemorrhage hit. He would have died there, with familiar smells and his own duvet, with dawn and birds starting outside the window. Instead he had died in that hellhole hospital, being mauled and probed like a cut of meat amid the reek of disinfectant and piss and other people's deaths, because he had shielded me.

Somewhere in there my mother came over, to pick out clothes for Hugo to wear and to bring me my black suit, which she had collected from my apartment. I got the vague impression of intense activity going on out there, among the rest of the family: Phil was in charge of the arrangements, Susanna was picking out the music and she was sure Hugo had liked Scarlatti, did that sound right? did I want to do a reading? because my father was organising those, and he thought maybe I would—

'No,' I said. 'Thanks.'

We were in Hugo's room, which I hadn't gone into since the hospital. It was a nice room, mismatched old wooden furniture, a huge teetering stack of books beside the bed and a faded photo on the wall of my great-grandparents in front of the house. It smelled like him, a faint comforting scent of wet wool and dusty old books and smoky tea. On the mantelpiece was a vase of yellow freesias that Melissa had brought home, on a day that felt much too long ago for them to still be alive.

'OK. It's up to you.' My mother was going through shirts in Hugo's wardrobe. She was doing it gently, but still, the casual invasion of it set my teeth on edge. 'You'll be a pallbearer, though, won't you? Your dad and your uncles, and you and Leon and Tom. You're OK for that?'

What with your leg and all. 'Yeah,' I said. 'Of course.'

'It won't be swarming with reporters, anyway, or at least it shouldn't be. His name hasn't been in the papers.'

It took me a moment to figure out what she was talking about – I had been asleep when she knocked on the door. 'Right,' I said. 'Good.'

'So far, anyway.' She unhooked a white shirt and examined it, turning it to the light. 'I don't know if the Guards are just being considerate, letting us get the funeral out of the way—'

'I don't think they do considerate,' I said. 'If they're keeping quiet, it's because it suits them.'

'You could be right. Maybe they just don't want to have to show up and keep photographers and gawkers away from the graveside. Either way, I'll take it.'

That – *graveside* – pulled something out of the foggy tangle in my brain. 'He wanted to be cremated,' I said.

My mother turned sharply from the wardrobe, shirt dangling from her hand. 'Are you sure?'

'Yeah. He said it, back in—' I couldn't remember how long it had been. 'A few weeks back. He wants his ashes to go in the garden.'

'Shit. I don't think Phil knows that. He was talking about your grandparents' cemetery plot— I'll have to ring him.' She turned back to the wardrobe, in more of a hurry now. 'This tie? Or this one?'

'No,' I said suddenly. 'No tie. And not that shirt. That one, the striped one' – a faded flannel thing that Hugo had worn around the house – 'and the dark-green jumper, and the brown cords.' Hugo had always hated suits; at Susanna's wedding, grimacing, running a finger under his collar— This much at least I could do.

'Oliver won't be happy. He said the blue suit—' My mother narrowed her eyes at the shirt and tie in her hands. 'You know what, Oliver can get lost. You're right. You pick out whatever you think; I'll ring Phil about the cremation thing.'

She went out on the landing to do it. Going by the careful soothing note in her voice, Phil was up to ninety. 'I know, I know, but we can ring them and . . . Because it didn't occur to him till now. He probably thought you knew— Yes, he's positive . . . No, Phil. He's not. What, out of nowhere? He's not . . .'

Her voice faded down the stairs. Bleak autumn sunlight fell across the floorboards. After a while I went over to the wardrobe and started taking out clothes and picking off lint and arranging them, very neatly, on the bed.

•

The day of the funeral was grey and cold, wind blowing long sheets of rain back and forth in the street. My black suit was baggy on me; in the mirror I looked ridiculous, lost in some stranger's clothes and some stranger's very bad day. Someone had organised long black Mafia-looking cars to ferry us from place to place, funeral home, church, crematorium, all of them out in unfamiliar bits of west Dublin, in no time I had lost my bearings completely and had no idea where I was.

'Where's Melissa?' Leon asked, in the car on the way to the funeral home. His rush-bought suit was too long in the sleeves so that he looked like a schoolkid, and he smelled faintly but un-mistakeably of hash. Our parents either hadn't noticed or had decided not to.

'She's not here,' I said.

'Why not?'

'I didn't bring umbrellas,' my mother said, leaning over me to peer out the window. 'I knew there was something.'

'We'll survive,' Oliver said. He looked awful, face sagging where he had lost weight, shaving cuts in the folds. 'Not like we'll be out in the cemetery.' He threw me a baleful look; apparently I was in his bad books about the cremation thing.

'But if it gets *worse*,' Miriam said, a little wildly. She was wearing a drapey black cape thing that, when she came out of their house into the wind, had looked like she was about to take off. 'Waiting outside the church, there's always all that standing around—'

'No worries,' the driver said peacefully, over his shoulder. 'I've umbrellas in the boot if you need them. Ready for anything.'

'Well then,' Miriam said, triumphantly and obscurely. 'There you go.'

No one had anything to say to that. Leon was still eyeing me. I turned my head away and looked out the window, at bare scrawny trees and boxy little houses whipping past.

The funeral home was spotless and neutral, nothing that could possibly make anyone feel any worse, every detail so discreet that it slid out of my mind the second I looked away. Off to one side of the room, shining in the tasteful soft light, was the coffin.

Hugo looked, bizarrely, more like himself than he had in months: hair smooth and neatly trimmed, cheeks filled out and ruddied by techniques I didn't want to think about, the look of unruffled absorption he had worn when he was at work and on an interesting trail. A flash of memory hit me out of nowhere, Hugo bent over my finger with a needle and that same absorbed look, digging out a splinter. Cold sunny day and his hair all dark back then. *Yes it will hurt but only for a moment – look, here it is, that's a big one!*

My father and the uncles, faces fixed in grim remote endurance, moved around shaking hands with people I half-recognised. A big bosomy woman cried, 'Oh, Toby, you look dreadful, you must be *devastated*,' and enveloped me in a fragrant hug. I caught Leon's eye over her shoulder and shot him a panicked stare; he mouthed *Margaret*, which wasn't a lot of help. 'Toby,' my father said quietly, in my ear. 'Time to go.' It took me a moment to understand what he meant.

The sheer weight of the coffin was stunning. Up until then the day had felt completely unreal, just another bad dream to be stumbled through – I hadn't even considered taking this on without Xanax – but the bite and grind of the wood into my shoulder was savagely, inescapably real. My leg shook and dragged, I couldn't stop it, a jagged catch in the slow march, everyone watching— Sliding the coffin into the hearse, rain driving down my coat collar, I tripped and almost went on one knee on the tarmac. 'Whoops,' Tom said, catching my arm. 'Slippery out here.'

Ugly concrete church, long faux-homemade banners hanging everywhere, stylised images and smooth soundbites about harvests. It was fuller than I had expected, mostly older people – I recognised some of them, they had visited Hugo – and there was a constant muffled buzz of shuffling feet, coughs, murmurs. Over the grey heads I caught a flash of gold, and my heart leaped: Melissa had come.

Hymns rising in the cold air; only the old people knew the tunes, and their voices were too thin and ineffectual to fill the vast space overhead. The priest's voice had that awful unctuous fall that they all pick up somehow. Wreaths propped at the foot of the coffin, candles guttering in a draught. Phil read out something from a sheet of lined paper, presumably a eulogy but his voice was hoarse and almost inaudible and the acoustics blurred it so that I caught only the odd phrase: *always at the heart of our . . . went down to the . . .* Something that made everyone laugh. We *knew he would . . .*

Hugo in firelight, looking up laughing from his book, hair falling in his eyes and a finger on the page to mark his place: *Listen to this!* Beside me my father was crying, silently and without moving a muscle. My mother had her fingers woven through his. 'He was,' Phil said, louder and firmer, raising his head defiantly, 'possibly the best man I have ever known.'

In the foyer afterwards – people milling about, everyone lining up to shake hands with my father and the uncles – I cast around wildly till I caught that gold flash again, and practically shoved people out of my way getting to Melissa.

She was on her own, pressed back against a wall by the crowds. 'Melissa,' I said. 'You made it.'

Sober navy-blue dress that made her look paler and older, hair pulled back in a soft twist. There were mascara smears under her eyes where she had been crying, and it went straight to my heart; every cell of me was howling to put my arms around her, hold her tight while we sobbed into each other's unfamiliar grown-up clothes.

'Toby,' she said, holding out both hands. 'I'm so sorry.'

'Thanks,' I said. 'I'm really glad you came.'

'How are you doing?'

'I'm OK. Getting by.' Her hands in mine, so small and so cold, I almost breathed on them to warm them. 'How are you?'

'I'm all right. Sad.'

Did she mean about Hugo, or about us? 'Me too,' I said. And then, with a thump of my heart: 'We're going back to the house, afterwards. Come with us.'

'No. Thanks, thank you, but I can't, I have to—' She was half a step too far back from me, as if she thought I was going to hug her or grab her or something, what the hell was that about? 'I just wanted to come and tell you how sorry I am – and your family, them too. He was a wonderful man; I'm lucky that I got to know him.'

'Yeah. Me too.' I couldn't bring myself to believe that this was it, goodbye, here in a crowded church foyer. I almost said it, the way I would have if this had been a normal breakup: *Please can I call you, can we talk* . . . It took everything I had to stop myself.

She nodded, biting down on her lips. 'I should go find your dad,' she said, 'before you have to leave for the, I don't want to miss him—' Just for a second she squeezed my hands so tightly that it hurt, and then she slipped past me into the crowd, weaving through it deftly and delicately until even that flicker of gold was gone.

Hoist up the coffin again, back to the hearse, load it in – everyone but me seemed to know by instinct where to go and what cues to wait for; I did whatever my father did. Back into the car. 'Those painkillers you had,' Leon said in my ear, when our parents were deep in discussion of what to do with the flowers. 'Have you got any on you?'

'No,' I said.

'Back at the house?'

'Yeah. I'll get you then.'

'Thanks,' Leon said. For a moment I thought he was about to say something else, but he just nodded and turned to stare out the window. The coffin had left a sharp line across the shoulder of his suit.

And, at last, the crematorium. It was a decorative chapel on the grounds of a cemetery: shining wooden pews, elegant arches and clean lighting, everything perfectly gauged and sympathetic. Scarlatti playing softly. More speeches. Phil crying, eyes closed, finger pressed across his mouth.

Hugo, testy, glancing over his shoulder at me sprawled on the study floor, pushing up his glasses with a knuckle: *Toby if you're just going to play with your phone then go somewhere else, you're distracting the rest of us.*

All day I had been steeling myself for the big moment: the wall opening wide, the slow measured slide of the coffin into the darkness; the clang of the heavy door behind it, the great muffled roar of fire. It had run through my dreams. Instead the lights over the coffin gradually dimmed, like a stage effect, and a curtain came to life and inched across the chapel, cutting off the coffin from view. Everyone took a long breath and turned towards each other, murmuring, shuffling out of their pews, buttoning coats.

I was so stunned that I stood there gaping, waiting for the curtain to open again, until my mother linked a hand through my elbow and turned me towards the door. *But wait*, I almost said, *hang on, we haven't—* Surely that had been the moment at the heart of the whole day, the reason for all the suits and hymns and handshakes and ritual, that moment was what all of it was about? Where had it gone? But before I could put words together my mother had steered me down the aisle and out the door.

In the car park Susanna was leaning against a wall, watching Zach and Sallie chase each other in circles through the spitting rain. Zach had found a stray lily and was whacking at Sallie with it; her laughter had a rising note of hysteria. 'They wanted to come,' Susanna said. 'I don't know if I called it right. I figured if they need to do this, then OK; Tom's parents can take them home if it gets to be too much. But the actual cremation – yeah, no.'

'There wasn't anything scary,' I said. It was still playing over and over in my head, curtain closing demurely across the coffin, the end, off you go home. 'You didn't see it go into the furnace, or anything.' The open space of the cemetery gave the wind room to build momentum; it came charging across the car park and slammed into us like a solid object. Deep inside that greyish building, Hugo was burning to ash. The bemused crease between his eyebrows, his quick smile.

'Huh. I thought we'd see it.' She pulled her collar tighter. 'They probably needed a run around anyway. Zach was getting fidgety.'

'They must have changed things in the last while. We saw Granny's coffin go in, didn't we? And Granddad's?'

'Granny and Granddad were buried,' Susanna said. 'Up there.' A flick of her chin towards the cemetery, crowded headstones stretching on and on, rise after rise of them. 'Don't you remember?'

'Oh,' I said. 'Right.'

'I fucking hate this year,' Susanna said suddenly. She shoved her hands in her coat pockets and headed off across the tarmac towards the kids.

•

The food-and-reminiscence part was at the Ivy House. I had been dreading it – invading crowd, noise, meaningless chitchat – but actually it was such a relief to be home that I almost slid down into a heap on the hall floor. Instead I went up to my room, took another Xanax and leaned my forehead against the cool wall for a long time.

When I went back down the house was packed and buzzing. I went looking for Leon – I had a couple of Xanax in my jacket pocket for him – but he was telling some story in a corner of the living room, surrounded by old people. My mother and the aunts were passing around wineglasses that had materialised from somewhere, along with platters of whimsical miniature sandwiches involving brioche buns and improbable ingredient combinations and fiddly bits of greenery. Zach had found an unsupervised plateful on a side table and was licking every sandwich and putting it back. 'Toby,' my mother called over – I was still standing in the doorway, trying to work out what I was supposed to be doing about any of this – 'I'm running out of white. Could you find a couple more bottles?'

There was already a sizeable cluster of empty wine bottles in one corner of the kitchen. My father was at the table, peeling back cling-film from another massive platter of winsome little sandwiches. 'Good turnout,' I said, which was what everyone in the church foyer had kept saying to everyone else.

He didn't look up. 'Do you know what I've lost count of?' he asked. 'The number of people who've asked about Hugo smoking. "Did he smoke?" "But, but, I thought he didn't smoke?" Which of

394

course he didn't, not in the last twenty years at any rate, and anyway it wouldn't be remotely relevant if he had; this type of cancer isn't linked to smoking. It's just a, a, a random vicious bastard. Hugo just had bad luck; a bad roll of the dice. But we're so desperate, aren't we, to believe that bad luck only happens to people who deserve it. People genuinely can't take it in that someone could die of cancer *without bloody well smoking.*'

The platter was overloaded; without the clingfilm holding them in place, cascades of sandwiches kept falling off. He tried to poke them back in. 'I mean, *Miriam* for God's sake, and she knew Hugo how long, thirty-odd years? not just some acquaintance – she's spent the last few months gabbling away about toxins from red meat and processed foods, and people who do yoga every morning and live to be a hundred, and I don't know what the *hell* she thinks she's on about but at this point I can hardly stand being in the same room with her.'

His hands were trembling; the sandwiches wouldn't go right, he kept fumbling them. 'Here,' I said. 'I'll do those.'

He didn't seem to hear me. 'And these detectives. Do you have any idea what they've got planned? How much they're going to tell the media?'

'No. I haven't seen them.'

'Because if everything comes out, those same people, the ones with the smoking, they're going to be absolutely convinced that Hugo died of cancer because he killed this boy. A punishment from God, or karma, or negative brainwaves from guilt, or – no, let's be honest, they won't even think it through that far, will they, they'll just make some vague mindless self-satisfied assumption. And nothing in the world will change their minds. And I know it doesn't make any difference to Hugo, but it's so bloody *frustrating*—' The sandwiches tumbled back onto the table. 'And these, *damn* these *things*—'

I collected them and started stacking. My father leaned back against the sink and wiped his hands down his face. I couldn't tell whether he thought Hugo had actually done it. There was no way I was going to ask him.

'I keep telling myself it could have been so much worse,' he said.

'You should remember that, too. For someone who'd had such a terrible piece of luck, Hugo was lucky. All the things the doctors warned us about: dementia, pain, seizures, incontinence, paralysis. He didn't have to go through any of that. Or' – he pressed his fingertips into his eyes – 'with the way things were going, jail.'

'He wanted to be at home,' I said. I couldn't hold it back. 'Not in that shithole.'

My dad raised his head and looked at me. His eyes were red and swollen, and someone with magenta old-lady lipstick had given him a big kiss on the cheek. 'He chose to ring the detectives, you know,' he said. 'It's not like they came after him. Yes, probably he assumed he would be coming home; but he must have known there was a possibility he wouldn't. And he did it anyway. I have to believe that he had his reasons, and he thought they were good ones.'

I couldn't tell whether there was a message in there, or a question, carefully layered so I could ignore it if I chose. 'I guess,' I said. The sandwiches looked OK. I went to the fridge for the wine.

'I don't know whether he would have talked to me about it,' my father said, 'if he'd had time. I hope that he would have.'

The fridge was jammed; I had no idea how to get anything out without the whole lot falling on top of me. 'He didn't say anything to me,' I said.

'Hey,' Susanna said, coming in with Sallie clamped onto her skirt. She was wearing a well-cut little black dress and heels, with her hair brushed sleek; she looked tall and striking and unexpectedly elegant. 'That old guy in the saggy tweed jacket just lit up a pipe. Mum and Miriam are freaking out and getting into a whole thing over who should tell him to take it outside, but I figure feck it, pipe smoke isn't even on our top hundred worries list today. As long as he has an ashtray – Sal, let go for a sec, I need to—' She pulled herself up, one knee on the counter, to grab a cracked bowl from a high cupboard shelf. 'This'll have to do. Who is that guy, anyway?'

'I think that's Maurice Devine,' my father said, rubbing his neck with a grimace. 'Social historian. He used to help Hugo out when people wanted more in-depth things. Reports. Whatever you call them. It's incredible, how many people showed up. I didn't realise Hugo was so—'

'It's a great turnout,' Tom said with an air of originality, sticking his head in the door. 'Su, have you got that ashtray? He's using the fireplace, and your mum's about to lose the plot altogether.'

'I'll talk to her,' Susanna said, straightening her skirt. To my dad on her way past, tapping her cheekbone: 'Lipstick, right there. Tom's mum got you.'

'Any more sandwiches out there?' Oliver demanded, over Tom's shoulder.

'On the way,' my father said, and he straightened up and carefully picked up the tray and followed them out to the living room.

•

That day felt like it lasted weeks. But finally, finally, the sandwiches and the reminiscences had all been got through, the guests had trickled away, Susanna and Tom had swept the yawning complaining kids off home, my father and the uncles had cried while they picked out a memento each, my mother and the aunts had (over my protests) tidied everything up and loaded the dishwasher and wiped down the dining-room table and debated at length over who should return the glasses to the caterers and God help me hoovered the entire downstairs, and I had the house to myself again.

I didn't cry for Hugo, over the next few days. This felt shameful, a spit in the face of everything he had done and yet another marker of just how fucked up I was, but I couldn't do it. I actually tried – put on his favourite Leonard Cohen album, broke open a leftover bottle of wine and thought about everything he had lost, the fact that I would never see him again, all of it – but nothing happened. His absence was enormous and tangible, as if a part of the house was gone, and yet on an emotional level his death didn't seem to exist.

My mother had been right about the detectives only keeping their mouths shut through the funeral. Two days later it was all over the news websites, via a neatly worded press release: Hugo Hennessy, the man in whose garden the remains of eighteen-year-old Dominic Ganly had recently been found, had died of natural causes; detectives were not pursuing any other lines of inquiry in connection with the case. The websites padded this out with lavish bumph about Dominic's rugby achievements, generic quotes from classmates, and whatever info on Hugo they could scrounge up, some bits more accurate than others. One website had misheard and had Hugo down as a gynaecologist, which led to frenzied hysteria in the comments section when someone wondered if he had been performing kitchen-table abortions and Dominic had threatened to report him after Hugo operated on his girlfriend. Within hours this had turned into fact, to the point where even a correction from the website didn't change people's minds (*So what it doesn't take a Dr!!! And we already no he was a murderer not much of a stretch 2 think he wd murder babies as well! He got off 2 litely shd be rotting in jail* and a bunch of angry red emojis). The other comments sections weren't much better ('Oh, God, comments sections,' Susanna said; 'cesspits. Never read them'): the general consensus seemed to be that it was deeply suspicious that Hugo had never married, and that he had murdered Dominic after Dominic rejected his advances.

I thought a lot about what my father had said, that week. Back in the hospital I had been convinced that I needed a plan, either to protect myself or to turn myself in and make some kind of deal, but now I couldn't remember why. The thing about not pursuing other lines of inquiry: that might have been thrown out there to lull me into a false sense of security, but either way, it didn't seem like there was a lot Rafferty could do to me. Even if he found some hard evidence, surely a confession from someone else would count as reasonable doubt? And it didn't seem like handing myself in would make the world a better place in any way. On the contrary: the situation was hard enough on my family as it was, I couldn't even imagine what it would do to my parents if I went to prison for murder. The reason I had been considering it to begin with had never been out of some noble urge to sacrifice myself on the altar of justice, anyway. Partly it had been because of Hugo – only a total shit would have let him spend his last couple of months in jail; but letting a bunch of internet douchebags spin bullshit that he would never see was a completely different thing. And, like my dad had said, Hugo had chosen this. His mind had been eroding, but not to the point where he didn't know what he was doing. He had done this deliberately, and he had done it to protect me. Throwing that away would have felt like a really impressive level of ingratitude.

The other reason I had been considering turning myself in had been because why not? What was left to protect? Even when most other stuff had gone by the wayside, I had hung on to the idea that at least I was a decent guy, one of the good guys, but the over-whelming likelihood that I was a murderer put a fairly big damper on that. But it was surprising how fast I had got used to the idea. Not that I liked it. I had never had fantasies of being a badass dan-gerous outlaw; basically, all I had ever wanted to be was normal and happy. But with that off the table, and once the initial shock had worn off, badass outlaw at least felt better than contemptible useless fucked-up victim. In a weird way, it actually went a step or two towards cancelling out the victim thing; it made the fact that I had let two scumbag skangers kick my ass a little more palatable. At least somewhere along the way I had, apparently, done some ass-kicking of my own.

All of which was to say that I wasn't going to be handing myself in to the cops. Rafferty could go fuck himself. I didn't need a plan; all I needed to do, if by any chance he showed up, was keep my mouth shut.

The big question, the one I hadn't really thought about up until then, was what I was going to do instead. I couldn't just drift around the Ivy House for the rest of my life, appealing though that sounded; in fact, there was no reason I should still be there at all. There was my apartment to deal with – I was still paying the mortgage, and my savings weren't going to last forever – there was work, there were all the things that Hugo had given me an excellent excuse for ignoring. Now Hugo was gone, and there they all were, lined up to jab at me more insistently by the day.

It seemed to me that it came down, in the end, to why I had killed Dominic (*if* I had, *if*, sometimes that slipped away from me). I didn't buy the implausible out that Rafferty had dangled in front of me, the scare gone wrong – if that was all I had had in mind, why not just jump Dominic and throw a few punches, or wave a knife around? Why the baroque hassle of learning how to make a garrotte, never mind how to use one? No: that had to have been because I wanted to kill him. And the reason mattered.

I went through it in my head step by step, methodically, pacing back and forth between rooms and talking out loud to myself to make sure I had things straight. If I had done this because Dominic was giving me grief that summer (plausible, given how shitty he had been acting in general) or because of some dumb hormone-fuelled bullshit over a girl (who had I even been into, that summer? Jasmine Something but not like I had been madly in love, same for Lara Mulvaney and basically every other remotely attractive girl I knew – I couldn't believe I would have garrotted anyone over any of them, although clearly what I believed meant less than nothing) – if it had been that kind of petty tantrum, then that didn't seem like something I could just gloss over. Not that I felt the need to do penance by dedicating my life to serving the poor, or anything, but aiming for a pretty white picket fence didn't seem like an option either. It was the wrong kind of dangerousness – volcanic, unpredictable, horrifying; something that didn't belong around, say, babies, or Melissa.

If Rafferty was right, on the other hand, and this had happened because I was somehow protecting Leon, then that seemed like an entirely different thing. That felt like someone who would deserve what Hugo had done for him; someone who had the right, or maybe even the responsibility, to reclaim whatever he could of life.

I don't know how much hope I held out. I had never seen myself as some white knight, either, charging recklessly into battle to save the oppressed, but I did still want to believe that at some level, at least, I had been a decent guy. Leon talked like I was some tremendous douche who had never lifted a finger for anyone except myself, but I had got rid of other bullies for him, after all, I had chased off the wanker who was hassling Melissa, I had stayed here at the Ivy House with Hugo right to the end; surely it wasn't too much of a stretch to think that, if I had somehow found out the full extent of what Dominic was doing to Leon, I might have been protective?

By this point I didn't trust my own mind enough even to bother trying to remember. Anything I dredged up would more than likely be bollocks, thrown up by the same batch of scrambled synapses as my grandparents' cremation. While Leon and Susanna clearly didn't know for sure that I had killed Dominic, they seemed like the most likely people to know – even if they hadn't made the connection – about whatever tangled set of circumstances might have brought me to that point. And so, one more time, I put on my Toby the Boy Detective disguise and I texted the two of them and asked them to come over some afternoon.

Probably it would have made more sense to leave Susanna out of it. With Leon I could cajole, guilt trip, needle till I got something out of him. But even before my mind had been hit by a wrecking ball, Susanna could have run circles around me; if she wanted something kept from me, I would never get within a mile of it. I never even thought about leaving her out. The two of them were, after all, wound around the roots of my old, my own life. Somewhere deeper than thought, I believed that if anyone could open up a route back to that life, it had to be them. I suppose I could say, and in spite of everything it wouldn't be a lie, that I needed them both there because I loved them.

I thought I was being cunningly casual about the invitation, but in hindsight it's obvious that they knew. They showed up anyway. I'm still not sure, even after all this time, whether I should be grateful for that; whether they at least thought, one or both of them, that they were there to do me a favour.

•

After all that time on my own sinking into the silent house, the energy of them came as a shock. Susanna had brought a bunch of sausage rolls, which she threw into the oven with a slam and a clatter of baking sheets, Leon had a big bag of mini Mars bars – Halloween was coming up; I had forgotten, till I saw the cartoon ghosts and vampires leering from the packet – and I had all the wine left over from the funeral do. 'Classy combo,' Leon said, kneeling on the living-room floor and shoving aside drifts of paper and jumpers and plates so he could shake out the Mars bars onto the coffee table – it was cold, I had lit a fire, the living room was the only room that was warm. 'You can say what you want about us, but we've got style.'

'Next time we can be terribly civilised and do tea and cucumber sandwiches and scones, if you want,' Susanna said, nudging him over to put down the plate of sausage rolls. 'But we've all been in emergency mode for so long, what we need right now is comfort food. Tom and the kids and I have been living on pizza and Chinese takeaway. I'll go back to being Organic Superfoods Mummy at some stage, but for now, fuck it.'

'What's the problem?' I said, pulling the cork out of a bottle of red. 'I like sausage rolls, I like Mars bars, I like wine, it's all good. Red goes with pork, right?' I had prepared for this by drinking an awful lot of coffee and I was kind of on a high, a precarious brittle one that felt like speed cut with something dodgy.

'You look like shite,' Leon said to me, anxiously, leaning forwards to examine my face. 'Are you OK?'

'Thanks, dude.'

'No, seriously. Are you eating?'

'Sometimes.'

'You've got every right to be pretty ragged,' Susanna said. 'You got the worst of this. And you've been a trouper, all through.'

'And here you guys were giving me shite about not being able to handle it,' I said. 'Remember that?'

'I know. I take it back. I'm sorry.' She thumped down on the sofa and reached for a bobbled woollen throw. 'If I'd known how things were going to go, I'm not sure I'd have asked you to move in here.'

'I wouldn't have come. Believe me.'

'We owe you.'

'Yeah. You do.'

'Have some of these,' Leon said worriedly, pushing the sausage rolls towards me. 'While they're hot.'

'No thanks,' I said. The smell of them was turning my stomach. What I actually craved, weirdly, was the Mars bars; I've never had much of a sweet tooth, but I wanted to cram them into my mouth three at a time. 'Here.' I passed around wineglasses.

'To Hugo,' Susanna said, raising her glass.

'To Hugo,' Leon and I said.

We clinked glasses. 'Ahhh,' Leon said. He settled on the hearth-rug, leaning back against the armchair opposite mine, and kicked off his trainers and socks. 'Excuse my feet, but I stood in a massive puddle and I'm *squelching* wet. I need to dry these.' He draped his socks over the hearth rail.

'Those had better be clean,' Susanna said.

'Don't be giving me shite. You're there in your socks—'

'Which don't stink—'

'Neither do mine. Clean as a baby's bum. Want to smell?' He waved a sock at Susanna, who mimed puking.

'You look good,' I said to Leon. He did. The pinched look had gone out of his face, his hair was gelled up and his stupid edgy wardrobe was back, which I didn't personally consider a plus but it seemed to be an indicator that he was feeling better. 'A lot less stressed.'

'I know,' he said, stretching out his feet to the fire and wiggling his toes happily. 'I feel so much better. Is that awful? I can't handle waiting for the other shoe to drop. Now that it's actually dropped, I can deal with it.'

'What are you going to do now?' I asked, through a Mars bar. 'When are you heading back to Berlin? Or are you heading back to Berlin?'

He shrugged. 'I haven't decided yet.'

'What about your job?' Susanna asked, taking a sausage roll. 'And Carsten?'

'I don't know. I haven't decided. Leave me alone.' To me: 'What about you? When are you going back to work?'

'I don't know either,' I said. The creamy rush of the chocolate was hitting me as overwhelmingly and rapturously as coke. I took another one. 'Give me a break. It's only been like a week.'

'You should go back,' Leon said. 'It's not good for your head, being stuck here on your own all day.'

'Speaking of which,' Susanna said. 'How's Melissa?'

'Fine.'

'Where did she go, after the church? Did she have to be somewhere?'

'Melissa's moved back to her place,' I said.

After a fractional pause: 'Is it her mum?' Leon asked, hopefully.

'Nope,' I said. 'I'm pretty sure she's dumped me. I haven't heard from her since the funeral.'

'But,' Leon said. He had sat bolt upright. 'She was here the last time we were over. That awful night, two days before Hugo had the—'

'Yeah, I know. And when I went up to bed that night, she wasn't here any more.'

Susanna was picking crumbs off her jumper; I couldn't tell what she was thinking. 'Was it . . . ?' Leon asked. He had a sausage roll suspended in mid-air, halfway to his mouth. 'The stuff we were talking about, that night. Was that what did it?'

'No shit, Sherlock. It's kind of hard to blame her.'

Susanna said, 'Does she think you killed Dominic?'

'I'm pretty sure she does,' I said. 'Yeah.'

'Told you,' Susanna said, to Leon.

'Oh, no,' Leon said. He looked stricken. 'I *like* Melissa.'

'Yeah,' I said. 'So do I. A lot.'

'She was good for you. I thought you were going to *marry* her. I was hoping you would.'

'Right. Again, me too.'

Susanna asked, 'Did Melissa ever actually say that she thinks you did it?'

'She didn't need to.'

'So maybe she doesn't,' Leon said. 'Maybe that's not why she left at all. I mean, all the stress, with Hugo, that can't have been—'

'The thing is,' I said, and cleared my throat. This was all, not harder than I had expected exactly but so much stranger; I was about to ask them why I was a murderer, and it seemed impossible that my life had landed me here. 'The thing is, it sounds weird but I think you're kind of right, that's not why she dumped me. I think she could actually handle me having done it – I mean, I know that sounds crazy but like you said, Melissa is pretty special, she's – I think she might maybe be able to deal with that, depending on why it was. Only she doesn't know. That's got to be really scary for her. It could have been because I'm a, a total psycho, and I just hide it really well most of the time. And the thing is, is that I can't tell her. Because I don't remember. Any of it. So I'm pretty much fucked.'

There was a silence. I took a big swig of my wine – I only realised when I lifted the glass that my hand was shaking. Susanna and Leon were having some complicated exchange of eye signals.

'If you remember anything,' I said, 'anything that could, could make sense of why I might have— That's all you owe me. To help me straighten this out. Melissa only ever got into this because you wanted me to come here. If I hadn't—'

'OK,' Susanna said. 'We're going to tell you a story.'

'Su,' Leon said. 'I still think this isn't a good idea.'

'Relax. It'll be fine.'

'*Su*. Seriously.'

Susanna regarded him across the coffee table. She had her jumper sleeves pulled down to her fingertips and her wineglass cupped in both hands, like it was a cup of tea. In the firelight the whole scene looked almost impossibly cosy and idyllic, the worn red damask of the armchairs glowing, warm flickers catching in the dinged copper kindling bucket and making the old etchings stir and ripple. She said, 'It's only fair.'

'No it's not.'

'It's as close as we're going to get.' To me: 'If you ever tell this to anyone – and that includes Melissa – we'll say it's complete bollocks, you must've hallucinated the whole conversation, we just came over tonight and had a nice sentimental chat about Hugo and went home. And they'll believe us. Are you OK with that?'

'Do I have a choice?' And when Susanna shrugged: 'OK. I get it.'

'I'm having a smoke,' Leon said, pulling himself up off the rug. 'I don't care. Where's that ashtray?'

'He's still kind of wired, isn't he?' Susanna said, when he had gone out to the kitchen. 'It's because he's trying to decide what to do about Carsten. I hope he sticks with him. They're good together.'

'Su,' I said. My heart was going hard. I hadn't expected it to be this easy. I couldn't tell whether I should worry about the fact that she had come here already planning to tell me this story.

'I know.' She leaned over the arm of the sofa to dig in her bag for her cigarettes. 'Want one of these?'

'No thanks.'

'Have you got a light?'

'*Su.*'

'OK, OK. I'm figuring out where to start.' She stretched out her legs on the sofa and rearranged the throw, getting comfortable. 'So. Sixth year, I guess was the beginning. Sometime in March; the Easter holidays. Our parents had gone somewhere, we were staying here, we were studying for the Leaving Cert orals. Remember that?'

'Yeah.'

'Our mates used to call round and study with us? Including Dominic?'

'Yeah.'

'It was horrible,' Leon said, coming back in with the cracked bowl Susanna had dug out after the funeral. '*Here*, for God's sake, where it was supposed to be *safe*, and all of a sudden there's that arsehole, swaggering in and swiping all my books onto the floor and laughing like a hyena.'

'At first I wondered what he was doing here,' Susanna said. 'It's not like you two were that close. But then he started sliming up to me, all smiley, asking me for a hand with French. I wasn't impressed – he'd always acted like I didn't exist, and suddenly when he needs help he's all over me? But I was big into giving people a hand, back then. Community responsibility and all that shite. Jesus, I was a self-righteous little snot, wasn't I?'

'We loved you anyway,' Leon told her, moving more stuff off the coffee table to make room for the ashtray.

'Thanks a bunch. Anyway, I thought fine, whatever, I'll try and get a few irregular verbs into Dominic's thick head. Which went OK for a day or two, until one evening – right in here, actually, I think you two and your other mates were taking up the kitchen table – he started rubbing my thigh and told me how sexy I was.' She reached out a hand; Leon threw her the lighter. 'Which, yeah, right. I assumed he was just taking the piss – I still think he was, actually. Like, he and his buddies had a dogfight going or something. Did you?'

'No! Jesus Christ, Su. What do you take me for?' I was pretty sure I was right to be outraged, I wouldn't have got involved in something like that, would I? 'And' – definitely true, this part – 'no way would I have let him drag you into it. No fucking way.'

'Well,' Susanna said, 'I knew he was setting me up, one way or another. Maybe it wasn't a dogfight or a bet, maybe he just thought I'd be an easy shag because I'd be so flattered by having someone so totally awesome wanting little old me. Or maybe he thought he was doing me a favour in exchange for the study help. Anyway, I took his hand off me and said I wasn't interested. Which he clearly wasn't expecting.'

Leon snorted. 'Why did he have to be setting you up?' I said. 'Or looking for a quick shag? Maybe he was genuinely into you.'

Susanna threw me a look, over the click of the lighter. 'Oh, come on. You know what Dominic was into. Cara Hannigan. Lauren Malone. Gorgeous popular super-groomed blondes.'

'You shouldn't underrate yourself,' I said, idiotically. 'You're beautiful. Not everyone likes the same—'

'Toby,' Susanna said, half amused, half exasperated. 'It's OK that I'm not gorgeous, you know. It's not some kind of deformity that you need to tiptoe around and pretend you don't notice.'

'I'm not—'

'Anyway, I wasn't into Dominic, so it doesn't actually matter whether he was genuinely into me or not. Although of course that's not how he saw it. He told me to relax, and put his hand back on my leg. I was done with the whole thing. So I told him to get off me because I'd rather eat my own puke.'

'Oo,' I said, wincing reflexively. Even after all those years I could feel, with a quick zip of adrenaline, exactly how little Dom would have liked that.

'Yeah, in hindsight, that may not have been a great call. Live and learn.' She stretched out a foot, hooked a toe under the edge of the coffee table to pull it closer so she could reach the ashtray. 'He actually acted like he was taking it OK. He made a big deal of jumping back and holding his hands up, laughed a lot, some stuff about how I needed to chill out and what was I, a lezzer, cliché cliché. I got up to go and he was like, "What, you're not going to help me out any more?" I said no, we're done. Well.' She raised an eyebrow. 'He was genuinely *outraged* about that. "What the fuck is your problem, I was just having a laugh, you're crazy . . ." I left. I was a bit shaken up, but I thought that was the end of it.'

Leon started to laugh. 'I know,' Susanna said. 'Bless my innocent little heart.'

I was – deplorably, maybe, I didn't care – thrilled by the way this story was going. I hadn't been sure about Leon, but Susanna: there was no doubt in my mind that I would have protected her if she needed it, no matter what that took. My heart was going like I was on a roller coaster, rising towards that dizzying peak, ready for the unstoppable plunge.

'After that,' Susanna said, 'whenever I ran into him, like when everyone was hanging out in the park after school, he'd get in some comment about me being frigid or uptight. Someone would crack a dirty joke and Dominic would be like, "Whoa, better keep it clean, Mother Superior's here!" And plenty of people would laugh. I tried telling him to shut up, but that just made him worse: Ooo, someone needs to grow a sense of humour, she must be on her period, she needs a good shag to loosen her up . . . And everyone would laugh harder. So after a while I just kept my mouth shut.'

I was trying to remember this. Everyone had flirted with every-one, mostly very badly, everyone had slagged everyone, a lot of people hadn't known where to stop – we had been kids, after all, seventeen, eighteen. Even if I'd been there for this stuff, it sounded close enough to normal that I might not have registered it at all.

'At that stage it wasn't a big deal,' Susanna said, as if she had read my mind. 'I mean, it pissed me off, but it was just your bog-standard bullshit; it wasn't *scary*. After the orals, though, it got worse. Dom-inic knew he'd made a total bollocks of them, and he figured it was my fault, because I'd quit helping him. He wasn't slagging me off to get a laugh, any more. Instead he'd get right in close to me, lean over and say stuff in my ear – "You think you're smart, you stupid bitch, you think you're smarter than me? Someone should put you in your place," crap like that. And the inevitable stuff about how he wanted to see just how good I was at oral.' She mimed a rimshot.

'He was like that with me too,' Leon said, turning to toast the other side of himself at the fire. 'All the clichés. Arse jokes. AIDS jokes. If you're going to put all that time and effort into being a douchebag bully, then at least go the extra mile and be original about it.'

'I don't know,' Susanna said, considering that. 'Things might have been a lot worse if he'd had any imagination. But he didn't. You know what, I think that may have been his real problem all along. As well as being an arsehole, obviously.'

'And a psycho,' Leon said. 'By then he was starting to get that look – I mean, he'd always been a psycho, but it was starting to be obvious that there was something really wrong with him. He'd walk up to you out of nowhere and punch you right in the stomach, and then just stand there staring and laughing. It was *creepy*.' To me: 'How you and your pals never even noticed—'

'In fairness,' Susanna said, leaning forwards to stub out her cigarette, 'none of us were at our most observant right then, what with the Leaving. By that time it was like May, the written exams were coming up – which meant Dominic was getting more stressed, which meant he was getting nastier. The stuff he said was sounding more and more like actual threats. "You're too ugly to fuck face-to-face, I'm going to do you from behind . . ." '

'Jesus, Su,' I said, wincing.

'Yeah, sorry if that bothers you. It wasn't fun for me, either.' She settled back into the sofa, tucking a cushion behind her. 'And he wasn't just talking any more. At first it wasn't sexual, exactly; just weird. Like one time I started to say something to him, and he shoved his finger in my mouth – I should've bitten it off him, but by the time I figured out what was happening, he was gone. Another time he pulled out the back of my top and spat down it.'

'He was an animal,' Leon said. 'One time he pissed on my shoes.'

'It turned sexual fairly fast, though,' Susanna said. 'One day he walked up to me – I was just *standing* there, outside that little shop beside the schools, waiting for my friends – and he looked me in the eye, grabbed my arse with both hands and gave it a good squeeze. Shoved his crotch up against me while he was at it. And then walked off.'

'You should have said it to me,' I said, as naturally as I could, and waited for it. I wasn't breathing.

Susanna's eyebrows went up. 'I did,' she said: coolly matter-of-fact, almost amused. 'Of course I did. That's exactly when I went to you. My lovely cool cousin who would sort it all out.'

'Aah,' Leon said, to the fire. 'Bless.'

'I was eighteen. I was stupid. So sue me.'

There was something wrong here, something I wasn't getting. 'What?' I said. 'What was stupid?'

'He doesn't even *remember*,' Leon said.

'Do you?' Susanna asked me. When it was obvious I didn't: 'Don't worry, you didn't laugh in my face or anything. You were very nice about it. You explained to me that it was actually a good thing that guys were starting to fancy me, it wasn't something to freak out about, I'd have a lot more fun and be a lot more fun if I got a boyfriend instead of spending my whole life saving Tibet. And it was probably a good call not to go for Dominic because he was kind of a dick, but maybe someone like Lorcan Mullan? And then you got a text from someone and forgot the whole thing.'

'I didn't—' This didn't sound right. 'I must not have got that it was serious. I wouldn't have—'

'Nope,' Susanna said. 'You definitely didn't think it was serious. Which, in fairness, was partly my fault. I was too embarrassed to tell you all the gory details. I just gave you the general gist.'

'Well there you go,' I said. A quick arse-grab and a few douchey comments wouldn't have sounded like a huge deal, Susanna always had liked getting herself worked up, probably a week earlier she had been throwing a wobbler because she had got an A– on some test . . . 'If you'd told me—'

'Well, I kind of expected you to take my word for it. But no. I asked you would you at least tell him to leave me alone, but you said that would make things awkward with the guys. You were a little miffed at me for asking. I think you felt like I shouldn't have put you in that position.'

Then when, how, how had I— Maybe this was what had done it? anger at myself, as well as at Dominic, when I found out what I had let him get away with – could I have needed to make up for that, taken it too far? 'Shit,' I said. 'I'm really sorry.'

She shrugged. 'Water under the bridge.'

'What did you do? Did you tell someone else?'

'My mates, sort of. They knew he was giving me hassle, but I didn't give them all the details either. I felt weird about it. Dirty. I wouldn't now, but hey: eighteen.' A philosophical shrug. 'And it's not like they had any idea what I should do, any more than I did. "God what an arsehole, maybe if you ignore him he'll stop, maybe you should tell him you've got a boyfriend down the country—'"

'I meant like your parents,' I said. 'Or that English teacher you liked.'

With an arch of her eyebrow, over her glass: 'You mean did I Tell A Trusted Adult? Nope. Probably I should have, but I was embarrassed. No one wants to tell her parents how some guy felt her up. And I wasn't sure whether I was making a big deal out of nothing – he was so casual about it, you know? Like it was all just a laugh. Plus, if I talked to a teacher and Dominic got in shite with the school, then everyone would find out and it would be total hell.'

'It would've been,' Leon said, turning his socks on the hearth rail. 'Remember when Lorcan Mullan ratted out Seamus Dooley for hiding his glasses? He was a *leper*. For months.'

'And anyway,' Susanna said, 'Dominic was smart about it. The worse he got, the more careful he was. He'd grab my wrist and pull my hand onto his dick and tell me I was going to suck it, but he'd only do it when there was no one watching. He'd come up to me in the park with a video clip on his phone – because of *course* he always had the fanciest phone, remember? – a video of some woman getting shagged in some creative way, and he'd be like "This is what I'm going to do to you," but he wouldn't send me dick pics or anything. I couldn't prove anything had happened at all. If I'd told anyone, all he would've had to do was say he didn't know what I

411

was talking about and I was a crazy bitch. Overall, it didn't seem like there would be much upside to talking.'

'I felt exactly the same,' Leon said. 'That's what he relied on. God, he really was ghastly, wasn't he?'

'And at that stage,' Susanna said, 'I still felt like I could handle it. I mean, not like I was handling it *well*. I was jumpy as fuck. I was rearranging my life trying not to go anywhere Dominic Ganly might be, and whenever I went out of the house I was whipping around every two seconds to check for someone coming up behind me; every part of me felt like it was about to be grabbed, the whole time. But it still wasn't the centre of my universe. I was studying like crazy; most of my mind was on the Leaving, and that was where I wanted it. The last thing I wanted to do was make the Dominic mess blow up even bigger.' She reached for another cigarette. 'Looking back, I don't think I was handling it as well as I thought. Somewhere around there was when I started thinking about killing him.'

The breath went out of me. Of course I should have known – no, I had known, except I hadn't been able to believe it. I had known I didn't have it in me to come up with the idea for that kind of planned, meticulous killing. And I would have known, if only I had been able to think about it clearly for thirty seconds, exactly who did.

'Well, not in a serious way,' Susanna said, misreading the look on my face. 'It was just a thing to make myself feel better, like sticking pins in a doll. I was daydreaming about blowing him away with a machine gun and coming up with some smart-alec line that would be the last thing he heard on earth, that kind of crap.'

' "Yippee-ki-yay, motherfucker," ' Leon said, grinning.

Susanna blew smoke at him. 'The point is, I still thought I could cope. I figured all I had to do was grit my teeth for a few more weeks: we were about to leave school, right? Once we'd done our exams, why would I ever have to see that arsehole again?'

'If only,' Leon said.

'Right. After the Leaving, it actually got worse. While I was living at home, Dominic couldn't exactly call round and demand to be let in; but once we were all here for the summer, he was over like every other day. He waited for me outside *work*, a few times – I don't even know how he found out where I was working. I definitely didn't tell him.'

Side-eye at me. I had no idea; I might have said something, how would I have known that was some terrible crime? A lot of this felt hugely unfair: I was being blamed for stuff that I hadn't done and had had no way of knowing about. 'Anyone could have told him,' I said. 'It's not like it was a state secret.'

'Well, someone did,' Susanna said. 'He'd walk me to the bus stop, pinching various bits of me and describing all the details of what he was going to do to me. I kept telling him to leave me alone, but he'd just laugh and tell me I could quit bullshitting, he knew I loved it. I don't know if he was just saying that to wind me up, or if he genuinely had himself convinced.'

'Who knows what the fuck went on in Dominic's head,' Leon said. 'Frankly, who cares. The whole reason for this was so that Dominic Ganly's horrible little mind wouldn't be our problem any more.'

'I think, deep down,' Susanna said, 'he thought I was a jinx. He'd always got everything he wanted, without even having to try for it, right? And then there was me. And then straight after that there was the Leaving. He knew he'd crashed and burned, and the only course he was going to get offered was like basket-weaving in Sligo Tech. Whatever life plans he'd had were pretty much fucked – which was my fault, for stopping helping him – and I doubt he had a Plan B; it had never occurred to him that he might need one. And I think he felt like it had all started with me.' She considered that, head cocked to one side against the arm of the sofa. 'Maybe not a jinx; more like an albatross. And if he could shoot me down, put me in my place, then everything would go back to the way it should be.'

'Or else it was nothing deep,' Leon said. 'He just liked making people scared and miserable, and he liked shagging girls, and you looked like a perfect chance to do both.'

'I don't know,' Susanna said. 'I think he was really seriously crazy, by then. I don't mean mentally ill, not in any way that would have got him a diagnosis. I just mean wrong; gone off the rails. Basically everything he'd ever been – the big success, the king of the castle, the stud – it was all gone. And it broke him. He must've been pretty fragile to start with, if that was all it took.'

'Oh, for God's sake,' Leon said. 'He wasn't *broken*. He'd always been a total shit. Any of us, if we'd crashed and burned in the Leaving, would we have started making rape threats to random people? No, thanks very much, we wouldn't have.'

Susanna thought about that, tapping ash. 'Maybe,' she said. 'Maybe it was more like he didn't break; he just broke open, and you could see what was inside. Which was basically the same, only more so.'

It had occurred to me, a little late, to wonder how exactly Leon fit into this. *Su I still think this isn't a good idea—* Clearly he knew the whole story, had for a while; what the hell did that mean? Had we all been in on it together? I wouldn't have put it past Susanna to come up with some byzantine Orient Express thing— I took another Mars bar.

'Anyway,' Susanna said, 'he kept getting worse. This one day he showed up outside my work and walked with me to the bus stop again, only there was no one else there, which I knew right away wasn't good. He shoved me up against the bus shelter and started groping me. I smacked him across the face, and he smacked me right back, good and hard, without even stopping what he was doing. My head bashed off the bus shelter; I had a big lump for days. When I stopped seeing stars I tried to push him off me, but he was *strong*. He got both my wrists in one hand and held them above my head, and stuck the other hand up my skirt. I tried kicking him, but he just laughed and slammed his whole weight against me so I couldn't move. I couldn't even get enough breath to scream. If a bunch of old women hadn't come along, I don't know what would've happened.'

'But that's assault,' I said. Her tone – cool, detached, she might have been describing a trip to the shops – was bothering me; this was Susanna, for God's sake, who could work herself into a passion about an injustice to someone in a whole different hemisphere, what was going on? 'Why didn't you go to the cops?'

'Way ahead of you there, champ,' Susanna said, raising an eyebrow. 'I did. After that happened, I told Leon the whole thing. Not that I expected him to jump in and put a stop to it, but I needed some-one to walk me to work in the mornings and meet me outside when I finished – which was pretty humiliating: like I was a little kid who couldn't handle the big bad world. And I knew Leon wouldn't think I was being a wimp, because he knew what Dominic was like.'

'Oh, I did,' Leon said. 'I knew exactly what he was like. He was still giving me some of the same old shite, by the way; he was well able to handle more than one victim at a time. Multitasking; he'd have done well in management. But at least I was getting a lot less of it. He'd only really ever picked on me when he had his buddies around – it was some kind of chimpanzee thing, displaying dom-inance for the other males – and now that no one wanted to be around him, he didn't bother as much. Just casual stuff, in passing. Knocking my coffee down my chest, that kind of thing.'

'But,' Susanna said, with a glance of real affection, 'Leon was horrified. Outraged. "That bastard, we're not going to let him get away with this . . ." I think if I'd let him he would've rushed right out to teach Dominic a lesson, and that wouldn't have ended well – no offence, Leon—'

'None taken,' Leon said cheerfully. 'He'd have eaten me for breakfast.'

'Instead Leon convinced me to go talk to the cops. I took some convincing, but seeing how furious he was . . . that made me twig that yeah, actually, I wasn't overreacting, this genuinely was a big deal, and it was about time someone stuck a spoke in that fucker's wheel. And like he pointed out, we weren't in school any more; I didn't have to worry about everyone finding out and me being a leper.' She was smiling over at Leon. 'He went with me and held my hand while we waited, and everything.'

'I'm so ashamed about that,' Leon said, covering his face with his hands. 'God. Every time I think of it, I want to ring you up and apologise. I don't even know what I thought they'd do. Go give him a stern talking-to. Scare him into backing off.'

'It's OK,' Susanna said. 'Seriously. I actually expected them to do something, too. Pair of middle-class spoilt brats that we were.'

'What, they didn't?' I said. 'Like, nothing at all?' This sounded completely bizarre. Martin and Flashy Suit had been pretty useless, but at least they had made some kind of effort.

'Laughed in my face,' Susanna said. 'They wouldn't even take a statement, or a report, or whatever they call it.'

'Why not? What was their problem?'

She shrugged. 'I didn't have any evidence. The lump on my head was gone by that time. No texts, no emails, no notes, no witnesses. Just she-said-he-said, and apparently what she said didn't count for much. In fairness, I don't think it was just because I was a girl. Dominic was a rich kid from a fancy school, his parents would've gone ballistic and hired big-shot lawyers and filed a million complaints . . . The cops didn't want to get into that mess, not with zero evidence. So they patted me on the head and told me he was probably just having a laugh, and I should go home and concentrate on having a nice relaxing summer, instead of getting myself all worked up about fellas.'

'Which seemed a teeny bit insensitive at the time,' Leon said, shaking another cigarette out of the packet, 'but actually it was the best thing that could have happened. If there had been a report on file . . .'

'So that was that,' Susanna said. She put out her smoke and pushed the ashtray across the coffee table to Leon. 'If the cops wouldn't touch it, then there wasn't much point in going to my parents, either, even if I had wanted to – what were they going to do, grab a cop and march him out to arrest Dominic? go talk to his parents, so Mummy and Daddy could be outraged at the thought that their precious prince had done anything bad? And the school wasn't even involved any more. I was pretty much out of options.'

'You were about to go to college,' I said. I knew it might come out wrong and piss her off, but I needed to hear that I had had no choice. 'You could have got in anywhere. Hadn't you applied to Edinburgh, or somewhere?'

'I had, yeah,' Susanna said, unruffled. 'And I was pretty sure I'd get in. I was thinking about going – I didn't want to, I wanted to stay here, but anything to be safe, right? Except then Dominic came up to me in the kitchen, one day, and he went, "So I hear you're thinking about Edinburgh" – who knows where he heard that.' A wry eyebrow-lift at me. 'I babbled something, and he said, "Cool. I've always wanted an excuse to spend some time in Edinburgh." And he shot me the finger guns and wandered off.'

Shrugging: 'I mean, maybe he wouldn't actually have followed me. Maybe he'd have forgotten I existed. But by that stage he was crazy enough that I believed him. God knows money wasn't a problem for him, and it wasn't like he had anything to stay here for. Even you guys were pulling away from him – not that I blamed you, believe me. He didn't have any real friends, did he? Plenty of dudebro types all ready to hoot and cheer when he did something moronic, but no actual friends. Not like you had Sean and Dec.'

'I guess not,' I said. I had never thought much about it, but I couldn't remember Dominic ever hanging around with one or two people; he had been either at the centre of a whooping crowd, or else – towards the end, mainly – sloping around on his own, with a fractured, roving glitter in his eye that made you want to stay far away.

'So he wasn't going to stick around Dublin just to hang with the lads. And I was so fucking terrified all the time, and so exhausted from being terrified, I couldn't think straight. I was positive he'd track me down, and it would be even worse because I'd be away from home and my family. By that stage he didn't feel like just some douche; he felt huge. Like a demon. Something that could find me anywhere.' With a glance at me: 'You figure I should've gone anyway, and kept my fingers crossed. I hadn't done anything wrong, but I should've headed off to Outer Mongolia because some arsehole couldn't handle not getting his way. Would you have?'

'I don't know,' I said. The calm of her – of both of them, really, Leon lounging on the hearthrug and poking experimentally at one wet shoe – was unsettling me more and more. It wasn't that I wanted them trembling and sobbing, but given where all this had led, it felt like they should at least be tense or jittery or *something*. 'I don't know what I would have done.'

'I was pretty crazy myself, at that point,' Susanna said. 'It was like being in a nightmare, that feeling where you have to get out but you can't move fast enough and you can't scream. I was cutting myself a lot. The only thing that made me feel any better was day-dreaming about killing Dominic. I still wasn't even considering actually *doing* it, but I had got a lot more realistic. Riddling him with machine-gun bullets felt stupid; like dropping a cartoon anvil on his head. I needed something that could be real.'

'I didn't know,' Leon said, to one of us or both, I couldn't tell. 'I mean, I knew, but I had no idea it had got that bad.'

'It took me a while to find a way that would work,' Susanna said. 'Dominic was twice my size, and I didn't want anything where he would bleed because the cleanup would be too complicated, so that ruled out most stuff. I thought about poison, but it's too dicey. Even if I managed to get something into him, most poisons take ages; he would've had time to go to the hospital, get treated, tell someone about me . . . I don't even know how much time I spent reading true-crime websites, checking out methods. I know how to poison someone so it won't come up on a tox screen – if I could have got my hands on succinylcholine – I know the best ways to drown someone, which would have been great if we'd had a lake in the garden . . . *Finally* I found out about garrottes. At first I couldn't believe it was that easy, but I kept reading about it, and bit by bit it dawned on me: *Holy shit. This could actually work.*'

And again, I should have known; I had known. It would never have occurred to me to go researching garrottes. It was, on the other hand, exactly Susanna's style. My mind felt like it was turning inside out. I could have trusted myself, all along.

'It was a good feeling,' Susanna said. 'Not that it made any actual difference, but I'd been so totally fucking powerless . . . After that, when he'd grab my boob or whatever, and give me that big shitbird grin like *What are you going to do about it,* I'd be thinking *Mother-fucker I could garrotte you any time I want.*'

'Oh my God, your *face,*' Leon said, to me. 'Don't look so shocked. I'd been daydreaming about feeding him into a wood chipper for years. And so would you have been.'

My apartment, step and drag, unstoppable fantasy loop where I tracked down the burglars and karate-kicked them off tall build-ings a thousand times a night. 'I'm not looking shocked,' I said.

'You've got nothing to be self-righteous about.'

'I know that. OK?'

'And then,' Susanna said, ignoring this, 'it got to August, and the Leaving Cert results came out. I only skimmed mine, you know that? I should've been over the moon with myself, but the only results I cared about were Dominic fucking Ganly's, because if he'd done OK then he might pull himself together, but if he'd bombed then I was in deep shit. And of course he'd bombed.'

'I got to tell her,' Leon said, on a stream of smoke. 'When we went down to the school and got our results, I headed straight off, remember— What am I saying, of course you don't, you were too busy jumping around making orangutan noises with Sean and Dec. But Dominic was just off in a corner, staring. He looked like he was about to pull out an AK-47. I barely even looked at my own results. All I could think was that now I had to tell Susanna.'

'I figured my only option was to lock myself in my room for the rest of my life,' Susanna said. 'Except even that wouldn't work, because Leon's birthday party was coming up like a week later, and of course Dominic was going to be there. I was *petrified*. I thought about saying I was too sick to go, but what was I going to do instead? Stay up in my room, where he could get me on my own any time he wanted? Hugo always put in earplugs for the parties, he wouldn't have heard anything, and I could hardly stay in his room all night – I mean, I guess I could have, if I'd told him the whole story, but it felt like things had gone way past that. I could have gone back to my house, but the thought of being all on my own there scared the shit out of me.'

She rearranged herself more comfortably, curled on her side, elbow propped on the arm of the sofa and her cheek leaning pensively on her hand. 'But in the end,' she said, 'it was totally fine. I dodged Dominic the whole way through the party, and he didn't even come after me. I was *so* happy. The college place offers had just come out like two days before; I thought maybe there'd been a miracle and he'd actually got in somewhere decent, and that had sorted his head out . . . Only then I asked around and found out: nope, he'd got nothing. No offer at all. He'd only applied for the big-shot courses, no safety backup stuff for him. So that wasn't reassuring.'

I remembered that, awed hushed voices, *Shit he got nothing at all?* and the odd snarky joke about McDonald's. Except at the party Dominic had seemed totally fine, louder than ever, bellowing with laughter, leaping off the kitchen table. I had meant to keep my mouth firmly shut so I didn't get a punch in the face, but down at the bottom of the garden, the coke making me jabber: *Dude that sucks about college, no I mean that really sucks, what are you going to do?* And Dominic staring at me, eyes white-ringed in the moonlight: *Like you give a shit. Like anyone gives a shit. I know you're all laughing your arses off about this. You bunch of fuckers.* And then he had laughed at the flash of fear on my face, punch in the arm that sent me staggering, *Relax dude I'll be fine, have some more of this!*

'And then,' Susanna said, 'I found out he'd spent the party nicking the garden key.'

She sighed. 'That was what did it,' she said, 'in the end. It meant he could get to me here, any time he wanted. *Here.*' An iron spike of outrage through her voice, a jerk of her head to the house, and for a moment I saw it the way it had been: warm, shabby, happy, us noisy and tangled in our fort and our contraptions, Hugo calling *Dinner!* up the stairs through a fog of savoury smells.

'And he did, too. A couple of days later Hugo sent me out to the garden to get rosemary, for something he was cooking. Remember where the rosemary bushes were? Right down the back? The second I leaned in to pick a bit, something came *barrelling* out from behind that oak tree and rugby-tackled me. I went flat on my face in the strawberries. I got the wind knocked out of me and there was this huge weight squashing me flat, I couldn't turn my head to look, but I knew who it was, obviously. I knew the smell of him, by that time; that shitty body spray, eau de jockstrap. He started fumbling under me, trying to undo my jeans. I was flailing around trying to dig my nails into him, but he got his other hand on my throat and started squeezing. And everything started to go all grey and fuzzy and faraway.'

She examined her glass, picked something real or imaginary off the rim. Her face hadn't changed, but it was a moment before she went on. 'Luckily for me,' she said evenly, 'right then Hugo stuck his head out the back door and called me. So Dominic rolled off me and grinned and whispered, "Rain check," and pulled my hair and oozed back off behind the oak tree.'

'You know,' Leon said tightly, 'sometimes I wish you'd picked a different method. Something slower and more painful.'

'Hugo spotted that I was covered in dirt and bits of grass,' Susanna said, 'but I said I'd tripped and he didn't guess, because in fairness, who would. I did think about telling him – I was pretty seriously shaken up. To put it mildly. But . . .' A small shrug. 'Hugo, you know? What was he going to do? He was hardly going to rush out and beat the shit out of Dominic. He couldn't have if he'd tried.'

You should have told me, I wanted to say. 'Jesus,' I said, instead.

'She didn't tell me,' Leon said. 'About that. Not then.'

'You'd have gone for him,' Susanna said, 'and got beaten up, and that wouldn't have done anyone any good. I needed to end this thing. Dominic was well capable of killing me next time, and he had been waiting for me out there. I couldn't tell myself he was just grabbing opportunities when he saw them, and I'd be OK if I managed to keep out of his way. He was coming after me. Even if I'd managed to get Hugo to change the lock, it wouldn't have made a difference. Dominic had plans; concrete ones. So I needed concrete ones too.'

She said it so simply, as if it were the most obvious thing in the world. 'I spent a lot of time thinking it through. I knew actually killing him was going to be the easy part; the hard part was how to make sure I didn't get caught. I think I did OK, for a kid.' Glancing up at us: 'It startled me, you know that? how well I did. I'd always thought of myself as kind of a spacer, book-smart but not practical-smart, but once my back was up against the wall . . .'

'You did great,' Leon said, a little sadly. 'You were amazing.'

Susanna took a sip of her wine. 'The first thing I did – apart from staying out of the garden, obviously, and double-checking that the house was locked up at night – was start playing down Dominic's bullshit to my friends. They didn't know the whole story anyway – like I said, I was ashamed and embarrassed and all that good stuff – but they knew some of it, and I didn't want anyone telling the cops, afterwards, that I'd been having problems with him. So I started making jokes about it, rolling my eyes, *Oh God that idiot, it's like having someone's stupid puppy jumping all over you, you can't really get mad about it but you totally want to smack him on the nose with a newspaper* . . . And I started dropping sympathetic little comments about how the poor guy was really messed up about his results, he seemed like he might be having an actual breakdown, I hoped his parents would get him to see a therapist, you hear all these news stories about people killing themselves because they don't get the course they wanted . . . And of course when you're that age everyone loves drama, so within a few days there were rumours all over the place about Dominic being in counselling because he'd tried to hang himself.'

'I was so disappointed when I found out that wasn't true,' Leon said. 'Wouldn't it have made everything so much simpler? If he'd just done the job himself?'

'The other thing I needed to clean up,' Susanna said, 'was the computer history. Back when I'd started thinking about real ways of doing it, I'd used Hugo's computer to do the research. So there were "how to make a garrotte" pages all over the browser history. And if the cops started poking around, I definitely didn't want them finding those.'

'I think we all had things in that browser history that we wouldn't have wanted anyone finding,' Leon said, arching an eyebrow.

'I had a big piece of luck there, though. I hadn't wanted Hugo finding weird searches in his history, either. He used Internet Explorer for his browser, right? the way most people did back then? So back when I started doing the research, I'd downloaded Firefox and used that instead. Which meant that, once I was done, all I had to do was uninstall Firefox, run a cleaner, and boom: computer clean as a whistle. Which was nice.'

She finished her wine. 'Still, though, I knew if there was a full-on murder investigation, I'd be screwed. The cops aren't stupid; if they started seriously looking, there was no way I could cover up well enough to be safe. I needed it to look like suicide, right from the start. That was doable – Dominic was such a mess, no one would be too surprised. But for that to work, the body couldn't be found, at least not till it had decomposed enough to get rid of the garrotte marks.'

The calm of her, explaining it point by point, like she was going through a problem from our geometry homework. The whole scene seemed unreal, wavering on the air, ready to dissipate and leave us fourteen and sprawled in front of the TV, with Hugo in the other armchair humming over his book. 'I thought about doing it up the mountains, somewhere good and remote, and just leaving him there. Or on Howth Head or Bray Head, and shoving the body into the water. But the problem with anything like that was that it relied way too much on luck. Up the mountains, you've got dog-walkers and hikers and poachers; someone could have wandered past at the wrong moment, or tripped over the body the next day. In the water, even if I got the tides right and he didn't wash up, he could have been spotted by a boat. I don't like relying on luck.'

She tilted the wine bottle towards me; when I shook my head, she shrugged and topped up her own glass. 'Once I thought about it long enough,' she said, 'I realised the safest way was to keep the whole thing under control, as much as possible. Which meant keeping both the murder and the body in a place that I had at least some control over. Which meant' – a lift of her chin to the house, the garden – 'here.'

'Here,' I said. 'You decided to use the Ivy House.' I knew this didn't say anything good about me, but this was the part that actually shocked me.

'Well, the house was out, obviously, because of the smell. It had to be the garden, and as far down the back as possible. I thought about burying him, but digging a deep enough hole would have taken forever, and I wasn't sure it could even be done – remember how Hugo kept running into hard ground and rock, when he was digging for the rock garden? Plus, if anyone ever found him buried, that would put the kibosh on the suicide angle – he couldn't exactly have buried himself. And then' – a little smile – 'I remembered the wych elm. The hole. I climbed up there, one day when all you guys were out, and got down inside it. And sure enough: room for two of me. It wouldn't eliminate the luck factor – the wych elm could have been taken down by a storm two weeks later – but it would minimise it.' She leaned over to pour for Leon. 'The only thing was, I'd have to get Dominic in there. And for that I was going to need help. I'd have been happier getting it done on my own, but . . .'

And finally, finally, here it was. I could barely breathe. I said, 'So you came to us.'

They both stared at me, utterly blank-faced.

'Me and Leon.'

The silence felt wrong. The cigarettes and the fire had built up a thick pall of smoke in the air. 'What?' I said.

Susanna said, 'I went to Leon.'

'Then when—' I didn't know how to ask the question: when had I got involved, how? 'How did I—'

'Toby,' Susanna said, gently. 'You didn't do anything. You never even knew about it.'

'But,' I said, after a very long moment. My mind had been knocked totally blank. It wouldn't go in; was she lying, how much of this whole story was made up, why would she— 'You said. When we were stoned. You said you went to my room, that night, you said where was I—'

'Yeah, that was probably shitty of me. But the way you were going at Leon— We were all just about keeping it together as it was. If you'd kept hammering at him, and he'd cracked and spilled everything, specially with Melissa there . . . I had to shut you up. That was the only way I could think of.'

'And when you, after that, then you said Leon thought I'd done it. That was just to, that was, what the hell was that?'

'You did?' Leon demanded. 'Why? You said *he* thought *I'd* done it.'

'Look,' Susanna said, irritated. 'I was doing my best, on the fly, with what you have to admit was a total clusterfuck of a situation. I was just trying to keep everything under control. The two of you were winding each other up; I needed to keep you separated till things settled down. And I needed you both on your toes. The last thing we needed was you' – me – 'getting all chummy with the cops, and you' – Leon – 'getting into a row with him and letting something slip.' To me, when I didn't answer: 'I'm telling you now.'

'Right,' I said. Both of them were looking at me with a kind of curious pity. 'OK.'

'You didn't do anything. I swear.'

I knew I should be practically collapsing with relief. No life sentence hanging over my head, no lurid stain on my soul, I could go back to Melissa with clean hands . . . All I could feel was, absurdly, devastated. I had got attached, more than I had realised, to the idea of myself as the dragon-slayer. With that gone, I was right back to useless victim.

But it was more than that. Susanna and Leon had known me since we were born. They had known me since long before we were capable of masks or concealments; since we were our first, our pristine and unaltered selves. They had seen in me, all that time ago, something that made me unfit to be the dragon-slayer, unfit even to be the squire on the sidelines holding the spare swords; fit only to bumble about in the background, to be wheeled out if a convenient distraction was needed and then steered off into the wings again.

'But,' I said. 'Why not?'

'You wouldn't have been on for it,' Leon said. 'Dominic hadn't done anything to you.'

'Well but,' I said, 'but that wouldn't have mattered. He was doing stuff to Su. If you'd told me—'

'She'd already told you once, remember? You hadn't been a whole lot of help. Why would we bother trying again?'

'She hadn't *told* me told me. Not properly. She'd just, she *said*, she only—'

'It wasn't even that,' Susanna said. 'Even if I hadn't tried telling you before, I wouldn't have brought you in at this point. I mean, we were talking about *killing* someone; one of your mates. That's pretty extreme, and extreme isn't really your style, is it? Let's face it, there's like a ninety-nine per cent chance you would've been horrified. You would've said I was totally overreacting, I was out of my mind, I should go to my parents or go to the police, or just go somewhere else for college—'

'All the things you said just now, in fact,' Leon pointed out dryly.

'—or else you would've wanted to beat him up, and by that point that wouldn't have done any good. Dominic was way past being put off by a few punches. He would've just blamed it on me – the jinx again – and been even more set on taking me down.' And, with a cool glance at me: 'And I couldn't take the risk that you'd decide to wreck the whole thing. Warn Dominic, or—'

'I wouldn't have. I wouldn't have done anything to get you in trouble. I'd have—' I had no idea what I would have done.

'Take it as a compliment,' Susanna told me. 'I knew you were too pure of heart to make a good killer. Leon, on the other hand—'

'I didn't even have to think about it,' Leon said. 'I mean, I did, because I didn't fancy going to prison; but as soon as I knew Su had a proper plan, I was *delighted* to be in on it. I just wished she'd decided to do it years earlier.'

'I should have,' Susanna said, 'with the stuff he was doing to you. But it honest-to-God had never occurred to me before. I don't know if I was just too young, or if I needed to be pushed right to the edge before I could think of it. It's probably good, though. When I was younger I would've fucked it up. Not prepared enough, and got us caught.'

'We were prepared, all right,' Leon said. 'We practised. Remember those rocks Hugo had got in, for the rock garden? One night you were out with the guys and Hugo had gone to a dinner party, and we loaded a bunch of those rocks into a sack till it weighed about the right amount. Then we got a rope out of the shed and tied it around the sack and threw it over a branch of the wych elm, and then I pulled on the rope while Susanna stood on the step-ladder, beside the tree, and heaved the sack up. Between the two of us, we got it hauled up to the hole in the trunk.'

'It wasn't easy,' Susanna said, 'but we got there in the end. After that I had us lifting weights every day – well, Hugo's rocks again – to build up our upper-body strength. And we trained with the garrotte, too. Everything I'd read said it was OMG sooo dangerous, you can crush someone's trachea before you know it, so I made practice garrottes out of jacks roll, so they'd break if we pulled them too tight.'

426

'We did it in our bedrooms with the lights off,' Leon said, 'so we'd be able to do it in the dark. And out in the garden, so we'd be used to doing it on grass and rocks. I think I could've done it in my sleep.'

'All the garden stuff was at night, obviously,' Susanna said. 'Not just because of you and Hugo and the neighbours; because of Dominic. He'd used the key before; it wasn't a big stretch to think he might use it again. We didn't want him popping in some afternoon and catching us in the middle of garrotte practice.' Leon snorted. 'That would've been awkward. At least in the dark, even if he showed up, he wouldn't be able to see us.'

'I think he might have been hanging around, actually,' Leon said, glancing up at her out of the corner of his eye. 'A couple of nights, when we were out there, I heard noises. Something moving, out in the back laneway. Scraping, against the wall; a thump, one time. I didn't say anything because I didn't want to scare you – it might have been just foxes—'

'I heard it too,' Susanna said. 'And a few mornings there was stuff moved around. The garden chairs would be turned upside down. Weird little piles of branches on the terrace. I don't know what the fuck that was about.'

'That could have been foxes too. Or the wind.'

'It wasn't,' Susanna said, taking a sip of her wine. 'I saw him a couple of times, out my bedroom window, in the middle of the night – I wasn't sleeping an awful lot. He'd wander around the garden. Break bits off the plants – one time he chewed on some of the rosemary and then spat it out. He'd push his face up against the dining-room windows, try the kitchen door.'

'Jesus Christ,' I said. All this craziness bubbling and fizzing in every corner, while I snored a few feet away, happy and harmless and useless. The room was dim and uneasy with shadows. I wished I had switched on the lamps.

Susanna shrugged. 'It didn't make much difference, at that stage. I just pushed the chest of drawers in front of my bedroom door at night, and never went out of my room when you guys were all in bed.'

'You should have told me,' Leon said reproachfully.

'You didn't tell me about the noises. I didn't want to scare you, either.' To me: 'Once we had the moves down, I made the real garrotte. I needed something that wasn't too thin, so it wouldn't slice him and get blood everywhere—'

I said, 'So you decided my hoodie cord would be perfect.'

She lifted an eyebrow. I wanted to slap that unbothered look right off her face, see it shatter into shock and pain. 'It worked, didn't it?'

'You didn't have any hoodies of your own, no?'

'Oh for God's sake,' Susanna said, exasperated. 'I wasn't trying to *frame* you. I just didn't particularly want to go to jail over this, thanks very much. I figured *if* the cops found Dominic, and *if* they twigged that someone had killed him, the only way I could get us out of it without dumping anyone else in the shite was by making the whole thing as confusing as I could. Mix it up, get a load of people in the frame; if they couldn't narrow it down, they couldn't do anything to anyone. My DNA was going to be on him. Leon had a motive – it would've taken the cops about ten minutes to find out about the stuff Dominic had done to him. I was going to wear one of Hugo's jackets and make sure to get some of Dominic's DNA on it. I had a few other random bits to throw down the tree – some hairs of Faye's, and a couple of cigarette butts and a shopping list that I'd picked up on the street, and a tissue where your mate Sean had blown his nose. I kept them in a sandwich bag, in my underwear drawer. I wonder if the cops found them.' A nod to me: 'And your hoodie cord. It wasn't *personal*.'

'And you made sure you had a photo of me wearing the hoodie,' I said, 'before you robbed the cord. So you could whip it out to give to the cops if you needed to. What did you take the photo on?'

'That camera you got for your birthday. My phone wouldn't have been clear enough.'

'Right,' I said. 'I figured.' The anger was much too vast and too cold for shouting. 'So once you knew Hugo was dying and all this was going to come out, you needed the camera.'

Susanna stared at me, eyebrows pulling together. 'What?'

The confusion looked real, but I knew her too well by now to think that meant anything. Yet another thing I should have copped, of course Leon would never have been able to plan something like that, but Susanna— 'The break-in. That was to get the camera, so you could give the photo to the cops. I should have figured that out ages ago, shouldn't I? Did you have a good laugh at what a moron I was?'

'The *break*-in?'

'At my place. The, when I— Was this how you wanted it to go? Because I didn't sort out Dominic for you? Did you want me to end up like this, like a, a—'

'Toby,' Susanna said. 'I uploaded that photo and emailed it to myself the same day I took it. Why would I just leave it on someone else's camera?' When I couldn't answer: 'You thought the break-in was *me*? You thought I got you beaten up?'

Leon let out an extravagant snort. 'That's all they took,' I said. My heart was going in great erratic thuds. 'Besides the, the obvious stuff, the big stuff, the telly and the car. Only the camera. Why would they, who wants a shitty old—'

'Jesus Christ, Toby. *No*.'

'Then what, why would they, *why*—'

'Listen. That was in *spring*, the break-in. Right? Hugo wasn't even sick yet. I had no idea any of this was coming. And even if I'd lost the photo, you think I would, what, put an ad on the internet for *burglars* to ransack your place and hope the camera was in there somewhere and the photo was still on it after ten years? Instead of just calling around and asking if you still had that old camera, oh look at all these great photos can I borrow it and put them on my computer?'

I felt much too stupid to exist. Of course she was right, blindingly right and anyone with half a functioning brain would have thought of all that, but then that had been the problem for a while now, hadn't it. 'Right,' I said. 'Of course. Sorry.'

'Jesus, Toby. For God's sake.'

It seemed a bit rich for her to get miffed over being accused of burglary, given the rest of the conversation, but I wasn't getting into that. I felt sick; too many Mars bars, the sugary residue of them flooding my mouth with saliva like I was about to throw up. 'OK,' I said. 'I get it. Leave it. What did you do next?'

Susanna stared me out of it for another moment, but then she gave me an exasperated head-shake and let it drop. 'So,' she said – resettling herself under her blanket, getting back into the swing of the story – 'that was everything basically planned out. All I had to do was get Dominic in the right place at the right time. A few weeks earlier it would have been easy enough to set up a meeting, he was practically squatting here, but since Leon's birthday party he hadn't been around as much – at least not during the day. And I knew I didn't have a lot of time. He wasn't going to be happy with wandering around the garden forever.'

I wanted to get up and walk out, away from the two of them and this godawful wreck of a conversation. I couldn't remember why I had ever imagined this would be a good idea.

'So,' Susanna said, 'I had to get creative. I hadn't been going out in the garden by myself, but I started doing it every chance I got. Pruning rosebushes, stuff like that – I know fuck-all about rosebushes; I probably killed them. But it did the job. After a few days of that, I was out there one afternoon when something shoved right up against my arse, hard, and Dominic asked if I liked it like that.'

'That guy,' Leon said, taking another sausage roll, 'watched way too much bad internet porn.'

'I nearly went face-first into the rosebushes,' Susanna said, 'which could have ended badly. I got lucky: I grabbed hold of a bush and got my balance back. Ripped up my hand on the thorns, but I didn't even notice till later. When I turned around to Dominic, he went, "Surprise!"' With a wry twitch of her mouth: 'I swear he was grinning at me. Great big satisfied grin, like he'd done something clever and he was expecting a medal. He went, "Happy to see me?"

'I said, "I don't like surprises." He thought that was very funny. He backed me up against the rosebushes and stuck his hand up my top. I said, "Hugo's in the kitchen." Dominic didn't like that. He took his hand back and said, "I'm gonna surprise you big-time, some night. Soon."'

'Complete fucking psycho,' Leon said, through a mouthful. 'Do you still think Su should have just headed off to Edinburgh? Without her around to lead him into temptation, abracadabra, Dominic would have transformed into a nice normal guy?'

'Up until then,' Susanna said, 'I hadn't been positive I'd actually be able to go through with it. But that made it easy. I said, "OK, I can't stand this any more. You win. If I give you a blow job, will you leave me alone?"

'His jaw hit the floor. He looked like he genuinely couldn't figure out what was going on, but after a second he went, "Are you serious?" I said, "Yeah, as long as you swear on your life that afterwards you'll never bother me again." You should've seen the grin on his face. He was all, "Yeah, totally, I swear!" – which was bullshit, of *course* he was planning to keep hassling me – "Like, *now*?" I said no, we'd get caught, Hugo would be out any minute. He'd have to come back late some night, like maybe Monday? And he said yeah, no problem, Monday night, deal. I said half-one in the morning – I thought he might kick up a fuss about that, but he would've said yes to anything.'

She checked the level in her glass against the light. 'So I made the most of it. I made him promise to walk, in case anyone saw his car. I made him promise not to tell anyone; I said if I heard even the tiniest rumour, then the deal was off. And if he texted me or rang me or anything, the deal was off. He was all, "Sure, babe, no problem, swear on my life" – he was obviously planning to tell the world afterwards, but I was OK with that. He went, "I don't need to text you, because you know you don't get to change your mind. And you don't need to worry about letting me in, I'll be here." And he waved the key at me and winked, and headed off.'

In the window behind her the sky was dimming, rusty leaves hanging heavy with rain on the chestnut trees. 'He was never even the smallest bit suspicious,' Susanna said, 'you know that? I made sure I looked totally terrified and disgusted – not that that was difficult – and he was getting such a kick out of that, he didn't have room for anything else. Sometimes I wonder what would have happened if he had.'

The room was getting chilly; the fire had burned low. Leon reached over to the pile of firewood and tossed in a log, sending up a soft crunching sound and a shower of orange sparks.

'So then,' Susanna said, 'all we had to do was wait till Monday.'

'You were our big worry,' Leon said, to me. 'Hugo was always in bed with the lights out by half-eleven, like clockwork. The factory was still being turned into apartments, there was no one living there yet, and the neighbours were all about a hundred and ten; they went to bed after the nine o'clock news, and even if they got up and looked out the window, they were mostly blind as bats. But if you'd decided to stay up late, surfing porn or whatever you used to do on Hugo's computer, we'd have been in big trouble.'

'Well,' Susanna said, tiny smile over the rim of her glass. 'Not that big a worry.'

'What?' I demanded. I had sat bolt upright. 'What did you do to me?'

'Oh my God, relax on the jacks,' Leon said, eyebrows arched. 'We didn't do anything.'

'We just got in a bottle of vodka, Sunday night,' Susanna said. 'And a bit of hash. And the two of us didn't have very much of either one.'

'You didn't even notice,' Leon told me. 'You got ossified. At one stage you were swinging from a tree branch, giggling and telling us you were Monkey Man.'

'And we made sure you were up bright and early for work on Monday morning. It wasn't easy, but we did it.'

'You were in bits. Green. I think you were actually puking. You wanted to pull a sickie, but we wouldn't let you.'

'So by eleven on Monday night,' Susanna said, 'you were just about falling over. We were in here, watching TV, *Newsnight* or something there was no way you would hang around for. You were bitching at us to switch over, but we wouldn't, so eventually you gave up and headed off to bed. We were pretty sure you'd stay there.'

'Well that's good,' I said. Not even the bumbler on the sidelines; just an object to be got out of the way so they wouldn't trip over it in the middle of important business, an irritating toy that needed its battery run down to keep it inert while the action went on. And I had trundled off, with barely a nudge to start me going, down the path they had mapped out for me. They had known me so well. 'I wouldn't have wanted to, to, to cramp your style.'

'You didn't,' Susanna assured me. 'You behaved yourself perfectly. Everything behaved itself, actually. My other main worry had been rain – the last thing I wanted was Dominic trying to bring things indoors—'

'He wouldn't have,' Leon said, licking flakes of sausage roll off his fingers. 'You think he was planning to stop at a blow job? No way would he have wanted to be anywhere you could scream for help.'

'True enough,' Susanna said. 'But he might not have shown up if it was raining; he might have wanted to reschedule. That would've been a pain in the arse.'

'Having to get me out of the way all over again,' I said. 'Bummer.'

'We'd have managed,' Susanna said. 'But we were lucky. It was a lovely night. Chilly, but not even a cloud. As soon as you and Hugo stopped moving around, we got ready—'

'I think that was the worst bit, actually,' Leon said. 'Su putting on Hugo's jacket and making sure she had her sandwich bag of bits to throw down the tree – that bag was disgusting, do you know that? It looked like a DIY kit for a voodoo doll.' Susanna snorted. 'And me finding dark clothes so Dominic wouldn't see me, and putting the garrotte in my pocket and checking like eight times to make sure it wasn't tangled . . . The whole thing felt impossible. I was positive that any minute I would blink and it would all be gone, and I'd be waking up in my bed like, *Oh my God, that was the weirdest dream!* But it kept on and on being real.'

'My worst part was the waiting,' Susanna said, taking one of Leon's cigarettes. 'Once we were in place. I was hanging about at the bottom of the garden – we didn't want Dominic coming too close to the house, just in case anything went wrong, or you or Hugo looked out your windows. And Leon was behind the wych elm. And all we could do was wait. It was terrible.' With a glance at me, over the lighter: 'I know you don't like that we did it here. But I picked the garden partly because I thought being on our own turf would help us keep it together. We're making this whole thing sound like a breeze, but it wasn't.'

'I don't think either of us had eaten in days,' Leon said. 'Or slept. People kept having to say things to me three times because I couldn't take them in; I couldn't even *hear* them. Anything that made it even a tiny bit easier . . .'

'Except when it came down to it,' Susanna said, 'the garden wasn't actually all that comforting. All these little rattling scraping sounds – leaves falling off the trees, probably, but—'

'But always right in my *ear*,' Leon said, shuddering, 'so I was leaping about like I was on a *pogo* stick. And the branches made patterns like things up in the trees, birds, people, *snakes*— I'd catch them out of the corner of my eye, but when I looked properly of course there'd be nothing there.'

'Our blood must have been about ninety per cent adrenaline,' Susanna said. 'My mind was *speeding*, what if he brings his car what if the garrotte breaks what if he's told someone what if this that the other . . . There was a second when I thought, really clearly, *I am going to lose it. I am going to start screaming and not be able to stop.*'

She blew a careful smoke ring and watched it waver upwards. 'Which sounds pretty wussy,' she said, 'unless you take into account what the last few months had been like. Anyway, I didn't lose it. I bit my arm hard enough that it shocked me back together – I still had toothmarks like a week later. And a couple of minutes after that, the garden door opened and there he was. Strolling in, hands in his pockets, looking around like he was there to buy the place.'

'Wait,' I said. I was a couple of steps behind. '*Leon* had the, my, the hoodie cord? *Leon* did it?'

'That,' Susanna said, so sharply that it startled me, 'was not the original plan. I was going to do it. Wait behind the tree, pick a moment when Dominic had his back to me, and bang. Leon was *only* supposed to help with the cleanup.'

'But once we talked it over,' Leon said gently, sitting up, 'it was

434

obvious that wasn't a good plan. It would have been way too risky; way too much chance he'd turn around at the wrong moment, or he'd never get into the right position at all. It would have been stupid.'

'I should have known from the start,' Susanna said. 'The way I was picturing it, all clean and arm's-length – literally: I wouldn't even have had to touch him till he was dead – it doesn't work that way. What we were trying to do, it's not small stuff. If you want something like that, you have to get messy.'

I wasn't sure how drunk she was – only a glass and a half, but I had gone heavy on the pour, I had wanted the two of them nice and loose. In the firelight her eyes were dark and opaque, full of sliding reflections.

'I never wanted you to get messy too,' she said to Leon. 'I didn't want you to be stuck doing the dirty work. But I couldn't think of any way to make it work the other way round.'

'I didn't want you doing your half, either,' Leon said. They were turned towards each other, intent, intimate; for a moment it was as if they had forgotten I was there. 'But we didn't have much choice.'

Only, I wanted to say, of course they had had a choice. If there had been three of us, the three of us together, we could have come up with something— Even this had seemed better to them than letting me be part of it.

'What?' I said, too loudly. 'What happened?'

They turned to look at me. It occurred to me that maybe I should be frightened. A pair of murderers, spilling their guts to me; in a TV show I would never have left that room alive. I couldn't find a part of me that cared.

'We did it together,' Leon said. 'It was much safer that way. One of us to get Dominic into position under the tree, and keep him still and keep him distracted—'

'That was me,' Susanna said.

'And once she had him where we needed him,' Leon said, 'I snuck up behind him. That part was awful – I had to go slowly, because if he heard me we were *fucked*, but I didn't want to leave Su there a second longer than I had to—'

435

'It worked perfectly,' Susanna said, cutting him off. 'I'd say he never even knew what hit him, except there was definitely a moment when he did. I saw it. I was basically eye to eye with him; as soon as he went down, I got on top of him and shoved a big wad of my jacket – well, Hugo's jacket – into his mouth. As far down his throat as I could get it. Probably we didn't really need that, the garrotte would have been fine on its own, but I wanted it so that neither of us would ever be sure who had actually got the job done. That felt like the least I could do for Leon. And I wanted Dominic's DNA on that jacket anyway.' She glanced over at me, cool pale face, a wisp of smoke rising past her cheek. I thought: *What am I listening to? What is this?* 'And, if I'm honest,' she said, 'I wanted to do it.'

'I couldn't believe how quick it was,' Leon said. 'I'd had these awful images of it taking forever, you know in horror films where every time you think the baddie's dead they come back to life and attack again? I was terrified I wouldn't be strong enough— But all it took was a minute or two. That was it.' He held up a finger and thumb, a fraction apart. 'This much time.'

'It was ugly,' Susanna said, 'but it was fast. Once we were sure his heart had stopped beating, the next thing was getting him into the tree. We tied the rope under his armpits and did the pulley thing we'd practised. I got him kind of draped over a big branch, and then the two of us climbed up and manoeuvred him down the hole.'

'He was a lot more awkward than the sack of rocks, though,' Leon said, leaning for the wine bottle. 'We put on gardening gloves, so we wouldn't get DNA all over him, but they made us all fumbly, and we had to get the rope off him without dropping him, and his arms and legs kept going all over the place and his shoe came off—'

'Well, it wasn't fun,' Susanna said, seeing the look on my face. 'But if you're going to get the vapours, I don't think that's the part to focus on. It's not like anything we did made any difference to him at that point.'

She had misread me. It wasn't that I was horrified. I just couldn't get hold of it, my mind kept snagging – *eye to eye with him, it was ugly but it was fast* . . . I wanted more, wanted every detail, to squeeze tight like broken glass. I couldn't find a way to ask.

'It sounds awful,' Leon said, topping up Susanna's wineglass, 'but honest to God, he didn't feel like a person any more. That was the freaky part. Dominic was just *gone*. The body, that was just a *thing*, this huge floppy object that we had to get rid of. Sometimes for a second I almost forgot why; it was like some bizarre impossible task out of a fairy tale, and if we didn't get it done by sunrise then the witch would turn us to stone.'

'God,' Susanna said. 'It was a million times more hassle than the actual killing part. It felt like it took *forever*. I couldn't even think about what we would do if it didn't work.'

'And then that fucking garrotte.'

'Oh God, the garrotte. We finally got him stuffed in there, right? we were still up the tree? and Leon took out the garrotte—'

'I'd put it in my pocket while we did the hoisting bit—'

'We were supposed to undo the knots and put the cord down the hole in the tree,' Susanna said. 'Only the bloody knots wouldn't come undone. They must have tightened when we did the job.'

'The gloves didn't help. After a bit we got desperate and took them off, but it didn't make any difference, those knots were like *rocks*—'

'The two of us sitting on a branch like a pair of monkeys, working away at one knot each, going frantic—'

'—fingernails breaking off—'

'And finally,' Susanna said, with an exasperated glance, 'Leon bloody panicked and threw it down the hole anyway.'

'Well, what were we supposed to do with it? We couldn't exactly put it in the bin, the cops could have come searching, and it wouldn't have burned properly, it was that nylon-y stuff—'

'Dump it in a bin halfway across town. Throw it in the canal. Anything. That garrotte was the one thing that showed he'd been murdered. Without that, as long as they didn't find him for a week or two, he could've killed himself, OD'd, just fallen in because he was drunk and an idiot—'

'Rafferty thought I had killed him,' I said. 'Because of that garrotte.'

'Yeah, sorry about that. Like I said, it wasn't the plan.'

'Oh well then. That makes it all OK.'

'We *tried* to get it back out,' Leon said. 'I stuck my arm down the hole and *rummaged* – it was disgusting, my fingers went in his *mouth*, it was like being bitten by a zombie. But I couldn't find it; it must have slipped too far down. What were we supposed to do? Pull him back out and dive in there to find it?'

'In the end we gave up,' Susanna said. 'We climbed down and collapsed under the tree like we'd been hit by tranquilliser darts. I've never been that exhausted in my life. Not even after *labour*. We would have gone to sleep right there if we could have.'

'I think I did,' Leon said. 'I remember lying there with my face in the grass, panting like I'd been running, *pouring* sweat, and then next thing Su was shaking my shoulder and telling me to wake up because we had to deal with Dominic's phone.'

'That phone was the main thing I was worried about, actually,' Susanna said. 'I mean, it was also our biggest advantage – one text and we could point everyone towards suicide, just like that; faking a suicide note, back before phones, would've been a lot dicier. On the other hand, though, I knew the Guards could track it. Not precisely, not like now with GPS, but they could tell the general area from what towers it pinged off. That guy had been all over the news, the one who killed his wife and he got caught because his phone wasn't where he said he was, remember him? I did a *lot* of reading about that. I thought about telling Dominic to turn his phone off because I was scared he'd take photos of me blowing him, or something, but in the end I decided that was a bad idea. The cops would still track his phone to this area, but if it turned off here, they'd figure this was where something had gone wrong. If the phone went on to somewhere else, they'd know he'd been somewhere in this general area for a while, but they'd also know he'd left. They might figure he'd just been wandering around here trying to decide whether to do himself in or not – maybe he'd been thinking about the canal and then changed his mind, right? He knew other people who lived around this area, anyway; there was no reason the cops should tie it to us.'

That calm, absorbed voice, breaking down the details of an

interesting problem. 'Even if worst came to worst and they some-how tracked him to here, like if someone had seen him going down the laneway, I had a plan for that. I was going to burst into tears and confess that he'd come over to tell me he was crazy about me, and I'd turned him down, and he'd stormed off all upset yelling about how I'd be sorry. It wasn't perfect, but it'd have to do. Leon would back me up.'

'We had the story all rehearsed,' Leon said, 'just in case. I was really, really hoping we wouldn't need it, though. If they'd got that close, I don't know if I would've been able to keep it together.'

'You would've been fine,' Susanna said. 'Either way, though, that phone needed to go somewhere good and suicide-y. At first I thought about Bray Head – I mean, Dominic; there's no way he would've gone to the Northside, even to kill himself. But Howth Head is nearer and it gets more suicides, and from what I could figure out about the currents, it was more plausible that his body wouldn't be found if he went off Howth Head. So Leon headed off with the phone.'

'Why Leon?' I asked. Personally, given the choice, I would have trusted Susanna with a job like that over Leon any day. I would have trusted me with the job over Leon, but they had decided I was unfit even for that.

'Thanks a bunch,' Leon said.

'No one's going to notice a young guy walking on his own late at night,' Susanna said. 'A girl, though, yeah. Someone might have remembered me. I really didn't want to dump more stuff on Leon – I even thought about sticking my hair up under a hat and pretending I was a guy, but if someone had sussed me, that they *would* have remembered.'

'I didn't mind,' Leon said. 'Honestly. You made it so easy.' To me: 'She had everything planned out for me. Every step.'

'That's the *least* I could do. You got the shitty end of the stick, all the way.' Susanna was looking over at him with that glow of pure admiration and warmth that I had caught before, once or twice, and never understood. 'All the hardcore parts. And you handled every second of it perfectly. You were a fucking gladiator.'

'Because of you,' Leon said. 'The stuff you thought of, there's no way it would ever have occurred to me. I'd have got us caught in, like, a day. She said' – to me – 'I couldn't get a taxi from here to Howth, because the taxi man might remember me. So I walked into town and got a taxi to Baldoyle. I said something to the taxi man about "Jesus, everyone else is still going strong, I've got work in the morning" but apart from that I kept my mouth shut. I pretended to doze off against the window, so he wouldn't get all chatty. Su even had that planned out.'

'The cops were definitely going to try and trace Dominic's movements that night,' Susanna said. 'They'd want to find out how he got to Howth. They'd know he hadn't walked, by how fast the phone switched towers – ideally Leon would've walked the whole way, but it's three hours minimum, so that would've been cutting it pretty fine, and we couldn't risk him getting lost and having to ask for directions. I figured the cops would check taxis, and once they couldn't put Dominic in any of those, they'd figure either he'd hitched a lift from someone who didn't want to come forward, or else he'd got a dodgy taxi – a fake one, or an unlicensed guy borrowing his mate's taxi, or maybe someone who wasn't supposed to be working because he was on the dole or an asylum-seeker. That was all fine. But if they turned up a guy who didn't match Dominic's description, taking a taxi from here to Howth and back again in the middle of that night, they'd probably pay attention.'

'I walked from Baldoyle,' Leon said. 'I didn't go all the way up Howth Head, because in the dark? along that cliff path? No thank you. I just went up a little way, till I was sure no one could see me, and then I sent the text. I was terrified it wouldn't go through, the reception wouldn't be good enough, but it was fine. Once I saw "Sent" I wiped my fingerprints off the phone and threw it as hard as I could.'

'Even if it hadn't gone out to sea, that wouldn't have mattered,' Susanna said. 'Dominic could've ditched it on his way up the cliff path.'

'And then I just went home,' Leon said. 'I walked as far as Kilbarrack and picked up a taxi. On the way out I'd been wearing a white hoodie over a blue one, and on the way back I swapped them around and put on a baseball cap. So even if the cops went asking and both the taxi drivers remembered me, it wouldn't sound like the same guy.'

'Your idea,' I said to Susanna, who nodded, turning onto her side to watch Leon.

'I told the driver to drop me in flatland in Ranelagh – Su had the actual road picked out, I don't remember. This time I told him I'd had a fight with my girlfriend. And then I "went to sleep" against the window again.'

He turned his glass in his hands, watching the firelight slide along its curve. 'That was the weirdest part of the whole thing,' he said. 'That taxi ride. Up until then it had been all about getting things done: get this right, don't forget that, don't fuck that up, go go go. And then all of a sudden it was over; there was nothing left to do. There was just . . . the rest of our lives, without Dominic. With this instead.' He drew a long breath. 'The driver had some oldies station on the radio, really low. REM. David Bowie. It was still dark, but the sky on one side was just starting to turn the tini-est bit grey and for some reason that made it look like the earth was tilting. Like the taxi wheels were off the ground and we were float-ing. There was this one bright star, low on the horizon. It was beautiful.'

Susanna had her head down in her elbow on the arm of the sofa, watching him. 'I felt the same thing,' she said. To me: 'After he left I dumped my sandwich-bag stuff down the hole. I threw in a ton of earth and leaves, too, to cover up the smell. And I put the ladder and the rope and the gloves away, and smoothed out the holes the ladder had left under the tree, and hung Hugo's jacket back in the coat cupboard. And then I just sat in my room, with the lights off in case you or Hugo went to the jacks. I went over it all in my head, to check if there was anything I'd missed, but there wasn't. There was nothing else I could do. Even if I'd wanted to undo it all, I couldn't have.'

Her eyes had slipped away from us, to the fire. 'It was really peaceful. It shouldn't have been; I should have been climbing the walls on adrenaline, or losing my mind with remorse, or some-thing. Right? Me with all my moral crusades, and now I'd killed someone. But I just sat by the window and looked out at the garden. It looked different – not in a bad way; just different.' She thought about it for a while. 'Clearer, maybe? I wanted to put the rest of the world on pause and just sit there for a year or two, watching.'

Curled up like that, dreamy in the dimness, hair mussed against the faded red of the sofa, she should have looked like her old child-hood self, tired from a day of playing; Leon, propped against the armchair with his legs sprawled anyhow, should have looked like that sparky little boy, smudge-faced and scrape-kneed. They almost did. We had been so close, back then, a closeness too fundamental even to think about. I couldn't work out how they had got so far away.

'Finally my phone went off with a text,' Susanna said. 'And then I heard yours through the floor, and then Leon's – he had to leave it here; I didn't like that, because what if anything went wrong and we couldn't get in touch, but if the cops went sniffing around we couldn't have Leon's phone pinging in Howth. I gave it a minute before I looked – in case the police went checking times on phones and they could somehow tell what time I'd read the text; I didn't want it to look like I'd been waiting for it. And there it was.'

And I had slept happily through it all. I had barely turned over to stretch out an arm when the phone beeped, check the text, *What the hell?* and back to sleep.

'After a while Leon got home and told me it had all gone fine,' Susanna said. 'It was getting bright outside. We were both starving, so I made sandwiches and tea—'

'Whispering at the kitchen table,' Leon said, 'giggling like a pair of little kids sneaking down for a midnight feast. I was light-headed. The food tasted amazing; I don't think I've ever eaten anything that delicious.'

'And then we went to bed,' Susanna said. 'Probably we should have been tossing and turning and having nightmares, but actually I don't think I've ever slept that hard.'

'Oh, my God. Like I'd been hit with a *base*ball bat. I think I would've slept twenty-four hours straight, only Su came in and dragged me out of bed for work.'

'Well, we couldn't be late,' Susanna said. 'We needed to act completely normal. It wasn't hard. All we had to do was go along with everyone else: did you get a text from Dominic Ganly, OMG what was that all about, has anyone talked to him? Oh no what if he's done something stupid!!' She raised herself on her elbow and reached for another cigarette. 'From there on, it kind of did itself.'

I tried to think back to that autumn. It seemed impossible that I hadn't noticed anything; I had been happily wrapped up in college and making new friends and various sports clubs and going out but surely something would have registered, they had *killed* someone, surely I couldn't have missed that? Surely they should have been different, branded or haunted or something? 'Weren't you scared?' I asked. 'That you'd get caught?'

'Probably we should have been,' Susanna said, shaking Leon's lighter. 'But no, not really. You've got to remember, we were used to being scared. It was basically our default mode, by that stage. And "Oh noes, the cops might possibly figure out that Dominic didn't kill himself and they might possibly tie it to us and they might possibly get enough evidence to arrest us and we might possibly be found guilty" was a lot less scary than "Dominic Ganly is going to rape me or kill me any day now."'

'I was scared, off and on,' Leon said. 'When I thought about it too much. It wasn't like they would have had to look very hard for him – obviously – and once they found him, that would've been it for us. The only thing that saved us was that they weren't looking this way at all.'

'We were lucky,' Susanna said. 'Dominic thought he was so smart, never texting me anything dodgy, so I'd have no proof. But if his phone had been full of vile texts to me, the cops would have taken one look and *dived* on me.'

'But,' I said, 'the cops did come here. Didn't they?' At this point nothing my memory came up with felt reliable, but all the same I was positive there'd been an afternoon, I'd been hungover and heading out to meet up with the guys for a cure, two culchie-types in suits on the doorstep holding out ID and asking pointless questions, I'd forgotten all about it till now—

'Yeah, they did,' Susanna said. 'About a week in. They talked to everyone who'd known him, but I got special treatment – I guess one of my mates must've told them he'd been hitting on me, and the cops wanted to know the story. Thank God it wasn't the same guys I'd tried to report him to – those were just normal Guards, the kind with uniforms. The ones who came to talk to me were detectives, in suits, like Rafferty and Kerr. I mean, the uniform guys had probably forgotten all about me by that time, but still, that actually would've been scary.'

'Jesus,' I said. The world I had been blithely bouncing through had been so utterly unrelated to this one running along its dark subterranean track, I couldn't make the two of them click together in my mind. 'What did you say?'

Susanna shrugged. 'It wasn't bad. They were nice to me. It's not like I was a suspect; I was just number ninety-whatever on a list of friends and acquaintances they had to cross off. I basically told them what the uniform guys had told me: Dominic was just having a laugh, it was kind of a running joke. You could tell they believed it. I mean' – she held out her hands, matter-of-factly – 'look at me, and look at Dominic. Then I got all upset because OMG what if he genuinely had been in love with me all along and I just didn't realise it, and he couldn't take the pain any more? So I cried a little bit. And they told me it wasn't my fault either way and he'd been upset about his exam results, and not to be worrying about it. And then they went away.'

'And thank God you handled it that well,' Leon said, turning his head away from her to blow out a plume of smoke. 'My God. They'd taken about five minutes with Toby and me – no one must have told them about the stuff Dominic did to me; not wanting to give the wrong impression of such a lovely guy, probably, or something idiotic like that. But they were in here with you for half an *hour*. The whole time I was up in my room, shaking so hard I couldn't stand up. Pouring sweat. I was positive there would be a bang on the door any minute and we'd be hauled off to jail – I was wondering whether to slit my wrists while I still had the chance. If you'd let the smallest thing slip – if we had ever occurred to them as a possibility, even for a second – we would have been *fucked*. *Mega*fucked.'

'Oh for God's sake,' I said. For some reason Leon's drama-queen shtick infuriated me more than ever; it felt like he was making a huge deal of this on purpose, to hammer home just how much I had missed. 'It was self-defence, basically. Even if they had caught you, it's not like they would have locked you up and thrown away the key. It's not as simple now that you *left* him there for ten years, but if you'd just gone to the cops straightaway—'

Both of them started to laugh.

'*What?* What the fuck is funny?'

'Oh God,' Leon said, through a fresh gale of laughter. 'This is why we didn't bring you in on it.'

'Thank God,' Susanna said.

'What are you talking about?'

' "Excuse me, Guard dude, I've like totally got something to tell you, right, but we'll have to make it quick because I'm meeting the lads down the pub—" '

'Of course they would've locked us up,' Susanna said, like she was explaining something to Sallie. 'We had zero evidence that it was self-defence; the police would only have had our word for it. You think they would've believed us?'

'Why not? Two of you, both telling the same story, and your mates would have backed you up—'

'Teenage girls,' Susanna said. 'Probably hysterical or liars or both – the cops *already* thought I was hysterical. Why would anyone believe us?'

'And a queer,' Leon said. 'I wasn't out yet, but it would have taken them about two minutes to guess. Fags are hysterical too, you know, and vicious, not to mention morally bankrupt.'

'And on the other hand,' Susanna said, 'you've got a fine handsome upstanding young rugby hero like Dominic Ganly.'

'OK, so he'd been a bit depressed,' Leon said, 'but that was just because of his exam results and possibly because this ungrateful bitch' – Susanna waved – 'refused to appreciate him the way he deserved. It wasn't like he was mentally *ill* or anything. Nothing wrong with him but a bit of boyish high spirits. He was a good guy – you said it yourself.' A sidelong glance at me. 'Everyone loved him, or at least everyone who mattered. The papers were drooling over how *wonderful* he was, how full of *potential*, they made it sound like he was Cúchulainn come back to save the nation from itself . . . The whole country would have been out for our blood. They would probably have brought back the death penalty just for us. Of *course* I was terrified.'

'I wasn't,' Susanna said. 'Not for a second. Beforehand, yeah, I was absolutely petrified, but not once he was gone. I was . . .'

I waited, but after a moment she shook her head and laughed and put out her cigarette.

'Well, yeah,' Leon said, and I caught a hint of a smile in his voice as well. 'There was that, too.'

'There was *what*?' I demanded.

They looked at each other. The fire was burning low again, dull red patches pulsing amid blackened wood. The pall of smoke stirred idly, small eddies and swirls.

'We both went a bit off the rails, I guess,' Leon said, 'in different ways. Everything felt very weird; disorientating. The best way I can put it is that it felt like there was too much oxygen in the air, all of a sudden, and our bodies took a while to get used to it.'

'I wasn't off the rails, thanks very much,' Susanna said. 'I was just having fun. It had been way too long since I'd been able to do that. Not just because of Dominic, to be fair. Even before him, everyone had me pegged as the good girl, all smart and serious and well-behaved; I didn't feel like there was any way to break out of that, or even figure out whether I wanted to. And once Dominic started in on me . . . Jesus. It felt like if I did *anything* fun – like wore nice clothes, or went out, or got drunk, or had a laugh – that would be Dominic's justification: *You were off your face with your tits hanging out, obviously you wanted it.* Or if not Dominic, someone else like him. Afterwards . . .' She shrugged. 'That didn't feel like so much of an issue. I mean, obviously Dominic's opinion wasn't an issue any more, but other people weren't as scary either, because I knew

I didn't have to take their shit. Not that I was going to whip out the nuclear option any time someone cut in front of me in the bus queue, but just knowing I could actually *do* something made the world feel a lot less dangerous. And I definitely didn't give a shit that I was supposed to be the good girl.'

'I think you were well beyond calling yourself a good girl,' Leon said, grinning.

'Past redemption,' Susanna said cheerfully, raising her glass. 'So I just had a good time. Remember those hippies with the camper van? They took me to Cornwall and this guy called Athelstan was teaching me to play the dulcimer?'

'Your parents were freaking out,' I said. Everything about this was bothering me. 'They thought you were in a cult or something. Or abducted. Or losing your mind.'

'Every kid has a right to some rebellion. I'd been angelic all through school. It evens out.' Rolling over to stretch out on her back on the sofa: 'I'm still Facebook friends with Athelstan. He's living in Portugal, in a yurt.'

Leon got the giggles. 'Don't know what you're laughing at,' Susanna told him. 'Who was your mate who used to go around wearing the big purple wings?'

'Oh God, Eric! He was lovely. I wonder what happened to him. This one time, right, we were really stoned and we went into the Arts Block in Trinity late at night, just before they closed up? We were trying to get locked in for the night? Only the security guard spotted us and we were like playing hide-and-seek with him, all these masses of empty rooms and we kept hiding behind chairs, except Eric's wings stuck out—'

'Well, that sounds like a blast,' I said. My coffee buzz was long gone; I felt sick and headachy and miserably tired. 'I'm glad you guys had so much fun.'

'We're not taking it lightly,' Susanna explained. 'It's just that we've had a while to get used to it.'

'So how come you're not living in a yurt and playing the dulcimer?' I asked. 'If it was so liberating. How come you're Mrs Suburban Mummy?'

'Ooo,' Leon said. 'Someone's feeling bitchy.'

Susanna ignored my tone. 'The thing was,' she said, 'after a while I started noticing that it felt like what I did *mattered*. Like it had weight. I'd never felt that before. All those campaigns I got involved with in school, writing millions of letters for Amnesty and fund-raising for places that had droughts, and they never changed anything; the guy was still stuck in some hellhole jail, the kids were still starving to death. I used to cry about that.' To me: 'You caught me once. You thought I was a total idiot, but you were nice about it.'

'Right,' I said. 'That's good.' It occurred to me that I should be feeling some kind of sense of achievement. I had got what I was after, detectived my way to the answer that even big bad Rafferty hadn't been able to get his hands on. I couldn't work out why all of this felt like such an enormous let-down.

'In a way you were probably right. I mean, yeah, I genuinely was crying for the guy being tortured in Myanmar, but I was also crying because it felt like I was nothing. Made of fluff. Feathers. I could bash myself to death against things and they wouldn't budge an inch; they wouldn't even notice I was there.' She took a sip of her wine. 'Killing Dominic, though. Whatever you think about the moral issues, you have to admit it made a difference. A concrete one.'

'Yeah,' I said. 'That it did.'

'I wanted to do more stuff like that – I mean, not like *that*, but stuff that made a solid difference. Stuff with weight. Smoking Athelstan's hash and singing around campfires was too fluffy. It was light. I'd met Tom a month or two before I headed off to Cornwall, and he was obviously mad about me, but I hadn't even had room to think about whether I was into him. Except when I did think about him, he felt like he had weight. Getting together with him would be serious; it wouldn't be like snogging Athelstan for a laugh. I pretty much knew if I snogged Tom, I'd end up marrying him. So I came home and rang him.'

'Thank God,' Leon said. 'He was hanging off me like a puppy. Great big moony eyes, asking me over and over when you were coming back. I'd have been a lot nicer if I'd known you were into him. I told him you'd married Ethelbert in a naked Wiccan cere-mony at Stonehenge.'

'I know. He didn't believe you.' Susanna gave him the finger. 'Same for having the kids: not that it felt more important than get-ting a PhD or whatever else I could have done; it just felt more solid. A difference I could see, right there in front of me. We made two whole new people. It doesn't get more concrete than that.' To me: 'I know you always thought I was insane for getting knocked up so young. And I know you've never been crazy about Tom. But it made sense to me.'

Leon was watching her curiously. 'God, I never had any of that. The exact opposite, actually.'

'But you did stuff that mattered,' Susanna said, turning towards him, surprised. 'You came out, that autumn. I always thought it was because of Dominic. No?'

'Oh, totally. I'd probably still be in the closet, if it wasn't for that. I'd been agonising for years.'

'It wasn't 1950,' I said. 'You weren't going to get shunned and, and, tarred and *feathered*.'

'I know that, thanks,' Leon said, with a flick of asperity. 'I knew exactly what would happen. I'd hear even more shitty stereotype jokes, I'd lose a couple of friends, and Dad would try to convince me it was a phase. I could handle all that. It was the thought of people seeing me as something different. Not being just a person to them any more, not being just me, ever again; being *a gay*. If I said something snotty, it wouldn't be because I had a point or because I was in a bad mood or because I've always been a stroppy bastard; it would be because gays are bitchy. If I was upset about something, it wouldn't be because I had a good reason, it would be because they're so dramatic. I'm sure this seems like a non-issue to you' – me – 'but it wasn't to me. On the other hand, I wasn't mad about the idea of spending the rest of my life in the closet, either. I wanted to have boyfriends, for God's sake, hold hands in the pub, bring them home to meet my parents; that shouldn't be too much to ask. I just felt totally paralysed. I thought I'd be stuck that way forever, rock and a hard place. But after Dominic . . .'

He reached for the poker and stirred the fire, which shot up a ragged, gallant spurt of flame. 'The whole thing looked totally different. If people didn't see me the same way once I came out, who cared? I'm not talking about being brave, or some YOLO shite. Just . . .' He shrugged. 'They'd be out of my life soon enough anyway. Nothing lasts forever, and I don't mean that in an emo way, I'm being factual. Dominic was *enormous* in my life for years, this huge presence looming over every single thing, I went to sleep thinking about him and had nightmares about him all night and woke up in the *morning* dreading him. And then we did this one thing, it only took a minute or two, and he was *gone*. Just *gone*. It's hard to think of anything as permanent, after that. What you've got' – to Susanna – 'the husband and the kiddies and the mortgage, all that ever-after stuff, it's never felt like an option.'

'Do you wish it did?' Susanna asked. For the first time she looked worried, twisting on the sofa to peer at Leon in the dimness. 'Do you wish you'd gone like me, instead?'

Leon thought that over, nudging charred bits of wood delicately towards the heart of the fire. 'No,' he said. 'Not dissing what you've got, but it's not my style. I'm happy the way I am. It's got its downsides – I've dumped every boyfriend I've ever had, or else made them dump me, and I feel like a total shit every time. But I like the feeling that anything's possible. I could be in Mauritius, this time next year, or Dubrovnik.' He glanced up at Susanna, smiling. 'I love places, you know,' he said. 'I always have. The less I know about them, the better. The Yorkshire moors: don't they sound amazing? All that space and heather and Viking place names? And New York, and Goa, and . . . Once I get to know them a bit, the shine wears off and I get itchy feet, but this way, that's OK, because I'm not tied down. I don't have to pick one; I can have them all.' He grinned. 'And I also really like guys, and I don't have to pick just one of those, either.'

Susanna smiled back at him. 'Good,' she said. 'Send me postcards.' She reached out a hand; Leon wove his fingers through hers and squeezed them. In the fireplace a splinter of wood caught, flared.

They felt alien, as if they were made of some material I didn't understand and shouldn't touch. The curve of Susanna's cheek white and smooth as polished rock, under the layer of moving fire-light. The long shadow of Leon's arm skimming across the wall as he pushed back his hair.

'So,' Susanna said. She leaned back into the corner of the sofa and watched me. 'There you go.'

'Right,' I said. 'OK.'

'Not what you were expecting?'

'Not really. No.'

'Are you OK with it?'

I said, 'I have no idea what that would even mean.'

'You'll get used to it,' Susanna said. 'Give it time.'

Leon was watching me sideways. 'Tell us you're not planning to run to Rafferty,' he said: joking, except it wasn't a joke.

'What?' This had never even occurred to me. 'No.'

'Of course he's not,' Susanna said. 'Toby's not stupid. Even if he wanted us to go to prison, which he doesn't, it's not like telling Rafferty would make that happen. It would just kick off huge amounts of mess and chaos, and when that cleared, we'd be pretty much where we are now. Everything's fine as it is.' She lifted an eyebrow at me. 'Right?'

'Not if Rafferty still thinks I did it.'

'Oh, he doesn't. And even if he does, there's nothing he can do about it.' When I didn't answer: 'Seriously, Toby, chill out. It's all under control.'

'But,' I said, looking from one of them to the other. There were things I needed to ask, vital things, but I couldn't figure out what they were. 'Don't you feel bad about it?'

As soon as I'd said it, it sounded like a stupid question, sanctimo-nious and faux-naïve. I expected some barbed putdown, but they were silent for a moment, glancing at each other, considering.

'No,' Leon said. 'I'm sure that sounds terrible. But no.'

'Not for Dominic,' Susanna said. 'For his parents, yes. I didn't at first, because it had to be partly their fault he was such an entitled arsehole; but once I had the kids, yeah. But I've never felt bad for him. I've actually tried to. But I don't. Fuck him.'

'I mean, I wish it had never happened,' Leon said, 'any of it. I wish we'd never met him. But we did, so . . .'

'Do you?' Susanna asked, interested. 'Really?'

'Well, I wish I hadn't had to *kill* anyone. You don't?'

Susanna thought that over. 'I'm not sure,' she said. 'I don't know if I would've had the guts to have kids, if none of that had happened. It's not like Dominic was this once-off supervillain; the world's full of people like him. If there's absolutely fuck-all you can do about them except lie back and take it, and then listen to people explaining how it's not a big deal? Bring kids into that? Now' – reaching to flip the blanket over her toes; the room was getting cold – 'at least I know, if anyone tries to fuck with my kids, I've got a decent shot at taking them down.'

Her story about the doctor, me wondering through my hash-and-booze haze why she was telling it. A warning to me, I had thought, but of course I had got it all wrong. That had been for Leon, nothing to do with me, and it had been a reassurance: *Don't worry. Look what we can do.*

'It's not like "The Tell-Tale Heart",' Leon said to me, through another cigarette and the click of the lighter. 'We haven't spent the last ten years hearing skeleton fingers scrabbling inside the wych elm whenever we walked past it.'

'Every now and then there'd be a storm and I'd be like, *I hope that tree doesn't come down*,' Susanna said, 'but that's pretty much it. I saw the wych elm every time we came here, and nine times out of ten Dominic didn't even cross my mind. I've *sat* against it.'

'Although,' Leon said, with an exasperated glance at her, 'it would have been really great if you'd kept him in mind enough to teach your kids not to mess about in that bloody tree.'

'I *did*. I told them a million times. Zach was just looking for attention, he was all wound up because of Hugo—'

'Yeah, but you *knew* he was like that. You could've left him with your parents, or—'

'I didn't know Hugo was going to call some big meeting. And anyway, how would that have been better? Dominic would still be out there. We'd have to deal with it sooner or later. At least now—'

Bickering like kids, like someone had dropped someone's phone or spilled Coke on someone's homework. 'I don't get it,' I said, loudly enough that they both stopped and looked at me.

'What?' Susanna asked.

'You fucking *killed* someone. You're' – the pair of them looking at me inquiringly, interested, it was hard to stay focused – 'you're *murderers*. How—' *How are you not fucked up* is what I meant, *you should be fucked up, it's not fair—* 'how is that not a big deal? How do you not feel guilty?'

Silence again, and those glances. I could feel them considering, not how much was safe to tell me, but how much I would understand.

'Has there ever been someone,' Susanna said, 'who treated you like you weren't a person? Not because of anything you'd done; just because of what you were. Someone who did whatever they wanted to you. Anything they felt like.' Her eyes on me were unblinking and so bright that for a wild moment I was afraid of her. 'And you were totally powerless to do anything about it. If you tried to say anything, everyone thought you were ridiculous and whiny and you should quit making such a fuss because this is normal, this is the way it's supposed to be for someone like you. If you don't like it, you should have been something else.'

'Of course there hasn't,' Leon said. Something in his voice brought back the kid he had been, scuttling along school corridors, eyes down, huddled under the weight of his bookbag. 'Who would ever?'

'Has there?'

'Yes,' I said. For some reason it wasn't just the two men in my apartment I thought of – them of course, sweat-and-milky smell horribly close and the blows crunching in, but in a confused whirl it was also the neurologist in the hospital, the clammy pallor of him and the fold of his neck over his shirt collar as he stared blandly back at me: *It depends on multiple factors.*

What fac, factors? Thick-tongued and idiot-sounding. The near-concealed pity and distaste sliding across his eyes, the moment when he demoted me to something not worthy of explanations, branded and filed away, no appeal possible.

It's very complicated.

Yeah but but but, can you, can—

Why don't you concentrate on your physio. Leave the medical issues to us.

Kick in the ribs and something snapping, *stupid cunt think you're fucking great*

'OK,' Susanna said. 'What did you want to do to them?'

It stopped my throat. Not for anything in the world could I have put it into words, what I had wanted to do and how badly. I shook my head.

'And how did it feel when you didn't?'

The memory flared all through my body: fist throbbing where I had smashed it into the wall over and over, leg one great bruise where I had punished it with every heavy object I could find, head pounding blindingly from slap after slap. I couldn't breathe.

'Now imagine,' Susanna said. She was looking at me very steadily, through the smoky air. 'Imagine you did it.'

Air rushed into my chest and for an enormous light-headed moment I felt it: the impossible ecstasy of it, almost too huge to be survived, the vast lightning rush of power and my fists and feet thundering down again and again, bones crunching, hoarse screams, on and on until finally: stillness; nothing left but obliterated gobbets of pulp at my feet and me standing tall, streaming blood and gasping air like a man rising from some purifying river, into a world that was mine again. My heart felt like it would burst free of my ribs and soar like a Chinese lantern up and away, through the window glass and out over the dark trees. For an insane second I thought I was going to cry.

Susanna said, 'That's what it was like.'

For a long time no one said anything. Things wavered in a sly draught, flames and high cobwebs, pages of a book lying open on the coffee table, the soft edges of Susanna's hair.

Leon said, 'Aren't you happy?'

I laughed, a harsh astonished crack that came out too loud. 'Happy?'

'You didn't do anything wrong. Or anyway not anything that

could get you in trouble. That's not good news?' When I didn't answer: 'Should we not have told you?'

I said, 'I have no idea.'

'I didn't want to. I thought we were all better off just leaving it. But Su thought you should know.'

'I felt bad about making you think you might have done it,' Susanna said. 'But that seemed like the best way to handle things at the time. And I was right, wasn't I? It all worked out in the end.'

I let out a hard, breathless laugh. 'I wouldn't go that far.'

'It's over. The cops are gone. We can forget the whole thing.'

'Yeah. Melissa's gone, too.'

'That's just because all the fuckery and drama got to be too much for her. I don't blame her. Now you can go tell her it's over, you had nothing to do with it, the end. You'll be fine.'

'She'll be over the moon,' Leon said, peering earnestly at me through the dimness. 'She's mad about you.'

'Sweep her off her feet,' Susanna said, tossing her cigarette butt into the last of the fire. 'Live happily ever after.'

Rain swept softly against the window, the fire fluttered. I felt like there was something else they should be telling me, some crucial secret that would illuminate this whole story so that all its rotten shadows blazed to life with a great transforming meaning, but I couldn't for the life of me think what that might be.

12

It seems obvious that, just like Leon said, that revelation should have improved things. I wasn't a murderer after all; what could be better news than that? Plus – yay for Toby the Boy Detective – I had finally found out what had happened to Dominic, just like I had wanted to; and to put the cherry on top, it was pretty clear that Rafferty couldn't do anything to anyone, we were all home free and clear. Everything should have felt, within the limits of the situation, just creamy-peachy.

And yet, somehow, it didn't. I had no idea what to do with this new state of affairs. Just for example, probably I should have at least done a little bit of ethical debating with myself about whether or not to tell anyone (my father, for one, didn't he deserve to know that Hugo and I were both innocent?), but I didn't. I didn't have it in me; I had nothing left with which to debate this, assess this, think about this at all. It was like Susanna and Leon had dumped an enormous IKEA package in the house: presumably it would change the landscape if and when I got up the energy to assemble it, but until then it was just there, in the middle of everything, where I barked my shin or banged my elbow on it every time I tried to get past.

I went about my routine methodically: breakfast and a shower, then up to the study for my day's work. While I didn't go as far as actually cooking, I did take breaks at the proper times to eat random assortments of things I found in the kitchen – someone, probably my mother, kept it stocked up with lavish quantities of stuff that didn't need preparation. After dinner I sat in the living room with Hugo's laptop and clicked around the internet until my brain shut down, at which point I went to bed. You'd expect I would have spent the nights tossing and turning, racked by grief and moral dilemmas and whatever else, or at least having more of those gruesome nightmares, but actually I slept like the dead.

I was doing well with Haskins's diaries; now that I'd got the hang of his handwriting, I was ripping through them at a great pace. He went through a stage of trying to get the baby's father's name out of Elaine McNamara, who pissed him off royally by refusing to say. Haskins's voice had become very clear in my head: nasal, heavily emphasised, overwhelmingly genteel, with a triumphant little throat-clear every time he had made some irrefutable point. One time, when I had been working for too long on a little too much Xanax (I was taking a fair amount again, not because I was tense exactly – I hadn't gone back to pacing all night or beating myself up, none of that – but because it seemed like a much more sensible way to live), I asked him if he wanted coffee.

The only real change to the routine was the Sunday lunches, which by unspoken agreement weren't happening any more. Someone called in every couple of days, presumably to make sure I wasn't rocking and mumbling in a wardrobe or decomposing at the foot of the stairs, but I wasn't very good conversation and they never stayed for long. Oliver gave me some speech about how we were all grieving but life went on, which I had absolutely no idea how to respond to; Miriam gave me a purple rock that promoted psychic healing, which I promptly lost. Leon rang me a few times; when I didn't pick up, he left long, tentative, confused voice messages. I didn't hear from Susanna at all, which was fine with me.

In April of 1888 Elaine McNamara had her baby – a boy, just like Hugo had figured, presumably Mrs Wozniak's grandfather. She 'protested very vehemently and in great distress' when they took him away to give to the nice O'Hagans. Haskins explained to her that the way she was feeling was punishment for her sin, and she should be grateful that God still loved her enough to chasten her thus, but he didn't think she really got it.

The house was going downhill, gradually enough that I didn't notice it unless some chance thing caught my attention: weak wintry light picking out the cobwebs that festooned the high corners of the living room, a brush of my arm along a mantelpiece sending a swirl of dust motes into the air and leaving a thick streak down my sleeve. Light bulbs blew and I didn't replace them. In Leon's old bedroom a stain was spreading across the ceiling, and there was a growing smell of damp coming from somewhere; I knew a plumber should take a look, but it felt impossible to make that kind of arrangement when I wasn't sure whether I actually lived there or not, or for how long. No one had mentioned Hugo's will, but it lurked uneasily in the corners of my mind: had he ever made the one he'd talked about, leaving the house to all six of us? who got it if he hadn't? was someone going to be delegated to explain to me very tactfully that there was no hurry of course, so grateful for everything you did for Hugo stay as long as you like just with property prices doing so well and all the work to be done before we put it on the market . . . I thought of my apartment, tight-drawn curtains and stale air, alarm lights blinking and the red panic button hunched low beside my bed waiting for its moment.

I did think, a lot, about trying to talk to Melissa. Now that I hadn't killed anyone, there seemed to be no reason why I shouldn't. She hadn't left – incredibly – because she had stopped loving me; she had only left because I was poking around playing detective, and she had in fact been right that that was a horrible idea, but now I could look her in the eye and swear that I was done with all that for good, also that the next time she told me something I would listen. Somehow I didn't worry about convincing her I wasn't a murderer. It made me cringe that I had ever thought she would believe that. Melissa had been way ahead of me, the whole time.

And yet I didn't ring her. Because – when I got down to it, when I actually had the phone in my hand – why would I? What, from this dim house where ivy crisscrossed the windows and all my clothes smelled faintly of mildew, did I have to offer?

It was cold out. I didn't go outside much; popping to the shops or going for a walk felt like bizarre foreign concepts, and although I occasionally wandered around the garden with some vague idea about healthful fresh air, I didn't like it out there. My and Melissa's optimistic marigolds and whatever had mostly died off – probably we had planted them wrong, or it had been the wrong season or the wrong soil, who knew. A few patches of skimpy, diseased-looking grass had sprouted, and there were some tall muscular grey-green weeds that looked like dandelions on steroids, but apart from that the earth was still a bare mess. The gap where the wych elm had been bothered me; even when I wasn't looking that way it scratched at the corner of my eye, something essential missing and I needed to fix it, it was urgent— The sky was always grey, there were always crows flapping and conferring among the oak branches, the cold always bit straight down and sank deep, and I always went back inside within a few minutes.

It was cold inside, too. The heating system couldn't cope with the size of the house, I was running out of firewood and no one had thought to bring me more. Draughts surged up out of nowhere like someone had stealthily opened a door or a window, but when I went looking for the crack I could never find it. Spiders were coming in for the winter; I saw more and more of them, in corners and along skirting boards, chunky grey-brown things with vaguely sinister markings. Woodlice trundled around the crack beneath the French doors.

A few weeks after she had her baby, Elaine McNamara went home, much to Haskins's relief. He didn't mention her again. She didn't show up anywhere in Ireland in the 1901 census, but there was a woman in the right part of Clare who matched her mother's info, with six kids born alive and six still living, so it looked like Elaine had married or emigrated or both. I couldn't find any marriage record for her. Hugo would have known how to go about it, and about looking for the baby's father, running complicated software to compare various DNA profiles, but I didn't have a clue where to start.

Instead I wrote Mrs Wozniak a report. I didn't know the right format so it was short, just the bare facts and a few lines at the end, as close as I could get to what I thought Hugo would have written: *Unfortunately I don't have the skills to pursue this any further. Another genealogist might be able to do more. I hope this new information doesn't come as too much of a shock, and I sincerely wish you all the best of luck in your search.*

When I was done I read it out loud, into the empty air of the study, to the dusty books and the wooden elephants and Hugo's old slippers left askew under his chair. 'Hugo,' I said. 'Is this right?' I had started asking him questions occasionally – not that I had lost the plot completely and believed he would answer, just that it got awfully quiet in that house. Some days the silence felt like an actual substance, thickening subtly but implacably with every hour, till it got hard to breathe. I emailed off the report to Mrs Wozniak, along with DNA analysis results and scans of the most important diary pages, and didn't open her reply.

It was worse after that. With nothing and no one to keep me on a schedule, my body clock went completely out of whack. I had gone from sleeping too much to sleeping way too little – the Xanax weren't working any more, they just threw me into a nasty limbo where I couldn't go to sleep but I was never quite sure whether I was actually awake. I wandered the house in half-light, between rooms dense with blackness and pale rectangles that could have been windows or doorways. Occasionally I got dizzy – I was never sure when it was time to eat – and had to sit down for a while. When I groped for something to tell me what room I was in, my hands found only unfamiliar objects: a table leg thick with carvings my fingers couldn't decipher, a ribbed wallpaper pattern I didn't recognise, an edge of curled linoleum when there had never been linoleum in the Ivy House. Things turned up in strange places, a heavy old 1949 penny on my pillow, Miriam's purple psychic rock in the bathroom sink.

When I thought about Susanna and Leon it was, strangely enough, not with horror or condemnation or anger but with envy. They came to my mind drawn in strong indelible black that gave them a kind of glory; Dominic's death defined them, immutably, not for better or for worse but simply for what they were, and it took my breath away. My own life blurred and smeared in front of my eyes; my outlines had been scrubbed out of existence (and how easily it had been done, how casually, one absent swipe in passing) so that I bled away at every margin into the world.

I think Rafferty knew. I think wherever he was, miles away, pulling out his notebook at some murder scene or raising the sail on a rugged little boat, he raised his head and sniffed the wind and smelled me, finally ready.

•

He came for me on a cold late afternoon that smelled of burning tyres. It had somehow penetrated to my brain that it had been days or possibly weeks since I had seen sunlight, so I had gone out to sit on the terrace, and by the time I realised that dusk was starting to fall and it was freezing I didn't have the energy to get up and go back inside. The clouds were dense and winter-white, unmoving; under the trees the ground was thick with sodden layers of leaves. A squirrel was scrabbling and dashing under the oaks and the grey cat was back, crouched in the rutted mud, tail-tip twitching as he slunk towards an oblivious bird.

'That your cat?' a voice asked, behind me and much too close.

I was up and hurling myself backwards across the terrace before I knew it, a shout ripping out of me, grabbing for a weapon, rock, anything— 'Jesus, man,' Rafferty said, holding up his hands. 'It's only me.'

'What the fuck—' I was gasping for breath. 'What the fuck—'

'Didn't mean to startle you. Sorry about that.'

'What—' He looked taller than I remembered him, ruddier, strong high sweeps of jaw and cheekbone more sharply defined. For a moment, in the grey light, I wasn't positive it was him. But the voice, rich and warm as wood, that was Rafferty all right. 'What are you doing here?'

'I was knocking for ages, couldn't make you hear. In the end I tried the door. It's not locked. I thought I should check that you were OK.'

'I'm fine.'

'No offence, man, but you don't look fine. You look in tatters.' He strolled closer, across the terrace. He made my adrenaline spike and keep spiking. There was something around him, a buzz and thrum, a vitality that ate up the air like fire and left me with nothing to breathe. 'Can't be good for the head, being cooped up here on your own. Would you not go stay with your folks for a bit, something like that?'

'I'm fine.'

That got a twitch of his eyebrow, but he left it. 'You should keep that door locked. It's a lovely neighbourhood, but still: better safe than sorry, these days.'

'I do. I must have forgotten.' I couldn't remember the last time I'd opened that door. It could have been unlocked for days.

'We're after wrecking his hunt,' Rafferty said, nodding towards the cat. The birds were gone; the cat had frozen, one paw lifted, giving us a wary stare and deciding whether to run for it. 'He's not yours, no?'

'It hangs around sometimes,' I said. I was still shaking. I didn't actually feel any better now that he had turned out not to be a burglar. Like an idiot I had believed Susanna, *It's over, the cops are gone, we can forget the whole thing . . .* 'I don't know who owns it.'

'I'd say he's a stray. He's awful bony. Got any ham slices, anything like that?'

For some reason I plodded obediently into the kitchen and stared into the fridge. *He can't do anything to me,* I told myself. *He'll have to go away soon.* I had forgotten what I was looking for. In the end I spotted a packet of deli chicken slices.

When I got back outside, Rafferty and the cat were still staring each other out of it. 'Here,' I said. My voice sounded rusty.

'Ah, lovely,' Rafferty said, taking the packet from me. 'Now. You don't want to throw it to him, or he'll think you're throwing a rock or something, and he'll be gone. What you want to do—' Wandering casually down the steps and into the garden, face still turned towards me, talking evenly and calmly: 'Just get as close to him as you can, yeah? and leave it down, and then back away. I'd say—' The cat flinched, ready to run; Rafferty stopped instantly. 'Yeah. Here ought to do it.' He stooped and laid a slice of meat on the ground. The cat's eyes followed every move.

Rafferty straightened smoothly and meandered back to the terrace, dropping a couple more slices of chicken on the way, big clear gestures so the cat wouldn't miss them. 'Now,' he said, flipping back his coat-tails and taking a seat at the top of the steps, easy as if he lived there. 'Do that every day or so, and he'll keep coming round. Keep the rats down for you.'

'We don't have rats.'

'No? Something dragged Dominic's hand out of that tree for a snack. What was it, if it wasn't rats?'

'I don't know,' I said. 'I'm not a wildlife expert.' It came out sounding snotty. He was acting like this was a normal casual chat, and I didn't know what to do with that; I couldn't hit that note.

Rafferty considered. 'A fox'll climb a high fence, but they haven't really got the claws for trees. I've seen the odd one do it, mind you. Going after eggs, or nestlings. Got foxes?'

'I don't know. I've never seen any.' Dominic's hand, flopping under delicate busy teeth. Small bones rained deep into the earth. The garden felt like it had that terrible stoned night with Susanna and Leon, distorted and alien. I wanted to go inside.

'Could've been, I suppose,' Rafferty said. The cat was stretching its neck towards the meat, curious. 'Sit, man. He won't come closer while you're standing there.'

After a moment I sat down, at the far edge of the steps. He fished out a packet of Marlboros. 'You want one?' And, grinning, when I hesitated: 'Toby, I know you smoke. Saw them in your stuff when we were searching. I promise I won't tell your mammy.'

I took a cigarette and he held the lighter for me, making me lean towards him. Getting that close made all my nerves tighten. I couldn't figure out a way to ask what he was doing there.

Rafferty drew in a deep lungful, eyes closed, and let it out slowly. 'Ahhh,' he said. 'I needed that. How've you been getting on, you and the family? Is everyone all right?'

'As much as we can be,' I said, which for whatever reason was the standard response I'd found myself coming out with a few hundred times at the funeral. 'It's not like it came out of the blue. We just didn't expect it so soon.'

'It's rough, no matter what way it happens. Takes a lot of getting used to. Look at that—' Paw by paw, nose twitching, the cat was inching nearer. 'Don't pay him too much notice,' Rafferty said. 'Are you going to go back to work? Now you don't need to be here for Hugo?'

'I guess. I haven't thought about it yet.'

'They could use you, man. Your boss – Richard, right? – he couldn't stop telling me how great you are, how they're lost without you.'

463

'That's nice,' I said; and then, in case I had sounded sarcastic, 'It's good to hear.'

'He wasn't just saying it, either,' Rafferty said, with a grin in his voice. 'Have you looked at the gallery's Twitter lately? There's been maybe five tweets since the night you got attacked, and one of them says "Hello Maeve, could you check that these are going through? Thanks, Richard."'

I managed to laugh. I really hadn't thought about going back to work, not in a long time. It seemed inconceivable somehow, as though the gallery was in some inaccessible country or possibly a TV show I used to watch.

'You need to get back in there, save them from themselves. Is there seriously no one else there who knows how to work the internets?'

'Not really. I mean, they can check their email and shop online, but social media . . .'

'Huh,' Rafferty said. Lazy still, only half interested. 'That's mad. Because the other thing I noticed, about that Twitter account? Up until the week you got hit, there's a load of other accounts following it, tweeting to it, retweeting your stuff. Dozens of them. After that week . . .' He arched an eyebrow at me, smile-lines starting in his cheek. 'It's tumbleweed in there. Not a chirp out of any of those accounts. About the gallery or anything else.'

'Yeah, well,' I said, after a moment. 'You got me. It's pretty standard practice. Set up a bunch of ghost followers, whip up a bit of buzz . . .'

He laughed. 'Is it? I kind of figured that, all right; nice to know I was on target. I'd say it's good craic, as well.'

'I guess. It can be.'

'Ah, come on. All your imaginary skangers? Arguing about whether Gouger's dole'll get cut off if he makes it big as an artist?'

There was a silence.

Rafferty's smile-lines had deepened. 'You should see the face on you. It's OK, man: you can come clean. We already talked to your pal Tiernan. He was shitting bricks, but he calmed down once he realised we weren't about to arrest him for distribution of a counterfeit skanger.'

'Right,' I said. I had tensed up hard, although I wasn't sure why – what could he do to me, why would he care? Why was he even bringing this up? 'OK.'

'He's good, isn't he? I don't know a lot about art, but those paintings looked pretty decent to me.'

'Yeah. That's what I thought.'

'Any chance they'll ever get seen now?'

'I doubt it.'

'Pity. I suppose your man Tiernan can make more; still, but. I don't blame you for not wanting them to go to waste. Those tweets, were they all you? Or did you have anyone else involved?'

'No. Just me.'

Rafferty nodded, unsurprised. 'Fair play. They were good, those. Rang true, got you wondering what was the story with this Gouger fella, looking for updates . . . I'd have fallen for them myself. No wonder your man Richard wants you back. Look, there you go—'

He pointed his chin at the cat, which had reached the first slice of chicken and was wolfing it down in quick snaps that managed to be voracious and delicate at once. 'A couple of weeks and you'll have him eating out of your hand.'

'When did you find out?' I asked. 'About Gouger?'

Rafferty shrugged, leaning to tap ash. 'Jesus, ages back. A case like this, we look into everything about everybody. The signal-to-noise ratio is horrendous, but that's grand, as long as we pick up the odd useful bit in there. We figured Gouger was irrelevant – got a good laugh out of him, end of.'

'OK,' I said. 'I'm glad he gave you a laugh.'

'We take them where we can get them, in this job. There haven't been a lot on this case.'

'What happens now?' I asked. 'Like, is the case closed? Are you . . .'

What I meant was, obviously, *Do you believe Hugo did it*, and of course Rafferty knew that. He kept me waiting; played with a pile of conkers Zach and Sallie had left on the terrace, turned one of them in his hand, considering. The light was dimming, darkness sifting down like a haze of fine dust in the air.

'Put it like this,' he said, in the end, balancing the conker neatly on top of the pile. 'Hugo was top of our suspect list from the start. Before we ID'd the body, even.'

'*Why?*'

'First off' – Rafferty held up one finger – 'he lived here, full-time, and he worked from home. He had the best access to the tree. Any of the rest of ye, you were never here on your own; you'd have had to work around Hugo and each other, somehow get the body in there without being spotted. Hugo had plenty of time here alone.'

Second finger. 'He was a big guy. Even by the time we got here, you could tell by looking at him: he used to be strong. Your cousins, no way either of them could get an eighty-five-kilo body up that tree and down that hole, not on their own. But Hugo . . .'

He hadn't mentioned me. *I was strong*, I wanted to shout at him, *I played rugby, I was fit as fuck, I could have done anything*. My cigarette tasted of mildew. I jammed it out on the terrace.

'And,' Rafferty said. Third finger. 'The first time I was talking to all of you; in the sitting room, the day the skull turned up, remember that? There was one thing that stuck with me, out of that conversation. Your nephew, Zach: he said he'd tried to climb that tree before, but his mammy or Hugo always made him get down. And then, two minutes later, your cousin Susanna said your parents didn't let you climb the tree when ye were kids, but Hugo did. Meaning before Dominic was in there, Hugo had no problem with kids going up in that tree. After Dominic was put there, he did.'

Hugo had known all along. *I suppose the truth is that I've never been a man of action. Don't rock the boat; everything will come right in the end, if you just let it* . . . He must not have known which one or two or all three of us it had been, not for sure – that careful probing in the car, *I do feel as if I've got a bit of a right to know what happened* – but he had known enough.

'You didn't spot that, no?'

'No.'

'Why would you, I suppose. Not your job.'

'No.'

'And,' Rafferty said – four fingers waving, long pleasurable drag on his smoke – 'not to get too graphic, but it's hard to miss a decomposing body. There was a load of muck and leaves dumped in on top of it, so that would've masked the smell a bit, and it was cold enough that autumn and winter; but still. Hugo would've gone investigating, and got the shock of his life, unless he already knew exactly what was stinking up his garden.'

With a slow strange flowering in my stomach I realised: Hugo hadn't just known. All of us gathered in the living room, Zach buzzing around looking for trouble, and Hugo had beckoned him over and whispered something in his ear; and Zach had got a big grin on his face and shot off to the garden, where he had gone straight up the one tree he had never been allowed to climb.

I told him there's treasure hidden in the garden. More than that: he had told Zach exactly where to look. Maybe not in so many words, in case Zach ratted him out, but he wouldn't have needed to. *Out you go, we'll all be busy in here for a while, you can look anywhere you want, anywhere at all . . .*

Once the three of us started making noises about what was going to happen to the house, Hugo had realised: if he died and left that skeleton out there, it would be like leaving us with a live landmine in the garden. It needed a controlled explosion, and so (*It takes some great upheaval to crack that shell and force us to discover what else might be underneath*) he had quietly made his plans and set them in motion. His method struck me as being a bit hard on Zach, even if he was a tough little bastard, but I supposed Hugo hadn't had much option: he could hardly have gone rooting around in that tree himself, or sent anyone else, without arousing suspicion.

Obviously I should have done it years ago. But it would take a certain kind of person to do that, wouldn't it, and apparently I'm not that kind; or wasn't, anyway, until now . . .

He had nearly left it too late for the final step, the confession – I wondered if when we got around to clearing his things we would find a handwritten one tucked away, just in case. Even in that moment I had room to be glad that he had left it so long. Melissa and I had made him happy enough that he had wanted every day he could have.

'And then' – Rafferty held up all five fingers, like a wave or a salute – 'the DNA results came back. Remember that big old jacket we took, when we searched the house? The one Hugo said was his?'

'Yeah.'

'Dominic's DNA was on that. On the inside, right here.' Tapping his right side. 'Not blood, but then we don't think he bled. Could've been saliva. Now, anyone could've worn that jacket, or Dominic could've got his DNA on it when he was in the house sometime. But when you add it to everything else we'd got . . .'

God but Susanna had been good. Only eighteen and that sharp, that far ahead. When the suicide story finally fell through, her Plan B had been right there waiting – *Mix it up, get a load of people in the frame* – and probably Plan C and D and all the rest, too. I wondered what, exactly, she would have done if the cops had arrested Hugo back then, or me, or Leon; or if they had gone after her.

'So,' Rafferty said, 'when Hugo rang us that day, it didn't come as much of a surprise. And he knew details we hadn't released. We asked him how he got the body down the tree trunk, yeah? He said he tied a rope round Dominic's chest, threw the rope over a branch, used that to haul the body up till he could climb a stepladder and guide it down the hole; and right enough, there were rope fibres all over Dominic's shirt. And he told us one of Dominic's shoes came off along the way, he had to grope around in the bushes for it and toss it in after him. And sure enough, Dominic had one shoe off; it was in the tree, all right, but up somewhere around his waist. That's what we look for, when someone comes in confessing. Bits and bobs he wouldn't know unless he was telling the truth.'

Except, of course, Hugo could have known. A noise in the garden, deep in the night; muffled urgent voices, drag of the stepladder. Hugo waking, wondering, finally unsettled enough by some tension distorting the air that he got up and went to the window.

He hadn't gone out to them. Maybe he hadn't understood or believed what he was seeing, till the news about Dominic went round. Or maybe he had known straightaway, and for his own reasons – safest for us, safest for his own peace, years of observing from the outside (*one gets into the habit of being oneself*) – he had decided to stay where he was. I wondered how much I had ever understood Hugo.

Darkness, Susanna bundled in his gardening jacket, Leon probably in something of mine. He hadn't known which of us he was seeing. Hadn't wanted to know: he could have checked which of us were gone from our beds, but he hadn't done it. Creaks and rustles downstairs as Leon slipped out to make the trek to Howth; the long wait, the sharp pings of our phones as the *Sorry* text came in. More waiting, on and on. The soft key-rattle of Leon coming in, whispers in the dawn. Bedroom doors shutting. Silence.

In the morning Hugo had smiled peacefully at us all over breakfast, asked us what we had planned for the day. At the end of the month he had waved us off to college and new lives, *Good luck! Enjoy!* And he had gone back into the Ivy House and closed the door behind him.

Ten years, living with that in his garden. His gift to us. I wished, so violently I could have howled, that he were there. I wanted to talk to him.

'The only question,' Rafferty said, 'was motive.' He was playing with the conkers again, tossing one and catching it dexterously overhand. 'Hugo wouldn't say. Just "It seemed necessary at the time" and "Why do you need to know?" Claiming his memory was banjaxed, getting irritable when we pushed – "Do you know how much of my brain has been shoved aside by tumour cells? Would you like to see the scans? I can barely remember my own brothers' names, never mind things that happened ten years ago . . ."'

He was a good mimic. The specific fall and rhythm of Hugo's voice, all its warm rough edges, spread over the garden. The thickening darkness flickered like static in the air.

'Kerr thought it was about Dominic bullying your cousin Leon, but I didn't buy it. If it had happened a year earlier, maybe. But when you'd all left school? When Leon never had to see Dominic again in his life? Hugo wasn't the type to kill for revenge.' Glance at me: 'Or was he? Do I have him all wrong?'

'No,' I said. 'He wasn't.'

'Yeah. So that was a missing piece. Not a big one, not a big deal – we can close cases without a motive – but I don't like missing pieces. Look at that—' The cat had made its way as far as the second piece of meat and was crouching to eat, more leisurely this time, one wary eye on us. 'He's relaxing already. Give him a bit of time, and you've got yourself a cat.'

'I don't want a cat.'

'Cats are great, man. And a pet would take you out of yourself, give you someone else to think about. Do you good.'

'Yeah. Maybe.'

Rafferty found his cigarette packet and flipped out another, squinting in the half-dark to see how many he had left. 'And then,' he said, 'Hugo died – God rest. So it looked like I was stuck with that missing piece. That left me in a bit of a bind: close the case, or no?'

He tilted the packet at me. I shook my head; he shrugged, tucking it away. 'Only then,' he said, 'your cousin Susanna came to see me.'

What? 'When?'

'Two days ago.'

Chill out, it's all under control. Susanna made me so tired I could have put my head down on my knees and slept.

'According to her' – stretching out his legs, settling to the story – 'Dominic had been giving her a bit of hassle, that year. Nothing serious; just trying to convince her to go out with him, not taking no for an answer. She complained about it to Hugo. Probably she made it sound worse than it was, she says; teenage girls, you know how they exaggerate, something's the end of the world one day and they've forgotten it the next . . . Susanna feels pretty bad about that. She just wanted to blow off steam, but Hugo must've taken her up wrong. Thought Dominic was some kind of pervert predator. Hugo was protective of the three of you, was he?'

One golden eye slipping sideways to me, bright in the lighter's flare. 'Yeah,' I said.

'Yeah. I got that, all right. So there was the motive. And – just in case I had any doubts left – Susanna told me she saw him, that night. Out here.'

'What,' I said.

'She didn't tell you?'

'No.'

'Huh,' Rafferty said. 'I thought she would've. Something that big, she wouldn't come to you?'

'Apparently not.'

If Rafferty caught the bitter edge, he didn't show it. 'The night Dominic went missing,' he said, 'late. Susanna got woken up by a text on her phone: the famous "sorry" text. She couldn't go back to sleep. Then she heard a noise out in the back garden, so she went to her window to see what was going on. It was Hugo, dragging something big across the grass; too dark for her to see what, exactly. At the time she thought he couldn't sleep, so he was doing a bit of work on this rock garden he'd been putting in – apparently Hugo suffered from insomnia, did he?'

'I don't remember.'

'Well, either way. That's what Susanna assumed – sure, why would she think anything else? I asked her if it could've been you or Leon out there, but she said no, Hugo was much bigger than either of you and he had long hair back then, no way could she have confused you for him.'

Which was gracious of her. 'I asked could it have been someone else,' Rafferty said, 'and she said yeah, that was possible, it could've been some other big guy with long hair. She wasn't watching for long. She thought about going out and giving Hugo a hand, but she had work in the morning, so she just went back to bed. When she heard Dominic had killed himself off Howth Head, it never even occurred to her to connect it up with Hugo messing about in his rock garden – that's fair enough, sure, isn't it?'

He cocked an eye at me. 'I guess,' I said.

'She copped on when we identified the skeleton, though. She's no fool, your cousin.'

'No,' I said. 'She isn't.'

'No. But she wasn't going to say anything then, and wreck Hugo's last couple of months. So she just kept quiet. Threw us the odd bit of info that pointed to Leon, or' – wry sideways glance – 'to

471

you. Just to mix it up a bit, keep us from zeroing in on Hugo. She knew it wouldn't do anyone any harm in the long run; she's got faith in the Guards, she figured we wouldn't actually arrest the wrong fella – and even if we had, she could've just come forward then. Otherwise, she was planning to tell us after Hugo died.'

I just bet she had been. Only it had never occurred to her that Hugo might have plans of his own. She had taken him for granted, Hugo the way we'd always known him, gentle and dreamy, drifting with the current. She wasn't that smart after all. Susanna, of all people, should have realised how those great upheavals can crack bedrock, shift tectonic plates, transform the landscape beyond recognition.

'So,' Rafferty said, 'getting back to your question: everything's adding up nicely. At this point I'm just dotting the i's and crossing the t's, so I can file my report and close the case. I've been having a look into that story about Dominic chasing after Susanna, for example, make sure it checks out.'

Something, a flutter of something cold. Out in the garden, the cat – just a silhouette, now – flicked its head up sharply to stare, immobile, at some invisible thing in the air. 'Does it?' I asked.

Rafferty wavered a hand. 'Yes and no, to be honest with you. I mean, Susanna's mates all confirm that he'd been at her, but they're not consistent on the level of harassment. Some of them say it was just a laugh; some agree with her that it was a pain in the hole, but not a huge problem. A couple of them – the ones who were closest to her, funny enough – they say it was bad. Like, real bad.' With a glance at me: 'So I'd love to know. How do you remember it?'

This was it, what he was here for, what he wanted out of me? There was nothing about him I could trust, nowhere to get a grip— 'Like Susanna says,' I said, in the end. 'Dominic was getting on her nerves, but it wasn't a big thing.'

'Did you ever say anything to him? Tell him to back off?'

'No.' When Rafferty raised an eyebrow, surprised: 'It didn't seem like I needed to.'

Dryly: 'Looks like you might've been wrong there, man.'

'Probably,' I said. In the last of the light his face was layered with swoops and slashes of shadow. The smells of earth and sodden leaves and burning were strengthening in the air.

'Here's a thing,' Rafferty said – twisting out his cigarette, examining it carefully to make sure it was dead. 'Might be connected, might not; I'd love to know. There were a handful of emails in Dominic's account that were never traced. Anonymous emails, sent over the summer before he died. From a girl he'd been chasing, apparently. She was well into him, but she didn't want to let on in public in case he was just winding her up, so she'd been shooting him down – are you following this? But at the same time, right, she wanted him to know that actually she fancied the arse off him.' With a grin, shadows deepening: 'The drama, Jesus. Doesn't it make you glad you'll never have to be a teenager again?'

Waves of cold were sweeping over me, like something very bad was happening but I was too stupid to figure out what it was. 'Yeah,' I said.

'Back when Dominic went missing, the emails didn't seem like a big deal. Everyone agreed that all the girls were mad about him, no surprise that he'd be getting the odd love note, and he obviously wasn't so mad about her that he'd have killed himself over her. The lads looking into it didn't even bother tracing them.' An eye-roll and a humorous twist of his mouth to me, *Bloody eejits, would you believe it?* 'When Susanna told me her story, though, I wondered if those emails might've been from her. She swears no, she never emailed him, but the circumstances fit nicely: Dominic coming on to this girl, her telling him to get fucked. Adds up, amn't I right?'

Another pleasant glance at me, like we were colleagues discussing the case over a nice pint in some cosy pub. 'I guess,' I said.

'You figure it was her?'

'I don't know.' That cold was soaking into me, trickling deeper, something I should know here, something I was missing— 'If she was actually into him, why would she email him? Instead of just, like, hooking up with him?'

Rafferty shrugged. 'Maybe she was nervous he was taking the piss, like she said. Or maybe she was playing hard to get. Or maybe she wasn't into him, she was trying to make him slip up and do something that she could use as proof that he was harassing her – email her a dick pic, whatever. Or maybe she didn't even know what she wanted.' Grinning again: 'Teenage girls are mental, amn't I right?'

'I guess.'

'That's what everyone tells me, anyhow. So I wondered, at first. But then,' Rafferty said – easily, comfortably, leaning back on his elbows to enjoy the view of the garden – 'I remembered those tweets. I already knew someone – not Susanna – who thought it was great craic playing with made-up identities online, to mess with people. And who was good at it.'

Another wave of cold hit me. It was coming up from the ground, into my bones. I couldn't feel my feet.

'You sent Dominic those emails, am I right?'

'I don't know,' I said. 'I don't remember.'

Rafferty blew out air, exasperated and amused. 'Ah, Toby. Come on. Not that again.'

'I don't.'

'What, you sent so many fake emails there's no way you'd remember a few more? To a guy who *died* not long after?'

'*No*. I don't—'

'OK. Let's try it this way. Did you ever send anyone a fake email, back when you were a teenager?'

'Not that I remember,' I said. Actually I had a feeling that might not be true, me and Dec snickering at a school computer, *Nah we have to tone it down he'll never go for*—

'Huh,' Rafferty said. 'Remember a guy called Lorcan Mullan? He was in your class?'

'Yeah. What does he have to do with—'

'He says in spring of sixth year he got a few emails from a girl who fancied him. She wouldn't tell him her name, just that she'd seen him around and thought he was hot. Lorcan wasn't a big hit with the ladies – skinny and spotty, from what he says – so he was only delighted. She dropped hints that she was on the hockey team, stuff like that, so he'd know she was fit, right? And after a couple of emails back and forth she said she wanted to meet up. They set up a time and a place, Lorcan put on his getting-laid shirt and half a can of body spray; but when he got there, it was just you and your mate Declan, pissing yourselves laughing.'

It had been Dec's idea. Dec bored in computer class, buzzing for trouble, getting that dangerous glitter to him: *C'mere, let's see who we can catch* . . . It hadn't been just Lorcan; it had been three or four guys, carefully chosen for gullibility and desperation and general loserhood, but apparently only Lorcan had been thick enough to go the whole way. 'We were little shits back then,' I said. 'All of us were. I bet someone tried to pull the same thing on me, at some stage.'

'Ah, you could've been a lot worse,' Rafferty said, fairly. 'Even Lorcan admits that. He was expecting the two of ye to tell the world, and he'd be slagged out of it till he had to change school or maybe leave the country. But as far as he could tell, you never said a word to anyone. You weren't in it to destroy him, like some people would've been. You were just having a laugh.'

Only we had said a word to someone, actually. Sean, not laughing along like we'd expected; instead (at his locker, stuffing books into his bag) giving us a look of mild disgust over his shoulder: *Fuck's sake. Lorcan? You want to fuck with someone, pick someone your own size. Give yourselves an actual challenge.*

'So,' Rafferty said. 'Seems like you might've had the same kind of laugh at Dominic. He had been fucking with your cousins; he deserved it, right?'

Surely we would have lost interest after Lorcan, moved on to some other dumb way to get our kicks. That had been Dec's style; once would have been enough for him. And I would never have come up with the idea to start with if it hadn't been for him, surely I wouldn't have kept going on my own— But I had always cared about Sean's opinion. That look of disgust had stung. *Pick someone your own size.*

'The emails,' I said. I was so cold I couldn't imagine ever being warm again. 'The ones to Lorcan. Were they from, was it the same address as the ones to Dominic?'

Rafferty gave me a long curious look. 'You genuinely don't remember?'

'No.'

After a moment, relenting: 'We don't know. Lorcan deleted the emails as soon as he found out he'd been had, and the server doesn't keep data this long. Any chance you remember anything about the address you used? Even part of it?'

'No.' Dec had been the one who set it up, huddled over the keyboard, giggling manically, kicking me to shut me up when I opened my mouth.

'Pity,' Rafferty said, after a pause that felt endless. 'Declan says he doesn't either. He remembers the emails to Lorcan, all right – and a couple of others, by the way – but he says he never emailed Dominic. And I believe him, for whatever that's worth.'

I would have told Sean about it, surely I would have, if the whole point had been to show him I wasn't just picking on rejects? Unless: unless Dominic had vanished before I could say anything, and I had thought it might be – even a little bit, even just maybe – because of my emails. Dominic, already half off the rails because of his exam results, realising he'd been suckered like some idiot loser; not a big thing, but one thing too many . . . If I had thought there was even half a chance of that, I would have kept my mouth shut. Why upset people by coming clean? Not like it could do any good, not like we'd ever know for sure, not like there was any point in beating myself up thinking about it . . . *Oh, you. Anything you feel bad about falls straight out of your head.*

Rafferty sighed. 'Looks like we'll never know. And I'd only love to. Because, if those emails encouraged Dominic to keep chasing Susanna? And he got killed for it? Then no matter who did the actual killing, whoever wrote the emails helped to sucker Dominic into getting himself killed.'

I couldn't even come up with a flash of horror. Honestly it wasn't Susanna I was tired of, not really; it was me, wronged innocent, white knight, cunning investigator, killer, selfish oblivious dick, petty provocateur, take your pick, what does it matter? it'll all change again tomorrow, it's all up for grabs. This formless thing, boneless, grotesque, squashed like Play-Doh into whatever shape the boss of the day wanted to see: I was sick of it.

The garden was black and blue-white, trees swollen with ivy and still as monuments. The cat had slipped away somewhere. Birch seeds whirling weightless in the air, filling it like tiny flakes of snow or ash.

Rafferty's voice rang over and over, in my head. Still, it took me a minute to hear it: *no matter who did the actual killing.*

I said, 'You don't think Hugo did it.'

He didn't turn to look at me. 'I told you already. Everything points to him. And now I've got motive and a witness. If this went to a jury, I'd put decent money on a conviction.'

'But you don't think he did it.' I understood, in some distant lucid fragment of my mind, that I should be terrified. Even a year earlier I would have been no match for Rafferty; now, if he decided I was what he was after, he could take me apart methodically, piece by piece, until I confessed to killing Dominic and probably believed every word. All I could dredge up was a faint reflexive kick of animal fear.

The air was so still that I could hear Rafferty's small sigh. 'A lot of the time, in this job,' he said, 'you can tell what kind of mind you're up against. You can feel them, out there.' A nod to the garden. 'I could feel it strong, this time. Mostly it's just some clown, you know? Some halfwit scumbag taking out a rival dealer, some arsehole who got drunk again and hit her too hard this time. This was different, from the start. Someone cool as ice, thinking twenty moves ahead. Someone who was never going to get spooked, or confused, or strong-armed. It never felt like Hugo.'

I said, 'Then why the hell did you arrest him?'

A lift of one shoulder. 'Intuition's nice, and all, but I've got to go with the evidence. The evidence says it was him. If you know different, though . . .' He turned his head to me then. He was nothing but eyes and shadows. 'If you've got anything that says it was someone else, and you don't want Hugo going down as a murderer, you need to tell me.'

I said, 'I didn't kill Dominic.'

He nodded, unsurprised. 'But you wrote those emails – shush, man, we both know it. You're no holy innocent, in all this. Your uncle, unless I'm way off base, he was a good man. You owe him this much.'

So that was what he was here for. Not for me, after all; to convince me to rat out Leon and Susanna.

I almost did it. Why not? Fuck the pair of them; let them deal with Rafferty settling in on their terraces and offering them smokes and unpicking their seams, let Susanna wangle her way out of this if she was so smart. She had been happy to dangle me in front of him, look over here, shiny! But more than that, much more: they had left me out. I could have been like them, changed, tempered. I could have come to that night in my apartment as someone who could come out of it unbroken, if only they had believed in me enough to bring me along.

Except all of that seemed to matter less than the lack of surprise in Rafferty's voice. It had taken me that long to realise. I said, 'You never thought I had done it.'

'Nah. It never felt like you, either, whatever about that hoodie. I know' – raising his voice a touch, when I started to say something – 'I know that was ten years back, and I know about the head injury. But right deep down, past all that, people are what they are. And this thing didn't feel like you.'

'Even when you came with the photos. You made it sound like you were about to arrest me. You were just, you were—' Here I had been thinking of him as an opponent, the brilliant adversary I was somehow going to outfox, *en garde!* I hadn't been an opponent to him. I hadn't even been a person, only a convenient thing that he could nudge carefully into whatever position suited his strategy. 'You were using me as bait. To get Hugo to confess.'

A one-shouldered shrug. 'It worked.'

'If it hadn't? What would you have done? Would you have arrested me? Locked me up?'

Rafferty said, 'I want my man. Or my woman.'

That spike of terror went through me again. He was like a raptor, not cruel, not good or evil, only and utterly what he was. The purity of it, unbreakable, was beyond anything I could imagine.

And this is one of the moments I come back to over and over, one of the things I can't forgive myself; because a part of me did know better, a part of me knew I shouldn't ask. But it seemed to me that an answer from him would make sense of everything, would be absolute and golden as an answer from some god. 'Why me?' I said. 'Why not Leon? He was the one who was being, who Dominic was bullying. Why not—'

Rafferty said, simply, 'Because you were my best bet.'

My heart was going in great slow thumps. '*Why?*'

'You want to know?'

'Yeah. I do.'

'OK.' He rearranged himself, elbows on knees, getting comfortable to explain it all to me. 'So the thing is: I could've gone for Leon, all right. As far as evidence goes, I had as much on him as I did on you. But – just like you said that day with the hoodie, remember? – none of it was solid; it was all circumstantial stuff. And with a circumstantial case, a lot of it comes down to what the jury thinks of the defendant. Say we got Susanna up on trial for this. Right? Lovely middle-class housewife. Well-spoken, from a good family. Married her college sweetheart; so devoted to her kids, she gave up her career for their sake. Not gorgeous or done-up, so she's not an evil scheming bitch, but not ugly or fat or anything, so she's not a disgusting loser. Educated, so she's not a skanger, but not too educated, so she's not some uppity elitist. Strong enough that you take her seriously, but not too strong – because you can bet she'd play it bang on – so she's not an arrogant cow who needs taking down a peg. If we had no solid evidence, you think a jury would vote to convict?'

'Probably not.'

'Not a chance in hell. Now, Leon' – he wavered a hand – 'maybe we'd have a shot there. Dodgy lifestyle and all that. Plenty of people still think the gays are a bit unbalanced, and you know those artsy types, couldn't watch 'em. If we had even one solid thing on him – a witness, DNA, anything – then you're dead right: he'd've been my best bet. But we didn't. And same as Susanna, he's from a good family, well-off, nice middle-class accent; he's good-looking but not enough to come across as a smug prick, he's articulate, intelligent, likeable . . . Get him into a decent suit, get rid of the stupid hairdo, and he'd come across great. That nice normal boy, a killer? Ah, no.'

Rows of blank black windows in the apartment block; something in the light made them look broken out, jagged holes onto emptiness, dust thickening on ripped-down posters and overturned chairs. No sound anywhere, not a far-off motorcycle or a shout or a snatch of music.

'You, though,' Rafferty said, utterly matter-of-fact. 'I could get somewhere with you.'

This is the amazing part: for a split second I almost laughed in his face. Me of all people, for God's sake, who the hell would ever believe— Maybe I should see it as some kind of triumph of the human spirit: even after everything, there was some tiny fragment of my mind that really believed I was still me.

'The little stuff makes a big difference,' Rafferty explained. 'Like the eyelid, you know that thing it does, the . . . ?' – gesturing with a finger – 'And the limp. The way you slur your words a bit – only when you're under pressure, like, most of the time no one would even notice, but God knows you'd be under pressure on the stand. The way you get twitchy, jumpy. The way you stumble, get your sentences tangled up. And the way sometimes it seems like you're not really tuned in; that out-of-focus look you get.' Leaning in: 'Listen, man, I'm not slagging you. In normal life, with people who know you, none of that matters. But juries don't like that stuff. They think it means there's something wrong with you. And once they think that, it's only a wee little skip and a jump to you being a killer.'

The trees moving, tiny subtle clicks and shifts, where there was no wind. Branch-shadows scrawled violent as earthquake-cracks across the bare earth. Smell of burning tyres, stronger.

'And there's the memory,' Rafferty added. 'Susanna or Leon, they could get up there and swear they had nothing to do with what happened to Dominic; all they'd have to do is convince a jury they were telling the truth. You, man, it wouldn't matter whether you convinced the jury or not. We'd be able to prove your memory was cabbaged. Nothing that came out of your mouth would matter a damn.'

I said, much too loud, '*None of that is my fault.*' Which I knew was ludicrous but it came out of me anyway, ripped its way out— 'It wasn't my fucking *choice.*'

Rafferty said, gently, 'So what?'

'So you don't, you don't get to, to *use it* against me' – the rising anger was so overwhelming it tongue-tied me, fucking moron, way to prove Rafferty's point, wanted to punch myself – 'you don't get to act like it, it, it— That *doesn't count.*'

'It would've, though,' Rafferty pointed out matter-of-factly.

I couldn't answer that; I could barely breathe. 'I'm not saying I would've ever taken things that far,' he reassured me. 'I wouldn't've. Hand to God. I'm not in the business of sending innocent men down for murder. But the thing is, I didn't need to. I just needed Hugo to think I would. That's why I went for you over Leon. Because Hugo knew as well as I did, if you got into a courtroom, you'd be fucked.'

He said something else to me then. I can still see the equivocal spark of a smile lighting his face and I've spent hundreds or maybe thousands of hours trying to remember what it was he said but I can't, because just as he started saying it I realised that I was about to punch him in the face, and just as he finished saying it I hit him.

I took him by surprise. The punch connected with a thick smack and he went over sideways onto the terrace. But he rolled with it, and by the time I scrambled to my feet – strange light-headed lucidity almost like joy lifting me, *finally, finally* – he was up again and coming at me, low, hands out and taut like a street fighter. He feinted to one side and then the other, grinning when I leaped to follow, beckoning me on.

I charged at him. He ducked my wild swing, caught me by the arm on my way past, swung me around and let me go. I flailed backwards across the terrace and slammed up against the wall of the house. He came after me, pulled back a fist easy as that and jabbed me in the nose.

Something burst; for a moment I was blind, blood poured down into my mouth. I inhaled it, choked, and then he was on me. He grabbed me in a headlock and started punching me in the ribs.

I stamped down on his instep and heard his bark of pain. In the second he was off balance I got my foot up against the wall behind me and shoved myself off it.

The pair of us shot staggering across the terrace, still clasped together. We went down the steps to the garden tangling in each other's feet, overbalancing, and fell full length. Before I could get my bearings he was on top of me and shoving my face down into the dirt.

He was bigger and ten times stronger than me. Earth pressed on my eyelids, earth filled my mouth. I couldn't breathe.

I almost went with it. I almost relaxed all my aching muscles and let him guide me down, among last year's leaves and small winter-dreaming creatures, between long-lost treasures and tiny curled bones, into the dark earth. But the wild heat of him pressing against me, his breath harsh in my ear: that night in my apartment surged up inside me and all I could think was, with a roaring fury that ignited every cell in my body, *Not this time.*

I got my knees under me, heaved myself up and over onto my back, and spat a burst of blood and dirt into his face. He jerked backwards and I got a foot in his stomach, shoved him off me, scrabbled away and up. He twisted to his feet like a cat and came charging at me, but I dug my heels into the ground and somehow this time I stayed standing. I grabbed hold of him and clung on.

We lurched in circles in the near-darkness like some grotesque monster, many-limbed and grunting, fumbling blind. There was a nightmare slowness to it all, feet sinking and sticking in mud, hands clawing at hair and cloth and skin. My breath was bubbling and rasping; his was harsh as an animal's, I felt his teeth press against my cheek, and even through the blood clogging my nose I would have sworn I smelled his wild pine scent. He was trying to knee me in the balls and I was bashing uselessly at the back of his head but neither of us could get enough distance, or enough purchase on the shifting ground, for a proper blow.

He changed grip, grabbed me by the thigh and lifted me right off my feet. But I had an elbow around his neck, and when he slammed me down on my back I took him with me. In the same second that the wind was knocked out of me I heard his skull hit a rock, right beside my ear, with a terrible squelchy crack.

I lay still, fighting for breath. He felt like a sack of wet cement holding me down. High above me misshapen grey birds flickered against the black sky and I thought they were the last thing I would ever see, but at last I managed to gasp in a great whoosh of air. I flailed at him, scrabbling and shoving, till I heaved him off me and dragged myself onto my knees.

Slowly, inch by inch, he pulled himself up onto his hands and knees and turned his head to look at me. His eyes were huge and solid black, alien, and there was blood running down his face from a big gash in his forehead, spreading rivers of it, dark and glossy in the dim blue-white light. He made a deep snarling noise, lip lifting, and clamped one hand around my wrist.

I punched him in the face. His hand fell away from my wrist and I went at him with both fists, swinging with all my weight behind it, hammering at his head, grabbing his hair to slam his face into the ground. I didn't even feel my knuckles splitting; I could smash through living rock, I was strong as a god and in-exhaustible. He was still making the snarling noise and I was going to make it stop, he was never going to grab me again, he was never going to do anything to me again, never, never— Through the ferocious drumming of my heartbeat and the huge roaring silence of the garden I heard Susanna's voice: *Now imagine you did it.* The holy rapture of it, the painless lightning running in my bones. Rising on the far side of that river into a world that was finally mine again.

In the end, little by little, the lightning drained out of me and I stopped. My arms were weak as cloth, they fell to my sides like they belonged to someone else, and I was breathing in great snuffling gulps. I knelt there in the dirt, swaying a little back and forth.

He was huddled face-down, forearms wrapped over his head. I couldn't remember why we had been fighting. I had lost hold of any

idea who he was, or who I was. All I knew was the vast cold cob-
webbed darkness and us, two tiny sparks of warmth, side by side.

Birch seeds drifting down, hanging pale in the air, landing
silently on his dark back. He was making a strange snoring noise.
After a while he toppled, very slowly, onto his side.

I lifted one hand, heavy as granite, and put it on his shoulder.
One of his legs twitched rhythmically. I thought I should lie down
across him, so that the birch seeds wouldn't cover him like snow,
but I didn't have the strength to do it. My nose was throbbing, dripping big dark spots of blood onto my jeans.

Snarled black branches, scrabble of something on the roof. I
had only the foggiest idea where I was; the place seemed familiar but
only barely, something from a dream or a story. It was terribly cold.

After a while the twitching stopped. Then so did the snoring
noise, and I was alone in the garden.

I knelt there with my hand on his shoulder until I couldn't stay
kneeling any longer. Then I eased myself painfully down to the
earth and curled up with my back against his. I was shivering in
hard spasms, teeth clacking together painfully, but his back was
warm and solid and somehow in the end I fell asleep.

•

Thin grey light woke me. I was curled on my side, knees pulled up
to my belly and fists tucked into my chest, like some Iron Age
burial. My mouth tasted of earth and one of my eyes was stuck shut
somehow. I was stiff and sore from head to toe, damp all over, and
so cold I couldn't feel my face.

I managed to inch one hand up towards my eye, but the sight of
it startled me: it was covered in dried blood, blood grained into
every crease, knuckles ragged and swollen. When I spat on my fingers and rubbed at my eye, they came back smeared with brighter
red. Something bad had happened.

The earth under me was soft, but my back was up against something hard and very cold and I wanted to get away from it. It took
forever, every movement feeling like it ripped muscles or snapped
joints, before I made it to sitting. The effort and the pain left me

shaky, with an ugly red pounding behind my eyeballs. I spat dirt and blood, wiped my mouth on my sleeve.

The garden was monochrome and dormant under a veil of dew. Nothing moved, not a leaf twitching, not a bird hopping or an insect scuttling. The sky was a null grey that made it invisible. Drifts of birch seeds had settled in the little valleys in the earth.

They brought something back to me. Someone, another person, here with me— I turned around and there he was.

Birch seeds dotting the outflung wing of his dark coat, dew silvering his hair. His head was twisted sideways, face buried in the crook of his elbow, other arm stretched above his head. His hand looked the same way as mine, the blood and the knuckles. I tried to lift his elbow away from his face so I could check if he was breathing, but it wouldn't move; every muscle and joint was rigid, as if he was turning to stone from the inside out. His hand was even colder than mine.

After a long time I managed to get to my feet and drag myself inside, stumbling, hunched over like an old man. I lit the fire – old ash whirling up, sending me into a painful coughing fit – and huddled in front of it, as close as I could get.

It came back to me bit by bit, falling into my mind with a slow, irrevocable, wintry calm. It had seemed like a heroic thing, at the time; it had seemed to light the whole sky with its own savage blaze of redemption. In the bleak morning all that was gone. Rafferty was dead and I had killed him. Not to save Leon or Susanna, like I had believed I had killed Dominic, or even to save myself, but simply because my brain was fucked enough that I had thought it was a good idea. And now he was dead. Somewhere not too far away, someone was starting to wonder where he was, why he hadn't called, hadn't come home.

Moving flame-shadows making the walls ripple and buckle. Ragged heaps of books and dirty plates on the coffee table, spider bustling purposefully along the floorboards by my knee.

My face had thawed enough that I could feel it was coated with something; when I fumbled at it, pain went everywhere. I made my way to the bathroom, stopping a few times along the way to lean against a wall until the surge of dizziness subsided and I could see again. In the mirror my nose looked weird, lumpy and off centre, and my face was crusted with dried blood and dirt like a mask. I rubbed at it with a wet towel for a while, but it didn't seem to make much difference and it hurt too much to keep going. My legs folded under me and I sat down on the bathroom floor. I sat there for a very long time, cheek throbbing against cold tile.

I was waiting for the thing Susanna and Leon had talked about, the grand transformation. *Well yeah there was that too.* The steely power that had come to Susanna, no one will ever fuck with me again, I'm a superhero now; I'll haul in the burglars by the scruffs of their necks and throw them at Martin's feet, I'll spin some Machiavellian web that will have the shitbird neurologist sobbing at my feet and begging my forgiveness. The airy weightlessness that had risen in Leon, none of it matters, none of it can hurt me; I'll let this damaged life drop from my shoulders like a stained jacket, and off I'll go to find something new and perfect. In the firelight they had shone as if they were made of some strange element, unknowable and indestructible. I waited to feel my own flesh transmute, to rise from the floor with my wounds healing themselves and my scars vanishing and everything at last making sense.

Nothing happened. All that came to me was the thought of Rafferty's wife or girlfriend or whatever he had had, starting to be frightened, wondering whether to ring Kerr; his kids, maybe, dark rumple-haired boys thrumming with energy, dashing in from playing to ask where Dad was.

Small stirrings in the house as the wind nosed in. Cracks and damp-stains patterning the wall like the shadow of a great moss-draped tree. Dim light shifting across the grimed window, shower curtain drooping from a broken ring.

I remembered the emails to Dominic. Or I thought I did, for whatever that was worth; but it was clear as day. Sprawled on my bed at home supposedly studying, restless and itchy with unseasonable spring heat, one of those weekends when everyone was a pain in the hole: Susanna had gone off on me because I made an unflattering comment about some hambeast friend of hers, Leon kept going into long bitter rants about how we were all slaughterhouse sheep plodding obediently from school towards college and then straight into the corporate maw, and my ribs were killing me where Dominic had given me a just-messing punch the day before. Sean or Dec could have pulled me out of my foul mood, but Dec was working some shitty part-time gig to save up for college and was never around, and Sean was off somewhere with his hand up Audrey's top or whatever, not answering his phone. I wanted to piss someone off.

The email address Dec and I had used on Lorcan was *ifancyyou@* something, Hotmail or Yahoo. The password was *sucker*.

Susanna had been in a flap the week before about Dominic trying to hook up with her. At the time it had seemed kind of endearing – for someone so smart, Su could be such a total kid, losing her mind because a guy came on to her – but that day it just seemed like annoying drama, an excuse for self-righteous outrage. If she wanted one of those, she could have it.

Hey I know I went off on you when you grabbed my arse the other day but actually it turned me on soooo much ;-)

I didn't sign it – plausible deniability if it all came out and Susanna came gunning for me, my best injured face, *What? I never said it was from you!* Dom would put two and two together, and if he didn't, I didn't really care. Either way, his head was all over the place enough that he would totally fall for it. One more move on Susanna and she would rip his arm off and hit him with the wet end, or lecture him into a coma about consent and bodily autonomy. They deserved each other. I just hoped I was there when he did it.

Then something more interesting came up, I snapped out of my bad mood and forgot all about the whole thing for a few days. When I remembered and checked the email account, though, sure enough, Dominic had swallowed it whole. *So why did u act like such a bitch?*

I snorted and forgot about it for another while, till the next time I was bored. *I don't know I was embarrassed!! Like in case you were just messing with me. Anyway this way is fun too right? ;)*

A big grinning smiley back from Dominic. :D *That's so hot*

And then? What had I said to him? How many emails had there been? Those were all I could remember, but *a handful* Rafferty had said. Enough; more than enough.

Great big satisfied grin, like he'd done something clever and he was expecting a medal, Susanna had said. *He went, "Happy to see me?"*

Probably the memory should have hit me with a rush of shame, guilt, horror, but all I could feel was an immense, bottomless sadness. It had been such a small thing to do. Kids pulled worse pranks on each other every day, thousands of them. I had thought it meant nothing at all; it should have meant nothing at all. And yet, somehow, here we all were, and everything was ruined.

My bedroom looked like it had been abandoned for years, crumpled clothes in corners, dusty cobwebs swaying from the lampshade, weak slant of light through the crack between the curtains. I found my Xanax and my painkillers, tucked away at the back of a drawer, and spread them on the bed. There was a surprising amount of them left.

I had thought about it before, of course I had – in those terrible weeks pacing my apartment I had thought about practically nothing else. But when it came down to it I had never gone through with it, never even tried. I had believed it was because of Melissa, because of my mother, my father – I couldn't bear the thought of never seeing them again, couldn't bear the thought of any of them finding me. But it had never been that. It had been because of that tiny ludicrous spark, somewhere deep in the core of my mind, that had still believed things could turn around. Somewhere on the other side of that sheet of trick glass, my own life was waiting for me, warm and bright as summer, beckoning.

Always one more miracle, always one more chance. Pull me from the earthquake rubble, weeks in, dust-coated to a white statue and just one hand lifting feebly, parade me high in triumph. Pull me from the river streaming like a merman, work on me past hope, till the cough and splutter finally come. I'm lucky, my luck will hold.

Only now there was a dead detective in my garden and his blood all over my hands, and I couldn't see a single thing that luck could do for me. Even if I managed to scrape a hole in the earth and bury him, they would come looking. He would have told someone where he was going, he would have left his car somewhere nearby, they would track his phone. I wasn't Susanna who could spin cunning cover-up plans; there was no room here to play misdirection games, claim it could have been this or that someone else. I was going to prison.

And even if I somehow didn't: I had killed someone, and I always would have. It was always going to be like this. There was no undoing this, no talking my way out, no fixing it or apologising it away, no smoothing off the sharp edges or planing it down so it could be tucked away into some smaller, manageable box. Instead it would grind me away till I fit around its own immutable shape.

What I had failed to recognise after that night in my apartment – even though it had been right there, and crucial, the whole time – was that no one had been dead. That was why that spark had refused to go out: ruined, half-witted, staggering, I had still been alive. *While there's life there's hope*: banal enough to make you retch, and yet it had turned out to be true. Now Rafferty was dead and there was no place left for luck or miracles or last chances. This was the blank wall of rock, the final word against which there was no appeal. I was done.

I swallowed the pills with palmfuls of water from the bathroom tap – I thought about vodka or wine, just to make sure, a parting glass, but the idea made my stomach churn and I couldn't risk throwing up the whole mess. Then I stripped off my clothes – bloody, muddy, shedding trickles of dirt and birch seeds as I dropped them on the bedroom floor – pulled on a clean T-shirt and pyjama bottoms and got into bed. The sheets were freezing and clammy. I curled up tight, wincing as I hit bruised spots, and wrapped the duvet over my head.

I thought of Melissa, a time when she had had the flu and had sat up in my bed flushed with fever and chattering with daffy, determined brightness, while I brought her soft-boiled eggs and toast soldiers and herbal tea and read her *Winnie-the-Pooh* off my phone with her head on my chest. I thought of my mother sitting cross-legged on the floor playing Snap with me, ponytail falling forwards over her shoulder, hand hovering and an unconscious half-grin lighting her face; of my father leaning back in his armchair in lamplight to give some school essay of mine his serious, unhurried attention, *This is very good, I like the way you've constructed your argument* . . . I would have liked to lie there for longer; I would have liked time to go back through every good memory, all the pints and messing with Sean and Dec, all the wild college nights, the girls and the holidays and the bedtime stories, even the Ivy House summers with Hugo and Susanna and Leon. But I was exhausted to the marrow, body and mind, I was fading in and out, and as the bed warmed up and the pills kicked in I couldn't keep my eyes open any longer. The last thing I remember thinking is how terribly sad it was that it should be so easy, in the end, to go to sleep.

13

I didn't get the job done, obviously. Somewhere in there I apparently left Melissa a long meandering voicemail made up mainly of apologies and incomprehensible slurred gibberish. When Melissa heard it she rang my parents, who rushed over to the Ivy House, where they found Rafferty dead in the garden in a puddle of blood and me only mostly dead in my bed in a puddle of puke. I can't even begin to imagine what the next few hours were like. I woke up back in the hospital, feeling like I had the mother of all hangovers and had been kicked repeatedly in the stomach, with that sickness-and-disinfectant reek soaked into me all over again and a uniformed cop glaring grimly from the chair beside my bed.

At first I thought I was back in the aftermath of that night in my apartment, and I couldn't work out why the cop was so pissed off with me about it. The realisation that my head wound was healed to a scar sent me into such a panic – how long had I been here?! – that a nurse had to come and give me a shot. When a couple of detectives strolled in for a chat, I was so off my face that all I could do was stare dreamily at them and ask if they had found my car and if they would mind checking that my feet were still there.

It took a while before I got things straight enough to be questioned – which in practice, under strict orders from the fancy solicitor my parents had hired for me, meant saying 'No comment' an awful lot of times to a pair of detectives who, behind the careful blank expressions, clearly wanted to rip me to pieces and piss on the leftovers. But one of the few intelligible bits of that voicemail to Melissa had been something along the lines of *snuck up on me, thought he was a burglar, scared the shit out of*. . . and then more mumbling and *sorry I'm so sorry* (having to listen to that voicemail being played in a courtroom was, in the face of some stiff competition, definitely one of the worst moments of the whole thing). By the time I recovered enough to have any idea what had happened, the story had solidified itself, in basically the form that my defence eventually used at the trial: Rafferty calling by to see if I could back up Susanna's story; the open door (my mother and Louisa and the postman all testified to having found the door unlocked or even swinging open, over the previous few weeks; apparently the postman had lectured me about it, but he didn't think I'd taken it in); the startle on the dark terrace, the poor triggered PTSD sufferer flashing back to the attack that had devastated his life, lashing out in a frenzy of what he truly believed to be self-defence (expert testimony from the shitbird neurologist and from several psychologists, as well as some pretty crushing stuff from my family and Melissa), and then horror-stricken to the point of suicide when he snapped out of his trance of terror and saw Rafferty's bloodied face.

It had some kind of truth to it, I suppose, in its own tangled, oblique way. My solicitor took me through it methodically, relentlessly, like a strict old-fashioned tutor drilling a backward student in Latin declensions. At first I refused point-blank even to think about testifying. It wasn't only, or even mostly, what Rafferty had said – *If you got into a courtroom, you'd be fucked*. It was simpler than that. There were very few things left in the world that seemed like they would make me feel worse, but expanding on the finer details of my fuckedupitude to an audience consisting of my family and my friends and Melissa and assorted media and the entire world was pretty much top of the list.

But the solicitor kept banging on about how it was my only chance of avoiding a murder conviction and an automatic life sentence, so in the end I went with it. I think, or maybe I just want to think, that I did it mainly for my parents' sake. I couldn't shake the image of my mother stepping into the Ivy House, *Toby? Toby are you all right?*, the cold draught through the open garden door; the thing lying on the earth, the moment of horror, the dizzying confusion when she saw Rafferty's face; rushing through dusty rooms and up dark staircases, *Toby!* voice rising and cracking, *Toby!*; and, at last, me, doing my best to die right there in front of her, just not quite able to cross that final borderline.

So I got up there on the stand, stripped and splayed and did my little dance in front of the world. I shook and hyperventilated, right on cue, as my barrister took me through the burglary step by step. I stumbled through in-depth descriptions of every single humiliating aftereffect (*And what happened when you tried to go outside alone? And when the credit-card company asked for your middle name you couldn't remember it, is that right? And we can see that your eyelid droops, is that a result of . . . ?*). I lost my train of thought and had to ask for questions to be repeated. When someone dropped a notebook I jumped practically out of my seat. I stammered and slurred my way through Hugo's death, jammed up so badly that my barrister had to ask for a break when it came to the fight with Rafferty. I tried not to look at the jury's faces as they carefully assessed just how much of a wreck I was, at the pretty blonde in the front row and her big pitying eyes. On cross-examination the prosecutor went after me hard, trying to push the line that I was faking it, but he backed off fast when it became clear that I wasn't at all, that I was in fact on the verge of breaking down utterly.

The prosecution's version was that I had held a grudge against Rafferty over Hugo's death, and when he had shown up looking for info to cement Hugo's reputation as a murderer, I had lost my temper and gone for him. I suppose there was an element of truth in that version, too, but the jury – after almost three days of deliberation – preferred my barrister's. There was, after all, no arguing with the fact that I was comprehensively fucked up. I was the only one who got the irony: all the things that Rafferty had explained would work against me, the slurring and the jumpiness and the glazed look and the inability to focus, those were the things that saved me. The verdict (eleven to one: there was one big, shaven-headed guy whose jaded stare said he wasn't buying any of it) was manslaughter by reason of diminished responsibility.

The verdict meant, as my solicitor explained to me, that the judge could sentence me to anything he chose, from probation to life. I was lucky. The judge could hardly let me walk away from a dead detective, but he took into account my unblemished record, my immense potential to contribute to society, my supportive family (he knew my father and Phil professionally, although distantly enough that he hadn't felt the need to recuse himself), the fact that my mental state and social background were likely to make prison an unduly harsh environment for me. He sentenced me to twelve years, ten of them suspended, and sent me to the Central Mental Hospital, where I could receive the appropriate treatment to make sure I fulfilled all that potential someday. I didn't need Susanna to point out to me that, if I had been some track-suited skanger from a family of dole rats, the whole thing would have played out very differently.

•

Susanna came to visit me a few times, actually, while I was in the hospital. The first time I assumed she was there to suss out whether I was planning to rat out her and Leon to the shrinks. I wasn't. Not out of love or nobility or anything, and not out of the cheerful non-chalance with which I'd covered for Tiernan, *Hey why not? who's getting hurt?*; just because it felt like enough damage had already been done all around. If anything could be salvaged, I liked the idea of helping to salvage it.

Susanna looked good. She had come straight from college; she was wearing a pale-blue T-shirt and skinny jeans and old runners, and she looked young and energetic and studenty. In the visiting room – ratty armchairs splotched with tea stains and gum, bolted-down coffee table, vaguely unsettling art-therapy paintings of distorted flowerpots – she seemed like an alien beamed in from another world; but then, all the visitors did.

She didn't try to hug me. 'You look better,' she said. 'Like you're getting some sleep.'

'Thanks,' I said. 'They have pills for that.' Susanna still wasn't my favourite person. I'm sure she would argue that she had done her level best to keep all of us out of trouble and it was hardly her fault that I had decided to beat up a cop, but I had a hard time seeing it that way.

'How's this place?'

'It's OK,' I said. It sort of was, actually. The first few weeks had been bad. Suicide watch, which in itself was enough to make the most stable person suicidal: mattress on a bare floor, tiny hatch in a metal door, stifling heat, lights never off. Unreadable stares everywhere, all of them pulsing with danger, doctors who might decide to shoot me full of some mindfuck drug if I made the wrong move, patients who might decide I was the devil and needed my face ripped off. Constant noise, always someone shouting or singing or banging something, all of it amplified by the bare institutional acoustics. And the dawning realisation that this sentence had no end date; the judge's two years were an illusion, I was there until the doctors thought I was cured, which might be years away or might be never.

After the first shock wore off, though, I had settled in without too much trouble. No one tried to eat my face or drug me into catatonia. I had a room of my own (tiny, overheated, paint peeling) and I was considered low enough risk that I got to do stuff like go for walks in the grounds and do exercise classes. Even the indefinite stay had lost a lot of its horror once I realised that there was, really, nowhere else I particularly wanted to be.

'Tom says hi,' Susanna said. 'And the kids. Sallie and I made you cookies, but the nurse or guard or whatever took them away.'

'Yeah. It's in case you put drugs in them. Or a razor blade, or something.'

'Right. I should've thought of that.' She glanced up at the camera hanging, very obviously, in one corner of the ceiling. 'Mum and Dad send love, too. And Miriam and Oliver. Miriam says to hurry up and get better. She looked it up online and found out you can apply for a discharge after six months, so she's expecting you home by Christmas.'

'Yeah. Right.'

'I told her it doesn't work that way, but she says I'm underestimating the power of positive thinking. She's already made an appointment for you with some guru guy who's going to reiki the bad vibes out of your aura, or something.'

'Oh God,' I said. 'Tell her I'm getting worse.' In fact, I had no intention of applying for a discharge until those two years were up. Before that, even if I was approved, it would only get me transferred to prison. The hospital was no five-star hotel and some of the company left a lot to be desired, but the place was blessedly free from gang wars and shower-room rapes and all the feral nightmare that I (from my smug middle-class perspective, Susanna said in my head) associated with prison. All of us in the hospital had done various major shit, but with a few exceptions none of us were looking for trouble, and the seriously scary types were kept separate. A lot of people were schizophrenic, and they mainly hung out together, but there were a couple of depressives and a guy on the autism spectrum who were surprisingly good company. The autistic guy in particular was very restful to be around. All he wanted to do was talk for hours about *Lord of the Rings*, and he didn't require any input or even any attention from me; I would sit by the day-room window and look out at the gardens, wide lawns and decorous topiary and spreading oak trees, while his flat rhythmic monotone went on and on like running water.

'Are we allowed to go outside?' Susanna asked suddenly. 'In the garden?'

'I guess,' I said. We were, actually, but there were a few of the guys I would have preferred her not to run into, for my pride's sake more than for hers.

'Let's go. It's lovely out. Who do we ask?'

It was lovely out: clean brand-new springtime, a warm generous breeze that smelled of apple blossom and fresh grass, little white puffs of cloud in a blue sky. The lavender bushes on either side of the path were in bloom; birds were everywhere, loud and jubilant.

'Wow,' Susanna said, turning to look back at the building: immense and sprawling, grey, Victorian, with pointed gables and bay windows.

'Yeah. It's impressive, all right.'

'I think I was expecting some modern thing. Super-discreet. Something that could be a community centre, or a block of flats. This place is like, "Fuck you, we've got a madwoman in the attic and we don't care who knows it."'

I couldn't help it, I laughed. She glanced over at me with a half-smile. 'Do they treat you OK?'

'No complaints.'

'Can they hear us out here? I mean, it's not bugged or anything?'

'Oh for God's sake,' I said.

'Seriously.'

'They don't have the budget to bug anything. There's him.' I lifted my chin at the large nurse standing on the terrace, rocking peacefully on his heels and keeping one eye on us and the other on three guys playing cards on the grass. 'That's it.'

Susanna nodded. She turned and we headed down the path, gravel crunching under our feet, Susanna tilting her face up to catch the sun.

'How are my parents doing?' I asked.

'OK, as far as I can tell. Relieved. I know that sounds weird, but I think they were scared of things going a lot worse.'

'Yeah. So was I.'

Susanna nodded. 'There's one thing I wanted to tell you,' she said, after a moment. 'About Dominic.'

'Right,' I said. I didn't want to talk about Dominic.

'I didn't really clock it at first; not until a few months after we did it. Remember I told you how at the beginning of that summer, when I was just daydreaming about ways of doing it, I downloaded Firefox onto Hugo's computer to do the research, instead of using his Internet Explorer?'

'Yeah.'

'So he wouldn't find out I was searching for murder techniques.' Someone had dropped a Kit Kat wrapper; she picked it up and put it in her pocket. 'But I mean, Hugo: how often do you think he went through his search history? You think he would even have registered if "making a garrotte" popped up? We could all have been watching orgy porn on there every day of the week, and he would never have noticed. And anyway, if that was all I was worried about, I could have just stuck to IE and cleared the history and the cookies and the temp files at the end of every session.'

'Right,' I said. I wasn't sure what her point was. Susanna always had liked making things complicated; messing around download-ing pointless browsers was exactly her style.

'Except that that would have shown. Not to Hugo, but if the cops had gone looking through that computer, they would've seen that someone had wiped everything. They wouldn't have been able to tell what had been wiped, but it would've looked dodgy as hell. I could have come up with some story – forums for cutters, maybe – but once the cops got interested, I'm sure they could have subpoenaed records from the ISP or Google or somewhere. The big thing about downloading Firefox was that when I was done, I could just uninstall it, run a cleaner programme, and it looked like nothing had ever happened. Totally normal search history, right there on IE, no gaps or anything. Nothing to make the cops look twice. Which was a good thing, and I'm delighted I did it that way. But the thing is, I did that before I ever got serious about killing Dominic.'

'So?' I said.

We had turned into the walkway, a series of arches overgrown with trailing creepers so that they made a long tunnel. It was cooler in there, shadowy, bees humming around white flowers.

'So when I started planning it for real,' Susanna said, 'at first I thought I'd changed. Because of Dominic; what he was doing to me. I thought it had turned me ruthless. Not that I've got a problem with being ruthless – I don't think.' She considered that for a moment. 'Probably I should have loved that idea. It would mean that none of it was my fault, right? That wasn't really me, it was what Dominic made me into. But I hated it. That might have been the worst part of all: the idea that I was who I was because of some random guy I just happened to meet, and if he'd gone looking for study help off someone else, or if he'd done Spanish instead of French, I'd be a different person. Like anyone could turn me into anything, and there would be nothing I could do about it. It fucked me up, for a while. It might be partly why I went through with it, I don't know.'

She brushed away a tendril of vine, tucked it carefully into the trellis. 'But once I realised that about the browser,' she said, 'I was OK again. I'd been all ready to kill Dominic, and get it right, way before I ever thought about actually doing it. The stuff he did to me, the stuff that felt like it was turning me into someone else? It didn't actually change who I was at all. I was always ruthless. It was just a question of what it would take to bring it out.'

She watched me, sunlight dappling her face as we walked, midges hovering. I thought of her as a little kid, Zach's size maybe, sharing her M&M's with me because I had cried when I spilled mine in our mud wallow. 'Maybe,' I said. 'You would know.'

'I do.'

I didn't ask her the question that had been on my mind, which was whether I had been inside or outside that ruthlessness's range; whether, if it had come down to it, she would have thrown me under the bus to save herself and Leon. There didn't seem to be much point. I'm sure she'd only have told me there was no such *if*, it could never have come to that, she had had everything under control all the way; none of which would have answered the question. More to the point, I wasn't sure I really wanted to know.

Instead I asked, 'Have you told Tom?' I had been wondering this, too. 'About Dominic?'

'Nope,' Susanna said. 'Not because I'm scared he'd turn us in, or leave me, or anything. He wouldn't. But it would upset him and it would worry him, and I'm not going to dump that on his shoulders just so I can pat myself on the back about having no secrets in my marriage. And' – a cool glance at me – 'neither is anyone else.'

'I wasn't planning to.'

'You know what, though,' she said, a little farther down the walkway. 'Sometimes I think he knows. About Dominic and about that doctor, too. Obviously there's no way I can ask him, but . . . I wonder.' Another glance at me. 'What about Melissa?'

'I'm not sure,' I said. 'And I'm not going to ask, either.'

'Yeah, don't. Leave it.'

We had come out of the walkway; after the dimness the sun felt too bright, aggressive. 'Hugo's ashes,' I said. I hadn't wanted to bring this up around my father. 'He wanted them to go in the Ivy House garden. Did you, did anyone—'

'Yeah, your mum said. But' – breeze playing with a curl of her hair, she lifted a hand to tuck it behind her ear – 'all our dads, they felt weird about that. After everything. There's a lake where the four of them used to go for holidays, when they were kids? Up in Donegal? We drove up there, a few weeks back. We scattered his ashes in the lake. Which is probably illegal, but there was no one around. It's a beautiful place.' A glance at me: 'We would have waited for you, but . . .'

'We should go in,' I said. 'Our time's probably up.'

Susanna nodded. For a second I thought she was going to say something else, but then she turned around and headed towards the walkway. We walked back to the building in silence.

•

My parents visited all the time, of course, and Sean and Dec, and sometimes the aunts and uncles. Richard came once, but he was so upset that it just made both of us feel worse. He had got it into his head that the whole thing was somehow his fault, that if he had pushed me to come back to work then I would have recovered faster (not true, and I told him so) and, more confusedly, that if he hadn't been so angry with me about the Gouger thing then I wouldn't have stayed late at work that night and wouldn't have crossed paths with the burglars, or wouldn't have been awake to hear them, or something. That one obviously wasn't true either, but it came close enough to what a part of me believed that I had a hard time with it, which of course upset Richard even more. After that he wrote me every month like clockwork – scene gossip, descriptions of new artists he had discovered, wistful asides about what lovely things I would have done for the exhibition of found-object sculpture – but he didn't come back, and I was glad of it.

Leon wasn't around; he had moved to Sweden, where he was working as a tour guide and from where he sent me postcards of national monuments with a few perky, meaningless lines scribbled on the backs. Melissa didn't come either. She wrote me long, very sweet letters: lots of funny stories about the shop, like the ones she used to tell me when I was licking my wounds in my apartment; awful Megan the flatmate had finally managed to run her chichi café into the ground, which of course was everyone's fault but hers, and now she was setting up as a life coach; Melissa had run into Sean and Audrey in town and their baby was completely adorable, the exact same laid-back expression as Sean, they couldn't wait for me to meet him! In spite of the huge amounts of time and consideration and care that must have gone into the letters, there was something impersonal about them – they could equally well have been written to a classmate she hadn't seen in ten years – and I wasn't at all surprised when she mentioned (delicately, not making a big deal of it) that she was going to some concert with her boyfriend. I rewrote my answer half a dozen times, trying to make it clear with equal delicacy that I wasn't angry, that I wanted her to have every happiness and while I wished with all my heart that I had been able to give it to her, now that that was impossible I hoped she could find it with someone else. Maybe I got the tone wrong, or maybe the new boyfriend was understandably not crazy about the idea of me; her letters didn't stop but they got farther apart, shorter, more impersonal, more like letters to some guy she had picked off a charity website. Still, I was one of the lucky ones. A lot of the guys, especially the ones who had been there for a decade or two, didn't get letters or visitors at all.

Martin, of all people, came to see me too. I had been playing table tennis – there was a complicated, ferociously fought tournament that had been going on for something like six years – and when they told me I had a visitor I took for granted it was one of my parents. The sight of him – his back to the window of the visiting room, scanning the place like he was checking for contraband – stopped me in my tracks.

'Surprise,' he said. 'Long time no see.'

I couldn't think of a single thing to say. My first thought was that he had come to beat me up. The visiting room had CCTV, but I wasn't sure what to do if he suggested a walk in the grounds.

'You're looking in fine fettle.' He eyed me up and down, taking his time. He had got older, lines deepening, jowls starting to sag. 'Got your tooth fixed,' he said. 'My taxes at work, hah?'

'I guess,' I said. He hadn't moved from the window. Behind him, faraway birds looped across a grey sky; the lawn had the rich green glow of coming rain.

'Wouldn't want you having any trouble getting the ladies, when you get out.'

I stayed silent. After a minute Martin let out a small hard laugh and pulled something out of a manila folder. 'Got something for you to look at.'

He didn't sit down, or hand it to me; instead he tossed it onto the coffee table and let me go after it. It was a sheet of card with two neat columns of photos, numbered 1 through 8.

'Any of those fellas ring a bell?'

They were all chubby guys somewhere in their mid-twenties, most of them with greasy little skanger fringes. 'Who are they?' I asked.

'You tell me.'

I did my best: went through them carefully, one by one, but none of them looked even vaguely familiar. 'I don't recognise any of them,' I said. 'Sorry.'

'But then you might not. What with that awful brain injury and all.'

'Yeah,' I said. I couldn't tell whether he was being sarcastic.

'Life's a bitch,' Martin said. He threw me another sheet. 'Have a go of that one.'

These guys were younger and skinnier and halfway down the page he hit me like a jolt from a live wire. Rush of sweat and sour-milk stench, I would've sworn it was there in the room with me, clamped over my face like a chloroform rag.

Martin was watching me, expressionless. 'Yeah,' I said, after a moment. My voice was shaking, I couldn't make it stop. 'This guy.'

'Where do you know him from?'

'He was, he, he, he—' I took a deep breath; Martin waited. 'He's one of the men who broke into my apartment. This is the one who attacked me. Attacked me first. The one I fought with.'

'You're sure.'

'Yeah.'

'There you go. Told you I close my cases.' Martin tossed me a pen – too suddenly, I flinched and sent it flying, had to fumble on the floor for it. 'Write down what number you recognise, how you know him, sign it, date it, initial by his photo.'

'Who,' I said. I sat down in one of the armchairs – I was glad of the excuse. 'Who is he?'

'Name's Dean Colvin. Twenty. Unemployed.'

Which wasn't what I meant, what I wanted to know, but I couldn't work out how to ask— 'How did you find him?'

Another sheet, just one photo this time. Gold watch and chain, the worn lustre of the gold holding its calm old silence intact even against the harsh light and the glaring white background. Ornately curled initials, *CRH*.

'Recognise that?' Martin asked.

I said, 'That's my grandfather's watch. That he left me.'

'The one that was robbed from your apartment.'

'Yeah.'

'Write that on the sheet. Sign it and date it.'

I started with that one; I didn't want to look at the guy's face again. *This is a watch that my grandfather left to me.* The pen wouldn't stop skittering; my writing looked like a drunk's.

'Deano says,' Martin said, 'he won that off some guy in a game of cards, a year or two back. Doesn't remember the guy's name, of course. With your ID, we might be able to shoot that story down. Although' – shrug – 'an ID from you isn't worth all that much. What with everything.'

'How,' I said, again. 'How did you get him?'

'Deano liked that watch. Made him feel posh, he says.' A glance at my worn T-shirt and faded jeans: *Not that posh now.* 'So he never tried to pawn it or sell it – or we'd've had him years ago; just hung on to it. Only a couple of months back his flat got raided because his brother was dealing, and the lads spotted that yoke there on Deano's bedside table. They thought it looked a bit out of place. Brought it in, ran it through the system, your file popped up.' With a tilt of his chin at the paper: 'Having some trouble there?'

'No. I'm fine.'

'You'll get the watch back. When we're done with it. The rest of your stuff is well gone; they sold it straightaway.'

'So he was a, a criminal, in the end.' When Martin said nothing: 'You said, back when it happened, I thought you said if he was one of the, the regulars, you'd know who—'

'I did, yeah. We would've. Deano's got a few priors for fighting, minor stuff. Nothing for burglary.'

'Then,' I said. 'Why me?'

'He's the artistic one of the family,' Martin said. 'Oil pastels all over his bedroom walls. Not half bad, some of them.'

He waited. When I clearly had no idea what was going on: 'The exhibition you were working on, when you got bashed? Young Skanger Artists or whatever it was? Deano was one of the artists.'

I said, after what felt like a very long pause, 'What?'

'We're thinking maybe he spotted that watch on you one day, when your man Tiernan had him in to the gallery. Or spotted your car. Took a fancy to it. Got his brother or a mate in on the act, and they followed you home one night.'

All I could think was, flat and absolute and unbudging, *No.* Just bad luck, sheer dumb bad luck, pick the wrong day to wear my watch and end up here— 'No,' I said.

Martin watched me, blank-faced. 'What, then?'

Flicker of something, something I had known a long time ago and somehow forgotten, but I couldn't— 'I don't know,' I said, after what felt like a long time.

Martin leaned his arse on the windowsill and put his hands in his pockets. 'We had a couple of chats with Tiernan,' he said, 'back when you got hit. Just nosing around, looking for any problems, any grudges. He told us the Gouger thing wasn't your— Ah, fuck's sake, Toby' – with a glance of pure disgust – 'of course we knew. Took us about ten minutes to get the whole story. Tiernan told us it wasn't your fault, the whole thing had been his idea, you had practically nothing to do with it; he was delighted you still had your gig, because this way you'd be in a position to give him a hand somewhere down the line. He was convincing. So were Deano and the rest of the skanger kids: no clue about Gouger, no clue about you, no clue what we were talking about. And you kept on insisting no one had any grudge against you. So . . .' He shrugged. 'Looked like a dead end. But if Tiernan was bullshitting us; if he wasn't happy that your boss threw him out on his ear, while you just got a few days on the naughty step . . .'

I said, 'Tiernan set it up.' I should have been blown away, but it barely felt like a surprise.

'Maybe. Maybe not.'

'He did.' Tiernan. When I tried to picture him, the only image I could come up with was some show opening, Tiernan buttonholing me to be outraged about how one of the artists had turned him down even though he had never been anything but nice to her, bitching on and on with canapé crumbs in his beard while I went 'Mm-hm' and tried to edge towards the people I was actually supposed to be talking to. I had never thought of Tiernan as anything but insignificant and mildly pathetic; on the rare occasions, that is, when I had thought about him at all.

'Got any proof? He threaten you, blame you, anything?'

'I don't remember. Maybe.' Actually I was pretty sure I hadn't had so much as a text from Tiernan after Gouger blew up – I remembered those three days of boredom in my flat, trying to get through to him and ask whether he had ratted me out, nothing but voicemail – but I didn't want Martin to let go of this. 'Can't you talk to him again? Ask him, question him—'

Martin's face had gone even blanker. 'Yeah, we managed to think of that. Tiernan's sticking to his original story. Deano's sticking to his card game.'

'But they're lying. Tiernan's, he's a, a wimp, if you just question him harder—'

It was all clear as day in my head. From Tiernan's point of view, the whole Gouger fiasco would automatically have been someone else's fault, and I was the obvious choice. He had been slipping Gouger into the show as just another talented sob story; I was the one who had hyped him up into the star, got Tiernan to do a big new series of paintings, told him to give Richard daily updates on his phone calls with Gouger. Except Tiernan had slipped up, hadn't kept his story straight – my ear pressed to the office door, Richard yelling, something about a phone call . . . If I hadn't stuck my nose in, Richard wouldn't have been paying any special attention to Gouger, and everything would have been fine. Instead Tiernan had got fired, and I had got off scot-free.

So Tiernan had picked the craziest skanger in his bunch and filled him up with stories about the bad guy trying to scupper the show and wreck all their chances at being the next Damien Hirst: the rich bastard with a flash car, a big TV, a new Xbox; the smug prick who was asking for a few slaps. And sent him off.

'Deano's lying, anyway,' Martin said. 'Tiernan, I'm not so sure. *If* he is, we've got no way of proving it, not unless someone talks. Which they won't. They're not stupid.' With a small bland smile: 'Sorry to disappoint you.'

There was something dizzying about it, about the fact that Tiernan could never have dreamed where that would lead. It must have seemed like such a small thing, just a tasty little lollipop of glee to suck on when the world refused to feed him what he deserved; nothing more, just like my prank emails to Dominic had been nothing more.

'You'll have to testify at the trial,' Martin said. 'If it goes that far. We'll be in touch.'

'But,' I said. I had just figured out why all this sounded vaguely familiar. 'I thought of that. That it could have been Tiernan.' Way back, all the way back in the hospital, as soon as the worst of the confusion started to wear off, the first person I had thought of had been Tiernan.

'Congratulations. If you'd bothered mentioning it, maybe we would've got somewhere.'

Crazy stuff, I had thought, just more evidence of my broken brain, and shoved it away. I had been right all along. 'I thought it was stupid,' I said.

Martin watched me. Behind him the green of the lawn had intensified, radiant and unsettling. 'You're not going to get any ideas in your head about going after Tiernan,' he said. 'Are you.'

'No,' I said.

'Because that wouldn't be smart. You can get away with it once – apparently. Second time, you wouldn't be so lucky.'

'I don't want to go after him.'

'Right. I forgot. You wouldn't hurt a fly.' And when I stared at him: 'Sign and date. I don't have all day.'

I wrote down something, trying to breathe slowly and keep my eyes off that photo. 'If you think about it,' Martin said, 'whoever gave you that bang on the head did you a favour. Without it, you'd be doing life in Mountjoy.'

This seemed not just false but outrageous, but when my head snapped up I met his eyes, cold and speculative and cynical as a seagull's. 'OK,' I said. 'Here.' I passed him the sheets of paper.

'These two' – lifting the sheets – 'if they go down, they're not going to get off with a couple of years telling therapists their problems in a cushy joint with lavender beds and a *gazebo*.'

'Right.'

'So you're in no position to get your knickers in a knot about Tiernan not getting what he deserves. Are you.'

That cold seagull eye again. 'I don't know,' I said.

'See you around,' Martin said, flipping the folder shut. He made it sound like a threat. 'Behave yourself.'

'I am.'

'Good,' he said. 'You keep doing that,' and he stuck the folder back under his arm and left the room without looking at me again.

•

I did behave myself. I followed my individualised care plan, did my cognitive behavioural therapy to cure my post-traumatic stress disorder, went to occupational therapy to teach me to live an independent and productive life, did my physiotherapy for my hand and my leg, my speech therapy to get rid of the slurring. The doctors liked me; I think I made a nice change from the vast majority of the guys whose problems were inborn, to be managed like haemophilia or cystic fibrosis, with no expectation of any underlying improvement. With me, they felt like they could get places. Maybe they did; anyway they seemed pleased with my progress. When, on only my third try, I got my conditional discharge, all of them seemed genuinely delighted. I was one of their success stories.

By that time the Ivy House was long gone. My parents had hired me the best solicitor and the best defence barrister that money could buy (another reason, I'm sure Susanna wanted to point out, why I wasn't serving life as some roided-up smack dealer's bitch), and the sum of money in question was, unsurprisingly, eye-popping. The expert psychologists, who had spent countless hours asking me confusing and exhausting questions and running batteries of incomprehensible tests, hadn't come cheap either. The decision to sell the Ivy House to pay for it all had apparently been unanimous. It was, everyone agreed, what Hugo would have wanted.

My job was gone too, of course. Richard apologised for that, from the heart, as if I might have expected him to hold it open indefinitely on the off chance that I might be back someday. Even if he had, I don't know if I would have been able for it. The various forms of therapy had helped a lot – apparently nothing except surgery would fix my eyelid, but the slur in my speech was barely noticeable except when I was tired, same for my limp, my hand-grip still wasn't great but I had learned lots of inventive ways of working around it. But my mind still had ravaged places in it, gaping holes full of drifting things; I had a hard time holding on to complicated sets of instructions, I needed a planner full of lists so I didn't lose track of what I needed to do and what I'd already done, and even with those I occasionally lost hold of big chunks of time or couldn't work out what day it was. Just thinking about my old job – no routine, no one telling me what to do, deftly juggling a dozen balls at once – made my head spin.

I had to hold down a job to keep my conditional discharge, and for a while there I had visions of twelve-hour shifts loading pallets in a warehouse full of immigrants who would hate my guts and spit in my lunch, but by the time I got out my family had come to the rescue again. Oliver had pulled strings with a friend at a big PR firm and got me a nice simple job that could have been done, and probably had been up until then, by a fifteen-year-old on work experience. I went in there under my middle name (Charles, after my grandfather; I went by Charlie). I'm not sure it fooled my co-workers for any length of time – there had been a few tabloid snippets when I got out, 'INSANE' COP KILLER FREE ON OUR STREETS and a blurry God-knows-where shot of me being sinister by wearing sunglasses – but at least it stopped clients from having me thrown off their accounts in case I stalked them home and axe-murdered them in their beds. The work went fine. My co-workers were shiny twentysomethings with hectic social lives, and overstretched thirtysomethings with complicated childcare hassles; they were chummy, in a preprogrammed way, but none of them had the room to put much thought into me, which was fine with me. They invited me along to the Friday drinks sessions; sometimes I went, although the pub they used was loud and I mostly got a headache after an hour or so. There was one girl, a sparky, energetic redhead called Caoimhe, who I was pretty sure would have gone on a date with me if I had asked, but I didn't. Not that I was afraid I would pollute her innocence, or anything, I didn't get that far; just that I couldn't come up with enough emotional engagement to bother.

I had trouble feeling anything much about anyone, actually, not just Caoimhe. Small things could bring me to tears of what felt confusingly like loss – frost on a dark windowpane, frail shoots of green sprouting from a pavement crack – but when it came to people: nothing. I knew it had something to do with that night in the garden, of course, but I wasn't sure exactly how: whether that flash-over of fury had ignited everything inside me with a ferocity that had vaporised the lot and scorched the earth; or whether, while my suicide attempt hadn't managed to go the distance, it had taken me just far enough over the line that I couldn't find my way back.

The upside was that it turned out to be true, what I'd told Martin: I had no desire at all to go after Tiernan. I kept waiting for the rage, the urge to track him down and beat the living shit out of him, but it never came. Maybe it was just that emptiness, or maybe all those sessions with the hospital shrinks had done their job, who knows; or maybe it was that, deep down, I was less sure than I would have loved to be that Tiernan had had anything to do with the break-in. At heart Tiernan was intensely careful of himself. Sneaking a couple of paintings into a show had had him shitting bricks; just the thought of anything that might involve jail time would have given him a heart attack, and I wasn't sure losing a job would have been a big enough upheaval to change that. Whatever the reason, my overwhelming feeling about Tiernan was that I never wanted to think about him again. If I could have had a very specific lobotomy to slice every memory of his existence out of my brain, I would have done it.

My apartment was still there, rented out (by my parents) to a nice young couple, teachers or nurses or something like that. I had no intention of taking it back. The rent was enough that, even with my laughable salary, I could afford to live basically wherever I wanted, given that I needed very little else. In the hospital a big topic of conversation had been the things people were going to do when they got out (poker tournaments, island-hopping in Greece, escort services), but that had been mainly from the guys who were going nowhere; those of us who had an actual shot at the outside world had had a much harder time picturing it. Now that I was there, it didn't seem any more real or more accessible than it had from the hospital. I couldn't think of anything that I particularly wanted to do, except hole up in my new apartment clicking on random internet links and watching an awful lot of bad TV.

Somehow, though, I couldn't stay put. My PTSD had faded a lot – the cognitive therapy or just time, I don't know, but I didn't leap at loud noises or people coming up behind me any more. I could go out walking, even in the dark. The only thing that was still a problem was being home at night. When I first moved into a new place I would be fine, but over a few months – as if I could feel at the back of my neck some searcher gradually closing in, some tracking circle homing tighter and tighter – I would start to get edgy: first double-checking locks and alarms, then lying awake with my ears straining, then pacing my apartment till the sky paled outside the windows. At that point I would give the landlord my notice and find somewhere else to live, and the cycle would start all over again.

It did occur to me – somewhere deep in the core of those nights, pacing another cheap rental carpet, the silence crammed with the hum of too many people sleeping on every side – to wonder whether I ever left that first hospital. The Ivy House, when I think about it, seems heartbreakingly improbable, a murmuring haven from a battered childhood book, suffused in all my memories with a golden haze that has something frighteningly numinous about it; could that place really have existed, in this drab grinding vapid world of Twitterstorms and carb-counting, gridlock and *Big Brother*? and Hugo, wandering vague and shabby and benevolent through its rooms, could he have been real? did I ever have cousins at all? In the morning, jammed onto the Luas with hundreds of other commuters steaming rain and swiping manically at their phones, I know that's nonsense, but at night: I can't stop myself from wondering, with a stunning rush of grief, whether everything since that night has been no more than a last burst of light from a dying star, the last rogue fizzles of electricity along the shorting wires.

In the end, I suppose, it doesn't matter, or anyway not as much as you'd think. Either way, after all, here I am: in yet another apartment that smells of unfamiliar meals, too high off the ground, too many bare hundred-watt bulbs, too many locked windows and doors. And while sometimes I can't stop my mind from reaching for the alternate realities (pacing the wooden floorboards of that white Georgian house, drowsy baby snuffling on my shoulder, Melissa asleep in the next room) I'm very aware that, of all the possibilities, this is at least far from the worst.

Maybe this is why I still consider myself a lucky person: now more than ever, I can't afford not to. If I've realised nothing else, you see, in the long strange time since that April night, I've realised this: I used to believe that luck was a thing outside me, a thing that governed only what did and didn't happen to me; the speeding car that swerved just in time, the perfect apartment that came on the market the same week I went looking. I believed that if I were to lose my luck I would be losing a thing separate from myself, fancy phone, expensive watch, something valuable but in the end far from indispensable; I took for granted that without it I would still be me, just with a broken arm and no south-facing windows. Now I think I was wrong. I think my luck was built into me, the keystone that cohered my bones, the golden thread that stitched together the secret tapestries of my DNA; I think it was the gem glittering at the fount of me, colouring everything I did and every word I said. And if somehow that has been excised from me, and if in fact I am still here without it, then what am I?

Acknowledgements

I owe huge thanks to the amazing Darley Anderson and everyone at the agency, especially Mary, Emma, Pippa, Rosanna and Kristina; Andrea Schulz, my wonderful editor, whose enormous skill, patience and wisdom have made this book so much better than I thought it could be; Ben Petrone, who is just plain great, and everyone at Viking; Susanne Halbleib and everyone at Fischer Verlage; Katy Loftus, for her faith in this book and for putting her finger on the one thing that would make most difference; my brother, Alex French, for the computer bits and for sending me the link to the case of Bella in the Wych Elm; Fearghas Ó Cochláin, for the medical bits; Ellen at ancestrysisters.com, for genealogy help; Dave Walsh, for his enormous help with the intricacies of police procedure; Ciara Considine, Clare Ferraro and Sue Fletcher, who set all this in motion; Oonagh Montague, Ann-Marie Hardiman, Jessica Ryan, Karen Gillece, Noni Stapleton and Kendra Harpster, for talks, laughs, drinks, moral support, practical support, and all the other essentials; David Ryan, I'm vilifying you, for God's sake, pay attention; Sarah and Josie Williams, for being meeptastic; my mother, Elena Lombardi; my father, David French; and as always, beyond words, my husband, Anthony Breatnach.

Author's Note

As of 25 May 2018, Susanna's line on p. 145 is outdated: with the repeal of the 8th amendment to the Irish constitution, pregnant women will have the legal right to give or refuse consent to medical treatment.